You Hear Me?

You Hear Me?

A Novel

Ainsley Finn

Willow Weed Books

Willow Weed Books
712 Bancroft Road #123
Walnut Creek, CA 94598

Published in the United States by Willow Weed Books

"I'm Nobody's Baby" (1921) was written by Benny Davis, Milton Ager, and Lester Santly

Cover design by Damonza.com

Library of Congress Control Number: 2014940689

ISBN 978-0-9904125-0-2
eISBN 978-0-9904125-1-9

For the believers and the nonbelievers —
Peace.

You Hear Me?

Contents

1. Ordinary Days

2. Waking Up the Dead

3. Potholes

4. Townies

5. Storytellers

6. Drift

7. Romance

8. Chimes

9. Broken Things

10. Shadow

11. True Love

12. Extraordinary Things

13. Crazy Boy

14. Long Lost

15. Ties

16. Slip

17. Love Again

18. Thanksgiving

19. Apple Days

20. Ho! Ho! Ho!

21. Icicles

22. Christmas

23. Gift Giving

24. Love, Please

25. Panic

26. Going…Going…Goodbye

27. Godspeed

28. Ghosts

1

♦ Ordinary Days ♦

They were all here once. There were people in this house he never knew and only heard about. His mother's name was Aster and he is dreaming about her and about his father, Abel. In his dream, his mother is standing on the porch and he is riding on his father's back across the yard. There is a sheet on the clothesline and he swipes at it as they pass to make it move. Abel hefts him higher.

"Gettin' big, Jojo."

At the pond, he dog paddles in a circle, and Abel laughs and swims over. "C'mon. You can do better 'n that." He tries to swim away, but Abel catches him and throws him into the air.

In his dream, he remembers his arms coming open, swiping at nothing, and the sunniness of the day. In real life, the sun is never that bright or yellow up there and the sky is never that blue. He laughed though and then there was water in his mouth, filling him up and the world turned green and he felt Abel's fingers, and then he was flying into the air again.

"Up you go, Jojo!"

He knew Abel was there to catch him.

He had a family once.

His wife's name is Alison, but he only calls her Ally. At the moment, she is standing by the door to his sister's room with her fingers resting on a plastic doorknob that's supposed to look like crystal. On the other side of the door the room is the same as on the day his sister died. Ally always makes sure to put everything back in the same place when she cleans. The carpet in there is blue, and his sister's blue and pink robe rests in a pile on her blue and pink bedspread. Across from the bed is a dresser covered with the bottles of perfume, nail polish, barrettes, and bracelets that their father bought her on her last Christmas. They both died not long afterwards.

All of this Ally heard about at work. His family almost haunts the house. At first their reminders gave him a sense of realness, a connection to a life he thought was taken away from him, stolen on the day he went to prison. Years later, coming back here, the emptiness in the house almost had an echo that kept him company. He saw them everywhere, Sissy's doorknob, a cowbell on the kitchen windowsill that Jonah's grandfather gave to his grandmother, his mother's paintings, even the pots outside that Aster used to grow her geraniums in. Then Ally came and he began to watch her and grow quieter and more distant every day.

Now he lies still, waiting for her. It is dark out and quiet. He isn't sure if it was some sound she made or her quiet that woke him. In the dark, he thinks of Christmas Eve, Sissy on Abel's shoulders, setting Aster's angel on top of the tree, and Abel's big hands on her knees. Then a light goes on.

When Ally appears, he gets up and walks by her. She stoops and picks a towel up off the floor.

"Time is it?"

"Eight thirty."

Some days he feels almost blameless. She was always like this, a tremor in the air as he passed.

At the dresser he pulls on his jeans and looks back. She hugs her towel and smiles, a blonde with shadows the color of honey in her hair, eyes like a summer sky, in the lavender top he loves, barefoot like Aster and Sissy usually were.

"Anything to eat?"

"I can make you a sandwich."

"Whatever. Just somethin'."

On other days he is full of blame.

Alone, he pulls a tee-shirt on and sits down. Her purple top is the color of his grandmother's lupine. Once, before they were married, he took her to a restaurant called Marjorie's where he looked over at a spot by the blue wall where the black and white tiles on the floor stopped against the baseboard and said, "I'm not gonna be any good for you. I already know that." She surprised them both by the way she grabbed onto his hands and said, "I don't believe that. I love you, Jonah."

He felt frozen and didn't move. After a while she stopped holding his hands as often. She began to grow afraid of him, unsure that he really loved her, and more and more he began to see bits of Aster in her. He thought about the night he warned her. He could have said more, he guessed. He thinks he wanted her to leave, but he didn't do anything to make her. There were times when he was gentle. He remembers standing on her porch outside the fan of yellow light from the lamp by the door, hearing the buzz and snap of reckless insects, hugging her to him, holding his face against hers. He rocked her side to side, not letting go for a long time. At home, he swam in the pond and looked up where the wind blew in the tops of the firs. Half his body is blue with tattoos. He robbed a mini-mart a long time ago, a place called *Mom 'n Pop*, and shot a man in a shirt with Pop on the name tag.

"That you? Pop?" asked Jonah.

"That's right."

He opened the register when Jonah told him to, but then Jonah shot him anyway.

Ally looked at him with pity when he told her. The first day he hit her it was summertime and she put a radio on the kitchen sill to hear it while she hung clothes on the clothesline. It wasn't loud enough to bother him. He got up for a glass of water and watched her out the window, pulling sheets out of a plastic laundry basket. The basket was blue, slightly washed out looking in the sun. When she came back in, he said, "You woke me the fuck up," and slapped her. She put her whole arm up to her face and just stared at him while he took a step closer to her, then backed up, as if wanting to hit her again and not wanting to at the same time. She didn't move, and then he seemed to make up his mind, pushed her out of the way of the door and left.

When she got pregnant the first time, he didn't hit her at all; then after she lost the baby, and for a long time after that, he still didn't. This time he feels a strange sense of suspension, a feeling that something is waiting to happen. People said his grandmother, Clover, had visions, and for some reason his grandfather, Job, always thought she passed that on to Jonah. The only memories Jonah has of Job is of when he was dying, pointing his stick finger at him.

"You're just like your grandma. C'mere an' let me see you."

He wouldn't go near him though, and strangely, Abel never made him.

He doesn't think he ever sees visions really, except of things that have already happened and that he can never change. When Ally came out of the bathroom on the day of Dahlia's funeral, fright and happiness in her eyes at the same time, he didn't guess anything. For some reason, it surprised him when she said, "I'm pregnant."

"Are you sure?" She nodded, biting her thumb, looking at him expectantly. "You better stay home then," he said. "I don't want you taking any chances." He meant Dahlia's funeral.

"Maybe you should start working part time," he added.

"We'll see. I feel good now. I'm happy. Are you happy?"

"Yeah, I'm happy. Of course, I am."

At the cemetery the wind blew and threw cold bright lights across the grass where Fin stood by his mother's grave and made the clouds thin and wispy, reminding Jonah of the day Abel died. He remembered the way the paler clouds blew away before the darker ones came and the rain started and drowned out the sound of his voice.

"Pops!"

At the cemetery, the wind was silent. He only knew it was moving from the shadows.

In the bathroom, he puts his hair in a rubber band and looks at Aster's flowers and vines on the walls. It took her all day to paint them. At lunchtime he ate his sandwich sitting on the tub, watching her. Coming in on his way to the toilet Abel stopped in surprise and said, "Hell's that for?"

"Decoration."

Remembering, Jonah smiles dimly into the glass. He wears a beard that only covers his jaw and upper lip. His cheeks are bare and there are tiny white scars on one half of his face. He looks like Abel and Abel's mother, Clover, with Abel's dark blue eyes and Aster's light brown hair.

"You hear that, Jojo? Dec-o-ra-tion."

Abel's face was always smooth, so maybe he grew his beard to be different. That was probably why he grew his hair long too. Now it's just him. He thinks of change sometimes but without the will to actually make any. He can't even quit smoking. The thought of that makes him return to the bedroom and feel at the pocket of his shirt before putting it on.

Outside, it is dark and windless.

In the kitchen he looks briefly out the back door. Ally slides her feet on the cool floor and sips at her milk. Sitting down he looks up at the clock. It is white with a red frame and a different fruit or vegetable at every hour. All the cupboards are white with yellow knobs. Ally's feet slide on white linoleum with yellow flecks. On the windowsill, red geraniums, lupine, or wild carrot. She pulls her feet under her chair and smiles up at him. Sitting down, he pulls his napkin off his sandwich and looks up at the clock again.

"You have time," she says.

"Nine minutes."

"I bought some lotto tickets." He shoves half his sandwich in his mouth and stares at her, waiting. "We might win," she explains, her glass in her fingers, motionless, eyes open and blue.

His cheeks redden as he chews. "Sounds about right. All my OT goin' for lotto tickets."

She sips her milk and stares through the service porch at the dark outside. Jonah drops his eyes, pushes his plate away and says, "Well, I'm quittin' if we win."

Her face brightens. At the door, he kisses her lightly, patting at his pocket again as he gets in his pickup. Through the windshield, he looks back over at her, knowing she can't see him. She is leaning with her face against the doorsill. Up here she's aware of things, of spirits like Jonah's grandmother's at the gravel's edge, forever picking ghostly flowers, of wonder and worry.

Yanking on the steering wheel, Jonah spins away, gravel spewing in the pickup's wake.

Jonah's father and grandfather worked at the Sanderwood Furniture Company too. Once it was just a brick building that stood in a circle of dirt with tree stumps all around. After a while a couple of the firs grew back and now there are benches around them and planters with petunias on the patio by the front doors. Ally works in the offices on the top floor where a couple of lights stay on until morning. At the side of the factory, a door is open and people are going toward it across the parking lot.

"You're gonna be late," says one of them, slowing down with two others beside him.

He is talking to Kurt Otto, who is waiting for Jonah to arrive. Kurt looks over, not moving away from the side of his car.

"We have a couple minutes still."

"Got somethin' to talk to you about."

"What?"

"Gus needs some advice," says one of the others.

"Won't listen to me," says a man named Wes.

"I'm just not sure," gripes Gus.

Kurt shifts a little against the side of his car, wanting to go with them because he wants to fit in and never feels like he really does. A lot of that is because he wasn't born here, while Wes, Gus, and Jonah were. Jonah's family was one of the first to arrive in this area.

"Talk to you at break."

"Okay."

When he first came to work here Gus told him to "walk real careful" around Jonah. "Antisocial as all get-out." Then one day he and Jonah were put together on the glue rack and he began to sense after a while that Jonah was a lot like him. He was friendly enough; he just didn't fit in. Kurt thinks the reason he doesn't himself is because he never had a real family. This is the longest he's ever been anywhere and he doesn't want to leave. Plus, he likes it here. Jonah lives in a little town called Sandorville and Kurt lives in a town called Acropolis on the other side of the factory. He likes all the Greek names like the Doric Palisades and the Rhodes mall. He lives off the main road through town, Olympus Avenue, which everybody calls Oly Way, and the bar he goes to is just down the street from his apartment, which he never particularly liked, but now he's glad he has. It's only one room, but it saves him money, the people there are quiet, and he has a new neighbor downstairs.

Across the parking lot, Wes stops at the door and calls out again before they go inside. "Gonna be late!"

Kurt almost follows this time but then sees a pair of lights come out of the dark and swoop over firs and the tips of bushes, lighting the leaves with bright edges before swinging into the parking lot and going out. A moment later the engine stops too and Kurt starts over. "We're gonna be late," he says.

Jonah grimaces in the light inside the pickup before he slams the door. "Don't remind me."

"You know what we oughta do?"

"Tell me," he says.

"Unionize."

"Sure. Why not?"

"I mean it."

"Won't change a thing," Jonah says.

"You never know."

"It's a guess."

There's a long empty hall inside the factory with a flight of stairs up to the office where Ally works and another flight on the other side down to the basement where the ceiling is covered in acoustic tiles and the lights are bare bulbs inside mesh cages. They take the stairs down to the rows of lockers. In back, there are showers and storage cupboards. The lights barely illuminate anything below the tops of the lockers. Jonah stops at his, pulls out a pair of gloves, then says, "Wanna help me with some potholes on my drive sometime?"

"Yeah, sure. Just say the word."

"Keep ya in beer for the day anyway."

"Can't knock that."

"Nope."

He closes his locker and follows Kurt upstairs. At the top, Kurt grabs onto the rails for momentum and swings himself out into the hall where he bounces off the far wall and spins back around with a grin. His cheerfulness and energy annoy Jonah for some reason.

"Don't you ever settle down?"

"Got enough time for that any day," he says, pushing the brim of his cap up.

"Try now."

"I'm just wired. Noisy today. Couldn't sleep. You should see who's movin' in downstairs. Wow."

He whistles with an admiration he didn't feel at first because she woke him up when she started laughing with her friends out on the walkway downstairs. It was usually quiet in his apartment building so he was mad when he got up to look, but by the time he put his jeans on and went outside, there was nobody there but a little boy on a chair by the open door of the apartment below his. The boy just stared at him, so he scratched at his bare belly and stared back until she came out and pulled the boy inside by his arm.

"You'd like 'er," he says to Jonah, who is ignoring him, laying boards on a glue rack and looking up at the windows, already watching them for daylight. "Name's Joy." The moon is a gray wedge in one of the windows. "I don't think 'er kid lives with 'er though...."

Sandorville was called Pineville once, named by Samuel Hollycock and John Sparrow, according to Orly Squire, and before that it was called Green Meadows, according to Wilkie Waylon. Waylon's Market, originally Pineville Market, was the first building in town after the town hall.

"Only real meadow I know about's Ira's," said Orly.

"That's just the closest," said Waylon.

The Waylons were here almost as long as the Hollycocks and Sparrows. Orly's gas station came later, on the other side of the street from the market. Jonah used to work there and for a while Waylon's wife used to work at the lunch counter inside the market. She was young and good-looking and Jonah used to stop work to watch her. The girl in the silver Plymouth that blasts past him out of the shade at the top of the market's parking lot is her daughter. He doesn't slow or hear her complain to the boy at the wheel.

"You almost hit 'im."

"Saw me comin'."

She twists to look back at him as he jumps up the steps onto the porch of the market, but he doesn't notice, glancing sideways at Orly's instead. He started working for Orly after he quit school, but for a few weeks he just stayed home watching TV until one day his father got up from bed, poured himself a drink, and came out to sit in his recliner. Jonah was lying on the couch with a pillow bunched up under his head, hearing the ice in Abel's glass as he drank. It made him antsy and he shifted on the cushions, drawing Abel's attention. "School out?"

"No."

"You sick or somethin'?"

"No."

"So what's with you?"

"I quit."

"You quit? What the hell for?"

"Why not?"

Abel drank, the sound of the ice like cold, lapping water in summer. Jonah knew Abel didn't care about school, just about Jonah doing something on his own. Making him go back though would be too much trouble and Abel wouldn't bother.

"Well, don't think you're sittin' around here all day gettin' in my way. You better get a goddam job, you hear me?"

"I hear you."

On one side of Kurt's apartment building fir trees cover up all the windows, and on the other side a balcony covers up the windows below. Most of the upstairs are one-room apartments like Kurt's. Joy's is a one bedroom. Her TV is by the wall next to the window by the walkway. The sound of it is coming up through the vent beneath his bed where he's lying underneath the dusty rays of light that are pushing past his curtains. It doesn't matter if he cleans, there's always dust anyway because it doesn't have anywhere to go. He doesn't mind his little apartment anymore though.

I have plans, he thinks to himself and that's what he'll say to Joy when he talks to her someday.

He can picture her smile already, cool as her light blue eyes. Her hair is a thin, delicate blonde that almost touches her shoulders.

When her TV goes off, he sits up, then hears her outside and goes to the window covered by the firs. Glimpses of her come through the trees, her hair aglow, with her purse swinging loosely, in jeans and a top as pink as cotton candy, which makes him think of baloney, his favorite food next to pickles, so he grabs a piece on his way out, eating as he goes.

His car is parked under a fir at the shoulder of the road and he stuffs the rest of the baloney into his mouth and drags his arm across the hood as he passes, gathering up needles in its crook and spilling them off the side. After that, he stops and sniffs at a leak only he can smell, then wipes his fingers off, gets in, and drives away.

There's a bowling alley on the corner with a giant white bowling pin on the roof and he always ducks a little as he goes by to keep it in sight. Across Oly Way is his favorite bar, and further down the road is Marjorie's Restaurant. Then there's nothing but firs and bushes and quiet until he pulls in at work.

Inside, he goes up a staircase with a window on the landing where the stairs turn up the last flight. The glass in the window is thick and grimy, and it's always dark and stuffy here. His footsteps echo.

Through the upstairs door is a large open room with offices in back. Windows line both walls and the drifting light is cool and thin. A counter separates the lobby-like entrance from the rest of the open room. On the near side of the counter, Sully Church is talking to Ally, who is standing on the opposite side. Hearing Kurt, they both stop talking and look over. Ally smiles, brushing at her bangs. Sully's forehead knits in a frown, projecting that impression that he doesn't really like or trust anybody. Kurt doesn't like him for just that reason, but always smiles politely because Sully is part owner of the factory with Fin Sandor, the original owner's son. Kurt has never seen Fin, doesn't even know what he looks like, although there's a picture of his father on the wall by the offices.

"Just gettin' my check," he says, passing another man coming out of an alcove filled with cubbyholes. A moment later he's in the stairwell again, following Bob Connelly through the gloom.

In the hallway he takes his cap off, scratching at his hair, and Bob Connelly looks up as if he can see back into the offices through the ceiling, then says, "I think we're outta jobs."

"Whadda ya mean?"

"I just heard a little of it, Sully tellin' Ally that he was gonna be gone a couple days. That he needed a car an' that he didn't want any of our customers to know that he was away."

"So maybe it's personal."

"That thing about the customers? I was in a buyout once. I have that same feeling."

"You're nuts. I don't believe it."

"I'm hopin' I'm wrong."

"We'd still have jobs."

"A whole new crew came in."

"We have to talk to Wes. Wes'd know."

"Maybe."

"I can't lose my job."

"I can't either. I have kids."

"Plus, I like it here."

"Pays good too."

Kurt nods and falls silent until they go outside and start across the sunny parking lot. Then he muses, "Do you think it's cuz 'iz mom died maybe?"

"I dunno. Could be, I guess."

The funeral was private, but they took up a collection on the floor for flowers, and Sully brought in a picture so they could see what their money bought. The picture had gravestones in the background and Kurt thought that it was strange to take a picture in a cemetery. Besides, he was hoping for a picture of Fin. He imagined being somebody like that, somebody with a family that would leave him things. Fin is young and doesn't have to work if he doesn't want to, and Kurt wondered if he could see something of himself in somebody like that. He knows that Fin and Jonah were friends before Fin moved away and remembers asking Jonah about him once. But all Jonah would say was "Nothin' special. Just some guy we work for."

Occasionally, Kurt passes by a stone wall in front of ferns and dark shade where there is a house nobody lives in anymore.

At his car he stops to open the envelope his paycheck comes in and then looks over at Bob. "Shorted me again," he says.

"Your differential?"

"Yep."

"Maybe it's a hint. Want you on days."

"Maybe," he agrees, and then says, "Only if we have jobs though."

"Guess we'll see pretty soon."

"I guess so."

Bob is a worrier though. Maybe he doesn't know it, but he always takes the side of the worst possible outcome of things. Kurt knows Jonah doesn't like him, and doesn't even like Kurt to talk to him. "Just in case you tell 'im somethin' I don't want the rest of the world to know about."

Turning onto the street by home, he ducks to look up through the windshield at the shadow of the bowling pin as he passes underneath it again.

It is quiet out and Joy is sitting on her couch. Her door is open, her wind chimes shimmering in the pale sun. She is capable of long stretches of emptiness and sits almost blankly until a man with shaggy brown hair peers hopefully through her door before going upstairs.

Sandorville and Acropolis are populated by people whose families have almost always lived here. Gale Sandor was the first of his family and Fin will probably be the last. In the twelve years since he left, he's only returned once for his mother's funeral, going home to the old Victorian he lives in the day after. Sully wants him to buy a place, but Fin says that he's comfortable and doesn't want to look for anything else, even though the hot water doesn't stay hot for long and it's dark and creaky and the crystal chandelier at the top of the stairs is gold with grime.

At home, in the cemetery by the house where he grew up, a light slowly swings and shines on a pair of stone angels.

Gale's is gray, Dahlia's pure white.

In the old Victorian, Julius Gladdise stops behind Sully at Fin's door and says "I bet 'e dies."

The words cause Sully's heart to clench. He feels sick and angry and holds a palm up, stopping Julius as he slides closer to the door. "You wait here."

Julius is bouncing an imaginary ball on the floor. He dribbles it, hand to hand. "Bounced. Just like this," he says.

On the night Fin fell off the apartment building's roof, Julius was taking out the garbage. He didn't really see Fin land, though, because he was already running away by then, leaping down the steps to the corridor under the building.

"On second thought," says Sully, "you don't have to wait. I'm fine."

Julius ignores him though, stocking feet sliding over the threshold.

Sully advances almost cautiously, glancing around quickly for things he half expects to be there and won't want to see. The way other people live dismays him. In his workshop at home, wood transforms in predictable ways into familiar forms. His talent is reverent, his work an appreciation of purpose. The dining room in front of him is tidy, a light film of dust on the dining room table from a few days' absence. Nothing is different or out of place. Fin is a mystery to him though, passing his days with a lackadaisical boredom, a smile that is amused without being cheerful, and a faint flightiness in his eyes that Sully always assumed he'd outgrow.

Julius shuffles behind him.

On the coffee table, Sully sees a bottle he expects, empty, a glass lying on its side by the couch, a side cushion on the floor too where he imagines Fin lay drinking until he got up for a new bottle, then climbed barefoot to the roof. Years ago, on Thanksgiving Day, Fin came home with Jonah in tow and stood frowning at Sully, who was sitting on the living room couch with Fin's mother. Dahlia sighed quietly but didn't speak. She might have been slightly embarrassed, but she didn't really care.

Fin was unsteady, stumbled a little when Jonah nudged him. "Stores are closed," he said, almost nonsensically.

"It's Thanksgiving," said Sully. "Most stores are." Then: "Where have you been?"

"Jonah's."

Another nudge sent him to the liquor cabinet where he came out with a bottle of bourbon. Behind him in the dim winter light, Jonah dropped an arm across his chest and began to pull him backwards.

Sully was dumbfounded. He looked at Dahlia. "Are you just going to let him go?"

She shrugged slightly. "If that's what he wants."

To this day it was Jonah's expression Sully remembers most, a strange mix of victory and anger.

A moment later they were out the door, and a moment after that Jonah spun off in the gravel-spewing, red-neck way of driving he still has today.

Fin was all of his mother. Sully never saw any of his father in him.

Picking up the fallen glass, Sully sets it on the coffee table and catches the movement of Julius bouncing his imaginary ball.

"You can go."

Julius pretends to catch the ball, sliding backwards.

"Am-ne-sia," he says, rolling his voice over the syllables. "Am-ne-sia, scam-ne-sia." Julius's socks whisper backwards. "Ask me," he says, "amnesia's a joke."

"Now look here—" Sully starts, but Blossom, Julius's mother, drowns him out, yelling out the open door of their apartment across the hallway.

"Juli!"

Julius keeps sliding away. At the door he smiles again.

"Am-ne-sia...."

Across the hall, a warm light pools on the dark floor. Alone at Fin's now, Sully goes to a window where a dull street lamp in front illuminates the leaves of a cherry tree and drains into the dark above the lights of the shops and cars. Warm air mixes in with the cold.

Outside, the sky is starless with a dull yellow glow above the lights.

At Blossom's, a shadow looms across a wall, Julius sliding into her room. She is almost bedridden, swollen legs, worry burrowing in her eyes.

"Whachya doin', baby?"

"Just thinkin'," he says.

"About what?"

"Amnesia…."

Across the way, Sully leans out a window and stares up at the ledge of the roof.

2

✦ Waking Up Dead ✦

The building is blue with violet trim work. Inside, stairs lead up to two floors, and another flight of stairs leads underneath the building. The woodwork is dark, heavy, and worn with time. The gloom in the stairwells and dark halls is veil-like, a weighty presence that hovers outside the light of the windows. Above Fin's floor is another apartment that belongs to a girl named Ginny. At one end of the landing outside of Ginny's apartment is the staircase to the roof. On the roof, there are a couple of plastic chairs and chaise lounges.

Going upstairs one day, Fin stopped by Ginny's door and looked at the threshold as if for a light inside, but it was daytime and all he saw was a shadow and the dust on the landing. She wasn't home, and when he passed by, he pictured the backyard through her living room window. One of the apartments, not his or Ginny's, has a flight of stairs down into the yard, but everybody else has to go through the corridor beneath the building to reach the back. The door at the end of the corridor opens onto a concrete trough with the back of the building on one side and a retaining wall holding back weeds and bushes on the other. That's all the yard there is, weeds and bushes, shut in by other apartment buildings.

At the stairs to the roof that day, he stopped to look back at the footprints in the dust by her door. Maybe he thought she'd notice them crossing hers. He wasn't sure of that though. The door to the rooftop opened by a skylight that went down to his own kitchen window. The glass in the skylight was dull, and when he looked down through it, everything looked gray and watery below. He sat on a chaise lounge and saw pigeons and clouds in a bright blue sky. It was sunny and cold out. When it grew dark, he put down the bottle of Jack Daniel's he brought up with him and went over to the edge of the roof above Ginny's. There were lights on in most of the windows and a light below under a porch-like roof over the garbage cans. He could see another chaise lounge in the light, but he didn't see Julius. Maybe he heard him though.

"Superman!"

In the fall he saw a swirling of lights.

"I hear we're sellin'," says Kurt, dropping down on the end of his bed. His apartment door is open, fading sunlight wedging in across a strip of his carpet.

Drinking his beer at Kurt's kitchen table, Wes says, "Well, you know what they say. You can't believe everything you hear."

"I've only heard one thing."

"Let me ask around. I'm sure I can find things out."

Wes has worked for the factory almost as long as Gus and Bob. His hands are scarred and thick from years of handling wood, and his temperament calm and amiable from years of handling people. He's in his mid-fifties with a family. Kurt met his son once, a boy in his late twenties with cool but not unfriendly eyes. Kurt likes Wes, and if anybody has a way of getting information, it's him.

"That'd be good," he says.

Not anymore, but for a while, Ginny wore a string of bells on one of her ankles that jingled with a miniscule sound, almost inaudible sometimes. Coming in or going out, as she passed Fin on the stairs, she'd slow, as imperceptibly as the sound of her bells, and they would exchange polite and neighborly smiles. "Hi," he'd say.

"Hi," she'd answer.

On one occasion she'd see him with a girl, on another occasion another girl. Nobody stayed with him for long. One day, he came upstairs with her and they drank glasses of wine on the couch.

"What do you do?" she asked, pulling her feet up underneath her, asking because she really didn't know anything about him. "For a living, I mean."

He was sitting on the middle of the couch with an arm across the top, fingertips almost touching her shoulder. His smile was directed at the point where they almost touched. She knew that she was always attracted to the damaged, and that he was one of those.

"I invest," he said, looking back at her face.

"In what?"

"Things I like. A store like yours maybe." He meant the bookstore where she worked. "I like to get things going again."

"I don't think we've stopped," she said, and his smile returned.

"Just an example."

Sometimes he seemed close to her and sometimes far away. The next time he came over, it was still a little light out, and he leaned out her window and said, "I like this side of the building."

She saw the shadow of his eyes in the glass, not the misty firs he saw, the slow swing of the signal light between Orly's and Waylon's.

She guessed he'd be happier if she didn't live above him. Having her here wasn't the same as meeting somebody he never had to see again. She wasn't sitting on some bar stool somewhere and she didn't live on a street he never went down. She was right above him, hearing the sounds of his footsteps, oddly meandering footsteps, the sounds of somebody lost.

Once, he brought a bottle of bourbon upstairs with him and fell asleep on her couch. She was still sitting beside him when he woke up, watching him with an emotionless face. He pushed himself off the arm of the couch and sat hunched for a moment, scrubbing at his hair before he filled his glass again and sat back.

"Do you ever worry about your drinking?" she asked.

"No," he said, right away.

After that, she didn't see him for a long time, not even on the stairs, and then she came home from work one day and he was waiting at her door. She stopped in surprise, not sure she was happy.

Inside, he sat down with a drink and looked outside, and she remembered when he said, "I like this side of the building."

Sitting down too, she took the bells off her ankle and slowly dropped them into a silver pile on the coffee table. Without really knowing why, she never wore them again. "Where'd you grow up?" she asked.

For some reason he wasn't surprised by her question. "Sandorville."

"As in Sandor?"

He nodded. "My father started a manufacturing business there. The town was named after it. I own it now." .

"Oh."

"That's where I was."

"I was wondering."

"My mother died."

She wasn't sure at first that she heard him. His arm lay across the top of the couch again, his usual pose, fingertips almost touching her shoulder, drink balanced on his knee between swallows, gaze moving quietly around the room, lighting on one thing, then another. "She died?"

He nodded, took the glass off his knee and swallowed. "Stroke." His bourbon sloshed in dark gold waves. He spun it into a vortex, watching it swirl, and suddenly she clapped her hands around his and took the glass away.

"I'm not drunk," he said.

"You can't just say it like that."

"Say what?"

"Well....Didn't it mean anything to you?"

"My mother?"

"Yes."

He shrugged. "I don't know. I guess so."

"Fin?"

"What?"

She was lost, floundering in some awful empty place that he always brought with him.

"I'm sorry."

"Thank you." He wanted his drink back. She gave it to him and he said it again. "Thank you."

After Dahlia's funeral, cars pulled into a long driveway through firs that hid the house from sight. Jonah drove by on his way to Waylon's. He didn't need to see the house to picture its whiteness, shaded front window under the porch roof, the darkish rooms inside. For all the windows there was never a lot of light. Behind the house there is a garden all the way up to the firs, hydrangeas in shade, zinnias and dahlias in the summer. The dahlias are almost surreally colorful.

According to Fin, on the day Gale died, Dahlia cut all her flowers down and set them on fire. Hearing Fin tell it, Jonah tried to picture her standing by the gas-fed bonfire, a wobbly, unreal image through the heat-warped air. One summer day, he sat on one of the disintegrating concrete parking stops outside of Orly's, waiting for Abel to come pick him up while Orly was pumping gas into Fin's car. Jonah knew Fin by sight but had never talked to him. He saw Orly twist sideways and point at the auto bay where it looked cool and comfortable inside, but Jonah knew it wasn't, just dark and muggy. A moment later, Fin came back out with two bottles of Coke, and Orly nodded at him with a nod that was almost like a push, propelling him cautiously across the lot over to Jonah. Jonah watched him with the same kind of caution, but took the Coke that Fin stretched out to him. "Thanks."

"Hot."

"Yeah."

Looking back, he probably didn't like Fin at first. Probably imagined a life that was easy and always would be. He took classes at a college between Acropolis and Enders, drove his own car, never had to work.

Getting up to swipe under his arms with his tee-shirt, Jonah drank the rest of his Coke and then said, "Drive me home an' I'll get you a real drink."

He doubted he meant any good, but in the end he liked Fin, and because of him, he never liked Dahlia. He felt no sorrow at her funeral, no inclination to join anybody; he just wanted Fin to see him, so he stayed down the hillside, leaning up against the front of his pickup, legs crossed at the ankles, watching the shadows of the clouds blow by. Afterwards, he went to Waylon's, then he went home, and after dark he went to Fin's. There was a light on in the front window and one upstairs too. That's where he saw movement, a swoop of shadow on the upper pane.

Jonah had his window down, arm hanging out. Gravel popped quietly under his tires. He stopped beside Fin's rental car and got out.

The front door opened as he came up, and he rested an arm against the door jamb and just stood there, looking inside. His eyes saw things that hadn't changed from years ago: a mirror on the entrance wall, a table underneath, the long empty hall to the kitchen in back, a flight of stairs. He couldn't see the couches in the living room or the liquor cabinet but figured they were the same. Fin was and wasn't the same. Dahlia's face, her dark wavy hair, tiny silver hoops in an ear, a coldness in his eyes he seemed aware of, even amused by.

Straightening up a little, Jonah shifted his weight. "I came to pay my respects."

"You didn't have to."

"Wanted to, I guess."

He was looking away again to his arm on the door jamb, shirt sleeve rolled up, to a tattoo of black waves he wished were green like the water at Ivy's. All his time in prison he would dream of swimming there with the strange belief that he would be washed free of things if he could just go back. Aster's sister kept the place up for him and stocked the cupboards before he got home. That house had always been in his family. He didn't thank her because she didn't like him, saw too much of Abel, he guessed, but he paid her back as soon as he could. Then the house was his, the same and not the same, like Fin. He kept looking back at him, trying to find the things that had changed, wondering at the faint amusement in Fin's eyes.

"What?" he asked.

"What do you mean, what?"

"You look like you were thinkin' somethin'."

"I was thinking I wanted a drink. Long day."

"Come out with me. I'll buy."

"I have a bottle here."

"Come out anyway. It'll do you good."

Fin's amusement grew, but it was wry and a little sad looking. He took a breath, then let it out with a shrug and took his coat off a hook by the door.

They didn't talk. It was strange to be with him again, the same and not the same.

Arm out the window, paddling at his door with his fingertips, headlights barely lighting the road ahead, strobing through the trees, Jonah drove fast, tires whistling, not slowing until he saw the lights in town. A couple of signal lights down Oly Way, he pulled onto a side street and turned again onto a street behind a bar with a neon sign in the shape of a cocktail glass on the roof. The bar was called Mulligan's after Henry Mulligan, one of the owners.

Pulling into a gravel alleyway, Jonah stopped in front of a black Harley Davidson parked by the side porch of an auto shop. Light coming out of the shop's windows pooled over the bike. Getting out of the pickup, Jonah pointed at a black door in the side of the bar.

"Go in there."

On the other side of the door, a short hall, bathrooms on either side, a room beyond with booths in the corners and tables throughout. Behind the bar was the other owner, George Wytton, washing glasses in a soapy sink. Jonah rapped the bar lightly. "Couple Wild Turkeys."

"Over in a sec."

Fin sat at a small round table toward the back of the room. The air was hot and stuffy, but a cooler air seemed to come off the windows in back. Jonah joined him, kicking out another chair to stretch his legs. He seemed to be considering something, running a hand through his loose hair.

"Really. I'm sorry about your mom."

A muscle bunched in Fin's jaw, smoothed out again. "You know we didn't have much of a relationship."

"I know…." He looked around for George. "Still."

It was Grace, Henry's daughter, who brought over their drinks. Jonah saw Fin frown thoughtfully at her. "Pretty," Jonah said after she'd gone.

Fin nodded. She barely looked at them. But she was known for that, a shyness that even went past awkwardness.

Jonah drank, then said, "This isn't going to last," and went back up to the counter.

Grace returned again with two drinks and two shots. Fin's face was entranced but still slightly thoughtful. Her hair was strawberry, eyes gray.

"Ask 'er out," said Jonah.

"I'm going home."

"Right."

There was something in Jonah's voice that made him stare. "What does that mean?"

"Nothing."

They settled back in their chairs and drank a few more rounds. Jonah didn't feel drunk, but he could tell that Fin was. There was a sullenness in Fin's face, a moodiness in his look every time Grace came over with their drinks. Jonah kept shifting his feet under the table. The movement was annoying Fin, breaking the strange spell he seemed to be under. His face was angry—one of the ways he wasn't the same. He was compliant before, easy to be with. Jonah felt his own anger growing.

"You work?" he asked.

"Work?"

"Yeah. Work. You know. A job.

Fin squinted at him, half drunk, half angry. "I work. Not like that though."

"Not like what? Like me?"

"What are you getting at?"

"I just think it must be nice. No ties. Bail any time you want."

"Is that what you think I did? Bailed on you? You never could figure anybody else out."

Jonah was astonished. "Is that right? So wha' did I get wrong?"

Heads began to turn. Attention shifted.

"Can't you count? I was here almost ten months after Sissy died."

"Died? Is that what you call it?"

"What the fuck else?"

Across the room, George set a pair of glasses upside down on a towel and came slowly around the end of the counter.

"You didn't come see me. I was sittin' on my goddam ass in jail. No family. Just Orly."

Fin's jaw bunched again. "I didn't put you there."

"What the fuck does that mean?"

"You did that."

"You just fuckin' walked away! From all of it, from Sissy—"

"Not her. Don't you fuckin' say that!"

"I am sayin' it! I should've figured this. You haven't changed one fuckin' bit, you piece a—"

"Stop!" George was leaning in, both hands on their table. "You've had enough. I don't want this in my place. Do you understand?" He waited. Jonah was breathing heavily, a fuzzy blur squeezing in at his vision. Fin stared back at him. He heard George's voice again. "Jonah?"

"Yeah, okay."

The table rocked slightly as George stood up. Grace was there too, setting down mugs of coffee. "Drink up," said George. "Coffee's on me."

After a moment, they settled back again. Fin's flush was slow to fade and Jonah's face felt hot, sucking at the coolness from the dark windows. They didn't talk again, not even outside. Fin looked reluctant to get in the pickup, but then he did, and Jonah drove him back home.

The next day he was gone.

On the same night, Ray Wycowski was sitting at a table against the wall, tilting back in his chair, one boot up on the chair beside him, chewing ruminatively on a toothpick. His hair was dark and heavy, and he wore a blue stud in one ear and a twisted leather band around one wrist. Cameron, the man sitting with him, was droning on about something Ray wasn't listening to because he was more interested in Jonah. Jonah's face kept getting redder, and the hand he kept pulling through his hair pulled harder and harder. Jonah never struck him as expressive and it interested him to see him this way. The other man he could only see when he turned to look at Grace or George, his face just as red as Jonah's.

When Grace came over to pick up their empty glasses, Ray asked, "What's going on?"

"I don't know. An argument."

She didn't like him which just endeared her to him more. He grinned at her cheerfully. In a moment she came back with fresh drinks and the voices across the room rose. Even Cameron fell silent, twisting to look over. When nothing really happened though, Cameron sighed in disappointment and twisted back again.

"Anyway," he said. "I'm just feelin' squeezed out."

"Can't hurt tryin' your luck someplace else," said Ray. "Always works for me." Even though he'd almost always lived near the town he was born in; the times he'd moved away weren't usually good times. He said what he said though because he didn't particularly want Cameron to stay here either. Glancing away to the door that somebody opened up to the side alley to let the cold air in, he saw the lights on at his shop, the shine of handlebars over the short wall between his driveway and the bar's. He used to have a 1970 Barracuda, but he sold that when he moved up here. The plan wasn't to stay; the plan was to come up and collect a debt from a man named Aaron Toler. Then Aaron told him about a man named Will, and somehow he ended up with Toler's auto shop instead of the cash he came up here for. He didn't regret staying, but after he moved in with Will's girlfriend, Will didn't want anything to do with him anymore and that included anything to do with his friends. Aaron moved away, but Cameron found his spot in Will's orbit taken over by someone else. Before any of that, though, Aaron took Ray to a place called Candi's so he could check Will out before meeting him. Candi's was a diner with a domed façade and big bright windows. They sat in back, waiting, until Ray got restless. "You sure 'e's comin'?"

"Like clockwork," said Aaron.

So they ate their pie and waited. Then Aaron jerked his chin to the glass doors and Will came in with a man named Andy and somebody everybody always called Craig's cousin. All three were in their mid- to late-twenties, all ropy and loose-limbed. Following Will and Andy down an aisle, Craig's cousin suddenly looked over at Ray, fixing him with alert eyes and a mild smile, and Ray half laughed uneasily.

"Fuck was that?"

"Dude's psychic," said Aaron.

"Seriously?"

"That's what Will says."

Ray sighed and planted his arms across the back of the booth. "That's my competition?"

"Yep."

Ray laughed quietly and rapped at the vinyl booth top. "Like takin' candy from a baby."

Later, when Will and Ray met for the first time, Will pulled his shirt off to show Ray his back and said, "I got hella beat. Over a joke too. Just cuz Trev here used to guess my scores in school an' get 'em right. Pissed me off doin' that," he said, beginning to frown and stare off into space for a moment. Even though there were no marks on his back, something about him made people not mention that. Ray didn't mention it either, but that was because he didn't really look. "Anyway," Will said, starting up again, "Trev was gettin' a pool, one a those big pools, a doughboy, he said, an' I said 'No, man. I have a feelin'. I think you're gonna get a built-in. I bet ya.' An' Trev was like, no way, an' then one day when nobody was home, I went over, an' I figured a way to get a hose into their basement, filled it right up. Built-in pool. Can't beat that."

He laughed and Ray smiled at him. Ray's eyes twinkled because people and life amused him, and he was seldom overtly angry. He wasn't bigger than other people, and he was always friendly, and people liked him and always made way for him. But he gave off a certainty that something inside him was the opposite of everything that everybody always saw. He was intimidating in a peculiarly magnetic way.

Outside the bar, the air was blue from the neon sign and filled with misty little dewdrops. Switching off the lights in the shop, Ray got on his bike, pulled on a pair of gloves, and rode off. Outside the lights of town, he began to relax. A lamp was shining in the front window of his house, meaning his wife was home.

Hearing him come in, she got up off the couch, and he picked her up in a hug.

"Hiya, lady."

When Fin fell, he crashed through the roof over the garbage cans and then hit the chaise lounge beneath it.

When she heard the noise, Ginny ran to her window and saw other people leaning out of theirs. A garbage can was rolling slowly over to the door of the corridor under the building. Almost there, it hit the short cement ridge around the top steps and grew still.

In her room, where she could hear all the noise too, Blossom sat quietly. Then Julius was there, and she froze with a gumdrop halfway to her mouth.

"Wha'z all that out there?"

He fell sideways onto her bed and lay with his chin on his palm and she felt one of her premonitions of doom that always began with Juli. His eyes as he looked at her were as round and shiny as pennies.

"I don't like all this," Blossom said with the beginnings of a pout. "Go see who's out there."

"I already saw," he said and moved sideways to let her get her robe. She puffed like a bellows as she got up. "I dunno what you're gettin' up for," he said, following her in tiny, soundless steps. "You won't be in time."

A fact that was prophetic to Blossom, the idea that she would miss all the things that were really important. She heard sirens in advance and then suddenly Julius wasn't there anymore. She felt him run by and heard a laugh in the empty lobby. All the lights outside flashed in and out.

'SUPERMAN!"

Blossom was always aware of tragedy.

Startled by the commotion, Fin tried to get up, but something was holding him down. All he could see were oblongs of lights swirling around him, golden as bourbon in a glass. Then the ground seemed to rise and fall, and the golden lights turned as red as fire. The fire was burning him and he began to groan in despair.

At home, Kurt meets Wes at the door with a package of baloney, shoves a piece into his mouth, chews and asks, "Are we or aren't we?"

"We aren't."

Kurt peels off another slice of baloney. "For real?"

"I can't tell you what's going on, but I don't think it has anything to do with selling. Makes no sense. Clients like stability an' we just got a big new job—"

"Who told you that?"

"Ally. It's not a secret."

"You just asked?"

"Of course," says Wes.

Kurt eats another slice of baloney and mutters, "Well, somethin's happenin', that's for sure...."

Coming home from the book store, Ginny hears a TV at Blossom's and sees a light under Fin's door. There's dust in the grooves between the floor boards and she slows on her way to the stairs. She knows there's a rug just inside his door, thin and multicolored. Even when she was seeing him she never felt at home there. She isn't sure he is either. There's a picture of his mother on the mantelpiece beside a green and white vase that he brought home with him after she died.

"She was pretty," Ginny commented.

Like Fin, she had dark wavy hair, green eyes. When Ginny said, "You look like her," he leaned away from the mantel and didn't really seem to hear her. She thinks being here surprises him sometimes, that there are moments he can't believe the way things are.

A couple of days later, the sky is a sunny blue and a plastic bird is spinning its yellow wings on a porch across the street while a jack hammer is filling the air with noise.

Standing at a window in Fin's room, Sully turns to look back inside. Fin is staring at him with glum, red eyes.

"How are you?"

"Okay," Fin mutters.

Sully comes over to look under the lid of his breakfast tray.

"You didn't eat though."

"I don't like it."

"You have to eat."

He looks at the fluttering bird Sully was watching a moment ago. Yellow wings with a parrot's beak. The sun is shining at the windows, bursting into bright rays. It flashes off the bird's wings too.

He rolls onto his side and stares into an empty hall.

A lawn chair broke his fall. His spleen ruptured and a hollow metal tube from the chair impaled him, breaking a rib at the same time. He hit his head twice and almost bit through his tongue. A finger fractured and one heel was badly bruised.

Later, his head felt like it was in a vise and squeezed tears out of his clenched eyes. They gave him morphine and he slept.

Going through a signal light, Kurt makes a sudden turn into the bowling alley. He runs in through the doors and comes back out with a giant cookie in a paper wrapper that he stuffs into the bag with his pickle and baloney sandwich before he pulls out between the stone pillars at the exit without looking.

There are lights on at the bottom of the giant bowling pin. The shadows behind the lights remind him of something he can't place right now, but he's in a hurry anyway. He gets points off at every review for being late.

"I'm not always late," he says to Jonah. "An' anyway, I do the work a two guys."

"Never do mine," says Jonah.

Further on, he passes the bar with its blue neon sign and moonlit planters of dark petunias at the factory. Cars cluster under the haloed lamps: dark, inky colors, or luminous, ghostly colors under the glow; empty spaces all around except for Jonah's pickup parked by itself in the dark. Kurt hurries, hearing a few ticking engines. The hall inside is empty. Skidding up to the basement door, he stops at the time clock beside the wall at the stairwell, stares at it for a moment, then pushes his card in until it clicks.

On the floor, the shift manager, Rob Chilburn, waves him over and he starts to explain that he wasn't really late, but Rob is just waving him over to Gus.

"Partner with Gus tonight."

"Sure," he says. "Okay." He is looking for Jonah, pulling on his gloves as he crosses over to Gus. "Where's Jonah?"

"New hire. Wes is off sick, so Jonah's trainin' 'im. Showin' 'im around right now."

"You have seniority."

"That's why I'm not trainin' 'im."

That doesn't make any sense to Kurt, but he doesn't pursue it. He feels discombobulated. He's not good with change. He keeps looking at the clock on the wall.

"What time is it?" he asks Gus.

Gus looks up. "Twelve thirty."

"On your watch," says Kurt.

"Oh. Twelve thirty."

Kurt goes back to work, but his eyes keep straying to the clock. At lunch, he takes his carton of milk to stare at the time clock again. Jonah is pulling his pack of cigarettes out of his shirt pocket, heading outside.

"Wait a minute," says Kurt.

"What?"

"We're losin' time."

"Every minute," says Jonah, shaking a cigarette out of his pack.

"No. I mean real time."

"Okay," says Jonah. "Reeeeal time."

"I mean it. That clock sticks about two minutes worth. Check it out. I was watchin'."

Jonah puts the cigarette to his mouth, lights it. "Jumps the same amount it sticks. You aren't losin' anything. You're still gettin' your sixty minutes."

"Are you sure?"

Jonah starts walking down the hall. "Yeah. I'm sure."

Kurt follows him.

"How's the new guy?"

"New."

"Kinda weird they hired a new guy."

"How come?"

"You heard the rumors. We might be sellin'."

"So what does that tell you?"

Outside, there's a light on, glowing gloomily over a collection of white plastic chairs and a table on dirt and dead brown redwood and spruce needles. Jonah steps over a curb onto the pavement on his way to his pickup. In the hallway footsteps follow, sticky and slapping on the linoleum floor.

Kurt darts to catch up to Jonah, swings around the pickup to get in on the other side. The sound of voices floats over, the smell of microwaved food. A can of pop opens. Jonah takes a bottle of bourbon out of his glove box, drinks, and passes it over.

"Total losers."

Kurt agrees out of reflex. "That's for sure."

Jonah looks at the top of his cigarette. "I said I'd quit before the baby comes."

"Good idea."

The cigarette glows, smoke fills the cab, and Jonah takes another drink.

"We're definitely not sellin'. I would know."

"Maybe Ally wouldn't say anything."

"Are you kiddin'? She couldn't keep a secret like that." He can see her with her fingers at her lips, timid as Aster, slow as his grandmother. Clover was sunshine and rain and springtime flowers. "Those guys are nuts," he says. "Total losers."

Kurt nods. "Yeah."

At home, Jonah swims in a misty pond. Above him the sky is gray. In wintertime, mists roll out of the dark, and the damp clings to metal and glass. At Orly's he saw Waylon's wife come out into mists that blew away all around her. She hugged herself in wooly jackets and one day ran away.

Swimming now in the cool, green water, he thinks that that was the only thing about her that ever made any sense.

A ball of sun rises in a blue sky. It glitters on silver waves, a bird with a parrot's beak, orange and yellow poppies. At the Wash 'n Go Launderette, busy dryers toss clothes behind steamy doors that look like the undersides of glass bowls. Earlier, Fin stood outside in gusts of warm air. At the top of the stairs he heard a fly buzz, a TV go off. On the mantel there's a vase of flowers, a picture of Dahlia, Ginny upstairs, a woman named Jane on the other side of the skylight with a pink begonia on the ledge under her window. A white cat with blue eyes sitting on the sill. A bottle of Jack Daniel's underneath the window on his side.

He drank on the sofa as the sun filled the room.

At night, lights spin in slow, rhythmic circles. In the daytime again, he wakes up on cool tiles in the shade of the toilet. Over the rooftops the sky's a soft gentle blue.

"Juli!"

Julius glowers and backs away from the front door. It swings in slightly, changing the flow of light outside.

The TV in Blossom's room is on and dust motes float in the soft light. He tiptoes, laces following soundlessly. She isn't sure of him and stares where his shadow will first appear. Gumdrops tickle her fingers. Resentfully, she looks down and sighs. Blossom loves the sparkle of sugar and all the colors of the rainbow. She plucks up a pink candy and suddenly freezes. Juli is staring at her, standing in her doorway with a jug of milk. He takes a swallow, swipes at his mouth and says, "Superman's home."

His jug is already dripping on the floor.

She scowls. "Go look in the keyhole."

He chokes in response and says, "You can't see nothin' through a keyhole."

"Go."

He snorts but goes anyway.

Fin dreams that there are lawn chairs in a river, just under the surface of the water, and a cross on the muddy bank. He stoops to pick up the cross. It slips out of his fingers and drifts away between the feet of the girl in the river. Her eyes are gray. He reaches for her and she drifts away too.

Once, he opens the door on a boy in the hall. Julius, although he doesn't know that then. Chubby face, startled eyes.

The boy rises with a look of distain.

"I told that bitch."

After Fin closes the door on him, he pours himself a glass of whiskey and sits at the bottom of his bed. A cherry tree covers his window in shade and softens the look of everything around him. A door opens and he drinks again. Ginny is coming downstairs.

Shadows flutter like leaves on the wall. All he hears are footsteps but remembers tiny bells, a symphony on the stairs.

There are open places under the lights. Jonah always parks in the dark though. Kurt can see the sudden red of his cigarette a moment later and then sees him leaning against the side of the pickup, arms resting across the top of the bed.

"How come you were callin' all day?" Jonah asks.

He scowls and says, "Thanks for answerin'."

"Busy."

Afterwards, he thinks Jonah already knew. He didn't seem surprised at all when Kurt said, "I have some news about Fin Sandor."

They were coming up to the door and Jonah stopped and dropped his cigarette onto the pavement and watched himself step on it.

"Almost died."

Kurt didn't expect him to believe him, but after he said that Jonah just stared for a minute, picked a bit of tobacco off his tongue and said, "Car accident or somethin'?"

"Accident, yeah. Fell. From a couple stories too."

Keeping quiet for a moment, Jonah picked at his tongue again, not feeling anything though, and then said, "That's weird. Musta been tanked."

"Not the weirdest thing though."

He expected ridicule, for Jonah to start laughing and say Kurt didn't know anything, and it surprised him that he didn't. The reason was that Jonah was picturing himself up on top of his garage at home, looking down through a hole in its roof, wondering if he ever told Fin about that, but he couldn't remember.

"What's weirder?"

"Supposed to have amnesia," said Kurt, and that's when Jonah started laughing and went inside.

The next day Fin wakes up on the floor by the toilet again, mouth dry from the bourbon the night before. He's hot and his skin feels itchy and he doesn't move.

Later on, cars pile up at the corner outside, and Fin can remember a dusty black Chevy Chevelle he bought one day and the smell of the damp again. There were hills all around with dark, silent oaks and his footsteps were loud on the gravel.

The car he sees now is the same, a 1968 Chevy Chevelle SS396, with white stripes down its hood, idling on the corner. He doesn't want to turn around and look behind him at the glass bowl on the little table by the door where he keeps his keys. Not on a ring where other people keep theirs but loose, easy to fit into his pocket. A key to his apartment, a house key. His mother's house, he guesses. Other keys, smaller, to lock boxes or file cabinets, he isn't sure. No car keys though. Blossom gave Sully a spare to the apartment and he told Sully to keep it.

That car is his. He stares at it, but still sees the garage, the dry leaves on the floor, the dusty, neglected car, still feels the damp cold as he walked along the gravel driveway. And then the car starts off and slows again before it turns. He runs outside, stops on the street in the sunshine and then runs over to the corner where the car turned. It's at the top of a hill where the street dips down and then back up again. He passes through the shadow of a building on one side, slowing in the sunshine on the other. Getting out of the car, Julius catches sight of him and backs up.

The car has a black interior, and Fin knows that it smells dry and warm inside.

He grins at Julius. "Grand theft auto. That's a crime, isn't it?"

Julius snorts and his eyes narrow at him. "I was doin' you a favor."

"Toolin' around in my car?"

"Keepin' you from gettin' towed."

"Give me my keys back. You should've done that a week ago."

"Whatever."

In the car, Fin turns off the radio and watches Juli back away. It doesn't bother him that they don't like each other. It feels natural, in fact. As he sits there staring, he starts to sweat and wipes his face. His feet are bare and the rubber mat on the floor is sticky. He smiles at the smell and can't remember the smell of leaves in that old garage anymore.

At home he pours a drink. The sun is still high above the rooftops across the street, and the room is light and bright.

Downstairs, Ginny pulls the door to the street open and gusts of warm air blow in and fall still again. Then before the door can close, fingers catch onto it and she stares up at Fin, feeling her heart jump, nerves making her stomach flutter. He leans his head against the edge of the door, closer to her. She stares into a familiar face, at lips she used to kiss.

"Ginny?"

"Yes."

His eyes don't know her, want to. She can see the strain, the muscles in his face contracting, relaxing, giving him a strange look of shame she thinks a moment later she imagined. All she sees now is a rueful, slightly tired smile.

"This is awkward."

She smiles too.

"Can I buy you a cup of coffee?" he asks.

"Sure. I have time."

Surprising her, he takes her hand as they walk. Their fingers interlock.

"Thank you," he says.

"For what?"

"I don't know. I just feel grateful."

"You're alive. That's a great thing, isn't it?"

His fingers squeeze hers. "That part I'm glad I don't remember."

"I tried to come see you."

"I know. I didn't want anybody to."

"And now?"

"I'm going away now."

In the coffee shop she waits for her coffee, waits for him to stir sugar into his and then says, "Away?"

"Home."

"For good?"

"Maybe."

She sips her coffee, looking at him over the top of her cup. "You don't know me anymore."

"Just who you are. That you live upstairs."

"What's it like?"

He stares for a moment, and she can see him consider her question, and then he says, "I don't care a lot of the time, an' other times that's all I care about."

His cup is on the table, his fingers open on the rim. They are sitting by the window and the light on his face is thin and quiet and she can't see anything hiding in his eyes anymore.

"We broke up, you know?"

He smiles that rueful, slightly tired smile from before. "I know. But I don't have anybody else to talk to."

She doesn't know what to say to him and she is suddenly sad. "Please be okay."

Then his smile comes back and stays and she halfway believes he remembers her.

Juli waits in the hallway with his milk jug. The door to his and Blossom's apartment is half open and the light behind it is colorless. There are no features on Juli's face that Fin can see, just a sudden white smile.

"Lose your girlfriend?"

Fin turns at his own door and says, "I'm leaving, Juli. You can come get my key in a minute."

Juli stares, all of a sudden feeling the milk jug pull at his fingers. A moment later he goes in to tell Blossom, but all he does is stare at her too. She sees the surprise on his face and screws up hers in worry.

"Use a *glass!*"

A moon shines over Ivy's pond. Alone here at night, Jonah feels oddly homesick. The house below is lit, waiting for him, Ally washing dishes or watching TV.

"Hey, Pops," he whispers.

It's easy for everything to disappear. It can be in rainy winter or on a hot summer day.

The lights at the house shine in the trees, winking in and out as he goes down. Inside, he passes jars of jelly and cans of soup and pulls a towel off a pile on the laundry table.

His hair sticks to his shoulders. It's a little lighter than Abel's, more like Aster's.

His eyes are Abel's dark blue though.

"Have a nice swim?" she asks.

The dishes are done and the TV's on. She's sitting with her legs curled up in a corner of the couch, watching him, nervously, reminding him of Aster.

"Pretty nice," he says. On his way down the hall he pauses and says, "Open me up a can a soup, will ya?"

"Okay."

"No tomato though."

She buys tomato anyway just like Aster used to. Growing up, he and Sissy ate it every day with baloney or cheese sandwiches; sometimes Aster put milk in it, sometimes noodles. He liked it with noodles best. He even liked it after Abel stared into his bowl one day and said, "There's gotta be more than this at the goddam store. Goddam chicken noodle even."

Lying down on the bed for a moment, Jonah stretches his arm into the air. The waves move on his skin. He yells, "What kind?"

"Split pea!"

In the kitchen she scoops the soup into a pot and stirs it slowly. Then the water goes on and off, a thump in the pipes. A cool, damp smell comes out of the drains sometimes. The house is old and the floor creaks with the memory of other footsteps.

"Hey."

Surprised, she looks over and smiles. "Your soup's ready."

He pours it into the thermos and gives her the pot and comes up behind her. She grows still and he puts his face in her neck. His hair is still damp, cool enough to make her shiver. His breath though is warm. His fingers brush her stomach as he straightens up.

"Better get some beer. Kurt's gonna be comin' over. Help me with those potholes."

"Oh good."

He grabs his thermos and bends down for a kiss. "See ya."

Fin stops at a motel with a pool in the courtyard. It is empty and the water ripples soundlessly. There's a lounge off the lobby he plans to go down to. Right now, lights move across the ceiling and he lies there, watching them. They make him feel lonely though and after a while he gets up.

On the freeway, streams of white and red lights go by, and next door a TV goes on.

His motel room is like any other. There are two glasses in paper and a cardboard bucket on top of the dresser, tiny bar soaps on either side of the sink, the smell of cleaner that goes with motels. His bag is on a chair under the window and he puts on another shirt, looking outside while he buttons it. White lights turn into red. The passage of the cars disturbs him for some reason. He feels uneasy and doesn't want to think about it, picks up his keys, and goes out for a drink.

At lunchtime Kurt jogs downstairs and throws his gloves in his locker. A couple other people come down too, Jonah stopping halfway.

"I'll see ya outside."

"Okay."

Kurt is going home. "Gettin' a stomachache," he told Chilburn. Actually, he plans to go to Mulligan's.

Outside, Gus stops him at the picnic table. "Will you think about it?"

"Askin' for a raise?" he murmurs.

"More of us the better."

A cigarette glows in the dark over by Jonah's pickup.

"Sure could use it."

He can see the cigarette move away. When he goes over, Jonah's leaning over the other side of the truck bed. There's a hint of a smile on his face.

"Any new news?"

He shrugs. "Just the usual."

"Nothin', you mean."

"Gus wants a raise."

Jonah laughs and picks a piece of tobacco off his tongue. "Don't we all."

"I wouldn't mind."

"I'm not sayin' I would either."

"You could pave that road a yours."

"Just fixin' it's good enough."

"Guess I'll see ya then."

Jonah nods and leans his weight back against the side of the truck. There's something in the way he does this that makes Kurt feel sorry for him. He almost wants to stay now and moves away slowly. When he reaches his car he looks back and sees Jonah flick his cigarette away and start over to the factory. Gus stops him and a minute later Kurt hears him laugh.

He feels better when he sees the bar. On Oly Way, the light of the sign is a bright blue. It is dark in the alley by Mulligan's though and he doesn't see Ray until he comes off the porch by the shop and nods at the bar.

"C'mon. Have a drink with me."

"Okay."

They sit at the counter instead of the table against the wall where Ray usually sits. "Just about to call it a night," Ray murmurs. He's watching Grace, his smile growing. "How ya doin', sweet pea?"

"Fine."

"Good. Couple on me."

She nods and moves away. She doesn't smile at Kurt either. He thinks maybe Ray's the reason. She pours their drinks and starts back over and Ray wipes his smile off with his thumb and looks sideways at Kurt.

"So how come you're out?"

"Sick."

He looks at the drinks Grace sets down, picks up his and says, "Good for what ails ya, I guess."

Fin is sitting on the side of the bed in his motel room and a girl is standing at the window, looking outside. He met her in the lounge downstairs.

"Sally."

She doesn't move at first. The light of the lamp on the dresser shines around her and he imagines her in sunlight, turning pink all over, his hands on her belly.

"I like the freeway at night."

"Me too," he says and pats at the bed, coaxing her over.

"All the lights going away," she adds softly, looking around at him. She catches his frown and cocks her head slightly. He smiles and leans back on his elbows, waiting for her. He likes the lights coming closer and his sense of friendliness in her fades a little.

"Do you like being here with me?"

She scratches at her neck, her hand falling and swinging at her side like a little girl's. "I guess."

He laughs. "You guess?"

"All the rooms are the same," she says.

"I guess."

She presses against his knees, looking down. "You guess?"

He cups her bottom and brings her up to him. Her dress is loose, slipping off of her and her face is luminous, ashy, like a ghost's. He rolls her over and she slips away, just fingers and lips. He smells leaves and imagines strawberries. A bowl on a counter, sticky and sweet, seeds on a girl's tongue, knees as pale as angel's wings.

Asleep, he feels waves rolling underneath him. Awake, he sees a gray-eyed girl disappear under a starless sky. Alone, he watches color grow, as soft blue as the pool outside. In a room below a toilet flushes and he imagines a man in a warm, messy room, a salesman, he thinks, padding sluggishly across the floor, yawning and scratching at a hairy belly, going out for coffee and Danish in a couple hours, walking happily back, about to go home, steam rising from his cup, eating in his room where he packs up a bundle of sales brochures into the pocket of his briefcase, ready to go, pats at his jacket pockets, looking for nothing in particular, swallowing the last of his coffee, lukewarm and sour.

The room smells of her.

Fin gets up and pulls on his pants. Small bulbs in the ceiling of the walkway light the hall. At the end, a soda machine glows in the dark and he scoops ice into a cardboard bucket and goes back the way he came. He doesn't really want the ice. It's just something to do.

3

◆ Potholes ◆

It's the same as on the first day Kurt saw her. She laughs and it's an airy sound. Then somebody else laughs too and says, "Anytime." Lying on his bed with the glow of the sun coming in, Kurt stares at the ceiling, waiting to hear her again. It's quiet for a moment though. Then her wind chimes ring, tiny little bell sounds, and he pictures her tapping them with her fingers. She's waiting for something and he gets up and pulls on his jeans. His shadow flickers on the walkway below when he comes outside, a part of the quiet, pulling her eyes up. She lives here without her little boy. At the moment she's alone at the bottom of the stairs near her open door. He always peeks in as he goes by and sees a shadowy blur surround her in a dimness he can't penetrate. Her wind chimes always sound sad and wistful. At the top of the stairs he stops and she is looking up with her cool blue eyes.

"Hey. How ya doin'?" he asks.

"Okay."

"Sure pretty weather."

She nods and it's then that the sound of her voice from a moment before brushes over him like soft warm air. He feels sleepy and slowly sits.

"Waitin' for somethin'?"

It seems to him she is. She rocks on her toes a little and taps at her wind chimes again, looking back up through the flickers of color that slowly spin like a top. She is always slow and willowy.

"My TV," she says and looks off the down the walkway because somebody else at the end of it says, "Up a little."

Then she smiles and backs up and Kurt looks too and sees a giant cardboard box on a dolly.

"Wait a sec." A man appears from behind the box and starts to back up.

Her smile grows. Kurt rises. She doesn't look at him again. She's all eyes for the TV in its giant box.

The man behind it is peering around the side as he goes, the man in front guiding him. "Couple more feet."

At her door, the dolly stops and the man behind it swipes at his face. "Hot out for this."

"I have some pop inside," says Joy.

"That'd be great. I'd appreciate that."

Then they follow her in, leaving her giant TV outside her door.

At Waylon's, Jonah takes a swallow of coffee and stands up. A screen door in back slams with a bang. Outside on the shady stoop, Agnes, Waylon's daughter, is watching her bare foot slowly scrape at the edge of a cement step. It itches and makes her curl her toes. She looks like her mother only sometimes. Her face is round like Mavis's used to be and her father's still is. In a minute she'll stop Jonah outside and he'll look at her and see a face without a real shape. His thumb might even leave an imprint. He'll imagine his was probably the same way at her age. All of that is before she says anything about Ira though. When she does, he'll stop thinking about her.

Now he's pushing money under his plate, swallowing the last of his coffee. There's a dimness in the air that makes everything fuzzy, as dusty looking as the air smells. A blue Formica counter stretches away from the door, behind it an open kitchen area that leads to a storage room with a cooktop in back. The rest of the market is shelving and a large refrigerator unit beside a back door to the post office.

Orly is straddling a donut tray, palms flat on the counter.

"Are these fresh?" he asks.

"Every night," answers Waylon.

"This is morning," Orly reminds him.

Outside, on the stoop, Agnes scrapes at the dusty step while her boyfriend, Doug, stares at the groceries in the trunk of his car. He got this job because he drives an old Plymouth with a good-sized trunk. Waylon doesn't want the groceries in the back of a pickup where the wind blows. She scrapes at her other foot and looks back inside. Waylon's shadow fills the kitchen doorway.

"Got another box in here."

"Okay."

She rocks slightly as Doug brushes up against her on his way inside. Her arm is suddenly warm and she fills up with air, about to burst, and spots her brush on the seat of Doug's car. With a sigh she goes over. Her hair is wooly, wheat and honey, crackling like fire as she brushes it. Doug comes out with the other box and stares at her until her arm falls and swings at her side. He puts the box in the trunk and slams the lid down.

"Careful with those groceries!" Waylon bellows.

"I am careful!"

His face reddens. He is staring at her again. She isn't sure he always likes her. He looks at her sometimes as if she's in his way, stopping him from something.

"We better go," he tells her, but then she sees Jonah and says, "Wait a minute."

"What for?"

"So I can tell 'im."

She tosses her brush inside and Doug goes over to his door, opens it, puts his foot on the bottom rim, and stares at her over the roof. She isn't sure he won't leave without her. She looks away slowly, aware of him standing there motionlessly, and a moment later he moves, but only to put his elbow on the roof, lean sideways and watch her.

Jonah's almost at his pickup. She half runs, stops and puts her fingers in her back pockets.

"Hey, mister."

He stops too and looks over. She squints at him against the sun and her face is even rounder. His eyes aren't friendly or even interested. He just stares at her, beginning to frown. She looks at the tattoos under his rolled up sleeves, a split knuckle that she sees as he switches his keys to his other hand. His frown is growing.

"What?"

She scoots back a little and moves her elbow at Doug, fingers still in her back pockets. "On our deliveries yesterday, Ira Clivvikker asked us to ask you to go see 'im."

"Ira?"

She nods and backs up again and he stares at her bare feet with a frown. She blushes, scoots one foot over the other until his eyes come back up. Then she says, "I guess that's all," and turns away so quickly she doesn't see him nod.

Still leaning sideways against his car, Doug stares at him, but Jonah is already getting into his pickup. He starts it, but just sits inside for a while, one foot outside, staring through the windshield.

Away from the shade the sun shines down on dry rock and dusty bushes. At the bottom of a steep drop, a river goes by, only sound under the green cover. In other places it comes into sight, white and fast, other times dark and almost motionless. Below, it sounds fasts. There are birds in the bushes, flowers blooming. Fin's car is in the shade of a tree by a reddish boulder. The mountain is made up of boulders, some casting oblongs of shadow below. Cool and heat are clearly separate. His shirt is open and he rubs his thumb over a cross on his chest. In a picture he found in a shoebox at home, he saw the gray-eyed girl from his dream standing in a pair of denim overalls and a white sweater by a Christmas tree with a cross just like his.

After a moment he bends down and slips a finger underneath a flower. It has a faint dampness to it.

A sweet pea.

Her TV is on. A while ago, the same man Kurt heard the first time said, "Anytime," just like he did before; then came the sound of the empty dolly rattling off down the walkway. A moment later the TV went on. He sees its light on the side wall as he passes. A couple of other people have theirs on too.

TVs make him feel lonely when he's alone.

As he drives by the giant bowling pin, he ducks to look up at it through his windshield. It's almost shadowless now.

At Ira's Jonah knocks impatiently. Something about Ira always irritates him. He'd like never to see Ira again, never see his beat up old trailer in the meadow again. His feelings don't make a lot of sense to him. Ira never did anything to him. He thinks Ira even liked him up until the day he accused Jonah of breaking into his trailer. Then he came at him at Orly's, jabbing a finger at him, eyes filled with hurt.

"I hope you go to jail! I hope you spend the rest of your life in jail!"

But it was Ira who came over to him on his first day at the factory eight years later and said, "Welcome back, Jonah. Good to have you home."

He remembers the feel of the heat in his face, the anger that came out of nowhere.

Abel didn't like Ira either, said it outright almost every time they went by Ira's trailer. "Man's a damn fool."

Abel worked with him too though, so maybe there was a reason for his opinion. Maybe it was because Ira always liked him anyway.

After Jonah knocks, he waits, but Ira doesn't answer.

"C'mon, Ira. You wanna see me or not?"

Ira's car is there, sinking in the mud. He knocks again and goes inside. Ira's lying on his cot with a bottle of gin beside him. His curtains are pillowcases, stirring gently. Jonah jostles the cot with his foot.

"C'mon, Ira. I don't have all day."

His boot leaves a smear of mud on a sheet and he sits down with a sudden sigh.

The diner's on stilts covered by trellises covered by honeysuckle. There's a red and white checked awning over the front porch, shading the windows. Inside, tables are covered by white paper tablecloths and plastic carnations in white vases between the salt and pepper shakers. A woman in jeans and a white blouse points to a table and Fin drops onto a chair, stretching his legs out, feeling the cool drafts of air blow over him. His car outside is shining in the sun.

Through the window he moves his eyes across all the things he might have seen before if he ever came this way. This place, the cut out on the other side of the road, red painted garbage cans under oak and pine trees, two stone pillars with a driveway curving back to a white Victorian called Oak Glen Mansion. Only a corner of the house is visible, the rest obscured by oaks and eucalyptus. Under these trees, a different kind of cool, the singing of insects.

"Water?"

The woman in jeans and white blouse is standing over him, a pitcher in one hand, a menu under her arm.

"Please."

She pours, then hands him the menu. "Just wave me over."

"Okay."

He doesn't at first sense emptiness when he tries to remember. He feels walls pushing outward and up, squeezing out any thought at all. Then there is emptiness and he flounders in the dark, sensing things all around him, amorphous, unfriendly, remorseless things swimming with faraway dots of light that lure him, shimmers that attract but swim in a foggy distance, too far away to reach.

Even here, in the cool air, listening to the sound of silverware dropping into plastic bins, a door in back clapping shut, he feels the prickling of sweat on his skin.

He lied to Ginny about his memory. He cares about it all the time.

On a ridge of gravel where the weeds are sparse and tough, a white jeep slows and stops. There are gold stars on its doors and a light bar on its roof. The name of the man inside is Cotter Paine and he knew Ira even before he became sheriff.

"I'll be votin' for ya," said Ira one day with a quick wink as if that meant they were friends.

Sitting there, Cotter puts his arms on top of the steering wheel and looks outside.

It wasn't always called Ira's meadow. A long time ago Samuel Hollycock came here with Ivy, his wife, and John and Ellie Sparrow. They skipped by that meadow with its openness and calm. It didn't have any name and nobody lived there. Samuel Hollycock lived up above the meadow in the same house Jonah lives in and after Samuel died, Job cut down some of the firs and now there's sun that was never there before. Samuel made Ivy her pond, but she never swam in it. According to Orly, John Sparrow was really Job's father. According to Samuel, Ivy and John ran away together. John's wife used to come to Ira's meadow with its mirror-like pools of water and look for shadows under the surface.

In springtime, it's all weeds and pink and purple flowers.

At the trailer, Cotter knocks and waits. He thinks he can hear him and leans against the door.

"Ira? Are you in there?" He's sure he is. A car goes by and he knocks again, beginning to worry. "Ira. It's Cotter."

A pillowcase flutters in a window. Cotter peers through the glass. Sunshine drifts in, disappears as the pillowcases settle back again.

"I'm comin' in," he says and opens the door.

Ira doesn't say anything and Cotter stares at the pillowcases over the windows, white with red roses. They swell and settle in the breeze, Ira lying underneath. Cotter sighs then and pulls a hand down his face. Ira's dead, with a bottle in his arms. He has on gray slacks and a tee-shirt and his feet are bare. His hair is the color of mud, thin and stringy. His pants are unbuttoned and his tee-shirt pulls across his belly. Otherwise he's as skinny as he always was. Sunshine struggles in under the blowing pillowcases again. The carpet and counters are bright orange. There's a couch against a wall and benches around a table, two stools with green and orange seats. A stool by Ira's cot, mud on the carpet underneath. Cotter sighs, looking down at him again.

"Damn, Ira."

'TIMMONS. Pop. 24.' It appears suddenly. Around a curve all the scrubby trees disappear. It's dry and almost empty on either side of the road. After the Timmons sign, another says, 'WELCOME! Gas.' He turns in and rolls up to the pumps.

At a house beside the station, a door opens, slams shut, and then a boy in the mini-mart comes out, hands in his pockets, walking slowly. At Fin's car, he stops and nods. "Sweet."

"Thanks."

It's almost cool here under the overhang. The sky is deep blue, clouds puffy white.

"Windows too?"

"Sure."

"Warmin' up," says the boy, shaking drops of sudsy water on the pavement.

"Sure is."

"Soda machine inside."

"Thanks. I think I will."

A fan on the counter is blowing warm air. Outside again, he walks around slowly, drinking his soda, stopping at the edge of the lot where thistles start growing in the dusty ground. A laundry wheel next door is creaking in the sudden, hot breeze. There's another house down the road with a pickup in the gravel driveway, a chain link fence around the yard, nothing else.

"Pretty small town," he says.

The boy points at the house with the laundry wheel. "My house." Then at the house across the street: "My sister an' her husband's house. The minute I'm eighteen, I'm outta here."

"College?"

"Army."

"Good luck."

"Thanks."

He is pocketing Fin's money, heading back inside. Fin looks again at the solitary houses, feels just a pleasant buffeting from the warm, dusty wind.

Outside of weeds there's only soggy, weepy mud. A soft light rolls over the weeds like green waves. On every gust comes a dark, damp smell.

"C'mon over, Tom."

On a rim of gravel, feeling a windy tug, Tom's gaze skims over stomped down blades of green and weepy mud until it reaches Ira's trailer where Cotter is standing in the open doorway, watching him. "How'd you get over there?"

"Walked."

"On that?"

"You can do it."

There are still prints in the mud that belonged to Ira. On cold nights he'd come out on a whim, or out of a dream, or a memory, only to tug free with an odd restlessness and go back in again. The holes in the mud don't tell anything about him.

"Will you look at this?" says Tom, looking unhappily at his shoes.

"Got some mud on 'um."

Tom squints again, tiny crow's feet fanning out. "You think?"

"It'll wash off, Tom."

Tom climbs up on a step and scrapes the muck off on the edge. Ira's pillowcases are still blowing. It is cool and shady inside, and there's a cardboard box on the orange couch.

"You look in the box?" asks Tom.

"Cookies an' jelly."

He stomps off more mud. "Cookies, huh?"

"Cookies."

Oreos were Ira's favorite. In summer he used to sit on the metal doorstep with a bowlful. After a while he didn't go out so much, usually ate them out of the package with his gin and watched TV on the little set he put on the kitchen counter. Ira only drank after he got sick, struck by the ridiculousness of life to die of liver cancer when he never drank before. Drinking helped him to sleep though, and he liked gin's slightly piney odor.

"It's kind of like Pine Sol," he explained to Cotter, who gave him a slow and appreciative smile in return.

"I don't think I've heard a fitter description."

Inside the trailer, Tom sees the pancake mix Ira didn't open and a jar of jelly he did. Outside again, he sits on the top step the same way Ira used to and says, "Too bad."

Cotter nods. "Yes, it is."

He looks at the shadows growing on the grasses and the darkness of the trees and feels the coolness coming on. Ira died alone alongside people rushing by every day. At night, there is only pitch dark, distant lights hidden in the thickness of the firs. Nobody would have seen who broke into Ira's trailer all those years ago. Ira was convinced it was Jonah, and Cotter always thought so too. Ira didn't lose much, mostly just the ring that was his wife's.

Cotter looks down at the same time Tom looks up and says, "Ira had a wife, I heard."

Cotter nods again. "I heard that too."

The sound of the car comes from a long way away. It grows loud and faint and then loud again.

Jonah gets up slowly. The sun's on the other side of the house and he can see the reflection of his face in the window as he looks outside, waiting for the car to appear. Abel never liked people coming up to the house either. He was suspicious of everybody. Jonah remembered catching that suspicious stare of his sometimes too.

"Wha'da'ya thinkin' about, Jojo?"

"Nothin'."

"You sure about that?"

"Yeah."

"You ain't sure."

In the face in the window he sees eyes suddenly like Clover's—bottomless, eyes he's only seen in pictures, pictures where Job is hiding his smile behind his hands, snickering beside Clover's big and toothy grin. This place didn't scare her or cover her in darkness. In her pictures she was always happy, and when Jonah looks at them, he looks with Abel's probing stare.

"Whadda ya thinkin' about, Grandma?"

His own spurts of happiness unnerve him, never last.

Outside, Kurt pulls to a stop and Jonah carries a green and white cooler over to the pickup. With a twist, he swings it up onto the back of the dropped tailgate. Kurt's mouth starts to open, but Jonah cuts him off angrily.

"That new guy's a total fuckup."

"Oh, yeah?"

"I have to follow 'im around, redo everything he does."

"You're trainin' 'im."

"Wes should be fuckin' trainin' 'im."

"Have a beer," says Kurt, trying to cool him down.

"In a minute."

The cooler balances on an angle between the side of the bed and a pile of gravel. Kurt looks up at the sun. It's low, beginning to cool. "Joy's got a big TV," he says.

Jonah looks at him, almost expectantly, waiting for something else that will make sense of that. It doesn't come though and he rolls his eyes a little and says, "Christ, you're weird."

His truck door slams. Kurt gets in too and says, "You just need a night off."

"Yeah. About that—"

"I think I feel another sick day comin' on."

"Take some Pepto."

Kurt leans his head back against the warm glass, used to Jonah's moods. It is cool under the firs, and shadows play across the windshield as the pickup rolls around the curves. This is the one place Jonah drives slowly, almost reverently. At the bottom of the road where the firs thin out, the sun is shining down in yellow patches. Opening a beer, Jonah takes a swallow, sets the bottle on the rim of the truck bed and pulls his shirt off, swiping under his arms with it. Then he takes another swallow and pulls a shovel out of the back of the truck. Kurt takes his shirt off too and catches the shovel Jonah tosses to him.

"Maybe we should back up," Kurt suggests.

The pickup's in the road and he thinks he can hear a car coming. The sound of it fades in and out.

"I left room."

In the back of the pickup, Jonah starts shoveling gravel, tossing it over the side. The sound of the crunch and slush of metal and gravel fills the air. A car appears, but it's only Ally's, sliding along the curve of the driveway. Jonah leans on his shovel, breathing heavily. Sweat is dampening the top of his jeans. Kurt is leaning down to wave through Ally's window.

"How you doin', Ally?"

She waves back, accelerating away. Jonah's eyes follow her for a space, then he jumps down and helps Kurt fill the pot holes, enjoying the coolness as the sun starts to set. A faint breeze stirs sometimes and the sunlit sky above the trees starts to turn pale.

In the gray light, Jonah sits in the open door of the truck with a beer, Kurt on the rim with his. A low rumble down the road grows louder, fades out, grows louder again.

"Not bad," says Kurt, referring to the pot holes.

"Passable."

Through the patchy light a car approaches, almost invisible in the pallor. Kurt whistles. A '68 Chevelle, black with white stripes down its hood, almost hugging the pavement. Jonah ignores it, drinking his beer. The car slows as it goes by, speeds back up.

"You see," says Jonah, tossing his bottle in a bush. "I left room."

Ira's empty cot is the kind of thing Cotter won't forget, or the yellow dingy sheets, or the pillow with blue stitching, all lying in wait. Alone, he stands by his car and looks at the cinderblocks in the weeds. He can hear the rattle of Ira's door. With a sigh, he goes down to shove with his boot at a chunk of cement. It raises up on its side, a patch of mud in the weeds like a fresh grave. He stoops and the stink rises, the block in his hands cold and clammy like the bottom of a lake. He drops it on the metal stair by the door and goes away.

4

◆ Townies ◆

At night, the river sounds soft and faraway. In the daytime, it is almost soundless, though loud at Ira's where Jonah sat earlier, waiting for Ira to wake up while a cool, damp air blew at the pillowcases.

On the trailer wall at the head of Ira's bed was a picture of a trout in colored rocks Ira glued to a readymade pattern. Before that, the picture hanging over Ira's bed was a paint-by-numbers of a mountain by a lake that he threw out the trailer door when he came home and found all his drawers open and the little cash he had and his wife's ring gone. The box he kept her ring in was on a shelf in his little closet. The box was open on his bed and the paint-by-numbers was hanging sideways. He threw it outside with his pillow and blankets and the box that didn't matter anymore. This happened a couple of days before Christmas and he threw away the little fake Christmas tree he put on top of the Formica dining table too. All of the things he threw out he replaced later on though, one by one. The day after Ira did this, Cotter came in to see Jonah at Orly's and took him into the auto bay where it was just as cold as being outside and they could see their breaths. Jonah stomped his feet a little and Cotter said, "Proud of yourself?"

After that Jonah stopped moving, stared a moment and then looked outside and said, "I dunno what you mean."

"You know. Ira was robbed last night an' I think you did it."

He could hear the creak of Cotter's leather jacket and see the lights of Waylon's Christmas tree in the market window.

"So arrest me."

Cotter rolled his shoulders back a little, hands in his pockets. "Do you want me to?"

Jonah looked at him again and said, "Doesn't matter. You can't or you would."

"Not for Ira's, no."

"Not for anything."

There was anger and dislike in Jonah's eyes and a sudden amusement in Cotter's. Cotter moved in closer and Jonah's body grew tense, a flush rising up his neck. He waited, feeling the small pocked wounds in his face grow hot despite the cold. He couldn't resist. "Well? Are you going to or not?"

"I guarantee it," said Cotter. "Just not today."

Then he walked outside, crossing over to Waylon's. Jonah stayed in the dark until he disappeared inside. When he came out of the auto bay, he saw Orly in the office door, chewing gently on a toothpick.

Jonah always thought of Orly as being a lot older than he was, but he wasn't really. He was only thirty-five then. His hair was a wispy brown and his eyes were hard for somebody nobody thought was hard. He'd only been in town for about six years, bought the gas station from his mother's uncle. He was a fixture in town anyway, his history oddly intermingled with a history he didn't share; but all the hidden stories of the town he knew, and there was a solidity about him that made others believe that he had always been there and always would be. Jonah always thought there was something not nice about him underneath, something that made them alike.

"I didn't do it," he said and Orly nodded. "I believe you."

At home he looks out into the dark where he knows Ira's meadow is, remembering the paint-by-numbers picture and the Christmas tree and the lights Ira always hung up along the edge of the trailer's roof. Beside him on the porch, Kurt is lying down with a bottle of beer resting on his belly, staring up into the dim starlight. After a moment, Jonah glances sideways at him and says, "I saw Fin today."

Surprise makes Kurt bolt up, almost spilling his beer. He pushes back against the porch rail, facing Jonah. "You're just telling me?"

"No big deal."

"Where?"

"Down below. That sweet lookin' car goin' by."

"Are you kiddin'?"

"No."

"How come you didn't say anything?"

"I dunno. Guess I had to think about it."

"Think about what?"

Jonah shrugs. The way he tells it, Fin ran off and left Sissy alone when she was pregnant. The timing for that is off though, because Fin didn't leave town until he got the first of his money from his trust fund. It's just the way Jonah feels and maybe believes now. Kurt doesn't know why they stopped being friends. In some ways, Jonah likes to talk; in other ways, he never says anything at all.

"Weird name," Kurt comments, opening another beer.

Jonah nods. He asked Fin about it once.

"My mom picked it," Fin said.

"I figured that. I mean where'd she get it?"

"I dunno."

Jonah never thought Dahlia was sane. He figured that was the explanation for her. She didn't have to go out in the world and could be any way she wanted to be. She didn't look at Jonah unkindly, maybe even with a little curiosity, but she didn't look at Fin with anything in her eyes. Fin wasn't there, at all; just a bit of the dark that was the whole darkness of that house. The only window with its curtains open was at the top of the hall upstairs where it grew silver at dusk.

Dahlia didn't want Fin. A bleakness came over her as her stomach grew. The life she had, her disappearances into fir and spruce, quiet, lonely forays that stilled and calmed her, the beckoning lights at home welcoming her back to Gale would be gone. She heard cries from the basinet and her head rang with noise. She sat in the dark and tried to hear nothing. The emptiness inside her came out in silent almost unnoticed tears. Then one day Gale picked the baby up and gave him to her and said, "What do you want to name him?"

She looked confused.

"Do you want to name him Gale?"

The baby lay in the hollow of her lap, arms akimbo, looking like wings to her and that's when she said, "Finch."

On the porch with Kurt, Jonah stretches out his legs and says, "Middle name's Galeson."

"Sounds rich."

Jonah's laugh floats up a little. He's sitting with his head back against the screen door and Kurt looks up too, seeing all the stars above the smudge of firs.

"I knew a girl named Starling once."

"That's a good name."

"Angeline's even better," he says suddenly. "I heard that someplace. That's a real good name."

Jonah nods and picks a mostly empty pack of cigarettes up off the porch floor. He shakes one out and lights it.

"You're supposed to quit."

"I can't."

Kurt finishes his beer and gets up. "Well, anyway, think about it."

"Quittin'?"

"Angeline."

"Angeline," he murmurs and rests an arm over his knee, swinging his half empty bottle.

"That's a good name," says Kurt.

"Not bad," he agrees. His smoke makes a wispy gray cloud in the dark. "Thanks for helpin'," he says when Kurt steps off the porch.

"Thank Ally for dinner."

He nods again and then sits there, waiting for Kurt to go. After a while, he stubs out his cigarette and gets up. All he can see are the stars now, the firs are as dark as the sky. He stays where he is, opens another beer, listens to the sound of the TV inside.

"Angeline," he whispers.

She won't like it. He can picture her smile though, a little worried that he likes it, willing to do anything to make him happy.

He lights another cigarette and stares at the rim of the door, the grayish light inside. She's waiting for him to come in, sitting with her legs underneath her, her fingers holding onto one of her ankles and he backs up, still staring at the door, only looking sideways when the light in the living room window comes into view. He feels tense all of a sudden, just at the thought of her on the couch with the worry he always sees in her smile and he moves quietly away. She can hear him on the gravel anyway though and sits in stillness.

This is where Clover fell and died, surprising Job forever. In his dreams he would see her in her white nightgown, smiling her toothy smile. Underneath the gown she was warm and pliant and welcoming. On the kitchen windowsill is a cowbell Job gave to her one day. He came in and raised it up so she could see it, then set it down on the kitchen counter with a strange emphasis. After he went by her down the hall, she waited a moment, then picked it up and followed him into the bedroom where he already had his pants off and was lying on the bed with one arm under his head. One of his eyes came open when he heard her.

Later, he came back out into the kitchen with a hand down his shorts and shook his head at her. She was standing in a puddle of water she splashed out of the sink, wiping the dishes with a soggy towel while humming to herself. Seeing the cowbell on the sill he began to snicker and Clover looked over with a grin.

"Don't get it, do you?"

And then he yanked open her drawer of candy and threw handfuls into the soapy sink. "Eat that, you cow."

The sign on the bar is glowing into the sky. A plastic lantern in the gravelly weeds shines up onto Ray's sign. He changed the name of the shop to Wycowski's. When it was Aaron Toler's it was called Reliance Auto Parts.

Inside the shop, Ray finishes a beer, sets it in the sink and switches off the back light.

At first the idea of buying this place made him angry. All he wanted was the money Aaron owed him.

"You know how much you're into me for?" he told Aaron. "An' now you want me to add another fifty on top?"

"It's worth triple that!"

"Fuck, Aaron. Are you nuts? I don't have that kinda dough lyin' around." Although he could sell his house. But he didn't want to. "I like workin' on my bikes, bro."

"Just sell it off again."

"You sell it an' gimme my money. No damn Caspar's around here anyway."

Aaron knew Ray loved hotdogs because Ray made a point of telling everybody he met. "Caspar's. Best in the world."

He had a friend named Ed, who always countered, "White Castle's, Ray."

"White Castle's are hamburgers, Ed."

Aaron thought he heard a tone in Ray's voice that made him hopeful though. There were other people who wanted money from him too.

"I sympathize," said Ray, at that point not giving in much.

Aaron built the shop up from the little white house with a picket fence he tore down to a building he added on beside it. The building is metal, painted white like the little house, with corrugated doors that roll open on casters.

"Pretty good place to eat in Enders," said Aaron. "Giant Dogs. An' they mean it too."

"Not Caspar's."

The thing with Ray though was that he was always looking at things and people, seeing the ways he could fit in, make a place his. He was always at home even if he didn't feel it.

Aaron said, "I could introduce you to some people."

"What people?"

"Dude named Will."

"Why do I wanna meet a dude named Will?"

"Dealer."

"Nothin' to me. I don't deal.'

To Ray, he's not in the business because "weed's just weed, an' pretty much legal nowadays anyway," even though he somehow managed to slip across that line he drew without any real struggle a long time ago, and guns are "everybody's fuckin' right to carry." He believed this without ever thinking of it as his whole life. How it mostly became that, he isn't sure. Working legitimizes him and he has always had a job.

"This'll be your business," said Aaron.

"I'll tell you what," said Ray, after a moment. "I will try out this Giant Dogs place."

Afterwards, they stopped at a bar called the Jack of Clubs, and later Ray realized that Miri must have been working there that night, and it struck him as odd that he didn't notice her, and not altogether a good omen.

On the porch, Ray watches a tiny red ember by the side of a pickup glow and fade, listening to the weeds and rolling sore knuckles against a rough palm, pain in his bones. Across the street by the pickup the red ember erupts in a spray of sparks. Ray comes down the rest of the steps.

"How you doin', bub?"

"Okay," says Jonah.

It is noisy inside the bar, the air stuffy, faces amiably soft in the dull light. Dropping his jacket over a chair, Ray sits down, rubbing his eyes with his fingertips. The door on the street side opens without a breath of fresh air. He drops his fingers, stretches out his legs.

"I don't see you out too much," he says.

"Wife."

His eyes rise in a commiserating smile, fingers knotting up again. His father, Wayne, was the same way, arthritic early, popping swollen knuckles with a grimace. He dropped tools with angry curses until Ray started to help him and Wayne taught him everything he knew about cars. Before Wayne left, there was a burnt orange Camaro in the oil-spotted driveway, and for a while his mother used to sit on a chair in the driveway and watch them work, elbow braced on her forearm, unlit cigarette in her fingers. After Wayne left, Irene sold the Camaro and Ray remembered feeling a sour anger he didn't know who he was feeling it for. Wayne didn't leave Irene with much of anything, but her friend, Marie said, "You are so lucky, Ray, to have such an upbeat mom in spite of everything."

Then other people began to describe her that way too. That Irene, always upbeat.

He drums his fingers on the edge of the table, unswollen fingers, straight, strong fingers. The pain is a phantom, haunting his nerve endings, teasing him with its random appearance. Will noticed it, saw him sitting with white knuckled fists on his knees one day and said, "You okay, man? Looks like you hurt."

Will smiled and Ray smiled too. Ray knew that Will liked to think that he liked people.

"Cuz I have somethin' for that," Will added.

"What?"

"Oxy."

"Can't. Got any aspirin?"

Will shrugged but got up and came back with a bottle. After he swallowed a few, he looked back at Will, who was looking at him curiously, smiling quizzically at Ray's fingers.

"I busted 'um on a wall," he said.

"What for?"

The minute Ray said it, he regretted saying it, and laughed to defuse his annoyance. "I dunno. Tanked probably."

At the bar he says, "Sure could use a drink," and Grace gives him a frown as she looks down at him.

"I'm right here, Ray."

"How ya doin', sweet pea?"

"Fine." The street side door opens up and Ray pushes out a chair with his boot. "The usual?" asks Grace.

"Yeah. An' a beer for Craig here."

The man named Craig stops with a deer-in-the-headlights look. He seems bewildered, almost surprised to find himself where he is. Ray nudges his chair. "Sit down."

After he does, he looks at Ray and says, "I was just...just...just...you know...."

Ray shakes his head. "Not really."

Jonah is giving him a slightly bemused scowl. Ray has heard Craig talk before, didn't even know that he ever couldn't. The stammer came out of nowhere one day and surprised Ray into asking, "You stoned, man?"

Craig blushed and said, "I don't...don't...I don't—"

"Use drugs," finished his cousin.

"Then what's wrong with him?"

"Nothing."

He found out later that something bad happened to him when he was a little boy and it started then, but Ray could never figure out Craig's pattern. It wasn't sunshine or moonlight, indoors or outdoors, friends or strangers, beer or coffee. Craig could talk about a sale on socks and stumble over free pizza, go on for days about a girl he liked and choke up over a bad day at work.

Usually Ray likes Craig, but other times he won't offer any help. Tonight, he waits, relaxing with his bourbon, finally rolling his head against the back of his chair to say, "Wonderin' what?"

"Oh...you know...about...about my parts...."

"I got 'um. Go over with you in a bit. Quarter the price you were gonna pay."

Craig's startled looking eyes brighten and shine. "Thanks, Ray."

"Don't mention it."

After last call, Ray takes him to the shop and opens the door on casters, flipping on a light that spills out on the gravel and rims the blades of weeds with silver. Ringing up Craig's purchase, Ray listens to the slightly mournful sound of the cars driving away. The fading engines leave an echoing emptiness. After Craig leaves, he turns off the lights and stands in the dark open doorway for a moment. Across the way, the weeds in the lot make a sound in the breeze that seems to go forever.

Dreaming of a pond as blue as a marble, Jonah swims with orange and blue and purple fish and blows out orange and blue and purple bubbles.

Then the sun pours in where he's lying on the seat of his pickup. At his windows, there's a sunny blue sky, outside a white half-dome roof at Candi's with all the sparkle of glass and metal below and Kurt's giant bowling pin in pure white with its giant eclipse of a shadow. He sits up and sees its cool, dark shape on the road. It wavers and looks like water, reminds him of Ivy's and home and Ally. He didn't feel like going home last night and parked on Kurt's street instead. He doesn't feel like doing anything now either, but after a moment he picks an empty bottle off the floor and walks over to Candi's for a cup of coffee.

The counter and most of the booths are full. He goes straight to the cash register and takes a box of matches out of a basket on the glass counter top.

Outside, he stops to sip his coffee, then walks back to his pickup and sets his cup on the dashboard. Outside of town, the sunlight is softer and pale; it thins and cools as it comes through the firs. He passes Ira's, sunlit and peaceful, and sees Agnes looking back as she walks, feet bare, sandals swinging in her fingers, wooly, honey hair. He pulls over and stops.

"Wanna ride?"

At dusk, Kurt liked to come out and sit on the steps. All the soft, gray shadows slowly emerged and gently rose. In the courtyard, dark bird shapes, almost like little statues. In the daytime, occasional noise, but almost always quiet at dusk, until one day by the big planter below there was a birdbath and ceramic saucers full of seeds and peanuts, and a flutter of wings with cheeps and chirps the whole time he sat there.

And now there's a parakeet at Joy's. It sits on a brass hoop inside a yellow and white cage in her living room by her new big TV.

Lying on his bed, he stares at the ceiling.

It's her with all the birds outside. Of course, Joy can have only good things around her.

TVs.

Parakeets.

All the doves that coo and coo....

At the lunch counter, Orly sips his coffee, looks at Jonah, sips again and stares casually at the shiny surface of the ice cream machine. Jonah is eating eggs and potatoes, sitting with his arm on the counter, hunching over his plate, guarding it, Orly knows. He looks at the tattoos on Jonah's arms, reminders of years he'll never talk about. Between sips of coffee, Orly says, "You see anybody at Ira's?"

"Why would I see anybody at Ira's?"

There's a tone though. Jonah scoops up another forkful of food, looking sideways at Orly while he chews.

"I hear 'e died last night."

Orly felt something ease in him when he found out Ira died. He was pretty sure Ira felt that same ease.

Jonah finishes chewing, stares at the countertop, thinking for a moment before he looks back at Orly and says, "No way."

Waylon approaches with the coffee pot, agreeing with Orly. "That's what I heard."

"Are you sure?" asks Jonah, still looking at Orly.

"Sure enough."

"I just delivered a box of groceries too," says Waylon. "Must've all gone to waste."

It sat on the orange couch, a box of Sugar Pops on the counter, a bowl in the sink, floral pillowcases blowing on a soft, sunny day, a picture of a trout in tiny rocks.

Jonah pushes off his stool, almost angrily, dropping a ten dollar bill on the counter. "I don't believe it. I don't think you know anything for sure."

Orly stares at the slam of the door and then looks back at Waylon with raised eyebrows.

"Prickly."

Orly didn't really have a job for Jonah when he hired him. He wasn't looking for anybody. His customers were steady, coming and going by on the road every day, but he was never busy. He spent half the day at Waylon's and closed up for all of Sunday. He hired Jonah because when he came looking for a job, he had a bruised jaw and a bruise on his temple that was oozing into his eye socket.

"Who hit you?"

"Nobody."

"That so?"

"Yeah. That's so."

Orly considered him, shoved his tongue against the inside of his jaw as if he felt sympathy pains and said, "Well, you have no car so you don't need gas."

"I need a job."

"After school?"

"I quit school."

"Quit? Why?"

Uncertainty filled Jonah's eyes. Orly could see he didn't know how to answer. Then there was anger, embarrassment.

"Look. I just need a job. I don't need to tell you anything."

"Well, you need to tell me a little bit. Like how old you are."

"Sixteen."

"What kind of hours are you looking for?"

"Anything you want."

"You can't walk. That's not reliable."

"My dad'll drop me."

He had no intention of hiring him, but the questions began to rope him in, the curious pain in his jaw, the desperation just under the surface of Jonah's eyes, a dislike of Abel that gave him a sour stomach the first time he saw him. He stood looking into Abel's younger face, the same eyes, angry and hostile, thinking no good could come of him, and then he said, "I guess I could try you out."

Needles blow across the asphalt and make no sound. They grow still and then move in fits and starts again.

At his pickup, Jonah slides halfway in and stops. Agnes is sitting on the back stoop with a can of tomato juice, looking down at her feet. Mavis was all movement, her stillness abeyance. She looked up and out and faraway. He could sense her, see her floating off like a lonely cloud.

He drops an arm through his open window. "Waitin' for somebody?"

Agnes glances up, pulling her feet in. "No."

"Just sittin'?"

She nods and squeezes her ankles.

"Wish I had nothin' to do."

"I'm doing something."

"I dunno," he says, closing his door. "Looks like you're just sittin' to me."

She shrugs and looks down at her feet again.

"See ya, Agnes."

"Bye," she says without looking up.

It's quiet and still out. The only sound is a faraway engine. A river rolls out of the mountains above Sandorville and passes Ira's meadow, curving away from Jonah's, and meandering by Acropolis. Near Ira's, there's a stretch of the river filled with boulders and the currents hitch up in frothy furls before flowing away again. On a windless day, the sound is the sound of the wind on a windy day, a rustling of hushed whispers.

At home Jonah can hear the sound of the river through his open window, breathless warnings that don't do him any good. He stays in his warm truck, watching Cotter emerge from the empty garage. He didn't come out right away. Jonah saw him in there, saw his eyes on the rays of light straining through the slats of the roof. Outside, Ally's geraniums are blooming. There are tee-shirts and towels on the clothesline. Jonah can imagine the warm, sunny smell. In winter, the light up here is diffuse, pale, cool beams emerging from the firs. Jonah remembers one Christmas, though, years ago, when the sky took on a strange aluminum cast, and there were paper snowflakes in the living room window.

The warmth of the pickup is making him sluggish, but he forces himself to move after a moment, gesturing Cotter over to the house. The service porch is dark and cool. There are a pair of women's shoes just inside the door, a pair of flip-flops. The walls are covered with shelves, canned goods, boxes.

"C'mon in. I need a beer."

Inside, there's a cowbell on the windowsill with sprigs of yellow through its hasp.

"You want one?" asks Jonah, holding a bottle up over the top of the refrigerator door.

"No thanks. Early for me."

"I keep forgettin'. Workin' nights screws you up."

He rests against the counter and pops the cap off. Cotter sits down in the dim, gray light. In a vase beside the cowbell are pink and red geraniums.

"I saw you pull up at Ira's after I left," says Jonah, leaning up against the sink, crossing his legs at the ankle. His eyes are down, staring thoughtfully at the floor. Cotter sits quietly. "Orly says 'e's dead."

"Yes."

"I didn't even talk to 'im. I just sat there waiting for him to wake up, but 'e didn't."

"Why were you there?"

"Waylon's kid. Said Ira asked to see me. I almost didn't go."

"Why did you?"

"I couldn't help it. I was curious." He shifts his weight, recrosses his ankles, looking up at Cotter. "I swear if I thought anything was wrong...."

"I know."

He keeps seeing Ira's curtains blowing in and out, and that picture of the fish on the wall.

"I feel bad."

"Ira knew."

Jonah thinks about that, buying Oreos anyway, just in case. Ira didn't want to die, of course. Maybe he wasn't really sorry though, living alone. He has a feeling though that Ira was already dead and just took his time in realizing it. Occasionally, when he was little, Jonah used to dream that he died but could still walk and talk and see people. One time he dreamed it after his mother died. In his dream she was alive, but he was dead, and she couldn't see him, didn't know that he was right there beside her.

After dreaming that a few times, he decided it was worse not to just give in and go, and this reminds him of other things.

He doesn't say anything though until after they're outside again and he's opening another beer.

"I heard Fin's back."

"I think so," says Cotter.

Old feelings of anger and shame stir inside Jonah, feel like the prickling of tiny invisible needles. He knows it makes him irritable, that the irritation is on his face, but Cotter looks up at him placidly as if he has no memories of the things Jonah does.

"I saw him, I think, the other day."

"Are you okay with that?"

"Why wouldn't I be?"

Cotter smiles slowly, almost affectionately. "The way you think has always kept me on my toes."

Jonah makes a face. "It's not even my business."

"Just so long as you're okay."

He shrugs. "Yeah, I'm okay."

That long ago friendship with Fin occurred in somebody else's life, a life like the one people look at in yellowed old photographs, trying to remember that kiddie pool on the lawn, that car by the curb, that childish face squinting quizzically at the camera. Relaxing the jaw he's beginning to clench, he remembers being alone instead. Those are the memories that make sense to him.

He was alone when he went to a little market with the name *Mom 'n Pop* painted on a wooden sign nailed to the eaves. The sign leaned out a little like it had hung there for a long time. Inside, there was a man in gray slacks and a white shirt that reminds him of Ira now. He had grayish hair and was bald on top. There were homemade cookies in a big jar on the counter. It was late and the place was empty and he went up to the counter and said, "Pop? That you?"

"Sure is."

One day at Ira's there will be paler weeds and dimmer puddles and maybe Ellie's ghost will disappear. At night, a light goes on in a house that used to be empty.

After Cotter leaves, he sits alone on the porch and tips his bottle toward the meadow in the distance. "Be seein' ya, Ira."

5

♦ Storytellers ♦

A man is sitting on Ray's porch. He's scruffy and scrappy looking, ink on his neck, wearing a sleeveless tee-shirt and jeans that keep sliding off his skinny hips. He is waiting for something Will wants because Will won't come to Ray anymore, sends other people instead—Andy or sometimes Jimbo. Today it's Andy, sitting on the top step of the porch, leaning back into a little bit of shade.

The sun rises over the firs behind the lot across the road, settles over the shop midday. On hot days the air conditioner churns uselessly. The place reminds Ray of a house he had back home, white like this with a porch in front, stuffy, sticky hot in summer; not a home though, just a place where he slept, where people he knew or didn't know came over, until the day it changed. He lived there not because he liked the place but because it was cheap and close enough to his job. He worked with a man named Gus, whose talents with any kind of engine reminded him of Wayne. They were artists in the days before computerization. He liked Gus and he liked his job, but the house was just a house. Then one day the phone rang at Gus' shop, rang like always, Gus answering because Ray never did unless Gus wasn't there. Ray heard him walk up.

"That's your ex. Wants to talk to you."

Sitting on the desk with his feet on the chair, he said, "Hey, Kathy. What's up?"

"Goddammit, Ray! Why do you even have a cell?! You never answer it!"

"Hey, settle down. I was working."

"I needed to talk to you!"

"You are talking to me. Just tell me."

"Your son ran away."

It wasn't the first time and he felt his annoyance begin to grow. "My son?"

"You always get the easy part, Ray, an' I always get to take care of everything else. You don't ever do a goddam thing!"

"I'm tryin' to be nice here, Kath."

"I don't get to be nice, Ray. You get to be nice."

He sighed, feeling a pain in his head. "Want me to go look for 'im?"

"You don't have to. He wants to live with you."

"I'll talk to 'im."

"You know what he said, Ray? That I make him feel bad. That I make his life suck."

"Come on," he said gently. "You know 'e didn't mean that."

"Yes, he did. An' it's true. I yell at 'im all the time. I don't do that to anybody else, Ray."

He almost said, "You do it to me," but changed it to "So, what happened?"

"We fought. Like always. Nothing I say gets through. I make him unhappy."

"No, you don't."

"You aren't here."

"He's thirteen, Kathy. Thirteen sucks."

"Will you go home an' make sure he's okay?"

"Maybe you just need to cut 'im some slack."

"Is that your idea of helping, Ray?"

"Well, whadda you want me to do?"

"Go home."

"An' then what?"

She was silent for a long time, then she said, "Maybe he should."

"Live with me?"

"Maybe."

"It's your call."

"No, Ray. You get to make the call this time."

And then she hung up, not waiting for him to say anything else. He didn't go home right away, finished out his work day, stopped for some burgers that he brought home in a bag, and saw him sitting there, sitting almost the way Andy is, waiting for him. Crossing the overgrown lawn he gave him the paper bag and said, "Here. Take these inside."

He didn't know where the brown eyes squinting up at him came from. Neither his, nor Kathy's. The face was belligerent and lost at the same time.

"Can I live with you?"

"Yeah, sure. We can try that for a while."

A lot of the time, he thinks that those were the best days of his life.

Now, riding up the driveway, Ray stops in back under the shady firs in front of the back fence. Andy is standing, hitching up his pants, when he comes back around to the front.

Andy steps back. "How you doin', Ray?"

"I'm doin' okay. How about you?"

"Me too. You got a minute?"

"Sure."

Ray is opening the door, pushing it in on a muggy room, an old living room crowded with shelves. A string of bells clatters against the door as Andy closes it.

"Those are cool."

They are made of brass with darkish etchings of vines on the surface of each bell, strung one upon the other like rain catchers.

"Wife gave 'um to me."

The way he says it he knows Andy understands that Ray knows that Miri is the reason Andy is here. Without Miri, Will would be here. Without Miri, there would be no rift between them. She was Will's girlfriend before she met Ray. He calls her his wife because she feels like one to him. "Kismet. Us meeting," he said, because of the feeling that he has always known her. They even grew up in the same town without knowing it.

After a moment, the bells stop ringing and he rests his weight on the counter in back and says, "Okay, bub, what is it?"

"Are you comin' over?"

"What for? I already saw the dude."

He is talking about a friend of Andy's sister. When he saw him at Jack's Club he didn't go over, just stared, trying to place him, Andy thought later. The truth was Ray didn't know him and didn't want to. He just allowed the sense of familiarity he felt to wash over him, trying to understand it. "Seems like I oughta know 'im," he said.

"From where?"

He kept thinking about it but finally shook his head. "Not sure."

"Not up here."

"I told you. I'm not sure."

"Do you wanna talk to 'im?"

"No."

Now Andy's saying, "As a favor to Will," and Ray pushes off the counter with angry eyes. "What the hell's wrong with Will he can't figure out if 'e wants somebody around or not? You introduced 'im. I think that makes this your problem."

Andy puts his hands up. "I'm just askin'."

Ray relents, irritated at his own irritation. "Joe Clay, huh?"

Andy nods. "You talk to your friend?"

"No."

The friend is Ed. Joe told Will that Ed would vouch for him, but Ray is certain that Ed never told Joe Clay about Ray. Ed would think that Ray could guess what Ed meant by offering a good word about Joe to people Ray knew, that they lived on the same wavelength. Ray didn't think anybody lived on Ed's wavelength.

"You wanna beer?"

Andy looks surprised. "Yeah, sure."

He follows Ray into a little kitchen in back. A giant pine outside the window shades the room. Pine needles litter the windowsill. Andy opens his beer and sits at the table while Ray leans against the counter, drinking thoughtfully. "You can tell Will I don't like 'im," says Ray.

"That's it?"

"I don't want 'im around. Will can make his own choice. I just won't be around 'im. I can't place 'im an' I can't figure out what's off about 'im. I just have a real hinky feeling an' since Will's askin', you can tell 'im that. An' you can tell 'im that I don't owe 'im anything for my wife either. My advice is a fuckin' gift."

Andy nods. "Okay."

Ray finishes his beer, sets it in the sink and gestures to Andy. "Come on. I gotta open up for real."

After Andy goes though, he just sits on the porch, forearms across his knees. The sun is pouring down, glittering on the gravel walkway. On the corner across from the bar there's a house with a wood and brick carport beside it. The house is blue, the wood part of the carport white and they don't look like they belong together. The weeds in the lot stop where gravel surrounds the house except for a lawn out front and mirror plants in a row on either side of the front porch. The house and the lot belong to a man named Errol Flagg. It doesn't bother Ray to look out on an empty lot every day; in fact, he likes it that way.

On the weedy side of the house nearer Ray's shop, a staircase rises to the top floor where workers came one summer and made the upstairs rooms into two apartments. That's where Grace and two men named Carl and Scott live. One day he went over with George and passed the door to Carl and Scott's apartment. He looked in as they went by because the door was open and Carl was there on the couch watching them pass.

"Dying," whispered George. "Some kinda cancer. Twenty-three years old."

Then, on another day, Ray came outside and saw Carl's mother running up the stairs. Her name was Wendy. She was blonde and she wore a blue skirt and white blouse and heels and it was probably her outfit that reminded him of his mother. Plus, she paused at the top of the steps to light a cigarette and that made him picture Irene pacing on their porch at home, elbow on her forearm, looking restlessly into the dark for something that was nowhere near her.

As the day passes, the shadow of the bowling pin moves like a sun dial, ticking a slow circle back to Oly Way. The shade in the shady places deepens and the sun in the sunny places casts a bright, hot light. It sparkles on cars and window panes. It is only April, strangely hot.

Sweating sleeplessly, Kurt sighs in frustration and sits up. Joy's TV drones below. Bending a blind at his window he looks outside. Nothing is moving. Sometimes he feels like nothing himself, wonders if anybody really knows he's here. If he never said, "Hi," to Joy, she'd just keep walking by him, oblivious to the little space he takes up on the planet. He needs an anchor, something with a presence that will reflect through him, importance of some kind, a good job, even a good party. He thinks about that, a party with Jonah, and maybe Ray, but nobody from the factory except Jonah, which causes him to realize he doesn't really have anybody to invite.

An exciting job.

An adventure.

A reputation.

He likes the idea of a reputation. A reputation is good, a reputation like Ray's. A reputation is a story that people want to hear, that Joy would want to hear.

Getting into a cool shower, Kurt wonders how to get a reputation without actually doing anything. In the other room, he pulls on jeans and a tee-shirt and reaches for his keys on the dresser top, sees his work cap, a Sandorwood cap, a cap he could wear even if he didn't work at Sandorwood. The cap makes a representation. It gives people an idea. Outside, he passes the droning TV, hears the sharp snap of fake gunfire, a siren. That's an odd thing about Joy. Sitting on the steps in the cool evening he can hear the movies she watches on TV. Action flicks, squealing tires, cars crashing, not love stories. She is a mystery.

The shadow of the bowling pin is reaching toward his car. Swinging around on the road he passes through it, stops at the bowling alley for a donut that he eats in his car on the way to Mulligan's.

The street is empty, the air above it wobbly in the heat.

Ray is sitting on his porch, elbows on his knees, watching him come over with a slightly curious, friendly expression. Kurt likes to think that Ray likes him, but Ray is friendly to pretty much everybody so he isn't always sure.

"Hey, bub. What's up?"

"I wanted to ask you something."

"Ask."

Kurt looks around surreptitiously, then back again at Ray's

increasingly amused face. "I was wonderin'…Can you get me…" He quickly glances around again. "…a gun?"

"A gun? What the hell for? Are you crazy?"

Kurt almost blushes, unwilling to confess that he wants to impress a girl who thinks he's invisible.

"I want one."

"Go buy one. I sell auto parts."

"I don't want it registered."

"Why the hell not?"

The conversation isn't going the way Kurt planned because now Ray's both amused and annoyed.

Kurt shrugs and says, "I guess I could do it legal. I just don't like the idea of all that paperwork. Everybody knowing my business."

"You surprise me, bub, but I can't blame you for that."

"Well, can you?"

"Of course I can."

Kurt steps back, letting Ray get up. "I'd appreciate it."

"I know you will. Not gonna be right away though."

"Okay. Sure."

"I'll be over in a minute. You can buy me a drink."

The bells clatter as Ray disappears inside the shop and the air conditioner kicks in. At the bar, it is cool inside. Grace looks at Kurt without a smile.

"Can I have a beer?" She gets it for him, tilting the glass under the tap. Still no smile. Sets the glass down on a square napkin. Kurt smiles anyway and says, "How ya doin'?"

"Fine," she answers, turning on the TV. Then the side door opens and Ray comes in and sits down.

"Damn it's hot."

Grace pours him a beer too and sets it down on another napkin.

He takes a swallow, reaches over the counter, repositions her TV, then settles back on his stool again. "Couldn't see it."

"I didn't have it on for you," she says.

He doesn't watch it though, swivels sideways to look at Kurt and nods with his chin at the window at the end of the counter. "Check out that ride. '68 Chevelle."

In surprise, Kurt bounds up, cranes his head to the window. A shiny black car is parked outside, tilting slightly toward the culvert alongside the empty lot. There's nobody sitting in it, nobody nearby.

"Yeah. Sweet," he says in disappointment, settling back on his stool again.

"I got one of those clock signs," says Ray, "so people know when I'm coming back. Tryin' to convince my kid to come an' work. Save myself some dough."

"Wouldn't you have to pay 'im?"

"I already do. Kid has a full-time job livin' off a me."

Kurt rears up again, trying to see if there's anybody out there with the car now. The twin stripes down the hood are gleaming white in the sun. "You see the guy who was in it?" asks Kurt.

"In what?"

"That car."

"No."

Grace takes away their empty glasses, pours two more.

"Sure hot," says Ray.

Kurt nods, takes off his cap and sets it down. "I hate workin' on days like this."

"You work nights."

"Not tonight."

"Callin' in sick again?"

"It's Saturday."

"Oh, yeah. So it is."

Kurt cranes another look at the Chevy Chevelle outside at the same time that a dusty beam swoops through the opening door. He swivels, sees a man in jeans and a green tee-shirt come in and take the stool closest to the wall. Kurt stares. A moment later, Grace is getting the man a beer, setting it down by his keys on the counter.

Beside him, Ray leans sideways, elbow on the counter and says, "That Chevelle yours?" The man nods. "Sweet piece a machinery, man. Had a '70 'Cuda myself. Had to sell it."

"Too bad."

"Yeah. Well, I was movin'. One less thing."

Feeling oddly nervous all of a sudden, Kurt says, "I just want somethin' that runs."

"Helps," says Ray.

The man doesn't look anything like Gale Sandor. Gale's hair was a lighter brown and his blue eyes gave a direct stare. This one's eyes seem as nervous as Kurt feels. He keeps looking around, not resting on anything until he picks up his beer, then he settles in and takes a long swallow. He looks strong enough though, not anybody broken up in any kind of accident, not somebody with a name like Finch, Kurt thinks, and then says, "Angeline?"

He is looking at Ray who stares back at him and says, "What?"

"Angeline?"

"Where the hell did that come from?"

"I was just thinkin' of names."

Ray shakes his head. "I don't like it."

"You don't like it?"

"That's what I said. I don't like it."

"Whaddidya name your kid?"

"I didn't."

"No name?"

"Jesus," says Ray. "What the hell do you think?"

"So?"

"So what?"

"So what is it?"

"Son."

"Son?"

"Yeah."

Kurt is aware of the man beside him, of Ray grinning at him now.

"Yeah. Son," Ray says. "Lemme tell you about that."

He has stories to tell, thinks Kurt, stories that people want to hear.

"Things went sour with his mom an' me. We weren't livin' together anymore. She was living in this boarding house...."

A large old house on a dismal block. The woman who answered the door every time he knocked was named Sadie. A skinny, pretty-faced lush married to the owner. She never let him in for some reason, just took her time looking him over, slowly smiling at the grin she always brought onto his face.

"You gonna let me in or what?"

She never did, just shut the door on him. At first he used to wait for Kathy, then he just started going in, looking into all the darkish rooms until he found her. The last time before the baby came, she was out on the back porch watering a row of potted plants.

"What are those?" he asked.

"Parsley."

"Lotta parsley."

"I like parsley."

He didn't know that. There were a lot of things he didn't know about her. They broke up because she wanted him home with her, doing the things that would never worry her, like fixing broken faucets or mowing the lawn on Sundays and working a regular job like regular people. They fitted to each other, though, whispered things to each other, things he guessed he'd never tell anyone ever again.

"I was wonderin'," he said. "Will you go out with me on my birthday?"

"On a date?"

"Yeah, sure. A date."

"What for, Ray?"

"Jesus, Kathy. I dunno. To have some fun."

"What kind of fun?"

"Whatever you want."

"It's your birthday. It should be whatever you want."

She was at the faucet, bending over to fill up her water pot. She was wearing a pair of baggy jeans and a white smock that billowed loosely, showing him her vein-threaded belly.

"We can pick a name."

"I already have."

"I hate it, Kathy."

"I don't."

"You might as well call 'im fuckin' Daisy Mae."

"Well, maybe I will if we have a girl."

"We."

That made her roll her eyes as she straightened and went back to her plants. "I thought you liked Buzz."

"Yeah. Route 66. Cool car."

"I thought you liked the name."

"I do."

He watched her watering her plants. It excited him. He thought of mowing the lawn, making love to her with the smell of grass in the air.

"I really hate Davis."

"I really like it."

"Will you go out with me?"

"Okay."

They didn't though because that was the day she had their baby.

"Anyway," he says to Kurt. "I got 'er off Davis an' we named 'im Davidson. Which is okay. We call 'im Son for short."

He is taking a picture out of his wallet. A boy with fair hair and Ray's face, sitting on a motorcycle, looking at the picture taker with cautious eyes.

"Nice lookin'."

Ray nods and pushes it back in his pocket. "Old picture though."

"How old is 'e?"

"Twenty-three."

Kurt is twenty-nine. The thought makes him feel strange. He becomes aware again of the man beside him, of Grace leaning against the back counter with her arms crossed in front of her, staring fixedly at the TV she moved back to its original position. It's a talk show with the sound turned off.

Kurt feels uneasily unreal.

"Don't you want to hear that?"

She looks surprised to hear him talk, then turns up the volume until there's a faintly audible chatter.

"Is that better?"

"I didn't mean for me."

The unrealness is passing over him. Now he just feels sticky hot again, wonders if there's a breeze outside. Picking up his cap, he says, "I'm goin'. I'll see you guys later."

"Sure, bub. Take it easy."

Outside, there's no breeze. He fiddles with his cap, looking at the car across the street, parked near Kurt's green Gran Torino, a good car that isn't as good as Fin's, isn't as memorable, wouldn't catch the attention of Joy like a Chevelle with a pair of bright, white stripes would.

Clamping down on his cap, he crosses the sunlit street and drives away.

The mugginess in the bar grows as the sun recedes, pulling the shadows in deeper, but bringing no coolness. A car chugs by outside, stops on the strip of gravel in front of the shop.

"Guess that's me," says Ray, sliding off his stool.

After the clap of the side door fades, the man at the counter turns his keys in a slow circle. His beer is almost empty, the square napkin gray with moisture. He picks up the glass to use the napkin to wipe up the counter and the little puddle grows.

"I'm making a mess," he says.

Grace brings over a cloth, mops up the puddle, and stares at him without meaning to, trying to overlay his face with the grocery store, or the mini-mart, or a gas station, or the video store, but she cannot see him in any of those places. Then she drops her eyes, feeling his nervousness, the way his eyes move from his keys to the window, to the TV, settling there, watching a woman on the screen vacuuming an unusually dirty floor.

"What is that?" he asks.

"An infomercial."

"Oh."

He sounds disappointed, so she turns the TV off which seems to startle him. "I didn't mean you should turn it off."

"That's okay."

The sound of the side door opening is a strange relief. It isn't George though, it's Ray, who comes back in and drags a chair across the room, using it to brace open the door. Then he sits back down at the bar, looks at the man in the green tee-shirt and says, "I've seen you before."

"Here?"

"Was it?"

"I don't know."

Ray shrugs. "Guess it was."

"Do you want a beer, Ray?"

"No thanks, babe. JD this time. On the rocks."

"Me too," says the other man, pushing his empty glass over to her. She takes it, drops it in a bin under the sink and pours their drinks.

"This is buggin' me," says Ray.

"What?"

"Tryin' to remember."

The man smiles. "Sorry."

"Play me some pool while I think?"

"Okay."

"Name's Ray."

He takes Ray's hand. "Fin."

Watching them, Grace leans back on the counter, crossing her arms again. She wonders what it would be like to be as free as Ray, at home wherever she went. His good humor is overwhelming, like being in a room with too many lights. She wouldn't be able to see or think in such a room. She likes the quiet of this time of day, the gentle dimming of the light. The pool table is in an alcove across the room. Ray and Fin are shadows, Ray at the table, Fin standing at the wall, watching.

"Give me a hint," says Ray.

"I can't."

She can hear Ray's sigh. "You're no help."

Glancing away, she sees the sun still bright outside and thinks of George. She thinks of George a lot. She knows he's at Lois's house because Lois moved out of the house they lived in together and George got her a refrigerator from Comfort Appliances which used to be Anderson's Appliances where George and Grace's father used to work. Later, her father bought half the business and a while after that sold it to buy the bar with George and now it's Comfort Appliances. According to George, Lois's new house has a deck outside and blue carpets on the floors and a yellow kitchen. When they first split up, George said, "I wonder if the divorce has made her into a new person." And Grace wondered what George saw when he looked at Lois then. She didn't know if Lois was a new person or just the person she had never let herself be before.

George's bewilderment was always a balm to her. She liked that he wasn't secure or insecure, opinionated or indifferent, good or bad, gentle or mean. George was the in-between of everything, a suspension where she could bob in her own space.

"I guess it could have," she said of Lois becoming a new person. She had always loved George, but on the day the divorce was final he fell out of love with her and back in love with Lois.

"Why don't I feel new?" he asked, but she didn't have any answer for him, and it didn't really matter anyway, because now he is back with Lois again, getting her house ready to sell, swapping out her new refrigerator for the old one in the house they raised their children in.

The sign on the bar's roof looks like a metal bird during the day, throwing rods of shadow on the sidewalk and pavement below. There was a door onto Oly Way once, but it was sealed up a long time ago. The side of the bar is painted a dark blue. On the other side of the building, the cinderblock is gray, the doors painted black.

Fin remembered the place at night, shadows of neon, lines of cars bumper to bumper.

Earlier, at home, he opened all the curtains and the back door, and all the dust floated up and then slowly grew still. When he drove off, he wasn't sure where to go and almost went one way and then came the other way instead. He passed the factory without looking at it, a restaurant called Marjorie's, then firs again, and then suddenly came out onto a wide open town with a giant bowling pin against the sky and this bar with a sign on its roof. The sun changed the look of the place, but he could still remember it. Sitting in his car, he tried to focus, tried to see past the walls and doors, but that barrier in his brain rose up, clamping onto his head like a vise. He sat for a long time, squeezing his eyes shut until the pain went away, until the emptiness came, soothingly cool. Then he got out of his car and walked slowly around the block to the blue side of the building on Oly Way, signal lights up ahead, cars zipping through the shade of the bowling pin. Circling back again, he came in, and now he is leaning on the counter, looking at Grace, picking up the glasses she sets down.

"Thank you."

"You're welcome."

Her eyes are the color of rain. He feels light-headed all of a sudden, takes a swallow of his drink, hands Ray his glass and sits down in a chair by a table in the corner of the alcove. The sounds of traffic come through the wall, remind him of the river near his house. He goes there when it's hot. Once when he started back, he came up through the firs where the road began to curve and saw a faraway meadow and a trailer sitting on the other side. It wasn't a memory really, but the meadow was familiar like this bar and its sign.

"Remember yet?" asks Ray.

"No." Not wanting to. Not wanting to do this.

Ray sighs and sits down in the other chair. When he sits and tips backwards with a boot against the wall, he looks familiar too, like the sign and the meadow near home. His house feels the same way to him, full of a friendliness it never really had but is familiar anyway. Ray isn't anybody he'd usually know. He looks at the tattoos on his arms and the humor in his eyes and then he can see him sitting back with a boot on a chair, a glass balancing on his knee, smiling like he is now as if he's remembering too before he drops his chair to the floor and goes out into the bar with his glass.

"Hey, sweet pea. Little water in this."

The sun is low and the shadow of the bowling pin is giant and shapeless. It reaches out and touches the cars going by. Outside of Acropolis there's the shade of the firs and the darker shade of occasional boulders. The place where Jonah's father died is even darker than that. Water collects there all the time, dripping into a pool that never grows. Abel fell out through the swinging door of his pickup while it was tottering on the edge of a pit that was going to be Ivy's pond.

The water there is dark and cold.

Kurt slows as he goes by. Up higher, the firs thin out and there's sun again. Jonah's in the doorway, leaning against the frame, not looking irritated like he usually does.

"Whach ya doin'?" Jonah asks.

"Just drivin' around."

"Wanna beer?"

"Sure."

He sits down on the porch and stares at his car. He's thinking about that Chevelle. "Stopped at the bar," he says when Jonah reappears.

"Oh yeah?"

Then he stays quiet for a moment because the same kind of moodiness down below is up here too now, even in the sun. He scowls slightly and then just says, "Think about Angeline any?"

"What if it's a boy?"

"Angelo."

Jonah laughs, almost choking himself. "Jesus, Kurt."

There was a pile of weeds, dark and dry against the others growing in the yard where Dahlia's flowers used to bloom. That's when Fin thought about the house being friendly. He's pretty sure he was never happy in it. Now he is sitting here at the bar, waiting for Ray to remember.

He thinks about the sweet peas he found growing wild by the river and the angels at the cemetery and the room he found in the house with a knobless door that goes up to the attic. He goes up there a lot and stands at the open window, feeling the air come in.

He's afraid of being curious, of leaning outside into the open. Some things make him want to remember. Other times he doesn't want to and he thinks about sitting in his car, not knowing where to go and coming here, and then he hears the door open in back. The sun is slanting away, leaving a familiar, pale twilight, full of pin dots of dust and he can almost smell linseed oil and remembers seeing those sweet peas again, remembers Ray sitting with a boot up on a chair, laughing as she went by.

"Hey, sweet pea…."

The back row of windows, pitch dark beyond, a man with blue eyes leaning in. This isn't that kind of place. All of this he remembers, but he doesn't remember going home and looking at a picture in a shoebox again. It kept reminding him of something he didn't want to think about and he drank the whole time, staring at the pictures under the lamp until he couldn't see anymore anyway.

At home, with a bag full of groceries, Kurt stops at the bottom of the stairs. Joy is coming up the walkway, swinging her empty trash can. He hears his heart in his voice.

"Hi!"

She nods without slowing, smelling like flowers.

Now the man with the blue eyes appears, glancing into the alcove at the sound of people there, lifting a hand wrapped around his keys in greeting. He swings back to the bar, squeezing Grace's shoulder, pulling an apron out of a drawer under the counter. Tying it on, he looks up as they come over.

Fin sits, rolling the bottom of his glass on the counter top. He focuses on the color of the slowly spinning liquid. Sitting beside him, Ray raps lightly at the counter and says, "Hey, George. You remember this guy?"

Fin looks up, meeting the frowning blue eyes. George nods. "Yeah, I think so. Who are you?"

"My name's Fin. Fin Sandor. I own Sandorwood."

Ray looks surprised. "No kiddin'? That dude here earlier, Kurt? He works there."

"I don't really have anything to do with actually running the place though. I just moved back up."

"From where?"

"San Francisco."

Ray laughs. "Fuckin' small world, man. I'm from the Bay Area too. Born in Oakland, lived nearby most of my life."

Fin looks at them all, feels the glass almost boiling in his hand. He sets it down, pushes it away, then pulls it back and takes a drink.

"How long you been up?"

"About two weeks."

"Well, hell, I think I'd remember you from two weeks ago."

"I think I was here a couple months ago too."

"You think?"

He is aware of Grace and George watching him from the other side of the counter, of Ray sitting sideways on his stool, eyeing him curiously. This is the conversation that haunts him, that makes the wounds on his belly start to burn. His tee-shirt feels rough against his skin and he pulls at it absentmindedly, talking without really looking at anybody.

"I had an accident…fell…off a roof."

"Yeah? You look okay."

"I am. I was lucky." His shirt is sticking to his skin. His face feels hot and the ice in his drink is melted. "Can I have another one?" he asks.

"On me," says George, reaching for the glass only to pause in midair, point, and say, "Now I remember. You came in with Jonah Hollycock. Couple months ago. Got in a fight. I had to break it up."

"That's right." Ray pushes his empty glass over to George too. "I remember that."

Fin nods, a stitch of pain knotting up his side. He lifts the drink George gives him, swallows half of it. "That's my problem. I don't remember anything before my accident. I don't remember who I came in with that night. I don't remember anything."

Swallowing the rest of his drink, the stitch in his side slowly relaxes.

George takes his empty glass. "I didn't know that actually happened to people, not for real anyway."

Fin nods. "It happened to me."

"It happened to me too," says Ray, meeting their stares with innocent eyes. "What?"

"You lost your memory?" George's voice has a sour tone of disbelief to it.

"Couple nights of it anyway."

"A blackout?"

"Very funny. Pour me another drink an' I'll tell ya...."

The sound of Ray's story is a relief, cool air drying the sweat under Fin's tee-shirt, easing the vise that was starting to clamp down on his head again.

"Got in a rip roarin' fight over this girl. An' not the last over her either, come to think of it...."

Resting against the wall, Fin's eyes half close. Under Ray's voice, the sounds inside the bar are little echoes now, hollow sounding, and he imagines layers of forgetfulness like Ray's, "...came to on some dude's couch, dude just sittin' there, starin' at me," and other layers deep below, of other things forgotten even longer.

Opening his eyes back up, he looks into hers, rain gray or moon gray, eyes that recede the nearer he approaches. Then very slowly she smiles at him and he smiles back.

The couch Ray woke up on was Ed's and the girl was named Sherry. Ed's father was in a Barcalounger, trying to ignore Ed while he watched TV, Ed talking to him anyway until Ray woke up, lying there actually, not sitting yet, catching Ed's and Ed's father's curious stares. There was a party earlier and he came with a girl. He thought he was in love with her, at least as in love as a fifteen-year-old could be. She was sixteen and they came in her car. Ed seemed to be fascinated by him. He leaned over him against the back of the couch. "Who're you?"

"Ray."

"My casa, su casa, Ray."

The sunlight is paler now, the air a little cooler. Ray is looking under the hood of Fin's car. Old cars remind him of Wayne, of the orange Camaro on the driveway, orange popsicles, pain in his fingers.

"You keep 'er nice."

Fin smiles, leaning against his door. The car really means nothing to him. He thinks maybe it should.

"So what's the deal? You think you'll be stickin' around for a while?"

He nods and looks back at the bar, squinting a little because the sun's on the other side, hitting him in the eyes.

Ray looks over with a grin. "Cute, ain't she?"

The comment embarrasses him. Ray drops the hood with a bang.

At home, he drinks cold water out of a jug in the refrigerator and then takes a bottle of Jack Daniel's upstairs with him to the attic. He pulls a chair over to the window, rests his bare feet on the sill, and tries to remember the color of Mulligan's sign at night.

Waking up at Ed's, Ray knew there was nobody there but Ed and Ed's father. Sherry was gone, but he hoped he was just groggy, that she was in another room or that she was out buying aspirin for him, on her way back. He didn't know these people. When Ed said, "My casa, su casa, Ray," he leaned over and threw up all over the coffee table.

Across the room, Ed's father slammed his recliner down and said, "For fuck's sake."

Ed just got up and pushed the coffee table out on the front walkway. He shrugged at his father's stare. "I'll hose it off later." Ray just rubbed at his face, looking around.

"Who you lookin' for?" asked Ed.

"Sherry."

"Chick you came with?"

"Yeah."

"Left."

There was a sound that might have come from Ed's father.

Sherry looked surprised when he went over to her house a couple of days later.

"You just left me?"

"I have a curfew, Ray."

For a while after that, he didn't think he was in love with her anymore. But it didn't stop him from going out with her.

His wife reminds him of that day too, of waking up on Ed's couch in an ordinary living room with people he didn't know, going along with the situation until he could figure things out. The reality of waking up with Miri every day is still a mystery to him. He walked into it deliberately though, eyes wide open, entangling himself with emotional ties that are already suffocating him. Still, he feels that weakness at the sight of her, his resentment receding as he watches her come up the shop's walkway.

"Hey, babe."

She stops at the bottom of the steps and squints at him, getting the last of the sun in her eyes.

"Hi, Ray."

"C'mon up."

She does, with the beads on the fringe of her suede shoulder bag clicking against the steps. She wears sky blue eye shadow, the same color as the flowers she has in a pot at home. There's a pair of go-go boots in the closet and her favorite earrings are big silver hoops. There were pictures of his mother that looked like that. He remembers Will calling her "a hippie chick" and expected somebody Will's age, a girl with a decades-old retro look—not somebody who missed it by only a few years.

On the porch, she puts her arms around him. Her lips are warm, never like cherries or berries or wine. She rests there for a moment, up close, and then he laughs and pulls her inside.

"Wanna beer?"

"Sure."

She follows him with her fingers in his. He looks back. "Wade go?"

"Yes."

Her voice sounds depressed. After she left home when she was a girl, her brother came to live with her for a while and she thinks of him as her only family. She sends her mother birthday and Christmas cards though.

"Only mom you got," said Ray one time, thinking about Wayne. He knew Wayne never forgot him. He's sure he's still alive, wondering about him over a beer sometimes.

In the kitchen, she sits with a leg underneath her and looks across the hall into the room on the other side. It still has a bed and dresser in it and sometimes he still sleeps here. His eyes follow hers and he knows what she's thinking. He isn't always alone. It doesn't bother him and he resents that it bothers her. She goes through his things too. He's found things out of place, like a picture of Cora, his old girlfriend, jammed under the loose paper in his dresser drawer. When she looks away from the bedroom he smiles at her.

"What?"

"Nothin'," he says, lifting his beer up.

He remembers the time she told him that she worked as a stripper after the boy she ran away with disappeared. He always tries to picture her dancing around a pole in a dark, noisy bar, but always ends up seeing a girl like Sherry instead, swinging slowly by with a smile that doesn't mean anything and that he can live without.

6

✦ Drift ✦

There's a party at Will's. His house is almost by itself at the end of a dead-end street, junipers out front, scrubby bushes and trees between his house and his neighbor's on the corner at the front of the street across from the dead-end sign. Will likes it here, and as long as nobody buys any of the property around him, he's happy.

Tonight lights are shining in all his windows, above the garage out back, through all the open doors. People come and go. After greeting Ray, he pointed with both arms at the speakers he put on either side of the couch, looked back at him over his shoulder and yelled, "*Check those out!*"

Ray went over and turned the volume down. "Nice."

Not speaking for a moment, Will scratched at a bare shoulder and then said, "Just for this party."

"Sellin' 'um after?"

"No."

Now Ray is lying alone on Will's bed, and Will comes in quietly and waits for him to stir. He doesn't open his eyes though. The light by the bed is on and a spruce branch is scraping gently at the window. It isn't windy out and it's a light scrape as if the tree is sighing out there by itself. In here, Will is thinking about his father. He wishes Ray had been his father. It occurs to him that there are mistakes in the way things happen. He steps closer, staring down. "Want somethin'?"

Ray smiles. "I dunno."

A little cloisonné box that belongs to the woman Will lives with is on the dresser. Will wonders where she is and glances into the dark through the gap in the door. Once he had Miri here and now she lives with Ray. He gets the box and comes back over.

Ray is sitting up, reaching for the drink he put on the floor.

His fingers don't look damaged.

Everything about Ray, to Will, seems natural. His presence here is natural. Will's father is dead and Will didn't think about that a lot until after he met Ray. Then he began to feel ungrown and disadvantaged without his father. He doesn't really care about his mother.

After they first met, Craig's cousin said, "Man, your mom looks just like Mrs Cleaver."

Except she never wore pearls and she didn't understand him.

He comes closer and Ray just sits there now with his elbows on his knees, watching him with a slightly amused smile.

"Hurt bad?"

He puts a hand out, looks at the tips of his fingers and shrugs.

Will holds out the little box. "Oxy."

"Pisses my wife off."

"A woman in love," he says of the woman he used to live with.

The day after she left him, Ray said, "Chick's too old for you anyway."

Will felt chastised by that, embarrassed and belittled. Ray was even smiling that amused smile at him. Now Will has Susie.

"Workin' out though?" he asks now.

"Yeah," agrees Ray. "Forgives me all the time."

He finishes his drink and Will looks at his fingers around the glass, a couple of white scars on the knuckles. He knows about the rock wall at Ray's friend's place, but he also knows that Ray likes to fight. It's odd to him that Ray will seek out pain in that way while he can't stand the pain of a couple of bones he broke years ago.

Feeling almost mystical or psychic like Craig's cousin, Will says, "You could just be imagining it."

Ray's head shoots up, an unwelcome memory in his eyes. He smiles grimly. "Psychosomatic, you mean?"

"Yeah. Like that."

"That's what Ed said."

"Yeah?"

"Yeah. We were staying at this motel, about to leave town. Sold my place, quit my job, couldn't work anymore anyway."

Will tries to summon up a picture of Ed, big enough to hold his own with Ray, but not too big. In reality, Ed is whip thin and tough, with a good-looking, creased face and pale eyes.

"I told Ed to fuck off. Pain's pain, man."

Will picks up the cloisonné box again, offering it up like a sacrifice. With a sigh, Ray reaches in, but only pockets the two pills he took. "I'm drinkin' too much," he says.

"I'll watch ya," says Will, "if you change your mind."

"Thanks."

Will is happy to have Ray back. He wishes him the best. Susie is just as good as Miri. He feels no more anger. When he saw Ray in his doorway, he jumped off the couch, threw his arms open wide and yelled, "*I love you, man!*"

He was audible even over his new speakers.

"*Check those out!*"

That was after he tripped over a girl on the floor. There were other people on the floor too. The couch and chairs were all full and people were stepping over other people on their way through.

After he yelled "*I love you, man!*" he jumped off the couch with his arms still up. The girl on the floor saw him coming and rolled sideways, but his foot caught underneath her anyway and he grabbed at her hair and felt her continuing to roll. It tipped him over, but Jimbo caught him, almost in motion from the first moment, only a second before standing with a bottle of whiskey at one of the speakers. Jimbo caught him under the armpits and then after he settled, Will took Jimbo's bottle of whiskey, straightened up and said, "Goddam bitch," then a moment later said, "Come an' meet my old lady."

They never did find her. They went outside where the air was cooler and Will looked around with a growing suspicion on his face until he saw her car, still there.

"Met 'er at Candi's. Eatin' a coconut cream pie. That pie looked so good."

"So who're you datin'? The girl or the pie?"

Will held his faltering smile up. "That's funny."

"Yeah?"

"You need a drink."

They went back inside, looking for a bottle.

Will never knew about the day Ray was sitting in a booth at Candi's with Aaron Toler, waiting to get a look at him, but when Aaron said, "I have a guy I want to introduce you to," Will was angry.

"You think I wanna meet a guy? Why do I wanna meet a guy? Do I look like I wanna meet a guy?"

"Your town," said Craig's cousin, sitting there with him, arm around the waist of a girl Will had never seen before. "You should check 'im out."

But there was something in Craig's cousin's voice that told Will Craig's cousin wanted him to go see Aaron's friend, and that meant he wouldn't. He dreaded it the way he used to dread hearing his father come home. "Dude can come see me," he said.

But Ray never did. Instead he set up his shop and every time Will heard his name around town he felt diminished.

"Fucker's disrespectin' me," he told Craig's cousin.

"How?"

"Just bein' here."

On the day Will went to see Ray, he stopped at Craig's cousin's trailer and said, "Check this out," put his arms up and turned in a slow circle in Craig's cousin's little living room. He was wearing a pair of white jeans, white shirt, and tan leather jacket. His hair was almost the same color as the jacket and he wore a pair of dark-lensed sunglasses. Sitting on a kitchen stool in one of Craig's cousin's tee-shirts was a girl Will was pretty sure worked at Candi's. Craig's cousin was in a pair of pajama bottoms, leaning against the end of the kitchen counter, arms folded across his chest. He nodded with a slow long-lipped grin.

"You look like a fuckin' movie producer."

"Cool!"

Ray didn't say anything to him when he came into his shop, didn't even greet him, just walked off through a glass door into the other part of the shop. After a moment, Will followed and leaned against the side of the aisle where Ray began slipping packs of light bulbs onto metal hooks in a pegboard wall.

It was cool in there too, with bright lights in the ceiling.

"I don't know you," he said.

Ray's palm went up against the pegboard and he gave a long stare into Will's eyes. "Want an introduction?"

"No."

Then Ray shrugged and started slipping the packages of light bulbs back on the pegs again.

Will came closer. "What's your game anyway?"

"No game."

"Guess you know some people."

He straightened up again, resting his palm back against the pegboard. "A few."

"Me too. I'm doin' okay."

"Okay's good."

"Doin' things my way."

Ray smiled. "Like the song."

"Yeah."

"So I guess you won't be in the market for any auto supplies then?"

Will took a moment to consider this. His answer was slow. "No."

After that, Ray just shrugged again and went back to work. "Then I guess I won't be sellin' you any."

———————

Earlier in the night, Will closed off the kitchen and opened up the kitchen window. His speakers drummed thunderously through the house and the sounds of conversation and laughter filled the air outside. He was alone in the kitchen with Ray and another man. He could feel Ray's simmer, the anger that probably started up with the pain in his fingers, Will thought later. Out in their cages, Will's birds were awake because of all the lights and the people outside. Leaning suddenly over the sink, he yelled, "*Shut the fuck up!*"

Then for a while it was quiet.

"I give 'um for presents," he said of his birds. "Gifts of love."

The man sitting against the wall had a nervous twang in his voice. "That's cool."

At the sound of his voice, Ray raised his head up, stared.

"Got any plans?" Will asked.

"Plans? No. Just passin' time."

"Fuckin' Andy's sister?"

The man laughed, then stopped laughing when nobody else joined in.

"You know Ray?" asked Will, pointing across his body. He was sweating heavily and he could smell himself, a sharp metallic smell that made him feel strong.

"No. I think I know a friend a yours though. Ed?"

"Ed's not my friend."

Will made a clucking sound. "Well, that kinda sucks."

"Guess I heard wrong."

"What's your name again?" asked Will.

"Joe Clay."

"Yeah, yeah. That's right. Do you like birds?"

"Sure."

"Yeah, me too. Love 'um. God's Quaaludes."

Then Ray laughed and looked sideways. "You are a visionary, man."

Will nodded sagely. "Yeah. I have a certain view a things."

Now Ray is lying on Will's bed, feeling the drumming of the speakers coming up through the floor and in through the walls.

"Party's costin' me," says Will.

Ray nods, half asleep. "Reminds me. My kid wants a new bike. I keep puttin' 'im off for some reason."

Will shrugs. "Paid cash for my Camaro. Saw it an' got it. Almost don't wanna sell it. Wanna SUV though. Or a jeep. SUV for Susie an' a jeep for me."

"How old are you, Will?"

"Twenty-nine."

"Close enough to my kid. I remember cuz we have the same birthday."

"For real? That's sweet."

"Yeah. I was twenty."

"An' you were on your own, right? Supportin' yourself?"

"Sure."

Will nods. "Me too." He is without doubts, just like his real father was. His father always made sure he knew all the rules, and his mother too was always sure of her role. He recalls a house that looked like it came out of a TV.

Sitting up by Ray, who is still lying down, he says, "I really wanted you to see Susie."

"It doesn't matter," Ray murmurs.

"Matters to me."

"Some other time."

Will rolls a little, resting his weight on one arm and looks down. "Whadda you think?"

He watches Ray frown, trying to catch what Will means, then sigh as his anger rises back up. Will can see it in the hardening of his face, the alertness under the closed lids fighting against the alcohol. It amazes him, anger that doesn't come with the crack of a belt. This is his true father.

"I already told you. This is your problem."

"You don't like 'im?"

"No. I don't want 'im around. I mean it. I see that guy again, I'm gone. There's somethin' off about 'im, like he's not real."

Authenticity means a lot to Will. Truth isn't always what you see. Mrs Cleaver might have been a good mother to the Beav, but she wasn't any good to Will.

Watching the anger leave Ray's face, Will says, "Okay, man. I'll take care of it."

Ray nods sleepily. "Countin' on it."

The house Ray lives in with Miri has two bedrooms, a bath, a small living room and a kitchen. Their bedroom fits just the bed and a dresser with a mirror over it. The fir trees that grow in small groves around the house cover it in shade and keep it cool too. The door to the hall is open, TV on in the living room. Ray rolls over, feels at the empty side of the bed. His head is pounding and his eyes throb. He doesn't remember getting home. But he does remember Miri shaking him awake every time he went to sleep, making the room spin all over again. He thinks he remembers swatting at her, but it is very dreamlike. Now he yawns, stretches and sighs, not wanting to get up, but he can smell sweat and it reminds him of Will. After he showers, he gets dressed and goes out into the living room, squinting a little in the light, still feeling a little groggy. Miri is sitting on the couch in a tee-shirt and pink slippers, her face stiff-looking. He knows better than to say anything, but he does anyway.

"What was with you last night?"

"You weren't breathing, Ray."

"What the hell are you talking about? Of course, I was breathing. I'd be dead otherwise."

"You were high."

"Which is different from not breathing. An' no I fuckin' wasn't."

"You can't do drugs, Ray."

"I know that. I was drunk. Fuck. I didn't get any goddam sleep cuz a you."

"You don't drink like that."

"Well, I did last night."

"Okay. Fine then. Excuse me for trying to save your life."

"Jesus, Miri. If you were that worried, you coulda called fuckin' 9-1-1."

"I was afraid you'd get arrested!"

He stares at her for a moment, then mutters, "For fuck's sake," and goes into the kitchen. Of all the places he's lived, he likes the kitchen here the best, with its red chairs and red-flecked Formica. He likes the way it looks with the gray of the early morning light outside. Pouring a bowl of Cheerios, he leans against the counter to eat it, then leaves by the back door.

When he hears Ray's bike, Carl looks outside. One day he won't be sitting here on this couch anymore. All the people he sees come and go will keep coming and going without him because he won't be here. He won't even be thinking this. Often, he makes a game of it and after a while doesn't believe it's not really a game anymore. He likes that, believing it's just a game. He can't talk about it. If he does, Wendy says, "You're being morbid, for God sakes. Just take your goddam medicine."

"It's only for pain, Mom."

She looks put upon when he says that and waves her fingers impatiently at her smoke.

He wants to be Ray. He wants tattoos and he wants to jump up the steps at the shop and sit outside with a beer and be free and easy and careless again.

After a while, he gets up and sways a little as the shadows the curtains make flow across the floor; the light grows diffuse and reminds him again of not being here. Pausing, he stares at the crack in the door of the room where Scott's asleep, then gets his grape juice and goes slowly back to the world out the window.

Cars park on the street in front of Ray's, a couple pulling all the way onto the scrubby grass between the porch and the street. Nobody goes inside. They stand on the porch or sit on the steps. A Silverado squeezes in with the other vehicles and a man named Goliath gets out, followed by a man named Roger.

Andy nods. "Hey, Roge."

Roger is Andy's friend and sometimes Andy brings him over to Will's, but for some reason Will never remembers him, even though he screws up his face every time, trying to pull a name out of his memory until Andy finally says "Roge."

"Oh, yeah. Yeah. Roger."

Craig's cousin is sitting on the top step, Jimbo standing above him, staring down at Roger. Roger backs up against the bottom of the railing and lights a cigarette. Ray is sitting at a distance with his back against the front of the shop, legs stretched out on the porch railing, balancing a bottle of beer on a knee. He looks preoccupied and he is.

Occasionally Goliath glances at him, smoking too. Eventually Ray looks over and says, "I'm allergic to that stuff, you know?"

Goliath stares at the tip of his cigarette. "No kiddin'?"

"No kiddin'."

He lifts his beer up to drink and sees the curtains blow in and out at Carl's. A moment later he frowns as if trying to recall a memory. "Were you at Will's?"

Goliath is lighting another cigarette, turning to exhale. "No, not me."

"Not Roger either," says Jimbo.

"I saw Roger," says Craig's cousin.

Roger is surprised because he wasn't there. Will wouldn't remember to tell him there was a party going on and Andy forgot too. Jimbo's humor dissolves as he stares at Craig's cousin.

"No Roger."

"Yeah, man. I saw 'im."

Now Jimbo's uncertain. Ray is laughing without looking over. Roger just looks surprised. Then Jimbo points at Roger and says, "Then you saw me. I saved Will. Chick tripped 'im."

"No. That happened before," says Craig's cousin.

In the sun the weeds are the color of leaves at the tops of aspens or birches, aflutter with cool, pale light at the end of a cool summer day.

After all the cars at Ray's leave, George opens the door at the bar and starts sweeping out clouds of dust. Then he steps out on the stoop to sweep that too. At first he doesn't notice the weeds or the light and doesn't think about Grace or anything that changes. It's not until Fin's car comes up, stopping at the plank that crosses the ditch alongside the weedy lot. Then all of a sudden he can see it, a pale cool sun, its light like the light that filled all the empty rooms of his house after Lois left.

He stands there motionlessly for a moment, then calls across to Fin. "Comin' over?"

"Pretty soon," says Fin.

Then Fin is crossing through the weeds, going upstairs.

George can see her at her door. She'll be quiet. He remembers that. She was always quiet in the car when he took her home from babysitting. When he pulled up at her house, she'd grow suddenly nervous with her hand on the door handle and look over, almost with embarrassment. He knew that he was in love with her; she knew it too, he guessed.

"Night, George."

"Night, honey."

Mr Volvo, Carl's name for him, stops in a blue glow below. A white Volvo in the way of purity. A pristine color. On the other side of the bar's windows, people sit and drink. Mr Volvo waits. Then Ray comes out of the bar with Kurt behind him, heading for the shop. Slowing as he passes, Kurt darts a look at the dark windows of Mr Volvo's car, can't see anything, and then hurries to catch up to Ray. They go through the door with the bells.

"Wait here."

The only light Ray turns on is the one in back. Then it goes off again, and he comes back and pushes a white bundle hard against Kurt's belly. "You better not piss me off."

"No way. Never. I swear."

Mr Volvo's window hums down and Ray glances in as he passes. Kurt heads over to his car, slips in briefly, then jogs back across the street and disappears into the bar.

Across the street, Carl sits in his window, staring out at Mr Volvo's car. Pristine white. Clean and pure. Carl likes purple. Grape juice purple. He sips his juice and stares. Mr Volvo probably washes his car every week. A hand wash he pays for.

Behind him, Scott is tucking in his shirt. Scott can see Mr Volvo too. Then he finishes with his shirt and comes closer.

"Your friend's outside," says Carl.

"I don't see anybody."

Carl points and Scott shrugs. In the cool air outside, Scott stops and lights a cigarette. Above the dome of neon blue, a few stars are winking dimly. Then he goes over to the white car and gets in.

"Ready?"

"Yeah."

The furniture in the motel room where Ray stayed with Ed was a sandy veneer. The curtains and bedspreads were orange and the carpet was green.

"You think they decorated it this way on purpose?" asked Ed.

"I don't care."

"Looks pretty new."

Ed sat in a chair in the corner of the room.

Now Ray dreams about him as Ed sat there watching him, sometimes sticking a finger into the curtains so he could look outside, look back over.

"What's that word, Ray? Psychosomatic?"

"Fuck you, Ed."

They were always like that. They fought over hotdogs and hamburgers.

"White Castle's, Ray."

Waking up at home, he rubs his eyes and sits up.

The TV's on, news, good weather for tomorrow. Turning the set off, he takes his keys off the kitchen counter and gets on his bike. After he moved in with Miri, he made a point to go and sit with her at work sometimes. Once, when Otis was bartending, he asked him, "Jack of Clubs? What's that mean?"

"It's a contradiction."

"Okay. What are you contradicting?"

Otis gave him an under the eyebrow stare, lips twitching. "I think that's for every person to figure out."

Ray nodded. "Meaning that was the name of the place when you got it?"

Otis laughed.

Now Ray is riding onto a mostly empty parking lot. There's almost nobody here. He waits outside in the cool air, hears the door open, two customers walking out into the dark. They don't see him, pull out in their pickups, red lights glowing.

Stillness and quiet settle down.

He sits on the hood of Miri's car.

Warm yellow light tries to filter out though the shuttered windows. A wedge of yellow at the door, on and off.

He watches her swinging her beaded purse, eyes down. She's in jeans, and all he can really see at first is the white of her lace top. Inside, in the light, her chest is freckled, every man's eyes on her pushed-up breasts. He longs suddenly to take one in his mouth with a longing that's almost like love.

When she sees him, she stops and he slides off her car and goes over, tugging on a thin piece of blue ribbon that is holding her blouse together. It slips out of a button hole, but she stops him and pulls away. He follows anyway and picks her up, feels her legs around his waist, palms pushing at his shoulders.

The blue ribbon flutters and he grins and pulls it loose. She pushes at him and slips down, running away. At her car she drops her purse on the hood, leaning back against him when he comes up behind her, cupping her breasts in his hands.

"Don't run."

She turns and he picks her up again, sucking hard on a nipple.

"Oh, Ray...." Her fingers knot in his hair and he feels her heart pounding in his mouth.

A woman in love, said Will.

7

♦ Romance ♦

There's a small lake where the firs are thick and the air is damp in the daytime. Strings of lights traverse the trees around the lake and shine like a necklace at night. The road that follows it winds and twists among the firs. Houses appear, glimpses of A-forms and log cabins, long driveways, metal or wood gates, mailboxes. As the sun sets, ribbons of mist begin to float out of the trees.

It is quiet and Fin is aware of the loud roar of his car. "We'll come back out this way?" he asks.

Grace nods. "The road circles the lake."

"It's pretty here."

"But dark."

"A little."

He couldn't grow dahlias here. That's the one memory that keeps coming to him, orange and yellow and purple dahlias. He glances at Grace and smiles. "Thanks for coming out with me."

Her eyes drop. She fingers a spot on her jeans. "You don't have to thank me. I wanted to."

"I'm glad."

He slows the car, following the road into a curve that drops almost to the edge of the lake, dark and glass-like, dots of lights reflecting off its motionless surface. Other lights are winking in the firs and there's the smell of smoke in the air.

"I wanted to ask you out for a while," he says.

He surprised himself at her door, thinking he'd back out, surprised when she opened it and smiled.

"Why didn't you?"

"Scared," he admits.

He hears a laugh in her voice. "Scared of what?"

"Of you. I wasn't sure if you liked me." Although she talked to him and he didn't see her talk to many people at the bar.

She plucks at the spot on her jeans again.

"I liked you."

"Liked?"

"Like."

He can feel her nervousness. He likes it; it excites him. Her face is like the surface of that lake, or the golden liquid in the drinks she pours, light and depth reflecting inward. He can't see below the surface. Her eyes without smiles give him no contradictions. Underneath her shyness, he senses a dark place to hide.

"How old are you?" he asks.

"Twenty-one."

"How long have you worked at the bar?"

"Nine months. How old are you?"

"Thirty-two."

The silence isn't comfortable or uncomfortable, but he feels a momentary fear, a worry that he has forgotten something or not thought it all the way through. Away from the lake, pink-colored clouds billow in a bluish gray sky. He lets the Chevelle pick up speed and rolls down his window. He thinks of Ginny, pictures her suddenly, layers of happiness, sadness, worry, joy in her eyes, feelings that had no place in the moment, elements of her life before him, things she brought with her, things he was afraid of.

Turning onto Oly Way, he slows and stops at a signal light. Grace is pushing her hair off her face, smiling at him faintly. He smiles back. "Too windy?"

"No. I like it."

He likes her, her gray eyes, the lightly freckled face. A sudden desire for a drink hits him in the throat, a vise squeezing up a sour taste in his mouth.

The light changes, he accelerates, driving down Oly Way, past the bar, into the dark of the firs once again, then slowing at the lights shining out of Marjorie's Restaurant.

"I haven't been here before," he says, almost sure of that.

"You'll like it. It's nice."

He opens her door, pulls her up by the hand. Light from the windows pools on the gravel. There are flower pots on the porch, café curtains on the windows, square tables and a single booth in a corner of the dining room. They sit at a table by a window away from the door. The table is a heavy wood, glossed with varnish, the chair seats upholstered in blue paisley to match the blue walls. A candle flickers, a white rose in a blue vase.

"This is nice," he says.

"I like it."

"Are you seeing anybody else?"

"No. Are you?"

"No. I was…I think. We broke up."

"I'm sorry."

"That's okay. I don't really remember her."

"What was her name?"

"Ginny."

He touches her fingers with his, smiling again as her hand rolls slowly over and he slides his fingers onto her palm.

"I'm glad you came out with me," he says again.

"Me too."

Her palm is moist, fingers squeezing his almost spasmodically, pulling away suddenly, face flushing.

"Will you go out with me again?"

"Yes."

At home, she pours him a drink from a bottle of scotch. She doesn't drink, it isn't hers, but he doesn't ask. There is bright yellow wallpaper in the hall with big orange flowers on it. Inside, she has a fuzzy yellow chair decorated with giant-sized purple flowers, and a red and white check love seat under a window. Lace curtains, a round kitchen table.

He doesn't stay the night. He sees her again, drinks her scotch, brings her a bottle of bourbon to replace it. He pours his own drink, sits on her red and white sofa, Grace sitting sideways at the other end with her knees up. He rubs at a knee with a fingertip. Her hands squeeze her shins.

"Whose scotch was that?"

"Nobody's. I just had it."

She isn't looking at him. He is glad because he knows he'd see things in her eyes. "I know who," he says.

"No, you don't."

"George."

"No."

He leans over to kiss her knee. "That's okay. I don't care."

He sits back up, drinks, feeling the numb edges he's waiting for. She leans her knees against the back of the sofa. He gets up and goes into the kitchen, pours another drink. The empty bottle of scotch is sitting in a corner of the counter, proof of a life he doesn't really want to know anything about.

He wants her to be empty, to wrap him up in emptiness. He is ashamed. His blood grows hot, his neck flushing, and he feels a sudden, overwhelming desire to go home. The bourbon burns his throat, heats his belly. Then he hears her say, "Will you stay?"

Her eyes watch him.

He puts his glass down on the kitchen table and goes over, reaches for her hand. Her bedroom is dark, an oblong of white at a window, curtains stirring gently when the wind blows in.

No moon. No stars. Quiet, woodsy air.

Waking up in her bed, he is surprised. The night before is a dim gray memory that disappears in the growing light.

At first, the dots of red look like a pattern, little flecks on a tile floor. The floor is white, shiny, glossy all the way to white baseboards. Sand-colored, once white, grout. The tiny dots spatter the floor near the toilet, nowhere else. Fin breathes carefully, following the grout line just under his eyes. He is lying on his bathroom floor. The transom window is open and the air is cold, but he is hot. He is lying face down. Curling his fingers on the tile, he pushes up slowly, sits on a hip, shaking on his arms. The dots are tiny, like a mist, a single large drop. Blood. Stray drops on the toilet seat. Acid rises into his throat. He chokes it back, squeezing his eyes shut, breathing slowly again. Cold air stirs in the room. A bird alights near the transom, flutters against the glass. He lifts his head to look and the room swims, unbalancing him. Snatching at the toilet, he sprawls over the seat and throws up. His head pounds, fingers loosening. He slides back down to the floor, soothed by the feel of the tile against his face. This time, no blood. The fluttering of the bird above fills his ears like the sound of the wind in the firs, drifting away. Falling asleep, he stays on the floor until a ray of sun floats across the ceiling.

The bird is gone, the color of the sky out the transom bright blue.

He gets up, avoids the mirror over the sink, treads carefully down the stairs, squinting where the light shines on the front window, shiny bright with dust motes. Shadows will soon grow again, forcing the light back out. He pauses at the window by the door to look outside. His car is parked up close to the porch. He scrubs at his mouth, feels fear in his belly. He can't remember driving, can't remember going out. He looks for his keys. Fear is prickling sweat under his arms. He is suddenly afraid of not remembering, of becoming as faded as the old photographs he keeps looking at, trying to disappear into pictures he can't remember.

Upstairs he looks back in the bathroom, under a towel on the floor, catches a glimpse of himself, red puffy eyes, bone white face, a tee-shirt and sweats. He looks down at bare feet. Carefully, he goes to the window at the end of the hall and looks outside, down at piles of pulled weeds. The memory floods back. He was planting dahlias, holes already dug in the weedy patches. Yesterday morning he drank his coffee at the back door and saw a pile of weeds go up in flames. It was shockingly real. The air smelled of gas. He stood motionless, frozen by the sight of dahlias growing in the receding flames. Then it was just weeds again. Now, with a sigh, he rests his forehead against the window, his reflection a shadowy image against the glass. Sparrows peck at the ground where the weeds used to be.

At Grace's, he sits on the sofa drinking a beer, only beer with her now, a case in her refrigerator, bottles on the shelves of the door where other people put pop or orange juice or milk. His fingers roll the bottle on the arm of the sofa. He imagines other people as the day changes to evening. Other people who come home and cook dinner, play ball with a boy or girl, go to soccer practice or dance lessons. Other people take a dog out for a walk, mow the lawn, help with homework. They are people who live on the other side of the moon. They are like Grace. Grace, who lives on the other side of the moon too, all the way across the room where she sits cross-legged on her purple and yellow chair, eating strawberry ice cream out of a green bowl. Who wakes up with an open heart. Who smiles at him all the time now. She's never fallen into a dark, bottomless hole. Never caught herself at the edge, wanting to fall. Never drank a beer with her anger simmering inside.

He unlocks his gritted teeth, swallows. His nerves are raw. He can feel every flutter of the breeze at the window.

"Do you want some?" she asks, offering her spoon.

Cars pull up outside, voices drifting.

He gets up, bends down for a spoonful of her strawberry ice cream. It smells strong like strawberry shampoo or strawberry lip gloss. The air smells of it. It follows him back to the sofa, taints the beer. He gets back up, opens another bottle. Strawberries. Strawberries and fir trees. Strawberries and coffee. Strawberries and rain-wet gravel. A memory that isn't a memory. Sitting down again, he squeezes the back of his neck. "That smells strong."

"You didn't like it?"

"No."

Her face bewitches him. Her moon gray eyes. Strawberries and snowflakes. She lives on the other side of the moon with people who aren't like him. She is laughing gently. "Who doesn't like ice cream?"

"I like ice cream. Just not strawberry."

She's sitting in a shadow now, a moon gray shadow.

"Grace...."

She looks up. Waiting.

"I need some time."

The words surprise him too. He hears her spoon in the bowl. The bowl on the floor.

"I don't understand."

He puts his head back, drinking the rest of his beer, wipes his mouth. "I'm an asshole," he says. "I'm sorry. I shouldn't have gotten involved."

"Involved?"

"Not like this."

"Like what?"

"I don't know who I am. I need to get my memory back."

"You might never."

"This isn't working."

"Is that really it? It just isn't working?" Her voice is deep, her gray eyes shiny.

"I'm sorry."

"You're sorry?"

"Please."

She rolls up, sitting with her elbows on her knees, her forehead resting on her cupped hands. "You were here all day, Fin. You never said anything."

"I told you. I'm an asshole."

"That explains it? That makes everything okay?"

"Please don't do this."

She looks up. "Please don't do what, Fin? Care?"

"I care."

"You care but want to leave me?"

"I have to."

"You don't have to."

He sits with his elbows on his knees too, biting on a knuckle, smelling, tasting strawberries. "You're making this hard."

"You're breaking my heart, Fin."

"Don't tell me that."

"I can't help it."

"I don't want to go. I have to."

"You don't have to. You want to. You don't care—"

"You can't tell me that!" His anger is boiling up again. He can feel the blood in his face. "I have to remember!"

"You don't have to. You might never. You might only have this."

"I can't...I can't give in. I don't want to fight with you. I have to go. I don't want to. I have to."

He can't look up anymore. A humming sound seems to fill the room, or maybe it's just in his head.

She says, "I won't stop you," and her voice isn't really hers. "You can go."

"I don't—"

"I want you to!"

"Grace—"

"I want you to go!"

He bites down on a knuckle, pulls it out of his mouth and leaves.

———————

One day, he saw the dry piles of weeds go up in flames again and there were soft pink roses and yellow and purple dahlias on the other side. He thought of Grace's yellow chair with the purple flowers.

On another day, he went upstairs with a bottle of bourbon and opened a door without a knob in a room at the end of the hall where the hall turned to go alongside the front of the house. The room had a bed in it and a chest of drawers and a rocker with a cane back, a sewing table without a sewing machine, a stool with an upholstered top, an oval mirror attached to the knobless door. The door popped open with a push and showed another staircase into the attic. There was a light chain just inside the door, but he didn't pull it. At the top of the stairs a silver light shone, like the light that filled the window at the other end of the hall at the back of the house.

In the attic he sat in a chair at the window, put his feet up on the sill and drank his bourbon while the sun went down.

A long delivery truck rolls up along the gravel strip outside of Ray's warehouse, rocks popping and crunching under its tires, stopping with a hiss of brakes. Ray pulls the warehouse door open, walking it along its track. He sees Grace in the lot, stepping over heavy clumps of weeds. Her hair, thin and light, floats. She is watching herself walk, oblivious to everything else. He thinks of the embarrassed way Miri moves, awkwardly tugging her tee-shirt over her bare knees as she sits on the couch in the morning.

Metal bangs on metal, disturbing the little birds in the lot across the way. They flutter up and settle back again at a distance.

The delivery driver is named Ed, reminding Ray to call the other Ed. Ray takes a clipboard from him. "I can tell just by lookin' this isn't right. Way short."

"Check the slips. Could be on back order."

They go through this every time. Ray slaps the clipboard against his thigh.

Grace is crossing over a plank of wood that spans the ditch beside the lot. Weeds grow in the ditch too, almost as tall as the ones that grow outside of it. Her steps sound hollow, silent on the pavement.

"Hey, sweet pea."

She looks over in surprise, sees him with an expression that turns strangely accusatory. Her voice, though, is normal, indifferent.

"Hi, Ray."

His eyes follow her inside, then look back at the delivery driver coming down the ramp of his truck.

"Back order, huh?"

"Is that it?"

"Looks like it. Why is everything always on fuckin' back order?"

"Sorry. Don't ask me. I just deliver."

They go through this every time too. Scowling, Ray passes back the clipboard. He is sweating by the time the truck lumbers off, and he goes inside to stand in front of the beleaguered air conditioner. Unbuttoning his shirt, he leans against the top of the unit and calls Ed.

"Me."

"Saw your kid," says Ed.

"Yeah? Where at?"

"Boardwalk."

His lips twist in distaste. "Overrated."

"Yeah, I know. I just went with a kid I know for fun. Pregnant ladies can't ride on most a that shit."

Ray looks down, his shirt barely fluttering, and straightens back up, not sure of the importance of that restriction. Then he rubs his eyes. "Talk to 'im?"

"No. Too far away."

Crossing the room, he looks through the window in the side door, sees Grace again, coming up the steps with a Day-Glo orange trash bag.

"Call you back," he says.

"Okay."

She drops it on the porch by the door. He looks down at it and then at her. "Hell are you doin'?"

"That's your garbage."

She pulled it out of the dumpster against the back fence. There's a dumpster on Ray's side of the alleyway too, piled high with the lid braced halfway up.

"You are fuckin' unbelievable."

This is bothering him more than it should, he knows, but he's hot and irritated, and not in the mood for her. Grabbing the bag, he takes it back over to the dumpster and throws it in.

She follows him, and then stops when he comes back over, crossing her arms over her chest.

"For fuck's sake, it's just garbage. You can put your shit in mine if I have room, I don't fuckin' care."

"You can't just do whatever you want," she says stubbornly.

Ray cocks his head at her. "Are we talkin' about garbage?"

"We pay for that bin, Ray."

"Okay, fine."

Reaching into his pocket, he pulls out a quarter and tosses it to her. She swivels away, still with her arms crossed, lets it bounce on the gravel, and then disappears back inside the bar. Ray's chest heaves in irritation and he swipes a hand through his hair, walking over to the shade by the side porch where he sits down on the steps to call Ed again.

"That you?" asks Ed.

"Yeah."

"You okay?"

"This is a fucked up day," he mutters, leaning back on the steps. It is cooler here than inside by the air conditioner.

"Take a break."

"Thinkin' about it," he says, and then adds, "Have you seen Cora around?"

"Yeah. An' I was thinkin'."

"What?"

"That dude came with her."

Ed means Joe Clay. Ray can feel a headache start. "Great character reference."

Ed would consider this.

There is a silence while Ray watches George pull up, get out and stoop, come back up again and flip Ray's quarter in the air.

He sits up with a sigh and a moment later Ed says, "Probably not."

There's a fountain under a palm tree beside a sign for the Acropolis Inn, a Safeway, a Taco Bell, a Jack-in-the-Box, and a Subway before the firs start up again. Up above, a strip of dark and starless sky.

Along a windy road, a building appears, flat roof, barely lit, a dark parking lot crowded with pickups, bikes, and cars. On a wall of the building facing the road is a sign in dim red: 'Jack of Clubs.' Shutters cover the windows. Under the eaves there's a cement walkway, a door painted black like the rest of the building.

Backing his car into a space at the far corner of the parking lot, Fin gets out and walks over to where Ray is waiting. They go inside where the lighting is slightly better. The place is packed with square tables, thrumming with music blaring out of a digital jukebox. Ray smacks Fin on the arm with the backs of his fingers, points at the back of the bar. A cut-out in the wall leads into another room. More tables, quieter. A few people are sitting there. There's a window without shutters but it is painted black. Fin picks a table by the painted window. A moment later, Ray joins him, yawns, and rests his hands on the arms of his chair.

"Anything new?"

Fin shakes his head. "Not really."

"I had a bit of a run-in with your girl today."

Fin leans back in his chair, sliding down in it. "Oh, yeah?"

"Nothin' serious though."

"That's good."

Even in the dim light Ray can see his jaw bunch up, see him take a deep breath to relax, slide his legs out slowly.

"You aren't curious?"

"About what?"

"I dump my garbage in Mulligan's bin sometimes. Today, she's flippin' out about it."

"That's weird."

Ray laughs. "Yeah, yeah. I'd say so."

"You work it out?"

Ray nods, rubs at his mouth with his thumb. "You guys okay?"

The question brings a grimace to Fin's face. He runs a hand through his hair, looking out into the bar. "Not really. We broke up."

"How come?"

"Strawberry ice cream," he says.

Ray smiles. Fin is laughing at him, rolling his head sideways on the back of the chair.

"You didn't like it?"

"No."

"Ask her to buy vanilla."

Fin laughs again, pushing himself up a little. Miri is there, setting down their drinks, plus two extra shots.

"Thank you," says Fin.

Ray swings his arm around her, a hand on her hip, pulling her into the crook of his arm. "This is my wife. Miri, this is Fin."

Fin puts his hand out and Miri leans over to shake it. Her blouse barely covers her. Fin looks away and Ray gives him a wry smile, then pats her on the hip. "Bring us back the same in a couple minutes."

"Sure. Nice meeting you," she says to Fin.

"Thank you. Nice meeting you too."

Ray is still smiling at him. "You get a good look?"

"I wasn't trying."

"No worries." Ray recalls his mother's boyfriend, Matt, saying that to him one day after Ray came home to find Matt and a topless woman swimming in their doughboy pool out back.

They drink their drinks. "Your ice cream. Reminds me of this strawberry cereal I ate as a kid," Ray says. "You remember that stuff?"

"No."

To Ray, it isn't strawberries that's a problem; it's orange, anything orange: Kool-Aid, candy, Miri's orange juice cartons in the refrigerator, reminding him of popsicles and Wayne. The fact that he doesn't really like oranges anymore isn't really about oranges.

"Cuz you don't like strawberries?" he asks.

Fin almost glares at him. "That's right."

"Sorry about your girl."

"Thanks."

In a few minutes, Miri shows up with another round. "Keep 'um comin', baby." Her fingers trail off Ray's shoulder, little ribbons of electricity. He follows her walk back to the bar. It isn't Otis' night. The barkeep is somebody named Gerry, youngish, wiry. He is flirting with Miri. Ray sighs and looks away. "Why'd you really break up?"

Fin rolls his gaze up to the ceiling, head against the back of the chair. "I don't know." The ceiling is black too, a flat lightless black.

Ray can feel himself beginning to sweat. He knows Fin's getting agitated. He gets the point of the tomblike atmosphere but the stuffy air and the thrumming vibration to the walls is getting to him too. Then Fin sits up and says, "Where's the bathroom?"

Ray points. "See the phone by the bar? Down the hall there."

Fin finishes his drink. Picking up the empty glasses, Ray follows, veering over to catch Miri at the bar. She leans over for a kiss.

"You having a good time?"

"Dude just broke up with his girlfriend."

"Oh…that's too bad."

"I need to cheer 'im up."

She eats an olive out of a plastic tray below her. "I'll bring you over the bottle.

He nods and says, "Gimme one."

"Are you hungry?"

"Not really. Ate at Candi's."

"What?"

"BLT."

She pops an olive into his mouth.

"I'm gettin' fat," he says.

"No, you're not."

"Over my fightin' weight."

"You look good."

"Good lookin'?"

She smiles and he grins at her again.

"Good lookin'," she agrees.

"That's my baby."

"Wife loves orange juice," says Ray, pouring a drink out of the bottle Miri brought over. Fin is watching him with sleepy eyes, head against the back of his chair, keeping his glass close. "I hate it. Never drank it growing up. Hated milk too, except in cereal. So did my mom. We never had much after my dad left. Went to St. Louis, I think. I got a postcard. Bowling," he adds because he figures that's why Wayne went there. Wayne's home is someplace near the Museum of Bowling. In the summer, he probably sits outside with an orange popsicle melting over his greasy fingers.

At home, they had a pale blue doughboy out back and a lawn that was clumpy where the water splashed on it. The grass grew better further away from the pool and it was tall on the day Wayne left. Before that though, he brought out two popsicles, orange for him, and they sat on the back porch, eating in the hot sun. Wayne's fingers were grimed with oil he could never get out of the creases. His fingernails were pale, cuticles cracked, the half-moons bright white. His knuckles were swollen. Ray kept staring at his hands, watching him swipe popsicle juice off on his pants.

Looking out through the screen once, Ray's mother said, "Are you going to mow that lawn?"

"I said I would."

"I'm just checking."

But he didn't want to mow the lawn and after he finished his popsicle, he flicked the stick away and said, "We're outta popsicles."

"I can go get some."

"On your bike? They'll melt. Gotta think things through, Ray."

"I'm just sayin' I could an' they wouldn't melt."

Wayne looked down and shook his head at him. "God, you're like your mom. I'll go get 'um."

Then he popped inside for his keys, went back down the steps and never came back.

"I thought you two kinda fit together," says Ray. "Too bad you couldn't work through the strawberry ice cream thing."

Grimacing a smile at him, Fin sits up, bumping into the table. Ray grabs the wobbling bottle and pushes it over to him. He pours a drink, sloshing bourbon on the table. "Sorry." Then he sits back and takes a swallow. "Tha' was a joke," he says.

Ray nods, rubbing his mouth with a finger. "I know. I'm just talkin' outta my ass. Thinkin' about things." Things like orange popsicles and Irene's first boyfriend, Matt, and the bike Matt took him out on, and the cigarettes Irene never smoked, and the postcard from St. Louis, and Sherry, and the party at Ed's. He came with Sherry, but he lost her there for a while, and then she was kneeling beside him where he sat on the couch with some other girl who was a sweet-smelling blur through the tequila he was drinking. Sherry was shaking him.

"Ray, do something. That guy just hit on me."

"What guy?"

She pointed at Ed's father. He didn't know Ed's father, but he squinted at a man in a Barcalounger, trying to make him out in the blurry room.

"Him?"

Sherry sighed. "C'mon." She dragged him over. The cold air coming through the open sliding glass doors cleared his eyes a little. He saw a grown man, fortyish, giving him a stare.

"Wha'do you want?"

"My girl says you hit on her."

"So?"

"So. She's my girl."

"So keep 'er on a leash."

"You fucker!" Sherry shrieked and started slapping him in the head.

The man swatted her hands away and slapped her back. She wailed, "*Ray!*" and Ray slugged the man in the head, bouncing back when he got up. He saw the beefy shape tower over him and said, "Wait a minute."

But the man didn't wait. He knocked Ray down on the floor. Ed and Sherry dragged him back to the couch. He knows he woke up in the morning, but he doesn't remember a lot of that. He remembers the evening and Ed looking over at a man in a Barcalounger.

"I could go for some White Castle's."

"Ain't no White Castle's around here," said the man in his Barcalounger.

"They have 'um at the store."

"Not the same."

"There's Caspar's," said Ray, surprised at the sound of his own voice. Both heads turned to stare.

"Caspar's are hotdogs," said Ed.

"Yeah."

When he finally went home, Irene was sitting on the swing on the porch with her unlit cigarette.

"Where have you been?"

"I went to a party."

"A party?"

He didn't answer.

She looked at her cigarette, then back at him, got up and said, "Your face is bruised."

He followed her inside. She had been smoking in the house. There were glasses and cups in the sink. She saw him looking at it.

"I called in sick yesterday."

"You're sick?"

"No, Ray. What the hell were you thinking? You just disappear? Christ, you're like your goddam father."

He could see the expression on his face mirrored in hers. She looked away. "I have to go."

He heard the water running in the bathroom, but she wasn't singing. Usually she'd sing as she got ready. It went with the sound of water splashing in the sink.

"I'm nobody's baby…I don't know why…."

She had a good voice, he remembers.

The room isn't his, isn't any of the rooms in his house. Tipping his head back, Fin looks at a window covered in tan- and brown-striped curtains. He's lying on top of a narrow bed against a wall. A door is in the center of the wall opposite the window, with a bifold sliding door to a closet on one side and a highboy on the other. White walls, a wood floor with a brown and green braided rug.

He rolls to his side, sits up carefully. Which makes his head swim, so he drops it down on the palms of his hands, staring at his feet. Somebody took his shoes off. He rubs his head carefully, thinks back, clutches at snatches of memory, the empty bar, Ray shutting off the lights, Miri's solemn face, the air blowing in through his car windows, waking him up, Miri again, looking across the seat at him.

"Are you okay?"

Nodding, leaning back against the door, eyes closing. A voice, sorrowful and hopeless. "Sorry…sorry…."

Then the motion of the car lulled him to sleep. He doesn't remember waking up or going into the house.

Slowly, he reaches down to his shoes. A TV is droning softly in the other room. He feels hot suddenly and sits quietly, resting a moment, then gets up and goes into the hallway. A door on the other side leads into a bathroom. He enters, avoiding the mirror, flushes the toilet a moment later, then follows the sound of the TV into a bright living room. Seeing him, Miri uncurls her legs and sits up on the couch, looking at him expectantly.

He smiles. "Morning…I think."

She smiles back. "Are you okay?"

"Sure," he says. "I'm good. Sorry for putting you out."

"You didn't."

"Well, thanks anyway."

"Do you want some orange juice? Or I could make you something to eat."

"No, thank you. Where's Ray?"

"Work."

He rubs his head and almost winces. "I guess I better go." Then he pats his pockets. "My keys?" he asks.

"On the kitchen counter." She gets up, in Ray's boxers and a tee-shirt. "I'll walk you out."

"That's okay. I'm fine. Thank you though."

"You do that a lot," she says.

"What?"

"Thank you. I'm sorry. You were doing it last night too."

His surprise stuns him for a moment, angers him too, but he smiles, shrugs. "I didn't know that."

Her eyes are on his. His feelings for her are suddenly unkind. In the bright light, she looks washed out, gray skin under her eyes, a hum of worry that grates on his nerves. Her appeal to Ray eludes him. He can feel pressure building up in his forehead. Heat burning up his skin again.

He says it anyway without wanting to. "Well, thanks…." Then, "I'm sorry." And then with a sigh, "I don't know what else to say."

"That's okay." In the kitchen she points out his keys. "You remind me of Ray."

He wants to get away. "In what way?"

"He thinks he's a lot worse than he is too."

He is controlling his breathing, aware that his stomach is spasming. "Will you tell 'im I'll call 'im?"

She nods, brushes her hair off her face in a way that does appeal to him.

"You're welcome back any time."

The words come out angry. "Thank you."

At home, he makes a pot of coffee and sips a cup at the sink, looking through the window at the weedless yard outside. He put pansies and marigolds in pots. The sparrows still come, pecking at the dirt. Halfway through the coffee, his stomach lurches and he bends over, retching into the sink with a cool, peculiar gratitude.

At night he goes to the cemetery and looks through the gates. Angels gleam in the dark. A pair with wings rise above a block of granite.

At the river he sits where a rock sparkles with bright specks in the sun.

Once, on a day he doesn't remember, he stood at Abel's grave with Jonah and Sissy, and everyday afterwards Sissy came back with flowers.

One day, he sees a pop bottle on top of a gas pump, a man bending out of sight, and thinks about Grace sitting there in the cool, dim light with a bowl of strawberry ice cream.

Asleep, he sees another girl with a bowl of ice cream on a porch he remembers in his dreams. A gray-eyed girl wearing a small cross around her neck. The smell of strawberries fills the air. A moment later he's standing at a gas station with two pumps out front, a Coke bottle on top of one. A boy with light brown hair down his neck is coming over to him, swiping a tee-shirt under his arms.

And then there's the sound of a car coming closer and he sits up on the couch at home.

Outside, the sun is shining and the living room is cool and quiet. He knows it's Sully outside. Usually he meets him at Candi's and feels a hint of a memory every time he sees the palm tree at the Acropolis Inn out the window. But it's a rain-washed window he sees, a silver sunless light filling the diner. After they have breakfast, Sully always says, "Why don't you stop off at work with me?"

His response is always the same. "Later."

Once he stopped on the road above the factory's parking lot, idling in the shade, looking across the tops of sunlit cars and pickups at the squat brick buildings. The heat built up in the car and he pulled away, remembering nothing.

Now, opening the front door, he says, "I forgot."

"Overslept," says Sully, closing the door behind him.

He follows Fin, who stops at the bottom of the stairs. Sully looks into the living room, almost unchanged, except the cushions on the couch are in disarray. The pages of a newspaper are scattered on the floor, a paper plate on the coffee table, a bottle of whiskey. Inexplicably, tee-shirts, socks, a pair of jeans litter the floor too.

Sully looks away. "Your landlady sent some a your things up," he says. "They came to work."

"Oh." He's aware of the whiskey too now and rubs at his chest. "I have to get dressed."

"Okay."

When he's upstairs, he can hear Sully in the kitchen and then in the little bathroom across the hall and then in the living room again. At the upstairs window he looks out at the ground below. The distance seems to stretch out, not bottomless, just deep, dark, beyond his reach, someplace where piles of flowers burn and it rains a silent silver rain and suddenly fills the house with a cold dawn light. He's afraid to open the window.

"You comin'?"

"Yeah. Be right down."

Outside he feels relaxed. "Sun's nice."

"Pretty day," agrees Sully.

There are still wildflowers blooming in the meadow with the trailer.

"Ira's," says Sully as they go by. In the weeds there are little birds and puffs of dandelion plumes floating away. Then he says, "Agnes," and starts to slow. "Waylon's daughter."

A girl with brown wooly hair and brown eyes and who smells like strawberries. She came across Ira's meadow from the river and picked a flower with pink petals and a white center. The smell of strawberries wafts in through the window and Fin's head starts to pound again.

"Hop in," says Sully.

"Thanks."

Her flower is drooping in the heat. She scoots up, leaning on the back of the front seat.

"I'm Agnes."

"This is Fin," says Sully.

Fin looks back, trying to avoid the smell of strawberries. She's close and warm and the smell is strong.

He nods and Sully says, "We're on our way to your dad's."

"I thought so." She braces her flower with her fingertip and her face is suddenly solemn.

Now the town appears in its circle of fir trees and mountains. Puffy white clouds sit motionless in the sky. A crisscross of roads. A yellow signal light. A gas station on one corner, a market on the other with a half hidden building behind it, and a town hall further down the road, then firs again, reforming against the disappearing asphalt. The sun here is mild and pale.

Fin's eyes slide over buildings he doesn't remember, a sun bleached porch, the sparkle of gravel on the lot behind the market, dusty cars, a pickup backed into a corner.

Agnes scoots over to her door, dragging her droopy flower across the back of Fin's seat. Easing up against one of the railroad ties that line the parking lot, Sully shuts off the engine and Agnes jumps out.

"Thanks for the ride!"

The smell of strawberries lingers and Fin gets out of the car too, sucking in a breath of fresh air. It smells good outside, warm, dusty, astringent with fir trees, but his head keeps pounding, irritating him and making him squint. "Why here?"

"Why not?"

"I like Candi's."

He's comfortable there, comfortable at the mini-mart with the liquor store next door, comfortable at the gas station on Ash Street, comfortable at Quality Videos. He presses a thumb against his temple, following Sully reluctantly. Then, at the smack of the screen door in front, he stops, skin flushing; he feels a sudden sweaty panic, but the footsteps recede, fade away on the other side of the building.

"C'mon."

"I'm coming."

There's nobody on the porch and nobody visible through the darkish windows. Sully pushes open the squeaky screen and Fin follows. A room filled with shadowy shapes where pale faces look over. Inside, the air smells like coffee, eggs, maple syrup.

A man on a stool gets up. He has thin, brown hair, whip-like muscles, eyes that are curious, neutral and calm. He stops in front of Fin and looks him over.

"I was at your mom's funeral. I guess you don't remember, though. My name's Orly Squire."

His head is going to explode. "I don't remember," he says. "But thank you."

Orly's hand is dry and slightly rough. His eyes maintain their neutrality, never warm to his smile.

"C'mon over."

Sully is sitting down on a blue stool at the lunch counter. On one side of him is a man with a receding hair line and almost colorless eyes behind wire-rimmed glasses. Standing, he is thin and angular with spider-like limbs. His movements are strangely awkward and willowy at the same time.

"Eb Sanderson. This is Fin Sandor. I don't think you ever knew him."

"No, sir."

Fin shakes his hand, feeling a clamminess that is probably his own. "Nice meeting you," he says.

"No, sir. The pleasure's mine."

A pudgy man behind the counter scrubs his hands on a white apron. He is pasty white with thin ribbons of color in his cheeks that give him a clownish, made-up look.

"This is Waylon," says Orly

Waylon nods. "Nice to see you again."

A long-haired man at the end of the counter keeps eating, rocking up a little on his stool. His boots are planted on the foot rest below. He is in a washed out blue tee-shirt with holes in the sleeves and a pair of jeans. Orly raps on his shoulder.

"An' this is Jonah. Jonah Hollycock."

The eyes that turn to him are deep blue, almost purple, and Fin sees something, almost like a memory, a strange, surreal memory that just flutters like a piece of tattered cloth in a blue sky. The color blue fills his eyes, a deep, winter blue, enveloping everything until Orly says, "Hey. Whoa. Here you go."

He feels hands pushing him down onto the stool by Sully. His face is sweaty. The man named Jonah watches him with narrow eyes.

Wiping his face, Fin sees Orly shoot Jonah a look. "Wha' did you do?"

"Me? I'm just sittin' here eatin' my breakfast. Or tryin' to."

"That's okay," says Fin. "I just get a little shaky."

Waylon sets down a glass of orange juice for him.

"Drink that," says Sully, "an' we'll get some food in you too."

"How long since you've been outta the hospital?" asks Orly.

"Weeks. I don't know why that happened."

"Pretty traumatic."

"Might be if I remembered it." He laughs, surprising himself, sees a startled look from Jonah again too.

Orly says, "Well, at least you have a sense of humor about it."

"Must be nice," said Jonah. "Just to forget stuff."

"Why would anybody want that?" asks Orly.

"I bet a lotta people would."

"You?"

"We're not talkin' about me." There are scars on the man's face, scars that are growing red.

Sucking air through his teeth, Orly goes back to his coffee and donut, patting Fin's shoulder as he goes by.

"Well, it's good havin' you home anyway."

"Thanks."

The orange juice cools him down again.

Sitting in the kitchen, Agnes peeked through the door when she heard the commotion with Fin, saw Orly and Eb standing over him. Then she looked at Jonah, willing him to look over, but he didn't.

Now her father comes in to cook their breakfast and says, "Couple eggs for you too?"

"Scrambled."

"Okay."

She swings her legs, watching him spread frozen potatoes on the griddle, cracking sweat-beaded eggs into a bowl and splashing in a little milk.

"Mix these up," he says, giving her the bowl and a fork.

"Do you remember Betsy from school?" she asks.

"I think so."

"They had a garage sale the other day an' made a ton of money."

"A ton, huh?"

"Well, a lot. Why don't we do that?"

"What would we sell?"

"We have a lot of stuff we don't use. We can even sell Mom's clothes."

Now his movements become slow. He reaches out in slow motion for her bowl, slowly pours her eggs onto the griddle.

"Your mom's clothes?"

His tone makes her hesitate. "Or other stuff. The stuff we don't use."

He nods, pulling plates off the shelf above the griddle. Then he says, "You can have this for now," taking Eb's tip out of the pocket of his apron. "Just take the garbage out for me."

"Okay." Then she says, "I love you, Daddy."

"I love you too."

Agnes waits until she hears him come out, then starts across the parking lot with a bag of garbage. Seeing her, he comes over slowly, grabs the bag and tosses it into the bin. "That it?" he asks.

"That's the only one I saw."

"You're a real worker."

"Why are you always making fun of me?"

"Just making conversation," he says, wandering off to his pickup.

She stares at him, but he ignores her, leans back against the front of his pickup and lights a cigarette, flicking the match away. He takes a puff, crosses his legs at the ankles, shifting to get comfortable. She doesn't move though until he finally glances over.

"What?"

Then she whirls away and slams the screen door on her way back in.

At the counter, Fin shifts to get his wallet out of his pocket and sees Sully's head shaking.

"No, you don't."

"You always pay."

"That's the way I like it."

Fin sinks back, hearing the screen door slamming again. It's the girl, Agnes, dropping her forearms on the counter, rocking there with a slightly aggressive look on her face. Fin imagines he has seen that face before, an older face with a restless, dissatisfied sulk to it. Agnes is sulking too.

"Where's your flower?" he asks.

"I don't know," she says, straightening up in surprise. Then she turns and goes back into the kitchen. The screen door creaks again, a little partway creak.

"You ready?" Sully is picking up his keys.

Fin rises too, bracing his fingers on the countertop.

"Okay?" asks Orly.

"Oh, yeah. I'm fine. Thank you."

"You always were a polite kid."

He smiles and goes over to the door, looking angrily outside, breathing in and out slowly. Angry over friendliness. A kindness. Miri's curious worry. Hearing Sully come up behind him, he pushes open the door with his shoulder and smiles again at Orly. "Nice meeting you."

Orly nods, chewing easily on his toothpick. "You too."

Outside, he takes a deep breath and steps off the porch. The road is empty, the gas station is empty, no Coke bottle on the pump, no boy with light brown hair swiping a tee-shirt under his arms. Fin's anger suddenly dissipates into anxiety. He remembers this, knows the man smoking at his pickup was the boy with the light hair. The man shifts his weight, raises his arms back, and braces his palms against the edge of the hood, resting backwards.

"Don't look at 'im," says Sully. "That's what 'e wants."

"Why?"

"I didn't understand you two at the time. I don't know what came between you. Considerin' your ages, probably a girl." Opening his car door, Sully gives the roof a loud rap. "C'mon. We need to go pick up your stuff."

But Fin stares at Jonah a moment longer, meeting eyes that stare back and reveal absolutely nothing.

Alone, Fin goes upstairs to the attic. In the daytime the sun is orange on the window, lace curtains dingy and still.

He sits in the sun on his chair, shirt off, a cool bottle resting against his belly. It is stuffy up here and he drinks slowly, staring up at the ceiling. A cobweb gently stirs. He pictures a starless sky and lets his eyes fall to the window and its curtains of lace like Grace's and she appears, ghostlike, sitting on a yellow and purple chair, her green bowl full of strawberry ice cream.

In the living room, there's a box with a clock, vase, silverware, a glass bowl, china, Dahlia's picture, *Superman* comics. At the factory, he stayed in the car. A man he didn't know came out with the box. The presence of the comic books bewilders him.

At the window upstairs he rests his elbows on the edge, whiskey bottle in his fingers.

At home in a happy house.

It was Dahlia who was unhappy.

Up here he sees all the way to a lightless moon and veil-like curtains over a yellow and purple chair.

8

♦ Chimes ♦

At least he said, "Good morning," when he saw her and she answered him back. She even gave a partial smile. "Morning."

Today, Kurt looks at her wind chimes when he goes underneath them the same way he looks up at the giant bowling pin. Oftentimes, he feels motionless as if he's not going anywhere at all. It isn't a physical thing and he doesn't need to move anywhere. He just needs a purpose, a point to things.

On his way to work, he passes her closed door. Inside is a quiet that's utterly still.

In the morning, Kurt follows Jonah into the lunch room and leans up against the coffee machine and sees the plastic strips of ribbon that flutter in the air coming through a vent across the room.

"Wonder why they do that."

Jonah looks back and says, "What?"

"Tie on those ribbons."

"I dunno," he says and faces the machine again, dropping his money into the slot. "Tell when it stops, I guess."

"Guess so."

Kurt is looking at the front of the vending machine again. One of

Joy's wind chimes is made out of crystal icicles for noise and pink and blue and yellow ribbons for color. On some days, they don't make any sound at all even though he knows the air is always moving. Her wind chimes remind him of a model of the solar system he got for Christmas one year. The people he lived with had an apartment with Astroturf on the balcony floor and in the entrance hall too. A roof covered the hallway and on the other side there was another apartment. He remembers that it was always dark in there and that there was a funny smell. He wasn't sure if it was dry or damp. The insides of the apartments were dark too except for the living rooms by the balconies.

The solar system fit into his sense of non-animation, of feeling motionless and he thought he might start moving once he put the model together. He got a scooter too that Christmas, but it's the model he still thinks about. He imagines it had an effect on him he still isn't sure of. He felt after he left that place that he really did begin to move. He stayed with only one other family and then he was on his own for real.

He doesn't know where the model went, but he can picture the planets' slow spin. The other day when he came downstairs and slowed up because Joy was passing by at the bottom of the stairs, he suddenly had a clear picture of that model and he didn't think it was random anymore that his life was crossing the course of hers.

She glanced up at him and he felt full of purpose.

"Good morning."

Especially after a corner of her mouth lifted up slightly. "Morning," she said.

In the lunch room, he straightens up and stares with Jonah at the vending machine. It's making noise inside but nothing's coming out, not even a cup. And then the machine thumps and grows still and Jonah sighs.

"Fifty fuckin' cents."

Somebody once taped a piece of yellow notepaper to the side of the machine and wrote 'NO REFUNDS WITHOUT A CLAIM FOR LOSS FORM' in red ink.

"Wanna fill one out?"

When he looks over, Kurt gestures with a tip of his head to the side of the machine with the notepaper and Jonah sighs again while he thinks and then shrugs and says, "It ain't worth it."

Kurt pushes off from the other side of the machine. "Guess not."

It would depress him not to get his coffee. He remembers when he stopped off at Safeway once to get some baloney before work but they were all out and he didn't have time to go anywhere else. It depressed him. He felt rejected.

Now he shrugs as if it doesn't really matter and says, "Stop off at the bowling alley."

"What for?"

"Coffee. An' I can tell you about Gus."

"Just coffee."

"I almost went in for that raise," he continues as if he didn't hear him. "Tell you all about it."

They walk down the hall to the open door at the end. It's light outside and the air smells cool and the floor where the light comes in looks shiny and clean. Up close it's covered in dirty boot prints.

"You or Gus?" asks Jonah.

"Me," says Kurt, blinking in the light. He pulls his cap off, scrubs at his hair, settles it back on. "A bunch of us were supposed to go in." Jonah looks over. "I didn't think you'd want to," he adds.

"Thought right."

"Well, I didn't go either."

He shrugs and slows up as they reach his car. He's embarrassed suddenly at changing his mind about going in for the raise and pushes at his hood to give himself something to do.

"Good thinkin'," says Jonah.

Kurt feels vaguely dishonorable. "I was thinkin' about my reviews."

"They suck."

"Yeah. I really need to fix up my car," he says, sniffing at an odor of oil only he can smell. The sun bounces off his hood in warm waves. He pushes his cap up a little. "OT's comin'."

Jonah pauses to laugh before he lights his cigarette, cupping the match in the slight, warm breeze. He waves it to put it out, exhales and says, "Guess that's your raise."

"Guess so," he murmurs, back to sniffing at his hood again.

Just before they left for the bowling alley, Kurt said, "Smell that oil?" and Jonah shrugged. "No."

"I love this car."

"Ain't worth the upkeep." And that's when Jonah came up the idea of bumping him into a ditch on the way for coffee. "Collect the insurance."

When Kurt is almost at Marjorie's Restaurant he hears the roar of Jonah's pickup and sees it come out of the shade, growing bigger and bigger. The wind is blowing through his car but the roar grows even louder. He speeds up and sunshine flashes off the grill behind him. It fills his back window and he hunches up, waiting. There's a tap, jolting him up, he lurches and the pickup falls back, then he whips by Marjorie's Restaurant and the pickup is catching up again. A signal light appears, disappears. Kurt changes lanes, passes the bar and focuses on the bowling pin, flat and almost colorless in the sunshine, then guns the motor and races through a yellow light at the corner. Behind him, Jonah stops and Kurt slows down again. Now the sound of rocks popping under his tires seems unnaturally loud. The shadow of the bowling pin slips underneath him and he rolls to a stop at his apartment building.

A man under a car twists slightly, stares out, slides back under.

He reaches over to roll his other window up and feels the heat outside. He locks up his car now because he keeps the gun Ray gave him in the glove box.

He still isn't sure that the look of disappointment on Ray's face was real. After all, Ray has guns too. He didn't really think that it would make him bigger or stronger. Or that people would suddenly take notice of him. He could never think of a good reason to show it to Joy; it's not like he could sit there cleaning it on the steps one day, casually calling out "Nice day, isn't it?"

But he does like it. He likes the thought of it in the glove box, the thought that he has something that not everybody else has.

At first, he couldn't wait to show it to Jonah, but then when the time came, he didn't for some reason. He just looked at Jonah looking back at him and didn't. Now he gets out, locks up his car and waves at the man, who is looking back out at him again.

"How ya doin'?"

The bowling pin was the topper when he came here. Plus, there was a whole strip with Arby's, Jack-in-the-Box, Subway's, and Taco Bell, and the minute he got out of town the air was always cool and fresh. There are real restaurants too, like Candi's and Marjorie's.

Anytime he wants a donut, though, he always goes to the bowling alley.

When he reaches Jonah, he pushes him up against the glass doors and says, "Fucker."

Jonah just laughs and follows him inside. Kurt pauses at the snack bar as Jonah goes into the lounge. There are people bowling already and all the jelly donuts are gone.

"Any jellies in back?" he asks.

"Sorry."

He buys a box of Juicy Fruit instead.

It seems like the only light in the lounge is coming from candles in red holders. Even the windows on the alley are dark.

When his drink and coffee come, he swallows some of his candy and says, "I ever tell you about this accident I was in?"

"I don't think so."

"You'd remember. I just got off work an' this car in front a me kept slowin' down, almost stoppin', then speedin' up an' slowin' down again. Pissed me off. Anyway I wanted to get home, go back out, an' I got up real close, kinda pushin'."

"Sue you?"

"No. I didn't hit anybody. The car in front just up an' stopped again. I slammed on my brakes an' got hit by the car in back a me. The car in front just kept on goin'. Man, was I pissed."

Jonah laughs.

"I shoulda sued. I just let the guy go cuz I thought I was okay. No big deal. Couple days later though, I'm at this laundromat, bendin' down to get somethin' an' *pow!* I can't get back up again. Stop laughin'. I went home a goddam hunchback an' some fucker stole my clothes. Can you believe that? A cripple's clothes…."

Outside, he follows the shadow of the bowling pin out onto the street, stopping in the middle to look up.

Ally put a jar of jelly beans in crayon box colors on the counter with the stack of brochures by the door to the stairs the visitors use. She likes butterscotch too, just like Clover.

Jonah rocks against the counter and stares at her violets.

At home there are geraniums like Aster's and pansies on the shady side of the garage, weeds and wildflowers.

She doesn't see him right away, comes out of a room in back with her tea and then slows when she looks up and sees him. "Hi."

"How ya doin'?" he asks softly.

Later, on the way home again, Jonah pulls over where the road drops down into the pit that was going to be Ivy's pond. Ivy didn't complain to Samuel because it wouldn't have mattered to him, but she didn't want the pond here. The sun only shines up high. Underneath, it is always dusk.

Ivy liked Ira's meadow because the pools of water were silver and still in the spring.

The water here always seeps away.

Once Abel put on his best suit and Aster came out in a dress, and when Jonah went over to her, she said, "Don't muss me," but then in the pickup she pulled him into her lap and whispered, "Look," because she saw a grouse above the little pool of water. The drop to that pool looked very deep and the bird had a strange blue light to it in the dark. There was wonder in her voice too because he knows now the bird was a surprise to see. It was almost invisible in the shade the firs made.

After she said, "Look," Abel looked over too and said, "We're goin' to say goodbye to your gramps so you behave."

"I told 'im," Aster murmured.

"So I'm makin' sure. I just wanna get this damn thing over with."

She looked away and her reflection in the window appeared and disappeared as the light came and went. Jonah hugged her, wanting her to be happy. She was different without Job, nervous, with quicksilver smiles. She made him be quiet at home, holding a finger to her lips. "Hush now."

Abel was strange too, irritable and suspicious. In the pickup, he looked sideways at them and said, "Never minds you anyway."

Abel was already angry by the time they reached the cemetery and saw all the chairs up on the hillside. The wind was pulling at their clothes and the light in the open was bright and clear. Jonah knew Job was in the coffin and he looked at Abel, who didn't look at him, and then at Aster, who put a finger to her lips.

During the service, when Abel got up, he got up too, but then Aster pulled him back quickly.

"I wanna see," he said. But she put a finger to her lips again.

Abel stared at her for a long time after he sat back down. Later, they waited for him at the pickup where Jonah poked a stick in the dirt, then looked up at her and said, "Are we gonna go home after this?"

She nodded and crossed her arms over her belly. She was pregnant with Sissy and had to buy a dress for the funeral. Abel turned red when he saw it and said, "Like you're ever gonna where that again."

It was a dark blue dress with a white collar and cuffs and big white buttons.

After a while of waiting, Jonah started to squint at her from different angles. She smiled, then her smile got bigger until that was all he saw, then he opened his eyes back up, sighed and said, "I'm gonna marry you when I get big."

Her look was pleased and expectant. "Really?"

Coming over, he leaned against her and said, "I'm already big."

"Very big," she agreed.

Then he put both arms up, reaching for her face.

"This big!"

"Not yet," she said.

When Abel started down, she was leaning back against the pickup, swinging him from side to side. It made her face red, but she was laughing anyway. Abel saw people smiling at her when they went by. He didn't look at them, just went to the other side of the pickup and said, "C'mon."

On the way home, he pulled his tie loose and glanced over at Jonah, who got onto his knees beside him, trying to see into the pool as they went by. It grew windy again and needles blew through sudden rays of light, then shadows fell. Abel looked back at the road, then said, "Whadaya doin' there, Jojo?"

Swiveling back around, Jonah sat with his knees up and his back against Aster's arm. Then she moved and her arm came down across his chest.

"Nothin'."

"Just lookin'?"

"Yeah."

"At nothin'?"

"Yeah."

"You just all of a sudden got up to look at nothin'?"

"Yeah."

"At nothin'?"

"Abe—"

"Abe what? Answer me, Jojo. Were you lookin' at me?"

"No."

"You were lookin' at nothin'?"

"That bird."

"No bird."

He felt Aster's arm tighten, her breath warm air.

"There was, Abe. On our way down. I saw it too."

"Well, isn't that interestin'? Your gramps is dead an' you're thinkin' of some bird you saw. Your gramps, Jojo, was my pops. Just like I'm yours. You just think about that, an' you too, Aster. Actin' like you were at a goddam party."

At the house, he pulled to a stop, shifted sideways, draping an arm across the top of the seat and the other over the steering wheel, then stared at Jonah for a moment before he leaned closer and said, "Do you like playin', Jojo?"

Jonah thought about it, looking for some trick, and didn't sound sure. "Yeah." He was frowning, too, and his face began to look belligerent. Abel's was empty for a moment. "Time an' a place though. I wonder what people were thinkin', you an' your mom?"

Her arm tightened and Jonah tipped his head back to look up at her.

"I was big," he said.

There was a second of silence before Abel laughed and looked outside, rocking the steering wheel with his arm. He didn't look back in again until Aster moved. Then she stopped and just sat there. Her face looked empty. Then Abel leaned in close and almost smiled.

"You ain't that big, Jojo."

Washing away the coffee he drank at the lounge with a glass of bourbon, Jonah sits on the side of the bed, thinking of nothing. Coolness, quiet, almost nothing until a soft creak interrupts him and he whirls, facing emptiness.

There's silt at the bottom of Kurt's pickle jar. He gives it a shake and starts to feel hot. On one side of the apartment there are shadows and on the other his shades are orange. He can hear Joy's TV. He takes a pickle out and sniffs at it. He feels like a fish sandwich too, a salad with cucumbers and slices of tomato, pop or lemonade, and lawn chairs to sit in outside of Joy's door.

He can hear himself say, "Great dinner, babe," and see the way the corner of her mouth lifts up.

As a shadow fades, Jonah jumps up off the bed, bursting out into the living room. It is bright and homey with sunlight. Empty, the kitchen too. He goes outside and looks up.

"Hey, Pops!"

On the walkway below there are footsteps, maybe Joy's. Her TV went off a while ago and now he hears a wind chime ring as if somebody tapped it going by.

A little girl lives in one of the apartments below. Once, she drew hopscotch squares in pink and blue chalk on the walkway.

It isn't the little girl's footsteps though. After a while it's quiet again.

Angeline, he thinks, lying with his head on his pillow.

If he married her, she'd have to keep their little girl quiet. At work he could sit there with a sandwich and say, "Wife's real good about lettin' me sleep."

After a while he sighs and sits up to watch TV.

Earlier, when he stopped off at work, Jonah leaned on the counter and heard it creak. "Think it's gonna break?" he asked without moving.

Ally smiled because it was a joke. He could see the worry in her eyes though and she could smell the bourbon he drank.

"Take it outta my pay."

She made herself laugh. "You better not then."

"Need all we can get," he agreed, straightening up.

She reminds him of Aster now.

On the walkway outside the apartment building, Kurt pauses and taps at the wind chime with the ribbons. It looks cheerful swinging in the cool light.

9

◆ Broken Things ◆

On a side street off Oly Way, there's a mortuary by a laundry and a pawn shop. It's on the other side of a white barrier at the end of the street and there's a sign by the walkway between the lawns up to a porch with white posts that says 'Greenview Mortuary Services.' Carl knows this and knows there's a man inside named Mr Torch. When he wakes up one morning, he thinks about this and imagines the look of the light on the grass.

Outside it's sunny, cool and dim and quiet inside.

Quietly, on bare feet, Miri slips into the dark bedroom. Her toes curl on the edge of a shaggy rug. On the floor, Ray's boots, a pair of jeans, a shirt on top. She sips her orange juice, then sets the glass down. She likes the signs of him here, his tools and weight bench in the garage, the block of Lava soap, loose coins on the dresser top. She didn't live here alone for very long. She was still with Will and stayed mostly with him. Having Ray move in didn't really change anything because he's almost never home, but she feels less lonely thinking he'll always come back, that this is where he lives. At the bed, she sets her knee on the edge and slowly adds her weight. His eyes are covered by his arm. She thinks he's awake though. She moves closer and kneels at his side.

His arm muffles his voice. "Yeah?"

"Wake up."

"I am awake."

Swinging a leg over him, she bends closer, brushing lightly at the hair in his armpit. She feels him tense and stretch underneath her. His arm drops back onto the pillow and he watches her as she pulls her tee-shirt off and brushes her hair off of her face. Almost as the air touches her though, she grows nervous and settles back on him with her arms crossed in front of her. He watches her without expression and she isn't sure of him. She always pictures him with a woman who is loud and tough. But after a moment, he smiles up at her and rubs her arm with the backs of his fingers. "How ya doin', babe?"

"I'm good," she murmurs.

Once, when Fin was a baby, he fell down the stairs at home. Dahlia was asleep upstairs. Another time she forgot him outside and he sat frozen on the garden wall in the dark, afraid to move. His feet hung loose in the air. He was afraid of the things that might be crawling in the dark. He imagined impossible, formless shapes, changeable, awful things. The lights in the house were faraway. Then Gale came home and carried him inside.

When he looks out the back door now though he doesn't remember that. He only remembers that bonfire in the middle of the yard. The memory is really like a picture: just a soundless fire, his mother on the other side of it.

His thoughts make him restless, even though he just got home, and he doesn't want to stay in the house anymore. Getting back into his car, he pulls out on the road toward Acropolis again, driving with one arm out the window, passing a road with newly filled potholes, curves where a rocky wall of dirt rises up on one side, struggling ferns and firs on top. Then, on the other side of the road, there's a weedy shoulder that slowly drops down to the stretch of pavement and brick buildings of the factory. He turns in and rolls down a slope into the parking lot. There's nobody outside. He parks near the front building, knows that the back building, shorter and squatter, is the warehouse. There's a patio in front of the building with benches and planters filled with marigolds and snapdragons. A dark glass door reflects the light. The door opens on a closet-sized lobby with an elevator door on one side and a staircase covered in red carpet. There are wood railings on either side of the stairs and at the top there's a room with a counter and an open space behind it. Four desks occupy the open space. At the far end of the room, there is a row of offices, portraits on the wall. Violets decorate the windowsills and there's a jar of jelly beans on the counter. Behind him is a room with built-in cubbyholes and a coffee machine on a table with a little refrigerator underneath.

"Can I help you?"

The woman behind the counter sets down her cup of tea. She's in jeans and a big white smock with red pockets.

He is looking into an office in back where he can see a window with cool, clear panes. The sun is rising up higher, filling the other windows with light.

"Are you here to see Sully?" She smiles helpfully but he doesn't answer, asks, "What's your name?" instead.

"Alison. Ally."

He can hear people in the other rooms in back. "Ally."

She watches him come forward, rest his fingertips on the edge of the counter and look around again.

"I guess I am here to see Sully."

"Okay. I just need to make a call downstairs. Would you like some coffee while you wait?"

"No, thank you."

He ends up with coffee anyway, sitting in the office that used to be his father's, because the minute she picked up the phone, she looked back over, smiling at herself and said, "I forgot to ask your name."

"Fin." For a moment her eyes stayed on his and then she smiled again. After she called, Sully came up and said, "Coffee's fresh."

"In that case...," he said and now he's in the swivel chair behind his father's desk, coffee on a green blotter, another portrait of his father on the wall in front of him.

In the doorway, Sully rises up on his toes, settles back, nods his head and says, "Good to see you here."

It was probably a gardener's or a caretaker's house once. Two bedrooms, porches on both sides, living room and kitchen. She bought it from Otis' mother. Prior to that, she had an apartment that she didn't really like or dislike, but she gave that up to move in with Will. Then Will took over her life. She couldn't go anywhere without him. He even came to work, checking up on her, chewing on the inside of his cheek when she took drinks to her customers or smiled or laughed. She was always happy at work, almost never shy. Work was a relief, a shedding of her anxiety until Will showed up, drawing his brows down in a frown.

"Are you coming on to these guys?"

"No."

"That's what it looks like."

"Will, I'm just working."

"Well, I don't like it. Quit."

She only went out with him because on one of the days he came in he called her "the best decoration in this place." It felt like a compliment, a contradiction of her life flying by. She was thirty-seven and Will was twenty-seven.

"You hear me?" he asked.

"I don't want to quit, Will."

He said nothing to that, drank the beer she poured him, fingers twitching on the countertop, smile flickering up and down. At home, he threw her down on the bed and started slapping her with his bare hands. She curled up in a ball, and after a while he fell sweating on top of her and said, "I only do this because I love you." And then when she didn't respond, he tried to pull her head out of her arms and said, "You hear me? I love you!"

"I love you too, Will."

Then he sighed and settled down on her.

Sometimes it was Andy who came to check on her. Andy was quiet, almost gentle looking, but she had no illusions about him. Then one day Otis said, "Maybe I can help."

"Help?" she asked.

"My mom has a place you can live. Maybe you can even buy it."

"Really?"

But then Andy saw her in Sears one day, buying a couch, and when she got home, Will looked at her curiously and said, "We don't need a couch."

Will was sitting on the couch they had already and she was near the bathroom door. She moved back a step, said, "I'm moving out," jumped into the bathroom and slammed the door.

Will started yelling and kicking. "You aren't leavin' me!"

She yelled back. "I'm not, Will! I just want my own place!"

"You don't love me!" She tumbled out the window just as the door flew open. Will jumped out after her and pinned her against her car. "You don't love me!"

"I do, Will. I do." He had his fingers around her neck. She felt the pressure, saw the shine in Will's eyes, mesmerized, the muscles working in his face. "I love you, Will. I won't leave you. I'll stay with you all the time."

"That's right." His fingers flexed and relaxed; he watched himself do this, fascinated by it. "You have me."

"I'll only stay there when you want me to." The pressure on her throat grew. She could feel tears in her eyes. "Please, Will."

"Only when I say?" She watched the thought of that take shape in his eyes. He shook his head abruptly, sweat drops flying. "Only when I don't want you?"

She tried to nod. He tightened his fingers again.

"Does that hurt?"

"A little."

Then he just let go, pushed her hard against the car and said, "Teach you."

She never thought she'd escape Will until he didn't want her anymore. Then she met Ray.

A long time ago, Ray and Kathy stayed in a motel room they rented by the week. For a lot of that time, Ed stayed with them. One day, for a reason Kathy never understood, Ed brought home an artificial Christmas tree with a silver star on top and gave it to her with a smile. She could see a cool emptiness behind that smile, waiting for her reaction.

She tipped the tree away from her, holding onto the metal pole below the star.

"Why'd you get this?" It wasn't even Halloween yet.

"It was on sale."

"Oh."

Maybe it was the reaction he wanted. He took a beer out of the little refrigerator and sat down. Kathy put it where she could see it on either side of the sheet she put up to divide the room in half and began to pick up the clothes on the floor.

For a while, she lived with a friend's family and before that with her grandmother. Her mother died a long time before. Then she lived with Ray and Ed. Ed being there bothered her, but maybe Ed helped in a way too, because she couldn't be free with Ed there. Ed's presence was a vise that squeezed all her loneliness back inside her. A loneliness that was hers, that she didn't want to give even to Ray. He didn't need her. He had Ed and he was happy. She never was. He could walk away. Even though he worked on and off at a place called Gus' Bike Shop, he was really just a street corner drug dealer with a job he could take or leave. She couldn't count on him.

At night she lay awake listening to Ed snore on the other side of the sheet, feeling Ray's heat beside her, aware that she couldn't imagine any of the days to follow. Her friend, Alice, could picture her wedding day, her future home, her children; Kathy saw nothing.

One day Ray sat on the couch watching TV and there was something jittery about him, the way he was sitting with his ankle across his knee, foot bouncing lightly. Ed was out somewhere.

"Aren't you going to work?" she asked.

"No. Took a couple days off. Helpin' Ed's Dad."

She almost said, "You liar," and watched his face relax when she didn't. He went back to watching TV and then she said, "I won't be waiting for you."

His eyes moved over to her. "C'mon, Kathy. You do this every time I go anywhere."

"You don't care every time too."

"Care about what? We're talkin' about a couple days."

"I don't believe you."

"Yeah, you do. You just wanna start a fight like you always do."

"I called Alice."

"What for?"

"I can stay with her for a while."

"What are you talking about? We're together."

"I don't want to live like this anymore."

"Like what? This isn't bad. You love me, don't you?"

"I love you."

She heard the way that sounded, like the last echo of something, and knew that Ray heard it too. But all he did was look back at the TV, rub his mouth with his thumb and say, "This is bullshit."

He wasn't going to try to talk her out of it, not really, so she just said, "You'll be happier."

"Fuck that."

"I'm pregnant," she added and he didn't do anything at first, kept not looking at her, then his head went back against the couch and he closed his eyes. "Are you kidding me?"

"No."

"Fuck."

"You can go. You can do what you want."

A thin smile stretched his lips. "Are you keeping it?"

She sat on the end of the bed, pulling gently on a loose string on the hem of her blouse.

His head came back down. She was almost afraid to look at him, then she nodded and said, "I want to."

When she looked up, he nodded too. "I'll help you."

That was their last night together. He made love to her on their side of the sheet, very quietly so Ed wouldn't hear.

She left Ed's tree in the motel room.

After Son was born, Ed would sometimes come over with Ray to visit and once, after sitting for a while in the living room downstairs, drinking a beer she gave him while Ray and Son played Candy Land on the floor, he looked up and said, "Where's my Christmas tree?"

She didn't answer at first because it took her a moment to remember, but Ray laughed right away and said, "You are the weirdest damn dude."

Ed smiled.

She lived in the house where Sherry found her a job for most of her life. The attic was her room and now it's Son's. A room with a peaked roof, a round window on one side and a regular window with an air conditioning unit on the other. The space is open with support beams in the center, a well-worn floor with braided rugs.

There was a time when Ray was gone for four years. On the day he left, he came upstairs with Son, sat on his bed, and gave him a phone. "So we can talk," he said.

Son took it. There were splints on a couple of Ray's fingers, scabbed up knuckles. Son watched him rub at the side of his nose, look at the floor.

"I wanna come with you."

"I told you. I don't know how things will be where I'm goin'."

"Where are you going?"

"Knock it off, kid."

"You can send for me."

"You're better off here."

"I'm better off with you."

"Quit arguin', for godsakes."

"Fuck off, Ray."

"Don't call me that!"

Son felt his blood bubbling up, saw only red and flung his phone against a wall. It broke apart and fell to the floor. They both stared at it, Son panting.

Then Ray said, "Great," and got up, swung suddenly around behind him, clamping Son hard against his chest, and spoke into his ear. "I don't blame you. I know I screwed up. You listen to me, though, okay? You're better off than you think. I won't ever walk away from you. Not for real. But you need to stay with your mom. Graduate. I know this is bullshit. You can be pissed off all you want. I won't be gone forever though. I swear that to you, okay?"

Son struggled, pulling at Ray's arm. "I don't care."

"I love you, kid."

Then Ray kissed him hard on the cheek and walked away. Son didn't see him again until he was eighteen. When Ray came back, he didn't tell anybody, but it got around anyway. He was living in a two-story house with a gravel driveway and a staircase outside. There was a party going on, people coming and going on the staircase. At first, Son sat on his Harley in the driveway for a while, not sure he really wanted to be there. He was never really sure what he wanted though. Right then, he was angry and excited at the same time. He felt butterflies in his stomach and that made him angrier. Everything he had was Ray's, the bike, the boots on his feet, his clothes.

People passed around him, a girl with blonde braids smiled. He ignored her. Shadows stretched underneath the eucalyptus that surrounded the house. Music pounded out the open windows. He got off his bike, went to the staircase at the side of the house and looked up. Almost simultaneously Ray looked down. He was leaning up against the railing in his jeans, barefoot, bare-chested in the winter air, arms around the waists of a pair of women who sat on the railing on either side of him. A lot of the times when Son looked at Ray he thought of him as just somebody who used to come around to see his mother and happened to stay longer than any of the others. He often thought about the year he lived with him. That day a smile slowly grew on Ray's face. Then he spoke to one of the women beside him. She reared away, looking surprised, then Ray pulled his arms in, sweeping them both off the railing and they went away. His gaze came back down to Son and he was smiling again.

"Well, I'll be damned. C'mon up here."

He climbed slowly. He felt nothing all of a sudden. He just stopped at the top and stared. Ray smelled strong, unbathed. They could look each other in the eye. They were built the same, same face, one dark haired, one blond, twenty years apart.

Then Ray laughed and swung a sweaty arm around him, dragging him toward the house.

"C'mon. Time to celebrate."

He stayed until the party broke up a few days later.

Now, in his attic room, he sits on his bed, cranks open the window behind him and calls Ray.

"Hey, kid. What's up?"

"I thought about it. Guess I'll come up for a while."

"I don't remember givin' you a choice."

"I can stay here."

"No, you're comin' up."

"I need some money."

"No problem. I'll put a dime in."

"I don't have any transportation."

"Take a bus."

"Seriously?"

"Seriously. We'll take care of your transportation problem up here."

Son sighs, nods to nobody, and then says, "Okay. See ya in a couple days."

Lying down on his bed, he puts his arm under his head, staring at the sky through the gap in the window.

Gravel pops gently under the tires, weeds scraping the chassis. An engine in neutral, stopping quietly. A few cars are parked in front of Mulligan's, a pickup in front of the auto shop. The sun slants long rays and the shadow of the bar's sign traces the pavement.

Fin sits with his arm draped over the steering wheel, staring emptily through the windshield, willing his upset stomach to settle. A man comes out of Ray's, gets into his pickup and pulls away. The wind from its passing stirs little eddies of dust.

Crossing the lot, Fin reaches the stairs and climbs up. The bar's windows are dark and he can't see inside. On the landing, he leans against the railing and takes a deep breath. A vise is squeezing his throat. Closing his eyes, he swallows, grips the railing, then pushes away. Sunflowers on the orange walls glow surreally, draw him on to her door.

A rim of light.

She might be eating ice cream out of a green bowl.

At the squeak of a board in the hall, Fin stops and imagines her staring at her door, moving slowly, uncurling her legs at the same time she sets her ice cream on the floor by her chair and gets up.

She's probably waiting for a knock, fingertips brushing the wall as she comes closer, hesitating when the shadows grow out of reach of the sunshine outside.

He can hear the sound of Carl's TV and moves closer too. Her feet darken the light under the door. Then she opens it and slowly rests her temple against the edge.

"Hi," she whispers.

She wasn't eating ice cream though. He can see a pop can on the floor and a book open halfway through.

"Hi," he answers.

Carl's mother is dressed in white. On his way back to the shop, Ray stops to watch her. In white, she doesn't remind him of Irene. He can't remember Irene in white, but her car was white, parked in the driveway when he got home one day. He deserved that empty house, he guesses, for all the times he never told her where he was. Nobody else knew where he was either, and there was nobody waiting for him to come home. All the lights were off and he guessed he knew then, felt a sick kind of fear he'd never felt before, but he looked in all the rooms, pushed open her bedroom door, his own, clothes on the floor, unmade bed waiting for him. He remembers a sudden tiredness that almost drove him to that bed. He wanted to lie down and sleep forever. But he backed away because he knew that room wasn't really his anymore. The house felt empty in a way it never did before, an abandoned house, long ago given up. She wouldn't be at work because the office was closed, so he went to Marie's where people were sitting at all the tables, but not Irene. When Marie saw him her face went white and pitying, and he turned around and left. She followed though, running across the parking lot to catch up, grabbing his arm, enfolding him in hers.

"Ray...Ray...."

He tried to get her arms off of his. "What are you doing?" he said. People stared. His face felt hot; he thought it might be steaming in the cold. "What's going on?"

"Your mom is dead, Ray."

He couldn't seem to get away from her arms. He twisted, broke free, backed up. "Dead? Whadda you mean, dead?"

"In a car accident, Ray. She was in a car accident."

"Dead?"

When he looked at Marie's face with her plucked eyebrows drawn back in with pencil and her stricken colorless lips, he believed her, because the world was suddenly that kind of place, a place that wore out people like

Marie, a place that took things from people in a way only Wayne could before. Until that moment he was always like Irene, ironic, in control. Always happy, upbeat, he thought. But then all of sudden he wasn't in control anymore, wasn't strong at all. He was a seventeen-year-old whose mother was dead.

"You're lying."

"Ray...."

Marie gave him free lunches at the coffee shop where he sat with Ed in the same back booth Irene sat in with Marie every work day. She packed up Irene's clothes for him too, went through the pictures he didn't want.

"Take this one," she said. It was taken in the backyard, by Wayne probably: Irene in a swimsuit, reclining on a chaise lounge, Ray sitting crossed-legged on the patio beside her, both squinting at the camera. "You sure look like her," mused Marie.

He didn't want the picture, didn't take it. He has no pictures of Irene and sees nothing of her in him. His hair is dark for one thing. It's Wendy's skirts that remind him of Irene. She's full of the same anger too. He can see it in the way her heels keep sinking as she walks and he can guess the look on her face, but that wouldn't've been Irene's. Wendy's face is red. Her skirt is white, her blouse is white, her heels muddy. She tosses her head.

Irene died at Christmas and he met Kathy at a Christmas party a year later. Kathy didn't want to ride on a motorcycle and he borrowed Sherry's car to take her out. She wouldn't let him pick her up where she was living either. He met her on the stairs of a movie theater in a mall nearby, but they didn't see either of the movies playing there. They ate at the food court and then went to a movie in the strip mall where Wayne's favorite restaurant used to be.

At the food court, he asked her, "Why won't you ride with me?"

He wasn't sure if she shrugged or shuddered. "I just don't want to."

"Maybe you don't trust me," he said and realized that that bothered him.

"No." Her face was growing stubborn.

"No, you don't trust me?"

"No, I don't want to ride on your damn bike."

She did ride on it, though, but she never liked it. He thought he could see some strange animosity in her eyes. A look he remembered decades later as he circled the kitchen table at the shop, nerves raw, squeezing at the back of his neck. The beer he'd come in for open on the counter. He didn't hear the phone until he came out of the warehouse. The sun was up high, boiling the metal roof. Coming into the cooler shop, he breathed a sigh, shaking his shirt loose from his skin. Then the phone stopped ringing. He grabbed it off the counter on his way to the kitchen, saw Kathy's number, that she'd called twice before. He drank half his beer before calling her back.

"What's up?"

"Fuck, you drive me crazy, Ray! Answer your goddam phone for once!"

"I was working. I didn't hear it. You know I don't carry the damn thing around anyway. That's no fuckin' surprise. I'm tired of having this same fuckin' conversation."

"I don't call you just to talk! Goddammit, Ray! I told you, I fuckin' told you!"

"Told me what, goddammit!"

"That bike! I told you I didn't want you to buy it! I told you! I swear to God, Ray, I'm gonna—"

"Just tell me, goddammit!"

"Our son! He ran into a car an' you didn't answer your goddam phone!"

"I'm answerin' it now!"

A moment later, he had the story drummed into his aching head and then he yelled back at her. "You didn't have to tell me like this!"

"I'm surprised I could tell you at all. You never call back. You're too damn dumb to care."

"You know what? I called back. I did my duty. I don't need any more a your fuckin' static right now."

"Good. Goodbye!"

She slammed the phone down and he grabbed onto the kitchen table and flung it up into the air. Chairs crashed to the floor. He drank another beer, picked up a chair and sat down. The fact that he still loved her amazed him. The girl he saw at the Christmas party was shy and awkward. She blushed easily. Now she yelled and swore at him, and he swore right back.

Opening another beer, he took a couple swallows, then picked his phone up off the floor and called Miri. "Hey, lady."

"Hi, Ray. Where are you?"

"Work."

"Come have a drink with me tonight."

"I could use one."

"Are you okay?"

Her voice soft, pliant as her body. She was an easy place to rest. He could feel himself settling, muscles relaxing.

"Yeah, sure. See you in a bit, okay?"

"Okay, Ray."

He made her say his name sometimes, her lips against his, "Ray...Ray...."

He didn't know why that excited him so much. Kathy gave voice to every fear in her. He couldn't live like that, couldn't live afraid of things, hobgoblins that were going to get him eventually anyway. She said that Son had been going sixty-five in a thirty-five mile an hour zone, ran a red light, and plowed into the side of a Honda Civic. The bike flew up and threw him over the car. He landed on the other side and tumbled down a paved embankment onto a strip of lawn in the parking lot of an office complex. At the hospital, he was still dizzy and confused, the skin on his arms and back raw and bleeding. Kathy brought him home and Ray talked to him later.

"You okay?"

"Bike's fuckin' totaled." His voice was slurred and sleepy sounding.

"You sound totaled too."

"I'm in fucking pain." Loud now, belligerent.

"You're not taking anything though, right?"

"I'm jus' drinkin' cuz this is bullshit. I'm in pain an' nobody fuckin' cares."

"You're an addict, kid. Suck it up unless you like rehab."

"I'm not goin' back."

"Then don't do anything stupid."

"You don't know how hard it is."

"Yeah, I do."

"You take shit." Voice softening again, drifting.

"No, I don't, kid. I'm clean."

"This fuckin' hurts."

"That bad?"

"Road rash."

"Ouch."

"I can't do this."

"Yeah, you can. Like I said. Suck it up for a couple days. Then I want you up here with me. You'll be okay up here." Another sigh, then quiet again. "You hear me?"

"I dunno."

"Yeah, you do. I mean it. I need to see you anyway. You can help me out."

"I dunno," he mumbled again. Then a muffled sound and a groan. "Fuck."

"Kid?"

"Yeah?" Weary and distant.

"You okay?"

"Hurts."

"Go to sleep."

"I am."

For a moment, there was nothing and then a creak like a door and Kathy's voice. "Wait a minute," she said.

He heard more distant, muffled sounds, footsteps. She was going downstairs. There was still anger in her voice. His headache returned.

"Promise me, Ray."

"Promise you what?"

"You won't get him another bike."

"My mom died in a car, Kathy."

"Do not try to argue this with me."

"We have different ideas about this. The kid fucked up."

"Ray…."

"God, you are a pain in the ass."

"Do you want me to beg you, Ray? Is that what you want? Okay. I'm begging you."

"You really think I don't fucking care. You treat me like shit. Like I'm that kid's worst fucking enemy. You ever think how that makes me feel? I do have fucking feelings, Kathy."

"Ray—"

"You win, okay? You fucking win."

"Ray—"

"What?"

"I was scared."

That deflated him.

"Okay, okay. I get it."

The same fear he felt going into that empty house, looking into rooms that had stopped being his because it wasn't his house anymore. He stayed in it until it sold, sleeping on the couch in the living room with the Christmas tree in the corner. On Christmas Day, Ed came over and said, "Are you just gonna sit here all day? It's goddam Christmas, Ray."

He wanted to, but instead he said, "You got somethin' better to do?"

They went to Lyon's with Ed's father for dinner. The Christmas after that he met Kathy.

When he saw her, Ray knew that he wanted her, and it didn't matter that she was Will's girlfriend. Maybe he wanted her even before he saw her. There was no reason for him to go into Will's bedroom. They were playing cards in the kitchen, Will, Craig, Craig's cousin, and Andy. From down the hall came the muffled sounds of a TV. It was early morning, almost daytime, the black of the sky outside of the window beginning to turn a dark blue.

Getting up to pour another drink, he filled the glass with water from the tap instead, drank it, and set down his glass. "Back in a sec."

He saw light under Will's door, paused at the bathroom, then went the rest of the way down the hall and opened the bedroom door. She was half sitting, half lying on a pile of pillows, in a long tee-shirt she pulled down her legs as she sat up. She didn't speak and she didn't look surprised. There wasn't a mark on her, but she looked beat up, and hopeless about it too. She wasn't young, close to his age, he thought, with the evidence of life on her face. A thin face, pale with puffy half-moons under her eyes. Eyes that were blue, not bright, not dark, just blue. Her hair was blondish, or light brownish. She smiled, and her smile showed her teeth and filled her eyes. "Are you lost?"

It took him a minute to find his voice. "Yeah, I think so. I was looking for the can."

"It's behind you."

"Thanks."

Going back out, he tried to ignore Craig's cousin's smile. He poured a drink, sat down, occasionally looked at him. Craig's cousin always made him feel like he was Santa Claus with a bag full of presents just for Craig's cousin. It annoyed him, the thought that he was missing something.

It was Craig's cousin he called the next day though, and Craig's cousin who took him over to her. They went on a day people were meant to be outside: clear blue sky, sunshine and breezy air. But Miri was inside. Ray could see her though the living room windows.

"What you watchin'?" he asked after she opened the door.

"Soaps."

"Sure pretty out," he said.

She nodded and stepped back from the door, smiling at Craig's cousin, who put himself between her and Will whenever he could. Nobody else could do that.

"Do you want a beer?" she asked.

Craig's cousin said, "That'd be nice." Then he sat down, giving Ray that smile that didn't have anything to do with Miri.

"You look like the cat that ate the canary, man."

Craig's cousin laughed and opened up his arms. "It's a great day."

After a while, Craig's cousin got up and said, "Where're your birds, Miri?"

"Out back."

Will built her a little coop under a fir tree in the center of the yard. Nearby were chaise lounges and a white filigree table. The little birds swooped, cheeped, and fluttered. Sitting down with his beer on one of the chaise lounges, Craig's cousin closed his eyes happily.

Inside, Ray followed Miri into the kitchen and took another beer out of the refrigerator.

"You want one? he asked.

"No."

She was leaning against the counter, wearing cutoff jeans and a halter top. There were freckles on her legs, purple nail polish on her toes.

"Surprised to see me?"

She shook her head. "I knew you'd come over."

"You don't sound too happy about it."

"I'm not sure," she said, looking down at her feet. "You're Will's friend."

"Not really," he said.

"Business associate."

"Not really that either. Craig's cousin, what's he do?"

"Cleans chimneys."

"There you go. I run an auto supply store."

"Really?"

"Really."

"What about Will?"

She was looking him in the eye. He shrugged and said, "We might share the same interests sometimes."

"I didn't know anything about Will," she said.

"Well, you know something about me."

She made a slightly sour face at him and looked down at her purple toes again.

"Do you want me to go?"

"No."

"You sure?"

"No."

Her eyes followed him over. He swallowed his beer, put the bottle on the counter and rested his hands against the tile on either side of her. He was smiling, a smile that made his eyes twinkle, that made her smile, filling her eyes.

"You're crazy," she said.

He laughed and said, "Now you know even more about me."

Her smile turned wary. "Okay, Ray."

He bent closer to her, making her eyes come up, float across his face like fingertips. "Say my name."

She leaned away a little. "What?"

"Say my name."

Picking up his beer again, he drank it, waiting for her. She looked around, squinted back up at him.

"Your name?"

"Yeah. Say it."

"Ray."

He grinned, the twinkle back in his eyes. "Yeah. Yeah, I like that."

"You really are crazy."

"I just like the way you say it."

"Ray," she said again.

"Yeah. Just like that."

"Ray…."

"Yeah," he nodded. Then he bent down and kissed her.

The story Ray told Kathy about Ed's father was true. They helped him move his furniture into a new house and then went to stay with a friend of Ed's. A couple of days later he was lying on a mattress in a house full of police. There was a girl lying beside him with her eyes closed, waiting patiently. At one point she said, "I didn't know anything about any guns," to anybody that would listen, and then Ray put his face into the mattress and waited patiently too.

After he got out of jail, he went to Sherry's and when she opened the door he leaned in with a big grin and said, "Hey, babe."

"Go away."

In a minute though he picked her up and she wrapped her arms and legs around him in a big hug. Then she gave him a beer and slapped him on the top of the head.

"Where'd you go?"

"Jail."

"Are you out for good?"

"This time." Then he opened an arm for her and said, "C'mere."

She got on the couch beside him, legs over his, wriggled her bare feet under a cushion and cupped the back of his neck under the heaviness of his hair. "You were gone a long time, Ray."

Her fingers wound in his hair, pulling it a little.

"Ninety days."

She smiled at him. "I missed you."

"I missed you too, baby. You look good."

He was leaning sideways, trying to connect with her mouth, conscious of her fingers in his hair.

"You really can't fool me, Ray. I know why you're here."

Grabbing her neck too, he finally found with her lips. She let him kiss her, wrapped herself around him, smothering him with her mouth. Then she sat back and said, "Kathy."

A look of confusion met her smile. He squinted, trying to get his bearings back. "What?"

"Kathy."

"Yeah," he said, remembered his beer and drank it. "I have to go see her."

"I thought you broke up."

"We did."

"You don't know where she is."

He shrugged. "I'll find 'er."

"You don't have to." She wrapped her arms around him again. "I got 'er a job at my boyfriend's."

For a moment he ignored the thought of Kathy, took another swallow of beer, and then said, "You have a boyfriend?"

She nodded, her mouth back on his, breathing into him. His brain fogged up like the condensation on the windows and he went down onto the carpet with her. It was warm and almost dark inside. Tires sloshed in the rain. The air coming out of the heaters smelled slightly burnt. They pushed and pulled at their clothes. Ray slid into her with a groan.

"Your boyfriend doesn't mind?"

"I'm not going to tell 'im."

"Okay. Good."

She wrapped him up in her arms and legs, and the rain pattered, his breath puffing pants. He smelled her shampoo, her warm skin, pressure building inside him. Her tongue flicked, licking a drop of sweat off his chin. Then he shook and gasped out loud and lay with his head on her chest. She dug her fingers into his hair, his heart pounded, his body heavy. After a moment, he pushed up and sat back, buttoning his pants, a distracted look in his eyes. When he reached for his coat, anger flooded her face and she said, "That's it?"

He looked at her. "Whadda you mean? Didn't you like it?"

"You fucker, Ray. You just came here to screw me."

"I came here to see you."

"You were looking for Kathy."

"You're crazy, Sherry. You know I love you."

"I'm not doing this anymore."

"Okay. I get it. You don't have to."

"Your little girlfriend is on Elm and Linden. Three houses, all white. Hers is the first." Then she smiled, a happy, mocking little smile. "My boyfriend lives there too. Works at the gas station on the corner. Name's Seneca. Better be careful. Just in case."

The rain pitter pattered. The tires sloshed. The heater kicked in again. The air smelled of dust. Sherry lay on her elbows on the carpet, wriggling her feet. Ray smiled. His face was flushed though.

"You mean I'm gonna get my ass beat, is that it?"

She shrugged.

"Jesus, Sherry. You're supposed to be my friend."

A red flush rose up her face too. She rolled over, got up and said, "Get out."

He was amazed, infuriated. "Yeah, well, fuck you too."

"Asshole!"

The door slammed on him. He stared at the rain falling. The air was cold out here. It smelled like metal. He zipped up his jacket and stepped off the porch.

Sherry's boyfriend, Seneca, was a twenty-four-year-old who occasionally lived in the boarding house his brother ran and occasionally worked in the gas station and salvage yard they both owned together. They inherited everything from their father. The gas station was on a corner of the street adjacent to the salvage yard and the boarding house was across the street with a few other houses. It was an old neighborhood and very little wasn't decrepit. The sidewalks bubbled from the roots of trees long ago cut down. Only a few of the old deodars remained on the far side of the gas station. The driveways were cracked and pitted from rain and freeze. Most of the asphalt at the gas station had worn away, leaving rough and pebbly patches that grew tough, clingy weeds.

One day, Seneca looked up at the roar of a motorcycle coming closer and stared at the rider. It was a boy about twenty with dark, wavy hair and a spray of freckles across his nose that hadn't faded out yet. Sherry had told him what Ray looked like and that he smiled a lot, "like he's happy all the time," she said.

The boy on the bike wasn't smiling, but there was nobody outside to smile at either. So Seneca dropped his magazine on the floor and came out of the dark auto bay. Then the boy, who was probably Ray, grinned at him and asked, "Are you Seneca?"

Seneca pointed at the patch on his shirt. "Who're you?"

"Name's Ray. Ray Wycowski."

"Get the fuck off that bike."

There was no hesitation. He got off his bike, but he didn't lose his grin either. He put his hands up, palms out. "Look. I don't want to start anything. Just talk."

"Talk about what?"

"Sherry."

"There's nothin' to talk about."

"Just so you understand."

"Understand what?"

"I didn't know."

"You're a fuckin' liar."

Seneca watched Ray's grin transition into a different kind of smile, rueful and anticipatory. His hands came slowly down. "Gonna be like that, huh?"

Seneca didn't answer. He just swung and hit Ray full in the mouth. Ray's lips crushed and he went down onto his knees. Seneca followed, punching through the arms Ray threw up at him. Ray rolled and scrambled away, spinning back around to catch another fist in the face. He fell again and Seneca grabbed him by the back of his flannel shirt, running him halfway across the lot before flinging him away, watching him stumble and slide with his palms and face against the pavement. Coming to a stop, Ray said, "Fuck," and then pushed himself back up.

"You aren't makin' this much fun," said Seneca.

"You sucker punched me, man."

"Fuckin' my girlfriend was a sucker punch."

"I told you. I didn't know."

Seneca began to circle around him, making Ray circle too, wobbling unsteadily. But he was grinning with his puffy lips, holding his palms back up, pink and raw, little beads of blood beginning to form. His forehead was raw too and he was squinting from the grit in his eyes.

"You gotta lot more a this to take," said Seneca, seeing Ray deflate a little. He grinned at that, raised a fist and then saw Ray's coming up in a sudden arc. It smashed him on the cheek, grinding it against his teeth, and sent him flying backwards. Footsteps followed him, scraping on pebbles, the bottom of a boot kicking him in the back of the knee. He stumbled, his leg giving out, and rolled away, dodging Ray's stomping boot, then grabbed onto it and twisted him sideways. Ray arced over, air gusting out of him when he hit the ground. Scrambling over, Seneca got on top of him and began punching. He felt Ray's knees come up, trying to rock him off. A fist kept hitting him in the head, but there wasn't enough force to knock him off, and then a voice roared, "Enough!" and hands under his arms pulled him up and pushed him away.

"That's enough!"

He pulled free of his brother and wiped at his bloody mouth, but at least Ray was worse, trying to roll over, scrabbling with his boots, swatting at Horace, who bent down beside him and began to pull him up.

"Get...fuck away."

"Let me help you. Come on. Do you need an ambulance?"

"No."

He was drooling ropes of blood, pulling up his shirt to wipe at it.

"Come on over to the house. You can lie down for a while."

"That house?" he asked.

Seneca and Horace followed his finger. "Yeah, that house," said Horace, walking with him slowly across the street to the house where Kathy opened the door, said, "Oh, my God," and led him gently inside.

Still at the gas station, Seneca muttered, "Fucker," and poked cautiously at his puffy cheek.

That night Ray dreams about a carnival where he sees everybody he knows and Ed points out Son getting onto a roller coaster.

"Too far away," he says.

Ed agrees.

"Better off without you anyway."

That makes him laugh and he sees Gus working the Tilt-A-Whirl and next door to that there's the Snake Lady's tent where they go inside to watch her dance. Sometimes she has Miri's face and sometimes Kathy's.

"This is weird," he says.

But Ed is spellbound.

"I could really go for a woman like her."

Then she dances away and Ray can see that her face is sad.

In the morning he gets up and sits outside with his coffee and Carl comes out too and sits down on the stairs and stares at the sunlit weeds. Water is splashing in the fountain under the palm tree at the Acropolis Inn and Wendy is sitting at her kitchen counter, waving her fingers at her smoke while Mr Torch is smiling calmly at his dewy lawn. Carl hugs the railing, feeling the wood against his temple. Then Fin appears below and starts up, and Carl straightens, suddenly aware of his pajamas.

"Hi," he mutters, scooting sideways.

It's growing warmer now. Ray goes inside and opens up the shop and Carl gets up too. The lawn sprinklers at the mortuary start tossing spirals of glittery water.

A shadow crosses the curtain over the window of an apartment in a complex called the Palm Estates. This is where Seneca lives, lying lazily on a couch in the sunless living room. As the shadow passes, his eyes track it, then it disappears and a knock follows.

Getting up, he opens the door and Son strides in, dropping onto the couch with a grunt. "You aren't workin'?"

"No."

"Quit?"

"I guess you wouldn't know how this works, but generally, people get a day off every once in a while."

Son grins at him. "Whatever. You wanna do somethin' then?"

"Eat. How about you?"

The suggestion seems to surprise him and he grimaces, wrinkling his nose at him thoughtfully. "Yeah, I guess I can do that."

Seneca rolls his eyes, sits back down, puts on his shoes, takes his keys off the coffee table and says, "I dunno how you keep yourself alive, kid."

"I do okay."

"Sure you do."

Outside, no palms, only shady sycamores that erupt through the lawns along the walkway, reach up with green leaves that catch the sun in the high branches, rattle and fall into a tan carpet in the autumn. Seneca lives here with a woman named Clarissa.

The apartments have varying designs, but in every one there's a stone wall facing the door. Seneca knows that Ed once lived in one of these apartments, although he doesn't know which one. He knows about it because he knows most things about Ray. Coming home after that day at the garage, he saw Ray lying with his head in Kathy's lap and a towel on his face. The minute he came through the door, Ray pulled the towel off and gave him a bloody grin.

"Gimme a few an' I'll be ready for another round."

"You sure about that?"

"You sucker punched me. This time I'll be ready."

Seneca couldn't help laughing. "You're crazy. I'm not fightin' you."

Sherry was just somebody passing through his life, but Ray stayed. And there was Kathy and Son. Around Horace, Kathy is calm, breathing in his gentleness. Horace is like a spinning ball held aloft by its own motion. He is true. There is no artifice in him, no secrets, no puzzles, no masks. Seneca, like Ray, is all secrets. Without Horace nearby, Kathy slips into chaos, a place that is really a place of loss, and Seneca doubts that Ray ever helped her out of it. So he never thought about Ray when Ray asked him to watch out for Son while he was away but only about Son. "It's the fuckin' noise, man. All that yellin'. Really freaks the kid out." Yelling back at her only made it worse. A lot of the time all Seneca could do was pick her up and carry her away. He wasn't a good example of anything, but at least he didn't yell.

Outside, Son kicks a few dry leaves and Seneca glances at his raw, pinkish colored arms. "Your ink looks pretty good considerin'."

Son looks down at an arm, twisting to see his tattoos.

"Yeah. Itches like crazy though."

"You got lucky."

Son's eyes roll. "That's original."

"C'mon, you pissy bugger. My car's over here."

Coming home alone, Seneca passes through the sycamores' growing shadows.

10

♦ Shadow ♦

Once, at dusk, Jonah saw her come out of her apartment and start across the courtyard to the birdbath, then stop for a moment; and she looked in that dim light like any of the spirits he kept expecting to see at home and was sure Ally saw, because there were times when he didn't believe his family was really gone. Sometimes it didn't seem that they died that long ago. Whenever he sees Agnes, he knows that Mavis is gone. Whenever he sees Ally, he knows that he's alone.

That dusk, when he saw Joy down below, he lit a cigarette, waiting for her to become aware of him. Then, as if touched by his thought, she moved just slightly and looked up at him, met his eyes in the dark, and then moved on.

After another moment he exhaled into a colorless sky and went down the steps.

There is a little fountain under the palm tree at the Acropolis Inn and a bigger one made out of pinkish stone with a woman holding an urn on a pedestal above the bowl in the center of the parking lot of the Pink Lady. This is the place they come to on their anniversaries, a place not special to Jonah, and maybe not to Ally, he isn't sure. Maybe it's only a symbol to her of something she wants but that they don't really have. He washed the pickup for her though, and opens the door for her, liking the way her sequined sandals sound when she drops to the pavement.

Taking a deep breath of air before they go inside, he expels it slowly into the dim room. Crystal chandeliers catch the light. White table cloths adorn the tables. There are alcoves in the walls with statuaries of women. He recognizes that he is supposed to value Ally, and in a way, he does. He thinks that if not for the baby, he would be happy with her. He likes to come home to lights in the windows in the early dawn, the sound of footsteps he doesn't imagine.

Coming home after prison, he didn't know what to do with himself. The realization that there was no one to tell him what to do paralyzed him. The emptiness of all the rooms compressed him into the smallest space on the couch in the living room. All the seconds, minutes, hours were his. All the plates, the glasses, the pots, the pans, the food in the cupboards and refrigerator bought for him by his aunt were his, the rooms with chairs and tables, TV and recliner were all his. Every thought and memory, all his.

He couldn't stay there. He went to Orly's and slept on his couch. Orly gave him work to do, but he knew it wasn't real work. One day he went to the factory to pick up an application and she was there, upstairs.

"You have good timing," she said. "We're going to be hiring a new crew."

That she would say anything personal to him struck him deeply. It had been a long time since words were kind. Maybe that was all it took, a smile from somebody who didn't know him at all, who gave him the benefit of the doubt. Her blue eyes were beautiful to him, her blonde and golden glow. There was never a time he understood what she saw in him. Her house was the house TV characters grew up in. At twenty-six, she still had her old room. Her mother was a nurse and her father was a claims examiner. She had a brother named Scott. Their old bikes were still in the garage; they had a Weber grill on the back patio. Being in their house made him sick to his stomach with a dislike he kept swallowing. Now that they are married, he never goes home with her.

He isn't sure she still loves him, just that she wants to.

After they are seated, she leans over, smiling a smile that is too cheerful to be real, and he can feel himself pulling even further away from her.

"Why don't you get a glass of wine," she said. "That way I can have a sip too."

"You aren't supposed to."

"A couple sips won't hurt, Jonah."

"I don't like wine. I only drank it last time for you."

The seconds that pass are eternal. He swallows some of the water the waiter keeps pouring.

Sitting back, she brushes her hair over her ears. "That's okay. You're probably right."

She puts her chin in her hand and looks across the room. He follows her gaze. Between the statuary there are paintings on the wall: a woman in a room full of light and one of a woman sitting under a shady tree and one of a woman in the door of a house that for some reason makes him think of Clover and Aster. Then Ally looks back at him and murmurs, "All these ladies."

"Yeah," he agrees. "An' none of 'um pink."

After dinner, he stops in the courtyard to light a cigarette. The fountain at the motel looks pink too. There are lights underneath, shining up into the palm tree. He sees the fronds move, flicks his match into the fountain beside him and looks at the water coming out of the woman's urn, splashing gently into the bowl, and then at Ally with her loose wisps of hair. She is wearing a pair of black slacks and a white top with sequins in the shapes of flowers.

"Happy Anniversary," she says. She speaks in soundless waves of air. The water in the fountain continues to fall and splash without a sound too. He told her once that he couldn't hear all the time.

"Comes an' goes," he said.

Once, at Orly's, it began to rain, but he didn't notice until he looked outside and saw it bouncing off the asphalt and Waylon's roof in giant silver drops. At first, there was no wind, then the signal light began to whip and the rain fell sideways and began to flow.

When it stopped, he could hear it then, dripping off the roof and it was never like that again. Usually, it's just the wind he can't hear.

Standing in the courtyard he knows that the wind is the sound of voices.

Moving closer, he kisses her and then the sounds of the water slowly come back.

"Happy Anniversary," he says.

A long time ago Jonah used to picture a place he didn't know, any place, just some place that wasn't here and where he'd be one day.

When Mavis used to come outside and look off into the distance, he knew that she was like him. In the summertime, she came out with less energy, wrapped her arms around a porch post and stared off almost wistfully. She seemed sad, as if she thought those places she imagined were too far away after all. In the wintertime she put her fists in her coat collar and stomped a little on the porch and looked like she was really going to go this time.

There are pools of water that won't disappear all summer and some of the weeds still have flowers.

This is where Ellie came and where Clover drove by with bags of candy on the seat beside her. At home, Clover used to pause outside sometimes, once with a bag of groceries in her arms, and look up at the sky as if she heard something there.

"You doin'?" asked Job.

"Listening," she said and there was the sound of wonder in her voice because she was surprised he didn't know. He eyed her suspiciously. After she was gone he said, "Cloey always had one foot on the other side anyway."

It is quiet at Ira's and no cars go by. Ally, walking along the edge of the ridge, stops and stares at the flowers in the meadow the way Ellie used to. She can see it never changes. On the far side, the firs are cool and deep. Her car died. Occasionally, it clicks when she tries to start it, a staccato sound, like the battery maybe. But it always started up before. She told Jonah and he said he'd look at it, but he didn't. Passing Ira's, she saw a car parked on a rutted patch of mud and thought there was somebody inside the trailer and let her foot up on the gas, slowing to look. Then the engine made a thumping sound and stopped. She took her purse and began to walk.

She likes to walk and now, with the breeze coming off the cool, damp meadow, she feels good. She watches the sunlight roll like ocean waves and pictures a little girl skipping through the weeds.

Anne, she thinks, and knows not to say that to Jonah.

Then the little girl is a boy, switching the weeds with a stick.

At home, she comes up the final rise on the road and sees Jonah on the porch, smoking a cigarette. His head is down, arms across his knees. When he sees her he puts the cigarette to his lips and waits until she gets closer and then he drops it and gets up. "Jesus, Ally."

She laughs, waving her hand at her face, trying to defuse the anger she sees. His hand comes out suddenly and he pulls her arm down, his brows bunching up as he stares at her. The pupils in his dark blue eyes are large.

"Are you crazy? You're beet red."

She can picture her face by its dry, hot feel. His frown is deepening, a look of suspicion and confusion in his eyes.

"Sometimes, Ally, you don't have any damn sense. Come inside."

She goes, pulled up the steps, elbow locked in his fingers. "Jonah, let go. I'm okay."

"Go sit down."

She takes the chair by the refrigerator, relishing the coolness radiating from its side. She is beginning to feel foolish, feels tears prick ridiculously.

"I'm sorry, Jonah."

"You take stupid chances, Ally. What were you thinking in your condition?" He is standing over her with a glass of water. "Drink it."

"The car stalled," she says. "I couldn't start it again."

He is watching her drink, his expression still suspicious. "Why didn't you call?"

"I just didn't."

"You just didn't? What kind of answer is that?"

"I thought it would be nice to walk."

"In the middle of the summer? In ninety degree heat?"

"Please, Jonah."

She sits with the glass against her cheeks, feeling the prick of tears again, embarrassment, ridiculousness. Shaking his head, he leaves the room. She hears a doorknob hit a wall, lightly though, just the door swinging open. He is putting his boots on. A minute later he's back.

"Good thing it's my day off."

She slips her sandals off and gets up and follows him onto the porch, standing by the railing where there's a corner of shadow. He is drinking a beer he took with him, looking at her again with that slightly suspicious stare. She slips her hair behind her ears and leans sideways against the railing.

"Where am I goin'?"

"Ira's."

He stares at her stomach underneath her blouse, takes another drink and says, "Go on back inside. It's too hot out here. Hottest goddam summer, I remember."

She puts her hair over her ears again. He waits and she stares at the steps with her fingers at her ears until he says, "Go on. Watch some TV or somethin'."

Closing the screen behind her, she stares through the shadowed mesh, waiting for the sound of the pickup's engine gunning, the scatter of gravel, before she can breathe again.

Shadows are beginning to form in the meadow. In the sun the weeds are lime green. Jonah stops at a distance, lights a cigarette and sits back. There was a wooden walkway here once that Ira built after he married Becky Waters. Jonah doesn't remember it. It wasn't a lot, just wood he put across the mud like railroad ties and sticks he tied ropes to. Ira met Becky at a carnival. She worked in the concession stand that sold beer and peanuts, and Ira drank a lot of beer that day. Finally, he went to a snow cone stand, came back to hers and said, "I got every flavor cuz I didn't know your favorite."

She received teddy bears, cotton candy, corn dogs, but nobody ever bought her a multi-flavored snow cone before and stood there holding it up to her without any doubt that she'd take it.

Ira's face was pointy and his eyes were almost black like his mother's.

When he saw Becky, she smiled at him like she did at everybody who came up for beer and peanuts, but Ira didn't know that. "We can go out for ice cream later," he said and she agreed out of friendliness.

She grew to love him indulgently, and always liked him, and felt sorry for him too. Then she went away. After a while, the walkway began to sink and disappear like his mother's garden. Jonah can imagine that all of Ira's life is here, reforming into pools of silver or blue, cloudless or cloudy, always under flowers and weeds and empty sky.

There are a lot of things about Ira Jonah can remember, like another paint-by-numbers picture, this one of a clown that he brought in to decorate a wall in the lunch room.

"We need some art," Ira said and hung it next to the message board over by the microwave where everybody could see it every day.

That was when Abel was working there. Jonah remembers seeing the painting for a while after he started but now it's gone.

Anytime Abel had a chance he'd point at Ira's clown painting and say, "Whaddo you call that, Ira? A self-portrait?"

At Christmastime, Ira's lights went up, hanging in loose swags from the trailer's roofline. Jonah and Abel saw them every day, glowing like misty balls as they drove by.

A year or so after he first started working for Orly, Jonah bought a used pickup, but then it broke down and wasn't worth fixing so Abel drove him into town while he saved up again. That was when Abel told him he had to apply at the factory and get a "real job." The idea of working in the almost windowless building with Abel filled him with dread, made him break out in a sweat if he thought too much about it.

"Are they hiring?"

"I dunno. You put in your application and if nothin' happens in a few months, you put it in again. It's called persistence, Jojo. Bein' responsible. I mean, hell," he said, swinging his arm at Ira's, making Jonah half duck. "Even Ira's workin' a man's job. But, you? No. You have a piss-ass part-time job sweepin' floors an' washin' windows. So I tell you what. I'm gonna bring that application home an' you're gonna fill it out."

Jonah just stared at Ira's Christmas lights without speaking.

There was another picture Ira painted at Orly's. A couple days after Ira died, Orly took it home and put it over the fireplace. It was a picture of a barn in the countryside with lots of greens and oranges and little dabs of white on the side of the barn that were supposed to look like sunshine.

One day on the way to Orly's rain began to spatter the windshield and the inside of the pickup grew steamy and smelled of the coffee they were drinking. Abel didn't bother with the wipers. Ira's lights turned into colored halos.

"This reminds me. I want that tarp up on the garage roof by the end of the day, do you hear me? I told you to do it last week."

"I didn't have anything to nail it down with."

"There are fuckin' nails in the garage, Jojo. If they haven't all rusted from the goddam rain by now. An' why the fuck do you always have an explanation for all the goddam things you don't do?"

"I'll do it, okay?"

"Today."

"I said I will."

By the time that Abel dropped him back off at home and left for work, it was almost dark, but he climbed up onto the garage roof anyway, pulling the tarp with him.

The air was drizzly, almost stinging him with cold. He looked at the surrounding trees, choked with ferns and vines. Behind him, down by the river, there were a few poplars that turned lemon yellow in the fall. The holes in the roof were angular gaps, places where the boards had broken free. There were no shingles. Crouching down by one of the holes with the tarp dragging behind him, he felt suddenly dizzy and grabbed onto the rough edge of the opening, almost teetering over empty space. He could stare straight down to the floor below where the rain had pattered a depression in the mud.

For a long time, he couldn't move, then he nailed a corner of the tarp in place and crab-crawled to the other side of the garage, nailed another corner and crawled down the ladder. His legs shook and in the morning he still couldn't get warm.

At Orly's, he lay on top of a row of chairs in the office and went to sleep until Orly came in and said, "I found a ride for you."

When he sat up, he saw Ira's car and said, "That's okay. I'm not that sick."

"I'm not askin'," said Orly. "Go home."

Jonah thinks he might have liked Ira a little and acted as though he didn't because liking him would just be another thing to add to all the things Abel could turn against him. He used to think there was nothing Abel couldn't make him sorry for.

On the road Ira's headlights swooped like moons. Close to town, yellow lights winked in the distance.

It would smell like wood smoke outside, but Jonah could only smell dampness in the wind rushing into Ira's car.

"Aren't you freezin'?" asked Ira.

"I'm hot."

"You're sick. I hope you don't get me sick."

Jonah shot him a nasty look. "I'm not gonna make you sick. Just let me out here," he said when the road up to the house appeared, pitted and half hidden by ferns.

"Orly told me to take you home."

"This is good enough." He had a picture of Abel in his recliner by the TV, hearing a car he didn't want to hear.

Ira idled there uncertainly, moon lights wavering in the misty air. "I don't mind," he said. "I didn't mean that about making me sick."

"I told you," said Jonah, opening the door. "I'm not sick. An' this is practically home anyway."

He walked away from the idling car, through the diffuse glow of headlights, then out of sight before he heard the sound of Ira's car pulling away. Then it was eerily silent, even the dripping of condensation falling silently.

When he went back to work a week or so later, Abel pointed at Ira's lights again. They were new and bigger than the ones from before and looked frosty even on clear days.

"Santa ain't missin' those," said Abel with a laugh.

Now there's a woman at Ira's, who comes outside and puts a cardboard box in her car.

Once, at work, Kurt saw Ira come into the lunch room and look up at the Christmas tree in the corner where Jonah sat on the couch in back, staring at the pools of color on the floor.

"Cool tree," said Kurt.

"Good as fake," said Ira, thinking of things to save for Ida.

Kurt saw Jonah smile almost wistfully.

After the break in at his trailer, Ira came into Orly's almost every day to stare at Jonah with an expression of both outrage and sorrow. Over the days, Jonah's face would grow instantly red seeing him. Once, Ira sat on the curb outside the office, Orly standing over him with a cardboard cup of Waylon's coffee.

"An' at Christmas, too," he said with a tone of puzzlement in his voice.

After a while, Ira went home. That day, or a few days before or after, Jonah and Abel saw him come outside with Becky's curtains and the paint-by-numbers picture of the mountain and lake. In Jonah's eyes, the picture fell in slow motion, paint side up, bouncing lightly on top of the box where Ira kept Becky's ring. Then came the slow fluttering of curtains. Accelerating as they drove by, Abel sucked on his teeth with an uneasy shake of his head. "Man's a damn fool."

All day the pile grew. By morning, there was a little pipe cleaner Christmas tree on top.

The weeds are sunny, and the air is warm and sweet smelling, and Ira's pillowcases billow gently.

His daughter comes outside again and looks across the meadow, not really seeing anything, just looking. Ira must still be here the way Ellie Sparrow was sure that John and Ivy were always here.

Ira came into Orly's on the day he found out he was sick and said, "I got cancer, Orly," with a plaintive look that made Orly sink down onto the stool behind the counter and feel the loss of him even before he stood back up and said, "Nowadays, Ira, there have to be things they can do."

Except there weren't.

"I always ate real good too," murmured Ira. "Lots a tuna."

At first, he didn't really feel anything and sat out on the step with bowls of Oreos and water glasses full of gin because that made the thoughts he was thinking seem far away, and then he made a picture of a trout out of tiny bits of rock and put up pillowcases in place of curtains.

On the day before he died, he ate a piece of toast with strawberry jam and Jonah remembers the jar on the counter with the knife lying across it. Now he flicks his cigarette outside the pickup and pulls away.

Job thought Clover saw things.

One day after church, before they were married, Clover came up and said, "You aren't comin' back to Church again an' I just didn't want you to forget me."

She didn't mention that Samuel was going to die because his father was the only reason Job went to church. He'd have no occasion to come back after he was gone.

After the funeral he began to see Clover on purpose and then he married her. She was bigger than he was and he had to stretch himself up with his arm over her shoulders for their wedding picture.

"You gotch your grandma in you," he said once to Jonah and one Christmas he began to grin at him and said, "You know what you're gettin', donch ya, Jojo?"

"No."

"Sure you do." He pointed to the pile of presents. "You know every single thing under that tree. Just like your grandma. I don't even feel like openin' anything anymore. You took all the fun out of it."

After Jonah fixes Ally's car, he lights another cigarette and crosses his arms on the roof top. He took his tee-shirt off when he got underneath and now his back is sweaty and dirty.

Ida's gone now too and the weeds look cool and dark in the growing shadows.

He isn't like Clover. Standing there though, looking at Ira's meadow, he feels like he did a long time ago, sure that things couldn't go on. Yet everything did and it's all the same. Even Ira's, where the weeds bend and rise and he can feel Ira there, waiting to pass on.

After a while he drops his cigarette and goes home.

The dusk is turning the sky gray, blurring things, turning the shadows into places he can't see into. The kitchen light is a deep gold in the back of the service porch and moths land silently on the screen. He stays outside for a moment, wondering if there really are things he can't see in the shadows, things that Clover saw, and then when he goes inside and sees Ally at the sink, he thinks a wisp of something suddenly escapes into the air like Ira's spirit under the edge of his pillow cases, blowing quietly away.

11

♦ True Love ♦

The house is quiet, the street out the window motionless, the sky gray. In the attic, Son takes his cup of coffee off the dresser, picks up a duffel bag by the door and goes downstairs. Light rims the bottom of some of the doors on the second floor, but he hears no sound from the rooms. In the kitchen he puts his coffee cup in the sink. The back door is open, light spilling down the porch steps. Beyond the porch light, dark meets his eyes, the shapes of trees, a pale crescent of yellow in the gray sky.

This house has never been home, less home to him than to the parade of tenants living here through the years. The fact that he is surrounded by memories and familiar things strangely only intensifies the feeling that he is misplaced. The times he ran away weren't reactions, really, but embraces of being somebody without a place to be. The nervous energy running through him now, the sudden feeling of belonging, is and isn't about Ray. It started with Ray though, with one of his back-handed insults when he said, "I told you I wanted you up here."

"I'm okay."

"Who the fuck cares? I need your help. You can earn your keep."

His usual anger didn't materialize. He just said, "I'm already workin'."

"You have a job?"

"Yeah."

"Doin' what?"

"I'm workin' for Gus."

"That's not a job. That's charity. Are you workin' full time?"

"You're never happy, are you?"

"Was that a no?"

Then he didn't feel that strange, nervous happiness again until the day of his accident. The part where he flew over the car happened in an instant and his memory of it is just a jumble of color and motion. But he remembers hitting a patch of soggy, spongy grass, bouncing off to slide across the pavement, and the whipping kaleidoscope of sky and lawn as he rolled onto another slope of grass outside the office building. The just-watered lawn felt good on his burned skin. He thought he should move, but he also thought that he didn't really want to, so he just lay there. In a few seconds, people would come running over to him, but in those seconds, he felt an upwelling of peace and happiness he'd never felt before. And then a sense of excitement that made him want to jump up and run. It was an intense and wonderful feeling and he felt euphoric, almost drugged. It had something to do with Ray, but it wasn't Ray either. He didn't tell his mother about the feeling because he didn't want her to tell him that it was probably just a reaction to the accident. He knew it wasn't. He was being drawn away, and for the first time in his life, he wanted to go where he was going.

Footsteps pull his gaze around and Kathy appears in the doorway. His mother is small with a round face and blue eyes. Her emotions are bigger than she is, uncontainable, eruptive. She gives no appearance of that though. She smiles almost wistfully and says, "Well?"

"I'm ready." He picks up his bag and lets her pass him out the back door. They go around the side of the house to the driveway where he tosses his bag onto the backseat before getting into the car. "Supposed to be cooler up there, I think."

She nods, reversing onto the empty street. "How long do you plan on staying?"

"I told you, Mom. I don't know. I'm not making any plans."

She nods again, but he can tell she's gritting her teeth. There's a pulse in her temple. He slumps back in the corner of his seat with his arm on the window rim, rubbing his own temple.

"Well, will you think about Horace's offer?"

With no children of their own, there is no one to take over the salvage yard. Seneca won't want it. It's a livelihood he could never get any other way. A job until the day the salvage yard becomes his. He knows it's possible that he defeats himself out of spite. His reflection appears and disappears in staccato flashes against his window. Then they are passing a long row of storefronts, gas stations, a day care. He gives a slight nod. "I'll think about it."

The bus station is a square building with a flat roof that extends over the sidewalk. Glass doors lead to a small waiting room with plastic chairs in sets of five bolted to the floor. Vending machines cover one wall. It is light now, cars backing up at the signal light. A bus is running out back, chugging fumes into the air.

"Call me," she says.

"I will."

Grabbing his bag, he swings it over the seat and climbs out. Inside, he can see her car through the glass, idling at the curb, spraying early sunshine off its roof. After a moment, he turns away, glances at the vending machines, and goes on. Out back, a crowd collects. He waits with the others, then boards the bus a few minutes later and sits by a window.

At first, there are oleander bushes along the side of the freeway. The sky is deep and blue through the window, not the pale almost colorless sky of a real summer. The bushes toss as the cars and bus go by and cover the ground in pink and white petals.

He called Ray at the bus station, caught him sounding half asleep and annoyed.

"What?"

"I'm comin' up."

"Today?"

"Tonight."

There was a moment of silence, then an annoyed grunt, the sound of him sitting up. "Call me when you get in. I might be awake then."

"Whatever."

Now the oleander is gone. They're going by fruit stands and orchards and houses with satellite dishes on long green lawns. At Seneca's there is a painting of a house and apple trees that Clarissa bought and put over the table in the kitchen. It just fit the wall, almost too big for it. That was where she really wanted to live, a place with apple trees. Son had trouble imagining that. After lunch the other day, they stopped at a bar for a drink and Seneca said, "An' apple farm? For real? She never mentioned that before."

She told him that she didn't think about it until she saw the painting. It wasn't a painting that grew on her. She felt like walking into it right away. On the day she saw the sycamores at the Palm Estates for the first time she looked up at their leaves in a wind she couldn't feel, all that light and air out of reach, familiar to leaves that would one day pile under her feet. It wasn't long after that that she saw the painting and apple blossoms littering the ground like snow.

Son liked Clarissa in an odd way, although he doubted she liked him. Most people didn't and his good looks didn't help him because he was usually disagreeable and moody. With Seneca, though, he had no need of defenses, liked to be around him, and found that he liked to look at Clarissa, although he couldn't really say why. She was a fizzy-headed strawberry blonde, fair and freckled, with light gray eyes and a long lipped mouth. Her looks unexpectedly appealed to him. He found himself watching the way her mouth moved, the faraway look that was always in her eyes. He liked the way that she could project into the vast empty white space that was almost all that Son ever saw of the future.

Sitting on the bus, he leans the side of his head against the window glass, watching the freeway streak by below, a gray white unfolding.

A woman named Vicki came with Will to Craig's cousin's trailer. Ray came too, looking for Goliath, but Goliath wasn't there, just Craig's cousin, Will, Vicki, Jimbo, and a couple of other people who knew Craig's cousin, but nobody else. Windows were open and Craig's cousin braced the front door open too. There was a little porch outside, thin white paint in worn away patches, and a row of trailers with yellow lighted windows stretching down the slight decline of the trailer park. A small living room with a smaller bathroom and a kitchen with counter space wide enough for two stools comprised the main area. Behind the kitchen was a bedroom closed off behind a sliding faux wood partition. Craig's cousin was sitting on one of the stools, nursing a beer, watching everybody else. When Ray appeared Craig's cousin gave him his usual smile, that strange mix of gentleness and irony.

Ray grimaced in displeasure after his eyes scanned the small space. "Christ." Then he looked at Craig's cousin. "Goliath ever show up here?"

Craig's cousin shook his head. "Have a drink."

With another look around, Ray shrugged, poured a drink into a plastic cup, and went over to sit beside Will on the couch. Will was hunched up on the edge of the seat cushion, a console box in both hands, focusing intently on the TV. On the other side of him was the woman named Vicki. She leaned forward a little to look past Will at the feel of somebody else sitting down. Will only roused himself to yell, "Fuck! Outta my way!" when somebody walked in front of the TV. Then Jimbo came over to stand guard and Ray smiled up at him until Jimbo's face began to redden. He enjoyed unraveling Jimbo's tightly wound nerves. Then the woman named Vicki got up for another drink, climbing over the back of the couch with a flash of legs. She was wearing cut-off jeans and a white mesh top over a red camisole. Getting a drink, she came back the same way, smiling at Ray's following eyes. She was drinking something clear, water or vodka or gin. Her hair was brown with blonde highlights, eyes almost green. He liked her eyes, the dimple on her chin, her bare white thighs.

Ray leaned closer to Will. "Hey, Will?"

"Will's not talkin'," said the woman named Vicki, bringing her glass up to her lips. She drank with a slight grimace. Not water.

"Talk to me," said Ray. "Won't ya, Will?"

Will frowned. "Whadda you want?"

"Who's the chick?"

"Vicki."

Ray leaned back, looking at her across the couch. "See? He talks to me."

"Yeah, that's some feat," she acknowledged sarcastically.

Ray grinned at her, then leaned back up to look at Will again. "Hey, Will?"

"Yeah?"

"Whadda you doin'?"

"Video game. Zombie shit, man. Vicki's."

"My ex's," she said. "Collected sci-fi games. Gave 'im the dog for half."

Ray's eyes dropped back down to her thighs. She crossed them, causing an eruption of little dimples. Ray breathed in, smiled. "Havin' fun?"

"I've had better."

"Whadda you say we go someplace where they serve drinks in real glasses?"

She looked at her own drink, half gone, then at him again with a small smile. "I have glasses."

"No kidding?"

"Nice ones."

"In a nice place?"

"Nice enough for me."

"Feel like taking me there?"

She shrugged, set her drink down and said, "Sure. Why not?"

He gave her his hand, pulled her up over the top of the couch and heard Jimbo complain: "Hey. That's Will's girl."

All of a sudden distracted, Will looked over, eyed Vicki almost without recognition and said, "You aren't Susie."

"Who's Susie?"

Ray took Vicki's hand, fingers interlocked, pulling her up close before dropping his arm around her waist and moving through the little crowd of people he didn't know. Outside, he squeezed her in a hug and her voice came out with an edge of irritation. "Who's this Susie?"

Ray shrugged, smiling at her in the dark. "Damned if I know."

Son's phone call woke him up. Now at the shop, he sees Goliath's Silverado pull up and forgets about Son again. Goliath is a shadow through the porch sheers, stopping to tuck in his shirt and smooth back his hair. Ray has known Goliath for years; so has Ed. The older Ray gets, the smaller the world gets. He never knew Goliath was up here. The Goliath he knew from before was just small fish, dependable and unambitious. There is really nothing wrong with him now, but the coincidence of meeting up with him in Acropolis is suspicious to Ray. All coincidences are suspicious to him. It was

Goliath who introduced Joe Clay to Andy's sister. Ray likes things simple and doesn't return the smile Goliath comes in with.

Ray's voice is quiet, unfriendly. "You called my house."

"Cell first," says Goliath.

"I don't carry it all the time."

"So what's the big deal?"

"The big deal is, I said don't call my fuckin' house. That's my goddam house. My wife lives there."

"Jesus," he says. "Okay."

Goliath's words ring like the sound of her bells on the door, reverberations like pain.

Earlier, Ray found her sitting up in bed, hugging her legs with her arms. He'd go insane if she ever slept with anybody else, but he wasn't sorry about Vicki or any other woman he slept with. He didn't lie about that part of him. He loved her, but he couldn't go without other women. Her bundled up look of hurt wasn't fair to him. Coming home nowadays tended only to aggravate him and he knew he sounded rough. "You just wake up?"

"No," she said. "I was awake. Somebody named Goliath called."

For a moment, still thinking of Vicki, that threw him a little.

"Oh yeah?"

He was pulling his shirt off, putting another one on. He felt her stare.

"Where are you going?"

"Work."

"On Sunday?"

"Paperwork. Shit never stops. We have a game on tonight too."

"I hardly ever see you."

"I told you before," he said. "You can come with me tonight. I don't care."

She leaned back on her hands, pushing her heels in a pile of sheets and then said, "Okay. That might be fun."

He felt his jaw lock, a raw scrape at his nerves. Glancing at her in the mirror, he swore she looked amused, except that wasn't really like her.

"Sure. Eight o'clock."

"Okay."

Then he bent down to kiss her and left.

There's a woman at Joy's. Kurt saw her when he took his coffee outside to drink. She was quiet at first, just standing there at the door and then the door came open and she started to laugh and went inside. Now he's sitting a couple of steps lower than usual, waiting for her to come back out so he can see her. In all the time Joy's been here he's never seen any of her friends. He feels excited in a way and hears the woman's laugh again and then Joy laughs too and says, "You liked being married."

"I pretended to like being married. I actually hated it."

Kurt scoots down another step. There are spots of sunlight shining through her wind chimes onto the carpet by her door; sometimes a shadow covers them up and he stretches a little, trying to see inside where Joy's friend flops back onto her couch and says, "I like this place."

"It's quiet," agrees Joy, seeing Kurt's feet appear at the top of her doorway.

At first, Mr Torch used to stay at the mortuary. Carl never saw him. When Wendy went to see him, though, she wore all white, and now Carl sees him in a starched white shirt under his black suit coat.

He is decorous and mannerly. Even Wendy said that. "A total creep."

Carl doesn't like him either. He doesn't want him to be here, sitting in that chair against the wall. When he looks at Scott to see if Scott sees him, Mr Torch smiles a knowing smile, and when Scott says, "More grape juice?" he yells, "Fuck you!" He means Mr Torch, of course.

"Jesus, Carl. I was just asking."

Mr Torch's smile is sympathetic. Carl sighs and looks outside.

"I don't want any," he murmurs.

"Attached?" asked Vicki.

"Real attached," he said.

She was plucking at the hairs on his chest.

"Too bad," she murmured.

They were back at her place and he was lying underneath her with his head on his arm. Her question irritated him. Before he came up to Acropolis, he was living with a woman named Donna. He liked her because she was easy to be with and reminded him of Cora that way. She had her own life. Once, when she brought somebody else into the bar he was in, he went up to her with his arm over the shoulders of the woman he was with. They both laughed. Then he said, "I know you, don't I?"

"I don't know. Do you?"

"I think I do."

She smiled. "Small world."

"Yep."

He started to turn and then she said, "Don't bring anything home, Ray," and he had to tighten his hold on the woman whose name he can't remember now and said, "You either, babe."

But when she came home on the day he was moving out and saw that most of his things and his car were gone, she changed. Her eyes and mouth went wide and round. "What the hell are you doin'?"

"I'm leavin'."

It surprised him when she picked up a bottle and threw it at him. He had to push her into a closet and shove a chair under the knob just to get away. A friend went over later to make sure she got out.

Afterwards he laughed, the relieved laugh of getting out from under something. At Vicki's though, he thought of Miri and didn't feel like laughing anymore.

"Do you like hotdogs?" he asked.

She put her chin on his chest and shrugged. "I guess so."

"Caspar's are the best," he said.

She didn't know of any place called Caspar's, but it didn't matter either. He lifted up his head and brought his hands down to her and she began to smile.

"Okay," she said. "Caspar's."

There is snow on the mountain, but the pavement and sidewalks float and waver in the heat. Behind the buses, the air vibrates with exhaust. Passengers move into the chill of the bus station inside, drift into different directions. There's a little half-moon lunch counter with a chrome rim and spots of blue on the Formica top. The stools are chrome and blue vinyl, and there are blue plastic chairs on a floor covered in blue and white tiles. Son sits on one of the stools between a couple on one side of him and a lone man on the other. They came in on one of the earlier buses. He hasn't seen them before. The man and woman are eating sloppy-looking hamburgers and greasy French fries. The other man is drinking a cup of coffee. He is youngish with glasses and slightly curling brown hair. Glancing over at the same time, they meet each other's eyes, then look away.

The cook behind the counter is a gray-haired woman with dishwater red hands. She is scraping the grill clean with a spatula. On the other side of the lone man, there's a pie case against the wall and covered cake plates underneath the pie case. One of the cake plates displays a pile of donuts. Then the cook looks around, surprised to see him.

"Sorry, honey. I didn't hear you come up."

"That's okay."

The gray in her hair is slightly bluish like the flecks in the Formica. Or maybe it's just the light.

"What can I get you?"

"Coffee."

"Just coffee? How about something to eat too? A piece of pie maybe?"

He hadn't thought of it but realizes he's probably hungry. "Okay, I guess. Cherry?"

"That's the best," she says.

After he eats, he goes outside, leans on the wall in the heat, and looks at the snow on the mountains.

Ray's girlfriends are always blonde and blue-eyed to Miri, womanly, not skinny. They laugh and tease him. They stick out their tongues at him, come and go, appear and disappear and reappear. They welcome him back and let him go. They all look like Cora, a wavy-haired blonde with her tongue sticking out at the camera.

The pictures in Ray's drawer stay in Miri's thoughts all day, stacked together, rubberbanded, except for a loose picture of Cora. All stuffed behind his tee-shirts, thin and wash worn. Holes in the underarms. Her face in the warm, cottony smell of him. A ring that isn't hers or his. A wedding announcement beginning to yellow, Kathy's.

She pulls at his tee-shirts, piling them against the front of the drawer, reaches for the pictures in back, leaving the loose one under the corner of the liner, Cora's face surfacing into daylight. Miri lifts her eyes to the mirror. A pinched face, never fearless or brave. In loving him there must be some rising point of balance, a midway between knowing enough and living with a mystery. But all of his girlfriends look like Cora. A face that isn't hers.

A picture of Cora on her wedding day, hair in ringlets, a yellow house and a lawn. Cora in a car, leaning with both arms out the window, fingertips twisting dimples in her cheeks, a toothy, grimacing smile. A man at the steering wheel, too shadowy to see. Cora on a couch with a baby. Thin light streaming into the room, washing her out, shining on luminous eyes.

A man on a couch with his arms stretched across the top. Smiling a tilted smile at the camera. Creases from eyes to mouth. Reddish brown hair, curly, cut close to his head. The same man at Cora's wedding. Ed, Miri thinks. Good-looking in a thin, detached kind of way. His eyes have no light. He is wearing black slacks and a white shirt, sitting in a folding chair, legs outstretched. She knows that Ray took the picture, that the currency Ed carries in his life is no one else's.

Pictures of a boy who looks like Ray. A gloomy-eyed boy. In one, he is sitting at a kitchen table with the man she thinks is Ed. In another, he is standing in front of a white house with a girl beside him, arms around each other's waists.

Cora again, sitting on a man's lap, her arm loose around his neck. The man has straw-colored hair and an open-mouthed smile.

The pictures burn her fingers, fired with an energy that reaches out into real life, not a life in memory; his other life, his life without her.

At Joy's, ice pops out of a tray and flies across the counter. Even though he can't see it, he can picture it from the sound.

Joy mutters, "Shit," but her friend laughs. One of the ice cubes must've fallen on the floor because it suddenly comes flying out through her door. Kurt watches it bounce across the cobblestones.

Joy's friend laughs a lot; he doesn't like her now and likes her less every time she laughs. He feels moody and knows it's only because of her. Getting up, he goes inside and that's when he hears sandals on the walkway and her laugh sounding like it's floating away. He thinks she's leaving, but at the window he can see that she isn't. They appear at the corner of the building and then pass behind the row of firs out front and all he can see are snatches of color and then the snatches of color are stopping at a car, staying there and then coming back again. Joy's friend is swinging a bag as she walks and he can see her for a moment, blonde and bouncy.

Going back out, he sits again, waiting for Joy to look up as they pass by.

Jonah bought her a bottle of perfume for their anniversary. It smells like flowers on a hot day. He's sitting on the porch when she comes home and he smells her and catches her wrist and then gets up and puts his face into her neck. His whiskers tickle and she giggles and pulls away. "That's nice."

"You have a nice day?"

She nods and her eyes look quizzical instead of worried. He pulls her closer and starts to back up. She goes up a step and then he is sitting down again, pulling her with him and she feels her purse hit a step and then her knee's on another step and she is looking over his shoulder, feeling his arms across her back.

"Here?"

The worry's back in her voice again and he leans away to look at her. "Why not?"

"I dunno," she murmurs, but she sits beside him, leaning sideways with her weight on her palm, waiting until he leans sideways too and kisses her.

"You said I don't do that," he murmurs a moment later.

"You don't usually."

"Do you like it?"

"Yes."

He kisses her again, then pulls his shirt off and puts it down on the porch for her. She lies back, and then he undoes the buttons of her top and she holds him against her so he can't see her.

"You smell good," he says.

She thinks of him on their anniversary, standing alone by the fountain outside, staring at her while he smoked, looking at her curiously when she came over as though he didn't know what she might want with him.

She hugs him tighter.

"Okay?" he asks, rising up a little.

She is chewing her lip. "It's nice," she says.

At first he just stares, then his head lowers again.

"Yeah," he agrees.

Joy's friend is laughing again, this time on the walkway. She came out in a pair of heels that caught in a crack between the slabs of pavement and now she's standing with her arms stretched out for balance. It doesn't seem to embarrass her. She sees Kurt and laughs again. "God, I'm clumsy."

He almost says, "Yeah," but then Joy comes out and she's all he can think about. Her friend totters over.

"I think I'm smashed."

She's wearing something yellow, but all Kurt sees is Joy's blue dress. It's sleeveless with a scoop neck and her arms and legs are alabaster.

Then her friend says, "Okay," and holds onto her arm as they go, tipping sideways until Joy straightens her up again. "This is so great."

He hears Joy's laugh and remembers the sound of her voice on the day her TV came, feeling like warm air blowing over him after the sound of it had already faded.

It's like that now, pulling him down to the walkway to stare at the emptiness they leave.

After a moment he looks at her window and then goes over and cups his hands against the glass. It's a cool looking room, all cream and pale green instead of blue. She likes blue. She wears it a lot.

There's a brush on the carpet, the bag her friend brought in.

"I think 'er name's Angeline," he says to Jonah.

The Greenview Mortuary is spare and white and matches the dark green lawn out front. Its only decoration is the plain white pillars. The doors are white too and it looks like a cloud on green grass.

He tries to make himself feel at home.

"Carl?"

Scott is leaning over him.

"What?"

"I'm leaving."

"Oh."

He doesn't have to be there to see the sprinklers go on, arcing in slow circles.

"I don't care about that anyway," he says to Mr Torch, who is sitting in a chair against the wall. Carl doesn't even want to look at him anymore. He gets up and wobbles. The coolness of the air reminds him of sitting with Wendy on one of her lawn chairs outside the trailer they used to live in, drinking pitchers of lime Kool-Aid.

He shuffles slowly, following the shadowy walls to the door.

She didn't want him to move away. She acted nonchalant though, bought him towels and pots and pans.

He liked her trailer.

Now she lives in a house with a man named Al. It's small and dark with wood paneling on almost all the walls. They went over for Christmas last year, and right in the middle of opening presents, Wendy covered her face with her hands and began to cry. Carl just sat there, not knowing what to do.

Then she quit because nobody got up to comfort her. He isn't sure why he's still here. He has lasted longer than anybody told him he would. A thing to be happy about, for sure, but he isn't happy about the thought of another Christmas with Wendy. Maybe he'll die first, he thinks, and waits for the wave of panic to flood his throat.

But it doesn't.

It worries him now, that he isn't able to feel anything really.

Outside, he sits and leans up against the railing to rest and hears the weeds rustle. The air is cool and he tries to think of people he likes and closes his eyes, only coming up with Wendy and Scott.

The rustle in the weeds grows louder. At the mortuary the lawn sprinklers stop and the grass glitters in the last of the sun.

"Ever wish on a star?" he asks later.

Fin is sitting on the steps with him, looking out at the dark weeds.

"No."

The sign on the bar is dark, a dull glow inside. Weeds roll like the waves of a night sea. Just on the other side of the bar, cars pass on Oly Way, lights at the bowling alley, behind the curtains at the Acropolis Inn, at the auto shop, glowing through the sheers on the front door where moths swoop at the porch lamp. Inside, Ray is sitting at the kitchen table with his boots up on another chair, drinking a beer.

A phone on the table buzzes in a circle. He grabs it, looks, says, "Shit," and sits back up. He forgot Son again. Now even Miri won't be home. His stomach sours and he feels a vague annoyance, pretty sure it isn't at Son or Miri. Which annoys him even more.

"Hey, kid. Up already? Yeah? You know the address?"

He takes a swallow beer and rubs his mouth.

"I told you I'd be busy...Take a cab...You can't walk. We're twelve miles out...There's a key under a brick by the garage. Under the garbage can...The first brick up against the wall. Lift it up. Beer's in the fridge, booze in the cupboard. An' food too," he adds. "Eat somethin'. Make yourself at home. First room down the hall is yours, okay...? Okay...? Okay, kid. See ya in a while."

Sighing, he tips back in his chair again, beer bottle resting on his stomach.

The street is almost empty, just a pickup on the side of the road. Getting out of her car, Miri pauses to look at all the dark gray shapes around her and the bluish tint of the sky. A loose, free feeling surrounds her out here. She even imagines she is brave. Then she looks back at the shop and pictures Ray's expression when sees her, emptiness, a cessation of whatever he was doing, a slight jostling as he brushes past her on his way out. Then she moves, goes into the shop through the side door. Light spills onto the porch, illuminates Ray's bike in the back of the alley. He is sitting in the kitchen with his boots up on a chair, legs crossed at the ankles, waiting for her. She stops and smiles. She's wearing jeans and the top with the blue lace through the button holes, big silver earrings. For a moment, he's motionless, then he sits up, boots coming down on the floor, and goes by her on his way out. She follows, half smiling at her vision come true.

In the bar, Ray drops the jacket he brought with him over a chair before looking back at her. "Wine?"

She nods and puts her purse down. The chairs are up on most of the tables and the air smells like cleanser. A feeling of stiffness comes over her. She can feel her awkwardness like a visible thing.

Then Kurt says, "Hey, Miri. C'mon over." He is playing pool in an alcove with a big, long-haired man she doesn't know. But she does know Kurt, who knows Will for some unknown reason, although he almost never goes over to Will's house. Kurt is pulling a chair over for her, gesturing to the big man on the other side of the pool table. "Miri, this is Jonah."

The big man nods, dark blue eyes looking her over. She twists the necklace she's wearing. When Kurt sees it, he says, "Hey, I like that."

"I made it," she says, straightening it out so he can see. Pewter balls intermixed with multicolored beads.

"That's cool."

She sits in the chair Kurt pulled over, feels Ray coming up behind her and leans back, tilting her head against his belt buckle. His eyes twinkle.

"Hey, babe."

"Hi, Ray."

She takes her glass of wine and feels his fingers in her hair. He speaks over her head. "Wife let you out again, huh?"

The man with the blue eyes, Jonah, looks up, sends him a humorless smile. "I'll pay."

Ray laughs, fingers leaving her hair as he walks away and calls back, "I feel for you, brother."

She sips her wine and twists her necklace. She is sitting here in the middle of one of his other lives, not really happy that he brought her, feeling like a spinning top bouncing off of objects that just send her spinning away again. Everything that is normal and centered for Ray bottoms out beneath her. She gulps her wine.

Kurt smacks the floor with his cue stick and says, "Goddammit," watching his ball bounce lightly away from the side pocket.

"You suck at this," says Jonah, eyeing the table, walking around to the other end.

Miri looks without trying to. He's attractive to her, the kind of man who always gets her into trouble. As he moves by her, she's strongly aware of him, suddenly nervous, and gets up, looking for Ray. As if sensing her, he swivels against the bar, looking over. She's with him only because he wanted to be with her. Will complimented her, that was all it took. But in Ray's eyes, his smile, she sees it again, a part of him he hides from everyone else, shows glimpses of only to her. His smile grows as she comes up and she imagines an aura of love shining around her because he is different from the others. Never spoken, never admitted, she knows that he needs her.

His smile turns into a grin. "Hey again, babe."

"Hi, Ray."

George pours her another glass of wine, Ray's eyes beginning to twinkle again. "We were talkin' about Shirley Temple's."

Miri frowns over her glass for a moment, watching the amusement in his eyes. He looks at George, his amusement growing.

"Not the drink though."

She lowers her glass. "Shirley the girl?"

"Sort of."

George looks embarrassed and Ray rocks a little against the counter, enjoying himself.

"Guy came in here the other day, asked for one a those Shirley Temple's."

"Shirley," says George. "Not the drink."

She frowns again, waiting, and George says, "But I made a drink," and Ray says, "An' after George gave it to 'im, the guy looks at it an' says, 'Not Shirley the drink. Shirley the doll. You know,' says the guy. 'The Amazing Inflatable Shirley.'"

"You lie."

Ray is laughing, but George nods.

"You both lie," she says, sipping at her wine again.

Later she says, "I can teach you to make these," when Kurt starts admiring her necklace again. "I made my purse too."

Across the street, Carl is looking out of his open window, hearing footsteps in the weeds. A shape grows in the dark below, makes for the plank bridge over the culvert. Quiet steps.

It is Fin, walking with his hands in his pockets. He crosses the street without looking up. His walk is unsteady. At the bar, he stops for a moment, then stirs again and goes inside where he has the feeling that everything grows still and silent except for the hum of shock in his ears. His eyes meet Jonah's. There is no stillness, no silence though. Ray nods at him, "Hey, bub" and Jonah sets his cue stick back in its rack, smacks Kurt on the arm and says, "C'mon. I'm fuckin' starved. Let's get somethin' to eat."

Kurt looks surprised. "Now?"

"Yeah, now. I'm hungry."

Jonah gives him a look, so Kurt scowls and finishes his drink. "Yeah, yeah. Okay." Then: "It was nice seein' you, Miri."

"You too," she says.

Fin keeps his eye on Jonah. They circle away from each other, Fin to the table, Jonah and Kurt to the door. Ray is shuffling a deck of cards. His face is turning sour.

"I hope you plan on stayin', dude, cuz this isn't much of a fuckin' game otherwise."

"I'm stayin'," says Fin.

"Good. Pour yourself a drink."

Upstairs, Carl watches Jonah's truck spin a circle on the road and disappear.

At Candi's the parking lot is almost empty. There are lights in the planters underneath the ferns and lights under the fountain at the Acropolis Inn, shining up into the fronds of the little palm. Out back, behind the Pink Lady, it's almost dark. Carl pictures Scott on his break, pausing to brace the back door open with a trash can to air out the stuffy kitchen. Lighting a cigarette. Smoking in the middle of the parking lot where he can look over at the pool next door. Six years ago, Carl saw him swimming there and came running out of the front office. A moment later, Scott came to the side of the pool, draped his arms on wet cement, shook water drops out of his hair. Carl was aghast. "Whadda you think you're doing?"

"Swimming."

"In the nude?"

Carl never pictures anybody but Scott in that pool now. It is theirs.

Next door to the inn, the lady in the courtyard holds her urn up and the palm fronds rustle quietly. Then Carl hears footsteps again and looks at Mr Torch, but Mr Torch's chair is empty. Down below, George opens the door a little and Carl looks up at stars he doesn't wish on. Water drops sparkle on another lawn, looking like stars in another sky.

There are little urns in the trees that make sounds like bells.

At night there is music and sometimes Mr Torch will come out and listen. The lawns are out front and in back just the fir and spruces and a bell-like ringing.

12

✦ Extraordinary Things ✦

Tiny pinpoints of bright white light glitter in the sky, a blanket of stars, cold, damp air, the smell of fir, firs that stretch out from a bare patch of dirt and grass. An eerie quiet that isn't really quiet.

Son is lying on a chaise lounge near an empty bird cage. In the house, Miri is asleep. She came in cautiously, peering out the kitchen door at him. He was standing by the couch, TV on, hands pushed into his pockets, seeing no Ray with her, smiling awkwardly.

"Hey."

"Son?"

"Yeah." She looked giddy and it made him laugh a little. "Is this okay? My being here?"

"Okay? I love it. Of course, it's okay."

Her giddiness had an excited quality to it. He smiled again, still standing awkwardly by the couch. "Okay. Thanks."

She smelled like flowers and there were tender colored pouches under her eyes. She was skinny and her skin was smooth, but she wasn't like any of Ray's other girlfriends. She intrigued him and he felt that peculiar attraction toward her that he felt for Clarissa too. Her smile was shy and she made him feel good.

"Well, sit down. Have a beer?"

"Sure."

Now he is drinking outside, sitting on the cold chaise lounge, eyes on the circle of sky above the firs, slowly lightening.

The plastic arms of the chaise lounge are damp and the outside of his clothes feel damp too. The dampness reminds him of one of the times he ran away. The house where he stayed was just an ordinary two story house in an ordinary neighborhood people called the Fruit Bowl because the streets were named after fruits like apple, peach, and pear. The house he was in was at a dead-end street, set back off the corner. An A-frame out of keeping with the pseudo-Tudors on either side of it. Giant oleander bushes blocked off the view from both sides. Almost every day, he would walk up to the arcade in a strip mall a block away. That's where Seneca found him one day. There were pool tables in back and he thought that's where Seneca was going, but maybe he was really looking for him. It was quiet, even with the sound of voices and the clack of balls that came from in back. He liked it there.

Then Seneca leaned back against the wall beside him and said, "Lookin' good."

"This is an easy one," he answered and then when the game was over moved off to another one.

After a moment Seneca came too. "Wanna come home with me?"

"No." He felt his face grow hot because Seneca was staring at him. He fidgeted, feet moving underneath him, fingers quick. "I'd just take off again anyway," he said.

With a nod, Seneca crossed his legs at the ankle and then looked at the carpet at his feet. "Sure, I know."

The carpet was maroon with a pattern of blue diamonds. Son played until he lost, then smacked the side of the machine in frustration. Seneca took out his wallet, gave him a dollar bill. Son fed it into the machine, bouncing eagerly on his toes.

"Are you high?" Seneca asked. He didn't answer. Seneca leaned closer. "How are you payin' for it?"

He shot him a quick, angry stare, then looked away again. A moment later, Seneca was pushing money into Son's pocket, giving him a sharp shake.

"Don't do anything stupid. I mean it."

Son watched him cross the lobby and go outside, not really believing he was leaving until he was gone. Son didn't go back the next day, but the day after that he did and Seneca was there again. He was drinking a beer in back and when he saw him, he put it down and came over.

"Hey."

Son shrugged at him, said, "Hi," and started playing one of the video games.

"I don't get it," said Seneca. "Your mom loves you. C'mon home."

"I just don't feel like livin' there anymore."

"You like that pigsty you're livin' in now?"

That startled him. He felt a jolt of fear and betrayal. "You followed me?"

"Are you stupid? Of course, I followed you. An' you didn't try to lose me, by the way."

"You should mind your own business."

"You *are* my business."

"I'm not your business. I'm not anybody's business anymore. I can take care of myself."

"You mean you can take it up the ass for your drugs."

His stomach dropped and his face went white. "That's a fuckin' lie."

"Sellin'?"

"No."

"Runnin' errands maybe?"

"No." But his voice had begun to shake.

Seneca's face was cold, close to him. "Juvie will not be a good place for you, kid. You want money, you can have it. Your dad says for you to go home an' lay off the drugs. You do that an' you get a bike on your birthday an' we'll keep you in cash. The money's between us though. Your mom can't know."

"Yeah?"

"Yeah."

"You guys are buyin' me off?"

"Whatever."

He looked away, pretended he was thinking about it. He slept on a floor that was covered with a dirty, smelly rug. It was better than the couches though. Those were covered up with blankets because of the wet places and the smell stayed even with the windows open. In the morning his clothes stuck to him and he had to shake his shirt loose to try and let it dry before he put his jacket on. His toes felt squishy in his socks.

"A real bike?" He already had a motorbike Ray bought for Christmas right after he left.

Seneca nodded.

He scowled a little at the video game machine and then stepped back and said, "I have to think about it."

Seneca gritted his teeth. His lips under his handlebar mustache were white and bloodless. "Yeah, you think about it. Then you get your ass back here tomorrow, you hear me? Your dad will come back if you don't go home an' trust me, you will not be happy about that."

Son gave him a baleful stare, then went back to his video games. Then he bought some drugs and felt good for a while. He thought about staying away just to make Ray return but didn't. In the end he was afraid that maybe he wouldn't come back after all and he didn't really want to know that.

The bike he got for his birthday was the shiny red Sportster he rode into the side of the Honda Civic. The spiraling sky of that day comes back, the high-pitched shriek of metal on pavement, clouds and leaves and grass, and the burbling roar of a motor growing louder and louder. He drinks his beer, sets the bottle on the lumpy grass and waits.

The stars are dim little flickers in the grayish sky. A headlight appears, arcing wide, swinging in again. Son stays where he is, doesn't move until Ray is almost at the back steps. The chaise lounge tilts underneath him, clatters back down as he gets up. Ray moves back a step, moves closer, and then says, "Goddammit, kid. You scared the hell outta me."

"Sorry." He is smiling, not sorry at all. He moves into Ray's arms, feels his rough cheek, a hand pounding him on the back, pushing him away again.

"C'mon inside. Let me get a good look at you."

In the living room again, he shows Ray the patchy remains of the burns on his arms and the raw red half-moon scar on his elbow where they stitched him up.

"Well," says Ray, looking him over. "You don't look too worse for wear."

Son grins, touches a finger to his chin and tilts his face into profile. "Still pretty."

"Well, shit yeah," says Ray with a laugh. "You look like me."

Earlier, a light at Errol's was on, shining through the slats of the porch on the ground below. The light was gold and further out the lot was dark and the houses on the other side were dark too. Houses with people asleep inside. People ready for work and carpools and dance lessons. People who lived on the other side of the moon.

At Errol's, things moved in the dark weeds. Fin slogged through them. They seemed to suck and pull. On the road by the wooden plank, Ray stood in the dark too, slowly rolling his sore knuckles against his palms.

"What's wrong with you?" asked Fin in the bar.

Ray gave him a curious smile. "Nothin', really. Just gettin' old, I guess."

Then he flexed his fingers and retreated, didn't want to share, Fin thought, not with him, not drunk. But he wasn't drunk, not as drunk as usual. He drank water in-between, like Ray always did. He wasn't drunk at all. Ray's watchful presence across the lot irked him, made him feel pitiful, incapable. He felt the same anger he saw in Jonah's eyes earlier, the betrayal of a truce. A truce with living in the same town. A truce with drinking. He couldn't not drink. The thought was like the feeling of panic. Besides, he wasn't drunk, just loose, relaxed, not happy, not cheerful. Angry.

He glanced back at Ray and stumbled.

"Okay?"

"Yeah, yeah. I'm fuckin' okay," he muttered. He didn't feel sorry. He didn't feel grateful. He wanted a drink. A glass with ice, dark gold bourbon, caramel sweet, sharp, rough, warm in his belly. He was climbing the stairs then, Ray backing up to the road. He could hear the bell-like sound of a bottle against a glass, bourbon burbling over clacking ice, feel the glass growing cold in his fingers. The heat, the dry burn down his throat. He wanted that drink. But he still wouldn't be drunk.

Oddly, the stairs kept going, never reaching the starless sky, the landing above him. He gripped the railing, climbing in frustration.

Ray was halfway across the wooden plank again. "Hey, bub? You okay?"

He wasn't moving, he realized, just standing there, eyes on the landing, the dark doorway that yawned open.

Another step, his slippery palm on the railing.

No stars to wish on. Only a dull blue moonless sky.

The door was an open space to nowhere. On the landing he looked through it and saw a hillside with doors in it, open and dark like graves. The hillside was covered in tall green grass. "Chairs," he said, inexplicably, surprised. Then the doors in the hillside became lawn chairs. Suddenly panicked, he went through the dark doorway and down the hall, bracing himself with his fingertips against the walls, breathless and sweaty. He didn't calm until he had his drink in his hands, swallowing it, slowly and steadily. Then he collapsed onto the couch in the dark room with another drink, and by the time he finished it, he couldn't remember coming up there.

Stopped at a signal light on Oly Way, Ray stared at a lighted window at the Acropolis Inn. It was the window of a bottom room near the pale blue pool. He pictured the inside of it and it became a room he stayed in with Ed. There were two twin beds with a nightstand between them. His hands hurt. Three of his fingers were in splints and his knuckles still oozed blood into the bandages Ed had tied around his hands. He slept for a while, and when he woke up, saw Ed sitting in a chair in the corner of the room by the door, looking through a magazine. There was a round table next to him covered in Paper cups and empty pizza boxes. A TV was on top of the dresser with a mirror behind it and a picture of an ocean over the beds. He could see the picture in the mirror, green waves with orange lights that he guessed was supposed to be sunlight. He remembered that it was getting dark outside and that he heard somebody walk by. Then he said, "Ed. C'mere."

Glancing up, Ed dropped the magazine with a smack on the table, came over. "What?"

"C'mere."

"I am here. You okay?"

"Sure."

He looked at the splints Ed put on his fingers and then Ed bent down to look too and Ray grabbed him by the neck, trying to choke him, but his fingers didn't work and all he did was stick Ed in the Adam's apple with his thumbs. Ed choked though and there were marks on his neck. Ray felt apologetic, even a little scared because he didn't remember doing that.

"I blanked out, man. I'm sorry."

Ed didn't look all that upset, but he did say, "You know, man. I don't think you really trust me."

"You're the only human being I do trust, Ed."

After staring at him for a moment Ed sat back with another magazine and murmured, "Worm in the apple, Ray," meaning, Ray knew, that Ed thought he lost sight of the bottom line a lot of the time. It didn't matter that they might not see the same bottom to things. Ed always thought that Ray needed to focus, that he gave power to things that didn't deserve power anymore. Which was why Ed could come over a few days after Ray's mother died and say, "Are you just gonna sit here all day? It's goddam Christmas, Ray." Ed's basis focused on the practical. Irene wasn't anybody to him in the first place and there was nothing anybody could do for her anymore anyway. It was the same basis that made him look over at Ray in their motel room a couple of days later and ask "What is that word? Psychosomatic?"

"Fuck you, Ed."

At home, the memory was still a fog, a darkening wall around him. His fingers squeezed his keys, burning with a slight electrical sizzle, then he saw the shape rise up and he took a step back, looked again and said, "Goddam, kid. You scared the hell outta me."

But Son was smiling at him like the cat that got the canary and he was laughing back. The memory of Ed floated away.

On the day Irene gave him Wayne's postcard, Ray looked at the picture on the front and then said, "It's from St. Louis," because he didn't know what else to say. Of course, she knew it was from St. Louis. She must have had it for at least a day. It was morning when she gave it to him and he was still in bed, awake but lying there, listening to her get ready for work, which was different now without Wayne's voice and his footsteps in the hall, always the first to leave in the mornings.

She still sang over the water running in the sink though.

"I'm nobody's baby...."

He thought it was a strange song to sing in the morning. He didn't think going to St. Louis was strange. Irene did though. After she gave him the postcard she just stared at him, obviously waiting for some reaction. That's when he said, "It's from St. Louis."

She nodded and put her elbow on her forearm and her eyes narrowed a little while she thought about something. He remembers that she was wearing the lavender skirt and silver blouse he almost always pictures her in. After a moment she said, "You better hurry up an' get ready," and then she left the room.

He didn't look at the postcard again until later and maybe it was in the same place or maybe she looked at it and just let it fall almost exactly where it was before.

He'd never seen the Museum of Bowling, but he could picture Wayne on a set of wide stone steps looking up at the tall face of it.

He figured that's where he'd be, but maybe he was wrong, and maybe the museum didn't even look like that anyway.

"Hey, babe."

"Hi," she whispers.

All he can see of her is a lump under white Chenille. He pulls his tee-shirt off and sits down to take off his boots too. His skin looks gray. She touches him on the small of the back as he bends over.

"You're cold," he says.

"A little."

"A lot."

Her fingers recede.

"Did you have fun?"

"Yep." He gets back up and takes off his jeans.

"Win anything?"

"Nope."

She reminds him suddenly of Irene with the postcard, just standing there with something to say and not saying it, or maybe saying it later when he didn't know what it related to anymore.

After she scoots back, he lies down and rolls onto his side. She's on her side too, her face on her pillow, a shadow that reminds him of the times she brushes her hair in the dark, sitting on the side of the bed in a towel after her shower, looking at a mirror she can't see into.

Then he thinks of Vicki and it surprises him. He's glad that he can't see Miri's face and rolls the other way with a sigh.

"Night, babe."

The arch of Candi's dome roof sparkles with tiny specks of glitter. Inside, plates and silverware clink and clatter. The air smells like pancakes and butter and coffee. Coming inside, Craig's cousin looks around and takes in all the pleasant aromas, breathing out a happy sigh. Pots and pans clatter in the kitchen. Conversation drones. He loves this place and he knows he's going to love this day too. A waitress with tired brown eyes and cheerful dimples is making her way over to him. His smile meets hers, growing into a grin as he points at the wall of windows.

"A booth."

"A booth?

He usually sits at the counter where it is easier to talk to her. Her name is Debby and they went out for almost a year. He knew it wasn't going to come to anything, but they liked each other and had fun together. Now they are easy friends who still talk on the phone and see each other without regret. Grabbing a menu, she takes him over to a booth by the window, pours him a cup of coffee and says, "Back in a minute."

He sits on the side of the booth facing the door and drums his fingers on the table top, feeling light-hearted, happy. Through the window he watches the traffic on Oly Way, pedestrians walking on the sunny sidewalk. In the parking lot, a blue jay is hopping from car roof to car roof. Occasionally, laughter breaks up the drone of conversation.

"Are you ready?"

He squints up into Debby's dimpled face. "No, not yet. Couple minutes."

His smile grows at her look of mock exasperation. He knows she's never believed in his psychic abilities and probably thinks this is an example of one of those so-called abilities now.

"Okay," she says. "You let me know."

He drinks his coffee, looking back outside. Cars pull in and out. Debby pauses to refill his coffee cup. His gaze returns to the window in time to see another car pull in. Sun shines off its silver rooftop. Still watching, he sees Miri get out of the car. She's wearing a pair of white sunglasses and he begins to smile as she pulls the glasses down her nose to peer at a blond boy getting out on the other side of her car. Jeans, tee-shirt, twists of leather on his wrists. She is smiling at him and he smiles back. Inside, they stop and look around for a moment. Miri's wearing jeans, too, and a white top with orange and yellow polka dots. Her big white sunglasses take up half her face. Craig's cousin nods in appreciation.

"Cool," he says, loud enough for her to hear.

Seeing him, she grabs the boy by the hand and pulls him after her. Craig's cousin gestures to the other side of the booth. "Sit down. I haven't ordered yet."

She bounces in, scoots over. "You look happy today."

"I am, I am," he says, arms across the booth, smiling a long lipped smile. "It's a great day."

His happiness is infectious. Miri smiles happily too, hugging the boy beside her. "This is Son, Ray's son."

Craig's cousin nods. "I know."

"Craig's cousin is psychic," says Miri.

"A little," he acknowledges.

Son's expression is curious, uncertain, then he says, "Well, I'm not, so unless somebody tells me, I'm never gonna fuckin' guess your name."

Miri gapes and Craig's cousin laughs.

"It's Trevor," he says. "Nobody calls me that though…Well, one person."

"What does your family call you?"

"Okay. A couple people."

"Wonder how many people we'd get up to if we kept going."

"You sure got a mouth on you."

"Yeah," says Son with a grin, showing off a metal ball in the curve of his tongue. "That's one of my little problems."

"Got a lotta those, do you?"

He shrugs.

"A few."

Craig's cousin's smile widens and then he looks back at Miri. "Where'd you get those glasses?"

"Kmart."

"Definitely cool."

Will shops at Kmart. There are always things for him to buy. At the checkout counter his cart is always full of the sale items they put out at the ends of the aisles. It's the only place Craig's cousin knows of that really makes Will happy.

"I recommend the strawberry pancakes," he says after a moment. "That's what I plan to order."

Ray eats his Cheerios on the back porch beside the grass that only grows where the fir needles don't cover it. Miri keeps reseeding it for some reason. He thinks of his mother moving the sprinkler from spot to spot on the lawn out front, and the tall spotty grass out back that his father didn't want to mow, and marvels at all the emotion and work people put into these little patches of green.

"Fuckin' nothin'," he says out loud, then drinks the milk out of the bottom of the bowl, sets it down on the porch railing and goes to work.

Will is watching cartoons when he calls.

"Scooby Doo!"

"Happy for ya," he says.

"C'mon over."

"Workin'."

"Me too," says Will with his mouth full of Cocoa Puffs. "Stuff t' talk about. Called you yesterday."

"Where at?"

"Shop. Cell. You need a beeper. I got tons."

"I need a car," he answers and Will is suddenly silent, listening to the noise Ray makes as he rolls open the doors in the other part of the shop.

The Cocoa Puffs don't taste anymore and Will looks inside the box and then outside where the sun is shining over the top of his car.

At Ray's, there's a breeze that's beginning to blow. He waits for Will's response.

"I love my car."

"Said you're sellin'."

"I am," he answers and looks back into the box of Cocoa Puffs again and hears the sound they made when his mother poured them into a bowl.

"Eat your breakfast," said his father, never letting him wait until the milk made them soggy. He likes them best out of the box now.

"Be over in a while then," says Ray and Will nods into his box.

"Okay."

The weeds roll in sunny waves across the lot. At the bottom of Errol's stairs, Fin stops to look. They remind him of the piles he pulled in the backyard at home. In summer his mother brought her dahlias into the house and he suddenly remembers them on a table under the window upstairs where the curtains used to float in and darken the floor at dusk. He remembers a light at a window, growing brighter in the dark house and the dahlias growing colorless inside it.

It's the same light he thinks is already spreading along the baseboards there and up the wall by the staircase and back outside again.

The breeze is cooling his skin. The sun is warm though and the air smells like the weeds.

At the shop, Ray is leaning in the open door, arms crossed in front of him, waiting until he gets across the plank. Then he straightens and says, "C'mon in."

It's cool and almost dark inside. The front is empty. Fin can see light coming through the window in the side door and he goes into the hall in back where the light turns grainy.

Ray is in a room with a bed under one window and a dresser beside the other. There's a rug, half rolled up and when Fin looks in, Ray says, "Don't tell," and steps on one end of a board to flip the other end in the air. Then he stoops down for a box in the space underneath and takes it over to the dresser. There's money inside.

"Buyin' my kid a car," he says. "Came up last night. You'll meet 'im. Gotta warn you though, pisses off everybody he sees."

"How old is he?"

"Twenty-three, goin' on twelve."

Ray counts some of the money out and then puts the box back under the floor and taps the board into place. There are dusty footprints around the circular rug and the paint on the windowsills is beginning to peel away. It smells cool and dry here, like flowers or the memory of the flowers at his house. The dahlias are growing, but the weeds have grown back too.

Later, at home, he takes a beer outside with him and sits on a chaise lounge, gazing at the weeds trying to choke the bushy flowers. Then he takes a swallow of his beer, heaves it up on the patio, drinks again, and feels his stomach settle. After the beer, he drinks a ginger ale and all of a sudden starts to sweat. The weeds and dahlias disappear and he is looking at Orly's gas station, a Coke bottle on top of a pump. It is Jonah's, set there when he sees

Mavis come out on the market porch. She stays with her hand on the door, holding it open, then lets it clap back behind her. After a moment, Jonah moves, swipes his shirt under his arms again and says, "Jesus." Fin doesn't know if he means Mavis or if he's just hot.

After that Jonah takes his Coke and gets into Fin's car. His shoulders are burned and beginning to peel.

"You drink, right?"

Fin nods.

"Good."

That was the day he met Sissy, he thinks.

The shade is dark and the air feels cool. Agnes is looking out at the trees as they go.

Outside of Acropolis is a place called Willow Glen and there's a market called the Willow's Corner Store that rents out videos. This is where Doug's family lives. His mother works for the Acropolis post office and his father owns Miller's Duct and Chimney Cleaning where Craig and Craig's cousin work.

Almost every time Doug goes with Agnes into Willow's Corner Store he says, "Your dad should rent out videos, or put in a Red Box or somethin'." Today he came out and said, "I just asked about a job."

"You have a job."

Hearing her reminded him of his father when he found out Doug wanted to buy Will's car. He was talking to Craig's cousin and Craig's cousin said, "I know a guy sellin' a real nice Camaro." When Doug's father heard him, he said, "But you already have a car."

They gave it to him for his birthday and he liked it at first. Especially when he met Agnes and she liked it too. It smells old now. Remembering, he looks over at her sitting with her arm out her open window. Old wood from forgotten fences peeks out underneath the firs and ferns and vines. At Ira's there are weeds and flowers and nothing else. She looks back in and Doug looks away.

"Want me to drop you?"

She nods and says, "Up here."

"I thought you wanted to go home."

"I do. But I wanna walk for a while."

"Why? Are you mad I asked about that job?"

"No, I'm not mad. I just feel like walking for a while. I like it."

"God, you're spacey."

After the car stops, sliding a little on the gravel shoulder, Agnes gets out and goes down the slope to Ira's meadow. The ground is spongy in places and the weeds are hollow-stemmed and dark gold. Little birds fly away from her. She picks up a piece of glass near the bottom of the slope. It's a blue circle with a smooth rim like a piece in a glass table top. At home, Agnes puts the piece of glass on her dresser, resting it against the mirror.

Outside, she sits on a metal chair with a bottle of pop and her bare feet up on the wooden rail around the porch and waits for Waylon to come home. The sound of the gravel under his tires is a sound she hears every day. She likes to mark her life by things like that, things she's sure Mavis doesn't have. At the corner store by Doug's, there's a chain link fence in back with a rope at the gate. A weight on the end of the rope taps against a metal pole.

"I like that sound," she said one time. "I always know where I am."

She thinks Mavis is always lost.

When Waylon comes up, she puts her feet down and says, "Daddy? Am I spacey?" The question makes him hesitate in surprise and then he says, "No, honey. Just deep."

"Deep?"

He nods, relieved that it sounds right and gives her a pat on the knee as he goes by.

Agnes's piece of glass came from a bowl made of multicolored blues that Becky Waters bought to put apples in. On the day Ira saw Sissy by the river, he bought a coffee cup made out of pieces of blue ceramic at a church bazaar because it reminded him of Becky's bowl. The woman at the bazaar put newspaper inside of it and then rolled it up in more newspaper. At home, he unwrapped it and set it on the sill over Becky's bowl on the kitchen table. He didn't have any curtains or pillowcases up there and he could see straight across the meadow where a path cut through the firs to the river. A road follows the river and there are a few houses near Sandorville where the course of the river straightens out for a while. Near Ira's, the river knots, foamy around boulders, and the fir and alder come down close to the water's edge. On the day of the church bazaar, there was only the dark green of the firs and smoky mist hanging motionless.

Above the river, before Ira saw her, Sissy was home, awake in the dark house. Early light clung to the windows but didn't enter. She closed her bedroom door very quietly so it didn't even click. People said she never talked, but that wasn't true. In Jonah's memories she is always wordless. But she talked to Fin, sitting bundled up by the river where they would go to be alone. His loneliness seeped into hers like the river's damp into the fabric of their clothes. His breath was the pale essence of him and she breathed it in for sustenance. He was her only love, a boy who promised to marry her and who never could. He was afraid of the baby, afraid of her, afraid of Abel. Walking home with her, he said, "I'll tell 'im. You don't have to."

She heard the weight in his voice, but it grew weightless as they got nearer to home. She felt the same unreality that infected Jonah all his life, the uncertainty of the things around him. The vapor of their breath dissipating in the air was real. The feel of the drizzle on her cheeks. The warmth of Fin's fingers pulled at her, peeled at the soft, billowy world she had wrapped around her. A world as gray as dawn, as silent as fog, as numb as sleep. A world that saved her, that lifted her on its currents without any effort. As they came near the house she felt the spasms in Fin's fingers and looked up at him, feeling a boundless love for the love he felt too, for the baby inside her she wanted to be real but wasn't, was only a wisp of the unreal.

And then they were home.

On the day of the church bazaar, on the last day of her life, she quietly closed the door so it didn't even click. She listened but couldn't hear anything. She wasn't sure what Jonah did, but when he came into her room and woke her up, he was agitated, red-eyed, bone-white under her dresser lamp. She smelled liquor on him, saw the way his hair stuck to his sweaty skin. She sat up, dragging her covers up with her.

"Sissy…Sissy…."

She just stared, her heart pounding.

His head dropped on the edge of her bed and he moaned, "I'm so fucked," then lifted up his head again, darted a wild look at the shadowy walls, then sat back on his heels and scrubbed at his face.

She didn't know that he looked up into the camera lens over the counter at the *Mom 'n Pop* store that night with a dull, empty eyed stare and calculated the time it would take to find him.

In Sissy's room, he ran his hands over his head and she saw his fingers dig into his scalp. She touched him on the arm and he jumped, startled. Then he said, "Don't come out, okay? I want you to stay in here. I really fucked up. Sissy…God, I'm sorry. I don't want you to see anything bad happen to me." His eyes mirrored hers, growing wide and despairing. "God, I'm sorry, Sissy. I called Hilary, okay? Wait for her. Don't come out. I have to go now."

She flung herself at him, wrapped her arms around his neck, heard him breathe another low moan. Only she could love him.

He tried to break her grip. "Sissy…Sissy…."

Her arms separated. He pushed her down and ran away.

Getting back up, she dressed in her cold room, squeezed her plastic doorknob in her fingers. Jonah bought it for her and put it back on her door after Abel died.

At the porch door, she looked outside. The dark was fading into gray. The air smelled damp and musty. She looked at the gravel driveway, the garage, felt the emptiness of the house behind her and went outside. The screen creaked a little. She tried to close it quietly, but it creaked again.

She didn't see Jonah freeze on his way to the pond, catch that second, faint creak of the door and come running back down the slippery slope.

She stayed in the trees until the sun was a fuzzy disc overhead. The day stayed gray and misty damp. On the road along the river, she stopped at the sound of a car. Headlights blurred into a single ball of yellow light. The damp sound of the tires grew louder, the river like the rumble of the engine. Then the lights separated. It was Ira's car, a light blue Dodge Omni. She looked away, pushing through the bushes down to the river.

Tires whooshed above her.

It wasn't until Ira was home, looking outside over the cup he bought that a strange feeling came over him. He thought it was the moodiness of the rain coming. Afterwards he never told anybody about seeing Sissy.

The cup from the bazaar wasn't there when Ida came. Her mother's bowl fell off the top of a box she was carrying and broke on one of the cinder blocks outside of the trailer.

There is a circle of crumbling asphalt in the middle of Will's driveway. The rest is gravel with short, clumpy weeds. The asphalt is the first thing Doug sees. The next is Jimbo, sitting on Will's porch. Doug can tell Jimbo's mad because his face is red, but he laughs when Doug comes up and stares at the asphalt that was always hidden underneath Will's Camaro.

"Sold it," says Jimbo, enjoying himself.

"Sold it?"

"Yep. Ain't home either."

Susie's the one Jimbo's mad at and not just because she's always sitting in that chair of Will's she took for her own, never getting up to get him a beer. This time he went over to the building she works in because Will told him to go get her, but she saw him through the glass in the doors, sitting on the hood of his car with his arms crossed in front of him and ran back upstairs and down another flight that opened up by the garbage cans on the other side of the building.

Jimbo wasn't anybody she was glad to see.

"You ain't gettin' that car," he says to Doug.

On the day he bought it, Will saw himself going home where the lamp by the couch would be on and his mother would be cooking dinner and his father would crack the paper to keep it open and not look up.

"I bought a car," he'd say and his father would be silent for a moment and then say, "You earned the money."

Then his mother would come out, drying her hands on a towel with a border of pink and yellow flowers that matched the hem of her apron and he would smell their dinner and hear water bubbling and say, "Come out an' see."

And slowly, his father would look up and say, "I don't see why. You didn't ask my opinion before."

In real life he didn't say anything because he was dead.

"I think you have a mental block or somethin'," Ray said earlier.

He couldn't find the title to the Camaro. The house was full of laundry in big smelly piles and empty Cocoa Puff boxes and Jack-in-the-Box bags on the dresser.

"No, I put it in a safe place, man. Besides, I'm only doin' this for you. I wasn't gonna sell it otherwise."

"So I appreciate it," said Ray.

"I need Susie to clean this shit up."

Jimbo was supposed to make sure she came home. At the time, though, Jimbo was sitting in an almost empty parking lot, staring at the glass doors while Will kicked a pizza box over to the door and made himself not look at Son leaning up against the wall. He wore the same kind of boots Ray wore, scuffed at the toes, jeans and a gray sweatshirt with the sleeves cut off. The only good thing about him was the scab-lined places on his tattooed arms. Will clucked at the big patches of washed out color and raw pink skin.

"Man, I bet that hurt."

Son only pulled his eyebrows together in a slightly suspicious glower.

"Want us to come back?" asked Ray.

"No, man, we're doin' this."

Across town, Jimbo was looking through a pair of glass doors at a flight of carpeted stairs and a fichus tree in a brass pot. He rattled the door handle and pressed his face against the glass. There was nobody there and he stepped back and began to pound on the glass and then stopped to lean on one side and pound on the other, waiting for a janitor or somebody to let him in. Across the street though was Andy's apartment building, which he found himself staring at because of the way he was leaning. The thought of Andy seeing him pound on the door to get somebody to let him in made him stop and back up instead.

That night, he'll dream about breaking the glass in the door and seeing pieces fly through the air.

In the morning he'll lie awake, wishing he could go back, but Will won't care anymore. That is because he found the Camaro's title in a Jack-in-the-Box bag on the floor a couple of minutes before Jimbo started pounding on the office door. After staring inside the bag for a moment, looking almost confused, Will gave it to Ray and said, "Got it."

"This is your safe place?"

"Who'd look there?"

"True," said Ray.

Afterwards, Will sat on the porch steps at Ray's while Son straddled a chaise lounge he pulled off the lawn and Ray leaned up against the side of the Camaro and drank his beer. It was dark by then and a lamp was attached to the top of the Camaro's hood, lighting the interior.

"You can work like that?" asked Will. "In the dark?"

"There's a light, Will."

Ray wasn't doing anything then, though, just drinking his beer. After a while, Will got up for another one and then settled down again and said, "Wait a minute. I was callin' you for somethin' this morning. You never called me back."

He knew Ray was smiling behind the bottle he put his head back to drink out of. Will's beer tasted like water and he thought that about his mother's cookies, too, and remembered her apron with the pink and yellow flowers on the hem and the glasses of milk she poured to go with the cookies he couldn't taste.

13

✦ Crazy Boy ✦

One morning, Carl wakes up and Mr Torch is sitting on the arm of the couch. Carl smiles at him tentatively.

Errol is going out for ice cream. In his living room there are hints of light outside the curtains, dim in the shade of the porch, draining in very softly, a lucidless presence to Errol that will shift and appear in a beam under a table, a spot on the back of the couch, a veil against the wall, that shrinks and deepens and turns into a shadow.

If Carl knew this and thought about it, he'd think Mr Torch came in a different form to Errol. Mr Torch might be the passage of light or the change of seasons or the darkening of summer twilights.

In Carl's own life, Mr Torch is back in the chair against the wall again. One of the odd things to Carl is that he can't really define Mr Torch's face. He's sitting right there, but he won't be able to recall him. And maybe he doesn't really want to. He looks outside at the auto shop instead, at the welcoming cool dark inside the open front door. Mr Torch can see everything: Joe Clay at Andy's, sitting up on Andy's couch, Andy glumly eating his cereal, Craig's cousin at Candi's, dropping down onto a blue stool, eyeing the jar of maple syrup on the counter. After years of buttermilk or strawberry pancakes, he suddenly decides, "Maple pecan, whipped cream, and blueberry syrup."

Craig's cousin knows all the waitresses. This one is named Candy, not Candi. She barely hesitates, pulls a dollar bill out from under a coffee cup and says, "Your gut."

A few minutes later, Son sits down on a stool beside him. He's just starting his pancakes and looks over between bites. "They're outta cinnamon rolls," he says.

It seems extraneous, but the fact is that Son was just about to order one. Which is another strange thing because all he planned to order when he came in was a cup of coffee; but then the minute he looked at Craig's cousin, the thought of food occurred to him. Which irritates him.

"You're weird," he says.

Craig's cousin doesn't comment on that, just looks back at his pancakes again and says, "Coffee cake's good."

In his garage, Errol pauses because the light there is the same as the light in the living room. It shines with little dots that move slowly in the near stillness. Errol moves slowly too, sweeps gently at the dusty light as if to move it away. He remembers the storeroom in the first shoe store he ever worked in, a windowless room with racks that rose up to the lamps in the ceiling. There was real light there too in the shadows above the lamps. He made sure he found an apartment nearby and he always came in early and closed up at night, and that was the first store he bought. Then he bought another one, and after he bought the last store in Acropolis he found this house for sale. It was close to the Qwik Stop and the Dairy Queen and Safeway and there was a porch roof above the windows. Errol doesn't like to go out anymore and doesn't like to be alone. He likes TV and the sounds of Scott and Grace and Carl upstairs. Carl watches a lot of TV and sometimes Errol imagines that they are watching the same show and that they laugh at the same things.

In the garage, he sweeps the light away and puts his palms against the warm, dry wood of the door and begins to push.

They go to a place called Aphrodite's Deli where they eat sandwiches called the Mt Olympus and salads with cheese and purple black olives.

"Ain't as good as George's," says Ray, picking up one of his olives. He stares at it before he eats it. "It'll do though."

Fin nods, picking up his Coke. He grimaces with every swallow and the purple shadows under his eyes deepen with every grimace. Ray shifts his gaze to a picture of Aphrodite on the window by the door. She looks like somebody's version of the Venus de Milo, or maybe her more voluptuous sister.

She reminds Ray of Cora because he can picture her without arms. Cora's a living Venus de Milo, cool as stone, a woman without love. Voluptuous, enticing, empty. She also reminds him that he's bored. Or maybe not bored, but something is making him think so. "You look beat, man."

"Work," says Fin. "I have a lot of catching up to do. Tryin' to take the load off Sully. I should be there now."

"It's Saturday."

"I still have work."

"Take a vacation."

"I just started."

"I need a vacation."

It amuses Ray that he keeps thinking that his relationship with Son will improve, almost miraculously, a turn-about from the last time he saw him, with time being the only reason because nothing in their behavior changes. He knows that he's to blame, letting Son's moods turn him irritable. And it's not that they don't have fun. He liked working on Son's car, taking his time every day after work, feeling like Wayne, with a beer in place of a popsicle, Son sitting lazily on the chaise lounge he pulled over to the driveway.

"Comfortable?" Ray asked one night.

"Tryin' to be. You're sure takin' your time."

"What's it to you?"

"Nothin'. Take all the time you want."

"Thanks."

He drank his beer, analyzing the indulgence in Son's smile. He didn't get it. "What?"

"I think you're losin' your touch," Son said.

"You think so?"

"I think it's possible."

"An' do you think it's possible that you can do any better?"

Son seemed to consider the question, sprawling comfortably in the chair. Then he sighed and admitted, "Well, maybe not...considerin' you were my teacher."

Ray guffawed. "You little fuck."

He laughed though and thought about the day he met his mother's first boyfriend after Wayne left. He already had his postcard from St. Louis and was working on Wayne's Camaro in the driveway, taking up where Wayne left off. The postcard made everything real. Wayne wasn't just at work about to come home with a box of popsicles he'd lift up as he came through the door. "Can't forget these."

He feels pretty sure that if Wayne came home like that one day, Irene would just go on as if nothing else had happened too. But then the postcard came and he started to work on the Camaro Wayne left in the driveway and that's when Matt came over from a house across the street with a red motorcycle in its driveway and a black El Camino at the curb. Ray didn't notice him until he started to laugh, and that's when he looked up. Matt stood there with his hands on his hips and then leaned in with another laugh. "You have got to be shittin' me."

"What?"

"How old are you?"

"Eleven."

"An' you think you know what you're doin'?"

"You think you do?"

That got him another laugh. "At least I'm big enough to see inside."

"I'm big enough."

"Oh yeah? What's your name?"

"Ray."

"What's your mom's name?"

"Irene."

"Tell you what. Introduce me an' you can ride on my Harley."

Then Ray looked across the street at the big cherry red bike and felt his own grin split his face. "Yeah?"

"No lie."

He remembers Irene's smile when she came home and found Matt sitting beside him on her couch. She opened her purse, took her cigarettes out and smiled.

"I'll take an explanation from anyone," she said.

Ray always admired her.

At Aphrodite's Deli, Ray picks up his Coke and says, "Pissed my kid off again."

The little deli is filling up with light, shadows moving back against the Acropolis painted in gold on the wall. The floor is covered in black and white tiles.

"I didn't notice," says Fin. His red-rimmed eyes make him feel sleepy. He rubs them with his thumb, elbows on the table, musing on a conflict he doesn't actually see. Maybe it's about memory, not the present, because to him Ray and Son seem to get along. They joke and taunt each other but always end up laughing. He isn't sure that he likes Son, but he doesn't dislike him either. He isn't really a version of Ray. Ray's life is on his face, things revealed and secret; but looking into Son is a little like going into freefall. He isn't truthful, but he isn't a liar either. Squeezing the bridge of his nose, Fin realizes he feels a surprising alliance with Son, shares the confusion of living in his own life.

"I pissed 'im off with that thing about the joke book," says Ray. "Wasn't even that funny either."

"He laughed."

"That wasn't a laugh."

They were all at Mulligan's when Son brought up the fake tattoo of a daisy one of Ray's friends gave him after he had passed out drunk on Ray's couch. For some reason, Son was all of a sudden indignant about it. "You remember that?"

"How could I forget? It was fucking hilarious."

"Yeah. Hilarious."

"You have no sense of humor, kid. I'd buy you a book a jokes but I don't wanna blow a whole two fifty on it."

They all laughed. But now Ray says, "Yeah, that wasn't a laugh. I can tell that kid's laugh an' that wasn't it."

At the bottom of the stairs there's a circle of gravel and a gravel walkway around the house. On the other side of the house, there is a row of mirror plants. They are old plants that were here before Errol bought the house. Over the top of the plant closest to the corner of the house, Errol is staring at Craig's cousin.

This is after Grace came downstairs and crossed the walkway past the other corner and said, "Hi, Errol." He was standing outside the garage, about to open it, she thought, because his hand seemed to hover above the handle at the bottom of the door.

She paused and then he pulled his hand up and pushed it under his arm and said, "Goin' for a walk?"

She nodded, then he nodded too, thought for a moment and added, "Nice day."

"Pretty," she agreed.

Sometimes Errol pleased himself, but he didn't seem pleased then. Now he's behind the mirror plant, staring over at Craig's cousin and Grace is kicking at little rocks. It stirs the dirt but she likes the smell. It's sunny on one side of her and shady on the other side. She stays in the sun and looks back at Ray's. Fin's Chevelle is parked out front. She looks away, growing warmer in the warm air. Crazy impulses sometimes come over her. She wants to pull her hair and scream into the open air, squeeze her eyes shut and see nothing but sparks. Stomp and jump on the floor until it shakes. Not be that other girl who hides behind her shyness. A fearless girl instead. A girl who can save the man she loves. She wants to scream at Ray, but all he would do is stare in amused surprise. Fin is nothing to him, a diversion, because a friendship makes no sense.

"Do you really like him?" she asked, and regretted it, regretted giving Fin her worry and jealousy to think about. She was never jealous of Lois, never worried about George's absences.

"Ray? Yeah, sure. Why wouldn't I?"

"You have nothing in common."

"I don't know that, Grace. You keep forgetting I don't know a damn thing about myself."

There's always a look of anger when he says that and she wonders who he's angry at. George was never angry. George was sorrowful and kind. She was blissfully shy because George liked that about her. She thinks Fin is impatient, at least he looks at her sometimes with a restless energy she can't share. Ray shares it. She is like George. After he decided to go home to Lois, he wouldn't come up to her apartment alone anymore. He brought Ray, who she didn't really know. She amused him. She saw it in his smile, in the way his eyes laughed at her. Then he finally laughed out loud and said, "C'mon, sweet pea. Relax. I don't bite."

At home, she looks at her skinny face and wispy hair and thinks of the way she always blushes at Ray's grin.

"Hey, sweet pea."

"Pretty flower," said Fin one day, sitting in her yellow chair while she put on her shoes to go to work. "Sweet peas," he added when she looked over.

She could smell the whiskey in his coffee and see the flowers on his cup that must have made him think of that.

"I guess so," she murmured, thinking of Ray in her living room again.

At Ray's, Craig's cousin stops on the porch and looks back over at Errol by the mirror plants. Errol ducks down and Craig's cousin pushes his scratched sunglasses up higher on his nose and follows Son inside.

Later, when they come back out, Craig's cousin stares at the mirror plants again and thinks about the day he met Will, because the plants are almost motionless in a way that reminds him of the stillness of time. That's when he can see things other people can't, a sudden snapshot, an impression of other things. He knows that Errol's outside again and can see him come off the porch and slow at the corner of the house by the stairs. In a minute, Errol's going to peek out and see Craig's cousin looking back at him over the tops of his new sunglasses. His old ones are lying on the seat of Son's car and Son is leaning against the side of the car behind him. Craig's cousin sits slowly on the front of the hood, making Son look over at the movement.

"What are you looking at?" Son asks.

"Dude over there."

The glasses are Ray's. The rims and lenses are a shineless black. It was the last pair he tried on, finding them at the bottom of the plastic display case at the counter. The case was on a swivel bottom and had little mirrors at the top of each row.

"You know that dude across the street?" he asked Ray.

"Yeah. What about 'im?"

"Got punked."

"What are you talkin' about?"

"Couple kids. Put a lock on the dude's garage." Both Son and Ray looked dubious and Craig's cousin nodded, tugging another pair of glasses free of the rack. "Locked 'im out."

"How the hell do you know that?" asked Ray.

"I saw it," he said and grinned at him over the tops of the glasses. "You like these?"

"Yeah. Fine."

Then, after he put on the pair he's wearing now and said, "These?" Ray said, "Jesus Christ, man, just take a fuckin' pair."

"Yeah?"

"Yeah!"

"Okay."

On his way out, Craig's cousin caught a glimpse of his sheered reflection in the front door before Son opened it and turned back in for a moment. "Hey, look," he said. "Recognize me? Roy, man."

"Get out!"

Now he's sitting on the hood of Son's car and Son is staring out at the empty lot.

"There's no dude."

"Will be," he murmurs, making Son frown.

He is staring where Craig's cousin is staring, but he doesn't see anything. After a moment he goes back to drinking his beer and then turns around again and says, "Who's Roy?"

"Roy Orbison."

"I don't get it."

"Your dad's no fan."

That was Will's conclusion on the day Craig's cousin and Ray first met. Craig's cousin knew right away that he liked Ray. He knows he always will.

"This is a great day," he murmurs, waiting for Errol to pop up above a mirror plant.

On the day they moved into the house where Errol grew up, he saw a boy outside by the truck their furniture was in. When he went out, they stared at each other for a moment and then the boy said, "I'm Pauley."

"I'm Errol."

"We have pop," said Pauley, pointing at a house with its garage door open.

"Okay." Then Pauley ran off and Errol started after him but stopped when his mother came out and said, "Wait!"

"There's a boy over there," he said, pointing at the house with the open door. Then his mother seemed all of a sudden pained and uncertain, but she only said, "Okay," and waved him off.

She was being brave. That's what his father always said. She imagined things. Things that scared her.

The house the boy pointed at had a picket fence out front and asphalt strips on either side of the grass in the driveway. The yard was empty. Errol went all the way up the driveway to the garage and looked inside. It was dark with curtains on the windows in back. There was nobody there. Then a door at the house came open and somebody shouted, "Got ya!" and Errol ran away.

In town, he found a park with stores and a movie theater surrounding it. He looked in all the store windows and then came to a shoe store next to the drug store. In the shoe store, there was an X-ray machine with a gum ball machine on top of it. A man saw him looking at it and came over.

"Step up."

"Will it see through my shoes?" asked Errol.

"No, no. It's just an exhibit. Used to work though." Then he put a dime in the gum ball machine and gave Errol a shiny blue gum ball. Errol took it reverently.

The man laughed and took a shoe box off the counter. The box was a dark, glossy green.

At home, his mother was bone white and when she saw him, she grabbed him and wouldn't let go. It was dinnertime and the lights were on, throwing the shadows of the boxes against the walls.

She rocked him from side to side and whispered, "Oh, thank God, thank God."

"You scared your mother," chided his father.

After that, whenever he had to go by the house where Pauley lived he always ran by it.

Now he goes to the Dairy Queen for ice cream and the Qwik Stop for almost everything else. At Christmas, he goes out to look at Christmas lights and once almost stopped at the mall to look at decorations, sure that he was going to go inside—right up to the second that he drove on by.

"Next year," he thought.

After his mother died, he bought a grave stone that said, "Brave in Spirit", the store in Acropolis and the house he lives in. It isn't quiet anymore though. He was used to the noise from the bar, then Ray bought the auto shop and now it's not just customers coming by but Ray's friends too, voices booming, engine's revving. He is awed by Ray, the easy way he moves even in those boots, a kind Errol never sold, heavy and black, scuffed at the toes and worn in places into soft creases.

Errol wears slippers, even now, standing outside with a hammer he found in a kitchen drawer. After a while he moves and taps at the lock on his garage, a lock that isn't his, that just appeared. Earlier, he found keys in the drawer with the hammer, stray keys, little and big, brass and nickel, heavy and flimsy. He tried them all, dropping them one by one on the driveway, then stooping to gather them all back up again. It isn't his lock; he didn't do this. It's a joke, he guesses, listening for laughter again, waiting for somebody to run out and yell, "Got ya!"

All Grace said was, "Hi, Errol," and he stuck his hand under his arm and thought on a response and finally came up with, "Nice day."

"Pretty," she said and left him alone.

———————

Outside, the shadows are long and only a patch of weeds in the lot is bright and sunny.

At Will's, shade covers the yard and his birds make soft fluttery noises as they go by. Craig's cousin hears the footsteps behind him stop, looks back and catches Son's nervous stare. "No worries," he says.

"You sure?"

The house is dark. Will isn't home and Craig's cousin scoots up between a spruce and a window he knows he can open.

"I do it all the time."

The window rocks in its casement and the air smells damp in the shade and branches occasionally scrape at the roof. Then, a minute later, Craig's cousin grabs onto the sill and scrambles up. This window is higher than any of the others and he has to kick off the spruce tree to roll in. Will's bed is underneath him; he rolls off that too and then stands up by the dresser and mirror.

"Roy," he murmurs, admiring his appearance through his sunglasses. The room is mostly dark.

"C'mon in," he says and poses with an imaginary guitar. He's wearing a gray knit cap though and doesn't really look like Roy with the cap on. When he first wore it, Jimbo laughed at him.

"Candy ass."

Occasionally he takes it off. Other times he just stares at Jimbo with a tiny smile that gradually makes Jimbo's face puff up.

"Why the hell am I climbin' in the window?" yells Son. "Unlock the door."

Craig's cousin sees a bag of macaroon cookies that he takes with him as he goes. There are piles of clothes and garbage all the way up to the door.

Outside, the sun is sinking and it shines into the kitchen at an angle that lights up all the dust and grit on the counters. It's strange in a way. Will's mother never left a spot of dust anywhere. He opens the back door.

"Beer?"

"Okay."

The cobwebs are thin and gray in the light. The fixtures shine, but there's a sour smell. Son looks around. Craig's cousin can see the house Son lived in with Ray, its grimy mess until one of Ray's girlfriends cleaned it.

"What's 'e got here?" asks Son, going over to the door to living room, glancing back at Craig's cousin for an answer. But Craig's cousin just shrugs and Son starts looking in other rooms, opening up the bathroom cabinet as Craig's cousin follows him in.

"Are you looking for drugs?"

He says it in a voice that makes Son pause. "Yeah."

"I gave you a beer."

"I know." He is reading the labels on the prescription bottles in the cabinet.

"Susie takes those for real."

Son looks back at him. "So where's the other stuff?"

Craig's cousin tilts his head at a box on the nightstand. "Some there."

He says it as a comment, not an invitation, not permission, and Son goes over almost cautiously, as if the box might disappear before he gets there. Opening it, he looks back at Craig's cousin. "Will 'e miss any? I can pay anyway."

"You don't want any."

"Yes, I do."

"No, you don't."

Son stares into Craig's cousin's stare, a tug of war Craig's cousin knows he'll win. But Son insists. "Yeah, I do."

"No, you don't."

"No, man, I really do. I mean it."

"I mean it."

"Fuck," says Son, starting to get angry. "Now I really want it."

"No, you don't."

"What if I just take some? Will that be okay with Will?"

"Yeah. With Will."

"Not with you?"

"Not you either. You'd've popped those by now."

"Oh, you think?"

"Yeah."

"Really?"

"Really." He knows Son just wants a little help. That's all this is.

"Are you seein' this?"

"Yeah."

Son laughs nervously. "Well, fuck, dude, this is ruinin' my day."

Craig's cousin looks in the bag of cookies, takes one out, and pops it into his mouth. "No, man. It's a great day."

In grammar school once, Will painted a purple banana and gave it to his mother, who put it up on the refrigerator until his father came home and said, "Bananas aren't purple." Then he made him sit at the table with a piece of paper and a yellow crayon and said, "Do it over."

Without a word, his mother took the picture down. She had that tired look she started to give him more often after his father died and a lost look she got when she ran out of things to do.

After she took the picture down, she turned in a circle in the corner the counter space made, then suddenly smoothed out her apron and took a box of vanilla pudding out of the cupboard. That way Will could smell it the whole time he drew his new picture. He looked at his father at the other end of the table with his paper open across his dinner plate. The table was always set with napkins and flowers and nothing out of place. They were going to have potatoes and peas and meatloaf that night. After a while, his father looked up, frowned a little and said, "You can start anytime."

He drew a yellow sun and got another piece of paper and drew a tree full of yellow leaves, got another piece of paper after that and drew a big yellow flower. His mother was spooning pudding into glass cups and his father put down his paper, got up, looked at his pictures and said, "Go to your room."

He sat on his bed until his father came in and took his belt off.

In the morning, he drew a yellow banana on a new piece of paper, and afterwards his father nodded at his mother and she poured him a bowl of Cocoa Puffs.

"Rules are rules," said his father.

It doesn't bother him to come home and find Craig's cousin and Son on his couch. It bothers him that Susie isn't there too, so he's frowning the minute he comes in, nervously, because things aren't right. Susie keeps staying at work instead of coming home to take care of him. She never makes him any real food. He sees the bag of macaroons on the coffee table and takes a handful, looking at Son.

"Car okay?"

"Great."

"Cool...."

He's standing in front of the TV and its light glows around him, making him look like he just stepped out of it. It's growing gray outside, cooling off. He finishes his cookies without looking at Craig's cousin, meaning he wants something Craig's cousin doesn't want to give him. Craig's cousin sets his beer down and crosses his arms in front of him.

Now Will's looking right at him. He even points as if a thought just occurred to him. "You can do somethin' for me."

Craig's cousin's arms unfold long enough for him to pick his sunglasses up off the coffee table and put them on, but then the room grows too dark and he has to take them back off and set them down again.

"C'mon, Trev." Will's face has the same plaintive look his mother used to give him.

"I have other stuff to do."

Craig's cousin knows things Will never tells him, and Will knows that Craig's cousin doesn't have anything else to do. "You're just sittin'."

"I'm goin' in a minute."

The thought of Craig's cousin being special that way used to bother him.

Craig's cousin picks up his glasses again and brings them up to his face but not all the way. Will is frowning, trying to think of a way to be at Marjorie's and Goliath's house at the same time. At Marjorie's a man named Marty is waiting for him. He lives in a house without plumbing or electricity up in the mountains. Marty told him to stay "exactly on the road" and never go off the road and never come unless Marty knew he was coming. Will was offended by this.

"You should treat me better."

"Better than what?" asked Marty.

Marty didn't come into town very often and Will didn't want to miss him.

"Are you goin' out?"

"Maybe," says Craig's cousin, looking at him through his glasses.

"Jack-in-the-Box?"

"No."

Then Will looks over at Son and says, "I almost didn't sell you my car. I was gonna keep it for the memories."

Craig's cousin smiles.

"I gave you the first ride," says Will, looking back at Craig's cousin.

"Yeah."

Then they both laugh. "Taco Bell!" That was their first stop before Will drove aimlessly around town for the rest of the night.

Now Will says, "I just need a minute of somebody's goddam time."

"I have time," says Son.

Craig's cousin puts his sunglasses on and rests an ankle on his knee. "Roy," he murmurs.

Will looks over again. "You have time, too."

"Not me."

"You're eatin' my cookies."

"Stale."

"Yeah," he murmurs, beginning to frown, thinking of Susie again and Son at Goliath's instead of Craig's cousin. He eats a cookie almost tentatively and says, "C'mon. I have to meet this guy an' Goliath at the same time. That ain't gonna work."

"Bad planning."

"Trevor, you aren't being very helpful to me."

"Call Goliath."

"What for? You can make the delivery for me."

"Not me. You got others."

"Not available."

Will looks back at Son.

"Not him either," says Craig's cousin. Son tilts a look at him and Will lowers his eyes. "It's the fuckin' space age, Will. Pick up your phone an' reschedule. Same night. Same bat channel."

Picking up the bag of cookies, Will throws it at him. Craig's cousin gets up with it and takes one out. Son gets up too and Will sighs. "I am in demand," he says.

Craig's cousin nods. "Roy too."

———————

There are no street lamps here and Apollo Liquors is the only bright spot. All the other buildings are dark. At Andy's, Joe Clay parks in somebody else's spot in the covered garage and goes around the corner and through the ivy. The office building across the way has lights shining underneath the bushes out front. He starts to picture himself in a scene from a black and white movie, shadows separating out of shadows, coming closer, gliding through the misty circles of lights, appearing and disappearing.

It isn't misty out though. It's clear and almost warm and the sounds of the cars on Oly Way carry over.

Andy's drapes are closed, but there's a light on inside. It looks to him as if the curtains move but nobody opens the door. "C'mon," he says and goes over to peek in through the part in the curtains. All he can see are the frayed edges of the fabric. He is pretty sure Andy is in there, though, cutting him off like everybody else. Even Jade, Andy's sister, won't talk to him.

After this he goes to Craig's cousin's, but it's dark inside there too and he starts back to his car; he stops when a pair of lights swoop onto the driveway out front and cut across an open space between Craig's cousin's trailer and his neighbors. There are chairs out here for the trailer park residents. Purple vinca grows along the edge of the driveway and plastic lanterns cast up shadows and amber halos.

The car stops and the sound of crunching cinders fades away. Joe goes over to the car and leans in. The rim of the window vibrates under his forearms and the sound of the engine is low and deep. Craig's cousin pushes at the door, forcing him back.

"Whadda you want?"

"Just lookin' for a place to kick it for a while."

"This ain't it," says Craig's cousin.

On the other side of the car, Son is observing him curiously. Joe flushes a little and rubs the back of his neck.

"So maybe we go out. Get a couple drinks? Help me celebrate. I got a job."

About to walk away, Craig's cousin stops and looks back. "You got a job?"

"Yeah. I'm helpin' a guy fix up some property, a caretaker kinda deal. I get to live there, too. Pretty cool."

"Yeah, sounds it."

"So whadda you say?"

"Pick up some chicks, too?" asks Craig's cousin.

Joe brightens. "Yeah, sure. Now you're talkin'."

"No."

Nonplussed, Joe looks at Son. "What about you?"

"No," Craig's cousin says again.

That makes Son laugh as he slams the door shut and joins Craig's cousin.

"Jesus, you guys, am I a leper or somethin'?"

Craig's cousin doesn't answer, just walks away and opens the door to his trailer. Hands in his pockets, Son hops up the steps and goes inside too.

Joe stands there, almost immobilized. Lights go on in the trailer, spill out on shapeless shadows. The darkness beyond is like the pounding ocean in a place like Key Largo or Miami Beach, a dark, moving presence, sonorous and alluring. A promise of neon and cheap hotels, girls on the street corners, a place with palm trees and drinks in coconuts, valises full of money, a diner with a waitress who welcomes him, hides him out, gives him a new start. A scene that works out just like the storyline of a black and white movie.

"Well, shit," Joe murmurs, smelling fir instead of jasmine and jacaranda.

Waiting until he sees Joe walking back up to the road, Craig's cousin grabs a pair of glasses and a bottle, steps over Son's legs and sits down on the other end of the couch, pouring bourbon into the glasses. "Ice?"

"No."

Son drinks, looking at Craig's cousin over the rim of the glass. Then he wipes his mouth with his thumb the way Ray does and suddenly starts laughing. "No…no…no…."

Craig's cousin sets the bottle down, takes a drink too. "Dude's a fuck."

"I don't mean that."

"I know what you mean. The fact is, you aren't a good decision maker," says Craig's cousin, "an' I am."

Son's mouth drops. He laughs again. "Fuck…you."

"You know it. You don't want any a that shit Will sells. No pills. No crack. No Molly. Your dad would flip out anyway. I have a feeling he thinks he took care of your little problem."

After he says this, Craig's cousin smiles because Son is looking at him with real light in his eyes. His expressions are usually flickers on the surface of his face.

"My little problem," Son says. "That's the least of my little problems."

"Not a problem anymore."

"No?"

"No."

"I am one fucked up dude, you know? I have a lot of problems. One in particular."

"Oh, yeah?"

Son takes a long swallow of his drink, grimacing it down. "Yeah."

"Show me."

"Show you?"

"Yeah," says Craig's cousin. "Show me this little problem of yours."

He is smiling a long lipped smile, close-cropped strawberry hair peeking out under his knit cap. Son sets his glass down, rolls over, and slowly covers Craig's cousin's body with his own.

"You are my problem."

"No," says Craig's cousin, gently cupping Son's face in his hands. "I am your solution, baby."

Opening his mouth, Son leans in and Craig's cousin sucks on his tongue for a while, then finally pushes him away. "Come on," he says. "You're takin' a shower with me."

Son's body is pushing against him, sliding up and down, his face close, breath moist against Craig's cousin's cheek. "I don't wanna shower."

"Well, you're takin' one, you grungy thing. I want you clean before I start fuckin' your brains out."

"Oh, yeah?" Son's mouth is moving all over his face, the ball in his tongue pulling a trail of spit on Craig's cousin's skin before he rises back up and says, "I was hopin' you'd be goin' a little lower than that."

Craig's cousin grins at him.

"Anything you want, baby."

The leaves of the mirror plant shine in the dark. The light at Carl's scoops down the side of the house and stops above the plant at the corner.

Wayne liked mirror plants too and put a couple in a shady corner out front. Irene wanted flowers but the only flowers they had were rhododendrons and Wayne put the pool in front of them. After he left nobody cleaned the pool anymore and soggy petals covered the surface. In the mornings the color of the light turned pink.

When Matt started coming over he cleaned the pool because he wanted to use it. Even now, Ray can remember the smell of the liner and Irene's suntan lotion. After Matt stopped coming over, she didn't talk about him for a while. Then one day she said, "I thought you were friends."

He remembers shrugging, not wanting to tell her anything. "I thought you were," he said.

She smiled and took her cigarettes outside where there was a mirror plant by the porch that probably looked like Errol's at night.

At the shop, he gets on his bike and then gets back off and goes inside again. There are tool boxes in the newer building and he takes a screw driver out of one of the drawers and starts over to Errol's.

Sometimes when he worked on the car Wayne left, he made believe that Wayne wasn't really gone and was going to come out through the garage door any minute with a couple of sodas and say, "Gimme that wrench. Show ya somethin' new."

In real life, Irene used to pace out front with her cigarettes.

As he walks by, Carl's light goes out and the mirror plants fade against the house. He brought a lantern with him too, which he sets down on the driveway and then starts humming the song Irene used to sing in the mornings. He knew the tune a long time before he knew the words.

"What's it called?" he asked once.

She sang it for him.

"I'm nobody's baby... I don't know why...."

After the latch comes off, he puts it on Errol's porch, then goes back to the shop to lock up again.

14

◆ Long Lost ◆

Outside on the walkway, Kurt stops near Joy's door and sips the coffee he got at the bowling alley. He ate his Danish already. There were jelly donuts, but he didn't buy any. He sips his coffee with the lid half on, half off the cardboard cup and moves up a little. The shade in the courtyard is shrinking as the sun rises and the cobblestones have a cool, white appearance. He presses the lid back on his cup, then Joy is suddenly standing in her door in a pale blue robe, leaning against the sill with her arms crossed in front of her, staring at him sleepily.

She looks completely calm, at ease on a cool morning.

"I think they make these lids too small on purpose," he says.

She rolls her head on the sill and smiles at him a little more. "Why don't you just buy a commuter mug and then you can fill it up."

"Yeah, I should, shouldn't I?"

He thinks he's amusing her. She looks out at the empty courtyard, her foot rubbing at the threshold.

"I had fun last night," he says, and she laughs and raises her eyes to the bottom of the walkway above him.

"So did your friend."

Kurt laughs too, but he doesn't think it's funny and peels back the lid of his coffee cup again. This time he puts it into the back pocket of his jeans and goes over to sit down on the steps.

"Make myself comfortable, I guess."

She smiles again but doesn't invite him in.

Upstairs, Joy's friend slips into her sandals, sits down and leans over. "I had fun."

Jonah nods vaguely. "Yeah, me too."

She knows he wants her to go and pushes her hip up closer. His eyes flicker and she rubs his belly and smiles. "Call me sometime."

He pushes up higher on the pillows, pulling the blankets up with him. "You know I'm married, right?"

"You told me."

"Okay."

She sees him relax and smiles again as she rolls away. The bed shifts as he moves up onto his elbow, following her movements across the room. She picks up her purse, stops at the door and puts on sunglasses he can't see her through.

"Okay, big guy."

She thinks she sounds happy. She can't really tell. He lets his arm down and leans back. His hair is loose and messy and his eyes are impatient. She keeps thinking that she's going to find a man who looks like this and likes her too.

"See ya," he says.

She could look forever though.

"Sure." She pulls open the door. "Have a nice day."

"Yeah. You too."

Her hair bounces on her way downstairs and she winks at Kurt as she goes by. "See ya."

Joy smells like some soap he bought on sale the other day. The bars were the same color as her eyes, pale clear blue and there was a picture of the flower they smelled like on the cellophane wrappers. Kurt forgets its name, a girl's name. It made him think about all the flower names in Jonah's family.

Picking up his empty cup, he watches her disappear down the walkway. She wears him out for some reason. She's too busy and he still doesn't like her. She wears sunny colors and her eyes always shine. She even smells like lemons. Outside his door he stops and takes the coffee cup lid out of his pocket and puts it back on the empty cup and tries to think of the soap's name. Jonah might like it. Sissy's name wasn't a flower name though.

"What was your sister's real name?" he asked once and had to wait through a long, long stare.

Jonah's eyes were almost black, then he shook his head and said, "Anne."

It went through Kurt's mind that Jonah didn't remember right away. She was Sissy to everybody. Maybe she even thought of herself as Sissy.

Anne is calm and composed like Joy is in real life. He imagines that Sissy had a flower quality to her though. Ally isn't a flower name either.

"Jasmine," he says the minute he opens the door. "There's a name."

Jonah's sitting on the side of the bed, jeans on, about to pick up a sock. "Angeline's prettier."

"I thought you didn't like it."

"I don't. I don't like Jasmine either."

Kurt sniffs at the drain in the sink and then tosses his empty cup into the trash underneath. It smells sour in here. He stares at the cereal boxes and the bags of chips and pretzels on the counter.

"Do you wanna get somethin' to eat?"

"No."

Jonah has his boots on and he takes his keys off the TV. He looks like he's trying to remember something.

"Guess I have stuff to do too," murmurs Kurt, sniffing at the space between the wall and the refrigerator where he keeps his paper bags. It doesn't smell like anything though.

"Are you gonna work on your car?"

"Yeah. Wash some clothes."

Jonah opens the door, sees the flat blue coolness of the birdbath below. The air smells light and fresh outside.

"Clean up a little," Kurt adds.

On the steps, he stops to take his cap off, resettles it and starts back down again. The light is pale and lies over the gravel without any sparkle and the giant bowling pin's shadow is gone for the day. It's quiet out and their footsteps sound loud.

Jonah stops and rests his forearms on the side of his pickup while Kurt pulls a burlap bag off the hubcaps underneath.

"Pretty cool."

"Gonna polish 'um or what?"

"Paint 'um maybe," says Kurt. He can picture fresh white spokes under the green of his car.

Jonah just nods. Kurt guesses he's thinking about Ally or that girl whose name he forgets for a minute. When he remembers, he grimaces and then tries to hide his thoughts by blowing out a sigh as he stares at the hubcaps.

Jonah looks too. "Lotta work."

"I'll just spray on that anti-rust stuff first."

Jonah nods and Kurt realizes that they are standing there not talking about last night. It's not the first time Jonah's been with somebody else, but maybe it always bothers him like this. Jonah rocks a little against the pickup, then leans back and says, "I can't think of it."

"What?" asks Kurt.

He seems really bothered now. "Her name."

"Clete."

"Clete. Jesus. No wonder." He pushes off his pickup. "What the hell kinda name is that?"

Kurt straightens up, hubcaps bundled in burlap. "Well, it's no Angeline, that's for sure."

On his way home Jonah keeps thinking about Clete. He can see her at the door with her sunglasses on again, orange dress, and feel the coolness of her arm over his on the couch. They were already upstairs when he pulled away from her a little and said, "What's your name?" He must not have heard her though and just didn't feel like stopping again.

At home he goes up to the pond and washes off before he goes inside. It smells like paint in the house now. His old room is bright yellow with a sky blue ceiling she's going to paint fluffy white clouds on. It reminds him of Aster's flowers around the bathroom mirror and Clover's bell.

One day, right after Abel died, Jonah thought he saw him. He wasn't in his own room, he was sleeping in Abel's. His aunt was in his room, staying for a while to make sure they were settled until summer when Sissy would go live with her. When she said Sissy couldn't stay with him, he thought that Sissy shrank and faded even though he didn't know how it was possible for her to get any smaller. She was smaller than Aster at her thinnest and frailest, so light she could blow away.

They were sitting in the living room after Abel's funeral. Fin wouldn't come back with them, not with Aunt Hilary there. Fin was nervous when Jonah came to see him, came up to the house only once or twice, then not at all. Even Sissy hardly saw him. So he was gone really, and when the first hints of spring came, Jonah knew he was going to lose Sissy too. So he put an end to all of it, and when he looked up into that camera at the *Mom 'n Pop*, he didn't feel anything anymore. But on that day of Abel's funeral, he wanted Fin to come up, to go out and drink. But Fin wasn't there and Aunt Hilary was making iced tea.

Sissy turned on the TV, rhythmically switching channels, looking for cartoons. He thought he was going to explode. Jumping up suddenly, he started pulling off his shirt. It was Abel's anyway and it itched his skin. He yanked the jacket off, unbuttoned his shirt, pulled his belt out and dropped it on the floor, then noticed Aunt Hilary with two glasses of iced tea, staring at him. He dropped with a huff back onto the couch.

"Fuckin' hot."

She gave him his glass of tea, then said, "I'm okay with Sissy staying here until school's out, but she can't stay here after that."

He was stunned. He looked at his aunt with the sick fear in his belly of being completely alone in the house. He was sure he'd go insane here.

"Why can't she stay with me? We live here."

"Don't be silly. She's fourteen. She needs a stable home. At least she can have that now, so please don't make things difficult."

Aunt Hilary didn't care about him. He thought it had something to do with the day that Aster died, the way he acted maybe. She took his room then too, but he didn't want her around. She looked like his mother, but she wasn't his mother. Maybe it was the way he looked like Abel, a boy becoming a man, filling the shape and form that was waiting for him but wasn't him yet.

"How could I make things difficult?"

"By arguing with me."

"You didn't ask us."

"I don't have to. This is what's best."

"You don't know what's best. You don't live here. You aren't a part of us."

Her voice grew quiet, but she didn't budge. "This is exactly what I mean."

"I won't let you."

Then there was a look in her eyes, a look that made him hate her. "Yes, you will. I know you'll realize it's the best thing."

It occurs to him now that she would never call him by name. Maybe that would make him into somebody real, not somebody she could go away and forget about.

To Sissy, he said, "Don't worry. I won't let you go."

He put her doorknob back on her door and slept in his dead father's bed and saw him there in the room, or dreamed that he saw him. But it didn't feel like a dream. He sat up in the bed and forgot that Abel was dead because he looked real standing there in his jeans and flannel shirt, Sandorwood cap on his dark head. Then he just laughed and disappeared.

After that, Jonah kept waiting for him to come back and he caught glimpses of him, but only wispy things that floated away. He wondered where he went when he wasn't real. He wondered if his mother was there, and Clover and Job. Job thought that Clover came back from the dead: he told Aster about it one day while she sat in her rocker, waiting for him to die.

"I felt this draft first," he said. "Nice an' warm an' I was surprised at that. I was lookin' around for the window it was comin' through, but it was only Cloey."

His face had a sad and distant look because seeing her didn't really bring her closer. She was still dead and he had never meant for her to be dead.

After Jonah got out of prison and came back home, he was sure that they were all here. It didn't matter if he was inside or out. He caught glimpses of them and then they were gone.

"Jojo's like my Cloey," said Job, pushing his tongue into his cheek.

His skin was gray and his neck had cords sticking out and his stomach was full of air. When his chest rose in a breath, it would stay pushed out at first and then suddenly drop, and when he put his tongue in his cheek and looked at Aster, she was afraid of him. She saw him looking at Clover that way, laughing at her, without that whispery, raspy laugh he had then.

His fingers were like gray twigs. He waved at the door and she heard normal things like the TV and saw the last of the day's light. Then he said, "Surprised me. Bein' warm, I mean. I never did like bein' cold."

When Jonah was here alone, he was aware of his family because they weren't really here anymore and he couldn't get used to it. On the day he married Ally and brought her up here to live, he thought he felt the ground shake underneath him. He imagined cracks spreading from the center of the house, deep, dark ruptures, releasing something that had been dormant for a long time.

Outside, there are some towels and Ally's slip on the clothesline. He kicks the laundry basket through the door when he comes in. Aster's basket was blue too. Abel hated it.

"Why don't you get wicker like my mom's? That thing's a fuckin' eyesore."

Aster looked startled. They had Clover's wicker basket for a long time. Then it just disappeared. Abel didn't care about the flowers Aster painted on the wall, but he cared about the basket and the tomato soup she always made for lunch. Jonah can't remember now if she ever made anything else, but he thinks she probably did. Chicken noodle. Alphabet. Now all he remembers is tomato, Abel staring sourly into the bowl she gave him one day.

"Is this all they make? Tomato? Every damn day, tomato, tomato, tomato." Aster picked up the coffee pot and poured him a cup and he took it and drank, keeping his eye on her. "Is this the only kind, Aster? Name me any other fuckin' kind."

She had to answer. "Barley."

He nodded. "Goddam barley. So buy that from now on."

That was all it came to though. Over other things he'd hit her. Sometimes the way Jonah hits Ally, for something, he guesses, but not much. He slaps or punches her where nobody can see, misses sometimes and hits her face and then she stays home. He knows how easy it is to do things to people that nobody knows about. Aster didn't think anything she did was right after a while; she did everything almost sleepily, waiting for Abel's reaction.

He laughed at her flowers on the bathroom wall.

"Dec-o-ra-tion. Is that what that is?"

Jonah was sitting on the rim of the tub, eating a sandwich while he watched her paint. Then, after Abel came in, he watched her stare as if just noticing what she'd done. She slowly traced a leaf with her finger, then let her hand drop. She still bought tomato soup after that, and for a while Jonah used to pretend that he jumped up and yelled, "I like her fuckin' soup!" and that

Abel backed down. He liked the look of surprise he saw on Abel's face, but there was no look of surprise, of course, because he didn't do that.

Sissy's doorknob was in a salvage yard in a puddle that shone with oily rainbows when the sun broke through.

It was wintertime and he thought of Aster.

When the sun didn't shine on it, the puddle looked bottomless and he thought of the day Abel took him swimming at Ivy's and he sank almost to the bottom. Then when the sun broke through, everything began to shine.

He picked the knob up and put it in his pocket and didn't think about it again until he got home.

He remembers noticing the cereal bowls in the sink and a couple of Abel's glasses and the broom standing up in the corner where Sissy left it. Her cartoons were on and she was sitting on the living room floor without any lights. It was cold in the house and he kept his hands in his pockets. Sissy had a sweater on over her pajamas and sat hunched over. In a little while Abel would get up.

"Here," he said, going over to give her the doorknob. "It kinda looks like a diamond."

She took it in surprise and then he took it back and said, "I'll put it on for you." She went with him to watch. In the hall light it almost always looks like glass even though it's really plastic, but Jonah remembers it disappointed him anyway, not really looking at all like he thought it would, and he just said, "There," after he put it on.

He doesn't know if Sissy liked it. He had to take it off again the same day because Abel didn't like it not looking like all the others. When he put it back on again later everything was different.

He drops his tee-shirt in the laundry basket and goes outside.

"Need some help?"

Her purse is on top of her car and she's carrying a grocery bag up to the steps. She nods and he goes by, grabs the rest of the bags and follows her back inside.

She's already putting the milk away. He opens a beer and leans back against the counter. The curtains stir and shadows rise up the wall and a bird begins to sing outside. She opens the freezer and he listens to her arrange the bags of beans and peas.

"You could've come," he says.

"I didn't know anybody."

"You know Kurt."

She pulls a mesh bag of oranges out of another bag and he looks away and stares at the wall for a moment before he pushes off the counter. "Remember I'm workin' tonight."

"I remember."

A few minutes later, she hears the TV go on and puts the oranges in a bowl. When he returns, he has his boots and tee-shirt on. "Don't cook me anything. I don't have time."

She looks at the package of hamburger on the counter and says, "Oh."

"I have to get gas an' some oil."

"I can make you a sandwich."

He is looking at the bowl of oranges, and for a moment he doesn't move or say anything. Then he looks at her for another moment, picks up an orange and says, "No, thanks. I'll just take one a these."

The orange stays on his dashboard when he gets out at the river.

On the day she died, Aster made tomato soup and cheese sandwiches. They sat in the kitchen and in those days there was a spruce outside the window that made the room cooler and shady. He remembers she put sheets up on a clothesline that was in the same place as the one they have today. Then she came in and made lunch and began to pick up the rest of their clothes. Sissy kept kicking him under the table and he kept saying, "Quit it," until Aster looked in once and said, "Hush."

In the living room, she put her basket on the couch and picked a shirt up off the floor. She looked outside and didn't move for a long time. Sissy kept kicking and Jonah kept getting angrier and his voice kept getting louder. "*Quit it!*"

Then Aster came back and yanked Sissy's chair all the way to the other end of the table. She looked almost afraid to Jonah. Her fear was like a living thing that got into him and hid. He didn't like it and sat quietly, thinking he'd hear whatever made her afraid, but there was nothing but normal sounds, birds, a bee at the window.

"Be quiet now." She was looking at him. "Can you watch your sister without getting into trouble?"

He nodded.

"Okay." She breathed a sigh and there was an almost wistful smile on her face. "Thank you."

Then she took the laundry basket and went outside. Jonah sat watching Sissy dunk one of her sandwich halves into her soup, dripping red down her chin. He scowled at her, then he got up to look outside. He saw the laundry basket at the bottom of the steps, but he didn't see Aster. Bees buzzed in a golden shine above the weeds.

Looking back at Sissy, he said, "C'mon," and pushed on the screen. Sissy came readily, carrying the other half of her sandwich. The weeds were beaten down on the other side of the driveway, down the mountainside to the road by the river. He went down the trail with Sissy behind him. On the river road though, Sissy began to cry in the hot sun and Jonah took her sandwich and said, "Watch."

Then she stared forgetfully as he shoved the whole thing into his mouth and swallowed it. She blinked and shifted.

"Let's pick some berries."

Jonah knew there were wild strawberries around here because Aster used to pick them. He pushed Sissy over to a blackberry bush in the shade and went looking for the strawberries. Every once in a while he'd look back at Sissy making a pile of berries in the dirt. Then he slid down another path to the river. A dark green vine grew close to the ground and he looked for the strawberries but didn't find any.

Then he saw her in the water. She wasn't even floating. She was weighed down or caught by the debris that collected against the outcropping of rocks. Scrambling down, he grabbed her arm and pulled, but she didn't come up. All through this he was aware of silence all around him. The river flowed and gushed without sound. The birds flew and sang without sound. His mouth was open. His heart pounding, the blood hot in his ears. He ran, or scrambled, knees in the dirt, hands digging and pulling until he plunged, tripping and staggering onto the pavement. Then he saw Sissy, frozen by her pile of berries, mouth wide open. A soundless orifice of horror. *There must be sound! There must be sound!* Then he heard it. A roaring howl, a man's sound, belly deep and unending. Sissy clapped her hands over her ears. He weaved over, almost drunkenly, took her hand and pulled her home.

In the living room she sat with a can of pop, watching cartoons.

Outside, Abel sat next to Jonah on the porch and said, "You didn't tell your sis, did ya?"

"No."

He was aware of Abel's nearness, a knee touching his, Abel's stare, the feel of his breath like a warm breeze against his neck. The feel of him bending close.

"I wish you didn't see that."

Abel's voice was so tender Jonah almost started to cry, but he gritted his teeth and didn't. He kept seeing the loose, soft look of Aster's hair in the water. When he saw the bag of oranges at home he remembered another day and the way that Abel really was.

Before it was Waylon's, the store in town was the Pineville Market, but it was just the same as it is today. On the day Jonah remembers they drove down in Abel's new pickup, the one he would die in. Abel went in first, bracing open the door with his palm, but not looking back at Aster with Sissy on an arm and Jonah's hand in hers. After they were in, Abel went to the lunch counter and Aster did the shopping. When Jonah wandered over to Abel, Abel picked him up and set him on a stool and bought him a bottle of pop with a straw in it. When Aster was done with the shopping, he got up to pay. The owner of the market then was a man named Dennis Ingles. Jonah doesn't really remember him. He thinks he was old even then.

At the register, Aster was bobbing Sissy, who was pulling at Aster's hair, tangling it up in her fingers. Aster laughed and tried to unwind it. Her hair looked like filaments of gold, floating with static. About to help, Abel was distracted by Jonah blowing bubbles into his pop bottle.

"Quit that." When he looked back, Dennis had pulled Aster's hair free and pushed the grocery bags across the counter.

"There you go. Nice seein' you folks."

Abel grabbed both bags, and Aster and Jonah took a milk jug. Jonah was only seven and the jug was heavy. Aster gave him a big smile. At the pickup, Abel took the jugs away, set them in back and said, "C'mon. Let's go."

At home, after Aster got out of the pickup, Abel came up behind her and pushed her into the stairs. She dropped the groceries to grab onto Sissy and hit the stairs with her shins and sat down at the bottom with her face against Sissy's until Abel said, "Give 'er to me," and took her inside. Then she held onto her shins and waited for him. Jonah hid behind the pickup's bumper and stared over the edge.

The heat of the engine made a pocket of warm air. It was a cold day but bright out and he thinks the gravel on the driveway sparkled, but he isn't ever sure of the things he remembers. Maybe she didn't die in summer. Maybe it was cold out then and sunny this other day.

He thought he saw Abel's breath though when he came outside and the sound of the door slamming was loud and clear. Aster didn't make any sound, not even when Abel kicked her off the stairs. Jonah backed up to the side mirror, lay down on the gravel and scooted under the pickup. He saw Abel's boots and Aster leaning on her arm with her other arm over her head. Crouching down, Abel stared at her, then maybe Jonah made a noise because suddenly Abel looked over at him and a blanched look came onto his face, and oddly he looked underneath the porch steps as though Jonah was really there instead. After a moment, he hobbled closer, with a hand on the rail, and looked underneath again. But there was nobody there, nobody looking out through the slats of board. Nobody who might have seen Clover as she fell and broke her neck one day.

Rising up again, he went back to Aster, boots and jeans from under the pickup. He seemed to have forgotten Jonah. Then Abel went inside again but came right back out and said, "Get up."

When she didn't, he started to hit her with something in his hand, pulling her up by her hair at the same time. She grabbed onto his wrists and he pulled her over to the porch and pushed her down on the steps. The truck was cooling and the engine pinged but that was the only noise. There were oranges on the gravel and Jonah saw Aster sitting on the steps and Abel cutting off her hair. It looked like autumn gold floating in the air.

Afterwards, Abel got drunk and picked her hair up out of the dirt at the bottom of the steps and sat outside with it for a long time.

———————

A bird calls at the top of one of the fir trees and the sound carries across the sky.

Jonah thinks of the soft blue sky of morning and the fresh, clean smell of the air. It seems like days ago that he saw Clete slip out of the door with a wave and Kurt stood on the gravel with his hubcaps.

Now a light goes on in a house he can't see and the air is a soft gray color and the firs are clumps of dark.

When he goes back up to his pickup, Agnes is there.

Agnes remembers the day he gave her a ride. She used to dream about something like that happening, so she was nervous that it really was and sat close to her door, looking over at him, but he just drank his coffee and didn't look back at her or say anything.

At Orly's she said, "Thanks," and he said, "No problem," and pulled the nozzle out of one of the pumps and didn't look at her again. Across the street she turned back, but he still didn't look over. He looked up, looked at Orly's office, looked down the road, looked at the parking lot, even off to her side, all places but at her. She slid through the screen door, letting it close quietly, invisible behind the mesh. She felt transparent in the hazy light.

Today, at the Willow's Corner Store, she waited outside for Doug and he almost didn't see her in the shady back. There were boxes and crates in stacks against the back wall of the building and full garbage bags lined against the wooden fence.

She was standing by the metal gate with the rope and the weight that pinged against the pole. He looked past her at first and she was sure he was happy like that before he saw her again.

Then he said, "I got the job," and she put her hands in her back pockets, elbows out, and said, "Congratulations, I guess."

At home she got out of his car in front of the house, stood with her hands in her back pockets again and looked at the light behind the trees.

"See ya, Agnes."

"Okay."

The light was almost silver and the walkway to the water almost disappeared in the dusk. Crossing over, she walked barefoot on it and the planks of wood were warm and rough. It was cool out too though and beginning to grow misty. There was a pool made out of a scoop in the river at the end of the walkway and the water made almost no sound underneath.

She looked at the dark trees and the sky and that's where she saw him in the faraway shadows. Between them the line of fir trees began to curve and a faint sun lit some of their branches. She ran back up the walkway and soon the sound of the river grew louder and the air became damp and cold and she stood with her hands in her pockets and her elbows out, almost not nervous anymore.

"Hi, Agnes."

"Hi," she said.

There are lights on in the house now and he slows the pickup, seeing the walkway up to the porch and the railing lit across the top by a lamp shining out the front window. That's where the chair she sits in in summertime is. He pictures her bare feet up on the railing as she drinks her lemonade and looks over at her. "Not much of a ride."

"That's okay," she says and sits up, curling a leg underneath her.

He stops in front of a detached garage with its doors open and a car out front. "Looks like Orly's here."

"Checkers," she says, bringing her other leg underneath her. She's facing him on the seat.

"Live wires," he replies.

"Come on in."

He looks at the house for a moment and then says, "I dunno."

A light over the kitchen door is on and the window out front wraps around part of the side of the house and looks warm and gold.

"You want to," she says and gets out without waiting.

Halfway across the yard she stops and looks back and after a moment he follows her into the dark through the kitchen door. Once he's inside, he's alone. He hears her in another room, Orly's voice too, but he lingers in the dark, smelling the smells of other people, evidence of other lives.

"I don't see anybody," says Orly.

Then Agnes reappears, a shadow in the dark doorway. "Come in," she whispers.

Again, she doesn't wait for him. He hears her on the stairs. The light from the living room shines on a long floral rug and pictures on both sides of the walls. The dusty living room is floral too. The couch has a flowery fabric and there's a rug with a floral border on the floor and pillows with needle point flowers, all faded though. This was Mavis's room where she sat with her coffee and the sun pouring in.

Orly is sitting on the couch across from Waylon, who is hunched up on the edge of his chair over a checker board on the coffee table. Waylon's belly protrudes out between his knees.

"So what are you up to?" asks Orly. One arm stretches across the top of the couch and a toothpick bobs in his teeth.

"Not much. I was headed to work, but I saw Agnes. Gave 'er a ride."

Waylon glances up. "Thanks for that."

"Sure."

For a reason Jonah isn't sure of, he knows Waylon doesn't like him. It isn't just the general dislike of somebody like him but something personal. The only thing he can think of is Mavis, but that makes no sense because if he ever said anything to her, it was only in passing. But maybe it was something he gave out, a desire for Waylon's wife he never bothered to hide. That makes him nervous suddenly and he notices Orly's eyes on him.

"Coffee?"

"No thanks," he says, looking at a little clock on the window ledge. There's a pot of flowers on the porch rail outside, a pot of ivy, the clock, and a glass dish on the window ledge inside. The curtains are open, white with tiny red checks on the bottom and cover only the bottom half of the windows anyway. The flowers on the white couch are pink and yellow, and Orly has to roll and grab onto an arm to pull himself up out of the softness.

"C'mon. Give you a little get up an' go."

"Yeah, that's true," he admits, moving sideways to let Orly go by. "I guess I could use some a that."

The light at the top of the stairs is still on. He looks up and sees the edges of a painting on the wall and the shadow of the lamp shade. In the kitchen, Orly takes a cup out of the drainer and shakes it off over the sink. The cup has flowers on it too and he thinks of Kurt in the doorway that morning.

"Jasmine," he says, looking at the cup Orly gives him.

Orly looks too. "Look like violets to me."

"I was thinkin' of names," he says, following him back down the hall.

"I like both."

He looks back up the stairs as they go by.

"Your mom's name was pretty too," says Orly, pouring Jonah's coffee out of a pot on a trivet with a blue sailboat on it. "Lots of people stick to family names."

"Where'd yours come from?"

"Mother's uncle."

"That reminds me," Jonah says after he sips his coffee. "I met a girl at a party whose name is Clete."

"Like the spikes on a shoe?"

"Yeah."

"Could be a real name, I guess."

"I wouldn't name a kid that," he says, noticing a picture of Agnes on the mantelpiece.

"It's made up," says Waylon, picking up the coffee pot too.

"Well, I still like family names," says Orly.

"We were thinkin' of Aaron or Abigail."

"Those're good."

He takes his coffee to the mantel to look at Agnes's picture. The frame was a gift from her mother like the trivet with the sailboat. He can sense Mavis here and see her image in the faded colors. Agnes looks like her and the living room is the way she made it. She probably put real flowers in her vases and left the windows open to feel the air blowing through. She is always partly here, never wholly anywhere.

On his way out a few minutes later, he puts his empty cup in the sink and looks back into the hall. The light upstairs is out.

It is quiet and damp out and grayish strings of mist float by. On the ground there are shadows from the lights inside. The windows still look warm and gold.

Agnes comes out of the garage and waits until he closes his door and then comes over and curls her fingers over his open window. Her hair curls like springs in the damp.

"You look cold," he says and sees her look down at her fingers. They are tense and white. The light reaches over and he looks at the house again.

"Is she pretty?"

He feels surprised because he was thinking of Mavis and looks back at her with a frown. "Is who pretty?"

"Clete."

"Oh. Her." She is staring at him and he remembers that he used to think that she looked like a piece of clay he could press his thumbs into. "I made 'er up," he says and feels confused at that. He wants her to believe him though.

"Why?" she whispers.

"Cuz I'm lonely."

"But you're married."

He nods and turns the key in the ignition, not looking at the house anymore. After a moment she backs away. "Bye, Agnes."

"Bye," she murmurs.

At work, Kurt comes over and he lights a cigarette, not wanting to go in right away. Kurt leans against the wall by the door and Jonah looks out into the parking lot. He can't see Kurt's car and looks back at him.

"Get those hubcaps on?"

"Just started gettin' 'um cleaned up."

He nods and blows his smoke into the air, watching it drift away.

He remembers the moment now when he realized that he didn't know Clete's name. She was sitting on her hip, smiling at him as he lit a cigarette and then she leaned across him and took one for herself. He lit it for her and she blew her smoke out and smiled at him again.

"I love freebies."

Her eyes were blue like Aster's, and when he noticed that, that's when he realized he didn't know her name. She looked amused and he remembers becoming angry, stubbing his cigarette out and rolling on top of her. His weight began to suffocate her and she struggled and said, "Hey, c'mon." Then he rose up a little, but that was only to grab her wrist and hold her cigarette up while he stared at her, holding her down again.

Then he smiled and said, "Yeah. I like freebies too."

15

♦ Ties ♦

The air is mild and the days go from misty to sunny and back. Geese call across the sky. The light is pale and the glitter on the gravel outside the auto shop is bright. The door to the warehouse is open and the cool light shines in. Up the ramp, the inside of the shop is cool too, a window over the counter open where Son sits behind the register and stares listlessly at Ray, who is standing at the other end of the counter, squinting at a sheet of pink paper.

"You need glasses."

"Shut up."

Son yawns, gets up with a coffee cup, pours a fresh cup in the kitchen and returns.

Ray is leaning on his elbows on the counter, flipping over the sheet of paper, looking at the next one.

"What are those?"

"Packing slips."

"What are you doing with them?"

"I'm looking for something."

"Why don't you log them into a computer?"

Ray looks up irritably. "I do with the real invoices. These are packing."

"Okay."

He sips his coffee and Ray looks back up again. "Nice a you to offer me one."

"What?"

"Coffee."

Son's eyes roll. He slides off his stool and comes back again a minute later. Ray takes a swallow of coffee, sets the cup down.

"Is it always like this?" asks Son.

"Like what?"

"Boring."

Ray looks at him. "I'm surprised you could tear yourself away from your new pal long enough to give me one day."

"He's working."

"Working? Imagine that."

"Well, at least it's a real job."

"What does that mean?"

"Nothing. It's a real job."

"Well, good for him."

Ray is slapping the sheets of paper upside down one at a time, not finding the one he's looking for.

"What's wrong with 'im?"

It takes Ray a moment to remember what they were talking about. "Nothing. He's alright."

"You like 'im, don't you?"

"I said, he's alright. Whadda you care if I like 'im?"

"I don't. I'm just makin' conversation, tryin' to find somethin' to do. You're so damn busy."

"I am busy. I have business."

"Yeah, right, all kinds."

"You know, kid, you are beginning to piss me off again."

"Well, that's my special skill set, isn't it?"

Ray laughs. He doesn't want to, but he ends up laughing anyway. "Christ, you're a punk."

"Whatever."

Taking his coffee outside Son sits on the porch for a while. The flash of light off the gravel is almost blinding. He leans against a post, lounging sleepily, gets up as a car pulls in.

A few other customers appear and then it is quiet again. Ray is in the warehouse. Son yawns. Another car pulls up outside and Son leans across the counter, grabbing the outer edge to stretch his muscles, sits up again as the door opens, bells jingling.

At first, the man just grins. He has a wispy little cowlick in back that catches the light behind him because he left the door open. Son waits for a moment, then says, "Help ya with somethin'?"

The man doesn't answer right away, just looks around and then suddenly brightens. "Hey, yeah."

Then he seems familiar. Son frowns, trying to place him as he approaches with a pair of fuzzy pink dice he took off a display rack at the end of one of the aisles. "I wanna pair a these in yellow."

Son looks at the rack. There are blue ones, white ones, green ones, even a pair of orange ones.

"Those are all we have."

"Really?"

"Yeah."

"Yellow's my wife's favorite color."

His grin is still there, still bright. He's holding up the dice as if to be sure Son sees them. They sway a little like a hypnotist's watch.

Son shrugs.

"Sorry."

"That's too bad."

"Maybe someplace else."

"No. She'd like 'um comin' from here better." The dice are still swaying, but now he's grinning at them instead of at Son. "I always get her favorites." Then he lifts his chin at the open glass door that leads into the other part of the shop. "Any in there, you think?"

"No."

"You sound sure."

"I am sure."

The man's grin is utterly complacent as if nothing ever bothers him, or if the things that might bother him are always unseen and unrecognized. The look growing on Son's face is wary, uneasy, but the man just smiles; the look he sees is not unfamiliar to him. People often make a wide berth around him, or pick and poke at him with an almost hostile curiosity.

"I think I'll just check myself," he says, swinging the dice as he goes.

At the top of the ramp he stops and starts to grin again even though the warehouse looks empty. The bright light is moving away outside and a cool breeze is blowing in.

He swings the dice. "Hey, Ray!"

A moment later, Ray appears from outside, looks up and grins back at him. "Pete! Fuck, man."

"Yep."

Pete backs up into the shop again and slaps Ray's palm as he comes through. Ray is laughing. "Jesus Christ, man."

"Long time."

"Hell, yeah."

"You look good."

"You too. How ya been?"

"No yellow dice. Cora likes yellow."

"Cora loves yellow," says Ray.

Pete looks at Son. "That yours?"

"Yeah. C'mere, kid. You guys ever meet?"

"Sure. You brought 'im to our wedding."

With Ed, Ray remembers, at Cora's yellow house. They were married on the lawn out back. There was a table with a white lace tablecloth outside and a cake in the middle of it. When Ed saw the table and the cake, he said, "Wow, man, this is just like the Brady Bunch's wedding."

The house was left to her by her mother and her mother's boyfriend lived there with her and gave her away because she didn't have anybody else.

"Wonder why the hell I'd bring a kid."

Cora's dress was covered in little pearls and fanned out all over the grass. When she walked, she pulled up the front in her fists and her feet were bare because the heels of her new shoes stuck in the grass.

"Idiot Bobby," she said. "Watered the fuckin' lawn this morning."

Her cheeks were pink and her curly blonde hair was on top of her head and there were pearls on the ribbons that fell down her neck and later, when she cut her cake, there was a look of horror on her face.

"Raspberry! I didn't order fuckin' raspberry!"

Pete can tell the look on Ray's face has to do with Cora. He grins up at him again and says, "You better help me think of somethin' for 'er. These dice were perfect."

"Take your pick," says Ray. "On me."

"I need yellow."

"Piss on a pair a white ones," says Son, and Ray and Pete both stare at him. Pete looks like he's thinking about it. Ray looks surprised too, but then he laughs.

"Good one," says Pete.

The flowers at the wedding were yellow and the house was yellow and she had little yellow silk flowers on her garter belt. Her cake was white and red though.

"I ordered goddam lemon. Fuckin' yellow!" she said.

Son remembers the flowers on her garter belt because she sat on Ray's lap in one of the folding chairs on the lawn and made its back legs sink deeper into the grass. The hem of her dress was turning green and she pulled it up and pointed at her white garter belt and said, "Do you know what garter belts're for? Money. Money's traditional at weddings."

"So's kissin' the bride."

"Married now," said Ed.

"I guess that means you're outta luck, babe."

After that, she flicked her dress back down and almost got up before she noticed the ring on Ray's finger and said, "Hey." She wanted it back. She bought it for Pete but gave it to Ray.

Then Ray and Cora went inside the house and Son stayed with Ed. Pete stayed outside too and when Cora came back out again without Ray she threw her arms around Pete's neck and said, "Oh, Petey. I'm so glad I married you."

With his grinning face, he doesn't look like she ever disappoints him.

When George quit Anderson's Appliances because Lois told him to, Henry's brother, Ralph, got him a sales job with him at Wellesly's Liquor Distributors. It was a job Ralph's wife, Audrey, always liked because it gave her time off from Ralph, and when he came home, he always came home with stories that made her laugh. Ralph was a good salesman for a long time. With Audrey he was good too until he ran out of stories he could remember.

He has an idea that he was funny once and that nobody thinks he's funny anymore. He tried to laugh when Henry came over earlier that day. "Look. I gave myself a nose job."

Earlier, the owner of a market Ralph walked into called Henry because Ralph's face was bloody and he didn't seem to notice. He drove his car into the wall of his garage and afterwards got out to walk because he couldn't get the car to start again. Luckily he went to a market where the owner knew him.

"You know, there are easier ways," murmured Henry.

"That's the truth," said Ralph, lying in his recliner with a bag of ice on his nose.

Now Henry's back at the bar and Grace is sitting across from him at the counter with her fingers on the edge, sometimes pushing herself into a slow circle. "It's nice like this," he says.

She nods and looks outside, back in again, outside. Then sliding off the stool, she wets a dish towel at the sink and begins to wipe off the tables. She moves slowly, in no hurry, and Henry's thoughts go easily where hers go, to Fin, who he likes and doesn't like. Not drinking, Fin makes her happy. For a long time it was Ralph's drinking that made Audrey happy. Over the couch at Ralph's is a cuckoo clock he and Rose gave Ralph and Audrey for Christmas one year, mostly to Audrey though, like the crystal ball Ralph flung onto a neighbor's lawn after she left. Henry remembers her up on a chair with the clock, exasperated as the minutes went by and Ralph never seemed sure of the positioning. He couldn't really see by then.

"Up a little."

He swayed.

"Godammit, Ralph."

Then he made a mark on the wall and Audrey got down and he tapped a nail into place and then plowed a hole through the plaster with his next swing.

"Oops."

She stayed with him a long time really. Henry pictures Grace like Audrey, all those years of staying and loving and giving up.

She wipes the tables in slow, contented circles.

Drinking, Fin is like Ralph, collapsing slowly. Henry saw him really drunk only once, but he drank steadily, on task, focused on a job that was onerous but inescapable. As he drank, the anger rose, suffusing him with red. Sober, he is humorous, mild, pleasant. Sober, his eyes reveal a weakness that Henry fears, a look of retreat, of defeat in place of courage.

Yet, Henry does like him. That mild humor. And, looking at Grace as she comes back to the stool, twirling slowly, Henry likes to think that there is nothing really inescapable, and that a day can mean a whole new life.

Fir needles drop with tiny clicks on the roof of Pete's car. Without the sun the air is cool, almost damp, coming out of deep shady places.

"I think I pissed your kid off," he says. "I wasn't really trying to."

"The kid's moody."

"Is this where your wife works?" asks Pete with that grin of his again.

"Yep."

She's not at the bar though. Will is, letting his eyes slide over Pete. Pete's grin stays on and Ray grins too. "Hey, Will. How ya doin'?"

"Okay."

They don't stop. Ray just looks at Otis and Otis nods. They sit at a table against the wall and Ray slides down and stretches his legs out, lacing his fingers across his belly.

"Friend a yours?" asks Pete, meaning Will.

"Nope."

Pete rubs the arms of his chair, looking around for somebody he wants to look like Cora.

"So where is this woman a yours?"

"Comin' up on ya...."

At the shop, Son sits staring at the sheered front door. It's cool outside and a fly is bopping gently at a window. After a while, he begins to scowl, then suddenly lobs Pete's pink dice out of sight and goes next door.

George pours him a beer and sets it down. "So where's your dad?"

"Out."

George just nods, doesn't look angry or put out. Son flushes though and scowls guiltily at his glass for a moment. Then he drinks half of it and goes to sit at a table out of the way of George and tries to call Craig's cousin. He is supposed to tell Craig's cousin about things like this, things he regrets, things that worry him. Things that make him blow up at people who don't do anything to him. Craig's cousin wants him to talk about these things, so Son told him about the daycare his mother once took him to. Miss Emma ran it out of her own house. She had a big room, like a sun room, filled with round tables and toys and book shelves. Big colorful flowers decorated the walls. One wall was glass and he could see a lawn outside and a swing set in the middle of it. There were big trees and lots of shade. The minute he went into that place, though, he knew he didn't fit in. He was angry, angry at the children. He wouldn't stay. He ran after his mother. He wasn't afraid, he was angry, but he couldn't explain. Kathy wanted him to and made him stay in his room until he did, but he couldn't. He couldn't explain the hate, the outrage at a happiness he didn't share. But Craig's cousin just wants him to talk, not explain anything, and he doesn't have to make sense.

He chews his lip, looking at his phone. Craig's cousin doesn't answer. He finishes his drink. He doesn't have to worry with Craig's cousin. All he has to do is let Craig's cousin decide things for him and that's easy. He can do that, not disappoint anybody. Except Craig's cousin might be mad about George.

He chews his lip again and gets up for another drink.

"Thanks," he says when George sets a fresh drink down on a new napkin. "I appreciate it."

One day, Will's mother made oatmeal raisin cookies, but he couldn't taste them. Ordinarily, he wouldn't get any; he ran out of the house earlier when he got into trouble and his father had to come out looking for him. For a while, he was at Craig's cousin's, but he couldn't even sit still long enough to watch TV. Plus, Craig's cousin kept watching him, giving him a strange concentrated stare. Craig's cousin's red hair was long then, halo soft and curly, and he looked a little like some kind of religious zealot in the middle of a vision. Will kept imagining the lick of his father's belt. There were no gradations to his punishment and no adjustments for his behavior. All of a sudden it came to him like Craig's cousin's visions that it didn't really matter what he did, it was all the same. Realizing this, a feeling of intense liberty came over him. When his father saw him walking home, Will wasn't the same, and for a while his father was afraid of him.

Now, at the Club, Will can't taste his drink either. He doesn't tell people about things like this. It might be a sign that there's something wrong with him. After Ray comes in, he drinks curiously. It's not even the same as drinking water. When he ate his mother's cookies he couldn't even compare it to eating cardboard because he was pretty sure cardboard had a taste. His mother's cookies were just lumps, soft and crunchy at the same time. He thought she did it on purpose, but she never looked over, never tried to catch a reaction.

Ray isn't looking over either.

Will takes another drink because he doesn't want to leave right away. He's alone really, even his senses have left him alone. In the mirror, he can see Ray pulling Miri onto his lap and the man he's with keeps grinning at everybody.

Alone is the word that best describes him. He knew it on the day he ate his mother's cookies too. She didn't really make those cookies for him. He knows she only made them because she didn't think he'd get any. She used to say, "Nice people can stay up and watch TV," or "Nice people can go to the movies."

Cookies were for nice people. The way she kept the house was for nice people.

After he moved out, she never had cookies for him when he went home, so he stopped going.

After his drink, he gets up. They don't even look over.

At home, Susie stares at him suspiciously and he stares back suspiciously because he feels uneasily fond of her. She leans against the arm of her chair.

"What?"

"Nothing."

He grabs a handful of chips out of her bag and says, "You eat too much. You need to lose weight."

"I don't need to lose any goddam weight. I get looks all the time, Will. A lotta looks."

She regrets that the minute she says it. Will's lids sink down over his eyes and he's alone again, always alone. The chips, at first almost salty, are the same as his mother's cookies.

"Oh yeah?" She surprises him by feeling so light when he grabs a fistful of her hair and pulls her up.

"Ow!"

Then she's on her knees, potato chips underneath her, swinging at him while he laughs and pushes her onto the floor. She sits on her hip and clutches the top of her head while he squats beside her and says, "I think you look too."

She stares and ends up lying back on her elbow because he is leaning in, trying to see into her.

"You better not look. You better not leave me."

She looks at the carpet and rolls her shoulder up, trying to hide. "I'm not going to leave you, Will. I love you."

And then he sits on top of her and pushes her down.

"You don't love me."

The carpet is dirty and smelly and he is pulling her blouse off. She tries to push it back down. "I can't breathe."

He stops for a moment and his voice is surprised. "So?"

They are walking over to Pete's car. Small circles of sun shine on it. Everywhere else the firs drown the asphalt in pools of shadow. Miri is walking under Ray's arm, his wrist in her fingers. He likes the way she leans against him, her arm around his waist. He long ago realized he doesn't intersperse thoughts of sex with thoughts of other things. The thoughts of sex are constant, to greater or lesser degrees underlying everything else. Occasionally he wonders if that's a bad thing, but so far, he's still enjoying it.

At the side of Pete's car he drops his arm off of Miri's shoulders and says, "I didn't ask you, man. How're your kids doin'?"

"Great. You should see Laurel though. Looks just like Cora."

"Meanin' you're in for some grief."

"I was thinkin' of lockin' 'er up for a couple a years."

"Wouldn't blame ya."

Pete stays with his arms resting on the roof of his car, grinning as Ray opens the front door and Miri opens the back.

"Sit in front," says Ray.

"You sit in front. You can talk better."

"I'm not gonna be comfortable. Sit in front." He can feel himself growing angry. There is nothing about her that ever flows with him. He is beginning to think that life with her is like a bumper car ride. Her face is stubborn, but she gets in front anyway.

Pete raps the roof of his car and says, "Okay. Where to?"

"Pizza?"

"Sure."

Inside the car, Pete swings an elbow over the seat as he backs up. "Remember Quincy's?"

"Hell, yeah," says Ray. "Hard to forget."

Glancing over at Miri, Pete says, "My old lady had one of our kids there. Just sittin' around, eatin' pizza an' bam, has 'im right there on the floor."

"Sure did a number on my appetite," says Ray.

"No kiddin'. We named 'im Quincy after that place. An', man, is he a lot like Cora. Same fuckin' my way or no way attitude. I don't see any a me in my kids. Shit, if Quincy didn't look like me, I'd start wonderin'.'"

Ray sits in the center of the back seat, legs open, arms stretched out across the top. He laughs, looking out through a side window, thinking of Will. "A woman in love," he says. But that was Miri not Cora.

Pete is nodding as he drives. "I got lucky."

"Good lady," agrees Ray.

Cora is a Venus de Milo, a woman without arms. Ray isn't really sure about the love part.

Reflections of the trees slide over the side windows. Images of Cora and Miri's faces pass and slide over each other too. He remembers taking Cora to meet Pete, and sitting at a table in the middle of Jack's Club with Aaron Toler and never noticing that Miri was even there. Not until later, when he saw her at Will's, and she came up in his memory like somebody from a long time ago. After Cora met Pete, Ray took her out to eat and said, "Pete liked you."

He took her to Quincy's and they were semi-dancing near the jukebox, Cora's arms draped over his shoulders. "That's nice."

"Do you like 'im back?"

She was swaying her hips against him slowly while he was moving her back to their table where his beer was.

"Sure. I like 'im," she said. "Any friend of yours."

On any other day she'd just pass him by without looking.

"Well, Pete likes you a lot," he said and felt her weight grow in his arms.

She was leaning back, giving him a quizzical half-smile, thinking. "Are you askin' me to go out with 'im?"

"Yeah."

After she thought about it for another moment she leaned back in and said, "Okay."

The lights are on at Carl's and the shop is dark.

Fin is sitting in his car, engine off, staring at his fingers on the inside bottom of the steering wheel.

All day he thought about drinking in the sense that he didn't really want a drink for most of the day and was aware of that fact. He drank coffee and sat at the desk his father used to sit at. At home, he ate a microwave dinner, sitting alone in his kitchen, staring at a ring lying in the center of the table. He found it in the attic in a small blue box in the top dresser drawer. There was another rectangular box with cufflinks inside. He showed the ring to Sully, who took it in his blunt tipped fingers and said, "I remember. It was an anniversary ring. Your father showed it to me. Never got to give it to her. Where'd you find it?"

"In the attic."

"You know, it's a good thing you're living in that house. You can take your time going through things."

He nodded and took the ring back home, set it on the kitchen table where he could look at it. It was composed of sapphires and diamonds in the shape of a star, and he wondered if his father showed it to him too, if there was a memory of it somewhere, a memory of something he shared with his father.

After he finished his dinner, his stomach hurt. He wanted to throw up but didn't.

The other night he went upstairs to Grace's and found her sitting in her yellow and purple chair with her heels on the edge of the cushion and her robe pulled down over her legs.

"Were you waiting up for me?" he asked, sitting on the couch across from her.

The moment he sat down, she got up and said, "I guess I have to now."

At work he put the ring on the tip of his little finger and thought about his mother. He can't call his memories of her real memories, but he sees her, catches glimpses of a smile or a gleam in eyes so green they are almost black or her heat-warped shape behind a wall of fire. In the house she moves from room to room. He remembers rainy shadows on her face and sunshine in the mornings. She drank in rooms that fell silent and grew dark. He remembers her silhouette, a bit of the hall light on her glass.

That night at Grace's, he lay on the couch and thought of her in the room next door, lying awake too. At night he can't sleep. He dreams in the mornings of lawn chairs on a grassy hillside and other things he can't remember, and thinks about drowning, of swimming for so long he has no more energy, and of Dahlia with her colorless face and a robe like Grace's.

Now it's almost dark and the air is a soft blue and the lights at the bar are warm and yellow, and he imagines it's a painting and the people inside are sitting in frozen poses with their glasses halfway to their lips, and he thinks about going upstairs to watch TV like Carl or Errol and pictures the dark empty lot and the stairs and the orange flowered wallpaper and puts his head on the steering wheel. An acidic saliva fills his mouth and his tongue is tingling. He swallows repeatedly and his throat feels dry. He wants a drink. It's all he wants. He wants it more than he wants anything.

In the bar, George sets a napkin with a blue outline of a martini glass in the center in front of him.

"These are new," he says.

"You notice the napkins?"

"They come with the drinks," he says.

Will saw Susie for the first time at Candi's when a couple of her friends from work took her out for her birthday. They were sitting in the big booth in the corner and she clapped her hands and laughed when the waitress brought over a coconut cream pie. To Will, watching her, the pie was all she saw. Will didn't pay attention to the others because it was clearly Susie's birthday, so it was her fault that they were sitting there. It was Will's booth.

Like his mother, she didn't understand.

After her pie arrived, he left without eating and stopped at Taco Bell on the way to Andy's and saw her again at the building across the street from where Andy lived. He was going up Andy's walkway through the vinca and heard car doors closing across the street but didn't look over until he heard "Happy Birthday...! Happy Birthday!" Then he turned and saw Susie and her friends in the office building parking lot. Some of her friends went in one door and a few others went in another door. The party was over, but Susie was carrying a pink and white box from Candi's. At five o'clock she came back out without her box, but she was smiling anyway.

Will was sitting on a wooden bench against the wall by the doors waiting for her with a bouquet of flowers. "I got you these," he said after he got up and stopped her.

She was startled. He tried to imagine the scene from a window up above or on a screen. A man with a bouquet of flowers waiting for a woman. The woman didn't know the man. To Will, everything rode on Susie's sensibilities. She could be disturbed or afraid, or she could show sense and recognize that only a special man would wait outside her office building with a bouquet of flowers.

"Who are you?"

"Will."

"Do I know you?"

"Do you want to?" he asked, holding out the flowers. He saw her face go soft and wash away that silly, meaningless smile. She looked at him with something like awe. "For me?"

"It's your birthday, isn't it?"

"How did you know that?"

"I know things," he said.

He knew there was something soft about him, something in the color of his hair and his eyes, something soft that contrasted with the way he walked and the way he behaved. He wasn't sure he was irresistible, but he could tell that Susie liked him right away.

She wore pearls to work the next time he saw her and he said, "Those are nice," almost distantly though because he was picturing June Cleaver.

He took her to Candi's and they sat in his booth.

"We have to dress up," she said.

"Where at?"

"Acropolis Title."

"Oh." He wasn't really interested and her pearls began to distract him. She wanted to know about his job and he thought about it for a moment and then said, "I have a coin-op laundry an' a couple vending machines."

The coin-op laundry is Jimbo's and Andy once talked about buying some vending machines.

"Wow."

"Yeah," he said, liking the way she looked at him after that, and he thought about his mother and being married and respected.

He wants to be married someday. He always pictures Susie in pearls and frilly aprons, though, and he doesn't like that picture. Once he looked in all the kitchen drawers, pulling out towels and pot holders and recipe books, just to make sure she didn't have any aprons. She doesn't clean either. She's not like Mrs Cleaver that way. She doesn't cook. They don't sit at the dining room table with a pot roast and gravy and have polite conversation like nice people. They eat chips and Hostess pies, and go out to Jack-in-the-Box and Taco Bell. Which is what Will wants to do right now, waiting at the door for

Susie, who appears in a pair of black and white polka dot capris and a white top.

"You look like a fuckin' milk cow."

"This is my best outfit!"

"Fuck," he says and opens the door at the same time that Jimbo pulls up outside, lights shining through the juniper.

Will closes the door. "Stayin' in."

He drops back on the couch and stares at Susie, who tosses her purse onto her chair when Jimbo comes in and gives him a look. "Keep off," she says.

There is another set of lights sweeping by outside, the sound of the motor causing Will to grimace and mutter, "My fuckin' car." But he gets up anyway and opens the door. "Hey, what's up?"

Son steps in. "I was lookin' for Trevor. Said 'e was comin' over after work."

"Not here yet." Will points at Jimbo. "Call 'im. Craig an' Andy too. I got a new game. We're all gonna play my new game."

Jimbo throws Susie's purse on the floor and sits down in her chair. It sinks underneath him and he stretches out uncomfortably, seeing her shadow emerge from behind him. She swallows the chips she's eating and stands in front of him.

"I said keep off."

He picks up the remote and points it at her. "Do you mind?" he says.

"Yeah, I mind. That's my chair."

"Your personal chair?"

"Yeah. My personal chair."

"You brought it with you?"

"Maybe."

"I don't think so."

"I do."

Jimbo shrugs and says, "I could use a beer."

"Me too," says Will, coming over for some chips. "An' get that game," he adds. "This is a real cool game."

Susie likes it too.

"Magic Beads," he says, sitting on the carpet.

The chips he took are barbecue and he can taste the spices. He wipes his fingers off on his pants and leans back on the carpet. Susie steps over Jimbo's legs.

"Asshole."

Son takes off his jacket, drops it on the end of the couch and sits down, Will looking up at him. "I saw your dad. Who's the dude?"

"Just a friend."

"I figured that." He thinks Son looks irritated. He is sitting with an ankle crossed over a knee, tapping at the side of his boot. "Whadda you hookin' up with Trev for?"

Son's eyes drop and Will can see the irritation growing. "See a movie or somethin'."

"No. Stay here. We're playin' my game."

Susie returns with the beer and Will says, "We need snacks."

She huffs at him with a hand on her hip, but says, "Well, give me some money."

He lies back, lifts his hips, taking out his wallet and throwing it at her. "Bitch."

"That's real nice, Will."

She leaves by the back door, slamming it behind her.

"I don't have to be nice!" he yells back, then smiles at Son. "This game is too cool."

Miller's Duct and Chimney Cleaning has a fleet of raggedy camper shelled white pickups with black silhouettes of a chimney sweep on both the passenger and driver doors. Craig's cousin is driving the one that always sounds like it's dragging metal on the ground. Coming around the little lake with the strings of lights in the trees, he checks his phone again. There are places in the mountains where he can never get a signal. Growing up, he didn't carry a phone, of course, and his family didn't have a computer either. He never felt the loss of these things but being without his phone now upsets his equilibrium. The things he sees and worries about are sometimes far away and his phone gives him a sense of being close.

Coming into town, he looks at his phone again and sees Son's name. It's Son he's worrying about, but he doesn't know why. He doesn't actually see anything to worry about. He's getting too close to him, he guesses. But he's close to Will too and he can see everything about Will. Of course, that isn't the same. He saw everything about Son too, at first. Then everything went dark and now it's like having no signal on his phone. He's worrying over things he might not need to worry about. But he's never been in love before either and maybe love is like this. And maybe everything will return to normal soon, because he needs to see. He's almost certain that he needs to see.

After he drops off the pickup and gets in his own car, Craig's cousin heads over to Will's. Craig isn't there, just Jimbo and Son. No Andy either.

Craig's cousin comes in the back to get a beer on his way to the living room. Seeing him, Will throws his arms into the air. "Trevor!"

"What's up?"

"Playin' a game, man. Sit down."

Craig's cousin steps over Son's legs, making him move over so he can sit near Will. "What game?"

"New game."

"Yeah?"

"I made it up," says Will.

"I found it," says Susie.

"Shut up."

She found it at Quality Videos on her lunch break the other day. They had a whole table full of games on the sidewalk. This one had colorful glass beads in a blue velvet bag and a colored wood board. The box top was almost flat and there was nothing else but the board and beads inside. The dice came out of another game and Will made up the rules. The board is a multicolored checkerboard with hollows for the beads in each square.

"Color you want, Jimbo?"

"Red."

"Nope. That's me."

Beside him Susie pretends to laugh. Will won't let her be red either, though. Jimbo takes blue and laughs back at her. He pulled her chair up to the side of the coffee table. Will is at the end of the table and Susie is sitting between Jimbo and Will. Craig's cousin and Son are on the couch. Son picks out the yellow beads and Craig's cousin takes the green beads. Then all the beads are gone and Susie says, "What about me?"

"Guys night," says Will. "Stick to your own color. Playin' for money too. Jimbo counts."

Jimbo nods and scoots out of the hollow he's making in Susie's chair to line up his beads on the side of the board.

"You roll for points. You keep your points an' your beads by stickin' to your own color. Anytime you can't move to your own color, you lose a bead. Losers lose all their beads."

"Me first," says Jimbo.

"Red's first," says Will.

They play around the board before Craig's cousin gets up, stepping over Son's legs again. Son moves back out of the way with a sullen glare. Craig's cousin ignores his mood, taps his beer with his own. "Wan' another one?"

"Yeah, okay."

"Me, too!" yells Jimbo.

The kitchen smells almost sweet and it is vaguely clean. Craig's cousin looks around for the source of the smell. He can't see anything and opens the refrigerator. Coming in behind him, Susie goes over to the counter and opens up a tray of Danish. She peels one off, licking her fingers.

"Smells good in here," he says.

"Air freshener. Green meadow."

"Nice."

He takes a swig of beer. She leans against the counter and looks at him appraisingly. He's always known she likes him. Not enough to leave Will but enough to enjoy looking. He smiles back at her. "You can play my beads if you want."

That brightens her up. She smiles genuinely but shakes her head. "Will won't let me."

"You're a nice girl, Susie."

She blushes. "Thank you, Trevor."

In the other room Will yells, "Do over!" Then Son's voice, annoyed, sullen. "There are no fuckin' do overs."

Craig's cousin returns to the living room, passes Son and Jimbo their beers, climbs over Son again, and sits down.

"What's goin' on?" he asks.

"I'm doin' a fuckin' do over, that's what."

"This is fuckin' bogus," says Son. "I'm winning."

"Will's winning," says Jimbo.

"You can't fuckin' count."

Craig's cousin leans over to Son and gives him a look. Then he mouths, "Chill," and sits back again.

Son takes a swallow of beer, but Will is sitting up, pulling himself closer to the table. "Wha' did you just say to him?"

"Nothin', Will."

"You said somethin'."

"You're gettin' crazy, Will, okay? I didn't say anything. You don't fuckin' own me, anyway."

"It's my fuckin' house! It's my house!"

"Fuck, man. It was nothin'. I don't even think I said anything. Jesus, Will."

"You know what, Trevor. I don't like this, the way you are lately. You're my friend. My fuckin' friend, remember? Fuck is he to you?"

"You are my friend, Will."

"Then don't fuckin' talk to him anymore. You're only supposed to fuckin' love me."

"I do love you, Will. You know that."

"No, I don't. You're lyin' to me, Trev. I can tell. You know I don't like fuckin' rats!"

"You know what, Will. This is what's fucked. The way you treat me. Your only goddam real friend. I'm goin' home."

It surprises him that he isn't prepared for Will, who jumps up and grabs fistfuls of his shirt and starts to shake him. "You aren't fuckin' goin' anywhere!"

"Hey, you asshole!" Son bellows.

"You aren't fuckin' leavin' me!"

By the time Son is halfway across the coffee table, Jimbo kicks him hard in the hip and sends him flying back onto the couch.

"WAIT! WAIT!" Craig's cousin's arms are in the air. "Everybody back off. Fuck it. Fuck. I'm stayin', okay? I'm stayin'. Everybody fuckin' chill."

Son is up again and Craig's cousin holds out a hand to stop him. Son is breathing heavily, upset. "No," says Craig's cousin. "Don't."

Will is smirking at Son. "You can go, Wycowski. You don't need to stay."

Craig's cousin nods. "Good idea. Just go. This is gettin' too heated."

Son stares at him, works his jaw, then puts his hands up. "Okay. Fine by me. You fuckers have a good night."

At the sound of the door slamming, Will pulls Craig's cousin into a hug and rocks him back and forth for a moment. Then he lets go and Craig's cousin sits back down, picking up his beer with a shaky hand. Suddenly, pushing himself out of Susie's chair, Jimbo reaches across the coffee table and grabs Son's jacket off the arm of the couch, dragging it back with him.

"Cool," he says, patting at the pockets. He discovers money, drugs, "Blues," he says, dropping the pills on the coffee table. Nothing else.

"Those are expired," says Craig's cousin.

Jimbo stares. "What?"

"The blues. They're expired."

Jimbo grunts, standing up. "You don't know that."

"Yes, I do."

"I'll try 'um. I'll let you know."

"Whatever."

Jimbo tries the jacket on, but it sticks at his shoulders.

"Give it to me," says Will.

Craig's cousin watches Will and Jimbo playing with Son's jacket, but he doesn't do anything about it because he won't show that it matters.

When Ray first met Cora he didn't see anybody else for a while and didn't think she did either. A while after that, they stopped seeing each other, started up again, stopped and started until he took her over to Pete's. It didn't change anything really. When he saw her after she married Pete though, he usually had Ed with him and then she started up with Ed too. Marrying Pete was only about her and Pete, but it made Ed wonder out loud once.

"Do you think 'e knows?"

"About Cora?"

"Yeah."

That was at the carnival with the sideshow where the Snake Lady danced and where Pete and Cora just disappeared into the Love Tunnel. Ray grinned, thinking about what he'd be doing with her in there, but just said, "No clue."

Outside the shop, he is leaning into Pete's car, his forearms resting across the bottom edge of the open window. He blocks the light over the bar's side door and Pete's face fades in the dark interior.

"Love to see ya," says Pete.

He means Cora.

"I dunno."

"No yellow dice."

"Wal-Mart."

Pete sighs. "Okay."

Wal-Mart sounds like a good idea though. He has to get her something; anything yellow should make her happy for a while.

"I'll call ya," says Ray, pushing off the window. He feels slow and thinks he almost stops in mid-movement just to look at the ring on his finger. He wouldn't mind seeing Cora again. At the pizza parlor, Pete pointed at him between bites of his pizza and said, "You're still wearin' it."

"Yeah."

He felt Miri beside him but didn't look at her until he finished his beer. She was looking at a family sitting at the next table anyway. The woman was feeding her baby some cottage cheese from the salad bar off the tip of her finger. He thought about Son when he was little and the mess he made out of everything he ate.

"That was supposed to be mine," said Pete, still talking about Cora's ring.

"You blew it, bub."

But Pete just shook his head and said, "No, man. Not me. I'm married to 'er."

Earlier, they saw Fin coming out of the bar and Ray said, "C'mon over an' meet Pete." Then they went inside the shop and sat down in the little office just inside the porch door. There were filing cabinets, a computer on a desk under the window, a leather couch and two beat up upholstered chairs. Ray brought out a bottle and shot glasses and they drank until Ray said, "Hey, bub."

Fin was slumping sideways on the couch. Ray pushed him back up, said "Gimme a hand," and Pete helped pull him up. They took him down the hall to a bed in back. Then Ray found Fin's keys in his coat pocket and Pete said, "Just like me. Can't take it."

"You can't take a sip," said Ray.

Pete was drinking Coke.

Now Ray turns off the porch light and locks up. The cold makes him think about snow and a sooty city he lived in with Ed for a while and the Snake Lady's warm, stuffy tent and the cold when they came back out again.

"Do you think 'e knows?"

"No clue," he murmurs, hearing the weeds whisper as he walks.

Errol's house reminds him of the house he lived in when he came back home after living with Ed. The house was in Oakland. His life looked the same but wasn't. Then one day he came outside and saw Ed waiting for him at the bottom of the stairs. Ed was smiling, but there was something chiding in his voice when he said, "I knew you'd come home."

Upstairs at Grace's, he knocks once, then leans his elbow on the wood frame, eyes down until she opens the door. She's wearing flannel pajamas with a pair of pink slippers on her feet. She stares at him without surprise.

"I saw your light," he says and she nods and lets him in. She looks pale and her eyes are red and a little puffy. She was sitting on the couch under a fluffy blanket, not watching TV, just sitting there with the lights on, her windows half open. The cold from outside makes the flowers on her dining room table look out of place to him, a reminder of summer. She reminds him of Miri, sitting like that, and he starts feeling restless and looks over at her flowers, giving her time to get under her blanket again.

"What kind are those?"

"Mums."

"They're pretty."

She looks away. His restlessness always turns into anger sooner or later. Over by her chair with the big flower pattern he looks outside. It's dark and all he can see is the room behind him in the top pane of glass.

"I was thinkin' of a song," he says. "True Love Ways." One of Irene's songs. "Buddy Holly," he adds, looking at her flowers again. She looks too. The petals are white and yellow and the vase has a white and yellow design on it. She hates the way it matches and for some reason thinks about George going back to Lois and says, "I don't care about your songs, Ray."

"Buddy Holly's," he says again, picturing Irene at the hi-fi and Wayne on the couch with a beer. Grace looks away though and he shrugs and says, "Okay, babe." He sets Fin's keys by her flowers on his way out.

On the porch he sees his breath and thinks of Christmas.

Once, on Son's birthday, Ray took him to Ed's and his jacket was hanging on a hook Ed never used in one of the wood beams in his living room. His apartment was on the bottom floor of a dark green building that backed up onto a mountain of pine. It was always dark and gloomy there and Ed's always smelled like mildew. It was cold inside too, even though there was a heater rattling against the wall.

Ed gestured to the jacket, said, "It ain't mine," then went into the kitchen.

Son knew he was getting it because it was custom made, but he didn't think it was going to be ready on time.

"Surprised?"

"Yeah. This is great."

Ed tied a bow under the collar. Son pulled it off and put the jacket on and Ray sat on the couch after Ed gave him a beer and said, "You won't be gettin' anything like this again."

Ed nodded and said, "Only happens once a year."

"Like Christmas," said Ray.

Ed nodded again and Son ignored them.

A moment after that Ed said, "I forgot something'," and went into another room. Gray light seeped inside through the door he left opened. There were no curtains on the windows in back.

In the living room, Ray sat waiting for Son to say something but he didn't. On the day Son was born, he bought him a teddy bear in the lobby gift shop. He wasn't going to until he reached the elevators and saw the people with flowers and boxes of candy waiting outside.

He was at work when Kathy called. He didn't talk to her. She told Gus and Gus gave him a big slap on the back and said, "Congratulations, kid." He had a feeling Gus meant somebody else.

After he got the teddy bear, he went upstairs and found her in a little room by a window with flowers on a shelf across from her bed and a baby in her arms. She smiled and pulled the blanket away with her fingertips and he made himself laugh and said, "He looks pissed."

The baby was mostly covered and the part he could see was red and scrunched. Kathy looked happy. He gave her the teddy bear, perching it up against her hip and half sat on the edge of the windowsill.

"That's sweet."

He shrugged and said, "I just saw it sittin' there."

"Gus sounded happy."

"You know Gus."

She nodded and sank back into her pillows. Her face was pale and shiny.

"You look good," he said.

She smiled again.

"I can't believe it." She meant their baby.

"Yeah," he said, not sure that he was happy about it though. He couldn't tell and thought maybe he didn't believe it was actually real. After a moment he noticed that she was still smiling at him.

"What?"

"Happy Birthday, Ray."

Once in a while on his birthday he wonders if Wayne remembers but doubts it.

At Ed's he drank his beer and said, "We'll go out to dinner in a couple."

"No hotdogs," said Son.

"IHOP," said Ed, coming back into the room.

They went to Denny's instead, but before that Ed gave Ray a pair of fingerless gloves and said, "Happy Birthday, man."

Ray was surprised. "You never gave me a birthday present before."

"You never gave me one either," said Ed.

Ed didn't want to go to Denny's and stayed home and that was the last time Ray took Son to see him.

Inside the shop, it's dark. Outside, Fin can see shaggy tree shapes against the sky, Errol's with a faint lightness where the stairs go up. The weeds are dark and formless. He stops in the lot and stares at a faraway light behind the shapes of the trees, the tips dark and the sky with a tinge of blue.

Going upstairs, he remembers the stairs in his old apartment building and the skylight on the roof and the cool spring air. This isn't that day. It's growing colder now, autumn. He feels strange, moving with himself down the hall, opening the door, seeing the light growing inside. He lies down on the couch and the couch spins slowly. He's not unhappy even though he dreams that he's outside on Errol's stairs, going up to a roof with a skylight and a lawn chair where the sky is blue and full of pale, puffy clouds.

He circles the perimeter of the roof and the sky spins too and the clouds blow away. It is clear and crisp and windy. The sky is everywhere and he goes to the roof's edge and sees a staircase that goes down to the yard below. A grassy slope dotted with lawn chairs rises away into the blue sky. Abel and Sissy are sitting on the chairs, looking up as they wave. At the bottom, Dahlia smiles and starts up to the rooftop. She is young again. Her curly hair is loose and her face is soft and she smells like lilac and roses. At the top of the stairs, she stops and points at a bottle; he picks it up and gives it to her. She pours it out over the edge and the clear amber liquid falls slowly and bounces back up in shiny gold bubbles.

After that, she goes back down the stairs again and the bubbles bounce away.

Once upon a time in a land far, far away, everything was beautiful. The sky was sunny and the leaves danced on the trees and the birds sang and the flowers always bloomed.

Grace's mother, Rose, told this story.

It was about a beautiful princess and a beautiful prince who lived in a beautiful land until one day a storm came and dark gray clouds covered the sky and the winds blew and blew and the beautiful land became ugly with bare trees and silent birds and torn flowers and the beautiful prince and princess were alone in a dark, dreary land.

Rose only told the fairytale she made up when Grace was little.

"That's not a fairytale," Grace always said after her mother was done. "They have to live happily ever after."

Then Rose would purse her lips for a moment as if she were thinking about it, then say, "I just didn't make that part up yet."

She always thought her mother had a secret.

When she gets up in the morning the wind is blowing against the window panes and the pale sun is flashing against the flowing weeds. She goes out into the living room and Fin is asleep on the couch. She puts a blanket over him and sits down on her chair and looks outside at the pale, cool light.

Mostly asleep, Fin thinks he remembers the toasty smell of the heater going on and the steamy windows. Once, he sees her sitting in her chair across the room and remembers her eating ice cream out of a green bowl. Another time the chair is empty. Once she comes over with a cup and sits beside him.

"It's soup," she murmurs.

He drinks some and drifts off again. The room feels stuffy and he thinks he's lying on a cement floor and that people are looking down at him. Then Ray clucks his tongue and says, "I bet that hurts."

Pushing up on his elbow, he drinks the rest of the soup out of the cup on the coffee table. Then he sets the cup down, a cautious look on his face, and stays frozen on his elbow, then suddenly pushes the blanket off and gets up. In the bathroom, he throws up, crouching down by the toilet. Sweat pops out under his eyes and on the back of his neck. Perched over the bowl, he rests for a moment, then rinses out his mouth and goes back to the couch.

The TV is on, but he can't hear it and the house sounds empty. Outside, the sky is dark gray and the bottoms of the clouds are shiny. He can see rain bouncing off of dark graves and the sound of it smacking something heavy and plastic. He gets up and looks outside. Shadows cover the weeds and he can feel the air through the sash. It feels damp and he leans against the cold glass of the window and sees Errol looking up. Everything seems frozen for a moment and he remembers picturing the bar in a painting and sees Dahlia alone at a table, looking out a rain-washed window. Errol looks sad to him, but he thinks he's dreaming. A moment later, the weeds begin to bend in the shadows and the sky grows darker. He can't see Errol anymore and dreams about the bar in a painting and sees Dahlia and Abel and Sissy and Sally and Ginny. They all sit alone. Ray sits at the counter and nobody's moving. George is frozen with a cloth and a glass, looking at Grace, who's motionless with a tray of glasses under lamps that shine in big yellow circles. It looks like sunshine. He sees flowers grow and stares at the arms of the yellow chair he's sitting in.

Then he gets up and pours a drink. The glass was in the drainer and after he fills it, he picks it up and starts to lift it, looking at it, staring inside, then stopping, frozen in mid-drink, posed in a painting he wasn't a part of before. Except now he is, sitting on the other side of George, staring in the mirror at a roomful of people in pools of shadow that change and grow darker and remind him of the lawn chairs on the hillside and the cool, white gravestones in the cemetery. Then the smell of bourbon wafts up. Saliva fills his mouth. His throat squeezes and his mouth opens. He breathes into his glass, stirring up the smell again. He can taste it without tasting it. His hand shakes, his body. The glass clatters against the counter. He is bent over, resting his forehead on the palm of his hand, squeezing his fingers into bone. The only pain is in his throat, the burning of his tongue. He pushes himself up, moving shakily on weak legs.

After a moment, he can hear the sound of the rain on the roof and a TV he doesn't remember being on. The light in the living room makes a yellow circle on the chair and a half-moon on the window pane. The rain sounds louder; he goes back over to look outside again, remembers Dahlia and the shadow of the rain on her face and the smell of lilacs and roses and strawberry ice cream.

Ray sits on a stool beside a woman named Serena. The bar isn't Mulligan's, which was almost empty and depressed him like the rain and the half empty parking lot at Candi's. He put on a slicker and rode off, but all the lights stopped him, and his nerves grew raw. Outside of town, he saw the black square of Jack's Club take shape and kept going until the firs began to thin and change to ash and alder. In the distance, the lights of a strip mall and a restaurant appeared; he passed both and found a place called The Lucky Cups and pulled into a parking lot full of pot holes.

The woman named Serena is a blonde with the ends of her hair flipped up.

"Your name fits," he says.

She smiles without saying anything and he guesses she's heard that before.

"Do you live around here?" he asks.

"A couple blocks away. I was on my way home."

"Glad you stopped."

She smiles again with a pause like the other before she says, "I am too."

She is starting to interest him. "I've never been here before."

"Where do you come from?"

"Acropolis now."

She smiles. "That makes you sound so impermanent. The 'now' part."

He smiles back, then shakes his head at the thought and says, "Pretty close."

They drink until the bar closes and then he walks her outside.

"Call me," she says, slipping into her car.

"Sure, pretty soon."

That sounds vague and impermanent too though, and she smiles before she closes her door. Her lights shine on the dark puddles the rain left.

On the way back, he sees the strip mall again and stops at the Waffle Place across the way and sits at the counter inside. A few other people are sitting at the booths against the windows. A coffee-stained card advertising a Fried Egg Waffle Sandwich Special is attached to a plastic menu by a paper clip. The card makes it look like it's been a special for a long time.

"I'll try that," he says.

It comes with potatoes and a bowl of fruit he doesn't eat. On the back counter, there's a row of syrups in glass pitchers. He looks at all the colors and thinks of Cora.

After he leaves, he thinks of Serena.

Outside, the sky is just beginning to turn blue. The giant bowling pin is almost the color of the sky and the pool at the Acropolis Inn is the color of concrete.

At home, he goes in quietly. The sounds are familiar, a clock ticking, the creak of a floorboard in the hallway, always louder in the dark. The walls are gray, doorways darker. He can see her under the covers though. He stares at her for a moment before he pulls his tee-shirt off and goes over. Up close, he can see the way she's cupping her face in her palms. It gives her a strange look and he isn't sure she's glad to see him. It suits his mood though. He feels like they suddenly understand each other, especially when she rolls away when he comes to rest against her. He puts a hand on her arm and his chest presses into her shoulder. She grows still against him. He holds his breath, thinking.

"No?"

"No," she murmurs.

"Why not?" He is thinking about Serena again.

"I'm not in the mood. I'm sorry. I know you always are."

He waits to absorb his anger, then says, "That's the way I am. You want me to apologize for that?"

She shifts beside him, comes up on her elbow, twisting her head to look back at him.

"I just wish you'd be more sensitive."

"Sensitive?"

"It's not a dirty word, Ray."

"I don't know what the fuck it means."

"It means that you can't just explain yourself an' expect that to count. You have to try."

"I have to try what?"

"To be faithful."

He almost laughs, but he is too angry. "Fuck that. I am faithful. We're talkin' about two different things, Miri. I never lied to you. I've always been this way. I need it."

"What about me? What about what I need?"

He sits up, pulling his pants back on. "You should have thought about that before you took up with me."

"What are you saying, Ray?"

"I'm saying you need to think things out, Miri. I can't change. I love you," he says, pulling his tee-shirt on over his head. "Either that counts or it doesn't. You have to figure it out. You'll have time to think about this when I go down to see Pete."

"You mean Cora, don't you?"

He grabs his boots, face red with anger. "Yeah, whatever. You think what you want."

Outside, the day is clear and cloudless.

At Kurt's, Wes leans against the balcony with a beer and looks down at the cool, wet cobblestones. "We're bein' moved to days," he says and sees a dove flutter above a birdbath below, rise up, flutter again and settle back down on the edge of the bowl. "You an' me," he adds. "Just us."

Kurt grimaces and leans away, backing up against the shingles behind him.

"That isn't right," he says. "That just isn't right. I have seniority over Gary."

"Gary's new. Still trainin'."

"So what?"

"All new guys start on grave, you know that."

"What about you?"

"I'm the glue rack guy. Guess they need a good glue rack guy."

"Well, it still ain't right," said Kurt. "Nobody asked."

The air smells like the wet stones below.

At Jonah's, it smells cold and dry inside. He is sitting on the couch, staring at the corner of the wall behind the recliner, waiting because he saw Agnes a moment ago, a flash of her hair, streaks of brown, electric gold through the window. The porch door is open on the other side of the wall and he can picture the way it looks, the screen a dark veil, everything through it as thin and unreal as a dream. Then she knocks and he gets up and goes out to her. He doesn't open the screen though and she puts her hands in her back pockets and backs up a step. Her elbows stick out and she looks at the slats beneath her, waiting for him.

She's wearing denim overalls and a sleeveless shirt and it makes him think of summer. In his mind, even the puddles are gone.

"C'mon in," he says, pushing the door open.

After a while, there are high white clouds in the sky.

The grass at Mr Torch's Mortuary is dark green with drops of dew on every blade. The bells in the quiet firs ring with tiny, airy notes.

"Like angels," says Mr Torch, leading people down the hall. At the end of the hall is a window with diamond-shaped panes like the cuts in the grass outside. The shadows on the floor look like crosses.

Carl says, "Angels are dead people."

Mr Torch smiles over the toes of Carl's feet and Scott's shadow. "Are you okay?"

"My toes look like cocktail weenies."

Outside the sun is bright and silver, and the air still smells like water.

It grows warm and cools again like spring. At night, clouds come and stay gray in the day. The air grows cold and damp.

At Candi's, the windows are steamy and Ray remembers swiping a forearm across a window at a White Castle's to look out at piles of crusty snow.

"No sun," he murmurs, leaning back in the booth.

"I see it," says Fin, looking out through the side of the window where the glass is clear.

"It's gonna snow."

"Too early. It's barely October."

A while later, it's clear and windy. Sunshine rolls over the grassy hills and flashes on the wings of the angels at the top of the cemetery.

In the attic, Fin sits without a drink and looks outside. Firs surround the house. The sky above is pale blue and full of clouds now. The tops of the trees begin to bend like weeds. He sees lawn chairs in the daytime too. Going outside he looks up into a clear sky.

At the shop, Ray opens the doors and the sun lights up the dusty concrete floor. Will follows him in and pulls a chair at the counter over to the shade by the ramp. "My eyes're botherin' me," he mutters.

Because of the spruce outside his window, Will's room is always cool and shady.

When he woke up today, he thought it was dawn. The drapes were drawn and the bit of sky he could see looked gray through the tree branches. He was alone too. The house was dark and quiet and smelled like Fruit Loops and garbage. The walls and bedspread looked gray and the closet door was partway open, white on the outside and dark on the inside. It looked empty and Susie's little cloisonné box wasn't on the dresser anymore.

"Susie!"

She didn't answer. He got up and saw some of his dirty clothes on the floor and a can of air freshener on top of a big pile of Jack-in-the-Box bags on a chair. The smell of Fruit Loops grew stronger. At the closet, he slowly pushed at the door and saw her clothes inside. It didn't help though. She could leave without anything.

After he ate a bowl of Cocoa Puffs, he looked for her at Candi's, then at her mother's house. Then he drove by the office building across from Andy's after her mother gave him a strange look and said, "I just talked to her at work."

"Her work?"

"Yes."

"Oh."

He saw her car and pulled up behind it.

There was a board outside with a list of names on it and he stared at the board for a long time, but it didn't make any sense to him. The image of her mother's strange look came back to him. Inside the building, he smelled Fruit Loops again and began to look through the leaves of the fichus trees in front of the windows beside every door. The windows were tall and narrow and nobody saw him through the foliage. He couldn't remember where Susie's office was.

On the way upstairs, he thought of her mother again, and the strange look he saw earlier began to turn into amusement. He suddenly realized she was laughing at him because Susie wasn't here anymore. Then, pulling a fichus tree apart, he saw her through the glass and began to laugh too.

Outside, the sun was bouncing off the pavement.

At Ray's he sees the light coming closer across the floor and gets up. Ray is going back up the ramp anyway. It's cooler and darker in the shop.

"Wanna beer?"

"Okay."

He couldn't taste his Cocoa Puffs again. A minute later, he decides he won't be able to taste his beer either.

"I'm takin' a trip," says Ray, flipping on a light in the gray room. The refrigerator is small and white underneath the counter. "I can't locate my kid though."

Will looks at his beer, drinks it casually. "Are you takin' 'im with you?"

Ray swallows and shakes his head. He clearly can taste his beer and Will feels betrayed.

"No. I want 'im to work for me."

"Oh."

It wasn't until a moment ago that he remembered that he gave Son's jacket to Jimbo to keep. That disoriented sense he woke up with is back. He starts to wonder if he only imagined he saw Susie at work and he gets up suddenly and says, "I have to go."

Ray looks surprised. "Sure."

She's there though, at a big wooden desk in the lobby with another fichus tree in a corner and a fern in a shiny brass pot on a glass table.

At home, Fin goes up to the attic, but he can't stay there. Downstairs, he turns on the TV, sits down, then gets back up. He stares at the soggy weeds out back. A particular cupboard draws his eyes back in. He yanks it open, letting the door slam back into another door. But it is empty. The bottle is gone. Nothing else there. For some reason he wants to turn, to look at the basement door, but he doesn't. Upstairs, he drops his clothes on the bedroom floor, puts on a pair of sweats, and goes out to the garage. There is a weight bench and barbells against the back wall. He is shirtless, barefoot on the cold cement. He doesn't care. He lifts the weights until his muscles shake and he hunches up, rubbing his arms. He can feel his heart. He stares into the stillness outside. Saliva starts to fill his mouth again and he bites a tongue he almost bit off once. In the mirror, when he looks, he can see the scars, red depressions that match the outline of his teeth. The marks of bones. An animal's mouth. The thought always makes him panic, afraid of a dark without memory that will only grow darker and narrower and then become nothing.

Getting up, he jumps rope and then goes back to the bench. The blue day turns gray and it grows colder. He is sweating, his hair drenched; his skin turns to ice. Shivering, he goes back inside and takes a hot shower. Steam covers the mirror and beads the air. It is like breathing underwater. Downstairs, he turns on the TV again, lies down on the couch and rolls himself into a ball.

Ray pictures her in a tight silver spacesuit with the ends of her silver blonde hair flipped up.

She's really a librarian. When she told him that, he said, "Are you kidding?" and she gave him that pause and smile again.

"You're surprised?"

"Well, yeah."

"What did you think I do?"

"B-movies," he answered, grinning at her.

It didn't seem to bother her. She just pulled his arm up, settling underneath it as they went up the walkway to her apartment.

Now he is starting to like her and she is looking at him curiously. They are at her apartment. He is still breathing in the freshness of the air from the ride over.

"Come on," she says. "I'm driving."

He raises his eyebrows but follows her. In her car, he stares at her admiringly. She takes him to a place down an alleyway with a courtyard out front. The picnic benches outside are covered in red gingham tablecloths and there are white lights in the trees. The restaurant is under a stone archway down some steps.

They are sitting at one of the tables in the courtyard. Tall heat lamps radiate warmth.

"The food's Polish," says Serena.

"I'm Polish," says Ray.

She has a twinkle that's like his, but he feels it dim his mood for some reason.

Later, she sits on a stool at the corner of a pool table with a mug of beer on top of one of her crossed knees. He should be having fun, but he isn't anymore. Her smile is growing curious again. She takes a swallow of her beer and says, "C'mon," slipping off her stool.

After a moment, he shrugs and puts his stick away. Outside, she goes underneath his arm again, quiet until she sees her car, then she moves off a little and smiles.

"Are you married?"

She reminds him of Vicki: "Attached?"

"Very," he says.

"Impermanent," Serena murmurs, reminding him of the first time he saw her.

On the way home, he stops at the Waffle Place and looks at the row of syrups on the counter and finds the one he thinks is raspberry. Cora's voice fills his head. "Raspberry? I didn't order fuckin' raspberry!"

In the morning, the sound of Miri wakes him up. He's lying on the couch, staring at the light at the opening of the curtains. She passes by, sipping her orange juice. After a moment, he gets up and follows her. She's sitting in a mostly dark room and he stops in surprise.

"You cut your hair."

She nods and continues to brush it. Her brush makes a scraping sound and her hair doesn't lift up like it used to. It cups her head and then grows longer and thinner against her neck. Retro, like sky-blue eye shadow, peasant blouses, and hoop earrings. He saw the same style on Irene in a picture of her and Wayne. They were sitting on a Danish modern couch in the house they used to live in in Oakland.

"What is that? A shag or somethin'?"

"Kind of."

It makes everything about her look smaller. Sometimes he thinks she tries to fade away and wears her go-go boots and bright blue eye shadow because some other part of her doesn't want to.

"I guess I like it," he says, starting to undress.

After a shower, he goes out into the living room with a bowl of Cheerios and eats it standing up. He is making her uncomfortable and she starts to pull at the longer strands of her hair.

"Kinda spur a the moment," he says.

"I just felt like it."

He keeps eating, still staring at her. Her fingers reach the end of her hair and she doesn't look at him. He takes his empty bowl out to the sink and shakes his head at himself. He can picture Serena's pause and smile.

"Married?"

"Yeah, yeah, yeah."

Going back into the living room he stares at her again and says, "Yeah. I guess I like it."

A row of mirror plants used to grow on the other side of Errol's house too. Now the space between the side of the house and the walkway is bare dirt with bits of gravel that spill over the walkway's edge. Stopping to light a cigarette, Scott tugs at a lock on the garage's side door. They don't use

Errol's garage for anything, not even storage, but they do pay for laundry and the machines are on the other side of the locked door. There's a little window in the door he can't see through anymore because a piece of sheet or cloth is covering it up.

Moving on, he stops again on the driveway, stubs his cigarette out, then goes up to knock on Errol's door. It opens slowly, just enough for Errol's eye to peek out. Scott moves closer and Errol puts the tip of a slipper against the bottom of the door, closing it against a finger he lays against the jamb. Scott peers in. "The side door's locked. There's an actual lock on it."

"I know," Errol murmurs.

He found the lock on his front porch, appearing there as mysteriously as it appeared on his garage door. Seeing that lock earlier, a good, solid padlock on the latch of his garage door, sealing him out, filled him with an old sense of ostracism, the realization that he never really fit in anywhere. He lived in a world where people would lock him out of his own garage for no reason.

Inside his house, he put the lock on his dining room table and stood back to stare at it uneasily. It stayed there on a doily he used to put a bowl of fruit on for a long time and it seemed, like the movement of the light in the room, to always follow him. He thought of the world invading here like the light pushing through chinks and gaps. He walked around his house looking for ways in, saw the gray and opaque surface of the window in the garage's side door and the way the light bounced off it. On the inside though, soft and diffuse beams shone in. Taking a towel that was lying in a pile of laundry on the washer, he slowly covered up the window, tucking it up with a tatter of lace over the curtain rod. Then a quieter darkness filled the garage and he was relieved.

After that, he went to Grand's Hardware because it was closest to the Qwik Stop and entered into a dimness that was a little like a shoe store stock room. He bought another lock and a screw driver with a green handle that reminded him of the hard apple candies he used to eat.

At home, he took the lock off the doily and went outside with it, replacing it on the garage door and installing the new lock on the side door. Errol's relief was inarticulate, a warm wave of consolation sweeping over him. His garage door was locked shut again but locking him in this time. This way he could pre-empt anybody from locking him out, the way he hid away in his house to assuage a loneliness that only grew.

Now Scott stares at him, reaching for his cigarettes, lights one and says, "But we have to get in there, Errol. We pay for laundry."

"I don't have a key," says Errol, lying.

Scott frowns and there are shadows in his eyes like the passage of strange, unwelcome thoughts. Errol thinks of Carl and feels sorry for him. Scott is playing absentmindedly with his lighter, flipping it up and down. "Didn't you put it on?" he asks.

Errol nods again. Scott is looking at his lighter, snaps it shut with a faintly surprised look. Errol sees the shadows in his eyes scatter and disperse.

"Then you can take it off," he says, and Errol pulls his finger in his door and nods in disappointment.

"Okay."

There are shadowy shapes on the side of the house where the mirror plants used to be and shadows pool in the corners upstairs.

Carl starts to look away and pauses with a tiny smile at something Scott can't see. The wall is a dull, grayish white with an empty chair against it.

Taking a cigar box off the coffee table, Scott sits down with a sigh.

Carl looks over and watches him take a pipe out of the box and light it with the lighter Mr Volvo gave him.

"Nice," he murmurs.

Scott's eyes rise.

"Your lighter."

He nods, sucking in.

"Was it expensive?"

He shakes his head and gets up, giving Carl the pipe. "Not really."

Carl reaches for the lighter. It warms his fingers and he rests the pipe on top of the couch and smiles outside. Scott moves in the corner of his vision, disappearing into the kitchen, passing through the living room again. Busy, busy. Unlike Carl. Carl lights the pipe again and lies back. His curtains are a luminous white, close and faraway at the same time. A blue like cornflowers fills the sky. Mr Volvo's lighter is a warm bowl in his fingers. Scott smiles as he takes it away.

"Enough for you," he says, crossing in front of Mr Torch's chair.

At the shop, Ray sticks a stopper under the door and goes in back for a beer. The shadows outside are always deep and cool here. Then there are footsteps on the porch and he goes back out. A man comes over, leaving a woman at the display of dice and he thinks of Cora again. He feels tired out now for some reason.

"Need help?"

"Fuses."

"This way."

He passes the woman and looks down at her boots—soft suede with leather ties like her coat. It reminds him of the ribbons on that top of Miri's he likes and the red go-go boots she used to dance in. She didn't wear the red ones until after she met him. One night, he went out to a strip club with Cameron and brought Miri with him. Looking back he isn't sure why he'd do that, but they had just started seeing each other and he didn't really want to hook up with anybody else right away. So maybe having her there was security against picking up some other woman he didn't really need to have right then. Later on in bed, she sat on top of him and covered her chest with her arms. He smiled, admiring her.

"You don't have to hide. You look good."

She shrugged and moved an arm up to brush her hair away. Thinking about this, he decides he's going to miss her hair in her face. At the time it fell right back and he had to brush it away again for her.

"Did the strippers embarrass you?"

She shook her head. Her hair looked soft and light. "I used to do that."

He couldn't believe it and laughed. "C'mon. You don't even let me see you."

"I kept some things," she said and swung off him. She was wearing a pair of light blue panties. They looked a little big and slid on her when she moved. A minute later, she came back with a big white box she took out of the back of the closet.

He started to laugh again in disbelief.

"Pictures?"

"My boots," she said. Shiny red patent leather, silver hooks and red laces.

"You actually danced in those?"

"I was popular."

She put one on and then he gave her the other and she put that on too and stood there in her slinky underwear and red boots and nothing else.

"Well, you convinced me," he said and she began to blush and covered herself up again.

It's almost dark now. He closes up and goes outside. At the Acropolis Deli he sits across from Fin and says, "This place reminds me of Cora."

Fin looked around. "This place?"

"Yeah. That Aphrodite."

He is leaving for Pete and Cora's in the morning and he smiles at Cora's likeness in the window.

"Just somethin' about 'er."

At Errol's, lights shine on the weeds below. Grace crosses the plank and follows a path she doesn't need to see. The sunflowers on the orange paper upstairs always look bigger at night and she doesn't like them. Inside, she looks at Fin on the couch and kicks off her shoes. The light in the bathroom is on and it reminds her of George, buttoning up his pants in the wedge of light through the door. Watching him, she knew he wasn't coming back even though they never talked about it. She could see it in the way he stopped in the light to button up his pants before he came over to her.

Now she leans over and feels Fin's arms fall across her back. He takes a deep breath and sighs.

"You smell like strawberries."

"We ate some," she murmurs.

"We?"

"Me an' George."

"I love strawberries," he lies and she pushes away and pulls him up with her.

"They were sour though. It's not the right season."

He feels a coolness by the window, dull with shadows, inside the light coming across the floor. Her dress slips off and he kisses her, tasting strawberries too.

"You're so pretty," he murmurs and later sees strawberries in his dream, bowls full on the grassy hillside. This time the sky is a rainy gray and the grass is the color of slate. Shadows move and flashes of silver come through the clouds and light up the rows of lawn chairs.

Some have bowls of ice cream on their seats. He starts to run up the slope and the sky grows darker. Once he stops and eats some of the ice cream and it tastes like flowers. At the top of the hill, he sees Sissy rubbing some onto her knees. She's sitting on one of the chairs and the rain is washing it away.

Outside, the weeds look slate-colored like the grass in his dream and the sky grows cloudy and gray.

16

♦ Slip ♦

At work, Jonah sits on the vinyl couch in the break room and eats his lunch. It's just like it was before Kurt. Without Ira though, or all the other people he can picture but doesn't remember anymore. Then one night Gus comes over, casually slow, glancing backwards like somebody with a secret he doesn't want to share with anyone else. Jonah doesn't say anything, just watches him pull a chair over and lean in. He takes another bite of his sandwich, and when Gus realizes he's not going to encourage him, he rubs at his cheek to hide his mouth and says, "Interviews start next week."

"'Bout time," Jonah murmurs and reaches down for his coffee cup.

Gus sinks a little, waiting for him to sit back up. Jonah's face is blank though and he doesn't look upset. "I guess Kurt's not comin' back," says Gus.

"I guess not."

Gus stares and Jonah takes a swallow of his coffee and stares back.

"We sure need help though."

"Yeah," he says, putting his coffee back down. "That's for sure."

On his way to Waylon's, Jonah passes the empty meadow. It looks the way it looked when Ellie came here and stood at the rim of the weeds and saw the shadows of the clouds pass over the surface of the water. It was silent, he knew, and she could see the movement of the wind without hearing it.

She must have thought John and Ivy were there even though everybody else thought they ran away, that Ivy left her baby for John Sparrow. And maybe she did.

Aster left, went away as far as she could go, and Mavis left too and that makes him like Agnes, and that means there are things Ally can't understand. Ally would love her baby, though. She wouldn't leave, wouldn't lie down in the river.

Alongside yellow weeds he slows, then speeds up again and remembers the day Aster died.

Abel went to the place Jonah told him to, then came back and sat beside him on the porch. When Aunt Hilary came, Abel left again and didn't come back until late. Jonah was on the couch in the living room. It was dark and quiet. At first, there was a moon that made the room silver but then that passed over and it was dark. He felt cold and began to think that she was still in the water and that it was even colder there and that nobody was going to get her. Then he didn't think he could breathe and it hurt and a sound came out and he froze, afraid to wake Aunt Hilary. She looked at him the same way she looked at Abel so he put the top of the blanket in his mouth and thought about Aster getting colder and colder, lying there alone.

Later, he heard the pickup. It woke him up and for a long time, he just lay there listening because Abel didn't come in right away. Then he heard the door and footsteps and a creak at each step until Abel stopped halfway across the living room, knocked up against the coffee table and sat down beside him on the couch, one arm across the top. He seemed almost to hang there, almost asleep, then he shook himself a little and said, "Jus' us now."

He thinks of that on his way past Ira's and pictures the shadows of the clouds Ellie saw.

The trailer is cold, even though cool, sunny rays filter through the fir trees outside. Craig's cousin's trailer is always cold, even though it's a little place and should keep warm. The rooms are small and the hall to the bedroom and bath are narrow, but Craig's cousin likes fresh air and it always feels like a gale is blowing through the open kitchen window and back out through the transom in the bathroom. Ignoring the cold, Craig's cousin eats his cereal, leaning against the counter with his legs crossed at the ankles, already dressed, a Miller's Duct and Chimney Cleaning cap on his head. Sitting on the couch in just his pajama bottoms, knees bent, feet up on the cushion's edge, Son shivers, staring at Craig's cousin under lowered lids, scowling at him almost angrily. Craig's cousin is watching Son too, face a blank.

"You look cold," he says.

"I am cold," says Son.

"Put something on."

"You know what Miri told me? Where my dad went?"

Craig's cousin shakes his head, watching him. Getting to know people is the best part of living to Craig's cousin and Craig's cousin is waiting for Son to talk about the things he knows Son doesn't want to talk about. It bothers Craig's cousin that he can't really see inside of Son anymore. That took him by surprise. He can't explain the way he sees into other people; it's not like somebody's life plays out in front of him. He gets an idea, a feeling that time and thought make concrete. But he felt a change with Son, felt it the minute he pushed into him and stared down at his squeezed-shut eyes, his bitten lip, and saw only happiness and unhappiness, desire and grief, things that play on the surface, things that almost anybody could see. He almost couldn't breathe for the strangeness, its suddenness, its loss like a thing Son took away from him. He got rough then, angry, but Son just grabbed on and took it.

"You like this?" he grunted.

"You...," Son gasped. "I like you...."

The tenderness that rose up to drown him then was like warm water and that's all he feels now; the things he sees in Son, his shame and rage, are the things he first saw. That he barely knows Son occurs to him sometimes, but he never doubts that Son is his.

Watching him scrape his chin across a bent knee, Craig's cousin imagines the feel of that bristly chin pulling across his shoulder and wonders if Son's skin is warm or cold.

"So where'd 'e go?" he asks finally.

"To see an old girlfriend. How fucked up is that?"

Craig's cousin shrugs. "That's Miri's business."

"You don't care?"

"I know my business. You stick to yours too. You don't need to be worryin' about anybody else. You answer to me, baby."

Son shivers. "I know, Trevor."

Setting his bowl on the counter, Craig's cousin looks at him for a long time. He knows that Son likes to answer to him, and he also knows that Son only really feels in control of things when Craig's cousin gives him rules to follow. Allowing Craig's cousin to take charge of him makes him feel safe and whole, and Craig's cousin doesn't think Son can feel like that any other way. Going around the counter, Craig's cousin takes another bowl out of the cupboard, fills it with cereal and milk, grabs a spoon and takes it over to him.

"Eat this."

Relaxing, Son slumps back, knees open, sitting cross-legged with his cereal. Craig's cousin picks his keys up off the counter and heads outside. "See ya, baby."

Son mumbles over his cereal. "See ya."

A few nights later, Gus comes up again, pulls his chair in close. Jonah is thinking of Agnes, staring up at the stains on the ceiling. Gus leans in.

"All of 'um are applyin' for grave. Wes saw the apps."

Jonah stares for a moment longer, then lets his eyes move down to Gus's face. "Everybody starts on grave."

"But these guys want to stay."

"So?"

"So, I thought maybe we'd get Kurt back."

He looks back up again. "That ain't gonna happen."

At home he goes up for a swim and the cold is strange because of the sunshine. It only looks warm, sheds a thin, pale light on the ground, barely lighter than the shade.

Afterwards, he goes home to sleep for a while. When the light behind the shades begins to fade he gets up again.

At the bowling alley there are windows on either side of the doors and stone abutments on either side of the windows. Agnes is standing in a corner of stone and glass. It's Saturday and busy. The doors are open and voices buzz and balls and pins clatter and clonk. She flushes because it's cold out now and shuffles nervously with her hands in her pockets.

He goes by slowly, window down, arm outside and she moves away from her corner. It's quiet in the dark where the firs are even darker and still. He pauses by the walkway at Kurt's until he sees her. It seems like everybody's at home, lights spilling patches of brightness on the cement below. The water in Joy's birdbath glitters with it. He glances at her door as he passes and then hears Agnes's tiptoes coming closer. She pushes past him through the door before he can even turn the light on.

"Crazy girl."

"I almost froze out there." She hobbles in place on her cold feet and blows at her fingers. "Gosh, Jonah."

"It's not that cold."

He drops his keys on Kurt's windowsill. His voice is soft, the softness he always has with her, distant almost, surprisingly, because he thinks about her almost all the time, but the thinking of her sometimes feels closer than being with her.

She pulls her coat off. It reminds him of one Sissy had.

"Go in an' get a hot chocolate next time."

She doesn't reply. Opening a beer he took out of Kurt's refrigerator, he leans back against the counter and takes a swallow. She sits with a bounce on Kurt's bed, pulls her legs up, then just sits there, cross-legged, staring at him. Once he said, "Whadda ya thinkin' about?" and she said, "You," and it reminded him of Abel.

"What about me?" he asked.

But she didn't look sure, just gave him a pained look. He thought maybe she did know and just didn't know how to say it, the way he could never say why he really married Ally, or the way Mavis never said anything about the way she really felt except in the way she moved and acted. Back then he thought he knew everything about her, desired her pointlessly.

Agnes is still staring at him when he comes over and flops down beside her, punching up one of the pillows, then lying back with his head on the crook of his arm.

She sighs at him. "You didn't offer me anything."

"Oh. some pop, I think."

She scowls and gets up. A slightly green strip of brass separates the carpet in the living room from the kitchenette. The flooring is old linoleum and starting to peel up at the corners. It's a cream color with a design of faded brown flowers. She gets her pop and pauses to look around. Jonah follows her gaze to the little dish drainer and soap bottle by the sink, the sugar jar by the refrigerator, a cap on a peg by the door and the dresser with its comb and coins on top. He isn't sure who his affection is for, or his guilt. When she looks back at him, he just stares.

"I wish this place was ours."

Then he smiles and she sits cross-legged on the bed again and opens her can of pop. "You can come with me up to the pond sometime. That'll be ours," he adds and pictures her on a winter's day in a coat like Sissy's or the one her mother wore. When he looks at her, he can sometimes see Mavis and other times he can't. She lowers her face when she notices him staring and looks at him from under her eyebrows, making him smile again after a moment.

"What?" she asks.

"Nothing," he says, closing his eyes.

"You can't think nothing about a person."

"Why not?"

"You just can't. You can't think of a person an' think nothing at the same time."

"Try it," he says, opening his eyes to look at her. "Think about me an' nothing."

"I can't."

"Try."

"I don't want to."

He's upsetting her. Her face is solemn, her eyes mirrors, and he sees pain. His and hers. "I'm sorry, Agnes."

"You can't do it either. Nobody can."

"I guess not."

Images flood his head when he thinks of her. His eyes are never empty.

———————

At the shop, all the lights but the one in the kitchen go dark. Son is inside, setting an empty beer bottle in a bin under the sink. After he closed up, he took the trash outside, then came back in to empty the cash register into one of the green bank bags Ray keeps under the counter. There's never a lot of cash. After that, he sat quietly on the stool at the register for a moment, then got up, opened a beer, and started to look for Ray's cash box. Son considered the possibility of the warehouse but then eliminated that. He looked under counters, in the filing cabinets, behind the desk and the couch, in the backs of closets, in the toilet tank. Then he started to tap on the walls, pull on the edges of linoleum in the hallway, stare into the bedroom in back, lift the mattress, look at the floor, step lightly on a floor board, pull back a rug, and push with a toe of his boot on each board until one rose up. Then he smiled, sat down on the floor and opened the box. There was a Glock inside and stacks of cash. He counted the money, then put it back, set the box back in its hollow under the floorboard, rolled the rug back and got up.

He doesn't want any of Ray's money; he just likes to know where it is. He can't account for it, but it gives him a little thrill to visualize the money when he's with Ray and Ray doesn't know that he knows.

Switching off the lights, he yawns, wanting to get into Craig's cousin's warm bed and sleep. Staying with him makes him nervous, though, because he doesn't want Ray to know. The idea of Ray knowing fills his veins with ice water, which makes no sense. He can count the times Ray has ever hit him, an angry slap on the back of the head for some annoyance. With his mother, he would roll into a ball and clamp his arms over his ears to shut her out. All the rage he kept inside with her scorches the outside of him now, races like a current on the surface of his skin. His fear of Ray is peculiar.

Going outside, he yawns again, thinking sleepily of bed. It is dark at the bar, too, but George's car is still outside. Jumping down the porch steps he hears it then, footsteps crunching, a voice behind him: "Hey, baby Wycowski."

He whirls, heart racing, and Will, Jimbo, and Andy come out of the dark. "You fuckers. What are you doin' here?"

Will appears in the porch light, scowling at him. "You are so impolite."

"Whaddo you want?" His heart is steady again, sleepiness gone. Belligerence is filling his face with heat. He can feel his fingers clenching. Occasional cars whoosh by behind the fence. Jimbo is circling out around Will, coming closer to Son.

"Lookee," he says. "I have a new jacket."

"Give me that." Son swipes at it and Jimbo tosses it to Will.

"Fits me perfect," says Will, pulling it on, shrugging it onto his shoulders. "Look at that. I could take your place."

"What the fuck do you mean by that?"

"That I could take your place. Who needs you?"

"Bury you," adds Jimbo.

"Not if I cut your fuckin' heart out first."

"You think you can, you little shit?"

"Try me."

His fingers are tightening into fists now. His head is clear, vision focused on Jimbo.

Then Will says, "Do you want it back?"

His eyes shift. "It's mine, fucker."

"I tell you what. Get down on your knees an' ask me for it. Pretty please."

He swings in a blur of red rage and slugs Will just under the eye. Will flies back and Jimbo races up. Andy backs away. Son ducks under Jimbo's arms, darts away, swings back and punches him hard in the back. Jimbo roars: "Dead man!"

Andy climbs up on the wall between the bar and the shop, looking around anxiously. The side door of the bar opens and George looks out. He stares at Andy and Andy stares back. Then the door closes. Andy looks away. Will and Jimbo are on top of Son. Will is stomping, Jimbo punching. Then Son skitters sideways, pops up and plants a boot in Will's belly. Will flies back again, landing on a strip of dirt along the driveway that gives underneath him. Then Son runs at Jimbo, slugging up close, arms grappling, slipping and scrabbling on the gravel, panting loudly. On the dirt, Will rolls over with a groan, staggers up, and comes around in a wide circle. "Get 'im!" he yells.

Jimbo wraps Son in his arms, lifting him off the ground. The porch light moves in a slow orbit. Son kicks out as Will approaches, laughing at him, slightly bent over his stomach. Son's voice is hoarse. "You fucker."

Jimbo squeezes and Son sees lights, then Andy yells, "Wait!" and Will and Jimbo freeze. That's when they hear the whoop and chirp of a siren approaching. Will bounces back and up again, punching Son in the face with both fists, knocking his head back into Jimbo's nose. Son sags and Jimbo staggers, then Andy yells, "Get 'im in the car!" and Son thrashes in a sudden frenzy. It surprises Jimbo who almost lets him go. Son arches, kicking up and back with his heels, and then Jimbo yells and drops him. "Shit...You fucker!"

Son bolts, but Will is behind him. He is running for the back fence, but in the light of the porch, sees the gleam of the beer bottles he didn't clean up. Stooping through the rails he grabs one up and spins back, swinging it. Will runs straight up, ducks too late. The bottle slams down onto the top of his head and his knees bounce off the gravel. Then, with a look of surprise, he topples over.

Andy says, "Oh, man...Fuck, man."

Jimbo says, "Will...?"

Will doesn't move. Son drops the bottle and runs again. He jumps, grabbing onto the top of the fence, kicking his way up. Looking back, he sees Jimbo pick up Will as Andy runs for the car. Andy swings the car around, brakes squealing, siren louder. Jimbo gets Will into the back seat, jumps up front, then swings his arms and head out the open window, looking for Son. Jimbo can't see him in the dark, but Son can hear him roar.

"FUCKER!"

There's a light on in the window, dull gold, a square with a fir branch silhouette against the thin curtains. Tires sliding in on loose gravel, Kurt stops his car and gets out. The drapes were open when he left, he's pretty sure of that. The sight of the light in the window doesn't bother him though. He knows it's Jonah, sees his pickup as he crosses the parking lot. The curtains at Joy's are pulled closed too. He likes summer, he thinks, open windows, open drapes, the way that voices carry.

He takes his cap off as he comes up to his door, scrubs his head, puts his cap back on, steps inside and then steps back out again. Jonah isn't there. Instead, a girl he's never seen is sitting on his bed. On the walkway a wave of disorientation freezes him in place. He stares confusedly at the number on his door. Then a voice says, "Hi," and he steps back in. The girl is sitting cross-legged, resting a pop can on her ankles, both her hands around it.

"Are you Kurt?"

"Yeah."

His tone is cautious. Even before he got here, the night struck him as unreal. He drove all the way out to Jack's Club to meet Wes. Wes lives outside of town and the Club was closer for him than anywhere else. The parking lot was full and the shutters on the windows facing the road were pulled open. A cheerful light streamed out and the voices inside were loud and cheerful too. Wes wasn't there, and when Kurt sat down at the bar to wait for him, Miri came over with a smile that wasn't her usual smile. It wasn't real, didn't look real. The bar didn't look like the bar, and he guesses that he got the date wrong because Wes didn't show up, and now a girl with wooly brown hair and dark brown eyes is sitting here with a can of pop. He looks over at the half open bathroom door. The light is on but there's no sound inside. She smiles painfully, eyes going to the bathroom door too.

Then she says, "I'm Agnes."

"Oh."

The sound of the toilet seat dropping claps loudly and Kurt almost jumps. He gives an awkward laugh. Then the toilet flushes and Jonah comes out with a curious expression. For a moment Kurt wonders if he's supposed to be here. Then Jonah says, "We were waitin' for you. This is Agnes."

Agnes smiles at him again, this time drinking her pop.

"I wasn't expecting you," Kurt says.

Jonah is sitting down on the bed again. "Problem?"

"No."

"Good. Wanna pizza?"

"I can eat, I guess."

His phone book's under the phone on a shelf on a little table somebody gave away for free in the last town he lived in. They put it out on the sidewalk on garbage day with a bookshelf without shelves. He left that. The surface of the table has little chips and scratches that he left too.

He can feel Agnes's stare. He doesn't want to look over. When he does, it's out of the corner of his eye. He knows he looks suspicious. Then she leans over and Jonah says, "Hey, Kurt."

"Yeah?"

"Extra cheese."

"Okay."

She looks a little red, strawberry red, reminding him of a girl he almost completely forgot about until now. They both worked at Carrow's and always got off late. Once he bought a bottle of strawberry wine and they went out together, a girl he can barely picture now.

He orders the pizza, drops the phone book on the shelf. "Fifteen, twenty minutes," he says.

He can't remember her name either.

"How much?"

"Twenty-two fifty."

"Jesus."

"Workin' for pizza money."

"Just about."

"You guys busy?"

"You mean at work?"

"Yeah."

"So-so."

"Us too."

He's feeling worried and lifts his cap up again, scrubs at his hair and pulls it back down. Agnes being here worries him and Agnes looks worried too. She keeps staring at Jonah or down at her pop, taking occasional sips. Kurt can't wait for the pizza. Jonah drops back against Kurt's pillows, crosses his legs at his ankles and yawns. Wes could be at the Club by now. Maybe Miri is leaning up against the other side of the counter to rub at the backs of her knees. When Kurt was there, her space heater was glowing a bright orange.

"I can never get it right," she said in a way that made him think she was talking about more than her space heater.

He rests his elbows on his knees and rolls his shoulders up, staring at the strip of brass between the carpet and the linoleum. He's aware suddenly of how dingy it is, wonders if Windex would help. Then his eyes meet Agnes's and she looks over at Jonah and Kurt decides she looks more helpless than worried, like she's trying to say something but can't make anything come out. Jonah rolls his head with a slightly hooded expression. Then he pushes up on the pillows and looks back at Kurt. "Want us to go?"

"No."

"You're actin' like it."

"No, I'm not."

"Thinkin' too much then."

"I've got stuff to think about," he says.

"Won't catch me worryin' about stuff," says Jonah, lifting his head up enough to rest his arm under it. He recrosses his ankles afterwards, looking relaxed again.

Kurt scowls. He wants to talk about work and can tell Jonah doesn't. Agnes keeps staring between them, sipping her pop. He's glad at the sound of footsteps on the stairs.

"That was quick," says Jonah.

"Real quick."

Opening the door, Kurt smiles at a girl with two long brown braids and a warming bag she rests on the railing.

"Just in time," says Kurt, pulling his wallet out of his pocket. Behind him, Jonah almost murmurs, "No worries." His voice is a little loud for a real murmur. Looking back, Kurt can see Agnes staring past him. She is frowning at something, but all he can see is a grayish haze over the sky.

"Keep the change," says Kurt.

"Thanks a lot. Have a good night."

Stepping back in, he starts to close the door, then Agnes says, "You can't see the stars," and he stops and looks back out.

"Yeah, you can."

They're small and pale, but they're there. He stays still for a moment and it doesn't feel as cold as before. The sky has a blue, almost vaporous tint to it.

"C'mon," says Jonah. He's sitting up, reaching for Agnes's coat. "You too," he adds to Kurt. "There's some kind a mood goin' on in this place."

He can't disagree.

"C'mon where?" he asks, looking underneath the lid of the pizza box.

"I'll think of a place." Agnes is getting into her coat and Jonah picks up Kurt's keys too and opens the door. "I need some air anyway."

Kurt waits until Agnes is outside, then he closes the door and follows them. "I was gonna tell you about work," he says, passing through a patch of light at the bottom of the stairs.

"No thanks."

"This is new," he says.

"I told you. You think too much."

"I have stuff to think about," he says again.

Jonah doesn't answer until he reaches his pickup and opens Agnes's door. Then he hooks his arm over the top and says, "We're hirin'. I guess you know that."

Kurt gets in, closes his door and sticks his elbow outside. After Jonah gets in too, he says, "You heard that?"

"Yeah."

He smells strawberries again and remembers the name of the girl from Carrow's. It was Carrie and he drove her out onto a dark empty road with hills on both sides and a giant moon in a sky full of stars. The electrical wires made a dull humming sound and the wine was sweet. He can't believe he almost forgot her name.

"Want some beer?" asks Jonah. He frowns for a moment because the question doesn't make any sense to him after thinking about strawberry wine, and then he says, "Yeah, I guess so."

"Will you cheer up?"

"I am."

"You're thinkin' too much."

"Just rememberin' somethin'."

"You aren't comin' back on nights, you know."

Kurt can feel his jaw tighten. It irritates him now. He is thinking about Carrie and looking at the storefronts passing by. A lot of them are places he's never gone into.

"I was only on for one job," he says and thinks that the thing that bothers him is that he didn't choose this and didn't choose any of the families he had to live with either, and that worries him. He sees the liquor store Jonah always goes to coming up after the next light and remembers thinking that Acropolis was a town made for people to live in forever. He doesn't want anything that isn't already here and doesn't want things to change. The feeling reminds him of going to a new family who didn't know him and where he didn't ever stay very long.

"They oughta ask me next time," he says.

They are turning into the parking lot now. Jonah stops and looks over. "You crack me up."

Once, after she first met him, Kurt said, "You must have a trick," and Miri smiled curiously at him and said, "A trick about what?"

"About being happy," he said.

"Oh that." She wasn't impressed by it.

"That's somethin'," he told her.

"Not really. You can fake it."

"You don't look like you're fakin' it." His face looked sad.

"That's because I'm not," she lied with a laugh, brightening with his smile. She likes to make people happy. Expressing her feelings always dissolves into panic. She can see everything in Ray's face, but he never really tells her his feelings. He tells her stories, funny stories, or stories he remembers when he's half asleep, fuzzy-edged stories that might be true or not. With her head on his chest, she listens to his heart and wonders what he feels. Maybe he doesn't want her feelings any more than he wants to give her his. She started to play a game when he left for Pete and Cora's. She imagines him not coming back in exact detail and thinks of all the ways it might happen because nothing she exactly imagines ever really happens that way. She hopes she can bring him back by imagining all the ways he can stay away. One time she started the game by telepathically telling him to call or to walk through the bar door. That morning, he was supposed to call by the time she finished her orange juice, and when he didn't, she imagined him coming home to pack up his things and pictured herself leaning in the doorway, watching him open the drawer she was always going through. Then he showed her one of his tee-shirts that she liked to sleep in.

"Want this?"

It made her stomach hurt it was so real and she went into the bedroom and opened up the drawer just to see that everything was still there. She began to look at the pictures again, the stray earrings he never wore and maybe weren't even his. She dug a tiny gold hoop out of a dusty corner and then she went to call him, but he didn't answer. She called a couple of times and each time told herself to stop, but every call made it worse. She couldn't make herself stop. Then she called the house number he gave her and Cora answered. Sitting on the bed, she stared in the mirror, at the circles under her eyes, her wispy cut-off hair, saw Cora with her fingers twisting a smile onto her cheeks, sitting in a washed out light with a baby in her arms. Miri was spellbound, bewitched, imprisoned by Ray. She couldn't even imagine walking away, her freedom equal to his. She grew without growing, a shadow inside a shadow, her breath absorbed by his.

On the other end of the line Cora was laughing. *"Raaaay!"*

Then her laugh faded away and Ray was there, maybe sitting down in front of a TV, not really seeing it, elbows on his knees, not wanting to talk to her either.

She heard him sigh.

"Hey, babe."

"I called your cell."

"Battery's dead."

"Oh."

It was probably warmer there, windows open maybe, the sound of cars in the distance.

"I miss you."

He sighed again, differently, settling back.

"Miss you too."

He didn't though; Cora was probably in the doorway, arms crossed in front of her, a broad taunting smile on her face.

"Really?"

But she could see him sinking back on a couch with an arm across the top and his knees splayed wide, watching Cora coming slowly over to him.

"Yeah. Sure."

"I wish you'd come home."

"Pretty soon."

His voice was growing cooler like the breeze through the open windows, like Cora's arms wrapping around him. Then he said, "I'll talk to ya later, okay?"

"Okay."

She imagined him putting all his things in boxes and loading up her car to take them to the shop. He'd just live there the way he lived before. He'd even kiss her and smile.

"I'll give you a call," he'd say, and then he wouldn't.

At work, Miri keeps looking at the door and feels like she is dreaming, the way Kurt keeps dreaming about strawberry wine and summer nights long ago.

Sitting next to him, Agnes murmurs, "Stars," and Jonah's arm goes across the seat behind her. "Just for you," he tells her.

After the pizza, they take her home.

"Waylon's daughter," says Jonah after she's gone. "You know that market in Sandorville?"

"Oh."

Her house is bright with lights. There are other lights Kurt can see in the trees, but they all look far away. They let her out down the road and watched her run through the misty beams draining out of the pickup's headlights.

"I love the way she smells."

Trying to think of a good comment, Kurt says, "I think it's her soap."

"Strawberries."

As the air blows in, all he smells is fir though. Jonah is quiet, lighting a cigarette as they go. At the sight of the factory coming up, Kurt says, "I think somethin's up. Wes says so anyway. An audit or somethin'."

"Man, that's something they do all the time."

"Maybe this is different."

"Why would it be different? They move us around. We're fuckin' chess pieces. Nothin's different."

He falls silent and Kurt is silent too. Upstairs, Jonah lies down with the same pile of pillows as before, punching it up again. Kurt tosses him a beer and opens his, trying to think of something to say. He knows Jonah's thinking about her. His face is almost angry. After punching at Kurt's pillow again, he turns on the TV and lies back with his arm over his head.

Kurt pulls his chair over and kicks off his shoes, settling his feet on the corner of his bed. The TV's at an angle and the lamp beside Jonah is shining on it.

"I wonder what's up," he murmurs.

Jonah looks at him and then shrugs. "Probably nothing. They wouldn't count us in anyway."

"Never ask," he agrees, looking at the top of his beer.

"I don't even care."

"Probably nothin'."

"Yeah."

Then Jonah turns off the light and a shadow covers his face and Kurt looks away at the TV he can see again. Jonah's voice doesn't surprise him. It's natural for him to say it since even Kurt's thinking about it. He keeps smelling strawberries and wishes he didn't.

"I didn't go lookin', you know?"

"You don't have to tell me."

"I don't want you thinkin' that."

"I don't."

"It matters to me."

"Okay." Kurt's glad that he can't really see him. After a while Jonah gets up for another beer and he looks down at the empty one in his lap and says, "Me too."

Tires crackle on the gravel driveway outside as a car rolls by. In a while another follows. Son is vaguely aware of this. The trailer is warm, warm for him, he knows. Craig's cousin flipped the heater on earlier and the air is stuffy and dry. He slips in and out of awareness, heavy with an anxiety he can't place.

Outside, the sky isn't as dark as the dark at the windows. He rolls a glassy eye around the room, catching a movement at the door, a strip of gray, a twinkling light.

"Trevor?"

The panic in his voice startles him. He can feel himself frowning and a pain starts up in his head. Craig's cousin leans back inside, looking over at him.

"It's okay, baby. I'll be right back."

"Where're you goin'?"

"Just to make a call. Relax."

He nods. The door stays ajar. His head throbs now and his mouth is gummy. He drank until Craig's cousin took the bottle away from him. Then he screwed his face up plaintively. "Trevor...*please.*"

Craig's cousin just shook his head and put the bottle back in the cupboard, so he drank the rest in his glass and wouldn't look at him. His face pulsed in pain.

Sitting beside him, Craig's cousin said, "You wanna talk to me?"

He scowled, lying back against the arm of the couch. "They attacked me."

Craig's cousin stared and Son could see his own panic in Craig's cousin's eyes. He looked away. Craig's cousin wanted the truth, a truth that reared up out of a long ago dark he never looked into anymore.

"You can tell me anything," said Craig's cousin gently.

He shook his head, glared at him, then rolled away.

Now he is drinking a glass of water at the sink. The cold hurts his teeth. He sits back down and stares at the door, waiting. Craig's cousin returns, feet bare, blowing into his hands. "You want some coffee?" he asks.

Son moves his head back and forth. His voice seems lost somewhere all of a sudden.

After a moment, Craig's cousin sits down on the other end of the couch and says, "I talked to Andy. Everything's okay." He nods and Craig's cousin takes his hand in his, rubbing his palm with a thumb. "You wanna lie down again?"

His throat aches. "I was afraid to get in the car," he says abruptly, the suddenness of the sound startling him. The rasp in his voice makes it sound like somebody else's voice. The words are somebody else's too, coming from far away, not his words. This isn't anything he talks about or thinks about. Even though his breath is suddenly quick, shallow, panicked. Craig's cousin pulls on him gently, hugging him, lips against the side of his face.

"Baby."

"I didn't wanna get in that car," he whispers. "I did that. I did that before. I was so fuckin' stupid, Trevor. I got in a dude's car cuz 'e was gonna give me some Molly for blowin' 'im. Fuck. Fuck…."

"Just tell me, baby. You don't need to keep this inside."

"I want it to go away. I don't wanna talk about it. I was so fuckin' stupid…."

He tells himself that he is only telling a story, a story that is usually still dreamlike to him. And like a dream it slips away in real life, only partly remembered, affecting him in ways he never knows. He squirms, thinking about it, though, like bugs are crawling over his skin. His sweat wets his tee-shirt and he feels Trevor's thumb gently stroke his forehead.

"You're okay, baby. No worries anymore."

"I got into the dude's car," Son says. "Fuckin' stupid."

He didn't think about it though. He just got in the car, opened up the man's jeans and took him in his mouth while they drove. By the time he sat up, they were on the highway, but he wasn't worried, not yet. The man clasped him by the back of the neck, squeezing pleasantly. "You have a sweet mouth, kid."

"Thanks."

"How old are you?"

He felt himself smiling as he looked out the window. "Eighteen."

"Hell you are."

"Almost."

He was a year and two months away. It started to rain and he watched the water run across the glass, blown sideways as they drove. It grew darker, only occasional lights winking in the distance.

"Where we goin'?"

"I told you. My place."

He started to frown then, felt the cold coming in through the door. "You said another party."

"There is. At my place."

"With other people?"

He saw teeth flash at him. "Wouldn't be a party otherwise, right?"

"You aren't kidnapping me?"

The man laughed. "Suspicious fucker."

"I want my Molly."

"You do, huh?"

"I blew you. I drank it."

"Just relax, kid."

"What's your name?"

"You don't wanna know my name. I don't wanna know yours."

"Won't people tell me your name?"

"What people?"

"Look. I changed my mind. Let me out."

"Here? We're in the middle a nowhere."

"I don't care."

"I do. I'm not havin' a dead kid on my conscience. I'll take you back in the morning."

"No, really. Let me out."

"I said no."

"Please." There was barely any sound in his voice then.

"I like that. Polite."

"Please let me out. I'll jump."

The man laughed again and then Son felt his head crack against the window. Then fingers in his hair, yanking his head back, slamming him into the glass again. He slumped, sliding down to the floorboards. He sat with his head resting on the seat, very still, trying to hide from the pain. When the man pulled him out of the car, he went willingly, quietly. An arm held him close.

"That's a good boy," the man whispered.

There were no lights, nobody at the little house. Son thought they were someplace outside of Lodi, but he wasn't sure. He leaned against the man holding him, wanting his kindness, and the man seemed to know that because he gave him another gentle squeeze and said, "Bet your head hurts. I have somethin' for that, though, don't you worry."

The man kept him in a stupor and he was grateful for that. He knew he was cuffed to a bed and that he was there for a long time. The sex was strangely foggy. There were times he thought he was dreaming it or watching it on TV. Just plain sex, his legs up, the man's wet, hot mouth on his face. There was a pain though, and it kept growing, a knot in his belly, an ache that went deep into his spine. The man made him drink, water spilling out of his mouth, but he didn't feed him.

Once, pulling his legs up to his empty stomach, Son said, "Can I have something to eat?"

"Naw. You won't be here that long."

"Please."

"I don't have anything."

"Please."

"Stop asking. Fucking greedy bitch."

The man didn't hurt him though, just went away. The stupor deepened and he just floated in it, not caring. Then one night the man was pulling him up and he could stand. Bending down, the man helped him put his feet into his jeans, pulled his tee-shirt over his head, and put his shoes on him.

"Time to go."

He was afraid, but he couldn't find his voice and just leaned in, trying to put his arm around the man. A hand patted his shoulder.

"Like you too, but I can't keep you. Gotta get back to work."

His voice came out rough and garbled. "Don't hurt me."

"I haven't yet an' I don't plan on it." The man put him back in the car they came in and took him close to the house where they met. "C'mon. Get out. You can get home from here."

"Get out?"

"Yeah. Get out. Go." Then with a sigh, the man reached over and pushed open the door. Son fell out, scooting back on a cold sidewalk on an empty street. He thinks he said, "Wait," but then the car pulled away.

He thinks he says, "I'm sorry, Trevor. I'm sorry I did that," but he isn't sure. Not until Craig's cousin says, "You didn't do anything, baby. You were a kid. A fuckin' kid."

"Yeah," he says, thinking he agrees, but not really sure of that either.

He sat on the cold curb for a long time after the car pulled away. Then he got up and went back to the house he started out in.

At Joy's, Jonah stops.

At first the breeze is as soft as still air. In the courtyard he can see a blur of pale stone and Joy's wind chimes stir almost silently.

He whispers, "Pops," and hears a footstep break the stillness. On the gravel he stops again and his breath comes in soft clouds.

The breeze stirs, rustling out of the trees. He sees Kurt's car in the ghostly light and goes over, sliding his arm through a half open window to unlock the door. Inside, he rolls the window back up and takes a bottle of bourbon out of the glove box, sitting still for a moment, and then drinking slowly.

Outside, shapes are beginning to form, patches of light separating from the dark.

He feels a sense of laughter, Abel's maybe. Taking a last drink, he looks back into the glove box, then puts the bottle away and gets out. At the back of his pickup he pauses for a moment, whispers, "Pops," and hears a whisper in return, fir needles falling gently.

At Orly's, he gets out and looks over at Waylon's where the light in the windows shine out in warm, yellow tones on the porch where Mavis used to stand and look away at places she dreamed about and where she probably isn't living. Places on postcards she sends to Agnes. She's as restless as he was here and he looks back at Orly's where everything is the same. A trash can is holding the bathroom door open. He sits on the same turquoise chair against the wall of windows.

Orly peers at him over the top of his newspaper. "This is early for you."

"I was out. How come you're open?"

"Whaddam I gonna do? Watch TV all day?"

The pumps are the same too with their rounded edges. He looks out over the tops to Waylon's where Mavis is standing as if she never left and time never moved on. She bunches up the collar of her coat under her chin and Abel is up at the house again, asleep in front of the TV by the window where Sissy always hangs her snowflakes at Christmas. All he has to do is believe Mavis is waiting, scrunching up her collar, feel the coolness of the air he used to feel every day, see the puffs of smoke over the roof of Waylon's, and get up like always.

"You comin'?"

"In a minute," says Orly.

He smells her too as he gets closer, sweet like flowers, not strawberries, and then she laughs and disappears.

Inside, Waylon sets his broom against the wall and he says, "Couple eggs an' some pancakes."

"Coffee?

"Yeah."

His stool has a hole in its seat and he can feel scratches on the counter. A minute later, Orly comes in and looks under the lid of the donut case. Jonah looks out at the empty porch and sees the signal light now, swinging slowly. There is nobody outside.

"Stale," says Orly, scowling at the donuts.

"I got 'um just this morning," says Waylon.

"Stale ones," says Orly, setting one down on a napkin.

Sprinkles scatter on the scratchy countertop and Jonah thinks of Christmas lights all of a sudden. The signal light keeps swinging and the air under the door is cold. He eats his pancakes beside Orly sipping coffee out of his mug.

"This yesterday's coffee?"

"I always give you yesterday's," says Waylon.

Orly grimaces at him.

Pretty soon, Waylon's pot belly stove will light up the corner and there will be a Christmas tree in the front window almost blocking Waylon's way around the counter. Jonah watches him watching Orly at the donut tray and suddenly feels sorry for him, thinking about the day Agnes came in and he heard her talking about Mavis's clothes. All of a sudden, he doesn't like being in this half real, half dream-like world anymore. At least not without Mavis, or maybe only with Mavis.

He isn't even sure of Orly, who is picking out a donut covered in white icing now. Pushing his plate away, Jonah gets up and drops his money on the counter. He doesn't feel Orly's stare, but opening the door, he hears his voice following him. "G'bye to you too."

"Bye," he says and goes over to Mavis where she's leaning up against his pickup, waiting for him with a smile. Her arms open as he comes up.

"I was dreamin' of you," he says.

At home, he goes inside and sees Ally at the sink, looking white against the white of the wall on the other side of her.

It's light out now and the strangeness of the shadows is gone. Her palms are under her belly and she is quiet, just staring at him.

"Mornin'," he says.

She smiles a little.

"Morning."

In the hallway, he stops to look into his old room with its sunny walls and sky blue ceiling.

17

♦ Love Again ♦

One of the things that bothers Kurt is that Joy's little boy never came back. When she moved in, it bothered him that she even had a little boy, but all of his dread about footsteps racing up and down the stairs all day and the rattle and clatter of skate boards in the courtyard was for nothing. The apartment building stayed as quiet as usual. There was a little girl, but she didn't make a lot of noise. He saw her once, splashing her fingertips in the birdbath, but that was all.

The absence of the little boy, though, is strange.

On Halloween, Kurt stopped off at the store after work because he forgot to buy candy and passed up a boy in a Spiderman costume, at home a bride carrying a bouquet of flowers and a white bucket shaped like a pumpkin. It was already dark. Passing by Joy's, he saw a glass bowl full of Sweet Tarts and Tootsie Pops on a chair by her open door. Later on, a little girl in a light blue dress and bright red shoes came upstairs. Red braids framed a freckled face. She didn't really look like it, but he thought she must be the little girl who was splashing in the birdbath.

"What's your name?" he asked, dropping a Kit Kat in the pillowcase she was holding up to him.

"I'm Dorothy."

"Oh. Well, there you go, Dorothy. Happy Halloween."

She gave him a funny look and later he realized she was Dorothy from *The Wizard of Oz* and wasn't telling him her real name. When he was little, he always thought that Dorothy was lucky, envied her all her adventures. He didn't have a real home to miss and decided he'd just stay in Oz and live on giant lollipops. It was all about what people had to lose, he guessed, and kept hoping that Joy would come upstairs with her little boy.

At work, Kurt is sitting in the lunch room, thinking about *The Wizard of Oz* again.

Wes was upstairs in the offices, and now he's coming over to Kurt, pulling a chair over from the table beside the couch.

"Well, it looks like there's another guy starting tonight. Wally Cumberland. No furniture experience, but he's done assembly line work before."

Kurt's life is completely different from the way it was. He equates it with waking up to find his apartment building spinning through a storm on its way to Oz now that he doesn't particularly want to go there.

Giant lollipops don't have the same appeal as giant TVs or bowling pins.

"What about Gary, the other new guy?"

"I don't think they'll be moving him until the next hire."

"What hire?"

"Another five or six guys, I hear. Gus is retiring for sure an' Bob's talking about it."

"On days or what?"

"Grave at first. After that, I don't know."

He puts his pickle back into his bag and mutters, "That's such bullshit." He used to think he wouldn't live here for very long either.

"You can always put in to transfer back on grave. I'd think about it though."

Acropolis was just a stop-off. And then he found his apartment by the bowling alley and he knows that things like a place to buy jelly donuts right next door and a really good fish sandwich at Candi's and Jack-in-the-Box right next to Quality Videos aren't really big things, but they add up to make a place as close to a home as he thinks a home probably is.

"I want to be left where I was." At first, all Dorothy wanted was to get out of Oz. All Kurt wanted was to save up some money and get out of Acropolis. Things change. "They'll just put new guys into Gus and Bob's spots anyway," he adds.

Wes gives him a smack on the knee and gets back up. "C'mon. Cheer up. I like workin' days."

The kitchen is dark, but a lamp on in the living room spills a watery light on the linoleum floor. The door to the backyard is open, letting the cold in. Taking another swallow of beer, Ray listens for Cora. She's in the living room, waiting for him to give in, but he won't. He wants her to leave. Growing irritated, he sets his beer down and says, "Cora! C'mon. Get in here."

Her voice comes from down the hall. "You come to me, lover boy."

There is laughter in her voice. He pushes away from the counter and finds her in the bedroom, lying on the bed with her arms over her head. In a single step he is beside her, grabbing both her arms and yanking her up. His anger surprises and delights her. She rubs her arms with a laugh after he lets her go.

"Well, well, well."

"Cut the crap, Cora." He crowds her through the door and down the hall.

"You can at least offer me a beer."

"You need to go. I don't want my wife to see you. I told you that."

They are back in the kitchen, Ray leaning against the counter again.

"Your wife?"

"My wife. What of it?"

"You aren't really married."

"Maybe I will be."

The whiteness that comes to her face surprises him. "That won't change anything."

"Maybe it will."

"You get home an' all of a sudden you don't want anything to do with me?"

"We aren't livin' together. I'm not going anywhere with you. You need to go home."

"You know you love me."

"You're a friend, Cora. I don't love you like my wife. What the fuck is this anyway? You have Pete an' the kids."

"I told you! I can't do that anymore. I'm going crazy."

"That's not my fuckin' problem, Cora. We aren't together. Work it out."

"Work it out?"

"Yeah. Work it the fuck out."

"Like you, Ray? You get a little itchy an' think you can just screw little Cora for a while? Get it outta your system?"

"I have no problem not doing that anymore. That's your call."

She laughs and says, "You can't live with just one woman, Ray."

"You aren't the only option."

"I'm the one you like."

He shrugs. "We'll see."

Smiling, she moves back into the light coming from the living room and slowly starts to unbutton her blouse.

"Jesus Christ, Cora." But she doesn't stop and he doesn't stop her. He picks up his beer and takes a long swallow. Her blouse slides off her arms and she lets it drop to the floor. She is naked underneath and he takes a deep breath. "I didn't say I didn't like lookin' at you, Cora."

"You like more than looking," she whispers, slowly moving closer.

But he just shakes his head, goes to the refrigerator and pulls out another beer. "I'm not gonna tell you again. Get the fuck dressed an' get out."

"You piece of shit."

Opening his beer, he drinks half of it and says, "I don't really give a fuck about your opinion, Cora. I never said I was a nice guy."

"Who are you kidding, Ray? That meth you were supposed to bring up here? It's still at Ed's. The weed in my car you feel okay about? It's legal."

"Still a market."

"You aren't such a bad guy anymore."

"Fuck off, Cora."

"Look at me, Ray."

"No." He lifts his beer up, looking at the ceiling. In the light, she blurs and her arms seem to disappear. She is armless and hopeless and loveless. And he doesn't care. He just wishes all of her would disappear and leave him in peace. "Just go, Cora."

But she doesn't answer.

Ever since Jimbo came looking for her, Susie always checks the parking lot before she goes outside. Now it's dark after work and the parking lot lights make more shadowy than bright places. She moves nervously through the headlights coming on all around her, gets to her car and locks herself in. No Jimbo. He leers at her, even in the hospital when Will was hurt. It isn't a good leer either. Everybody is competition to Jimbo, but Susie is competition he doesn't fear. His leer is the leer of a fantasy that only involves her disappearance. She'd go home, except she can't leave Will. He needs her. Andy and Jimbo can't help him. Even Craig's cousin isn't any help. The other day when he came over, he pulled Susie's chair over to the couch, sat down on it, draping his forearms over his legs, and stared at Will lying there with a damp cloth over his eyes.

"C'mon, Will. Give it a rest. You aren't that bad off."

Susie gaped at him. So did Will, pulling the cloth down to his chest and bleating pitifully. "I could have fuckin' brain damage."

Craig's cousin just sat back with a sigh. "Not from this."

"You weren't there."

"You shouldn't've been there either, Will. What were you thinking? Ray's kid?"

Will almost pouted. "I was just gonna talk to 'im."

"You need to stop listenin' to that bozo crew a yours. Listen, Will." Craig's cousin was leaning over again, resting a hand on Will's leg. "You need to start thinkin' things through. You aren't on a good path. I'm tellin' you this cuz I love you. You know I have your best interests, right?"

"Am I gonna get a tumor?"

"Fuck, Will. Are you listening?"

"I have a headache, Trevor. I don't wanna hear this."

"I'm tellin' you, you're runnin' outta luck, Will."

Will peeked suspiciously over the top of the cloth he was pulling back over his eyes.

"Whadda you see?"

"Just what I'm tellin' you. An' this. You better lay off Ray's kid. I'm tellin' you this straight up an' honest. If you ever touch him again, everything I see for you, everything goes dark. That's it. Over. I'm not lyin' to you, Will. You are nuts if you think you can get away with hurtin' Ray's kid an' live."

"I called 'im." Will's voice sounded sheepish.

"Ray? What did you say?"

"Nothin'. Didn't answer. I left a message. Told 'im to call me."

"Well, don't call 'im again. Give this some time an' let Ray come to you."

"I got hurt, Trevor. Me. Me. Look at my head."

"I can see your head, Will."

"You aren't bein' very nice to me."

"I'm tellin' you the truth."

"I don't want the fuckin' truth! I want you to make me feel better. I don't have any goddam friends anymore."

Craig's cousin rocked Will's leg under the blanket. "Will, what would you do without me?"

Susie saw Will's face almost slacken, fix into an expressionless stare. "I better not have to, Trevor."

Craig's cousin sighed, pushed himself up and pulled Susie's chair back to its place. "I have to get goin'. I'm already late for work." His skin was pale again from the gray, cold damp, raw patches on his cheeks and knuckles. Susie smiled at his smile, watched him pull his cap down over his red hair. "Nice seein' ya, Susie."

"Bye, Trevor." She felt a longing in her, then looked at Will and sighed. "Poor baby."

"Nobody loves me," he moaned.

Sitting down on the edge of the couch, she lay the cloth over his eyes again and stroked his hair.

"I love you, baby."

Oly Way is a kaleidoscope of color, street lamps, headlights, storefronts, Candi's high arch streaming light down onto the dark leafed plants below. Shapes move behind the steaming glass. Susie pictures a fluffy crown of coconut cream pie and wheels suddenly across the intersection, bouncing over the curb into the parking lot. Inside, a waitress comes up, ready with a menu.

"Just one?"

"To go."

"Okay."

"Two burgers with grilled onions, two fries, an' a coconut cream pie."

"I'm sorry. We're all out of the pie. We have chocolate cream. Or strawberry."

Susie is crushed. "No pie?"

"I'm sorry."

A pieless dinner is flustering her. She wants pie. "Okay, okay," she mutters. "Just the rest then."

A few minutes later she's carrying a bag full of cartons out to her car where she stands squinting through the lights on Oly Way before she sets the bag on the back seat and drives away. Two signal lights later, she stops again, this time at the mini-mart next door to Taco Bell. Inside, she collects an armful of Hostess pies and drops them on the counter by the cash register.

"That it?"

"Yes, please."

Cherry, lemon, blackberry, all dropping into a big brown bag. It is amazing, the relaxation that comes over her. She swings a beatific smile to the front door, hearing a bell tone cheerfully. Then she points. "Hey. I know you. Kurt."

A hesitant smile comes onto the startled face, then broadens. "Yeah, yeah. Susie. Hey, Susie. How you doin'?"

"Great. I'm great." She is still basking in the pleasure of a bagful of Hostess pies. "Just pickin' up some desserts. Will's sick. Not sick, actually…more like…like an accident. I'm just tryin' to cheer 'im up." Then she almost jumps, smiles excitedly, and pulls Kurt over by the arm, bouncing a little on her toes. "Why don't you come over? We can't go out at all while Will's sick. We just stay in all the time. We're goin' crazy. Why don't you come over for a while? Are you doin' anything? C'mon over."

The look she gets is slightly bewildered. "I'm meetin' a friend in about an hour. I guess I could stop by for a few minutes, though."

"That'd be okay. Just a little bit. You can have a Hostess pie."

Kurt smiles uncertainly. "Sure. That'd be okay."

"Do you know where we live? No? Okay, it's easy. Keep on Oly Way until Larch Street. Halfway down Larch, turn on Sugar Pine Lane. We're the last house. You'll see our cars. Okay? For sure? You'll come?"

"Yeah, sure. I'll come over."

Impulsively she leans over and kisses his cheek. He blushes a fiery red and she laughs.

"Hostess Pies!"

At home Will stares at the boxes of burgers and fries. "Hostess pies too," says Susie, warily offering him a box. He takes it and she takes her own, dropping into her chair.

Will's day passes between the bed and the couch. A pile of pillows braces up his head. He's wearing pajama bottoms and a tee-shirt, a blanket wadded up around his feet. The house is hot, air blowing out of the heaters. He eyes her almost reverently, making her nervous. She eats half her burger, sinking into her chair. Will just looks at his, lifts up the bun.

"Aren't you going to eat?"

"I'm not hungry."

"You should eat. Kurt's coming over."

His eyes come up sluggishly, scowling at her. "I dunno any Kurt."

"Yeah, you do. Craig's cousin's dad's friend."

His scowl deepens, then a look of pain comes onto his face. "That hurts my head."

"You remember. We see 'im at Jack's Club sometimes. I asked 'im to come over."

"Why?"

"To keep you company."

"To keep me company? That's your fuckin' job."

"My fuckin' job? That's not my fuckin' job, Will."

He glares at her, reaching for his beer on the coffee table. The porch light is shining through the window. He complains about the TV light too, doesn't want any lights on anywhere near him. Everything about Will is making her nervous and she can hear the whine that keeps coming into her voice, the one that makes him grit his teeth. She switches on the lamp by her chair, leaning over the chair's arm to push the lamp against the wall.

"Don't do that."

"I can't see in the dark, Will."

"You don't need to fuckin' see."

"Yes, I do. That can't really bother you anyway. The doctor said you're fine."

"I'm not fuckin' fine!"

"Why don't you just eat?"

He lifts the lid on his burger again, eyeing it suspiciously. "Onions?"

"Grilled."

"I don't like grilled."

"You have to eat something."

"You never get it right."

He flops back on the pillows with a look of despair. She thinks of Craig's cousin, his vision of everything in Will's life going dark. "Do you want me to make you something else?"

"You don't care."

"That's not true."

She is eating a French fry, watching him carefully. He finishes his beer, looks longingly at his empty bottle, then sullenly at her. "You don't love me."

She pushes the rest of the French fry into her mouth, not otherwise moving. Will's eyes are fixed on hers, growing in liveliness, his body beginning to tense. She grabs another fry, chewing quickly, jumping up at the same time Will rises onto an elbow and Kurt pulls up outside. Slowly, Will sits up, but he makes no move to her, just stares as she goes to the door where Kurt enters uncertainly.

"Hey."

"Check this out," says Will, dipping his head down to the dim light. Susie crowds in too, seeing the same shaved circle, light red stitched spot on a bristly white scalp. Will's fingers flutter around the edges. He swears electrical currents jolt through his head at the lightest touch.

"Even air hurts," he says.

Kurt looks dutifully impressed, sympathy on his somber face. "Wow. How'd that happen?"

"You know that kid a Ray's? Came up behind me. *Bam!* Got me with a beer bottle. Fuckin' sneak thief."

Kurt looks amazed.

"Why?"

"We made a deal. I honor my fuckin' deals."

"Yeah, sure" says Kurt, fingers in his pockets, standing there awkwardly.

Will makes room for him on the couch. "Sit down."

Susie goes back to her chair, starting back in on her French fries. Will's fingers still flutter delicately over his scalp. At the hospital, he sat on the side of a bed behind a curtain with an ice bag on top of his head. Jimbo wandered in at one point, ignoring the looks of the nurses and orderlies. Seeing Will's ice bag, he looked at the ticking, beeping machine recording Will's heart rate and blood pressure, then back at the ice pack and said "Pretty high tech."

"Nobody fuckin' cares," moaned Will. "I could have fuckin' brain damage."

Afterwards, Jimbo went back out to the waiting room where Andy was sitting, sat back down and said, "Brain damaged."

Andy's face went white. "Are you shittin' me?"

"Hell, who's gonna know? Never uses that much anyway."

After Will was back home again, Andy told him what Jimbo said and Susie thought Will was going to have a heart attack. He clapped a hand to his chest with a look of real pain and his voice was a barely audible rasp. "Fucker insulted me?"

Then Andy withdrew a little, got the reflective look he always got when he was considering his current situation, ate half a donut he found in the kitchen and then said, "I'd think of it more like a compliment. You know? You bein' so smart you'd never notice."

Jimbo explained it that way too. "I was just commenting on you havin' a ton to spare, man. You an' Einstein. We only use like ten percent. But your ten percent, man, that's like fifty percent, that's what I meant. You can take a loss."

Susie watched Andy during Jimbo's explanation, smirking a smirk Will never saw, Jimbo reddening, puffing up, shooting a baleful glare at Andy's smirk.

"I'm still gonna set that fucker straight for you, though, Will. Dead man. You wait."

Andy guffawed and Jimbo's face went redder.

A lamp against the wall behind Susie's chair throws a high coned shadow up to the ceiling. The rest of the room is dusk-like. Kurt sits awkwardly on the couch near Will's blanket-strewn feet. Kurt gives him only quick glances. There are shadows under Will's eyes, an alert glitter in Susie's. She doesn't seem aware of him anymore. She eats the rest of her burger, goes back to her fries. Scooting up, Kurt starts to rise, then drops back at a blow from Will's foot as Will jams at the couch cushions to push himself up on his pillows. Grabbing his empty beer bottle, Will shakes it at Kurt. "You need a beer. Susie?"

She wriggles down in her chair. "I'm eating."

"I don't care."

"The doctor says you're fine, Will."

"I'm not fucking fine. Get up. We have a guest."

"You get it."

Kurt looks at Will's darkening face. His own feels like it's on fire. He looks longingly at the front door, imagines the cold, fresh air outside.

"Get uuuuuup!"

To Kurt, Susie looks frozen, pinned between wanting to get up and not wanting to.

"I work all day, Will."

"Get up!"

She does this time, rolling over the arm of her chair. Kurt swallows. Will is panting, staring foggy-eyed at the ceiling. Kurt watches the muscles in his face move, thoughts passing through his mind. Then Susie is there with a beer and a Hostess pie. She doesn't offer him the pie. Kurt takes the beer and swallows half of it. Will's eyes follow Susie back to the chair. He waits for her to sit down, then pushes himself off his pillows, resting his weight on his arms.

"Susie?"

"What?"

"Where's mine?"

"My fries are cold," she mutters, looking with distaste into the container.

"Where's my beer?!"

"You didn't ask me."

"I don't have to ask! You have to goddam guess!"

"I can't guess. Jesus, Will. I work. I do things."

"You don't love me."

"Yes, I do."

"You only love your goddam fries!"

"I do not!"

"Fuck your fries!"

"Well, fuck you too, Will!"

Kicking at the blanket on his feet, Will is trying to roll off the couch. Kurt jumps up, taking another foot in the thigh while Will scrambles furiously. "Wait, wait," he says. "I'll get it."

"You fucking bitch!"

Kurt races into the kitchen, grabs a beer and runs back. "Hey, here you go. Look. Nice an' cold."

Will settles slowly, kicks free of the blanket, pulls his feet up so he's hunched on the couch and says, "See, you bitch? That's kindness. You don't have any kindness."

Susie wails at him. "I bought you Hostess!"

"You don't care!"

"Yes, I do."

"Prove it. Gimme your fries."

"Eat your own."

"Gimme yours!"

"No!"

Will gets up, swaying, and Kurt jumps over the coffee table. "I have to go."

"C'mere!"

Susie jumps up too, running for the door with Kurt. She doesn't run fast enough though and Will grabs her by her hair and pulls her back. Kurt yanks on the door to get out and it bounces off his foot and slams back again.

"Shit!"

Susie's swinging underneath Will's arms.

"Goddammit!"

He punches her and she falls back onto her chair and Kurt claps his hands on his head and says, "Oh, man, don't do that."

Will circles unsteadily in front of him. The porch light sucks the color out of his face and the circles around his eyes are black. "No worries," says Will calmly, looking back at Susie. She rolls in her chair, squeezing the arms in both hands. Kurt is inching back in, working his way over to her. Susie bellows at Will: "You better not!"

Will takes a step closer. Her knees pull in and then her feet shoot out and kick Will halfway across the room. He pinwheels, bounces off the wall and swipes at the air. "I can't *see!*"

Kurt grabs him and he straightens up and blinks. Then he looks surprised and blinks again.

"You leavin'?"

Kurt nods, pushing him gently back to the couch. Will lies down, sleepily pulls his blanket back up and says, "Well, thanks for comin' by."

"Sure thing. Thanks for the beer. You guys have a good night."

At the door, he mouths, "Are you okay?" and Susie nods, sprawled almost listlessly in her chair. Then all of a sudden she brightens and says, "Take a Hostess pie."

"No, that's okay. Thanks though. I have to get goin'."

The air outside is like waves of ice cold water. Fir needles skitter and he takes off his jacket and feels the heat of the house blow away.

Kurt was with Wes at Jack's Club when he first met Will. They were sitting at a table near the back alcove and Wes looked across the room with a pained expression that made Kurt turn and look too. There were three men. The first one said something to the other two, pointing a finger at a spot on the floor before he started over. The other two looked at the spot on the floor, then one of them pushed his tongue into his cheek, looked at the other one, then shook his head and went over to the bar. The third man stayed where the first man pointed. When the first man reached Wes and Kurt's table, he gave Kurt a slightly aggrieved look before pulling out a chair and sitting down.

Wes said, "Will, this is Kurt. Kurt, Will."

Kurt said, "How are you?" and Will nodded at him, looking a little perplexed by then. After a few more meetings, Kurt began to get the impression that people weren't real to Will, just props, and the fact that they might move or talk was a startling surprise to him. After Wes's introduction, Will ignored him, leaning on the arm of the chair he pulled closer to Wes.

"I didn't know you came here."

"On occasion. It's on my way home."

"Yeah, yeah. Speakin' of that. Thanks for calling me. I meant to go over, but I never got a chance. Bozos I work with…." Gesturing with his arm, he looked over to where there was just one man standing at the spot on the floor he pointed to earlier. "Jesus, you see what I mean? I said stay put. That's what I get."

"Well, everything's okay now," said Wes. "A bit of a scare, but it's fixed."

Will grimaced at him. "It was a pipe or somethin'?"

"Gas," said Wes.

"Gas," he repeated, nodding slowly and sitting back a little. "Jesus."

"It's okay now."

Will didn't seem worried anymore though. He was gazing back across the bar and his expression seemed distracted. When he looked back at Wes, he frowned for a moment, concentrating, then said, "I sent flowers."

Kurt thought somebody died. It turned out he sent them to his mother and she wasn't dead, but there was a gas leak and it made him think about her dying.

"Tell 'er I'm doin' good, okay?"

"Sure," says Wes.

Kurt watched him cross the room, grab one of the men he came in with by the back of the shirt and yank him off a stool at the bar. The other man still standing at the spot on the floor smiled broadly. Then they all left and Kurt looked back at Wes who gave him an embarrassed smile.

"Will used to live next door. My kid's best friend."

Kurt had met Craig's cousin too and knew about his psychic abilities. He was friendly enough, but always detached, always looking at everybody from a cool distance. Under the friendliness, he was tough and speculative. But then maybe it wasn't any fun to see things; maybe he didn't like what he saw.

Once, Kurt went to an art show to look at something for his apartment and saw a painting that he almost liked. It was a scene of a country road with autumn trees and brown hills in the background. It was something he'd usually like and he looked at it for a long time, trying to find the thing that was wrong with it, but he never could. To Kurt, Will living next door to Wes was a little like that picture. Wes's house was in a neighborhood between Acropolis and Enders, with an Enders address. The lots were a good size, but the houses looked a lot like suburban houses everywhere with lawns and bicycles on the driveways and shady trees to replace the firs. All normal and calm. He could never picture Will walking home from school or riding a bike or playing ball in the street. Kurt pictures Will almost popping into being in a world already made up for him, maybe in the same way Will does.

At home, when he sees Jonah on the walkway talking to Joy, Kurt thinks of her little boy and that painting again. She is smiling in the light of her apartment with her parakeet on her finger.

Jonah looks over, hearing him, and falls back a step. "Hey, bubby."

Then she murmurs, "Have fun," and goes back inside and Jonah slings an arm over his shoulder and pulls him away.

"C'mon. I'm starved."

Kurt was going to stay at Joy's a moment and say something like, "I have a ton a candy left," and wait for her to smile and say, "Not me. I went out."

"Trick 'r treating?" he'd ask.

Maybe she'd have a picture of her little boy and he'd look at it and not see anything wrong.

"Cute," he'd say.

"We went all over town for that costume."

At his car, he stops, looks over at Jonah, and Jonah looks away, about to start laughing. Kurt wishes he didn't show everything he thinks because he is thinking about something else now too that he doesn't want to talk about. But maybe he isn't giving that away because Jonah just swipes his face on his shoulder to hide his laugh, looks back up again and says, "Chinese okay?"

"Sure."

Pete and Cora wrote their own vows, saying them on the wet lawn Bobby witlessly watered that morning, grassy water staining the hem of Cora's dress. She said her vows with her arms around Pete's neck, smiling her clownish smile at him. She remembered her vows, but Pete forgot his, screwed up his face, trying to remember, feeling Cora's antsiness, her weight shifting impatiently onto her hip before he said, "Yeah, the same for me too."

Cora hit him in the chest. "Are you high? Those are your fuckin' vows?"

"Well, I wrote something," he said, patting at his pockets again.

"Jesus Christ, I can't believe I'm doing this."

Then Pete shrugged with an embarrassed grin and said, "I can't believe I got this lucky."

Setting them up was a whim Ray suddenly doubts. Pete lit up at the sight of her and nothing she ever said fazed him. She didn't have to give up anything by marrying Pete and Ray didn't have to give up her. Occasionally, he thought about Pete and told himself that Pete had to know. It never made him feel bad though, and he doesn't feel bad now. Pete wouldn't have Cora without Ray and Ray never felt any inclination to back away. It was the way things were. But tonight, with Cora's bare torso lit like gold from behind, it isn't the way it's supposed to be. It's supposed to be easy, friendly, reliable. No strings because there never were strings before. All the other times, he just left her, met that lascivious twinkle in her eye with his own. Because he'd be back. He always was. He lives his life in ever returning circles, but here, in the kitchen, is a thing he never wanted: a woman in love. She is ending it, ruining it, cheating him out of it somehow by being somebody she never was before.

He stares at her silently for a moment. Her hair is beginning to wilt against her face and her chest heaves as she breathes, making him think of Venus in the spume. He feels tired and his whiskers make his face itch. When she moves, coming closer again, turning a dusky white, and lifts her arms, he takes her by the shoulders and pushes her away.

"You really are pissing me off, woman. Trust me. You are doin' nothin' to turn me on right now."

She swings, surprising him, befuddlement like a stupor. He doesn't even think to move, just watches her hand fly up and feels it connect with his face. His head rocks sideways, stills for a moment, then moves back again, his eyes on her face.

"Fuck, Cora." His tongue moves in his mouth. The inside of his cheek feels pulpy.

"You asked for it," she says.

"Actually, I was askin' you to leave."

Her shoulders sink. "Ray, c'mon. This isn't funny. Who's better for you? You know I am. I'm just like you."

"You just hit me."

His face almost stings, but the idea that somebody who is supposed to love him just hit him numbs it. Numbs him on the inside too. He can barely feel his face. Barely cares about Cora anymore. "I mean it, Cora. Go. Get the fuck out."

"You asshole."

She is balling up her fists, arms stiff at her sides. Remembering her blouse, he picks it up and throws it at her, grabbing one of her arms as she throws it up in surprise, forcing her out through the open door. She stumbles on the porch. Stepping back in, he picks up the blouse on the floor and tosses it over again, staring at her, tongue still exploring the inside of his cheek.

"You bastard, Ray. You're gonna regret this, I promise."

"I doubt it. Regret really ain't my thing."

He doesn't speak anymore, drinks his beer standing in the doorway to keep her out. She's leaning against the porch railing, buttoning up her blouse, flinging her hair back. Her face twists and he wonders how far she can go, but then she just whirls away, darting down the porch steps, looking back in the wedge of light spilling out her car door.

"I hate your fucking guts," she says.

He laughs and goes back inside.

At the shop, he calls Will and Susie answers. He likes her voice. It comes out in a Marilyn Monroe type whisper and he pictures her in a silky white robe with her blonde hair in curls until he hears the tiny snaps of the gum she's chewing. He laughs and she pulls the phone away from her ear.

"Hey, babe."

"Susie," she whispers.

Will is lying on the bed and she keeps checking the movement of his chest.

"I'm lookin' for Will."

She backs up into the hallway and then leans her shoulder against the door sill. There is no sound but the wind outside, no light but the dull seep of a night light out the bathroom door. She whispers again, her Marilyn Monroe impression. "Who're you?"

Ray feels slightly fascinated. "Wycowski."

"You can't talk to 'im."

The tinge of outrage in her voice intrigues him. "Why not?"

"You know."

He laughs, dropping a bottle of beer in a bin under the sink. "Okay, babe. I'll catch him another time."

"Susie," she whispers.

"Susie," he agrees.

Craig's cousin met Ray at a party at Will's. It was almost morning and Will was sleepless and starting to act nervous and then Ray came in and all Will's energy focused on him. Ray just sat there mostly while Will talked and Craig's cousin liked him just because he looked like he was about to start laughing any minute and always would. Will was starting to gulp at the air.

"Check this out," he said abruptly, pulling off his sweaty shirt to show off the marks on his skin that he didn't really have. "I got hell a beat."

Then Ray showed him his tattoo of a hotdog and Will talked some more and Ray told a story, and then he sat back with his arms hanging over the arms of the chair that became Susie's, looked around and said, "Man, this shindig is dead."

"I got my friends here," said Will, twisting at the waist with his arms wide open. He was shiny with sweat and his eyes were bright and his nerves were on edge. "I got Jimbo an' Andy an'…an'…."

"Roger," said Jimbo.

"Roger…an' I got *Trev!*"

"Minions," said Ray between swallows of his drink.

"Good word," said Craig's cousin. Debby was sitting on the arm of his chair and he sprawled backwards, smiling easily.

Will wasn't sure about that word, just stood there, rubbing his shoulder and beginning to frown. He looked at Craig's cousin to explain.

"Means subjects." Will still wasn't sure. Craig's cousin went on. "Roy, man. Roy had subjects. Roy was a king. Elvis was no king. No way. Roy was, man. King Roy."

Ray's lips parted and began to go up in an amused smile. Craig's cousin smiled too because he knew Ray didn't like Roy Orbison, although he didn't know how he knew this any more than he could explain the things he saw. He just saw things and knew things, the way he knew Ray's father wanted to name Ray Roy, but Ray's mother wouldn't let him.

"A goddam king," said Craig's cousin. "Elvis wasn't any king. Roy Orbison was a king. King Roy, man. Elvis wasn't even a duke. Duke Ellington was a duke. Elvis was—"

Ray yelled: *"Shuuuut uuuup!"* And then Will murmured, "Ain't a fan."

"Ain't a minion," said Craig's cousin and Ray laughed at that and saluted him with his glass. "Okay, bub. Your point."

Craig's cousin liked him.

Next door, Ray gets a drink at the bar, about to sit down until he sees Son and Craig's cousin at a table across the room. Then his stomach suddenly knots and he takes a long swallow of his drink before he continues over. Purple and blue bruises cover Son's face in giant splotches. Kicking a chair out with his boot, Ray sits down and says, "What the hell happened to you?"

Craig's cousin casts his eyes to the glass in his fingers and Son's face reddens. "Will. Jimbo. Andy."

Ray sets his glass down, then wiggles his fingers at him. "C'mon. Out with it."

"Out with what? They jumped me."

"Just like that?"

"Yeah. Just like that." Son's anger is turning the skin under his eyes white.

"No reason?"

"Yeah, a reason. Will started pokin' at me the minute I got up here."

"That's not jumpin' a dude for no reason."

"He stole my jacket. I wanted it back."

Ray wipes at his face, feeling his own anger. "Yeah, you aren't wearin' it, are you?"

"Fucker was baitin' me."

"You lost me on the stole your jacket part. That doesn't make any sense."

"He took it."

"Were you lookin' at the time?"

"I forgot it, okay? I forgot it at the house. I was pissed. We got in a fight an' I forgot it."

"Jesus, kid, is there anybody you don't fight with?"

Son gapes at him. "Look who's talkin'."

"With strangers. I fight with strangers. You can't get on with anybody except this dude here an' that's just because he likes everybody."

Craig's cousin takes a swallow of his drink. Son's jaw is working back and forth. "I want my jacket back."

"Well, don't look at me, kid. You treat it that way, you live with it."

"Well, what the fuck did you come back for?"

Ray gets up with his empty glass and kicks his chair back in, rocking the table. "Beats the hell outta me."

The lights in the ceiling start to move, a slow orbit growing wider, speeding up. Son swallows, leaning his head back against the chair, stretching his neck.

Craig's cousin leans in. "Take it easy."

"God, he pisses me off," Son mutters.

He can feel Craig's cousin lean back, feels his watchful stare, giving him what Ray never did. It makes him laugh to hear Ray remember things that he doesn't. He thinks Ray's life is so full because he just doesn't forget anything and imagines the clutter in Ray's head: piles of junk, collections of things he doesn't use, never will use, refuse and unopened boxes, stray tools and jewelry and tee-shirts commemorating every place he's ever been. Garbage bags full of tee-shirts. A hoard of uselessness crowding out the rooms of his life. It annoys him that Ray always seems to know where he's going though and amuses him that Ray remembers things that are fantasies to Son, like going to the Oakland Zoo on their birthdays for years when the only time Son remembers was when they were on a ride over the park and Ed was in the car behind them, rocking the cables.

They went to Caspar's a lot but that only reminds him that that's where Ray took him on the day he told him he was going away with Ed for a while and a while turned into years.

Now he lifts his head and says, "I don't feel good," and Craig's cousin pushes himself up and says, "You need to eat." He feels slightly woozy getting up, but steadies in the cold air outside.

Wayne put a mirror on the outside of their bedroom door to make the hall look brighter. When it was open Ray could see her bed without looking in, the puffy, pale blue comforter and her skirt lying on it, shoes below. She never put her skirt on until she was ready to go, came out for her coffee in her slip and blouse, looking in at him on her way by.

He liked it when she said, "I don't have any cash on me so come by Marie's," because that was where she always ate her lunch and when she didn't have any money her friend Marie always gave him a free hamburger.

"Too bad this isn't Caspar's," he said once.

Irene laughed the same way she used to laugh before Wayne left. Marie's is gone now and the drug store next to it too. He thinks of Cora stopping at a place like Marie's on her way home, eating anything without raspberries.

It's cold enough now to think about Christmas.

Outside of town the sky is crystal clear and full of stars. At work, fir needles always litter the hall floor and muddy water pools in the grooves of the mat at the door. Standing outside the fan of light coming through the open door, Jonah looks back inside. The hallway is empty, then Rob Chilburn and a man with a blond ponytail come out of the lunch room. Bending his head, Jonah lights a cigarette, sucks smoke into his lungs and breathes out slowly.

At the doors to the work floor, the man with the ponytail pauses and looks back, Chilburn waiting with a half-open door resting against his palm, Jonah motionless. Of course, the man can't see him, maybe just the tip of his cigarette.

Then when the doors close, Jonah goes inside, stopping in the lunch room for coffee. Gus comes over right away. "Have you seen 'im yet?"

"Who?"

"We have a new guy startin' tonight."

He puts his cigarette back between his lips and nods. "Good."

Gus stares. "You aren't supposed to smoke in here."

"So sue me."

Gus makes a face at him. "I'm just sayin'."

"I'm puttin' it out anyway," he says, tossing it into the sink.

Gus leaves and Jonah follows him. The blond is named Wally Cumberland and his hair is long and straight except where it's curly and ginger-colored at his ears. When Rob brings him over, he's chewing on a wad of pink gum.

"How ya doin'?"

Jonah tosses his coffee away before he answers and then says, "Stuff sucks."

Wally's hand comes out. Jonah takes it.

"Nice t' meet ya."

"Yeah. You too."

"Wally's new at this," Chilburn says.

"Just prefab before. Cookie cutter stuff."

His mouth is almost always open and after he chews his gum on one side a couple of times he switches over and chews it on the other side. He smells like ice cream or pop and makes Jonah think of the beer he just drank. He looks at Rob, who is staring back at him.

"I learn pretty easy," says Wally.

"Easy stuff," says Jonah, pulling on his gloves. Wally backs up then and he says, "C'mon," and takes him over to a wooden crate full of gloves against a wall. "Extras. Probably wanna get your own though."

"Definitely."

While he's looking, Gus comes over and tosses a glove in the crate. "Hole," he explains.

Jonah stares at him and then says, "Which makes it garbage. What'd you put it in there for?"

"Oh."

Wally sticks out his hand again. "Wally."

"Gus."

Jonah is standing with his weight on one leg, watching him go through the gloves again. "Prefab, huh?"

"Yeaaaah," Wally drawls as he pulls a glove on. Jonah frowns. "Kiddie toys," he adds.

"Like Big Wheels?"

"Yeah."

His gum pops from cheek to cheek.

"All the stuff I see's made in places like China."

"The good stuff, yeah. You want cheap, though, you come see Wally Ling-Ling. Cheap-A-Rama. Cheap Wally Ling-Ling." Gus's mouth opens in shock. Wally grins and goes on. "Ain't no fancy Big Wheels at Wally's. I buy cheap. You buy cheap. You come Christmas to Wally's. Ain't no cheaper! Wally give free candy canes, no warranties. Used stuff," he adds. "Good Will Specials. I used to work there too."

Irene, at Christmas, used to sing a song he can't remember. He remembers the other song she sang. That was the sound he woke up to, her singing in the bathroom. His room was next to hers at the back of the house with the doughboy pool just outside the window. She sang with the water splashing in the sink and she sounded almost happy unless she saw him, awakened by her song, sometimes looking in to see her sitting in her slip and bra, her blouse on a hanger on the knob of the closet door. It was always the same, every morning.

"I'm nobody's baby...I don't know why...."

Her smile was slow, almost loveless, like Cora's. Cora's voice, venomous. "I hate your fucking guts."

Or maybe she half loves him again in a place she found to stop at. A Denny's or someplace like the Waffle Place, eating anything with blueberries or peaches or apples, staring outside where it's dark or blue neon and starless.

Cora the Lonely.

He looks at Kurt, who's as happy as people at Christmas, and thinks about that city he and Ed had to live in, and the White Castle's there, and the sootiness that Ed never saw.

"It's fuckin' filthy here," he said.

Ed looked surprised. "No, it's not."

Ray knows he's drunk. He smiles and presses at his eyes with his fingertips.

"I don't usually get like this," he murmurs.

He wonders where Cora really is. She probably didn't stop anywhere. All she's doing now is probably trying to get home to Pete. A Venus de Milo he won't ever love again.

Kurt looks over when he laughs.

"Man, I'm tanked."

Errol's is dark and he can see outside the windows. It reminds him of the movies he used to watch with Wayne about atomic bombs that blew up the world and only a couple of people and mutants survived. The people were usually strangers and didn't like each other and somebody always had a secret.

He looks over at Kurt again. "Do you ever wonder about the end of the world?"

"Not really."

"A lot a parties, I bet."

Not for Cora though. She'll be at home, alone by her empty house, on the lawn where she married Pete. She didn't even look back at the house she was leaving yesterday. She just came out with her suitcase and stood on the porch, giving Ray a look he didn't really like.

"Are you comin' or what?" he asked and didn't like her smile either.

She drove and he rode his bike behind or ahead of her, beside her sometimes, pulling her eyes off the freeway onto him. Then he rode onto an off ramp and she followed him. He used to go to a place called the Coffee Tree on his way by here, but it was gone now.

They stopped for lunch at the Black Oak instead where he ate the rest of Cora's sandwich when she was done, waited for her outside, and saw her come out with that look again.

"Are you gonna clue me in?" he asked.

"What?"

"You've got somethin' on your mind."

She smiled over the roof of her car. "Maybe," she agreed. They started out late and only had a few more hours of daylight. At night they stopped at a motel and when he woke up once she was awake too, just watching him.

"You're beginnin' to creep me out," he muttered, rolling away from her.

At lunch the next day at a diner called the Crackle Cafe, she slipped her fingers under his where his hand lay on the table and he pulled away. "I need somethin' to drink."

They stopped at a nearby bar and he went in and she followed, taking a seat in back where she could see the rest of the bar. The place was almost empty, one couple at a table, a man at the counter. Ray sat beside her with a view on the door.

"I like this," she said.

"You like what?"

"This."

He shrugged, not knowing what she meant or not wanting to, and looked away. Then, when he was about halfway through his drink, she looked over and said, "I want to stay with you."

His stomach curdled. He burped loudly and said, "Fuck."

"That's it. You don't have anything else to say?"

"We were supposed to go to Caspar's, Cora. Shit. Why didn't you remind me?"

She sat back and drank her wine without talking. He knew she was trying to figure him out. The way Cora thought, he couldn't not want her. He almost dozed there, head back against the wall, glass in his fingers. Her awareness of him was almost physical. He could feel her. He pictured her in the red beret, the jeans with the laces in back that she was wearing the first time he saw her. She wore those jeans on their first date too. He took her to a friend's house and left her alone in the living room. It must have been for a long time, but she was still there when he came back out and pulled her up. "C'mon," he said. "Time for some fun."

They went into the city and ate on the wharf and then went to the wax museum and all the shops he hadn't gone into since he was little, and then back to that house where he said, "Be back in a while," and left her alone again, driving off with the people who lived there.

It was almost morning when he came back and she said, "I wanna go home."

She didn't look mad, just tired.

On the way, he pulled off the freeway though, and they rode underneath trees that were still dark although the sky through their limbs was growing smoky. He stopped in a turn out and when she got off, he said, "Down there." She went past a metal barrier where there was a picnic table somebody put under the trees. Alone in the dark, he pulled her top off and came at her with a grin she could see in the gray light.

When he first kissed her she almost pulled away, almost irritably, but he grabbed on and then she unbuttoned his pants and her lips never left his. There were cars going by and the air was cold.

Afterwards he laughed and said, "God, I love that," and moved his fingers over hers curiously. He could see her clearly then and the headlights on the freeway above were growing lighter. "You look great too," he added.

She looked marble white and he knew that this was the back of somebody's yard and that up closer to the house there was a statue that reminded him of her.

Now it's Venus de Milo he thinks of.

"Caspar's after this," he said.

Smiling, Craig's cousin feels little nips on his face, cheeks, chin, the tip of his nose, a flutter of lips on his eyelids, a tongue flicking the corners of his mouth, teeth nipping his bottom lip. Son's body hovers over his, mouth brushing his neck, nipping again. He rolls his head back, arms over his head, Son's face in an armpit, licking at his sweaty skin, a flutter of breath on his ribs, teeth scraping, a tongue in his belly button. Groaning, he swings his arms down, grabs Son by the hair and arches his belly up. Son's mouth moves, swallows him, hot and hungry. His head drops back, fingers pulling in Son's hair, airborne, soaring through clouds and space, happy.

Cora stops for gas, frozen in the cold, a mini-mart on a corner and a Carrow's on another and a big cement building on the other side.

Ray's picture of her is hers too. She's afraid her house is empty and the air feels colder, Christmas air, still and icy.

There's a ring around the moon.

———————

Outside the factory, Jonah lights another cigarette, Wally gumless, smoking too.

"Tryin' to quit," says Wally.

"That what the gum's for?"

"That's what the cigs are for."

At the bar Ray is showing Kurt a penny. It is dark out but still and silent. The air inside smells like bubble gum soap. Chairs are on the tables, glasses lying on cloths to dry. At the counter, Ray is leaning closer to the light, throwing his shadow over the penny. He stretches it out, marveling at the tremor in his fingers. Kurt leans over too.

"You use jus' a regular penny," he says, "an' the machine stamps a picture on it." He thinks he is slurring, but he isn't sure.

George looks at the penny too.

"It's a flower."

"A poppy."

Cora said that poppies were for remembrance. Later on, when he tells Miri that, she'll say said "Rosemary's for remembrance."

Kurt says, "Cool."

"Yeah." Ray squeezes his fingers around it.

George is flipping off the lights. Outside, Ray looks longingly at his bike, then Kurt nudges him gently and says, "Over here."

Sighing, he follows him to the green car with the shiny spoked hubcaps. "'Preciate this," he says.

"No problem."

The car lulls him into a peaceful stupor. The penny in his palm grows sweaty. Almost home, Kurt rolls down his window and the cold air rouses Ray a little. He sits up, yawning, and rubs his face. He keeps his eyes closed until the car rolls to a stop though, then looks at the dark house and pushes open his door.

"You're a good friend, Kurt." Halfway out of the car, he looks back and tosses over Cora's penny. "You keep it."

Then a light comes on in the house and he stops on the walkway, waiting for her. He sways a little bit, but the cold is waking him up. Then the door opens and she starts down to him, barefoot, and he can tell just by the look in her eyes that she knows everything about him and that none of it matters to her.

When she reaches him, he picks her up and carries her back up the walkway.

"Ray," she whispers.

"Don't worry, babe. You win."

The apartment building is waking up. Water pinging in the pipes. Quiet underneath him though. Kurt tries to imagine that Joy feels any worry, but he can't. Her cool apartment, cool in winter, cool in summer. Her easeful life. He tries to remember his dreams, but he can't do that either. He didn't sleep long, slapped off his alarm, distressed and sweaty. He sits up, dropping his head in his hands, and wishes for coolness, ease. He wonders if he has ever done anything right in his life. All the time fantasizing about Joy, imagining conversations they never have, impressing her with a gun she never saw and he will probably never see again either.

Struggling to move, he gets up and takes a shower. The heat makes him sick and he turns the cold on high. After he gets out he starts to shiver. When he got home from Ray's, he popped open the glove box to toss Ray's penny inside, then leaned over and pulled out the bottle of bourbon. His engine ticked a pleasant rhythm. The penny pinged somewhere in the back of the glove box. He pulled out a square of cloth, oddly warm and soft. Wadding it up, he put it to his mouth, then pushed it back into the glove box and came upstairs.

Outside, it's still dark, the sky almost cottony, starless, like something he can just reach up and touch. Dressed now, he pulls his cap on his head and hurries out to his car. He wants a cup of coffee, but he doesn't stop. The streets are almost empty, the signal lights long, but soon he's out of town, driving with his window down, cold air blowing in.

At lunch, when Wally jumped up on the edge of the pickup to sit, Jonah remembered Kurt's gun and turned around to rest his arms across the side of the truck bed and look down, but it was too dark to see. The fact of it still being there vaguely astonished him. When he took it, he told himself that he'd put it somewhere safe when he got home and wondered now as he hung over the truck bed if the reason he left it there was because he wouldn't be safe from it anywhere else. He took it almost by rote, barely thinking, just exchanging it for Kurt's bottle of bourbon. But afterwards, he thought about it, and he knew he'd think about it if it was anywhere in the house. He would have the same compulsion that made him take it in the first place and would sit quietly in the house when Ally was gone and contemplate the peacefulness of it, of putting it in his mouth and pulling the trigger. Then everything would end quickly and suddenly, a burst of light maybe. Swimming at Ivy's he sometimes sank, drifted down to a bottomless bottom, watched the light receding up above like an old fading memory until his bursting lungs propelled him up and he broke the surface with a pounding heart. He kept coming back, kept trying. His eyes moved away from the gun with the thought that it was strange that of all the things he'd done in his life, loving somebody might be the worst.

Now the sun is up and Cora is dreaming of home. She's sleeping in her car and it feels like it's moving. She pictures her street and sees her house. The grass is steamy and the light shines off the windows. She goes inside and hears the TV, but there's nobody there. The beds are all unmade. In the kitchen, she passes cereal bowls on the table with milk dried inside and realizes they've been gone for a long time. Then she wakes up and starts up her car again.

At the factory, Kurt stomps in the chilly air outside. His breath puffs and ribbons of mist come out of the fir trees. He thinks about Dorothy again, the scarecrow and the tin man and Glenda and the Great Wizard of Oz.

A little while later, Jonah comes out with a cigarette he's about to light and stops with a look of surprise. He isn't thinking about the gun anymore and it's been in the back of his truck for days now anyway.

"You're in early."

"Yeah."

He lights his cigarette with a frown and walks on. Kurt follows and they get into Jonah's pickup and sit without looking at each other. Then Jonah cracks his window and Kurt says, "Cold."

He nods, picks a piece of tobacco off his tongue and looks over. "I have some news for you this time," he says. "We got us a new guy."

"Oh."

"You didn't know?"

Kurt shrugs. "Wes said maybe."

"Wes didn't know."

"It's a good thing though. We need the help."

"Yeah."

Jonah leans over and takes his bottle of bourbon out of the glove box. The lid stays open and Kurt looks in. It's a lot like his except for a bottle of Ally's perfume. Jonah drinks and passes the bottle over. Kurt takes it and cracks his window too. It smells good outside and the sky is growing blue. He sits quietly, uncertainly, giving Jonah the bottle when he reaches back over.

"Ask Wes about me," Jonah says after a moment. "I need to know. I think Rob wants me out."

"No way."

He nods and takes another drink, eyes on the firs as the mists float out and blow away. Kurt's eyes move from the glove box to the floor. Jonah stares and frowns as Kurt scoots up and reaches under his seat with a slightly strained look on his face.

"Hell you doin'?"

"Thought I dropped the bottle cap," says Kurt, sitting back up again.

"I have it."

"Oh."

Jonah sighs and flicks his cigarette outside. The sky reminds him of summer and strawberries.

"Nice day," he murmurs.

At home he goes swimming and Kurt puts his bowl of Halloween candy on a chair in the courtyard and goes back upstairs to pack his lunch.

18

♦ Thanksgiving ♦

The lawn chairs are still on the hillside, wreathed in mists, dank cold water in the open graves. Once, Fin looks in one and a corpse's eyes snap open, flinging him up out of the dream. He sits with his knees bent, head in his hands, panting in bed. Outside, the wind patters at the window. It is dark, but Grace isn't home yet. Switching on the light, he gets up and looks outside, but he can't see anything. There could be graves out there, or just weeds. There is no alcohol in the apartment, nothing he can do with his restlessness. Dropping on the couch, he watches TV for a while, throat tightening, mouth filling with saliva. He gets up for a glass of water, feels its thinness, brackish and metallic. His gaze lingers on the cupboards, fingers rising to a knob. He opens them all, but there is nothing there, just dishes, glasses, cans and boxes.

A sudden thump of wind rattles at the glass, draws him away.

Scrubbing at his mouth almost angrily, he suddenly goes through the door, out into the sun-flowered hall, out into the cold. The air bites through his tee-shirt. He takes deep breaths, looking across the street, misty windows hiding the inside of the bar. Shadows move. The light looks warm. His heart starts to race and the cold feels good. All of a sudden, he is running down the stairs, feet on dirt and soggy weeds. He veers over to the pavement, feels the rough surface under his feet and begins to run away from Oly Way. The road leads straight into firs and darkness, then begins to rise and curve between steep embankments. He can't see. The stars are covered by clouds. There's a thread of fear that begins to wind tighter and tighter as he runs, following the road from memory. His breath is a cloud that breaks apart in the wind. He falls once, landing hard on a knee, pain sparking lights in his eyes. A bluish cast comes over the scene ahead, revealing a blur of firs on either side of him, wispy clouds thinning above.

He keeps running, in pajama bottoms and tee-shirt, skin numb. He isn't sure he can feel his feet anymore. The wind begins to blow again, rasping and wheezing to the rhythm of his own breaths. He's panting, ears ringing, head swimming. Then he is falling again, rolling into a needle-strewn depression on the side of the road. His heart is drumming in his throat and his mouth is dry. The pain begins to burn. In his feet, his knee, his chest. Groaning, he rolls over and staggers up, running again, slower now, hearing the slap of his feet, air bursting out of him. He slows, walking, feeling the cold seize him, shake him. The dark is thick and heavy, and the air feels like water in his lungs.

After a long time, a few lights appear, winking through the blowing fir branches, Oly Way. Mulligan's blue sign is dark, invisible, a dull light deep within. He feels the weeds under his feet. Nights have passed maybe, time churning away in a different dimension. He feels suddenly bereft and afraid and starts running again. The windows at Grace's are lit, bedroom and living room. He climbs the steps on legs that suddenly quiver. Opening the door, he hears her coming out to him, worried, eyes flying open.

"Oh, my God."

She grabs him around the waist and he begins to laugh. "I went for a run," he gasps. His face is red and cold radiates off him.

"My God, you're freezing," she says.

"I'm sorry."

She covers him with blankets, helps him stretch a bloody leg across the coffee table. The knee of his pajamas hangs by a flap, the skin of his knee raw and pitted. "Are you insane?"

"No," he says, shaking his head and smiling happily at her. "I feel good." His night's demon vanquished in the bitter cold outside. With his knee bandaged and a change of pajamas, he sleeps without dreams.

George is putting up a Christmas tree. All the chairs are upside down on the tables and there's a mop in a metal bucket in the dark hallway. A while ago, Ray was next door with Kurt where they could see their breaths every time they went near the open doors in the other part of the shop. Now Kurt is thinking about a tree that looked like it was made out of pipe cleaners on an Astroturf covered porch and Ray is thinking about Ed's Santa cap. The first time Ray saw that cap, he was waiting for Ed by a steamy window at a White Castle's where he pulled a clear streak down the glass with the side of his fist and saw Ed's car appear in the flurries of snow. It was a blue Nova and like most cars reminded him of Wayne and he imagined Wayne driving away in it.

"You eat already?" asked Ed when he came in.

Ray couldn't believe he was looking at Ed in a Santa cap. Or that it was Christmas. "No," he said.

He was sitting in a booth up front where slushy puddles led from the front door to the counter and he couldn't get warm because it was always busy and people kept coming in and out.

"White Castle's are the best," said Ed.

"Caspar's," he murmured.

Now he's watching George get up and stand back from the tree.

"Looks good," says Kurt with a yawn.

George picks it up and takes it down the dark hall. The bucket and mop go next, wheels creaking up to the door of the storage closet.

In a couple of days, the Christmas decorations will come out all across town, bells and stars on the light poles, pictures of candy canes and Santa's sleigh painted on windows, and lights that will stay on all night.

Tonight, though, it's dark.

At home, Ray sits down on the couch with the TV on, feet up on the coffee table, flipping through reruns, cooking shows, toy commercials. There's a Christmas tree glowing in a make-believe window. A car salesman in a Santa suit. Which makes him picture Ed again, sitting in a White Castle's in that stupid Santa cap of his.

"This place is fuckin' filthy," Ray said and that time he used his whole forearm to smear a clear streak across the window.

Ed looked surprised. "No, it's not."

"No fuckin' Caspar's."

Ed brought Caspar's back to the motel room before they left town. Ray gave up the little house in Antioch and quit his job. It was still warm out and he could swim in the pool at night. He didn't care about that at first though. He just lay on the bed with the TV on or stared in the mirror over the dresser at the picture of the ocean with its sunlit waves.

One time, he looked over at Ed in a chair in the corner of the room. Ed looked strange to him, and when Ed saw Ray, he leaned forward and smiled at him. "You went at me, Ray."

"Whadda you mean?" he murmured because he didn't remember anything and felt worried about that. It reminded him of the party Ed's father gave.

"You tried to choke me."

"Oh."

Their room had a kitchenette with a transom window on the back alley and there was a church on the lot behind them. On Sundays, the sound of cars woke him up, muted singing on the autumn air. All the time there he kept thinking about the place they stayed in with Kathy. One night after Ed poured a little bourbon into his glass and drank it, he came over and pulled Ray up off the bed.

"C'mon. Let's go for a swim."

There were lights on outside, almost like Christmas, decorations already in the stores.

He begins to hum a carol he can't remember the name to. "Hm…hm, hm, hm…hm."

Now it's almost Christmas again, Christmas in a sooty city with sooty snow and Ed. "Quit mopin', Ray. Kid's old enough for Christmas without dad."

Outside, he swam under the stars with Ed on the pool's edge, legs kicking gently. Or maybe he sank and saw the lights behind the brown and orange curtains slowly go out and maybe Ed swam over, smiling curiously at him.

"You laugh at the damnedest things," said Ed.

On the shallow side of the pool, he lay on the steps and Ed swam backwards, kicking gently.

All the giant lights behind the orange and brown curtains went out as he sank deeper into the pool and came back on again when Ed pulled him up. "We're gonna go gets us some White Castle's, Ray."

Someplace far away he didn't want to be. His fingers were splintless and ribbons of pink swirled in the water as he moved. Ed pulled him over to the steps on the shallow side. "Wish I had a pool at my place," said Ed.

"Why'd you rent there then?"

"Cool wall," he said without a smile.

It was a stone wall that faced the front door. The rocks were a reddish brown and some were smooth and some were rough and sharp. The last time he went over there Ed stood in the door with the wall behind him and said, "Quit your job?"

"I told you I would."

"Your boss was cool?"

Ray was angry. "I told you that too."

"Okay."

The TV was on and he saw dishes in the sink and thought about the house he just left and saw Ed watching him and said, "The hell you lookin' at?"

Ed just shrugged and went over to the refrigerator. He came back with a beer. "I don' wan' any goddam beer," said Ray.

"An' I don' wanna mix it up," said Ed.

"Mix what up?"

Ed just shrugged again.

Ray snorted. "You think you can take me?"

"I can take you."

So Ray slugged him and Ed stumbled back and caught himself, swiped at his mouth with a smile and said, "We can't fight, Ray. Cops can't come here."

But Ray swung anyway and Ed ducked and Ray hit the wall with the stones and pulled back, bending over the ball of his fist with a grimace. "Fuck."

"You're actin' a little mental right now, Ray. You know that, right?"

Ray laughed at him. "You're callin' me mental?"

There was no animosity in Ed's smile, no worry, no concern. Just curiosity. Ray was a bug under a water glass he might put out into the summer sun just to watch. "You should sit down, Ray. Drink your beer. Your hand's bloody," he commented.

Ray looked at it, flexed his fingers, thought of Wayne, St. Louis, his mother's boyfriends, swung back to the wall and slugged it again. Ed came up to him, leaned on the corner of the wall and watched. Ray swung with both his fists in a numb quick frenzy. When Ed stepped suddenly in front of him, a fist glanced off of Ed's shoulder and he fell backwards, landing on the floor with a grunt. He started laughing a moment later and sensed Ed crouching down beside him.

"You okay, Ray?"

There was some emotion in his voice then. Ed was tipping up the water glass to look curiously beneath it.

"Hell, yeah." He kept blinking and sweat kept pouring into his eyes. Then blinking again, he saw Ed's smile, slow and admiring. "You are one crazy dude, Wycowski."

Miri looked at Ed's picture after he called one day and asked, "This Ray's old lady?" She got goose bumps from the sound of his voice and forgot to say anything, just listened to the deadness of the air before he said, "Tell 'im Ed called." Then she said, "Okay," and went to look at his picture again. That was the one of him and a fourteen year old Son sitting at a kitchen table. The house was a small two bedroom, white stucco with a square of lawn out front that Ray paid a boy next door to mow until Son came to live with him.

"You can mow it now. Earn your keep," he said.

Sour grass grew in the shade under the porch roof, lemon yellow flowers out of the way of the lawnmower. One day when Ray and Son came home, Ed was there, sitting with his dusty boots planted on the walkway and his dusty bike on the driveway, chewing on a piece of the sour grass.

It was late and the last of the sun made its way across the porch. Ed spat out a piece of grass and squinted at him as he came up.

"Damn. Ed."

Ed nodded and began to smile. "Long time."

"Couple years."

Ed was supposed to follow after Ray went on ahead of him, but he never did. "You look good," said Ed with a strange appraising smile. "Nice little setup too. Are you renting?"

"Nope. Price was too good to pass up."

"You're sounding pretty settled."

That reminded him of Son, who was standing between Ray and Ed with a scowl Ray knew he wouldn't even be aware of. When Ed's eyes lifted, Ray pulled Son back and dropped an arm across his chest to hold him there. "You remember my kid. Livin' with me now."

Ed leaned back a little, out of the sun and smiled again. He was still squinting though, eyeing Son curiously. "How you doin'?"

"Okay."

"Looks like your mom," he said to Ray. Ray always thought so too.

"You wanna beer, Ed?"

"Sure."

He got up with a slight grunt and they went inside; Ed took his beer and went out into the living room. "Most definitely a nice place."

"Thanks."

"Remember Jessie's?"

"That last place we were at?"

"Yeah."

"Sure."

"Gone. I went by to see it before I came here."

"What for?"

He was looking through the kitchen door at him. Ed sat on the couch and put his arm across the top. "I dunno. Old time's sake, I guess."

Ray took a drink of his beer and stared at him, remembering. The house was in back of a Taco Bell on a court with woodsy green apartment buildings at the end of a short dead-end street and a Jack-in-the-Box on the opposite corner. They were staying in town longer than Ray wanted. He was working for Gus then too. Getting bored, he guessed.

"You like this girl?" he asked one day.

"Good enough."

"I don' wanna get in your way."

"Up to you."

In his house, with Ed back again, he realized that he couldn't recall the girl's name until Ed said it, or the color of her eyes, or the sound of her voice, or anything else about her. She wasn't important to him and he doubted she was all that important to Ed. Looking back, he guessed that Ed had some scheme he was into with people he didn't want Ray to know about and it was convenient for Ray to leave. Ed had never been that way before, but Ray found out later that most of their years apart Ed spent in prison. Ed didn't just forget him and Ray is still sure that Ed's girl didn't really mean anything to him.

When Ed said, "You wanna go, that's okay," he was surprised, but

Ed said he'd meet up with him again and he believed him. At the signal light, though, before he pulled away and rode through the intersection, he saw Ed still there on the sidewalk, watching him. He couldn't see his expression but always imagined he could, a look like shock as Ray really disappeared, a look that hardened into the long-lived memory of a score to settle. Ed set him up, handed him a test he didn't even look at until it was too late. He was never sure what the test was or why Ed wanted to put him to it, but he knew that he failed, and when Ed came back, he knew that it wasn't forgotten.

But that was years before. The house in Antioch was a place he might stay a long time, he thought, the restlessness gone. Ed liked it too, sitting on Ray's couch with a beer and an arm across the top. That was the pose in the other picture of Ed Miri found in Ray's drawer.

"Yeah, real nice," he said.

On Thanksgiving morning, the Qwik Stop is open, but it doesn't have Christmas tree lights.

"Try Kmart," advises the clerk.

"Today?" asks Errol.

"I dunno. Tomorrow definitely. Big sales."

"Oh."

He got the idea to decorate when he saw the lights on a house across the lot. By the time he returns home there's a big plastic Rudolph on its roof.

The weeds are flat and silver with ice and curls of mist float slowly over the corner of the roof at the auto shop.

Ice covers Joy's birdbath in silver. She cracks it like glass with the water she pours in.

On the other side of the apartment building, Kurt walks over to his car and stamps his feet, looking up in time to see the sun top the giant bowling pin. Curls of mist unfurl from its plywood edges.

It is quiet out, almost empty of cars. The dome of Candi's catches the pale white sun. At Ray and Miri's, soft beams come through the blinds and curtains. The heater's on and air blows out of the vents. Miri sips her orange juice in the living room and watches a parade on TV. She likes it when a man picks up a little girl who looks like a cherry snow cone in her puffy red coat and lifts her up. A giant Barney is bobbing by in the clear, cold air.

Under the covers, Ray thinks of Christmas. The sound of the heater reminds him of home. He remembers the leaves in the pool and Irene making Wayne go to the store for new filters, the warm toasty smell of the heater when it first went on, Christmas lights going up outside, and Irene playing that song that he can't remember. The hi-fi was on one side of the fireplace and the TV was under the window beside it, and when she was listening to a record the lid on the hi-fi stayed up and he remembers the soft gray shadow it made on the wall in the wintertime and Irene's soft, shadowy face as she went by, humming her song and smiling her smile at him.

Only now it's Miri's smile. "Morning, Ray."

He comes up slowly, pushing an arm out from under the covers and sees her put a knee on the bed and lean closer, sitting on her hip, not really touching him, strangely shy.

"Hey, babe."

She smells like orange juice and reminds him of the mandarin oranges in Irene's ambrosia salad, the only oranges he likes anymore.

One Christmas, Irene invited Matt over and he came with bottles of champagne. She wore a dress made out of brown silk and the pearl earrings Wayne gave her and put on that song Ray can't remember. Matt sat on the couch with his arms across the top and said, "C'mon, babe. Sing."

Her voice was a bell at Christmastime, clear and high and pure.

"Your mom's good."

"But unappreciated," she added after she stopped and went back to the kitchen. Matt always put money on her dresser or by his coffee cup when he left.

"Appreciation," he said with a grin.

She had other boyfriends, but Matt was the one Ray slugged when he came home from school one day and found him swimming in their pool with a couple of beers on the platform Wayne had built, a girl without a top bobbing in the water beside him. The grass was raggedy with yellow circles and patches of burnt brown. He thought of Wayne and the rusty lawnmower in the back of the garage. After Wayne left, Irene bribed him to mow and he still didn't do it. It didn't make any sense to him, but he felt sorrier for Irene over that lawn than over Matt. The woman bobbing beside him pretended to be shocked when Ray saw her, but she wasn't.

Matt laughed and said, "Get a good look?"

He didn't answer. "You're cheatin' on my mom?"

Matt just shook his head like it didn't even matter and said, "You can't cheat on a whore, kid."

The beer cans flew, Ray's arm swinging across Wayne's platform. With a grimace of annoyance Matt hopped over the side of the pool and Ray sank a fist into Matt's stomach.

"Oomph." Whooshing out air with an exaggerated stagger, Matt drew his breath back in and began to laugh. "You're a touchy little fucker."

Ray's face was blazing red. Matt didn't come back again after that and moved out of the neighborhood a few months later. When Ray was sixteen, they met up again at a party and laughed about that fight. Matt didn't ask about Irene and Ray didn't offer any information. When the party ended, it was morning and Ray rode with Matt to the Gilroy Garlic Festival where he went again with Ed and Son years later and bought a tee-shirt that Miri took to sleep in. Now, sitting on the bed beside him, she pulls off one with a teddy bear on it and folds her arms across her chest, reminding him a little bit of the girl in the pool with Matt.

———————

They are locked together with the sounds of the heater and the TV on in the other room. Hair and fingers tangle, her breath in his mouth, his heart drumming against hers. She rises up on him and her face is strained, worried. He sees her through a narrow tunnel. He can feel heat and the coolness where she was lying on him a moment ago. "Miri, what?"

"I want a baby."

His heart stops and the white outline around the drapes grows achingly white. In its brightness he sees the motel room he was living in with Kathy and the hospital with the gift store teddy bear and the flowers and the scrunched up angry baby face. Irene was pregnant when she married Wayne. Wayne always said they would've gotten married anyway.

When Cora got pregnant she was already married and he was afraid for a long time that the baby was really his. Once, when he was living closer to St. Louis, he thought about looking for Wayne. That's when he looked out of a White Castle's window and imagined him driving off in Ed's Nova. Going someplace warm maybe.

"Get off," he says.

"Ray…."

"Get off." She scoots backwards and Ray sits up on the edge of the bed, bent over, his head in his hands. His voice is rough sounding, angry. "Was this really the best time you could think of for this conversation?"

"No…I mean I wasn't thinking of a best time. I was thinking that I love you an' a baby's just a natural part of that."

His head tilts in her direction. "Is it? Does it go together for you, Miri? Because it doesn't for me. I'm real clear on that."

She leans closer, resting her weight on one arm. "Why, Ray? You love kids."

"I have a kid."

"I don't."

"Miri, listen to me. I can't do it again. I fucked up the one I have."

"No, you didn't. You don't give him enough credit."

"I know 'im. I don't give 'im any credit. Me, even less. I'm forty-three anyway. I don't have that kind of energy anymore. An' don't tell me about all these people who keep havin' kids at my age. I know what I put into it. I wouldn't give up havin' a kid for anything, but I was a lousy father an' there's no makin' up for that. I told you this shit, that I was outta his life for years, came back, didn't call 'im, didn't say I was home, partyin' for days when he showed up. I shouldn't've, but I let 'im stay. At one point he flat out asked me why I didn't let 'im know I was back. I said somethin' about gettin' settled, I was only back a week, blah, blah, blah. Well, he called me out on it, said he knew I'd been back a month by then. I just blew 'im off. I thought about 'im every fuckin' day. But the truth is I didn't think I could look 'im in the eye. I'm a fuckin' loser. I know that. An' I shouldn't've let 'im stay. I got rid of the drugs the minute I saw 'im, but why did I let 'im stay? Why do I keep bringin' 'im around drug dealers? He's a fuckin' addict. What the hell's wrong with me? You see what I mean, Miri? I hate talkin' about this shit an' I don't wanna try an' make good cuz I know I can't. I can't do it an' you better not put me in that position. You have no idea how fuckin' pissed off I'd be."

"You don't give anybody any credit, do you?"

He looks at her in annoyance. "Whadda you mean?"

"Do you really think I'd do something like that?"

"I'm just sayin' that if this is somethin' you want, I can't give it to you. I love you. I'm committed to you. I made the commitment you wanted me to make, but it's just to you. I don't want you to be unhappy. I don't want to think I'm makin' you unhappy."

She stares down at her hand on the bed, then looks sideways at the floor, the dresser with its drawer full of Cora, the mirror, not at him. She puts her tee-shirt back on.

"I guess I knew this."

He takes a deep breath, runs a hand across his face, looking sideways too, catching her out of the corner of his eye. "Are you okay?"

She nods, getting up. "I'm okay."

In the living room she sits down in front of the TV, pulling her tee-shirt over her knees.

The door is open at Grace's, airing out the muggy little apartment. The heater blows and the steamy windows are ajar. Grace looks askance at Fin sitting on the couch as she goes by.

"Come watch the parade with me," he says.

"You're wasting energy."

"With the TV?"

"The heater. The windows."

"Oh."

He likes the feel of cold and warmth at the same time. At dawn he went running again, sweaty and chilled, limping slightly on his sore knee. He's wearing jeans and a sweatshirt and when Grace comes back out of the bedroom in a dress the color of her eyes, she says, "You can't wear that."

"Do I have to go?"

"Yes. You have to get dressed. You have to pick up Sully. You don't want him to spend Thanksgiving alone, do you?"

"He always has."

The dress is shiny, darkens and lightens as she moves. He likes it, the black heels she's slipping on, fingers resting on the arm of the chair. Coming over, she bends down to him, face to face. "Your bad," she whispers, kissing him gently.

He feels himself flush and hears anger in his voice. "I never thought of it. An' anyway, I was alone too."

"Well, you aren't now. I want you with me, Fin. I don't want to be alone either. I don't like it."

"You'll be with your mother an' father."

"I'm alone without you. I want you with me," she says again.

He pushes himself up, wincing at his knee and follows her into the kitchen where she's emptying the dish drainer, setting glasses on a shelf. He flashes suddenly on a bottle of bourbon and leans almost dizzily against the sink.

"Why can't we be alone just the two of us?" He reaches over, feeling the fabric of her dress.

"That would make me sad."

"Why?" His eyes meet hers, the same lightening and darkening gray of her dress.

"I know you, Fin. Being alone isn't good for you."

His mouth moves, half smiles. "Is that so?"

"Yes," she says.

"You never used to talk to me like this."

"Like what?"

"Bossy."

She cocks her head at him. "Do you like it?"

"I kind of do."

"Good. Get dressed."

He sighs and limps away. Behind him in the living room is the sound of windows closing.

There's nobody at the mortuary. It's cold and Mr Torch's perfect lawns glitter with bits of ice. At Carl's, he sits against the gray wall, growing warm as the heater goes on. Carl looks outside, waiting for Scott to come back from the donut shop, and Kurt stomps his feet outside of the hospital and says, "We need somethin' to celebrate with."

Jonah is sitting on a wall that encloses a patio outside the cafeteria where there's an alcove with a vending machine for coffee and garden umbrellas leaning up in a corner and pots of primroses between the plastic tables.

Jonah lights a cigarette, drops his match and says, "We don't have anything to celebrate yet."

"Pretty soon," says Kurt, blowing into his cup of coffee.

Jonah shrugs, feeling the cold numb him. Being inside with Ally fills him with heat, a pressure that grips his chest and squeezes. He doesn't want to be inside with her. Her mother's with her. She doesn't need him. The smoke warms him and he flicks his cigarette away, wanting the cold back.

At the donut shop, Scott gets blueberry and chocolate donuts and

Will looks at Susie in their living room and says, "I feel like Jack-in-the-Box tonight."

"Jack-in-the-Box!"

"Yeah." She's in the terry cloth robe he hates and he's in the flannel pajama bottoms she bought him. "Dress up."

Holidays upset him. He isn't sure if he's happy or unhappy. Christmas is his favorite but all the carols and cookies and candies and decorations distress him. His anxiety jumps, nerves in his stomach, certainty of disaster. This morning Ray called him, said, "I'll be at the Club. Bring the jacket."

Which Will is willing to do. The jacket means nothing. But he wants it to mean nothing to Ray too, wants Son to mean nothing. Parading Susie on his arm is a statement to Ray. Will can already feel himself puffing up. Susie beats Miri. She's curvy and young and sassy. The sassy part he doesn't usually like, but as a comparison to Miri it is an enviable trait. He feels vaguely loving towards her. Then she ruins it.

"Jack-in-the-Box isn't special."

Meaning it's not Candi's and the Thanksgiving Day Buffet with candied yams and green bean casserole and coconut cream pie.

"It's special to me."

"C'mon, Will. It's Thanksgiving."

"*Dress up!*"

Even with Susie, meeting Ray worries him. He couldn't taste his Cocoa Puffs this morning and his feelings about Thanksgiving confuse him: he likes Jack-in-the-Box but doesn't like coconut cream pie.

"You don't love me!"

"I do toooo!"

On the same day Ed came into a White Castle's with a Santa cap on, Ray called Kathy, walking alone to a liquor store by the house they were staying in. The house belonged to Ed's family and it was old and narrow with dusty, faded carpets on the floor and stale musty air. Walking on the damp sidewalk, his breath a cloud, white and clear like the snow never was. He called her with one hand in his pocket, the phone at his ear, head down. In the distance, somebody was ringing bells. On the phone, he heard voices in the background.

"Hey, Kathy."

"Ray?"

"Yeah. Merry Christmas."

"Merry Christmas to you too." There was a pause and then she said, "Are you okay?"

"Yeah, sure. Just out gettin' some fresh air. Thought I'd call."

"Son said you called earlier too."

"Yeah. Checkin' to make sure he got everything I sent."

"You sent too much."

He laughed and said, "I might've got a little carried away."

"You don't need to do that, you know?"

"I like doing it."

"We miss you."

"You too?"

"Me too."

Then they didn't say anything for a while. Ray stood still on an empty street corner, breathing out clear plumes of air, staring down at the dirty brown piles of snow in the gutter.

"Well, anyway," he said finally. "I just wanted to wish you a Merry Christmas."

Her voice came back from far away.

"Merry Christmas, Ray."

When he came to Acropolis to look at the shop, he remembered thinking about snow. "Get a lot?" he asked Aaron. "I hate puttin' my bike away."

"We get some."

Going outside he sits down on the porch with his coffee and looks up at the sky. It stays soft and gray.

Andy doesn't feel like going out and that's when Jimbo calls and says, "Jack-in-the-Box. You, me, Will an' Susie."

Jack-in-the-Box isn't the kind of place Susie usually dresses up for.

After she puts on her eye shadow she looks sideways and sees Will looking in at her. A lamp above the mirror floods her face with light. Her eye shadow is a shimmery purple.

"You look like a goddam tramp!"

"I doooo not!"

All the lights in the windows look cool and closed in. Cars pass by with damp, lonely whispers.

At home, Miri wraps herself up in a towel and sits without lights and sees her face in the mirror, dim and featureless, a reflection of the other lights. She thinks of a baby eating cottage cheese off its mother's finger, Cora's babies, the empty place inside her.

Ray looks for her in the bathroom. Then he's there in the doorway.

"You smell good," he says.

"New soap."

"I like it." He leans on a dresser with a drawer full of mementos.

She sees herself in a soap opera, a happy wife with a secret other life until one day, at Christmas maybe, her real love disappears and she searches for him for a year's worth of episodes, and maybe at a Christmas party at the mansion of one of the soap's biggest characters, he suddenly shows up again in the doorway with a goddess who looks like Cora.

"I got it on sale."

He doesn't answer. She wonders if Cora ever saw this look. Or Kathy. As cool as the fingers he cups her face with, coming down onto the bed with her, eyes on hers the whole time, to settle on an elbow above her.

As cool as the surface of a photograph, or Ed's eyes, or dreams, or stars. She is liquid, warm, dispersing with the weightlessness of space, a dissolution coalescing in happiness, only in his arms, beneath his weight, sweaty, fragrant, familiar, hers.

"I love you, Ray."

"You an' me," he murmurs, slowly lowering his face into her neck.

At Candi's, Son is sitting in a booth opposite Craig and Craig's cousin. Craig's cousin points at the menu. "Check this out. Pumpkin spice waffles, maple syrup an' cranberry chutney."

"Costs…you know…costs a lot," says his cousin.

"I want it anyway. With blueberry syrup," he adds, smiling at Son's look of disgust.

"An'…you know…hot chocolate."

"Yeah."

At Andy's, Jimbo pulls up behind Andy's car. Andy's building is blue on light blue with a flat roof and planters around the posts for the upstairs walkway. Jimbo wants to come back the day after Andy moves out and shatter all the windows into the same silver blue shade.

Now he goes through the vinca out front, opens Andy's door, then slams it shut again.

"Not real keen on Jack-in-the-Box," says Andy.

At Carl's, Wendy sits oblivious to the figure standing at the edge of the road outside the window. Carl peers over the top of his glass of grape juice on the window sill to confirm Mr Torch's presence. A shadow of a shadow in a shadow. Carl pulls up his knees, curls to look away at the palm tree, gray and gloomy over water that doesn't splash. He can see, he thinks, into the lobby with a silver bell on the counter which rings like Ray's as the floorboards on his porch give under Mr Torch's weight. At the top of the steps, Mr Torch stops and smiles up at Carl.

At the liquor store across from a hardware store where a Christmas tree lot is already taking up half the parking lot, Kurt raps a bottle of champagne down on the counter and says, "Celebratin' my friend's baby."

"Oh, yeah?" says the clerk.

"A Thanksgiving baby." The timing impresses Kurt.

Outside, he breathes pine from the trees in the parking lot across the street. The gray sky is opaque with mist, soft and stinging at the same time. At the hospital again, he paces the parking lot, whistling through all the Christmas carols he can remember.

At Jack's Club, Susie follows Will in little black-buttoned white boots that slip in the damp. Inside, she grabs his wrist and he jerks it away and she spins on her slippery soles. Sitting by a wall across the room, Ray smiles. Joining him, Will pulls out a chair, drops a beeper on the table and says, "That's for you."

"What for?"

"Do you ever answer your fuckin' cell? Read a fuckin' text? Time is passin' you by, Wycowski."

"An' you're keepin' up?" Ray is laughing at him, at Susie too, laughing at her over his glass. "Who the fuck uses beepers?"

"Doctors. It's a modern convenience."

"You know what I remember, man? I remember my mom watering the lawn. We had one a those whirly bird sprinklers you had to keep movin' from place to place. An' you know what? That water in the sun looked just like pieces of candy. Pink, blue, yellow. I remember like it was yesterday. You're missin' out, bub. You an' your modern conveniences."

The sound of Ray's laugh puts Will on edge. His skin prickles and the hairs on the back of his neck stand up. He's pretty sure it isn't a good sign. He glances at Susie who smiles at him. Her lips are glossy and smell vaguely like coconut, which isn't really a Thanksgiving smell.

"Who the hell has coconut cream pie on Thanksgiving?" he asks suddenly.

Ray shrugs, unperturbed. "Whoever wants it, I guess."

"I want it," says Susie.

"There you go."

Will looks at Susie, who just shrugs. He feels lost and alone again. "We hafta talk," he says.

"Introduce us."

It doesn't register at first, not until he follows Ray's stare to Susie. She's wearing a pair of pants he hates.

"You look like a fuckin' mime," he said, really meaning a harlequin. Big white and black diamonds. Her blouse is white too with a vee at the top and bottom.

"Susie," he mutters, pushing back in his chair.

"Can I have a beer?" she asks.

He stares at her again. "A beer?"

"Yeah. Corona Light."

"In a minute."

She scowls and rubs at the arms of her chair, then looks up as Miri comes over and perches on the arm of Ray's chair. They sit without looking at each other, but his arm goes around her and his fingers tap gently at her hip.

"Couple on me," he says.

"Corona Light."

"No fuckin' priorities," mutters Will, grabbing Susie's purse off the floor as Miri crosses over to the bar. "I need some a your gum."

"I can have a beer, Will."

"You can shut the fuck up too. This isn't a goddam social call." He shoves the gum in his mouth. "I have problems. Tell 'im."

Susie nods. "That's right."

He thinks the gum tastes like grape, but he isn't sure.

"This grape?" he asks.

"Yeah."

"Sucks," he says and pictures the plastic fruit his mother set in a bowl on the dining room table. She put new placemats and glasses on the table everyday. He remembers the cupboards attached to the ceiling, cutting the dining area off from the living room, his father on the couch, his mother in the kitchen like a picture in a magazine.

His chest is a vacuum.

"This sucks," he says again, maybe of the gum.

"Too bad," says Ray, sounding tired now.

Will's father always sounded tired too and stood heavily in the doorway of his room. The smells of their dinner came in with him. He imagines his father took his belt off again before bed with a sigh of gladness that the day was almost over. Once when he took his belt off in Will's room, he said, "You could at least think of your mother." She didn't look upset at Will though. Not usually. She had ruffles on her apron, he remembers suddenly. A disappointed Mrs Cleaver. He feels almost close to her for a moment and grows aware of Susie's tasteless gum again. Stares at her because her arm is reaching past him for her beer.

"Thanks," she says.

He doesn't bother with his, just leans closer and moves his lips at her so only she can see. "You…don't…love…me."

She freezes with her beer halfway to her mouth until he looks away and pulls off the coat he's wearing and throws it at Ray.

"That's your kid's." He notices that Ray's face doesn't change at all, that it's still tired looking or maybe bored. "Nice," he adds.

Ray nods. "Yeah. Got for it for his birthday."

Will can't remember any of the things he got on birthdays or Christmases and thinks about the Christmas he didn't get anything. Then he thinks about Jimbo carrying him away the night Son hit him with the beer bottle and Susie in the emergency room with him, blowing her bubbles. When he looks at her again she stops drinking her beer and sinks a little in her chair.

Ray sighs.

"C'mon, Will. Talk."

Will stares at him. The jacket's on the table but Ray doesn't seem to care about it, which was what Will wanted before. But now he wants him to care and he complains, "You don' even care, man."

Ray is swirling the bourbon in his glass, tired, but relaxed looking. "About what?"

"About me! Jesus, I care about you."

Will imagines tasting things, even coconut cream pie or the big chocolate cakes his mother made on his father's birthdays.

"You did this," he murmurs, confusing Ray for a moment with his father in the doorway.

"What the hell are you talkin' about?"

Then it occurs to him that he doesn't really know. He feels lost again and when Susie whispers, "Will," he doesn't really resent her until she adds, "Are we gonna be goin' pretty soon?" because he knows all she's thinking about is coconut cream pie.

"You don't care either!"

Only Jimbo cares. Jimbo, sitting on Andy's couch. "Think we rate better 'n Jack-in-the-Box," he says.

Andy knows that as a rule Jimbo likes Jack-in-the-Box.

Susie likes Candi's.

After Ray says, "C'mon, man, let's get some fresh air," Candi's is where they go, sitting in Will's favorite booth.

Ray looks out at the steamy windows and slowly smiles, imagining a Nova outside, puffing soft, white plumes into the air.

Lights glow in store windows and wisps of mist float like wings in the gloom of the cemetery and a lightless sun slowly drops.

In the drizzly air Jonah leans against Kurt's car, smoking a cigarette.

The firs are a grayish green, slowly darkening.

Ray swipes his arm across the window. The giant bowling pin grows as gray as cinders. Carl sees Mr Torch get up off the chair against the wall and disappear. At the mortuary, it's dark and there is the sound of little bells faraway.

"I had fuckin' brain damage, man, an' they only gave me aspirin," says Will, remembering its chalky taste.

He feels unnerved at that and looks over at Susie's coconut cream pie because he can smell it and it smells like marshmallows. Susie looks at Ray, waiting for something to happen.

Ray just looks amused. He has Son's coat beside him, arms across the top of the booth.

Will is sitting like that too, not eating the plate of candied yams he got off the buffet. The yams made him think of his mother's and when Ray wiped the steam off the window, he could see the lights outside, blurry and colorful, and he swung his arm behind Susie's shoulder, making her freeze for a moment.

"Almost Christmas, man. I love Christmas."

Ray half laughed and then Will laughed too.

"Presents!"

At the cemetery, airy angels fly with pale stone wings and a cool, pale glow appears at the top of the giant bowling pin. Sitting in Jonah's pickup, Kurt pops the cork on a bottle of champagne and pours it into the plastic cups he bought at the liquor store. Jonah is smoking again, but now the smoke is relaxing the tension in his chest. He huffs a laugh at Kurt's excitement and takes another puff on his cigarette.

"C'mon. Drink," says Kurt, lifting his champagne. "To Angelino!"

"Asa," murmurs Jonah, emptying his cup in a swallow.

Back at the Club, Ray takes his drink with him down a dark hallway. The store room is unlit, but on the other side of the room there's a brightly lit doorway to the office in back. It's a cramped room with a computer on a metal desk, a metal filing cabinet and a Formica table set up with dishes of green beans, stuffing, turkey cold cuts, and a clear plastic bowl of ambrosia salad. Son is sitting there with his legs up on another chair eating the salad off a paper plate, glancing up at him, eyeing him wordlessly before returning to his plate. There are times that Ray isn't sure he likes him. He keeps looking for energy, happiness, enjoyment, the thrill Ray feels almost every day. The speeding blur of life is beginning to surprise him.

Sitting down, he says, "So how you doin', kid?"

"Okay. Miri make all this? She asked me to eat some."

"I think so. Or bought it." He sips his drink, sets it down on the table. "Call your mom?"

"Yeah. This morning."

Ray nods, fingers turning his glass on the table, eyes on Son, whose almost perpetual scowl begins to reform.

"What?" Son asks.

"Nothin'. Just wonderin' how you're doin'."

"I told you."

Ray grins, Son's anger amusing him.

"So whadda ya been up to?"

"Nothin'."

"Nothin'?"

"Yeah. Why?"

"You must be doin' somethin'."

"I don't keep a fuckin' record."

"You sure have a hell a lotta time on your hands, kid."

"I'm not usin', Dad. Is that what you're askin'?"

"I'm askin'."

"I'm not, okay?"

"No, it's not okay. I never see you. Don't know what the fuck you're doin'. I worry about it."

"Well, don't."

Ray laughs. "Yeah. Don't."

"I know I'm not anything you wanted me to be."

"For fuck's sake. Where the hell did that come from? I never told you anything like that."

Son shrugs. "I know it."

"You don't know anything. I worry about you. That's my fuckin' right. I don't want you usin' again."

"Kind of ironic, isn't it?"

"Yeah, yeah. I get the irony."

"Whadda my eyes tell ya? I'm sober, clean, hella bored."

"Sober?"

"Well...I have to do somethin'."

"No, you don't."

"Are you done lecturing me?"

"Not yet. I want you to put in a couple days at the shop from now on."

"I just did."

"You just did? That was almost two months ago."

"It's boring."

"It's a living."

Son sighs, scooping more ambrosia salad onto his plate. "I pick the days."

Ray raises a palm in consent. "You got it."

"I can't start until next week."

"Sure. You like that salad?" he asks, finishing his drink.

"Yeah, it's pretty good. What is it?"

"Ambrosia. Your grandma made it every Christmas."

"I could eat it again."

"You're doin' a number on that bowl."

"Yeah, well, it's Thanksgiving. I figured I'd come over, hang out with you guys...except we're not actually doing anything," he adds.

"So come on out an' sit with me. I need another drink."

"Me too. You're buyin'."

"Yeah, yeah, yeah."

In the morning there are bells up on some of the light poles, a giant snowman at Kmart and Christmas scenes in the store windows.

At the end of the street Ray turns onto there's a metal barrier and a mortuary on the other side. He sits on his bike outside Smiley's pawnshop and guesses that Wayne's probably still alive, still fixing Camaros and Corvettes, close to that sooty city he lived in with Ed.

"Filthy goddam place."

"No, it's not," said Ed, looking out at the piles of crusty brown snow through the smear Ray's arm made.

19

♦ Apple Days ♦

On clear days it is cold and crisp.

"Apple days," said Abel because that's what Job always said.

At the grocery stores there are wooden bins of apples outside and boxes of nuts and oranges inside. One year Aster bought a box of maple candy shaped into leaves. At work, a wish tree goes up, attracting Wally. It's in a corner of the lunch room across from the vinyl couch. There are presents underneath.

"Santa came for 'um last year," says Gus. "Gave 'um away in the church parking lot. We used to just put empties underneath before."

Wally laughs. "Cheap, cheap-a-rama."

Jonah stares at the tree with a dullness that's the same dullness he feels inside.

It is winter.

Outside, a world full of lights and cheerfulness.

"I can't wait for that Christmas party," says Wally. "I am goin' to that for sure." At the tree, he sets his hands on his hips and looks up. There's a star on top. Or an angel....

Outside, winter's voices whistle through the firs.

At Kurt's, some of the trees outdoors are decorated with Christmas lights. When he sees them, Jonah wonders who did it. Some have only white lights and some are multicolored like the one by Joy's birdbath. At night, colors glitter on the thin sheet of ice that covers the water and every time Jonah sees it he remembers Ira outside in the rain, putting up his lights that last Christmas Abel and Sissy were alive.

Grayness floats in the soft damp air.

At home, he sees Asa staring into space and looks at the patches of light with him, a window without snowflakes, a chair in the same place Abel's was, Asa's frown, Ally scooping him up.

The grayness outside is inside of him too.

It comes like this, fills him up and there's nothing he can do. He stares like Asa into empty spaces and Ally grows quieter. He hears her quiet more than any other sound she makes. He starts to listen for her. In the bedroom today, putting on his boots, he listened and couldn't hear her. He sat still for a very long time, then got up and felt his anger for no reason.

"What the hell are you doin'?!"

She was sitting on the couch, cutting out coupons. He saw her scissors and she saw them too. Her voice was almost a whisper.

"Nothing, Jonah."

In town, the giant bowling pin is wrapped up in red sashes like a candy cane. Agnes isn't there and he sits outside of Kurt's, waiting until he sees Joy passing by with a little Christmas tree, the handle of a big paper bag she's carrying in the crook of her arm.

The grayness is a drizzle now and hovers in the air.

Crossing the gravel, he follows her to her door. She opens it with a small smile and goes inside. He stops and leans against the sill, watching her set the tree in a corner of the room by the giant TV. She looks over and he says, "Naw. It looks lost there."

She picks it up and looks around. There's a bookshelf under the window and he comes in without her asking, pulls the book shelf away from the wall to make room and puts the tree down on top of it.

"Right here," he says. She shrugs and puts her bag down below it. There are boxes of lights and decorations inside. "Now you can see it when you come home."

She nods and looks up, cupping the back of her neck with her hand. "Thanks."

He's aware that the tree hides him now, that her parakeet is watching, that her coolness can melt, that he can melt it, undo her life here, put a hand over her face and push her back into a room he's never seen and afterwards walk away. She wouldn't tell anybody. She might even pretend it didn't happen, seal back up in her quiet and cool until he felt like reminding her again.

He smiles at her, reaching for her screen. "Anytime," he says.

———————

Outside, a bird lands on a garland, a gray ball in the gray light.

Agnes runs upstairs, a mitten pulling along the damp rail. It's dark inside. She goes in a door he didn't lock, turns on the light, and pulls his arms away from his face. Her cheeks and nose are red and her eyes are shiny. He's lying with his jacket on and boots off, legs crossed at the ankle. She kneels beside him and he pushes himself up a little and finishes the beer he set on the nightstand. After that, he sighs and lets his head rest back against the pillows and says, "All I think about is you."

Sometimes he tries to remember her the way she used to be and pictures her standing in Waylon's parking lot with her fingers in her back pockets, shifting nervously. He was angry then, he remembers.

Now he lies without energy.

He can hear Joy's TV, pictures her putting balls on her little tree, a star on top or a red cardinal like the one Agnes is talking about.

"We got it at a craft show. I wish you could come over."

He puts his arms around her and stares at the ceiling. Maybe Joy's decorating with tinsel. He thinks about that and feels the way Agnes is hugging him at the same time. He knows she thinks he's going to go away.

"I love being with you," she says into his neck.

He is hugging her with the remoteness of memory, almost not feeling her against him.

When he goes downstairs Joy has her tree lit and there's tinsel and multicolored balls with gold glitter. He can smell cookies as he goes on.

The drizzle is dark gray and heavy and the signal lights look like decorations.

When Aster was alive, she made tarts with white icing and Abel pulled the TV out of the corner of the room to make a place for the tree. Abel loved Christmas.

"All we ever did was go to the movies before," he said, referring to Christmases with Job.

At Aster's family's house, there were candy trays, plates with Christmas tree designs or holly leaf borders full of cookies, cakes and the little fruit tarts.

Ally makes her father's jelly omelet concoction with orange marmalade instead of her father's grape jelly in the center. Jonah eats them without talking, almost grudgingly.

He likes the day to be cold and clear. She makes cider and he thinks of apples in wooden bins and maple candy. There are pumpkin biscuits and cheese for lunch. They never have ham at dinner or Aster's parsnips with orange sauce or her spiced red cabbage.

Agnes is making pies from scratch.

He didn't tell her that he saw her picking out her pumpkin when he was at Orly's one day. He stood behind one of the pumps, and when he saw her, he set his arm on top and rested his chin on the crook of his elbow and watched her. There were baskets of pumpkins and gourds on the porch. Some were the yellow color of autumn leaves.

When she went back in the store, she let the screen slam behind her the way Mavis used to sometimes when she came outside and Jonah could see her breath in the air and it felt cold just to look at her. Waylon's Christmas tree filled the window with color and he knew that it smelled like hot chocolate and donuts and coffee inside.

Ally makes cookies in the shapes of angels and bells.

Once, she brought a fruit salad inside a scooped out watermelon for a picnic at work. There was always something in him that made him stay away from her and something else that made him finally give in. He liked her for a long time though. On the porch of her family's house he picked her up one night and hugged her, and she was happy and whole and hugged him back with strong, solid arms and smelled as warm as summer. She came to the house and put geraniums back in Aster's pots, flowers in Clover's cowbell. She lay beside him and her skin was like honey in summer. Then he put his arm across her belly and saw only her likeness to him. On windy days, she stood outside to see the clouds come and blow away. He thought of her one day when he drove out onto a dirt path weeds almost covered up, a meadow like Ira's, a house in the trees up ahead nobody lived in anymore, built probably by people who knew Samuel and Ivy and John and Ellie Sparrow a long time ago. He could almost see Ellie passing by, going to Ira's where she stood in the shadows of the clouds moving past, seeing the puddles in winter or the dry, whispery weeds in summer.

Ally was like that, carrying a silence with her he could hear.

At Agnes's, he sees ordinary things like a pot of ivy on the porch, a bucket by the door, a chair he pictures her sitting in, a metal chair that rocks, and a glass of lemonade on the railing, summers into the future.

After she left Kurt's, Agnes went to the mall with her friend Betsy, and now Betsy and her mother are dropping her off at home, waiting until she runs inside, lightly and happily, into a house that is warm and full of familiar smells, her shoes by the door, TV on, old spots on the carpet, a puddle of light in the hallway, Waylon leaning back in his chair.

"That you, honey?"

She kisses his cheek, quick and chilly. There are presents under the Christmas tree.

At Kurt's, she put on her cap with the pink snowball on top and spun in a giddy circle. Then breathless, she stopped, abruptly serious. "Will I see you?"

"Christmas Eve," he said.

"All day?"

"All day."

"Promise?"

"I promise."

She smiled and Jonah pulled the rim of her cap down over her face and thought about the day he wouldn't see her anymore. Then she rolled the cap back up and blew at her bangs.

"I love Christmas."

"I love this one," he said.

On the other side of the river there are Christmas tree lights on a big spruce, reminding Jonah of Ira's and the Christmas tree at work with its big frosty balls, apple days, pumpkin pie, little tarts with white icing.

At home there's a white car with a sheriff's star on its door, circles of red and blue and green lights overlapping on the window, a light over the porch door.

Jonah pulls up on the far side of the driveway opposite the house. Getting out of the pickup, he starts over to the porch, then stops at the open door of the garage. Cold air stirs like a quick breath. Looking inside, he can't see anything, not even shadows. Nobody's ever parked in that garage and he isn't sure why. It's mostly open space, hard packed dirt on the ground, tools and boxes stored on shelves against the walls.

A long time ago, Cotter came up here and stood looking into the dull light outside. His eyes swept across the dark house, the silent mist-cloaked fir trees. All around was the slow drip of moisture. Watching him from inside the garage, Jonah moved back a step, maybe wanted Cotter to see him because Cotter's eyes came round suddenly and saw his shadow back in the darkness. "Come on out," he said.

Jonah's voice was low and deep. "I didn't kill 'im."

"No," Cotter answered. "You didn't. He'll recover. You need to not talk anymore though. I'm going to cuff you an' then I'm going to read you your rights."

Earlier, the rain clouds broke and the sky was silver. Then the light was thin and gray and Cotter was preternaturally pale, caught in the day's final gasp of life. Inside, Jonah was standing by another beam of light that was coming through the back of the garage where some boards were missing.

"I need to find Sissy."

"We'll do that," said Cotter.

Coming closer to the door, he looked in. Jonah shifted sideways and the gun he was carrying shone in the dull light. It was the same gun he took to the mini-mart with him the night before

"You Pop?"

When Cotter said, "I mean it. Come on out," Jonah jumped through the gap in the back of the garage. A moment later, Cotter squeezed out of the gap too, hopping to pull a foot free when Jonah swung at him, gun in hand.

Surprising him, Cotter dropped down and Jonah's arm swooped through empty space. Staggering sideways, he saw Cotter rise up and he leaned over to slam a boot into Cotter's stomach, sending him sprawling backwards. Then he ran for the tree line. Behind him, Cotter rolled up, yelling after him.

"I told you about this day, Jonah! You knew I'd come!"

Maybe he did. But all of a sudden he didn't want that, wanted to escape and ran partway up to Ivy's, then plunged back down through the trees and bushes to the river. The sound of the rushing water obliterated his raspy gasps. The sun was dropping behind the firs and the mist was thickening. About halfway to Orly's, he heard a car coming up fast and dashed across the road up into the trees. Brakes squealed and then the car went in reverse. He stumbled, dragged his heavy feet up and ran again, staying in the trees. White vaporous plumes escaped his mouth, dissipated in the cold air. Dropping back down to the road again, he ran past Waylon's house, came up upon the curve that led up to the main road, and cut away into the firs again. Up ahead came flashes of yellow from the signal light and then he broke out of the trees and ran over to Orly's. The lights were still on and Orly was still there.

In Waylon's lot, headlights came on and Cotter drove slowly across the intersection. No one else. Just Cotter. Cold and grim. With a groan, Jonah felt his knees give out, just like that. His arms barely broke his fall. He lay flat on the pavement, feeling Orly's hands under his arms, trying to lift him, then Cotter's calm voice.

"Step back, Orly."

He couldn't breathe, his lungs were on fire. He sucked at the air, clawed at the pavement.

"Arms at your sides."

He lay his face down, saw Orly crouched nearby, staring at him. He didn't look sorry or upset. That struck Jonah as odd, and he stared back, oblivious to the feel of Cotter's hands on his, the cold of the handcuffs. In that moment, Orly was just there, a witness, absorbing with him in silence an enormous loneliness that came swooping down on him. Gravity intensified. He was crushed underneath it, frozen to the pavement. It surprised him when Cotter could lift him. Then Orly rose off his haunches, watching him without a word. The whistling of the wind deafened him, a banshee wail, battering at the signal light. In the sky was a starless dark, wisps of smoke colored clouds moving swiftly over the tops of the trees.

Sitting down on the porch steps, Jonah lights a cigarette. He knows he should go in and socialize, pretend there was ever any mercy in Cotter's eyes; but he stays outside instead, sucks smoke into his lungs and breathes it out again. Ally laughs, her nervous laugh because she knows he's outside. Cigarettes usually relax him, but now his whole body hurts. He is tense all the time, his muscles like rocks under his skin. He listens to the wind, the movement of things he can't see. All of a sudden, he is acutely aware of his seven years in prison and reaches up with a hand, digging his fingers into his tight shoulder muscle. Ally laughs again and he jerks. Dropping his hand, he puffs on his cigarette, feeling a tightness in the skin around his eyes. A band of pain develops around his head. He wants a drink, but he doesn't want to go inside, doesn't want Ally to see him drinking before work. He grits his teeth, making his jaw ache. The creak of the screen door behind him is a kind of relief. He shifts slightly, tucking the side of his face against his shoulder as he looks behind him.

"Hey."

"Hey, yourself." Cotter's voice is quiet, calm. He has nothing to worry about.

"Come to see Asa?"

Cotter descends the steps, leaning back against the stairwell at the bottom. "I was on my way home, decided to stop by. I hope that was okay."

"Sure." Jonah takes a final puff on his cigarette and grinds it out on the step below him. "What do you think about that name?"

Cotter is quiet for a moment. In the fading light from the porch Jonah thinks he looks amused. "I think it's a good name. Why? Second thoughts?"

"No. I picked it."

"You did?"

"You'd think I'd break with tradition, wouldn't you? Give up the bible names."

"Nothing wrong with tradition."

"I dunno," says Jonah. "I could see there might be different points of view on that."

Cotter's arms cross over his chest. His head cocks quizzically. "What's going on?"

"Whadda you mean?"

"You seem a little out of sorts."

Jonah sighs. "I'm not." He debates saying nothing, just letting the moment pass, then adds, "Christmas just isn't my best time of year."

Cotter nods.

"I can see that. You aren't alone that way."

Jonah shrugs. "My problem. I'm lucky."

Cotter nods again, just eyeing him for a moment. Then he says, "Nice looking little boy."

"Yeah. Good too."

He thinks of the way he stares off into space, mesmerized by lights and colors and things Jonah can't see. He follows Asa's gaze wonderingly. His eyes fall on strange, unwelcome things. A garland of Christmas cards over the window where Sissy's snowflakes used to be. Ally bought Asa a snow globe that plays Jingle Bells and an ornament of a baby in a crib. Her mother made Asa a blanket with pictures of candy canes and little bluebirds carrying holly branches on it. At the hospital, she came outside and he saw her look over at him where he leaned against Kurt's car, smoking in the drizzly air. She reminded him of Aunt Hilary and he stared back at her without going over.

"Well," says Cotter, pushing off from the railing, "I better be going on home."

Jonah rises to see him off, listening to the sound of the car until it disappears, replaced by just the wind, not a sound in the house. Cotter's home, Jonah knows, is a house on the other side of Acropolis by a meadow like Ira's with a creek running through it. His wife's name is Fay and his boys are named Benjamin, Owen, and Clay. It always bothered Jonah that there was a life in the depths of Cotter's eyes that he never let on to Jonah. All Jonah ever saw was a flat gaze, once a lot like dislike, that only seemed to bounce Jonah's emptiness back at him. Cotter never gave him any glimpse inside and Jonah always felt oddly lost not knowing about that life. Even with Asa he doesn't know about it, any of the truth of Cotter's life with his family. Maybe knows it even less now because of Asa.

Sitting down again, he smokes another cigarette. The tension in his body stays. Pains in his neck start shooting into his brain. He grimaces, his nose burning from the smoke, flicks the cigarette onto the driveway, and goes inside.

In the kitchen, he stops to pour a cup of coffee, takes a sip, then sets the cup down, standing very quietly. The tinny sound of Jingle Bells rings cheerfully in the air. Asa's snow globe. The sparks of pain in his neck flash red in front of his eyes. He squeezes them shut and more sparks flare, multicolored like the lights on the tree. Opening his eyes again, he moves into the hallway. The light makes Sissy's doorknob look shiny, not like the dull, 'cheap piece a crap' Abel said it was. A floorboard creaks underneath him. There is a moment of blissful silence. He looks in and sees her at the dresser, winding up the snow globe again. Cheerful little notes peal out.

He roars at her. "SHUT THAT UP!"

In summer, he can swim and be happy again. Agnes will glide by like a slippery fish and beams of sunshine will sparkle like rainbows. At work though he's sitting on the vinyl couch in back, staring at the light on the floor.

Coming through the door, Wally stops suddenly, then runs on tiptoe up to a pink bakery box on the counter, peeking in excitedly. "Hey, cookies!" He eats one and waves one in the air, laughing over the one still in his mouth. "Man, this is like Kiddie Land. Sugary crap everywhere. I took my little girl yesterday. Ate nothin' but cotton candy an' kettle corn."

Jonah rouses curiously. "You have a kid?"

"Yeah. Chrissie. Wanna see?"

Gus is coming over too. He took a picture of her on Halloween before they went out. "I got 'er first. My ex took her out after." She was wearing a pink dress and pink slippers and a tiara with rhinestones. "Cinderella."

"Cute," says Gus.

"Got a ton a candy too," says Wally, grabbing another cookie on his way out. "Kiddie Land!"

At the glue rack, Wally pulls his gloves on and says, "I got a Christmas tree yesterday too. Artificial. On sale. I let Chrissie pick. Any tree you want I said. Any tree. Five fuckin' hundred dollars. You know what she was pickin'? The damn decorations. Which don't come with the tree. I'm fuckin' broke…Watch this," he says to Jonah. "Hey, Gus!"

Gus stops.

"You goin' to the Christmas party?"

"Yeah."

"Cool. Me too. Gonna be fun." Gus nods and starts off again, waiting for a joke he knows is coming. "Goin' with your mom?"

"I can't listen to you," says Gus. "I have a job to do."

Wally sticks his tongue out at him and pulls on his gloves. They start to work and Wally is quiet for a while. Once, he runs over to Gus and then back again, leaning in so Jonah can hear over the noise. "Said I'd let 'im borrow Chrissie's tiara."

Jonah nods and keeps working. He is thinking about Ally. She couldn't get the music to stop in the snow globe and he took it outside and threw it at the garage. It hit with a crack and ricocheted somewhere out of sight. Then he went back in, backing her into a corner of the living room. She put her arms up, blocking his punches, then she rolled into the corner of the wall and sank into a ball and he grabbed her by the neck, feeling her fingers on his wrists. Rocking, he hit his head against the wall and sparks of red blinded him. He let go of her and she scrambled away. The room spun with light, red and yellow and blue. His head was pounding. In the dark outside, he could hear Jingle Bells playing in a strange, disjointed rhythm; on the factory floor, tiny persistent notes. The song fills his aching head. Wally doesn't seem to notice. He's pointing at Gus. "You can borrow her slippers too. Pretty in pink!"

All of a sudden, Jonah leaves and goes into the lunchroom for a can of pop. Then downstairs where the noise grows quieter. It's cool here and he puts his coat on. The floor is cement and the benches wood. He can feel the cold coming up from below. He puts his can on the floor and sits with his elbows on his knees and rubs his hands together. One of his thumbs is scarred. One day after Abel died, he took some wood up to fix the garage roof. Then his thumb started to hurt and he saw a splinter in it. At first it was just red, then it got hot and puffy and even his wrist began to hurt. He started to feel sick and that was the day he woke up and saw Abel, even though Abel was dead.

Upstairs, the noise stops and it's quiet for a while, then there are footsteps, quiet again, and then Wally is coming downstairs.

At the bottom he stops with a wink at Jonah and then looks back up. "I can get 'um," he calls out.

Chilburn follows partway, bending down to see into the dim room. Wally's boots thump as he runs. Jonah hears him in back behind the lockers. Picking up his pop, he moves closer to the stairs. Chilburn's still there.

"You feelin' okay?"

"Headache," he says.

"Take some aspirin?"

"Yeah. It's just kickin' in."

"Good."

There's a box in back of the basement full of the empty Christmas presents they used to put under the tree before they bought real presents to give away.

When Wally comes back, he's carrying the box on top of his head. "We need some stuff to stay under the tree after the kids get theirs," he says.

"Just remember which is which," says Chilburn, disappearing up the stairs.

After his footsteps recede, Wally laughs and says, "Chilly, Chilly," referring to the nickname he gave Rob. It started when he saw a couple of holes in the lunchroom walls just above the floor and said, "I bet Chilburn lives here. Morphs into a mouse or somethin'." Gus smiled politely. "Seriously though. Any a you guys ever seen 'im outside a here?"

"Once," said Jonah.

"Out lookin' for cheese, I bet."

"Cheetos in the vending machine," said Gus.

"Hey! Cheetos! Chilly Cheetos!"

Upstairs, Wally drops the box by the tree and starts tossing empty presents underneath.

Later, at the glue rack, he nudges Jonah's arm and says, "Check this out."

Jonah waits. Wally flips the switch on and off and the machine starts and stops. "I made Gus go out an' listen. You can hear it in the hall." He flips it on and off and on again, grinning at Jonah's frown. "Early Chilly warning," he adds, pulling on his gloves. His voice is louder now over the cover of the noise.

"Chilly…! Chilly…!"

In winter, Jonah swims with slivers of ice and a cold that makes him flex and gasp.

Upstairs at Kurt's, he rests against the door and relaxes. It is dark and quiet and Kurt stays asleep.

Wally kept talking and he can hear him laughing as they worked.

"Couple kids…couple raises…couple movies…couple big juicy steaks…*Weekends*…! TV…A vehicle ain't a luxury. I don't count that. An' we work cool hours for washin' clothes an' shit. Just sit around, read my paper. I don't have to *have* a washer an' dryer. I *need* a TV. A big screen TV. Relaxation time…."

It's growing lighter now and he can see something on top of Kurt's refrigerator. Up close, it turns into a glass bird the color of Joy's eyes. There are whitish smudges where its wings are. He pours himself a drink and leans back against the counter and looks at the bird again. He thinks Agnes would like it. He can't think of anything else to get her. On Sissy's last Christmas, Abel gave her a box of things he bought from the drug store, perfume, lip glosses, costume jewelry, tied up with a messy red bow. Fin gave her a cross with a tiny ball of turquoise in the center. She lost it on the day she died and Sarah Sparrow found it later and wore it to Waylon's one day where Orly saw her and bought it back and kept it for him. By the time Jonah got it, it was dull as a nickel. At home, he sat on the couch with it and remembered when Fin gave it to her, there in the living room with Abel drinking his drink, watching a Christmas movie, not even paying attention.

He keeps the cross in the same coffee can he keeps Kurt's gun in.

On the way home, he buys Ally some flowers and brings them inside. She sees them and stares as he comes over, leaning slightly away. She's sitting on the couch in her robe, not doing anything. It's quiet and the lights are off.

"I bought you these."

Then he gets down on his knees and puts the flowers beside her. The damp and weedy smell reminds him of the day she found Clover's cowbell and put it on the kitchen window sill, picking flowers to put through its hasp. There were no pictures of that, no reason for her to do it the way Clover did. He remembers his feeling of bemusement, the first worry that he was losing his place in this house. Another time, when she put her coat on for a walk, Jonah got up and said, "I'll go with you," and that's when he took her up to the pond. When they got there, he sat on his heels and waved his fingers through the water. It was dark and cold, not green like he always said. It wasn't really quiet either. It sounded more like there were things trying to be quiet, wanting to be alone again. When he looked up at her, he could see her unease and it made him happy. This was his place, Ivy's, where he was always at home.

Now she opens her arms and he lays his face in her lap.

20

♦ Ho! Ho! Ho! ♦

HO! HO! HO!

Carl sits with his arm on the windowsill, elbow outside, just below the bottom of the sash, numb in the chilly air. At the bar, strings of lights are blurry balls under the eaves and there is fake snow on the window ledges.

HO! HO! HO!

He smiles dreamily. Scott comes out on tiptoe. Carl's dreams are more and more real, as real as a stool across the street where he sits and drinks eggnog and brandy and there's a dark green garland over the mirror and all the faces are wide with smiles and George is singing Jingle Bells in a voice like Carl's.

Scott smiles at him. "Okay?"

"Sure."

Under this dreaminess there are other dreams.

One day Ray came through the kitchen into the living room, stopping to grab Miri in his arms and swing her into a quick dip.

"Merry Christmas, babe!"

On another day, she came home from work, slipping her shoes off at the back door. The house was dark and his voice surprised her, coming quietly out of the bedroom. He was singing a song she'd never heard before, stopping suddenly when he sensed her in the doorway. Then there was a yawn in his voice and she heard him stretch. "Hey, babe. Didn't hear you come in."

His voice was warm with deep, round tones. At Christmas all things are possible.

The other morning, when she heard him pouring cereal in the kitchen, she asked loudly, "Can we get our tree on my next day off?"

She was wearing one of his tee-shirts, fuzzy socks, watching TV with her glass of orange juice. After the pouring sounds stopped, he came out to the kitchen doorway with his bowl of Cheerios and a frown. "Tree? What tree?"

"Our Christmas tree."

"Oh. That."

He returned to the kitchen and didn't come back out. She heard the door half slam behind him a while later.

Will sat up to catch a blue velvet box Ray pulled out of his pocket and tossed over to him. "Check those out. Couple rocks for my baby."

A pair of diamond earrings glittered on a blue background. Will was impressed. "Fuck, dude. Those are good sized."

"Yep."

Ray leaned sideways to put the box back in his pocket, eyes still on Will's face. Will forgot him though. He was staring at the tree, all the presents underneath it. Store-wrapped, a few in ribbon-tied tissue paper. Susie's to Will. Will's face took on a look of focused panic. The Christmas tree was pushed into the corner and the lights collected in big splotches on the wall. There was a wreath on the door, a Santa doll on the couch. When Ray came in, he gave it a pat as he sat down.

"You guys are really into this thing."

Will looked hurt. "Christmas is cool!"

"Okay. Hm...hm, hm, hm...hm..." He hummed it. "Do you know that?"

Will pulled himself away from his reverie. "What?"

Ray hummed it again. "Do you know this song?"

"No."

Will's face screwed back up. Ray kept humming, smiling at Will's peculiar antics. Then Will's face suddenly colored with joy and he bounced in his chair, clapping his hands on his knees.

"A mink, man! A fuckin' mink!"

Ray nodded. "Yeah. That would do."

"Diamonds are old school, man."

Ray grinned, draped his arms over the top of the couch, humming again. He thought of a cool and sunny Christmas in a living room with Irene.

He could see her in the living room with the lid up on the hi-fi, TV on too, orchestrating with her fingertips as she left the room.

Hm…hm, hm, hm…hm….

HO! HO! HO!

Now Ray's sitting on his porch, a bandana in his hand, scrubbing at his hair. It feels good in the cold. All the roofs with reindeers on top, Christmas trees inside and out.

Party time!

At Will's he gave him a jab of his finger. "Big blowout, man. You remember. I expect ya. Christmas Eve."

Except for those years in that sooty city with Ed and his goofy Santa cap, Ed scuffing in his slippers across the carpet, static electricity in the stuffy, overheated room shooting off his fingertips. It was a narrow, long house with two stories. Stairs rose just inside the front door. The living room where Ray was sitting was alongside the stairwell wall. A door on the other side of the living room led into a dining room, which led into a kitchen which opened onto a narrow, scruffy yard with chain-link on either side. The walls were dingy, paneled behind Ed. Ray just sat there, slumped on the couch, tense and hot, cool looking to everybody but Ed.

Ed stuck a finger out. "Shock ya."

Then Ray pushed himself up. "Wait a minute." Ed stopped and just smiled as he came over and pushed a pillow up his pajama top, then pushed him away and took a look.

"Santa!"

Upstairs, a moon of clear glass appears in a misty window, Carl scrubbing his breath away. He can feel Scott's stare, out there in the real world, pulling him back again. Scott always stares. Scott is all eyes. He can't see a lot though. He can't see Mr Torch. Carl can. Mr Torch is real. A part of the real world. He laughs suddenly and Scott's eyes grow bleak. Mr Torch works in a white building with a white portico and a clean white walkway between two deep green lawns. His lawns are frosty now and there's a wreath on his door. His white building is almost like a house. A Christmas tree glitters with calm white lights in a dark corner of the foyer. It smells like fir trees inside and other things underneath.

Carl doesn't like it there. He likes Mr Torch to sit here in a chair by the wall where he isn't real.

In his house, calm and gentle, Mr Torch is real.

"Oh, that, that!" yells Carl, pointing at the TV.

Scott flips back a channel. A great spirit of pure light glows and pulses.

"Mr Magoo!"

———————

"Hm…hm, hm, hm…hm…."

The melody is familiar but not like a memory. The act of remembering for Fin is a physical process. Pressure grows in his head, the dark inside of his eyelids all he sees. And then he's swimming in darkness, pain encircling him, growing tighter. He floats with those amorphous shapes in the dark, memories he won't go near. He panics there, near those shapes. The walls rise up, clicking into place, exiling him again. He does remember some things though. Usually after he gives up trying, or when he wakes up in the morning, or when he runs and slows to a walk to catch his breath, a picture will float up in his memory. Opening his eyes back up, he looks at Ray who's leaning up against his car, looking at him expectantly.

"Hm…hm, hm, hm…hm…?"

He shrugs.

"Goddammit," says Ray. "My mom used to sing it all the time. Now I can't get the damn thing outta my head."

A light at the shop fills the glass panes with color, Christmas tree lights reflect off the bar's windows, George's snow-like flock on a tree inside. At night all the colors will dance in the dark.

"Hm…hm, hm, hm…hm…."

One of the things Fin remembered one day was a box in the back of the basement under shelves filled with years-old canned goods. The box is still there, a flimsy wood crate that never moves anywhere. It stays where it is, attached to the wall and shelves by cobwebs. And as long as the cobwebs remain, he hasn't disturbed it. But he knows it's there, his mother's gin in sky blue, dust-covered bottles. Sometimes, on seeing the crate, he pauses and goes over, even stoops down, readying to pull it out, grab the bottles, and go upstairs. But the fantasy isn't to drink it, even though his mouth waters and his throat tightens. He wants to pour it out, rinse the sink clean again, and toss the empty bottles out. He doesn't want her gin anymore and resentment stabs him every time he sees it. Then he reaches down, his fingers near the cobwebs and sees himself in the kitchen, opening a bottle, the smell of gin knocking him backwards. His legs shake and it's hard to get upstairs. So the gin stays there under its fluttering cobweb cage.

Ray is humming again. "Hm…hm, hm, hm…hm…."

There is no tree at his house. At work, he goes into the lunch room and looks at the tree there, almost envious. It's covered in shiny, multicolored bulbs. Presents pile up underneath. Once, he sat down on the vinyl couch and squeezed his eyes shut, trying to remember a tree at home. Then the pain came and he opened his eyes again. Later, at Grace's, he ran up the long road past the houses on the other side of the lot. He ran for a long time, listening to the slapping of his shoes and his breath. This was one of the times that he remembered when he slowed to a staggering walk, then bent double to catch his breath. Straightening up, there were lights in front of his eyes, resolving quickly into darkness again, but an after image of lights remained, a shape grew, a Christmas tree in the foyer. It took up most of the passageway into the living room and covered up the tall windows by the door. He saw his mother in the downstairs room his father stayed in before he died. It's a den now, across the hall from the living room. The Christmas tree was visible from the doorway and he could see the portable record player that sat on the dresser and hear Christmas carols playing.

He can remember other carols, but not Ray's song.

"C'mon, bub. Hm…hm, hm, hm…hm…?"

"Sorry."

On the tree he remembers there was a light that didn't blink, a white one, deep inside.

Ray slaps the roof of his car and pushes off with a scowl. "Damn song."

A Christmas carol like Silent Night or Joy to the World. Fin frowns, trying to recall the song, his eyes on the Christmas tree at the bar, white-tipped, white lights behind the glass.

"HO! HO! HO!"

Mr Magoo is Scrooge in a Santa suit and Carl is lying on the couch, smiling at Mr Torch, who's sitting in that chair by the wall. Carl is happy to see him.

"Jingle bells…jingle bells…." Scott is staring at him again. He smiles back. "Jingle, jingle, jingle bells…."

He is back again on a starry night with a fountain splashing below. Underneath doors and between the curtains, lights glowed softly and his indignation is just a dim remembrance. It was wonderful to feel the air and the shower of warm water splashing up at him. He brought over a big terry cloth towel and ducked his eyes. A bare-skinned Scott was laughing at him.

"I did this to meet you. Aren't you flattered?"

He was suspicious actually but interested too. "You could've just come into the lobby…In clothes."

"An' miss this?"

Carl wouldn't have missed it either, not for anything. He stares resentfully at Mr Torch.

"Jingle bells! Jingle bells! Jingle, jingle, jingle bells!"

Wendy gave Mr Torch her nastiest looks the whole time she was there. "A total creep," she said as her fingers flew at her smoke. She went to see him all in white, her hair in her motherly bun. "You aren't going to die anyway."

One long leg crossed over the other, crossed back. She lit another cigarette. He looked at the ashtray. "I am though."

"Oh, for crissakes!" She scooted up then, all tense, reaching over, fingers in the arm of the couch, a sudden brightness in her eyes. "Just take your goddam medicine!"

"That's for pain, Mom. For godsakes, I'm going to die. You act like I want to. I have fucking cancer an' they can't do anything to stop it. I'm fucking twenty-five an' they can't do anything for me!"

As his voice rose, Wendy calmed. She moved from her chair to the side of the couch in a quick, graceful twist, bending down over Carl's face. "Sweetie, don't you worry. I'm going to be right here with you. We're not going to care about anything else or what they say. You're my little boy." She brushed his hair back and kissed his forehead. "I don't want you to worry anymore, do you hear?"

"Mom...."

"Okay, sweetie?"

"Okay," he agreed with a sigh.

Mr Torch looked into her though and there is always now a picture of Mr Torch that overlays everything.

"An' God, that name." Her fingers were flying a mile a minute. "Mr Torch! Wouldn't you think he'd change his name?" she said again when Scott came in.

"Or change professions," Scott countered.

She laughed at that, a laugh which was as close a communion as she'd ever have with him.

"Mr Torch," she said in a softer voice as her eyes drifted away. Mr Torch came to life for Scott too, just as he did for Wendy, who left Carl with a quick kiss.

"See you, sugar."

Easily, casually, without a care in the world. All in white with her hair in her motherly bun. As virtuous as patience.

Mr Torch nods.

Scott is a ball of energy about to blow. In a way, he's a lot like Mr Torch. Carl can even see through him at certain times of the day. A shimmer of light like stardust will fill his eyes and even float inside him. Scott, in the room, passes by on the other side of a pale veil and Carl hears his voice like the last roll of an echo and calls out, "Juice!"

Other times, Scott is real and present, just like now, swinging two bottles of salad dressing at him like plastic pendulums.

"Creamy or garden?"

A garden of stone fountains splashing pink water like punch, shimmering like that stardust, with a pool for Scott and chaise lounges for Wendy, all white, white towels for her hair, sunlit cement and palm trees fluttering up at the bluest of blue skies....

Or a real memory.

"Creamy," he says.

They were out of gas, stopped in the middle of nowhere, waiting for a car to come by. Scott said, "It's too hot to walk." So they waited and Carl remembers the brown of the hills, the oak trees and the waves of heat in the air, the crisp sound of the dry, dry weeds and the feel of Scott's buttons popping open. Then at the last button they could hear the sound of an engine growing louder.

Scott groaned.

"That figures."

Carl scoops a spoonful of noodles off his plate. There's a pea in a puddle of white.

Wendy white.

"See you, sugar."

I LOVE YOU!

It's the force of passion. Scott is looking at him. Sandy freckles, spots of green in his eyes, just like always, a home for Carl's love.

All he remembers and invents is just a parade for Mr Torch.

"Will you kiss me?"

He sees Scott's head go back, grief awakening in the shadows. Then he half smiles and comes over, arm across the back of the couch, leaning slowly. It takes forever, a million, million forevers. His lips are soft and give just a little. Carl's heart leaps in bliss.

Mr Torch is smiling.

Merry Christmas, Mr Torch! Merry Christmas!

A car pulls up outside, a Camaro. Ray pictures Wayne getting out of it. He's sitting in the house he grew up in again and he can see Wayne through the living room window. It's Christmas Eve and that song's playing on the hi-fi.

Hm…hm, hm, hm…hm….

Then Wayne is opening the door and Irene squeezes by from behind and smiles at Ray on her way to the kitchen. "Caspar's."

"Cool."

Christmas lights under the eaves, Caspar's on paper plates.

"I'm sick a goddam White Castle's," he said to Ed after another Christmas away from home.

They were sitting in the same booth they were in the first time they ate there. Ed thought he was referring to lunch, but he really meant what he said in an allover sense. He meant it so much that he suddenly got up and left. A couple of days later he was home. Then he saw Ed again, standing at the bottom of the stairs when he came out of his door one day. Ed wasn't mad. He just smiled up at him and said, "I knew you'd come home."

It is cold and windy out. Fir needles clitter and the windows rattle.

A bell somebody hung in a tree is ringing, clattering noisily as the wind picks up. In Craig's cousin's trailer, the little Christmas tree on the kitchen counter is the only light. But there are other lights outside, glowing through the rectangular window in the trailer's bedroom. Craig's cousin is lying with his head on a bent arm, his arm on his pillow. He can see the outline of Son's face on the pillow next to his.

"Are you asleep?" he asks.

"No."

"Are we going to your dad's party?"

"I guess so."

"You don't want to?"

"Yeah, I want to. It's just Christmas, I think. Not a good time for me. I really wanna hit a somethin', you know, but I'm stayin' away."

"I know."

"I think about it though."

Craig's cousin feels for Son's face in the dark, brushes his hair off his forehead. "You're doin' good, baby. I'm proud a you."

"I wouldn't bother without you, Trevor."

"I'd want you to. I want you to be okay."

Son rolls away onto his side and pushes back under Craig's cousin's arm. "I was usin' a lot for a while. I told you I was in rehab twice, right? I don't even know why I'm still alive, the things I did. An' the other stuff," he adds in a voice Craig's cousin can barely hear. Then, after a moment he asks, "Do you know about my dad's friend, Fin? About his accident?" Craig's cousin nods against his shoulder. "I don't think he fell. My dad says he didn't anyway. Says 'e jumped. This was off a three-story building. There was an overhang or something that broke his fall, so it was really just two stories. Not exactly a sure thing. I guess maybe he didn't really wanna die after all."

"Why are you thinking about this?" Craig's cousin murmurs.

"I don't think I wanted to die either."

"What did you want?"

"I dunno. I think maybe to get back at people. My mom an' dad. Me. To make 'um pay attention. I wanted 'um to hear me."

"Hear you say what, baby?"

"That's the thing. I didn't really know. I was okay. I got away from that guy an' I was jackin' my own self anyway. How do you fix that? My dad couldn't. I think about that, you know? What did Fin want everybody to hear? What do you want everybody to hear, Trevor?"

"Only that you love me."

"You know that."

"Out loud."

"I love you, Trevor."

Craig's cousin sighs and rises up to let Son roll beneath him. "You know I don't mean it that way. Out loud."

"Trevor. My dad. I can't."

He is silent for a moment and then says, "Okay, baby. I can wait for a while." It bothers him that Son is afraid. He can feel the fear in the air and he wants it to go away. "Show me though," he whispers.

"Show you?"

"Show me."

Son's lips touch his, warm and soft, and he can feel Son's breath filling him, a living, breathing spirit that permeates his being, coils quietly inside his heart.

"I love you," Son whispers.

"I love you too, baby."

"I ain't gettin' you no misfit toys!" yells Will.

It is morning and the TV's on. Susie feels like tiptoeing by. She's in awe of all the piles of presents underneath the tree and Will's strange mood. He hides in closets or behind doors, once behind her chair, leaping out suddenly, flinging money at her like green confetti. The first time she ducked, swatting at it, then he picked it back up again and eyed her seriously. "Green is for Christmas."

Numbly, she took his money and then he began to bounce up and down, eyes sparkling.

"Go on, baby, buy me anything you want! I don't care how fuckin' expensive. I am worth it! I want goddam cookies! An' fuckin' roast beef! An' goddam Brussels sprouts! Christmas, baby!"

She keeps waiting for him to go completely insane.

"Cool! The Grinch! I am totally watchin' that."

A big lead in to a gigantic disaster.

"What about our moms, Will?"

A look of worry comes onto his face. "Moms?"

"Aren't we going to see our moms on Christmas?"

His eyes turned to tin. "No."

She's at the mall now, carrying bags full of Will's presents. She found a motorized car she won't put out until he goes to bed on Christmas Eve. She pictures him like a little boy, playing with it under the tree on Christmas morning. She remembers a pink bike she got once, leaning on its kickstand in the living room, a fire popping in the fireplace, stockings on either side.

She wants him to be happy.

One of her bags bobs against the edge of a bay window. She stops and people push by. There's a crafts show in the middle of the mall. The sound of all the voices and the Christmas carols coming out of the speakers in the ceiling fills her ears. There's a snowman in a window with a blue shirt and red ski cap. She taps the glass.

He has a big smile and a carrot nose.

She can put him by the big Santa on the couch under the mistletoe Will ignores. She pulls him under it and points up. "Mistletoe."

"So?"

"Kiss me!"

"I always kiss you."

She sniffs and pushes closer to the window. People are smashing up against her. She yanks her bags away and goes inside the store.

There are candles and candies on the counter. Greeting cards and ornaments cover the shelves. It smells like chocolate and cinnamon and the air is warm. She goes over to the snowman again, puts her bags on the floor and looks back out at the crafts show. There are tables and glass displays, cloth walls covered with paintings, shelves full of pottery, and displays for wind chimes and sun chasers and crystal necklaces.

A man in a ponytail is talking to Miri. Susie can't see her face from here. A moment later, Miri leaves and Susie feels a strange, lonely love for Will.

At home, she runs into the living room with a loud, "Merry Christmas!" and flings a bag's worth of chocolate kisses into the air. Will ducks, curls up, unrolls, swipes one off his lap and yells, "I'm watchin' the fuckin' Grinch, *godammit!*"

Carl giggles. Mr Torch smiles. Mr Volvo's all in Christmas white.

"An angel," he whispers to Mr Torch.

Except he isn't really. White doves will not come down to lift him on high. In his car is a present for Scott with eternity Christmases and Christmases away.

Scott comes over, buttoning his shirt and suddenly drops to the couch. "Shit."

Mr Volvo's coming over. Scott stares at Carl. Carl stares back. Mr Torch sits patiently.

"I'm not here," says Scott.

Carl shrugs.

On the porch, Mr Volvo puts out his cigarette, walking slowly between the giant orange flowers on the walls. He stops and knocks.

"Go away!"

"Carl!" Scott hisses.

Carl shrugs again.

Merry Christmas, Mr Volvo.

Mr Volvo returns to the side of his car and looks up at Carl. He lights another cigarette while Scott puts on his coat and slips Mr Volvo's lighter into a pocket.

Merry Christmas, Mr Volvo.

Merry Christmas, me.

Merry Christmas, Mr Torch.

Merry Christmas, Ray.

Ray is giving Mr Volvo a stare. Mr Volvo puffs on his cigarette and Carl glances at Mr Torch. As he passes by, Scott dims and blurs, only real again outside of Mr Torch's sphere. His lips brush Carl's cheek.

"See you later."

Carl feels a Christmas chill blowing in. It whistles softly and Carl smiles.

Jingle bells, jingle bells....

As cold as snow, as cold as ice, as cold as a star in cold, cold space.

As cold as Wendy's nights.

As cold as Mr Volvo's heart.

As cold as lights in the dark.

As cold as deep, black water.

As cold as you, Mr Torch.

As cold as Christmas and mist and damp....

And Ray's laugh in the wintry air, as magical as icicles.

Kurt is following Ray out of the shop. In the bar, they get a drink and sit down. A luminous yellow glows out of some of the lamps, cherry red out of others, or blue or green. On the inside of the front door there's a big red bow and candy canes in glasses on the bar, glittery glass snowflakes splashing red and yellow and blue lights. Coming through the door is Andy's friend, Roger. He called Ray earlier and after a long pause trying to remember who he was, Ray said, "I'll be at Mulligan's tonight," and disconnected.

Now Ray kicks a chair out for him and Roger goes over, skirting a snow-flocked tree without any presents. At Will's there were presents all over, under the tree, on the couch, a stack in a corner. Will was happy, gesturing at the Christmas-festooned living room. "I got shit for everybody!"

Then he looked at Roger and began to frown until Andy said, "Roger," and Will said, "Oh, yeah. Yeah." Then: "Oh, shit, man. I forgot you."

"That's okay."

"No, no, man. It's Christmas." He put a hand on Roger's shoulder and tapped a fingertip against his lips, staring glassy-eyed at him for a moment. Then his face brightened and his other hand came down on Roger's other shoulder and he said, "I know. You can do me a favor."

Roger agreed. "Sure, I can do that."

"Cool."

At the bar, he scoots up and says, "I got this memorized." He went through it with Will, who kept jabbing a finger in the air at every point.

"Number one...." Jab.

Ray sighs and lets his eyes close.

"I love you, man. I totally love you...." Jab.

Will was in a red robe, blue and white check pajama bottoms, kingly to Roger, as he spun in his living room or paced back and forth, eyes aglow. Will was a little crazy too.

"A visionary," Ray always says with a laugh. Which was part of Roger's attraction.

"Number two. You an' me. We're a force!"

One of Ray's eyes comes slowly open, a laugh twinkling inside. "You know I just saw 'im, right?"

Roger pauses. "No."

"Well, I did," says Ray. "Coulda told me this himself. Just so you know. Cuz I dunno what the fuck this is all about."

"Well, maybe you will," says Roger. "I haven't finished yet."

"Yeah, yeah," says Ray, leaning his head back against the wall behind him. "You were on number three."

"Number three. Mega bucks. You an' me can make bank. Number four. You are key. I look up to you, an' nobody, nobody's gonna say Will ain't that fuckin' big. Cuz I am. I am totally without jealousy. I rule in my circle. You an' me. King to King."

"You memorized this?"

"Well, yeah...."

Number three made Roger smile, which caused the blood to drain out of Will's face and then fill back up again.

"What the hell are you smilin' at?"

"You. I mean, you give real good speeches."

"I wasn't fuckin' done either, an' now I lost my goddam place!"

"Number four," said Andy. "You're a king."

"Oh yeah. Yeah. An' I'm in *pain!* Number five," he added.

At the bar Roger hugs himself like Will. Will was dramatic, lit up by the Christmas tree, full of passion. Roger's arms fly open.

"I need *love* an' your kid, man, number goddam six is a fucking asshole...Sorry. Sorry. Like I said, this is Will talkin'...I gave up a woman for you. You owe me this. King to King. I want a goddam safe zone."

And then Will's arm, fist at the end, rose in glory. "I—WANT—JACK'S CLUB!"

At Will's, Roger applauded. Will bowed.

At the bar, Ray leans over and points at him. "I got one for ya. Hm...hm, hm, hm...hm...."

Wendy used to make gingerbread houses at Christmas. Once she made one with icicles of sugar, a gumdrop pine tree, coconut snow.

"I might do that again," she said with her fingers waving in the air.

At Mr Torch's, there was a bowl of candy canes and red and green peppermints. "With the goddam urns!" she yelled, fingers in motion. Cranberries and popcorn in the trees outside. "I just about puked."

Carl got a plane with a real engine for Christmas once. His father liked it too and put half of it together under the tree before Wendy finally came out with her knife buzzing angrily and said, "Godammit, John!"

"Do you remember that plane I got for Christmas one year?" asked Carl and she laughed at the memory of John yelling back at her, "Fine! I'll make my own goddam plane!"

"Fine!"

After Christmas he filled up the garage with piles of sheet metal and she couldn't fit her car inside anymore.

"I have a present for you," she said when she got back from Mr Torch's.

It came in a big box wrapped in gold paper with green Christmas trees all over it. Inside there was a blanket as red as cranberries or cinnamon candy.

"Merry Christmas, sugar." Her lips were cool, slightly remote. She was pulling away, out of Mr Torch's sphere. Mr Torch was real now. Mr Torch sold urns.

Carl giggles out loud and thinks, *Scorchin', Mr Torch. You can't touch these prices!*

Orange and green and red halos floated slowly on the walls. "Like a fuckin' disco ball!" yelled Will.

Susie stood there in amazement as Will pushed a remote control button and the Christmas tree began to spin. "I love it!" he yelled, as bubbly as Miri at the arts and crafts show. Susie forgot to jump in delight or clap or cheer or—

"I bought it for you!"

"Oh."

"You do it."

He gave her the remote and stood there in his underwear and a tee-shirt with a wreath on it. She felt numb and stared back at him.

All of a sudden, he brightened up again and pushed a little ball on the wreath on his shirt and all the other little balls began to flash and glow.

She suddenly began to laugh. "Hey, that's cool."

She even began to like all those globes of color on the walls. It was like being at the North Pole in Santa's house with the whole world's presents under one giant tree.

Will grabbed her and spun her in circles.

"Christmas is cooooool!"

A flurry of tiny snowflakes appear and melt in the shiny dark. The lights in town keep glowing.

At the Club, Ray and Miri are dancing an almost motionless dance. He sees Otis smile. There's no music. The bar is empty, chairs up on the tables. The only sound is the click of the glasses Otis is putting away and his own humming. "Hm…hm, hm, hm…hm…."

He pictures Irene on Christmas morning, sitting on the couch in the light of the tree, sipping her coffee. Outside, sunshine, crisp and bright and clear.

"Hm…hm, hm, hm…hm…."

He always had to wait to open his presents, wait for Wayne, eating slices of banana bread until Irene sighed and said, "Go on an' get 'im." Then Wayne would come out with a robe on over his boxers and tee-shirt.

Christmas was always good though. After the banana bread she'd bring out a cheese ball covered in nuts and put that record on the hi-fi.

"Hm…hm, hm, hm…hm…."

A silver, snowy night. A night full of silver bells swinging in the trees….

"Just like urns," says Wendy.

Carl can see them, catching the moonlight, brightening, coming closer and closer, silver bells, sleigh bells…Christmas bells!

Mr Magoo!

A very merry Christmas….

Mr Torch is absent. Suddenly Carl is awake and he can see the empty chair.

Outside, bells ring and he feels like he is floating. George and Henry's sign is across from him and lights pass by underneath. Suddenly he's at the Acropolis Inn, standing in the parking lot near the palm tree where silver glitter sparkles on the surface of the pool. He's in his pajamas, his feet are bare, and when he looks at the lobby the light inside suddenly goes out.

He jerks and wakes back up and sees Mr Torch again. Mr Torch looks like Mr Magoo. He's in a red Santa suit. Carl looks away. There's a light on under the bedroom door. He can hear Scott and somebody else. Mr Torch is going over there. He's carrying a sack and suddenly Carl knows he's going to put Scott in it. He is laughing Mr Magoo's laugh.

"Noooo!"

Mr Torch stops and backs away.

Scott comes out and Carl kicks at the blanket Wendy gave him until Scott falls on top of him and says, "Carl, shush…."

Carl gasps. He wasn't breathing. He looks over at the light in the door. Scott sinks down beside him. "Jesus, Carl."

He can still hear the bells and Mr Magoo's faraway laugh. "HO! HO! HO!"

Mr Volvo's successor comes into the light at the door. He is putting his coat on. Mr Torch is a chill in any room. It takes more than a bright Christmastime. It takes more than gumdrops and candy canes.

It takes palm trees and cool, blue water and TV and Wendy's pink slippers and Mr Magoo and Ray's bells and Christmas tee-shirts and Christmas lights that float in the air like—"Disco balls!"

And a tee-shirt that glows in the dark with Will inside it, looming over Susie with a luminous face.

"Santa's here!"

And Christmas parties!

And "Jingle bell! Jingle bell! Jingle, jingle, jingle BELL!"

Hm...hm, hm, hm...hm....

Silver bells and mistletoe.

Hm...hm, hm, hm...hm....

"Kiss me!"

And cool, cool winter's light, goose bumps, and cartoons. "An' fruitcake!" yells Will. "I want fruitcake!"

And Scott lying beside him.

And Mr Volvo a million miles away.

And Santa Claus.

And Santa's laugh. Ho! Ho! Ho!

Ho! Ho! Ho!

HO! HO! HO!

21

◆ Icicles ◆

In the liquor store, there's a cardboard cut-out of a giant Harvey's Bristol Cream bottle. It's visible from outside, between the end of the counter and the door, and has a rope of brass sleigh bells around its neck. On the windows, covered up on the inside with shelves full of real bottles, there's a picture of Santa and his reindeer over mounds of snow and the tops of red brick chimneys. In the open door, Kurt appears and shakes the bells he took off the Harvey's Bristol Cream bottle.

"Rudolph!"

A minute later he's trotting back over to the car.

Jonah is sitting inside, staring at the Christmas tree lot he can see in his side mirror, picturing Santa and the liquor store reindeer landing in that winter wonderland across the street. The entrance is a giant plastic igloo with a candy cane walkway leading up to it. Strings of lights shine down on the fake snow.

It's probably colder over there just because it looks colder.

After Kurt gets back in the car, he takes the bag and Kurt swings his arm across the seat and backs out of the parking lot.

"Got some extras."

"What for?"

"Presents maybe."

Jonah doesn't say anything to this. He didn't get Agnes a present because he couldn't think of anything that was special enough for her. Then he realized he was really thinking of something that she could remember him by and he couldn't even look after that.

At Kurt's he takes a Harvey's Bristol Cream gift box and a fruitcake in red cellophane out of the bag.

"Don't give me this."

"Naw."

It's the only thing that even looks like Christmas that Kurt has besides the snowflake glasses he pours the whiskey into.

"I got my pops' old pickup for a present once," says Jonah, remembering Aster's tarts with the white icing.

"That's a good present."

He nods and feels a chill, the memory of a cold day. That Christmas Abel bought a new pickup, but didn't tell anybody about it, left it at the dealership in Enders. Jonah's present was Abel's old pickup. Its blue paint was sun-bleached and the underside of the roof was bare metal. Worse, though, the door on the driver's side wouldn't stay closed anymore so Abel tied a rope through the side and back windows. Then the side window wouldn't roll all the way up to the top and the back window wouldn't slide all the way shut. The cold always blew in and the rope always loosened and had to be tied up again. But it ran, so he guesses it was a good present.

After a moment, he notices the glass he's drinking out of. "Where'd you get these?"

Kurt puts his feet up on the bed, leaning back in his chair. "Kmart." Then he adds, "I got some good presents too," in a tone that makes Jonah pause and then ask, "At Kmart?"

Kurt stares at him. "Christmas. I got a scooter once."

"Oh."

Jonah didn't really like the pickup Abel gave him but not because of the door or the beat up interior. It worried him because he wasn't sure what it meant or what might come after it. When he quit school, Abel didn't seem mad, just annoyed. Then a few weeks later when Jonah came into the kitchen through the service porch, his head seemed to suddenly explode. He fell against the doorframe, confused and scared until his sluggish brain began to work again. Abel had hit him. Then he saw him coming up again, slamming a fist into his temple. His head bounced off the doorframe and he grabbed onto it with both arms to keep upright. A moment later Abel put his lips against Jonah's swollen face. "That's for quittin' school without tellin' me. An' I meant it about gettin' a job."

The shock made him feel sick for the rest of the day. Abel's logic could take weeks to surface.

That whole last Christmas was strange to him. There was no tree and almost no food, just the cans on the service porch shelves. Sissy's snowflakes always took him by surprise. That morning, before he got the truck, Abel woke him up and he went out into the kitchen where there was a gold box tied up with a red bow on the kitchen table. He thought he was dreaming. It was still dark outside. Abel was pouring bourbon into his coffee and he just waited, thinking he'd wake up.

He felt that way a lot and sometimes found Orly staring at him when he wasn't looking. It started on the day he came to work sick and Ira drove him home. He remembers that his throat was sore and his skin was hot, but he didn't really think about it. He went home because Orly told him to. He didn't come back for almost a week. Even then, he hurt, but he didn't know if he was still sick. Every pain blurred into one. When he came back to work he kept his head down low. Abel dropped him off in the early dark and he skirted the light coming out of the office, got the mop out of the storage closet and started to scrub the bathroom floors.

Afterwards, he stayed out back and smoked a cigarette.

Then he ducked his head down again, went out to the front and stepped up the single step into the office. Nothing from Orly. Then the silence finally drew his head up. Orly was still sitting, elbows on the counter, hands pressed hard across his mouth. The surrounding skin was bone white.

Jonah's stomach dropped. He felt sick and guilty. "It's okay, Orly."

Orly's head moved. His hands came down slowly. Jonah knew what he saw, the lingering puffiness, purple and blue face, the holes in his cheek, scabbed over like poisonous black pustules. "Why?"

"It was my fault."

"Your fault?"

He nodded and Orly listened to his story about the roof and the tarp and the cold that made him sloppy. "I slipped. Fell."

Orly's face blanched with anger. "You really expect me to believe that?"

"It's the truth!"

He was grateful for his belligerence, grateful that it was still there, that he wasn't numb all the time. He didn't want to talk about the times that Abel beat him up, not even to Orly. He was twenty years old then, sixteen the last time Abel had hit him. And he was ashamed. Ashamed that it marked him in some way, that he was somebody that other people could do that to, that he deserved it. But then he thought that if that's why his mother didn't stay with him, he didn't deserve her. Then he thought of her flowers on the bathroom wall, her tomato soup, her plastic laundry basket, all the things that aggravated Abel.

"I told you. It was my fault. I shoulda done it before it started raining."

Orly put up his palms as if to ward him off. "I'm not listening to this."

He was better by Christmas, but he didn't really feel better. Outside with Abel that day, he crossed his arms in front of him and only realized he forgot to put his shoes on because the gravel felt like ice. He looked down in surprise. Abel was grinning in anticipation. "See it?"

The question made him angry for some reason. "See what?"

"Your present."

"No."

There was nothing there that wasn't always there and the cold hurt his ears, or at least he thought it was the cold, and he began to shuffle on the icy gravel while Abel kept on grinning.

"C'mon."

"Just tell me. I'm cold."

Abel's voice rose a little, his face flushing too. "You're taking all the fun out of this, Jojo."

"There's nothing out here."

Abel swallowed some of his coffee, took an exaggerated look around, and then looked back at him. "I see it."

"Christ," Jonah said. "Now I don't even want it."

He did though. It was Christmas and that's the way it was supposed to be. It was cold and there was no fire in the fireplace. Aster was dead and he felt sorry for himself and just wanted to go inside.

Sissy looked frozen too, standing there in her nightgown with her box in her arms.

A moment later Abel's keys hit him in the chest.

"Merry fuckin' Christmas, Jojo."

There are sounds in the walls, a tremor of voices, TVs. A door opens and footsteps approach, drum down the steps and fade away. A car starts up a while later. Joy's is quiet though.

Yawning, Jonah sets his empty glass in the sink. "I'm too old to be stayin' up nights."

"You work nights," Kurt reminds him.

"I can't sleep anymore."

"Why not? Asa?"

"Yeah. Ally's mom's gonna watch 'im for us when she goes back to work."

"Too bad she has to."

"Never make it on what we make."

"No kidding. Wes says we're gettin' raises though."

"Why do you listen to that guy?"

"Because he knows stuff. I dunno how."

"You're an easy mark, man. You shouldn't believe 'im."

"Why not?"

"People lie all the time, you know."

"I don't."

Jonah feels a jolt of surprise, then he realizes it's probably true. He takes his keys off the kitchen table and eyes him with affection. "You're the last of the good guys, Kurt."

"Laugh if you want."

"I'm not laughin'."

Pulling on his coat, he kicks at Kurt's chair where he's still sitting with his feet on the bed, eyes closed. Kurt opens one sleepy eye, the other squinted shut.

"Truthfully," says Jonah, gesturing with his chin to the glass bird on top of Kurt's refrigerator. "Are you really gonna give 'er that?"

Kurt's other eye opens up and he drops his feet to the floor. "I was." His tone is suddenly suspicious and he can see himself giving it to her early when she comes out to break up the ice on her birdbath.

"Truthfully?"

His face twists into a resentful scowl. "Well, no, I guess not. Why?"

"I didn't get Agnes anything."

Kurt sighs. He thinks Christmas is the best time. Christmas would make her friendlier. She wouldn't really ignore him on Christmas. Then he says, "Oh, alright. Go on. Take it."

"Thanks, bubby." Jonah slips the little bird into his pocket and taps Kurt's ankle with the tip of his boot. "See you Christmas, okay? An' no fruitcake."

Kurt guffaws, then moves over to the bed and lies down as the door closes. It wasn't really like she was going to invite him in for champagne or anything.

At Ira's, Jonah stops and stares as the light grows on frosty weeds and pools of starlight.

He remembers Ira's misty lights, Sissy's snowflakes, Waylon's Christmas tree and a pot belly stove that blew out hot air, and Orly's bowl of peppermints on the counter. At home, the tarp was a pool of blue on the gravel and the rain made a smacking sound as it bounced off the plastic. He lay over a hole he almost fell through and saw the rainy sky grow as luminous as silver.

At Ira's now there are only weeds and misty firs. A pale day that gray birds disappear into. This is the way it was before Ira, when Ellie Sparrow came here, just weeds and the movements of the wind. In the summer, bugs spun in golden halos. Now a 'For Sale' sign is hanging from a post beside the road. It twists his stomach to think something might change.

Lighting a cigarette, he rolls down his window and pulls away.

The signal light sways slightly and the firs and the buildings around the intersection begin to take shape. A ghostly bluish tinge appears in the sky.

In the parking lot at Waylon's, Jonah stays outside his pickup, smoking in the dark. The smoke warms his throat, soothes him. He has quit before, but it's his fingers more than anything else that grow antsy. Then his antsiness grows into irritation, and then the irritation becomes anger. He can smoke until his throat feels raw, drink until his throat feels raw, and nothing ever stops him. On early mornings, his headlights occasionally catch a figure running up ahead of him. It always leaps off the road into the firs until he passes, dropping back onto the pavement in his side mirror. He recognizes him, never slows, never moves over. He's always been naturally strong the way Abel was, big muscles fed by anger, probably. It wouldn't occur to him to take any special care of his body. The thought is strange and he tries to imagine running like that, coughing his lungs clear again. Smoking is a reflex, a habit of his fingers, a comfort to him. Putting his cigarette up to his lips again, he inhales deeply, exhales slowly through his nose.

At Kurt's earlier, he passed Joy's darkened apartment and thought about the day he came in and set her tree in the window for her. She attracted him and it wasn't her looks or proximity. He had to think about it and concluded it was her utter lack of energy. She bought a Christmas tree and decorations, but he could tell that she didn't really care. She was going through the motions and his attraction to her grew. He could take her and she wouldn't resist. He could upset her whole life with hardly a ripple for anyone to see. She was like him, he thought. A lot like him. The idea of leaving no ripples in the world bewitches him. The pull of Ivy's where he can sink into a silty otherworld. His home with no one there but ghosts. Ally could be happy again and Asa only needs her. He could disappear and only Kurt and Agnes would really care.

Taking a last drag on his cigarette, he tosses it away. Kurt's little bluebird is pressing into his hip. He's happy he has a present for her now, but she has a lot of other presents.

"A ton from my mother," she told him.

"Does she get you good stuff?" he asked.

"Pretty good."

She said it thoughtfully though because Mavis didn't really know her anymore. All the things she bought her, she could probably buy for any other girl as easily. Mavis spent three Christmases with Agnes and Agnes said she remembered her last one. "I got up real early an' my mom picked me up an' we went downstairs in the dark. That's what I really remember. The lights on the tree were so bright, that was all I could see, just those lights, so pretty an' colorful. I guess there were presents, but I only remember a doll, a really big doll," she said with memory-bright eyes. Jonah could only look at her with a feeling of helplessness while she talked. He would never have thought it true that even Mavis could leave a ripple.

When Orly's tree starts shining in the window, Jonah puts Kurt's bird in the glove box and leans back against the side of the pickup again. A car with a tree on its roof goes by, disappearing.

Thinking of Agnes's Christmas with Mavis, he remembers his own last Christmas with Abel and Sissy again, although he didn't remember that it was Christmas at first. One minute he was asleep and the next there was a shape in the dark, looking down at him. His door was open and there was a tinge of gray in the hall. Then Abel bent closer and whispered, "C'mon. Get up."

He already smelled like bourbon. The room was beginning to grow lighter. Jonah stared at his familiar dresser but the strangeness didn't leave.

"An' be quiet," Abel added. The living room was silver with beams of brightness coming through Sissy's snowflakes. "I got this for your sister."

Abel was still whispering. The gold box was on the table with the red ribbon in a lopsided bow Abel pulled loose again. Jonah went over to the coffee pot, then Abel took the lid off the box and Jonah said, "It looks like you robbed a drug store."

"Yep. Went in an' cleaned 'um right out."

Then, after he tied the ribbon back on, less lopsided this time, Abel said, "Getch your sis."

She came out in a flannel nightgown and a pair of blue slippers. The present made her nervous, or maybe it was Abel's eagerness. Her mouth opened in surprise, though, and she pulled everything out in a rush, went around the kitchen table to hug him, and then put everything back in the box again, hugging it close to her. Jonah's skin felt cold and shivery. He couldn't look at them, drank his coffee with his eyes half-closed. Later, Fin came over and they went out and brought home a pizza. That night, Jonah dreamed that he was driving in Abel's old pickup and couldn't stop it. The road was a blur of twists and turns, and he pumped at the brakes, tires squealing. Then the landscape changed even though the road kept twisting. It rose above the timber line and there were steep drops on either side. Then the tires began to wobble and the steering wheel jerked out of his hands. In the next moment, his door popped open and he was suddenly airborne. Below, there was nothing, no trees, no houses, just ragged boulders, scrubby weeds and scree. He saw the ground come up, tiny, sharp-edged rocks glittering in the cold white light. Then suddenly he woke up, panting loudly, feeling at his pitted cheek, doubt dissolving at the awakened tenderness. Sometimes he didn't believe until his fingers felt it or he put his face up close to the mirror. Over time the red rawness washed away. The scars now are just dim reminders until his temper flares, but he remembers lying on the carpet one day with Agnes kneeling beside him, a look of pain in her eyes.

He grew uncomfortable because he knew she was looking at his scars.

"I fell," he said. "Messed up my face."

"Fell where?"

"Off the garage roof."

"I always wondered how you got those," she said and leaned her hip against him. Then she cupped his face and kept staring.

He imagined that his scars were turning red. "You don't scare me anymore," she told him and he laughed at that at first and then stopped. He felt the moisture growing between her palm and his cheek and moved his face away. She rested her weight on her hip and said, "I don't like to think about you being hurt."

"Me either."

Sometimes his story becomes real to him and he sees himself up there, sliding on the slippery boards, trying to grab on.

"You were lucky," she said.

"Yeah, I was."

He didn't break anything. He didn't even really fall. The memory isn't always there, but there are times he freezes outside the garage, unable to make himself go in. Other times, he can enter without really thinking about it. This year, though, he told Ally he couldn't find the Christmas lights because the thought of going in that garage made him sick. Ally was standing on the porch, hugging herself in the cold, her breath frosty and pale.

"I don't know where they went," he said. "Probably tossed 'um accidently."

"I think I saw some on sale," she said.

"Where at?"

"Safeway."

There was nothing in her voice, but the Safeway was next door to Candi's, a block away from the bowling alley; he thought of all the times he met Agnes there. He wasn't being careful anymore, not really. "I should look again first," and he finally went into the garage.

The light was faint over the dusty rafters and thin strings of cobwebs moved in the air. The hard packed ground had a dry and musty smell and he looked down on it for the signs of a stain, some evidence of where he lay bleeding into the earth, but there was nothing. Then he looked up again at the boxes on the shelves, imagined finding decorations from years ago, went back out without the lights and said, "Never mind. We can't afford the damn electric bill anyway."

It's called the Elysian Fields Mobile Home Park.

Craig's cousin lives there now; Mavis once lived there with her mother. They had the last lot in the park next to a hedge the trailer park gardener always cut down to window level even though the hedge belonged to Dinna, who lived in the house on the other side. Dinna wasn't happy about having a trailer park next door or about the garden art Mavis' mother used to make out of pop cans. Dinna's kitchen window was right across the hedge with chintz curtains and ceramic salt and pepper shakers on the ledge.

One day, when Mavis's mother threw a pop can into a garbage pail she kept outside by her work bench, Dinna said, "Yes, ma'am, that sure is trash, alright," loud enough for Mavis's mother to hear.

Mavis's mother smiled at Dinna with mock politeness and said, "Trash is in the eye of the beholder, my dear."

Dinna slammed her window shut and one day later on yelled, "I'm not payin' property taxes just to live next door to a bunch a trash!" That's when Mavis's mother finally lost her temper and yelled, "Well, I'm not payin' to live next door to a bunch a trash like you either!"

That Christmas, she rolled her cans in glitter and hung them outside as decorations. That was the Christmas Mavis met Waylon and saw a real house for herself, a bigger TV, a car, and a honeymoon in a place with a beach and a moonlit dance floor, and pearls and diamonds and champagne.

Her real honeymoon was at a casino by a lake, her real life was Waylon's market, and Waylon's house, and the lunch counter, and Orly with his toothpicks and donuts and checkers, not white, empty beaches or champagne at night or sunshine and dance floors, but the yellow signal light and Orly's gas station and Ira's meadow.

She isn't really faraway because she always thinks of Agnes.

At Christmas, she pictures Agnes drinking hot chocolate by Waylon's pot belly stove. She bought her a lava lamp this Christmas, remembering one in her mother's trailer. She pictures empty pop cans with glitter every time she sees the Christmas lights in the courtyard of her apartment building. She lives where it never snows and almost never rains. She sees a man who buys her diamonds and champagne, just like she always used to dream about. At Christmas, on brightly lit streets, she always thinks of Agnes.

The tree on Orly's counter looks bigger from outside. Its blurry lights glow on the frosty glass.

After Aster died, winter came, and then Christmas, and Abel sat watching TV. They didn't have presents or ham for dinner. That whole day Abel thought about Aster's tarts and Christmas with her family, all the cookies and candies he ate, and the ham and her parsnips with orange sauce.

One year, Sissy cooked ham slices and scalloped potatoes for dinner. Before that though, she made her paper snowflakes for the first time. Abel was already sitting in his chair with a drink before he saw them in the window above him. A grayish light came through the thin paper and there were patterns on the floor. He looked at Sissy sitting cross-legged on the carpet watching TV and said, "Are those yours, baby?"

She nodded, paper pale like her snowflakes.

She must have talked, Jonah realizes, but when he thinks about it, he can never recall hearing her.

After Abel fell asleep, Jonah gave her her coat and put a finger to his lips. Then they went outside and got into the pickup. Inside, she sat tentatively, perched almost, with her fingers around the handle. He let the truck roll, staring out the back window, listening to the gravel popping underneath.

He remembers it was cold and clear out.

He didn't care if they were stopped. They didn't have a tree and that was Abel's fault. Even Sissy's snowflakes didn't make Abel think about getting a Christmas tree. He just went to sleep with their shapes on his chest.

"I have Aunt Hil's birthday money," he said, looking sideways at her. She was staring at him watchfully. She waited on everything that happened around her. "You can pick the tree if you want," he said. Then she relaxed a little and folded her hands in her lap.

The day was cold. Clouds came and went and made shadows over the straw-covered Christmas tree lot. The air smelled woodsy and good. Except for one family, there was no one else there. The woman in the family kept pointing out trees and the man kept picking each one up and shaking it. Needles fell each time. Once, the man said, "Nice an' fresh," but then he put the tree down anyway and kept looking.

Jonah followed them for a while, not sure why. They had two boys and a girl. The girl looked his age, the boys younger. He wandered off before they found their tree, walked along the perimeter of the lot by the sidewalk, then found Sissy near the kiosk next to a tree with a strangely wide and bushy bottom and spindly branches near the top. For no particular reason he picked it up and shook it. Needles fell.

"This one?"

She made an "uhm-hm" sound and went back to sucking on the candy cane he bought her. After he paid for the tree, he had only a dollar in change, so he bought another candy cane for himself, put the tree in the back of the pickup and drove off.

At home, Abel was waiting with his coffee on the porch. Sissy got out of the pickup and edged away from her door but didn't go over. Jonah saw her looking behind her, looking for him. Then Abel took a swallow of his coffee and came down a step. Jonah stayed on the other side of the pickup.

"C'mere," said Abel, but Jonah didn't move. "I don't recall you being old enough to drive. Got yourself a license, do you?"

"Nobody stopped us."

Abel went around the back of the truck, looking down at the tree as he circled around to Jonah's side. Jonah sidled away, keeping the same distance.

"Your money?"

"Yeah."

"Didn't ask."

"You were asleep," he said. Then, when Abel put his cup on the roof, he bolted up the porch steps and slammed through the door of the house.

"Godammit, Jojo!"

Inside, he skidded across the cold, gray floor. The TV was still on, the shadow of snowflakes on the carpet. In the hallway, he stopped, wondering where to go. Then he heard Abel coming up the steps, went into the bathroom, locked the door, and got up on the edge of the tub underneath the transom. He heard Abel in the hallway.

"C'mon outta there."

The glass in the transom was a pale bubbly blue and the trim was painted white like the walls and beginning to peel. He opened it and put his arm through and jumped up, soles squeaking on the slippery tile.

Outside again, where Sissy still stood by the pickup, Abel passed underneath the spruce by the kitchen window and jumped the rest of the way up to catch Jonah's arm before he slipped back in.

"You break that window, you're in goddam trouble."

"Let me go!" he yelled, stuck between the transom and the sill.

Abel pulled on his arm and he felt it pinch and started to squeal. "That hurt?"

"Yes!"

"Good."

"Let me go!"

"Only if you come out, you hear me?"

"Okay. Okay."

After he dropped down, he waited there a while, squeezing his pinched arm in his fingers, then went slowly into the living room. It was getting dark and the snowflake patterns were gone.

Outside, Abel was waiting by the pickup with the little tree on the gravel. When he saw Jonah he said, "Take it inside. Then come help me with the decorations."

A few minutes later he found Abel in the garage and stood in the doorway, rubbing his pinched arm. Abel was on a ladder, pulling boxes off the shelves.

"C'mere an' take this." Jonah set the box on the ground, then took two more. When he was done, Abel jumped down off the ladder, set a box in Jonah's arms, put a hand on top of his head and gave him a light shake. "I'm surprised, Jojo. This was a pretty damned good idea."

Then Abel picked up a stack of boxes and they went inside.

The light is growing and mist rises off the firs. The air is damp and a hint of something sour wafts over from the garbage bin behind Waylon's back door.

Now Jonah is crossing the dark parking lot toward the spill of light out Waylon's windows. He saw Orly come over from the gas station a few minutes ago. Inside, he is sitting at the counter, jabbing a toothpick at Waylon as he sings, "Four bags a cranberries, three tins a cookies, two homemade pies, an' a thousand fruuuit cakes!"

Jonah takes a seat beside Orly. Waylon's mouth opens. It's a game they play every Christmas.

"On the fifth day of Christmas USPS gave to me...."

Orly waits. Waylon stops and Jonah half rises, reaching over the counter for one of the mugs stacked beside the coffee pot.

"You lose."

"I do not. I was just about to go," Waylon says. "You cut me off."

Reaching now for the coffee pot, Jonah murmurs, "Five Christmas trees," before sitting back down again.

"Hey," says Orly.

"Five Christmas trees! Four bags a—"

"You helped."

"Just gettin' my coffee."

"Three tins a—"

"Stop!"

"Two homemade pies—"

"I quit!"

"An' a thousand fruuuuit cakes!"

It is growing lighter and lighter outside, filling the windows like mirrors.

At school, the auditorium is still decorated with aluminum stars and green paper garlands. On the day of the Christmas dance, Agnes stopped to look inside and heard sounds in the cafeteria but didn't see anybody.

"Are you goin'?" His voice surprised her and she jumped and looked around at Doug. "Sorry," he said.

"That's okay."

"Are you?"

"No."

"Me neither."

She waited, but he didn't ask her. She thought he wanted to. She pictured the dresses and dim lights and gave him another quick look. His eyes were pointed toward the floor and there was a slightly defensive look on his face. Not belligerent really. Misunderstood, she thought. Maybe he thought that she expected things of him, but looking back she couldn't really say that he wasn't any of the things she expected. She felt sorry suddenly about Doug and the dance she wasn't going to. The sight of the decorated auditorium gave her a pang. She wanted to go with him and be the way she used to be, smell the smell of his familiar car, talk about things not worth remembering, little everyday things, but she heard herself say, "Betsy's mom's picking us up," and saw him nod. For a moment though, he gave her a long, almost gentle look, then said, "I'll see you, Agnes."

A moment later, the corridor was empty. He went through the door at the other end and she pinched her nose, feeling it suddenly burn, and blinked her eyes, feeling tears well up. Then, after a moment, she sniffed and looked back at the auditorium. She made herself think of Jonah and the leather wrist band she bought him for Christmas, not sure if he'd ever wear it. She made his face appear and made herself feel happier.

Walking back down the corridor, she picked up her speed to a cheerful pace. In the parking lot, waiting by her mother's car, Betsy waved and Agnes went over with a smile.

On the day that Agnes came up to the house for the first time, he held the screen door open just enough to let her slip by. Then, in the living room, he sat down on the couch, picked up the remote, put it back down again and rubbed his face.

"Is this where you grew up?" she asked and he thought of Mavis for some reason.

"Yeah."

She sat down on the couch with some space between them, looking at him while he stared at the carpet. Then she said, "Is that an angel?"

He looked down at the angel tattoo on his arm and nodded. "Yeah."

"I like tattoos."

"Yeah?"

"They're like wearing memories on your skin."

He gave a short laugh but smiled at her. "Not all the time. Guess so for me, though."

"Are you really lonely?" she asked.

It took him a moment to remember telling her that he made up Clete. "Yeah, I guess. A little anyway." Then she came closer and he whispered, "Agnes, don't." So when she slid next to him, he didn't look at her again for a moment. It was cool out, not summer, but he closed his eyes and smelled strawberries, and then he looked back at her and said, "I wish you didn't come here."

"Do you want me to go?"

"Yes. No." He dropped his head against his folded hands, rocking himself on the edge of the couch. "I swear to God, Agnes, you're gonna break me into a million pieces."

"I just want to be with you, that's all."

She sounded plaintive and he felt angry. "You just don't get it, Agnes. I'm about to ruin everything. You. Me. I have a wife, Agnes. I have a wife."

Her voice was small. "Do you love her?"

"Yes. No. I don't know for sure." He lifted his head off his hands. He knew his face was red. He looked at Agnes's face, her eyes brimming with tears. "Why me?" he asked.

"Because I love you," she answered.

Inside, he felt the silent breaking apart of everything he was. On the outside, he just leaned back against the couch and said, "C'mere, Agnes."

Then he kissed her, felt lips as soft as an angel's. Then he put his tongue in her mouth and felt her hand on his cheeks, smoothing at the roughness of his scars. His skin felt cool in the wake of her fingers. Then she sat up for a moment, staring at him, astonishment shining on her face.

"Aren't you afraid?" he asked.

"No."

"Have you ever done this before?"

She shook her head and her skin flushed bright red. He touched her cheek with his fingertips and said, "I won't hurt you."

But he was lying and the lie tasted like salt in his mouth.

The pale sun is up, wisps of mist disappearing. The air is damp and still, firs motionless, the gray drizzly sky without clouds. Wishing for sun, Jonah pulls up at the house near Ally's car. He remembers snowy Christmases, white flocked firs, a snow dusted world, but it seems a long time ago. He found Asa's snow globe still in one piece under a bush by the garage and wound it up in surprise. The same tinny, small notes of Jingle Bells rang out. In the baby's room, he picks it up off the dresser and shakes it, watching the cloud of white specks swirl and drift. He remembers snow in Abel's headlights, swirling and drifting, just like that.

One year, Aster made stockings out of pieces of felt and leftover fabric. He remembers it especially because he came out for a drink of water one night and she was there under the lamp, working in secret. Tiptoeing up behind her, he saw a red and white sailboat on his. His name was stitched on it, but the fabric was from a dress she made for Sissy and he came out from behind her and yelled, "That's for girls!"

She jumped and the pieces fell and Abel spilled his drink and yelled, "Goddammit, Jojo!"

He doesn't remember what Abel did after that, he just remembers the look on Aster's face, a look that seems to slide over Ally's face, a smile covering her worry.

"Hi," she says, picking up Asa. "I didn't hear you."

He sets the snow globe down. She was slipping blue booties onto Asa's chubby feet. He looks like a snowball in his puffy white jumper.

"Hi." She is taking Asa home for the day. "I might put those lights up while you're out," he says.

"You don't have to. We have a lot of other decorations."

"I dunno. I might anyway."

He knows that there are lights at her house, icicles, a blow-up Santa in the front yard. Three Christmas balls hanging from the branches of a maple tree outside. Their Christmas card was a picture of their house. Wishing You Christmas Joy All Year Long on the back. "Not much of a wish," he commented. "Year's almost over."

Ally didn't respond. He looked at the picture of the house as if it might tell him something about her. But he didn't think of her for long. Their house could be Aster's with hydrangeas instead of irises. He remembers his mother's childhood home because he went there with Abel and Aunt Hilary after she died. He didn't really know his grandmother, who was still alive, because Aster stopped going to see her. Looking back, he realizes he never thought it was strange that she didn't go back home. He didn't really look past his own family, the house on the empty, quiet property they lived on. He only went to his mother's old house the one time; he doesn't like going to Ally's either.

Walking outside with her, he feels that fleeting wish for snow again. "Be careful," he says. "Roads are probably slick."

She nods, looking up through her open window at him. He glances back at Asa, red-faced, over-heated in his puffy jumper.

"You look tired, Jonah."

His eyes shift back in surprise. "Aren't you?" he asks.

She smiles. "A little."

"You don't look it though. You look good today."

Her smile turns wistful. "Thank you."

He nods, his hands on her door, straightening up. "Say Merry Christmas to your folks for me."

"I will."

He backs up, waiting on the driveway until she's gone, knowing it won't snow.

Inside, he stares at the tree again, Aster's wingless angel on top, remembering the bushy little tree he got with Sissy. Abel put it on top of the TV cabinet and Sissy began to decorate with the balls Jonah gave her, while Abel got himself a drink, then sat down in his recliner and said, "Go on, honey, that looks real nice."

When she came back for another decoration Jonah found Aster's angel with one sheer wing at the bottom of the box. Jonah gave it to her and she took it to Abel, sat on his lap and watched him try to fix it. The angel had a deep hole in one shoulder where the wing was supposed to attach by a hook. There was something gruesome about the hole and Jonah looked away, putting more balls on the tree. They weren't pretty decorations, just thin, colored spheres, some frosty. The other boxes had plastic looking snowflakes and fake candy canes. He found a few stray bells that he liked and a red cardinal that he attached to a branch with a wire. Once or twice he glanced back at Abel, furtively watching him try to push the wing back in place. Every time Abel took his hand away though, the wing fell off. Sissy swung her feet, waiting patiently. She didn't bother Abel at all. About to return to the boxes for more decorations, Jonah stopped when Abel said, "I know", and looked back in time to see him pull the angel's other wing off, and like Mavis, who never wholly left and can imagine the lives here that never really change, he smells Sissy's candy cane again and all the dust as he dug through the box of decorations, and sees her sitting on Abel's shoulders to put Aster's angel on the tree top, and then again on her last Christmas with her lip gloss on and the cross Fin gave her, standing for her picture in front of the window he sees Agnes out of, running up to him with her cheeks as pink as the ball on her cap, as cool as green water and sunlit rainbows. Inside the house, his arms open wide and he laughs as he catches her.

"Merry Christmas, honey."

22

♦ Christmas ♦

Swags of colored lights up Errol's staircase blur in the mistiness, icicle lights twinkle, and Rudolph's nose is glowing on a rooftop across the way. The sound of Christmas carols fills the air at Ray's. Across town, Andy stops in his door as Joe Clay is coming up the walkway. Andy backs up. He was on his way to Ray's party. Now he just stands in the open door as Joe comes in and pulls a beer out of his refrigerator.

"Want one?" asks Joe.

"I was just leavin'."

"I'll come with ya."

"You aren't invited."

He doesn't mean anything by it, but Joe looks put out anyway. "C'mon. It's Christmas Eve."

Andy closes his door.

Cars line up on both sides of the street at the shop. Lights pour out through the open doors and windows. There are people inside and out, laughing and talking loudly. In the dark, bluish clouds of breath appear in the air. The shop is almost empty of everything but people, a couch, and folding chairs. Closing early, Ray started to clear out the shop. Then Son came over and together they emptied the shelves and put everything in the warehouse below. Afterwards Ray said, "Feel like a pizza?" and Son said, "Yeah. I could eat." Ray bought a pitcher of beer, and when their pizza came, he said, "I hear you been keepin' my wife company."

Son gave him a sly smile. "Worried?"

He shrugged with a blank stare. "About what?"

Not long after Son came to stay with him, Ray was lifting weights in the garage. Lying on the bench he could see a shadow on the wall, but he didn't stop until he finished his set. Then, after he racked the bar, he rested his hands on his chest and looked sideways. Son had a strange expression on his face, sort of speculative and amused.

"What are you starin' at?" Ray asked.

"You."

"Any particular reason why?"

"I was just wonderin' if I could take you."

Ray laughed and rocked his head. "Are you shittin' me, kid? Not on your best day."

"I reckon in five years."

"You think?"

"We'll see."

"You bring it on, baby boy."

Then they both laughed, grinning at each other. At the pizza parlor, Ray said, "Maybe you should find yourself a girlfriend," and Son said, "Maybe I already have." They both laughed again.

Son drank the rest of the pitcher of beer, and by the time they got back to the shop, he was already a little drunk. He started in on bourbon as everybody began to arrive. Now, going outside for some air, Ray leans against the side of one of the cars on the far side of the street out of the reach of the light. The cold air dries his sweaty skin. He starts to feel chilled, but he doesn't move. Son is on the porch, leaning back against a cushion from Will's Goodwill couch that he brought outside with him. Will likes the concept of a Goodwill.

"Good Will. Get it?"

Ray grinned at him, glad to have the couch though. "Sure, Will."

"I want it back after. Sell it. Make a little somethin'."

"Sure."

Ray watches Son adjust the cushion, twist sideways to punch at it like a pillow. Inexplicably, he is drinking wine now, grimacing at every swallow. Craig's cousin is sitting on a step above him, elbow on his knee, head resting on his palm. Occasionally, he says something and Son's face twists angrily.

Ray starts to hum his mother's song. "Hm...hm, hm, hm...hm...."

Another car arrives, parks on the street. Jimbo's. He gets out, rolls his shoulders, then starts up the walkway. Watching him, Ray can't say that Son actually sees Jimbo, but he slumps down suddenly and stretches his legs out across the step just as Jimbo reaches the porch. Jimbo stops and then backs up a step. Ray can hear him.

"Comin' up!"

Son rolls his head, stares a moment, then takes a swallow out of his bottle of wine, not moving. Jimbo tries again.

"Comin' up I said."

Even from a distance Ray can hear Craig's cousin's exasperation. "Step over 'im."

"Fuck that. I want some fuckin' courtesy."

Craig's cousin sits back, lifts a boot and stomps on Son's leg. Jumping, Son pulls his knees up and glares at him.

"You happy, Jimbo?"

"No fuckin' rules," Jimbo complains on his way inside.

Ray sighs and looks back up at the dark sky. All the lights below are blotting out the stars. There might even be clouds up there, thin and grayish, collecting raindrops or snowflakes. Christmas clouds, invisible from below.

That morning it was cold and gray out for a long time. Waking up, Fin felt the cold but didn't turn the heat on. He went downstairs in his bare feet, laced up his shoes on the porch, then started to run. The air hurt his lungs at first, sharp and damp. At the end of the driveway, he turned toward Sandorville and picked up speed. His shoes slapped the pavement, but otherwise it was quiet and he felt alone. Mist cloaked the firs. He heard nothing, not even birds. Without thinking—he is sure he didn't think about it—he crossed the road into the trees, slowing up as he made his way through ferns and saplings to the river. The sound of rushing water grew louder and louder. He went sliding down an embankment and came out by the river. On pavement again, he ran faster, his breath growing hot in his throat, the drumming of his steps vibrating up his legs. There were cascaras and alders with the firs, a few with dead sodden leaves still attached. The dampness of the air clung to his skin. The road curved alongside the river and finally he could see lights in the distance where there was a final curve in the road before it connected with the main one. For some reason he didn't want to pass the house he saw up ahead, slowed down, ran backwards a step or two, then turned and continued back the way he came.

Everything was the same in reverse. Dampness. His breath. The lonely, lingering leaves. He caught glimpses of the river through the trees. Passing the spot where he came down the embankment, he saw her, a girl with pale reddish hair at the edge of the road. She was a vague misty figure and he knew she would soon disappear like the mirage she was. Up close, there was nothing there, not even a shadow. Doubling up, he braced his hands on his knees, waiting to catch his breath. His heart was pounding and he could feel it knocking against his breast bone, flooding him with waves of a fear he hadn't felt in a long time. Straightening up, he ran his hands down his face, looking at his palms, the clouds of his breath. He glanced around him and the familiarity was there, the place where she disappeared revealing itself to him. Hidden behind the firs, a flat rock stretched out above the river. He could see her sitting there, looking behind her and up, maybe at him, waiting for him, smiling her welcome. Her gray eyes swam in his memory. He was afraid of her. He was afraid of dying without the life he lived, of never remembering. Sweat prickled his skin and he grew cold. Then a feeling of intense shame flooded his skin with heat. His sweat dripped and suddenly he was cold again. He wanted to remember. He didn't want to be afraid anymore.

Walking slowly, he made for the spot where she disappeared. He pulled a branch aside, felt the sponginess of the ground underfoot. Then he was stepping on rocks and he came out from between the trees and saw the flat gray rock above the water. Waiting, his breath coming in strained hitches, he saw nothing that wasn't there, the rock, the water slipping by underneath, the trees crowding the river's edge, rocks on the other side of the river, a mirror image. Then the image grew cloudy and she appeared on the rock and he was sitting beside her, holding her hands, bent over, lowering his face into her palms. She closed her fingers on him, then leaned backwards, drawing him down with her. Then he saw himself lying on his side next to her, eyes closed, lying peacefully. Going over to the rock, he lay on it again, wanting it to feel warmed by the sun, but it was frigid like a block of ice, carrying nothing of life in it. He closed his eyes and imagined her, but knew he was alone.

Fin remembers Christmas with Sissy, fastening the cross he gave her on her neck. She was wearing overalls and cherry lip gloss, barefoot in the house. The heater was on and the living room was warm. There was no tree, but the cold light coming through the window made shadows of the snowflakes. He drank with Jonah. They ate pizza for dinner. Abel was quiet, almost amiable.

He didn't want to go home. There was a tree there, Sully, a Christmas dinner. The thought of home distressed him. He was nervous and anxious, and the bourbon made him sullen and unhappy. He stayed the night, sleeping on the couch. In the morning he went home, crept upstairs and got into his own bed. His mother said nothing to him when he came down later, barely glanced at him. He wasn't sure she even knew he was gone.

But Sully knew. There were presents under the tree for him.

Other memories come to him, but not the ones he fears, the ones that float in the dark outside of his reach. He remembers the apartment he lived in while he was going to school, a plain white building, anonymous spaces. He wasn't sure who he was. A detachment built up in him and he liked it, and it made him very different from who he knows he is now. His memories of Jonah just circle him. Glimpses of his younger face, angry purple eyes. He remembers Sissy's face, the luminous shine in her moonlit eyes. Kindness. She was kind to him, stronger than he was, although he doesn't remember what she was being strong about. He remembers Christmases in his apartment in the city, no tree there either, the faces of women he spent the day with but can't otherwise remember. He felt safe in his detachment until the alcohol began to erode it. Now he feels the raw nerve-endings attached to every emotion and thought he has. He doesn't know if anything about this is like the way he was before except that he wants a drink.

Sitting on the couch at home, he thinks about the gin in the basement below him. His throat locks and he swallows at the sour taste in his mouth. Jumping off the couch, he runs upstairs and brushes his teeth, spits in the sink and pictures himself lying on the floor by the toilet. Then he looks in the mirror and stares at his face, at his eyes, the same unfathomable green of his mother's, the color of standing water, algaed and still. He rubs his fingers over his stubble, sees her chin, his father's nose, sees Gale drinking a beer in the backyard, smiling down at him. "You keep lookin' at this. You want a try?"

His father held the can. He took a swallow and recoiled, pulling a sour face. His father laughed. "I guess it takes a little getting used to."

Another memory comes and he closes his eyes, holding onto the sides of the sink, resting his forehead against the cool glass of the mirror. His father is lying in a hospital bed in the room downstairs. A nurse comes every day. Maybe not the same nurse. He won't go downstairs to see. When his father came home, Sully took his hand and said, "Come an' talk to your dad with me." But Gale couldn't talk. His face pulled down, slack and useless. His hands only trembled. When Fin saw him, he tried to run, but Sully held him, pulling him back.

"Whoa. Wait a minute now. Just relax."

But the closer he got to the door, the more he panicked, yanking at his hand, falling backwards, kicking frantically and bawling in hysterics. "No...No...No!"

Sully looked panicked too. All of a sudden he could see that panicked look, hear his mother, "For God's sake, stop him. Stop it, Fin! Stop!"

Sully let him go. He ran upstairs and hid between the wall and his bed, crying until it got dark and he finally fell asleep. Somebody picked him up and put him on the bed because that's where he woke up in the morning. And he remembers now that he didn't consciously remember the day before, but he stayed away from the door to that bedroom and his mother never asked him to go in.

He doesn't remember when Gale died because he wasn't there. But he remembers the funeral, holding Sully's hand, and he remembers the flowers Dahlia burned in the back yard, and her funeral with Sully by his side again and Jonah down below, leaning against the front of his pickup until it was over. And he remembers Abel's funeral, Sissy's numb face, Jonah's blank and stark. The headstone came later, but he remembers that too. It just had Abel's name, "Husband and Father", the years he was born and died. He was only thirty-eight.

Straightening up, Fin looks at himself in the mirror again, frowns slightly at his image. A feeling comes to him that he has always been waiting, and always for the wrong thing. The memories don't really matter. He can remember them or change them and he will never know if any of it is real. He tastes the toothpaste in his mouth and thinks of the gin again and that is real. In the bedroom he packs a duffel bag, grabs his keys and leaves.

At Grace's he hears the party across the street, runs up the lighted staircase, and trots down the hall. There's a light under her door. She looks at him in dismay.

"You aren't ready. We're already supposed to be at my parents'."

"Give me fifteen minutes." He is pulling his clothes off on his way to the bathroom. "God, I'm glad to be out of that house."

"Why? What's wrong?"

He is turning on the shower, his fingers in the spray. "Why didn't I decorate?"

"Honey, I don't know. You said you didn't want to."

"I'm an idiot."

"Honey, are you okay?"

He pulls his hand out from behind the shower curtain and comes over to her. "I'm an idiot. It's Christmas Eve an' I'm naked."

She laughs. "So?"

"Will you marry me?"

"Fin." Her voice is hushed and uncertain.

"Will you? I don't have a ring an' I didn't plan this an' I know it isn't a very good proposal. I want it though. With all my heart."

A smile grows on her face, lighting her moon gray eyes. Her arms wrap around his neck. Kindness, he thinks. She is kind to him, undeservedly kind. Her chin touches his and she says, "That's okay. I like the naked part."

He feels his lips moving too, smiling back at her.

"Will you?"

She nods, still smiling. "Yes, Fin. I will. Now will you take your shower, please, so we can go? We're late."

He kisses her gently. "Yes, ma'am."

The inside of the shop is crowded, thick with smoke and heat. People talk, laugh, yell over the sounds of the Christmas carols. The doors to the rooms in back are locked, but people crowd into the kitchen and sit on the railing and steps of the side porch. A row of silver tubs filled with beer line the wall between the shop and Mulligan's. People are sitting on the wall too.

Out front, Craig's cousin and Son sit alone, but people keep coming and going down the steps. Son's irritation is growing. He doesn't look at

Craig's cousin, but Craig's cousin stares at him, growing angry himself. He knows Son isn't as drunk as he's acting, not as drunk as Ray thinks he is. He was drinking bourbon when Craig's cousin arrived, but the glass was only half empty and stayed that way until Craig's cousin said, "I have to go in a little while."

Then he finished the glass and pulled a bottle of wine out of the refrigerator because there wasn't any beer there and it was easier to take the wine than to go outside for a beer. Now he's outside anyway, but only occasionally sipping out of the bottle he's holding. It doesn't account for his attitude, the aura of antagonism he uses to keep people away. Craig's cousin knows that isn't really Son. The real Son is funny, big-hearted, and thin-skinned. His mood right now is for Craig's cousin.

With a shake of his head, Craig's cousin moves his foot down a step, getting ready to get up. He can see himself walking away without a word. But Son turns his sullen face to him before he does and says, "Aren't you goin'? You said you were goin'."

"You are such a shit."

"I'm just sayin', go if that's what you wanna do."

"I wanna be with you, but that means you comin' with me."

"I can't."

They look away from each other. Goliath thunders up the steps. Craig's cousin looks back. "Why the hell not? You just come to my house an' meet my folks. I know Ray."

"You knew 'im before. That doesn't count."

"What's the big deal if my parents know?"

"I don't want anybody to know!" He seems abruptly surprised at his loud voice.

Craig's cousin speaks quietly. "Are you fuckin' embarrassed by us?"

"No. You know I'm not."

They both fall silent again. A few more people come down the steps, voices breaking apart in the air as they walk away.

"I need you, Trevor. I need you to make me."

"I'm not going to. Not about this. You come with me cuz you want to."

 "I can't tell my dad."

"An' you don't want anybody else to know either."

"You dated girls. Pretty good cover."

"I like girls. I like guys. I never hid that from my family. Just from these other bozos."

Son leans over, mouths the words, "Trevor, I love you."

"Say it out loud."

Son leans back, staring sullenly out to the street again.

"I just did."

It's not Son he's worrying about, not really. His worry is becoming anger but his anger is just a surface feeling. Son's attitude is annoying him, but he's not really that upset. He knows Son's afraid of Ray's reaction, afraid of Ray, of losing him for good. Making sure that people know what Craig's cousin already knows isn't that important to him. He'd like to take Son home and he knows he will, but the thing that's annoying him is that he still can't see the way he used to. He knows there are things he's supposed to be seeing, things about Will and Son, and a feeling about Jimbo that is making him nervous. The anxiety is like a pain that he can't get rid of and he wants Son with him.

"I'm going," he says.

Son won't look at him now.

"Go tomorrow."

His anger flares again. He puts a hand on Son's knee and levers himself up. "You fuckin' come with me or shut up."

Son's face turns red. "Asshole."

"Fuck you."

He is flooded with heat. It warms him in his coat. He isn't worrying that something bad will happen to Son. He doesn't feel that; it's not the problem, but he doesn't know how to live without seeing the things he sees. The idea of living this way forever is disturbing to him.

Walking away, he lets his eyes rise up, feeling something almost like a prayer rising inside. The smoky starless sky looms above him, giving away nothing.

Rain fell at Ed's. Silver needle-sharp drops that bounced off the roof and formed into dark, mirror-like puddles. Light struggled into the gloom inside the house. Heavy shadows lay over the walls and at the windows the rain was luminous. A Christmas tree in the corner, lights muted in the dimness. The Christmas before Irene died, Ed went to Ray's house. Ed's father had a girlfriend that year and the girlfriend had Christmas at her house. Ed wasn't sure he wasn't invited, but he wasn't sure he was invited either. He liked Christmas at Ray's, mainly because of Irene. He liked her sardonic eyes, the little smile she gave him. She didn't like him, but Ed didn't care. He liked to look at her. He remembered watching her pick a piece of tinsel up off the floor and let it flutter out of her fingers onto the tree. He was sorry that she died, but he didn't dwell on it the way Ray did. The next Christmas, Ray came to his house and they went to Lyon's for dinner. It didn't look like Christmas at Ed's because nothing was decorated, but Ed's father bought himself a Beer Meister and sat it in the windowless family room, in a brown case to fit the brown and beige couch, the brown carpet, the brown recliner, and the brown wood coffee table with the chipped edges always covered with cups and paper bags from Nation's because Ed's father couldn't go to White Castle's. Ray asked Ed about that once, why his father didn't just move near one.

"Too close to my mom," said Ed.

Earlier, sitting on the couch by the darkish tree, Ed called him. He called every Christmas that Ray wasn't with him.

"Almost time," he said.

"Yep."

"Kid still there?"

"Yep."

"You remember my dad's Beer Meister?"

Ray laughed. "Oh, hell, yeah. I remember it now."

Later, Ed started to look for his Santa cap. The rain had stopped and the trees just dripped. The air had a silver sheen to it. He felt a vague disturbance at the color, then he shrugged and went back to looking for his Santa cap.

All the windows at Errol's are dark, dark at the houses across the lot too, but the cheery sound of Jingle Bells fills the air anyway.

Ray is humming. "Hm…hm, hm, hm…hm…."

He watches Son get up and go inside, come back out again, kick Will's couch cushion off the step, knees sprawled, elbows across his thighs, sitting with a bottle of bourbon he drinks out of between long stares at the gravel walkway.

Ray sighs. He likes where he is, against the damp, cold car, out of the smoke and activity. He didn't used to be this way. There was a time he was the center of every crowd, every party he gave or went to. He remembers the party he gave when he came home again, the blur of days, the jolt of pleasure and pain when he saw Son at the bottom of the staircase. He was standing at the top, he remembers, with a girl sitting on the railing on either side of him. Seeing Son he looked at one, nudged her and said, "Go inside an' tell everybody to put their shit away. Nothin' illegal from now on." She gaped at him and he pushed her. "Are you fuckin' deaf?"

Maybe he thought he was doing the right thing, at least going through the motions; there was no way to keep Son away from the drugs though, not there. He was doing too many himself. Even now he can't remember separate days. He can't remember all the women he took to bed, a blur of faces and bodies, people coming and going through the room, and he didn't care who saw or who stayed.

Wiping a hand down his face, he sees Miri appear in a window, lean out with her forearms on the sill.

He pushed one woman off him to roll onto another. He loved it. Smiles even now thinking about it. Miri is a mystery to him because he cannot understand himself with her. She is the life he never lived. The other life, the life he doesn't think he ever would have had, even if Wayne didn't leave and Irene didn't die and he never met Ed. It's too easy to think that he ever would have paid attention. He was happy, is happy in the life he picked. She just isn't a part of it, even here. But he can't live without her.

Now she is sitting on the sill and her arms to Ray are as white as any statue's but Venus de Milo's.

He looks up again, humming that song. "Hm…hm, hm, hm…hm…."

His mother wore the same dress every Christmas that he can remember. Miri is wearing purple velvet and lavender silk. Rhinestones cover her spike heels and there are diamonds in her ears.

Yesterday she came out into the living room where he was watching TV and said, "Ray?"

"Yeah."

"Are these yours?"

He looked over. The earrings were on her palm. He gave it a moment and then said, "No."

They stared at each other for another moment and then he began to laugh and she pursed her mouth up at him and said, "I know they are."

"Think what you want," he said.

She gave a sprite toss of her head and disappeared. A moment later, she came back with the diamonds in her ears. They sparkled like all the icicles hanging from everybody's eaves. He looked at her without expression. She put a finger behind one of her ear lobes, showing him.

"Are they pretty?"

"No."

Her finger fell. "No?"

"But you are."

She smiled almost shyly and he felt that jab of passion for her.

"Thank you, Ray."

"Merry Christmas, lady."

The back hallway is narrow and white. The window at the end is open but dark. There is no light and the long wall of the warehouse outside seems to absorb and deepen the dark. All the doors are closed, white walls, white doors.

Sitting on the back porch, Will squints and the hall looks like an endless tunnel to him. Then there are people in it, blurred discorporate shapes. He blinks, then one of the shapes turns into Miri. He brightens.

"Hey, babe. C'mere."

She hesitates, her eyes moving back to the shop, then she comes closer, pausing in the doorway, not stepping out to him. He slides off the rail and crosses over, leaning a shoulder against the doorsill. She slips past him, out into the cold air.

"Nice earrings. Present?" She nods, touching one with her finger. "I got Susie a mink," says Will.

Miri doesn't say anything to that either and Will pushes away from the doorsill and leans against the railing beside her. Jimbo appears at the row of tubs full of ice and beer. She leans back into the corner of the porch, facing Will. Some of her hair is coming out of the pins she put it up with.

"You look nice," he says.

She still doesn't say anything and he edges closer to her. She's prettier than Susie, even though she isn't really pretty at all. There's just something about her. Susie's tougher and younger, more like he is. Susie understands things.

"You oughta come over, try on Susie's mink."

"That's okay."

His Christmas tree is plugged in, waiting for him to come home, and some day he and Susie are going to have a baby. He can't wait to buy it toys and never take its Christmas presents away. "I can't wait for tomorrow," he adds.

She is staring at him with an expression that isn't quite gentle but almost. Will only remembers the good times. He smiles at her. "Yeah," he says again. "You look real nice."

Will doesn't notice Andy isn't there, but Andy wouldn't be surprised at that. Andy isn't thinking about Will either though. It's Ray's party he wants to get to. Other than that, there's really nothing special going on this Christmas. Jack-in-the-Box or Taco Bell maybe, but he doesn't count that. The only thing close to a decoration he has is a picture on the bathroom mirror of a girl dressed up like Santa's helper and the only thing special about that is that she forgot to wear her panties.

He's aware that he doesn't have a lot going on, but at least there's a party to go to. He looks at Joe Clay, sitting on his couch with a beer, looking expectantly at Andy, waiting to go out somewhere, to do something, something friendly, festive, convivial. To drink and be merry.

"Get the fuck outta my house!"

The moisture in the air makes Errol's icicle lights look like glass. Jimbo is standing in the alley with his empty beer bottle. On the side porch, Will is talking to Miri and Son is still sitting on the porch out front. Jimbo squints and the lights glitter. It reminds him of that day at Susie's office building when he pounded on the door and the glass wobbled and he stood back, waiting for it to break.

There's other glass though.

He looks at the cars, Son's especially. He dreams that he almost caught him here that night with Will and Andy. He imagines he remembers the feel of Son's shirt just before he got loose. In the dream he always yells, "Got ya!" but then Son is suddenly gone.

The more he thinks about it, the more his face begins to puff. He looks back at the house and bellows, *"No rules!"* Outside, Son and Ray both look to the side. Ray gives a sour grimace and shakes his head. Now Jimbo is staring at a man in a pair of reindeer ears at the tubs. He moves closer and reaches for another bottle, still staring at the man, who glances back at him as he starts into the shop because now Jimbo's following him. He's in no hurry, but there's a look on his face that makes Ray call out, "No trouble, man. I mean that."

Will yells too. "You hear that, Jimbo?"

Jimbo slows and looks back at Will, seeing Ray appear in his line of vision instead, a hand stretching out. Ray pulls Miri down the steps and now Will is alone too. Jimbo goes back out.

"I want those ears," he says.

Will agrees. "Pretty cool."

When Andy finally arrives, Jimbo has the ears. "I'm givin' 'um to Will," he says. "Christmas present." Andy looks upset. "Wha' did you get 'im?" asks Jimbo.

"Nothing."

"Dork."

He laughs and heads back inside as Andy goes over to the tubs for a beer, then saunters back up front again. The Christmas lights across the lot are bright and festive, halos of color. People come and go, and Andy is enjoying his beer until Jimbo reappears without the ears and pushes him over to his car, wanting to leave.

Andy complains. "But I just got here."

"Like I care."

Two Christmases earlier, Miri was living with Will, but Will didn't bring her to Ray's party. At the time, she didn't know that she had ever seen Ray. When he appeared in the bedroom door at Will's, she didn't really know him then either, but she thought that she had seen him before somewhere. She had no reason to connect him with the name then. She knew of somebody named Ray from Will, but she had never met him. Then, when she saw him in the doorway, she knew who he was. She liked the humor in his eyes, the heaviness of his wavy hair against his neck, the easy way he stood there, his small smile. But there was something else. Something in him that she knew was waiting for her. Now he is leaning up against her car and she is standing barefoot with her heels beside her, looking up at him. He begins to smile. She likes his smile. He looks like he is laughing about everything.

"What're you thinkin' about?" he asks.

"You."

"Do you like me?"

She smiles and shrugs. "Maybe."

His arms are over her shoulders, fingers in the hair that's coming loose. In the silence she wonders if he ever thinks about Cora or sleeps with other people on the nights he doesn't come home, even though he says he doesn't anymore.

"Do you like me?" she asks, feeling his fingers on her cheek.

"Sure."

She sighs and leans in. His arms cross behind her. They are on the side of the street by Errol's house and the noises from the shop seem to carry and suddenly sound lonely. "Ray?"

"Yeah?"

She leans back, looking up. He pulls his hands down his face, yawning. Miri takes one of his hands, rubbing the softened skin on his little finger. "Where's your ring?"

Cora's ring. He takes his hand back, flexes his fingers with a shrug. "I dunno. Lost it, I guess."

"You never take it off."

"I must have." He shrugs again like it doesn't matter to him, but he's worn the ring as long as she's known him, for years according to him.

"You're a strange man, Ray Wycowski."

He grins at her. "You think?"

She leans in again, palms on his chest. "Merry Christmas, Ray."

"Merry Christmas, lady."

They paid ten dollars each to see the Snake Lady exhibit. In a tent reminiscent of some Depression era side show, golden with light, straw on the floor, rows of folding chairs, they sat down with their beer and waited. The place filled up, the lights went down and she appeared, a red head painted green, color fading as it reached her pale, freckled shoulders. Those freckles bothered Ray for some reason. He drank his beer and when it was gone he was annoyed. Ed was almost hypnotized. She undulated on the straw-strewn floor, rose and swung lazily around a pole in the center of the stage. Her face was freckled too and her eyes looked pain-filled and glazed. Ed leaned up against his shoulder as she made her circuit of the tent, trying to get a closer look at her as she came down the aisle. Maybe it was the shadow Ed cast, but when she passed by, Ray could see the details of her skin, pitted and scored by scars, tough scaly patches that gave her a rough, reptilian appearance. He didn't know what it was, but he guessed the pain was real. Looking back, he thinks there might be medicine for her now, but maybe she wouldn't take it, wouldn't know how to make a living any other way. He thinks he knows a little bit about that.

He still dreams about her sometimes, still gives her Miri's face, the look of old pain at home in Miri's eyes.

Now he's standing where her car was, staring at Errol's icicle lights. They are a cold, icy blue. He hasn't left her even though everyone else before him has. After a while, he starts back over to the shop. Will's in a pair of reindeer ears and he can see somebody through the window climbing up on one of the racks inside.

She attracts people who almost never stay in love with her.

Inside, he unlocks the room where his bed and dresser are, half-closing the door and pulls a jacket out of the closet.

She reminds him of the Snake Lady, dancing up and away, a sight people buy a ticket for and then leave after they see.

It is hot because of all the people in the shop. Some are beginning to leave though. He closes the door behind him. In the shop itself, there's the man he thinks was wearing the reindeer ears earlier, but now he isn't so Ray isn't really sure.

"How ya doin'?" he asks him.

"Good…good…."

The man looks confused though, so maybe it was him. Maybe he's looking for his ears. People are sitting on the windowsills and somebody is sitting on a bean bag he never saw before. It's a bright blue vinyl patched with tape.

Outside, he pokes Son in the shoulder with the toe of his boot. "Are you alright?" He nods but doesn't speak. Will's couch cushion is lying on the walkway. Son is still sitting on the top step, drinking out of his bottle of bourbon. His face is drained-looking, unhappy. Ray closes his eyes briefly, then drops the coat on the step beside him and goes back inside. Except for the other night, decorating a Christmas tree which he forgot all about, didn't go with Miri to pick out, he almost never sees Son at home anymore. It surprised him when he found out that Son went home all the time, just not when Ray was there. One day, a week or two ago, he came in and saw a bowl of popcorn on the coffee table and a couple of empty bottles of beer. He ate some of the popcorn and found Miri in the tub, soapy feet up on the tile wall. She was pink where he could see her over the soap suds.

He dropped the lid on the toilet seat and sat down. "Good popcorn."

"Kettle corn."

She sank a little under the suds, making him smile. He let his eyes move over her, saw her toes curl against the wall. "Looks like a party or somethin' out there." She shrugged slightly and the cloud of soap suds shivered. "Who you with?"

She smiled and he leaned over, resting a palm on the side of the tub. Her eyes looked sleepy and he breathed in the smell of her soap. The damp heat made his hair stick to the back of his neck. He shook his head to free it and she brought a hand up, sliding it between his hair and his skin. The water felt good, slippery and cool.

"Is 'e good lookin'?"

She pulled her hand back, slipping lower in the tub. "I guess so."

"I bet."

Her hands moved, fluffing up the bubbles.

"You an' my kid," he murmured, pushing up his sleeve and sticking his hand underneath the bubbles. She looked startled at his touch even though she saw him coming.

"I have to go to work," she said.

"Later."

"We got a tree," he says to Will on the porch.

"About time. I'm keepin' mine up 'til Easter."

Will is sitting on the railing with his reindeer ears on. The air outside feels damp, mixing with the warm air inside. Ray leans back and drinks his beer. He can finally remember that song his mother used to sing. It came to him at home when he saw Miri take a batch of cookies out of the oven and found a Christmas tree in the corner of the living room. He dropped down onto the couch with a laugh and said, "Man, I feel like I'm in a goddam Christmas card."

He could picture warmly lit windows and people inside by the Christmas tree. His mother had a frosty ball she used to hang on a hook in the ceiling with a scene like that inside. The ball was hollow, two Styrofoam halves glued together and spackled with glitter. Inside the ball was a scene of a living room with a little fireplace, a rug on a wood floor, a woman in a rocker, a man decorating a Christmas tree, a boy and a girl playing with their toys on the floor. Attached to the top was a plastic sleigh and reindeer. He guessed he sold the ball at the garage sale Marie helped him with. Remembering it again, though, he suddenly remembered her Christmas song too, and laughed out loud.

"Oh, Come All Ye Faithful!"

"Christmas spice," said Miri with a plate of cookies.

He sat back up after she set them down and stared at the plate, white plastic with little gold stars on the edge. He ate some grudgingly and then she left again and Son took an empty cardboard box out to the garage and he began to hum Irene's song until Miri came back with a beer and sat down beside him and he picked up a cookie and murmured, "You an' my kid," making her smile.

She rested underneath his arm with her head on his shoulder. "I love this."

The lights were twinkling on the tree, then he heard the back door open and Son came back in with another box of decorations. He brushed his lips against her ear and took a drink of his beer.

"It's not so bad," he agreed with her afterwards. He was thinking of Pete and Cora though and the night at their wedding, dancing with Cora out of reach of the paper lanterns she hung in the trees.

"Fancy," he said.

"You only get married once," Cora replied.

"Supposed to, anyway," he agreed.

A long time ago, he used to wonder about the way things might've been if Wayne had stayed. Or the way things might've been for Son if he had never left. Nowadays, he doubts that any of that every really mattered, but back then it was one of the only times in his life he couldn't laugh things off. He even laughed the day Ed came over after Irene died and said, "Are you just gonna sit here all day? It's goddam Christmas, Ray."

And there were those other Christmases with Ed's mother's family and the White Castle's they went to where he sat in a booth across from Ed and swiped at the window and imagined he saw Wayne get into Ed's Nova and drive it away. "What?" asked Ed.

"I was just thinkin'."

"About what?"

"Goin' to St. Louis."

Ed nodded, ate his White Castle's and then said, "You're better off without 'im. Your kid too," he added and Ray tried to pretend that what Ed said didn't matter and swiped again at the steamy window.

"Guess it's good I'm gone then."

"Yep."

The sky is a dark, sooty gray and the Christmas lights have a cold, lonely look. Will's murmuring, "Santa's comin', Santa's comin'..." all the way to his car.

In the doorway, Ray listens to the sound of Will's footsteps. It's quiet otherwise. After a moment, he steps back out, grabs Son by the back of the jacket he's wearing, and gives him a yank. He lurches up, then twists sideways to get his feet underneath him. Ray lets him pass by. The shop feels cold now and he turns up the heat, liking the sound of it coming through the vents. In the back, he gives Son a push through the bedroom door, pulls the jacket off, and waits until he sprawls face down on the bed. Son's phone rings, a muffled tune Ray doesn't recognize. Lying down on the couch in the other room, he closes his eyes. It is preternaturally quiet, just the sound of his breaths. Then the phone again. It rings for a while, stops. He thinks he sleeps, comes up groggily to the ringing phone, gets up and goes down the hall. Son is still lying on his face on the bed. There's nothing in his pockets. Ray looks around, turns and grabs the jacket Son was wearing off the chair by the door. Digging in a pocket, he finds the phone and takes it back with him to the couch. The minute he lies down, it starts ringing again.

"Fuck," he mutters, looking at the screen. Trevor. He answers it. "What do you want, Trev? It's four in the morning."

There's a pause, then: "Where is 'e?"

"Here. Crashed. What you should be."

"Okay. See ya."

"Jesus," he says, finally falling back asleep.

On Christmas morning, Joe Clay wakes up and stares at a gray ceiling in a room at the Acropolis Inn. He feels vaguely unsettled and envisions himself in a movie with a clock ticking louder and louder, lying in a lonely motel room without hope, waiting for the door to crash open and guns to grow giant-sized and fill the screen. That's all anybody can see, black guns in the light of the door. It's a black and white movie. He pictures it fading out and then gets up and goes over to the lobby for a Danish. There's a tub of candy canes on the counter and a gold wreath under the counter ledge and a man named Frank, who comes out of the back room and watches him pour his coffee.

"Merry Christmas," he says.

Frank nods. "Yeah. Merry Christmas."

Awake now too, Carl lies under a fluffy red blanket pulled up to his chin and Scott stirs a cup of hot chocolate with a candy cane.

Mr Torch has candy canes on his tie.

Carl smiles dimly.

The air is frosty cold and it's quiet out until the door at the shop opens up. Glass clinks and clatters. Carl looks. Ray is picking up empty bottles, dropping armfuls into an aluminum tub in the alleyway. The sound is sharp and loud.

After a while, Ray goes back inside and Carl looks away.

In the shop, light puddles on the cool linoleum floor. "I feel sick," murmurs Son.

"Make some coffee," says Ray, lying back down again.

At home, Craig's cousin is eating scrambled eggs and ham. He misses his pancakes at Candi's. He wonders what the special is today. Cranberries maybe. Growing up, he almost always ate breakfast with his father because that's when he got home from work. On Saturday mornings, his father always brought donuts home. Craig's cousin likes the blueberry and maple bars the best. His mother is scooping more eggs onto his plate.

"Do we have any jelly?" he asks.

His father looks at him over the top of his newspaper and his mother purses her lips at him, but she pulls a jar of strawberry jam out of the cupboard and brings it over. "Will this do?"

"Yeah, that's great.'

"How's work?" asks his father.

"Busy. We're gettin' customers from all over."

"How's that? You advertising more?"

"No. Not really. Customer service, I think." He looks at his mother. "A customer wrote in about me last month. I didn't really do anything but whatever."

His mother makes a face at him. "I doubt you didn't do anything. Nobody takes the time to write in about somebody doing nothing."

"Do you still like it?" asks his father.

At the same time that his mother murmurs, "Wes," Craig's cousin says, "I've been workin' there ten years, Dad. I'd hate workin' at the factory, you know that."

"I'm just asking. I'm not saying. How's everything else?"

"Whadda you mean?"

"How are you?"

"We hardly see you anymore," his mother adds. His father is giving him a long look over the paper again.

"I'm okay. Why?"

"You look a little...I dunno. Rattled, maybe." After he says that, his eyes drop back to his paper.

"Whadda you see?" asks Craig's cousin.

His father shakes his head. "Nothing. Don't worry."

He does worry though. Nothing is what he sees too. A feeling of panic stirs in him, exposure, like a weakness he doesn't want anybody else to see. His mother didn't ruin his father's gift. He can still see. He wonders if his skin is red. In winter, he chaps and his knuckles sometimes crack. He changes the subject. "When's everybody comin' over?"

"About ten."

Craig grew up in this house and Craig's cousin's sister, Kate, lives nearby with her husband, Sam, and their two daughters, Katie and Debbie. Kate is a fixture because Craig's cousin's mother watches her girls all the time. Now that Craig's cousin's father works days, he and Sam bowl together and play golf on the weekends. Craig's cousin doesn't like bowling or golf. But that isn't the problem, any of the things that keep him at a distance. Kate can't see. She is blissfully fearless in the dark. Craig's cousin looks like her. They look like their mother. But there is a buffer between him and his family, a zone of non-belonging. And some of that, he knows, is because of the people who are his friends, the life he leads because of them, the things his family thinks he overlooks. But it isn't overlooking, it isn't thoughtlessness. He knows that even the lost need hope. But these are not people he is close to either. He's only close to Son. There is nothing Son hides, no dark between them, only light. And even though he can't see anything, he feels a wave of worry wash over him and grows anxious to get away.

"Do we have to wait?" he asks.

His father looks at him again. "Wait for what?"

"Presents."

They all look at each other. His father lifts his shoulders in a shrug and says, "I don't see why. They're going to be late anyway."

"Cool."

Craig's cousin scoops another spoonful of strawberry jam on the last piece of ham, picks up his plate, and heads for the Christmas tree.

———————

Golden bubbles rise up, fizzing at the top. Apple or grape juice, he isn't sure. He drinks it because they want him too, Henry and Rose and Sully, Ralph staring at his glass with a glum disappointment. The lights on the tree wink against the window. A fire is crackling in the fireplace and there is wrapping paper on the floor. A Christmas picture where everyone freezes with their glasses rising, apple or grape juice, flavor and fragrance, but not lifesaving, not numbing, not poppied forgetfulness. His nerves jerk, but he drinks and smiles, feels Grace's fingers slide against his. He leans back on the couch, pulling her into the circle of his arm and kisses her temple with his eyes closed.

"I love you," he whispers.

Christmas carols play: Silent Night, We Three Kings. Outside, the mist is frozen in the air, the sounds of cars and cheerful voices carrying. The night before he dreamed it was raining and daylight broke through the storm clouds, silver gossamer beams shining on a grassy hill. Lawn chairs interspersed with gravestones. He saw angels at the top of the hill and Jonah leaning against the side of his pickup. Sissy sat on a chair near a grave with her face up to the rain. Once he saw snowflakes falling too, delicate edges growing gray like wet paper, a blue tarp laying out on the grass, and Sissy again, with the wings of the angels in the cemetery behind her. When he woke up, he lay frozen, trying to see. The room wasn't completely dark. There was a thin, watery light on the ceiling. He let his eyes move. Not his room, Grace's old room, with a white dresser and mirror, a white and pink striped duvet, soft, feathery warmth. She was standing by the window, looking back, her face in shadow.

"I think it's going to snow."

Now Sully is picking up wrapping paper and Rose is reappearing with a new bottle of apple or grape juice. "Leave that, Sully."

"No, no. I need to stretch my legs anyway."

"What is this?" asks Ralph, eyeing his glass suspiciously.

"Martinelli's," says Rose.

Apple juice.

His heart is slowing. Maybe Grace can feel it. She lifts her head, smiling at him, her thumb rubbing his chin.

"Okay?"

He nods, whispers back. "This is nice."

Her smile widens. "Really?" she mouths.

He mouths it back. "Really."

His arm tightens around her and he looks out at a wintry day far away from home.

Will's mother always made the best Christmas cookies Craig's cousin ever saw. They looked just like bakery cookies.

"You could sell these," he said to Will one day.

There were bells with green icing, stars covered in powdered sugar and gold balls and angels with white icing.

"Yeah," murmured Will, getting a look in his eye.

He took a tin full she made for the Christmas party at school but sold them during recess instead. That got his Christmas presents taken away and he never really liked Christmas again until he moved out. After that, he could never feel happy enough. At home he runs out into the living room in Jimbo's reindeer ears. Susie's on the couch, eating cookies with pink and white sprinkles. Will is poking at the presents underneath the tree.

"Me first," he says. She ignores him, taking another handful of cookies out of her bag. "Christmas is cool," he adds.

She doesn't respond. Her mouth is full.

Where Son's mother lives, the sun is shining and the skies are blue. She makes a pomegranate jelly they always have on Christmas and bakes little cakes with nuts and candied oranges.

"Hey," he says when he calls her. "Merry Christmas."

There are other sounds coming from the living room where the Christmas tree covers the window next to the hydrangeas.

"Merry Christmas, honey."

He's alone in the shop, looking for his keys in the dresser. A few moments ago, he felt in his pockets, even the pockets of the jacket Ray had given him to wear. No phone or keys. He looked in the kitchen, heard Ray's bike start up and ran out. "Hey!" Ray paused. "Where're my phone an' keys?"

"Phone's on the coffee table. Keys in the dresser. Top drawer."

"Oh." He turned away, saying nothing else.

"Hey, kid."

"Yeah?"

"Merry Christmas."

He could hear the antagonism in Ray's voice, but he just shrugged and said, "Yeah, okay. Merry Christmas." Then he turned away again and Ray rode off with a burbling roar. The quiet that came after had a slight ringing sound to it.

Son didn't really like Christmas. At home, Horace played Santa, giving out presents and Son always had a feeling when he took his that everybody was trying to make him feel like he fit in, meaning that he didn't.

They weren't his family. Only Kathy was.

He liked birthdays better and that made him think about his jacket, and for just a moment while he was standing outside in the cold, he was sure Ray was thinking about it too. He remembered Ed and that Denny's.

In the shop there are no lights, no Christmas decorations. On the floor, empty bottles and cans and ash trays. Out the window, the shady light grows without brightening. The bedroom is almost dark, but a patch of yellow in the dresser drawer catches his eye. He pockets his keys, then takes out the piece of yellow paper. It is a slip like the tear-off from the bottom of a receipt. There is a number and a date on it and the name Smiley's Pawn Shop. His knees seem to give way. He sits down heavily on the bed and says, "Mom, I have to go."

She sounds surprised. "Well, okay. Merry Christmas, honey. I love you."

He nods, says, "Yeah, Mom. I love you too."

Then he sits in the dark, staring numbly at nothing.

At the intersection by the bowling alley, the light turns and Ray rolls to a stop and looks up at the candy cane-decorated bowling pin.

Across town, Will is in his Christmas wreath tee-shirt, bouncing up and down on his couch. Christmas paper covers most of the floor and some Elvis carols Susie bought at Kmart are playing. She's still eating her cookies, wearing her mink now.

Andy and Jimbo arrive, Andy yawning, Jimbo rising up and down on his toes. Will points. "Check it out!"

They look at the presents and the paper and the cookies and the cheese ball and the box of Ritz crackers.

"I got stuff! Susie too," he adds, pointing at the glittery orange shoes she is wearing.

The Christmas tree is spinning and the room looks surreal. Will is sweating and his eyes are as glittery as Susie's shoes. His breath comes in quick little pants. Then, abruptly, he stops bouncing and points again. This time at a yellow car with big rubber tires.

"Check that out!"

Joy's old home where her little boy still lives is on Ash Avenue. Now that Kurt knows that he marvels at the way things work. When he first moved up here he almost rented a converted garage there. He might have been living next door to her or across the street at any rate. The reason he didn't want to live there though is the reason he can picture her house so clearly. The houses remind him of the apartment with the veranda he used to live in. There's Astroturf on the cement floors of some of the porches and no mats at the doors, chairs with the paint peeling off their seats and wind chimes hanging in a row along the front of the porch roofs.

Kurt wouldn't like it there.

The chairs rock on metal springs and he pictures soda cans on the railing in summer and plastic Christmas trees. Outside, at the bottom of the stairs of his own apartment, a little girl is rolling in noisy circles on her new skates. Kurt rode his scooter all day when he got it. It was sunny cold and the scooter puffed exhaust and rumbled in the cold air. Joy is at her old house where Santa probably brought a pile of presents for her little boy, maybe skates too. They click and clack on the cobblestones.

Clickety clack, clack, clack....

She rolls in circles in a birdless courtyard. He can see Joy's cool blue eyes looking over roofs and distances to settle here as pale as vapor.

Clickety clack, clack, clack...Clickety, clomp, clomp, clomp....

Now she's on the walkway and he can hear her giggle, clear bell-like sounds. She has her hands over her mouth and she hops sideways by the stairs, grabs onto the banister and rolls in a slow half circle. She is giggling at Ray.

"Shoot, girl. You almost ran me over." She rolls away, hands over her mouth again and he points at her as he goes upstairs. "I got my eye on you."

Kurt is surprised. Ray's never been over before except outside once to work on his car. Coming in, he goes into the living area, stops and looks around as if there's something to see, but there isn't.

"Cute kid out there," he says.

Kurt nods. She came as Dorothy for Halloween. He's embarrassed when he sees her because he remembers thinking Dorothy was her name. Now he thinks it's Jennie, but he's not sure.

"Wanna beer?"

"Sure."

Kurt gets it and Ray sits down and leans back, one foot up on another chair. He is noticing Kurt's clothes. He has on brown corduroy trousers, brown suede shoes, and a red shirt with a gold paisley design. The shirt reminds him of Christmas paper.

"I was gonna invite you to the Club, but I guess you got plans." Kurt nods. He even smells of cologne. "I'll get outta your way right after this," says Ray, taking a drink of his beer.

"That's okay."

Clickety clack, clomp, clomp, clack....

The cologne smells familiar to Ray. It might even be the kind Miri bought for him once. He can see it with its dusty top in a corner of a shelf in the medicine cabinet. A brand she probably gave Will too. Irene bought English Leather for Wayne. He didn't know if Wayne liked it, but he got it every Christmas, unwrapping presents in his shorts and robe. He never got dressed until after breakfast, but every Christmas he poured some cologne on a palm, rubbed his hands together and then patted his neck.

"I smell good now."

"Those are the cookies," Irene always said.

Hm...hm, hm, hm...hm....

"Great party last night," says Kurt.

Ray smiles and takes a chance. He can't remember him. "You left pretty early."

"Yeah."

Clickety, clack, whoosh, clack....

She stops suddenly, wobbles sideways, gasping in soft, pale puffs.

People are coming up the walkway. "Merry Christmas!" She smiles and swings in a circle.

On that first Christmas when Ray stayed with Ed's family, he went to buy Son a motor bike and Ed came with him in his Santa cap. He remembers the misty shadows on the floor from the sooty light outside.

"Cost ya to ship," said Ed.

"I don't care. I feel like blowin' it. Celebratin'! Open invitation. A goddam party," he said and Ed grinned. "Ho! Ho! Ho!"

Now he says, "Anyway…," (clickety whoosh, clomp, clomp), sets his empty bottle down and stares at the ring on his little finger. It isn't Cora's and it doesn't fit. He rolls it up until it stops at a knuckle and clenches his fingers into a ball.

"I bought champagne," says Kurt.

"Oh yeah?"

"On sale," he says, opening the refrigerator door to show the yellow bottles full of pink champagne.

"You goin' to Hollycock's?"

"Yeah."

"Good deal."

He doesn't really mean it. Christmas always depresses him. He can picture people sitting around the TV with bowls of nuts and crackers and cheese on those decorative plastic plates even Miri buys. She put her cookies on one with little stars and a green Christmas tree on the bottom.

"Oughta be fun."

Just add a sooty sky….

They are sitting around the Christmas tree, Kate on the arm of Sam's chair, the little girls on the floor. Katie has an Erector Set, Debbie an Easy Bake Oven. Craig is drinking champagne. Craig's cousin hates champagne. He wants a real drink. Trying to catch Craig's attention, he finally does and tips his head imperceptibly toward the front door. Craig nods, a quick staccato motion. When Craig was about six years old, his stepfather swung him around by the ankles and let him go. He hit a wall head first. When his mother got home and found out what happened she gave him baby aspirin and put him to bed. In the morning, he couldn't walk, so she took him to the hospital. Craig's mother is Craig's cousin's mother's sister, and when Craig's cousin's mother decided that her sister needed a break from Craig, Craig's mother didn't really object. It was hard for her to look at Craig for a long time. Now, though, Craig sees her all the time and holds no grudges. He's one of the kindest people Craig's cousin knows.

Swallowing the rest of his champagne, Craig sets his glass down, about to get up. Then Craig's cousin's phone starts ringing and he sits back down again as Craig's cousin goes over to the sliding glass door to the backyard and says, "Hey, hi. Are you still mad?"

"No."

Hearing his voice, Craig's cousin murmurs, "Wait a minute," and goes down the hall to his old bedroom. It's still the same room, plaid bedspread, pictures of Roy Orbison on the walls, a corner desk where he did all his homework. He drops down onto his bed, lying back. There was a tone in Son's voice. "What's wrong?"

"I have to see you."

"No problem. I'm leaving. I just have to stop by Will's." Son doesn't say anything else. Craig's cousin puts a hand on his forehead. "What's wrong?"

"He pawned my jacket."

"What?"

"He pawned it. My fucking jacket."

"How do you know that?"

"I found a ticket. Some place called Smiley's."

"So what? It's a pawn ticket."

"I know what 'e did."

"I don't think so."

"Trevor. That jacket was really important to me. It was the best thing I ever got from him."

Craig's cousin knows everything Ray gave Son and he isn't sure why the jacket was the most important thing, but he knows it is to Ray too. "Baby, don't flip out over this. You don't know anything. You know how worked up you get."

"I'm not worked up. I'm fuckin' pissed."

"That's what I mean. I don't want you to say anything until I'm with you. I really mean that."

"I don't wanna wait, Trevor."

"A couple hours. I'll meet you at the Club at two o'clock."

"Jesus, why would 'e do somethin' like that to me? I mean, fuck, I didn't do anything to him."

"Stop thinking about it."

"I can't."

"Yes, you can. Go get something to eat. Have you eaten anything?"

"No."

"Are you hung over?"

"A little."

"Go eat. You need to do that. Get somethin' sweet. Get those pumpkin waffles at Candi's. Think about me an' relax, okay?"

"Okay. Okay, Trevor."

"I love you, baby."

"Always, right? You always will?"

"Always. I told you that. I always will. Okay?"

"Okay."

Afterwards, Craig's cousin just lies on his bed for a moment, pressing his phone against his forehead. Then with a grimace he rolls up and heads back out into the living room.

Outside, Ray stops at the bottom of the stairs and Jennie rolls away, giggling again. Then she stops herself by grabbing onto one of the posts and rolls back up.

"Havin' a good Christmas?"

"Yeah."

Her voice sounds surprised at him and he laughs, guessing that he didn't need to ask.

"Yeah. Me too."

It starts to snow, flurries spinning outside an unshuttered window at Jack's Club. Miri stops to look. She doesn't move and it looks like a photograph in the pale light outside. Otis goes over too.

"Look," she murmurs.

The snow melts, disappearing in the deep, dark trees. Then she takes her drinks to a table across the room and goes back to the bar a minute later. Outside, the snow stops and the air grows damp and misty again.

Otis is washing glasses in a sudsy sink, lulled by the loud drone of happy voices, steamy warmth surrounded by silent snow, a mesmerizing white in the opening of the door. Cold whistles in, disappears again. He watches Ray walk up, lean on the counter.

"Hey, bub."

He smiles at Ray's cheerful grin.

"Merry Christmas, Ray."

They see the snow when they run outside. Inside, there is a hole in the wall where Will fell against the door and put the knob through it.

Craig's cousin knew something was wrong the minute he stepped inside. He felt Craig stop behind him and looked at the Christmas tree and the paper strewn floor and the blinking wreath on Will's tee-shirt and let his eyes go empty. Against the gray wall of his vision, he saw it and looked back at Will, who was sitting on the couch between Andy and Jimbo, pointing the remote control at the motorized car, about to say, "Look at this." Then Craig's cousin looked into Will's eyes and Will went suddenly white. "What?"

"Your birds."

"I brought 'um in," said Will, plaintively, not wanting to know what Craig's cousin knew. Craig's cousin was torn between happiness at seeing again and unhappiness at what he saw.

"Your birds are dead, man."

"What the fuck?" said Jimbo.

Will's voice was hoarse. "Dead?"

"Yeah."

Then Will got up slowly with a dull look on his face and they all made room for him. When he looked in the back room he remembered the Christmas he didn't get any presents. Jimbo, Craig, Craig's cousin, and Susie crowded up behind him. Then Susie pulled her mink over her mouth and backed away. Jimbo said, "Fuck," and Craig's cousin said, "Man, that ain't good."

Will looked at Craig's cousin and said, "I don't get Christmas."

And Craig's cousin felt like he'd just been slugged in the stomach. He even bent over a little and grimaced. "Fuck, Will. I'm sorry."

"Dead," he said. "Dead." Then he spun away and ran outside.

Jimbo and Andy ran out with him, then Craig and Craig's cousin followed and Susie came after, hugging her collar up under her chin. Will ran in circles on the grass and his breath made pale puffs in the misty air. A car was pulling up at the house on the corner. People with presents got out of the car. The people in the house came out and they all laughed. The sound was light and airy and floated over. Will stopped running, then Susie came down a step as he looked over. The wreath on his tee-shirt was still blinking and Elvis was singing Christmas carols. Then his gaze found the reindeer ears that fell off when he ran outside and then Susie's heels caught between the boards on a step and she almost fell before Craig's cousin caught her by her coat. Her arms flapped at him and then Will began to run again.

"No Christmasssss!"

At home, Ray put some Old Spice on and felt it sting. When she gave it to him, she said, "I got this for you, but it's not really a present."

It didn't look like a present because she didn't wrap it, but it was almost his birthday. Even so he said, "So what is it, a hint?"

It didn't depress him the way things like presents usually did and she made light of it anyway, wrapping her arms around him and moving in a way that made him think of her dancing around a pole.

"I love the way you smell."

His Christmas present is wrapped though and he gives her a look of disgust over the drink Otis just poured him and says, "What did I tell you about that?"

"You gave me earrings."

"I didn't give you any earrings."

He looks away but sees her in the mirror, leaning in to sniff at his neck. "You smell good."

"I took a shower."

His present's on the bar. He picks it up and looks at it, drinking with his other hand.

"I had it made special."

"Oh yeah?" He remembers the fingerless gloves from Ed and the coat he gave Son. His face grows sour when she starts to pull on him. "Where we goin?"

"In back."

"I can open it here."

Then she shakes her head and moves backwards, fingers gliding along the edge of the bar. "I might have something else," she murmurs, drawing him down the hallway with her. He likes to watch her from behind, the way she twists to look back at him, her eyes lazy looking, the way she gets when she wants him. They pass through the store room into the office in back. Thin gray light seeps through the windows. There's a coat rack by the door with Miri's coat on it. It reminds him of Son's again and he sits with a sigh. She rests her hands on his shoulders and stands between his legs with one knee on the edge of the chair.

"Open it."

He shrugs and pulls the bow off.

"Remember after we met? When you came over?"

"Not especially," he lies.

"I said your name."

He looks up and thinks of the way her hair used to fall over her face before she cut it.

"Ray," she murmurs.

After Craig's cousin left, he jerked his thumb back at the TV and said, "Why don't you turn it off an' come outside with me."

"My soaps are on."

"Oh. Soaps."

Instead of going out, she gave him another beer. He liked her kitchen, its color and the oldness of everything. "Nice place," he said.

"Thanks."

"Where you work?"

"The Jack of Clubs…Jack's Club."

He frowned then because he couldn't remember her there. "I know that place. Been there a couple of times."

"You should come in again."

"Yeah. Definitely. I have a feeling about us," he added, lifting up his beer. At that moment, he fell in love with her. But he doesn't think about that and would reject it if the thought ever arose that he could fall in love with a woman for things other than sex or affection or comfort. Because the place where he could fall in love like that, almost at first sight, is a place he won't admit exists in him. It's a place of faith where things are forgiven. It's a place where he might be washed clean again and he won't admit that that's even possible, that he could ever deserve it. But that's what she gives him, even if he won't think about it, thinks instead about her awkwardness, her dependency and occasional resistance, and wonders more comfortably what her appeal to him is. He remembers getting up to go over to her, his fingertips on the edge of the counter on either side of her, the sound of her voice. "Ray."

When she went to the Acropolis Arts and Crafts Show, she saw a man on a yellow and white lawn chair behind glass display cases. He had a gray ponytail and pale blue eyes that reminded her of Ed's and made her hesitate until he said, "Yeah?"

"Are you Jake?"

He got up. "I'm Jake."

She took a picture of a garden tile with a sun and wavy rays on its surface out of her purse.

"I want a belt buckle like this picture."

"I can make a buckle like that."

It came later on a piece of sky blue felt, a golden sun with wavy silver rays.

After he puts it on, he gets up and pushes her slowly out into the chilly, snowless air, gray and ghostly, stopping at her car where she puts her arms over his shoulders and he touches her hair and she starts to blush without anything to hide behind and almost looks away before he grin and says, "You have great arms."

The air is still, soft and misty, and the firs are dark, almost indistinct. Occasional snowflakes swirl. Smoke is coming out of the chimney of the house on the corner. It's Will's Christmas picture and Craig's cousin remembers Will's mother in her apron on Christmas morning when he went over one year. She gave him a present that was waiting for him under the tree, a Pierre Cardin gift package that was always on sale at the holidays. He doesn't remember her in the way Will does. She always looked frustrated and tired and disappointed, though he didn't think it was at Will. He thought of her as Mrs Cleaver just because she always made everything look so good when it wasn't.

Standing in the doorway to the porch, Craig's cousin feels the cold against his chapped skin. It stings and he takes a tube of Blistex out of his pocket and rubs it across his lips.

Craig is waiting in his car and Will is sitting on the porch, inside of Susie's arms. Two days ago he came home with a present he bought for himself and showed it to Susie. It was a bird, white and orange. In the cage with the other birds, it fluffed itself up and looked as soft as a cotton ball. Will called it Creamsicle. When they looked into the back room today, Creamsicle was the only bird anybody saw at first. Then the rest of the room came into focus; Susie backed away and Craig's cousin said, "Man, that ain't good," and Will saw all the bodies on the bottom of the cage. Creamsicle puffed and preened and then resumed pulling out their feathers. Will couldn't breathe at first. His lungs made wheezing sounds.

"I don't get Christmas."

To Craig's cousin, Will seemed almost bemused by the thought and Craig's cousin wondered if Will was remembering the Christmas he sold his mother's cookies.

Now Susie pats his shoulder and Jimbo kicks awkwardly at one of the porch steps and asks, "Want me to kill it for you, Will? We can run it over with that cool car Susie gave you."

Will is silent. Probably considering it, thinks Craig's cousin. Stepping outside, he goes down to the walkway and looks back at Will. "Don't do anything dumb, Will, okay?"

"Like what?"

"You don't want to feel worse, right? Creamsicle has mental problems."

A sluggish frown pulls down Will's face. "Really?"

"Well, that wasn't fuckin' normal."

But then Will's look of malice and resentment returns. "I want my money back."

"No kidding. Take it back to the store."

"Run it over," says Jimbo.

Craig's cousin looks at him carefully. "Fuck off, Jimbo."

"Fuck you, you freak."

Animation returns to Will's face. "Don't you fuckin' talk to Trevor like that."

Jimbo grouses back at him. "I was just tryin' to help."

"I have to think," says Will, shrugging off Susie's patting hand.

"I'll call you later," says Craig's cousin.

"Where you goin'?"

"I have a couple more stops."

"Mr Popularity," sneers Jimbo.

Craig's cousin smiles. "Don't worry, Jimbo. You might grow a personality someday."

Will laughs, a quick hiccup of a sound. Susie giggles beside him. Uncertain of who's on his side, Jimbo flushes and looks around. Leaning against the side of the house, Andy tries to avoid his gaze.

Jimbo puffs up. "Who're you lookin' at?"

Andy shrugs. "Not you, man."

Craig's cousin raises his palms, backing off down the walkway. "See you later, Will."

The house where Miri grew up was green with brown trim. There were junipers out front and a maple planted by the developers. The front and back yards were big. When they moved in, there were no fences out back, but those were put in quickly. Children played outside until the streetlights went on. When Miri told Ray about it, there was the shine of recognition in his eyes. He knows where she lived, a street where all the maples are tall and shady now. She lived with her father, mother, and brother. In middle school she was a pom-pom girl. Her brother, Wade, was quiet, quietly failed in school, quietly found the wrong friends, quietly slipped almost away. She never took drugs and always imagined she loved every boy she ever slept with. She was never the one to leave. Up until her father's death, they were a perfect family. She can't recall if her mother and father ever kissed or ever held hands. They sat in the same living room and watched TV. They didn't fight; they didn't even really talk. There was a strange tension in the house even though nobody ever seemed angry.

When she tells Ray about her life, he looks at her with a slightly bemused expression as if she's leaving something out. She can't explain the strange feeling of suspended animation that she had, the stillness that only love could seem to release. She knows that she barely struggles, that it's something Ray doesn't particularly like about her, but waiting is the way she lives.

Like her, her brother Wade just waits, patiently immobile in the flow of things, but unlike her he has no illusions that happiness will ever be part of the jetsam that floats by. He lives on the streets in the town where they grew up, for Christmas rented a room in a hotel. There used to be a drive-in movie theater across the street and a catalog store next door. Now there's a shopping center with an indoor theater and no catalog store. He left a message on Miri's phone and told her where he'd be. As he's leaving his room, he hears the phone in the office ringing and smiles at the feeling that it's her, but he doesn't pause. He walks across the damp parking lot and starts down the street, hands in the pockets of his dirty jacket. He has her thin face, slightly freckled skin and sandy hair. He is thirty-five, five years younger. On the posts of the street lamps, white banners with red berries and green holly leaves flutter in the soft gray air. Cars pass him by.

He can't hear the phone anymore. He remembers perfect Christmases with perfect trees and perfect presents, Miri in a new coat with her hair in a ponytail, toys under the tree, going to his mother's family's house to sit in a row on a stiff white couch with paper cups of store bought eggnog.

As he walks away, a bell rings like a faraway toll and he smiles at the image.

He smells Chinese food and donuts in the cold air and remembers a farm by the freeway and the irrigators in the rows of green, water twinkling like dewdrops in the warm, sunny air. Now there are office buildings, apartments, and little shops he never goes into. Like perfect Christmases, all the things he grew up with have disappeared. Up ahead, he hears the bell again, Christmas carols traveling through walls and the misty gray to reach him. Cars whistle by and he smiles as he walks.

People are sitting out on their porches at the trailer park, stomping their feet in the cold and drinking together.

Craig's cousin parks his car beside his trailer, then jogs back to Craig's car idling on the road above the driveway. He cups his hands in front of his mouth, waiting to get warm again. His nervousness surprises him. He glances at Craig, who keeps glancing at him, catching his nerves. After he met Son and stopped being able to see, without telling his father about it, he asked him if there was ever a time that he couldn't see, and his father looked at him with slight amusement and said, "Twice. When you an' Katie were born."

Craig's cousin was hoping he'd say, "When I met your mother," because he thought that losing his sight had something to do with falling in love, but he didn't think it likely that his father loved his children more than his wife. His father's smile grew as he watched him, then he said, "I didn't like either of you right away, actually. I know. That sounds terrible. I didn't dislike you. I just don't think I knew what to make of you. I loved you quick enough though. Maybe because you were my second I was a little more used to it. Everything corrected though. I wouldn't worry."

"I wasn't talking about me," he said, feeling strangely defensive.

"Course not," his father answered.

Seeing Will's birds let him know that it isn't gone, but he isn't seeing anything that he wants to see now either. At Jack's Club, Craig idles at the door, not parking. "You're not coming in?"

"No, I…You know. I…You know…Need to see my mom."

Craig's cousin nods and gets out. Then he stomps his feet like the people in the trailer park and blows into his hands again. His knuckles are red. He sucks on one, stalling, then sighs and goes inside.

The warmth is heavy, pleasant, the noise level at a comfortable low drone. Standing still for a moment, his eyes swing to the back of the room where he sees Ray sitting alone at a table in the alcove. Ray doesn't look surprised to see him, not happy to see him, not annoyed. Stopping at the bar, Craig's cousin gets a drink, sipping it on the way over. It feels good going down and his nerves start to settle.

Ray is giving off a good and not good feeling at the same time. The good feeling is stronger, but Craig's cousin feels confused too, as if he's somehow misreading things.

He sits down and Ray says, "What's up, Trev?"

"Not much."

"You don't do the Christmas thing with your family?"

"I was there." He eyes Ray and says, "We need to do the Christmas thing here. No Christmas music."

He watches Ray's eyes begin to twinkle. "Allman Brothers, man. Don't ya like 'um?"

"Sure. But it's Christmas. I want Christmas carols."

"Too bad."

"Yeah. King Roy on Christmas. Elvis sang carols. Will's got an album. Only ones I have are Roy's. King Roy. No Christmas carols though."

Ray's eyes are laughing. "You are a fuckin' freak, you know that, Trev?"

He nods. "Jimbo told me."

Ray laughs. Craig's cousin knows Ray likes him. He wants him to remember that. He finishes his drink, quicker than he wanted to. Then the door opens and his heart starts to race. His nerves are back and he feels sick. A moment later Son is beside him, dropping a jacket over the back of a chair, sitting down with a drink. He looks at Ray for a moment, opens his mouth, then scowls and looks under the table. Craig's cousin pulls his foot back. Son looks at him, then back at Ray and takes a swallow of his drink. Craig's cousin waits for him to finish it while Ray looks for Miri. When she comes over, she gives Ray a kiss, straightens up and says, "How many?"

"All of us," says Ray. "On me."

"Comin' right up."

Son puts down his empty glass and then starts to look restless with nothing to do.

"I bet Otis has a radio," says Craig's cousin.

Son frowns at him. "What for? There's a jukebox."

"Christmas carols."

"I don't want any fuckin' Christmas carols."

"Well, it is fuckin' Christmas," says Craig's cousin.

Son shrugs and twists his empty glass. "So go ask 'im for a radio."

"I don't give a fuck anymore."

"Yeah, you do," says Son, leaning over. "You're gettin' all pissed off about it."

"I'm not pissed off."

"Yeah, you are."

"Whatever."

Son scowls at him and slumps back. "Yeah. Whatever."

Craig's cousin sits back again too, pushing at the arms of his chair. Ray is staring at the ceiling. There is a slight squint to his eye. When Miri arrives, Craig's cousin drains half his glass in one swallow. Son follows suit, then stares at Ray again. Ray stares back. Then Son takes another swallow of his drink, looks back again and says, "Smiley's. Ever hear of it?"

"Pawn shop," says Ray.

"I used to go all the time," says Craig's cousin. "Date money."

Son glares at him. "I wanna talk."

Craig's cousin's mouth twists in irritation, but he nods. "Yeah, okay."

Son looks back at Ray again. "I found a ticket at the shop."

Ray shrugs. "So?"

"So wha' did you pawn?"

"Hell, kid, I don't remember."

"You don't remember?"

"What did I just say?"

"Who doesn't remember somethin' like that?"

"Me. Why the hell should I?"

"You fuckin' pawned somethin', that's why."

"What the hell are you saying?"

"I'm not saying anything. I'm asking."

"I didn't hear you ask anything. I heard you tell me I'm lyin'."

"I think you fuckin' remember. I think you remember exactly what you took there."

"You think so?"

"I fuckin' know so."

"You tell me, kid."

"I'm not gonna tell you. That's bullshit. You think I'm gonna give you any fuckin' satisfaction?"

"Well, you know what, kid? Satisfaction's not exactly what I'm feelin'. What I'm feelin' is you should get the fuck outta here."

Craig's cousin can feel his blood warm while the red in his knuckles flares. He is resting an elbow on the table, rubbing his forehead with his fingertips and looking between them.

"The hell I am. This is chickenshit. You better fuckin' tell me."

"I better?" says Ray, straightening up angrily.

At the same time, Son starts to rise and Craig's cousin drops a hand on his arm to stop him. "Wait a minute for fuck's sake. This is Christmas. I don't want to deal with this shit on Christmas." He leans over to Son and his voice is low. "You don't need it. I don't need it. This is a dumbass thing to be talkin' about right now."

Son sits red-faced, glaring at Ray. He is frozen with anger and Craig's cousin knows that Son doesn't know how to get out of this situation.

"I want you to wait outside for me," he says and Son gets up with a sudden lurch, kicking his chair back, knocking it over. Ray just stares at him. When Son is gone, Craig's cousin puts his hand on his head, clenching his fingers. "You didn't have to do that."

"Says who? You dunno what I have to do."

Craig's cousin shifts sideways, removes his wallet and says, "I'm payin' for us."

"Us?"

"Why'd you do it?"

"Why'd I do what?"

"His jacket, man. Why?"

"He showed no respect."

"That's bullshit. It was situational. You weren't there. Things got heated."

"They always get heated with that kid. You just saw that. There's nothing he doesn't manage to fuck up. Like I said, no respect."

"That's bullshit."

"I heard you before."

"God, Ray."

"Whatever."

Craig's cousin gets up and goes outside. A shadow moves beside him and Son grabs him by the front of his jacket and tugs him around the side of the building out of sight. He leans back against the wall and Son pushes up close. "You see?"

Craig's cousin rests his hands on either side of Son's neck and then Son is leaning into him, pushing his tongue in his mouth, breathing heavily, pressing into him. Craig's cousin pushes him away and then pulls him back in again. After a while he can feel Son speaking against his lips. "You love me, don't you, Trevor?"

"Yeah, baby."

Then Son almost slumps against him and Craig's cousin says, "You went in there lookin' for trouble, though, an' that's not okay. You really messed things up."

"I know," murmurs Son. "I fucked up."

"Royally. I don't want you thinkin' about it right now, though. We're gonna go eat an' relax an' have a Merry fuckin' Christmas."

Son half laughs at that, his body heavy against Craig's cousin's side as they walk away. "Yeah, okay. I guess we can do that."

Snowflakes drift through the air, melting on the pavement. The shutters are pulled back on one of the windows at Jack's Club and a cozy orange light struggles out into the dim day. Joe Clay pulls into the parking lot and gets out of his car. Outside, he can hear the whistling sound through the firs and recalls the sound of the wind in movies, singing over desert sands and through abandoned houses.

This morning he went to Andy's and Andy said, "Head's up, man. Jimbo's out lookin' for ya. Will's orders."

He laughed a little, staring at Andy's carpet, and put himself in a movie again where he ran away because people who wanted him dead for some reason nobody was willing to tell him were chasing after him.

Andy looked uncomfortable. "I mean I don't care."

Then when Joe laughed again and said, "You guys gonna kill me or somethin'?" Andy looked pained and Joe felt embarrassed.

At the door, he sees the golden shine of a bell on a Christmas wreath and goes inside. At the bar, Ray looks over at him without expression, only smiling and laughing when he turns back to Otis.

At this time of year even palm trees rustle in a cool breeze and the deserts at night are icy and moonless.

After a moment, Otis comes over and pours a drink that he picks up and takes with him, sitting down at the end of the bar. Ray is leaning sideways now, looking at him again and then back at Otis.

"It's called inflation," says Ray. "Pump fees."

Joe pictures a McDonald's by a pure white beach where he can work up to night manager and eat a free burger out under the moon and make enough one day to buy a boat and sail away. He drains his glass and sets it down.

"I like mine already inflated," says Ray with a wink at Otis. Otis gives him a mild smile and lets his eyes drift to Joe, too. Joe watches Ray approach, sit down beside him. Otis comes too, pushing over a plain white napkin before he sets a drink on it.

"On me," says Ray.

"Thanks." Ray smells like cologne.

"We were talkin' 'bout Shirley Temples," says Ray.

After a pause Joe asks, "The drink?" and Ray laughs.

"Otis. The man wants to know. Shirley the drink?" Otis smiles too. "Cherry sweet," says Ray, lifting his glass for a swallow.

He's in jeans, a plain knit shirt with his sleeves pushed up, tattoos on his forearms, the smell of that cologne, and his eyes are cold and remind Joe of the way Ed looked at him. At first, Ed was just vague, barely remembering that he met him at Pete's, not really caring. Then one day he turned cold like this. Even though Joe was always with Cora and thought that she ought to bring him some kind of credibility. He thinks of that word because he knows that's what Ed didn't see in him. Credibility. A thing that was there at first and then suddenly gone. He knew there was nothing anybody could say against him and he remembers staring into his own eyes in a mirror, looking for some fissure that showed the life underneath. He wanted to live a life like the ones in the movies. Cora with her moppy blonde hair fit in easily into every scene. She was fun and made him feel good. Then Ed's eyes turned cold and he knew it was time to go. He told Cora about a friend in Acropolis and she laughed and said, "Wait until I tell Ed. We have a friend there too."

He didn't want Ed to know, didn't appreciate having him appear at his apartment and tell him to look up a friend, who wasn't Ray, but Goliath. "Tell 'im I sent you. I'll be waitin' to hear you did that," he said and his eyes appeared a little less sub-zero. He even smiled. But everything down there came up here. He is like the hero who started a new life only to have the old one destroy it.

Looking sideways, he sees Ray's slightly amused gaze on him again. "You keepin' busy?"

"I was. Outta work again yesterday though."

"On Christmas Eve?"

He smiles into his drink. "Yeah."

"Cold."

Then Ray picks up his glass and looks into the mirror over the bar. Joe looks too and can see Miri in her green jumper in back. She's picking up glasses in her fingers, stopping at a table where she puts her free hand on her hip and somebody laughs. Catching a glimpse of Ray's gaze in the mirror he doesn't see any love in his eyes. Even for her, he is cool, speculative, *scoping out the angles*, thinks Joe. Then Ray murmurs, "I guess you didn't get the word," and Joe feels a coldness inside that his drink isn't warming.

"You mean to leave?"

"That was the word I remember."

"I don't understand. What the hell did I do to you?"

"Nothin'. I just don't like you. It's nothin' personal."

"Not liking me's pretty personal."

"Not really."

One day, after he makes it to night manager at McDonald's, Joe will sail off without any luggage at all, and sit on deck with Shirley Temple the drink and follow the wake of the sun, and Ray will go out with Will and Andy and Jimbo, and laugh with Otis, and go home to a cocktail waitress, and work at the shop, and do the things that he won't let Joe be a part of while Joe sails away with only seagulls and Shirley Temples for company.

"I thought this was a fuckin' free country," says Joe and Ray looks askance at him.

"Are you shittin' me?"

At Candi's later, Joe eats a slice of cherry pie in a booth under a green plastic garland. There are poinsettias on the counter, and a waitress named Candy, not Candi, pockets her tip with a smile and stops him at the door.

"Hey!"

He looks back in.

"Merry Christmas."

"Merry Christmas," he says.

On Christmas Eve, Miri's father stomped across the roof and she shook Wade and looked excited. "Do you hear it? Santa Claus!"

Wade still believed in him a little. She still remembers his doubtful expression, eyes rising up, wanting it to be true, but not willing to believe it. Even then, that was the difference between them. Willingness. Miri trusted blindly because of what she wanted. Wade refused to take a chance on what he wanted. But he was little then and they both listened to the stomping on the roof with eager smiles.

After they went to bed, she remembers looking at the light under her door, listening to the whispers in the hallway, the sound of footsteps going back and forth, the muffled thumps of things hitting the wall. That was one of the few things her mother and father did together with the sense of really being together. Even Christmas morning, after all the presents were open, they went to their separate spaces. When Ray listens to her stories he says, "Sounds nice," and she knows compared to his life it was. There was nothing wrong, nothing at all. Except it was just a picture with nothing underneath it. There is life in the pictures in Ray's dresser drawer, Cora's leering smile, Ed's far away stare. Ray's cheating made his life with her unreal. She was living a picture life, an image of people who are together. He gave more substance to Cora, more life and happiness. She isn't easy to make happy and knows that Wade isn't either. She pictures him sitting up against cold cement by a canal full of reeds and dark, cold water with the sounds of traffic nearby under a clear, starry sky. She imagines him always looking for things he won't believe in anyway.

She remembers her father going outside to smoke in the side yard under the eaves of the roof. After a few minutes he'd drop the cigarette in the dirt and grind it under his shoe. Half-smoked cigarettes collected there like relics. He died at work, on a cool, sunny day, smoking on the lawn under a redwood tree. She guessed he could see the birds flying by and hear the sounds of the traffic and smell the mustard in the field by the buildings. It was quiet there.

Outside, the snow starts falling again, lying white on the ground. Spruce and redwoods emerge from the dark like ghostly phantoms. In the back of the bar, Ray sits with his elbows on his knees, looking at the ring on his little finger. He is thinking about Cora's, feeling a vague surprise that it isn't there anymore. It never really meant anything. It was Pete's, and when Cora wanted it back, noticing it at her wedding, he kept it just to play with her. The second time she asked for it back, they were dancing, or moving in slow motion, on the still damp lawn. His hands rested on her swaying hips and he was smiling at her. She turned her head sideways and rested her face against his shoulder.

"Are you happy?" he asked.

"Just peachy. Thanks to Bobby, this dress is for shit." Green from the newly mowed, newly watered grass stained the hem.

"Take it to a dry cleaner."

"You can't fix this."

"Cora, babe, I think you're missing the point here."

Her head tilted back. "I get the point. Pete's the point, right?" Her hair was coming loose, thin, buttery tendrils sticking to her flushed face.

"I think you need him. I think Pete's the right guy for you."

He reached up to brush her hair away and she caught sight of the ring again and grabbed him by the wrist.

"Oh, yeah. Give that back."

"Give what back?"

"My ring."

"It's my ring now. You gave it to me."

"I already told you. I didn't give it to you. I threw it at you."

His smile broadened. "I remember that. Anyway, I'm keeping it. I want a part of this. I deserve it."

Her arms slipped off his shoulders and went around his waist and she leaned in, chin on his chest, looking up at him, her clownish mouth temptingly close. "Will it make you think of me?"

"I don't need a ring for that, Cora."

"Promise?"

He shook his head. "No."

He wasn't surprised when she pushed him away from her, yanked up her dress and stalked across the lawn. He never made promises because he never doubted he'd regret them afterwards. Having Son was a kind of promise he knows he's never lived up to.

Sitting back in his chair, he watches the bar empty out, Otis rinsing out the last of the glasses. When Miri starts wiping down the tables, Otis says, "Don't worry about that. We can clean up tomorrow."

She nods and goes in back. Lights switch off. The perimeters of the bar contract, pull in toward the abandoned tables and chairs in the center. A feeling of loneliness comes over him. He wipes his mouth with his thumb and finishes his drink. Miri reappears and says, "Go home, Otis. I'll lock up."

"You sure?"

Ray's voice floats out from the back. "Go, Otis. Leave us alone."

"In that case," says Otis, pulling off his apron, "I'm outta here."

After he's gone, Miri starts wiping off the tables anyway. When she draws closer to Ray, she says, "Do you want another drink?"

"Yeah, I guess. But I'll get it."

He pours half a glass, watching her from behind the bar. Her earrings are shiny little Christmas balls that keep shooting off sparks of light.

"Play something," she says, scooting a chair in before she starts back.

"Anything in particular?"

"You pick. I want to dance with you."

He half laughs at her timing, his memory of Cora.

"What?" she asks.

"Nothing."

He slips his money into the machine and waits for her. She approaches, smiling, and leans into him. He barely moves, just rocks against her, relishing the feel of her. His face rests against hers and he breathes in her scent. It is so familiar, so strangely calming. "I'm getting old," he says.

She laughs and tightens her arms. "You're crazy."

"Crazy somethin'."

She tilts her head back, smiling at him, her moves mimicking Cora's, giving him a strange, disorienting feeling that he likes. The emptiness of the bar, the dull orange light, the song floating into the room enhances it. Resting his forearms on either side of her neck, he pulls the ring off behind her, then drops his hand, grasping hers. A surprised look comes onto her face and her fingers squeeze his.

"I don't want you to say anything about what I'm gonna do," he says. "I know you're gonna want to so I'm tellin' you now. I don't want to hear it.

You can keep what I'm gonna give you or take it off. I don't care. I'm guessin' you're gonna wanna keep it, but I don't wanna hear about it. I don't want you to say anything, okay?"

"Ray—"

"No," he says. "You're gonna fuck it up. Don't talk."

She curls her other hand against his chest and her eyes are open and serious. "Don't worry, Ray. It's okay."

He smiles at her, bemused and nonplussed. "You really don't listen to me, do you?"

"I listen."

"Shut up." She nods and her hand opens on his chest, fingers pushing gently. He lifts her other hand, kisses her palm, then slides the ring onto her finger. "No talking."

Amazingly, she doesn't speak for a moment, doesn't look at him with surprise or excitement or happiness either. The song suddenly ends and there's just the echo of it. He feels good, smiles at her silence and murmurs, "That's my girl."

"You talked."

"I'm allowed," he says quietly, bending for her lips. They push against his and he feels her tongue and opens his mouth, pulling her against him, feeling her arms wrap around him, her fingers in his hair. After a moment, she pulls away, but she holds his face in her hands, smiles into his eyes.

"Merry Christmas, Ray."

He smiles back at her. "Merry Christmas, lady."

23

◆ Gift Giving ◆

The bowling pin looks like a candy cane, the banners on the street lamps droop in the damp air. Mr Torch is sitting peacefully, listening to the faraway sound of bells in the trees at the mortuary.

There are lights on at the trailer park, porch lights haloed in the cold. The driveway into the park drops down an embankment, then makes a slow half-moon curve into the distance. Cars crowd each side of the road, Craig's cousin's car down by his trailer. Son wedges his Camaro into a space at the top of the driveway, the rear end of his car sticking out.

"Nobody better hit me."

"You're not that far out."

Lights pop on inside the car, then snap off as the doors slam shut. The cold seems to contain the sound. Even the soft crunch of their shoes on the gravel seems to carry no further than their steps. There is no other sound, no wind whistling, no Christmas carols. At his porch, Craig's cousin lingers outside, letting his eyes roam.

Son hesitates in the open doorway. "You okay?"

He nods after a moment. "Yeah, I guess so."

There are no figures out there, no waiting shadows. He follows Son inside, switches on the little Christmas tree on his counter, the radio in the bedroom, hearing the Christmas carols he wanted to hear all day. In the bedroom, the shower goes on and he shucks his clothes too and follows Son into the steamy stall. They don't talk, just wash, get out again. Craig's cousin pulls on his pajama bottoms, grabs a comb off the sink and says, "C'mere."

Son scowls, but follows him. In the kitchen, he gets a drink first, then he sits down on the floor between Craig's cousin's knees and feels the comb in his hair. He never combs it with anything but his fingers. His hair is like Ray's, thick and heavy. In some ways his looks don't really matter to him. He wears tee-shirts with holes, jeans that are too big for him, boots he never cleans. He doesn't always bathe, annoying Craig's cousin, won't comb his hair, just ruffles it with his fingers and shakes it into place. But the ink on his body is beautiful and he can tell Craig's cousin the story behind every tattoo. A spill of red rose petals drips to his wrist like drops of blood, marking the day he didn't kill himself.

"I was going to. I had the rope. I was standing on the fucking chair. I could hear kids playing outside cuz I left the window open. I heard the cars. I played like that once. I remembered it. I just couldn't remember why it stopped. I wanted to remember why so bad I got off the chair an' sat down on it to think. I couldn't remember though an' I started bawlin' like a little kid. I didn't want my mom to find me anyway so I didn't do it."

"Why would you in the first place?" asked Craig's cousin, ruffling his hair with his fingers in the way he knew calmed him.

"Oh, my God, Trevor. I was blowin' guys for ten bucks a pop. They could bang me for twenty. I got in a car with a psycho. I hated my life. I hated me. An' I was so fuckin' pissed off."

On his back is a sun, glowing yellow with orange shaded rays. "A present from my dad. We both got the same tat on our birthdays. I was twenty-one. Went out an' got fuckin' wasted afterwards. That was probably my favorite birthday."

An address on the inside of his thigh in black calligraphy. "You know what's funny," he said, fingers digging into Craig cousin's back while Craig's cousin slowly traced the address with his tongue. "My dad's seen it. Never asked about it, though. We lived on that street, but it wasn't our address. It's where the boy who popped my cherry lived. Ray used to pay 'im to mow our lawn before I moved in."

The angel over his heart is because it was the only thing he could think of that was pure. "Water, I guess, but I couldn't see that working. Or a baby, but then people would think it was my baby. So I got this angel for purity. That's what my mom's name means. Pure. Kathleen. You know what Raymond means?" he asked, putting Craig's cousin's hand over his heart.

"What?"

"Protector."

Craig's cousin's eyes came up. "For real?"

"Yeah. Protector. Your name means prudent."

Craig's cousin laughed. "You're kidding?"

"No."

"How do you know this?"

"I looked it up. My name though? My name doesn't mean a fuckin' thing. They made it up."

But Craig's cousin moved his hand over Son's shoulder and found the sun on his back, rubbing it with his finger. "It means this," he said. "Life."

The burning in Son's eyes pulled him in. He took the rest of Son's clothes off, then pushed him down on the bed and took his own clothes off, watching Son's face the whole time, seeing a glassy look come into his eyes, his mouth open, his breaths quick and shallow. He began to arch his back and then he said, "C'mere," and Craig's cousin got onto the bed with him, kneeling between his knees. Son's fingers dug into his waist, pulling him down. Craig's cousin grinned, laughing at Son's excitement, grabbing his wrists when his arms flew above his head, fingers clutching at the bed sheets.

Around a bicep, four twisted strands of barbed wire. "One for every year my dad was gone."

There is more ink on his other arm, the outside of his other leg, the small of his back. His ears, nipples, tongue, and belly button are pierced. His body is his, decorative and disposable, but his life isn't. He gives everything that isn't Ray's to Craig's cousin, relies on him, lives off of him, obeys him. Craig's cousin knows that Son's love is real and he isn't afraid of losing him. He's afraid of the dark that Son lives in, the way it closes in on him, the way he lashes out at it, cornered and furious.

Thinking these thoughts, he runs his fingers through Son's hair, then gently pulls his head up. "Okay?" he murmurs. Son nods. "I didn't hurt you?"

"No."

Getting up, he throws a handful of loose hair away, then goes over to the window and looks out. There's nothing to see. The dark is like a cloak. Crossing over to the door, he goes out onto the porch and looks down the long empty road. Lights are off everywhere now and the cars from earlier are gone. It was windy earlier in the day, but now it's still out.

"What's wrong?" Son is leaning against the door behind him.

"I don't know."

There is nothing to see, nothing out there, nothing against the lids he closes for a moment, but when he opens his eyes, he sees pieces of ice glittering everywhere in a snowy cold. His worry is contagious. He can feel Son's nervousness.

"Come fuck me, Trevor. I don't wanna think about this day anymore."

Turning around, he cups Son's cheek in his hand and gently pushes him back inside.

Outside of town, a low moon casts a bluish glow through the clouds.

Mr Torch can see it at the mortuary, looking up through floor to ceiling windows at the end of the entrance hall. The tiny bells are silent. Behind him, Christmas lights shine in the dark. Outside, it is all dark, no light from the moon.

Quietly, Jonah pushes through the slightly squeaky door to the porch. He has sneakers without laces on his feet and can feel the cold through the soles of his shoes. The patches of snow are faintly luminous. He can feel his feet growing numb. The idea of the water scares him slightly. He expects pain, a shock to his lungs and heart. Fir branches brush against him. He can't smell anything but water. By the time he reaches the pond, the moon is behind the trees and a faint hint of light is growing in the sky. He lights a cigarette and leans against a tree, staring at the flat expanse that he knows is the surface of the pond.

Yesterday, he went outside with Kurt, lit a cigarette and drank a beer. They were quiet at first and then he said, "I think she knows."

He was calmer than Kurt, who looked back in, afraid she might be there. "You sure?"

He puffed on his cigarette and looked inside too. "No. Not really." Maybe he just wants it over with.

At the pond, kicking off his shoes, he pulls his clothes off too and walks straight into the water with his cigarette in the air. The cold sucks his breath away and he tries to gasp. Pressure builds in his head, then slowly eases. He rolls over onto his back, still buoyant, even though he feels like concrete. The cigarette comes to his mouth in shaky fingers, but the smoke warms him, lulls him into a feeling of comfort. He floats, numb and pain free, waiting for a light to come on below.

No bells ring at the Greenview Mortuary. A light in the building seeps out a window and glitters like icicles.

Warm air blasts in Jimbo's car and steams the windows. Swiping an arm down the windshield, Jimbo thinks of glass.

"Fuckin' hot in here," says Andy.

"Roll your window down."

Jimbo is taking Andy home. They drive by a Christmas tree lot with its lights still lit, a cardboard sign leaning up against a garbage can. A brightly lit Taco Bell glows cheerily up ahead. "Want somethin'?"

Andy yawns. "Not me."

"Fuckin' weird day."

"No kidding."

Jimbo's energy is still running high. He's tired, but not. He wants his girlfriend, but doesn't. He'll probably end up over there anyway because he can't think of anything else to do. Unless, after he drops Andy off, he crosses over to Susie's office building and breaks her glass door in. But he probably won't because it's probably alarmed.

"Why didn't you go to Jade's?"

"Boyfriend."

"Joe?"

"Hell, no. I made 'er break off with him."

"Shit taste."

Andy can't argue. He's never really liked any of Jade's boyfriends. But he likes Jade and doesn't like Jimbo talking about her. Crossing his arms, he looks out his open window, sees the Elysian Fields Trailer Park slide past into the dark. "Dead out," he says, then jerks forward as Jimbo suddenly breaks, throws the car into reverse and backs up. "Hell you doin'?"

Jimbo rolls back, past the entrance to the trailer park. Then he stops again, drops his arm over the steering wheel and peers out into the dark with a white toothed smile. "That's interesting."

Andy sits back up, hearing the sudden glee in Jimbo's voice. "What is?"

Jimbo points, raising the hand he has dangling over the steering wheel. "Whose car is that?"

Andy squints. "Son's. So what?"

"Fuckin' faggots."

"Huh?"

"Faggots."

"Are you shittin' me? Not Craig's cousin, man. No way."

Jimbo opens his car door. "C'mon. Keep quiet."

There is no sound, no wind, no lights on anywhere. Their footsteps make a barely audible hush. Jimbo moves to the edge of the driveway where the ground is soft, Andy following, and there is no sound at all. Weaving around Son's car, they follow the embankment down to level ground, then pass a pair of dark trailers before they reach Craig's cousin's. Jimbo places a finger to his lips, points at Andy, at the ground, then moves quietly across the driveway. He looks at the darkened windows, notices one open near the back, high up and narrow. The ground here is covered in needles. Jimbo makes no sound. He creeps to the open window and his toothy smile returns. He cackles soundlessly and creeps back across the driveway, pats Andy on the arm, pushing him back up to the road. Andy looks back at him questioningly. A moment later, Jimbo pulls up at Son's car and his soundless cackle becomes an almost soundless giggle.

"Fuckers are gettin' it on in there."

Andy looks back. "No fuckin' way. Not Craig's cousin."

"This is too rich. I can't wait to tell Ray."

"Are you fuckin' nuts? You can't do that."

That shuts Jimbo up for a moment. He stands in the dark, thinking, while Andy begins to stomp his feet in the cold.

"Quiet," whispers Jimbo, staring at Son's car, smile beginning to grow again. "C'mon."

Andy follows him up to the road. At Jimbo's car, he says, "You're crazy. The kid's just crashin' here. I see 'im here all the time."

"Bingo, you rocket scientist."

"You've got a screw loose, Jimbo, you know that?"

"You know what fuckin' sounds like, right, Andy? At least when other people are doin' it?"

Andy doesn't say anything else. He just rubs his forehead, beginning to wince. Starting the car, Jimbo turns back the way they came. A little while later, he pulls over again and says, "I knew I saw that."

He's stopped by a Christmas tree lot with a sign for FREE TREES leaning up against a garbage can. Jimbo pops the trunk, circles around the front of the car, grabs a tree, and proceeds to the back of the car. There he stuffs the tree in the trunk, then comes back up with a blanket and a crow bar. At the sight of the crow bar, Andy says, "Hey, that's mine. You never gave that back."

"I wasn't done with it."

"What're you gonna do?"

"You're such a pussy, Andy."

Andy squeezes his forehead. They stop again, pulling into the empty parking lot of an almost empty mini-mart. Andy stays in the car, watches Jimbo through the glass. He stops at the counter and the man behind it points at an aisle near the middle of the store. Jimbo reappears with an armload of plastic bottles. After he gets back in the car, Andy leans over the seat and pulls the bag over to look inside it. Drano. Liquid Plummer. "Fuck," he says.

"This is gonna be good."

Andy rubs his face. Jimbo squirms in his seat. His excitement is a living thing. He can feel it in his toes, his burning ears. He switches off the car engine before they reach the trailer park and they roll up almost silently.

"Faggots are probably asleep by now. All fucked out."

"You better be careful what you say to Will about Craig's cousin."

Andy's words are like a bucket of cold water. The thought of Will scares him, but his brain is on fire, only briefly sputtering in the chill of Andy's negativity, clicking along like it never other times does.

"I won't tell 'im anything," he says. "Won't have to. I'm gonna make Wycowski do it."

"How you gonna do that?"

"I'll tell you after."

"After what?"

There's unhappiness in Andy's voice. Jimbo's excitement starts going again. "C'mon."

Andy sighs and gets out of the car. They walk along the edge of the road again, dipping down the embankment to Son's car. Nobody passes by. Jimbo hands Andy the crow bar, sets the bag of drain openers on the ground and lays the blanket over the windshield of Son's car. Giving the crow bar back Andy wraps his arms around his head and squints. Jimbo swings the crow bar and it smacks against the glass with a muffled pop. Stopping, he listens. Andy too. There is no sound. No lights go on. The crow bar rises, catches strange sparks of light, whistles back down again. After a few more blows they can see the blanket imploding into the car. Jimbo pulls it out, lays it over the back window. Swinging the crow bar up again, he stops, feeling suddenly generous, and points the crow bar at Andy. "You want?"

Andy takes it, looks around, swings. Jimbo grins, liking the look on Andy's face. Andy swings again. A hollow in the blanket grows deeper. Andy swings back and Jimbo grabs his arm. They stand still, listening. There is still nothing, no cars on the road, no movement from the trailers. Yanking the crow bar away, Jimbo flings it up, clutching it in both hands, swinging it down like an axe. The glass gives, collapsing, and Jimbo jabs at the window with the end of the crow bar, knocking it onto the seat. Collecting the blanket, he shakes it out and gives it to Andy, pointing at the side window. Andy holds it up against the glass, wincing as Jimbo swings. The window breaks quickly, pieces of it dropping onto the ground in a quiet shower. Jimbo jumps up and down on it, then he opens the car door, pops the hood and picks up a bottle of Drano. He pours a bottle into the radiator, letting it gurgle up and overflow. Andy pours a bottle inside the car, Jimbo over the engine and hoses. Then Jimbo trots back up to his car and brings back the Christmas tree, settling it inside the ruined engine compartment. He wedges it between the hoses so that it stands upright, tip bent under the hood, then tosses the empty drain opener bottles back into the bag, gestures at the blanket Andy picks up, grabs the crow bar, and returns to the car.

On the road he grins at Andy. "What I tell ya?"

Andy shrugs grudgingly. "Yeah. That was okay."

But Jimbo doesn't take Andy home. Instead he heads back into town again. Warily, Andy says, "Now what?"

"I need my bitch's phone. It's blocked."

"So?"

"So I'm tellin' Ray an' I don't want 'im to know who's callin'."

"Won't answer," says Andy, knowing Ray better than that.

"I'm plantin' the idea, Andy. That little faggot's life up here is over."

Jimbo's mood is rapidly changing. Now that it's over, he feels depressed. It wasn't what he thought it would be. But then he realizes he couldn't see the glass shattering. The image of glass blowing into tiny bits is almost orgasmic to him and there was no glass, no real climax. "Fuckin' faggot," he says again.

Andy keeps quiet.

A wind picks up, blowing bits of paper, freezing the crusts of snow. It blows at the loose sash on the bowling pin and pushes the signal light in Sandorville into a slow swing. It blows away the mist at Ivy's pond and scatters fir needles and litter across empty parking lots. It whistles through cracks and rattles at doors. Awake, Ray listens to it. He lies with an arm out of the covers, bent around his head. His skin feels chilled and he can't sleep. The air is vibrating, dancing to the wind, or it's something inside him. He tries to sleep, closes his eyes, rests a hand over his face but imagines he can feel the absence of Cora's ring on his finger, a difference in the skin, a sensitivity that keeps reminding him of Miri. He listens to her breathe, feels her warmth next to him. Then the wind thumps restlessly at the window and he feels alone. The dark promises no light. The wind outside is creeping in, moving like fingertips across his exposed arm. He stretches his body, trying to release the tension in his lower back. Miri stirs beside him. He rolls over to her, pulling her closer. He feels her wake up.

"Just lie there," he whispers, already pushing into her. "Go back to sleep."

She stays on her side, doesn't move except to brace her hand on the bed. He breathes on her neck, bites her shoulder, feeling the tension inside him growing. He groans and he can hear pain in it. She grasps his arm then, squeezing it close.

"Miri," he whispers, thrusting into her. A moment later, he stiffens, releases a long breath and goes slack against her. She stays still and he kisses her gratefully before he gets up. Closing the bathroom door, he leans against the sink before he looks up into the mirror. It surprises him that it is him looking back. The same hazel eyes, just a little bleary. The same cheerful laugh lines that aren't even deep. No bags, no pouches, no soft spots. He isn't old, but the sound of the wind at the window is the sound of his life blowing away. All because of that ring he gave Miri. He splashes water on his face, uses the toilet, grabs his clothes off the chair in the bedroom and dresses in the dark living room.

In the kitchen he opens a beer and takes his phone out of his pocket. The display is the only light, an eerie bluish white that doesn't really illuminate anything except the tips of his fingers. He swipes at the screen, frowning at it, drinks some more of his beer. He doubts he should be drinking a beer this early in the morning, but it feels good in his belly.

The only call came in at three thirty. He looks at the red-framed clock on the wall. Six fifteen. The voice is a man's, garbled and fuzzy sounding. He pictures somebody with a mouthful of socks. The voice mutters: "Your kid's jacked up. Needs you. Trevor's." Then the call disconnects. The way it's supposed to, it raises the hairs on the back of his neck, but it angers him too. He calls back but only gets an automated message. Then he calls Son and gets voice mail, tries Craig's cousin and gets the same thing.

"Goddammit."

He doesn't know if he's worried. He's angry though and he drinks another beer to calm down.

Outside, a faint light is filling the sky.

Coming out of the trees, there is nothing but darkness, an empty looking house below, just like it used to be. Jonah hesitates on the lawn by a dirty brown clothesline that's rotting in the damp. A movement, almost like light, passes over the kitchen window. He goes inside and she puts the kettle on the stove and moves away.

"Mornin'," he whispers.

At Will's, the tree is motionless and the room is dark. There are still boxes and ribbons and Christmas paper all over the living room floor. The cheese ball and crackers are still there too. Will goes down the dark hall, slowing by the spare back room. It isn't light enough to see inside. Susie is waiting for him, sitting in her mink coat on the side of the bed. The bathroom light is on. That's all he can take. When Son hit him with that bottle he saw stars, real stars, shooting like fireworks. Afterwards, there was just a blur until the hospital with its bright sun-white lights snapped into place. Needles stabbed him in the eyes. Then a nurse gave him a Motrin and ice pack and left him sitting there with Susie. He was almost overcome with hurt. "Those fuckers don't care." His voice sounded horrified. He heard it with dismay and looked at Susie, but Susie just blew a big purple bubble that wobbled in the currents of cold air. "I could have fuckin' brain damage."

Now she just bunches her coat up under her chin and Will opens up his arms when he appears in the door and says, "That's it. No more Christmas. Christmas sucks."

The lawns are frozen at the Greenview Mortuary. Mr Torch enters through a door in back. Shadows are everywhere, moving gently. In the lobby, Mr Torch is opening the front doors. He does this every morning, ritualistically, grabbing onto each knob and slowly backing up, revealing the glossy floor and the long hall with the windows at the end, welcoming people who never want to enter. After the doors are open, he goes out onto the porch and stands there silently for a moment and then retreats, closing the doors again just as slowly.

Carl's Mr Torch is never solemn. In the growing light he comes over and sits on the arm of the couch.

Outside, a mist clings to the weeds in the empty lot and Errol's lights are still lit, icy blue and frozen looking.

Mr Torch moves and Scott sits down in Mr Torch's place.

"How 'bout some donuts?"

He is growing more and more solicitous. It irritates Carl and he almost says, "You never asked before," but notices Mr Torch's smile. It's wry, almost disrespectful, includes Carl and excludes Scott, which isn't fair. They aren't supposed to be alone in anything. "Okay," he says.

That's the worst part, being alone.

Mr Torch's smile grows softer.

The Christmas tree is spindly and half dead. Needles litter the gravel below. It is strangely quiet here. Ray can hear the hiss of a car's tires on the pavement above, but the driveway through the trailer park is empty, nobody out, no lights in the windows. He grits his teeth, climbs out of Miri's car and walks down the incline. He can hear his bootsteps, the sound of another car. As he gets closer to the trailer his stomach clenches and his anger grows. His neck is sweaty under his hair, but his face and hands are cold. He climbs up onto a porch. There's nothing on it, as if nobody really lives here. Up and down the row of trailers, there are porches decorated with lights and statuary and whirly-gigs and pots planted with all kinds of flowers and greenery. Some people have awnings over their windows. There are curtains on Craig's cousin's windows, plain brown and beige, the same on every window, except the small one open in back. He tries to remember the inside of the place, but can't, besides there being a couch and a TV. There's no sound inside. He knocks loudly, but only once. When the door opens, he's surprised by the little Christmas tree in back. For some reason, it makes him feel sad. Craig's cousin just looks at him, sleepily, but not surprised. He's in pajama bottoms, nothing else. After a moment he seems to realize he's cold because his arms cross in front of him and he shuffles his feet.

"My kid in there?"

Craig's cousin nods, shuffles back in. Ray waits.

A beige carpet, blue and brown checkered couch. Coffee table, lamp, nothing special. Ray looks through the open door at the Christmas tree again. Voices murmur in back, then Craig's cousin reappears.

He still doesn't say anything, rubs his bare shoulder with a bristly chin.

"Tell me somethin', Trevor. Just so I'm clear on this. Are you fuckin' my kid?"

Craig's cousin's chin gives a last swipe at his shoulder. Then he looks at Ray, eyes meeting his, and nods slightly.

Ray lifts his head up. "Christ. This day is really shapin' up."

"Whadda you want?" asks Craig's cousin.

He still sounds sleepy, out of sorts, a little angry, or scared. Ray isn't sure. He doesn't like the fact that Craig's cousin can see things. It's not the way things should be, gives him a strange, helpless feeling sometimes. Maybe that's what Craig's cousin is feeling.

"What I want is to know why you two idiots didn't hear anything. Or why this whole brain drain of a trailer park didn't hear anything."

"Whadda you mean?"

"Where is 'e?"

Craig's cousin looks back, makes some kind of expression on his face that Ray can't read, then a shadow takes shape behind him, blotting out the Christmas tree.

"Get out here."

Son approaches slowly. "What?"

"I said, get out here." He steps out on bare feet, in a pair of jeans, arms crossed in front of him like Craig's cousin's still are. They give off an air of suspicion and worry. Ray points at the driveway. "Go take a look. Maybe you can explain it to me."

Son passes him cautiously, walks gingerly on the gravel, stops suddenly and yells "Fuck!" He whirls back. "What the fuck?!"

"You tell me."

Craig's cousin is coming down now too. He stops at the driveway and looks back with a grimace.

Son is still yelling. "How the fuck can I tell you anything? You fuckin' tell me. You're the one here. You couldn't leave me any fuckin' happiness, could you?"

"What the hell are you talkin' about? I swear to God, kid, you are wearin' real thin on me."

"You asshole."

"Me?"

Then suddenly Son is running up the driveway. Ray takes a step after him, stops to watch him for a moment, then yells, "Hey, careful, kid, there's—"

Son yelps and hobbles back.

"—glass."

He can hear the weariness in his voice and pulls a hand down his face. There are people out now, coming closer. He looks behind him and says, "Get the fuck back," in a voice that stops the movement. They don't go away, but they don't come closer. Son is making a wide circle of his car, hobbling back again. Ray looks at Craig's cousin, just standing there still, staring at him.

"What?" asks Ray angrily.

"Don't do it."

The intensity of that stare annoys him. "I'm not doing anything." He points back up the driveway. "I'm the one that bought that vehicle. Seems to me that makes me the one with the loss."

Son is back, hopping, trying to pull a piece of glass out of the bottom of his foot. Craig's cousin goes over to him. "Give it to me." Son holds onto his shoulder, balancing on one leg. "Jesus, Son. You were walking on it."

"Get it out. It hurts."

"Hold still."

"Ow."

Ray looks up, staring at the gray sky. The clouds are thickening again, soft and billowy, moving with the wind. He sighs and looks down. Craig's cousin is tossing a bloody piece of glass under the trailer, swiping his fingers on his pajamas. Now Son is approaching him, limping, leaving bloody marks on the gravel. Behind him, Craig's cousin shakes his head. Ray frowns at him, then looks at Son.

"Who would do this, kid?"

"That's a laugh. You're askin' me?"

"Yeah. Who've you fucked with lately?"

"You!"

Ray stares at him. Son's chest and face are flushed red. His dark eyes burn. "Are you fucking nuts?" He articulates every word, asking him. "You really think that was me?"

"You're always fuckin' with me. You give me things an' then you take 'um away. I'm a fuckin' joke to you. When you have nothin' better to do you can just screw me over, get a good laugh cuz I'm so goddam stupid. I'll just keep comin' back for more."

"You wanna know what you keep comin' back for? My money."

"I don't need your money. I know how to get money."

"Yeah, I bet you do."

"What the fuck do you mean by that, you fuckin' drug dealer?"

"What did you just call me?"

"You're a fucking drug dealer."

"Not exactly. An' what I do, you live off a that, kid. An' real happily too."

"You see, you asshole. You never get it. You never fuckin' get anything. You do this shit to me. You do it. You fuckin' get off on it."

"Jesus Christ, kid. Just shut the fuck up. I don't even know what you're talkin' about anymore."

"You don't fuckin' care."

"Okay. You're right. I don't fuckin' care."

Son steps back, then swings at him. Not like with Cora's slap, Ray is ready for him, almost expecting it. The thought makes him sad, like the tiny happiness of that little Christmas tree inside makes him sad. Son's fist rises up, swinging slightly sideways. Ray catches it and closes his fingers, squeezing at it. Startled, Son tries to pull away, but Ray holds on. Son's breath is hot and damp in his face. Ray pulls him closer. "You wanna play with me?"

Ray's finger bones feel like iron under his frozen skin, metal joints ratcheting tighter. He is surprised at his strength. Son pulls at him, worrying, still angry though. "Let go."

He's too close to get in another punch. Ray can feel the bones in Son's hand give and move. He doesn't feel anger, but he doesn't care either. He sees panic filling Son's eyes and feels his bones grind together. Son's other fingers are trying to pull Ray's loose. "Let me go!" Now a wail is working its way into his voice.

"Ray!" Craig's cousin is suddenly there, grabbing Ray's wrist. "Stop it.

That's it. I let you make your point. Ray! Goddammit, Ray, let him go or I'm gonna hurt you."

His eyes shift to Craig's cousin.

"You don't want to do this," Craig's cousin says quietly. "You really, really don't want to do this."

Son's face is red, bunched up. He is angry, pulling angrily at his hand. "Let me go!"

Ray shoves him suddenly, releasing him to stagger back. Clutching his fist, he bolts inside and Ray drops his face into his hands, runs his fingers through his hair. "Fuckin' Christ," he mutters.

Craig's cousin shuffles. "I'll talk to 'im."

"Talk to 'im? About what? None of it makes any fuckin' sense."

"It makes sense to him."

Ray almost laughs, pulls his hands down his face again. "This is fuckin' great."

"I'm not gonna be sorry about this, Ray. About us."

"Did I ask you to be?"

"I'm just sayin'."

"Well, don't. I'm not in the fuckin' mood."

He turns and walks away. Behind him, the door closes. As he's heading back up to the road, he keeps his eye on the splotches of blood on the gravel. At Miri's car he puts his back against the door, slumps down until he's out of sight, puts his head between his knees and throws up. Sweat instantly chills his skin. He still feels sick. His hands are shaking. Slowly, he pushes himself back up and leaves.

There are patches of snow under trees and porches. Mist moves aimlessly through the firs. The day is a peculiar gray color as if tiny fibers of metal permeate the air. Vapors of breath hold still, dissipate slowly.

At Craig's cousin's, voices come and go, a gathering outside. But it is cold and they don't stay. It grows quiet again. The lights on the little Christmas tree flash. There's a box of chocolate-covered cherries on the counter. Craig's cousin sits on a stool and eats one slowly. He is waiting for Son to relax. After a while, he gets up and approaches the bedroom. Son is lying on the bed with his arms over his face. Craig's cousin stops in the doorway, leaning against the sill, gaze on the carpet.

"Are you okay?"

"I have to go. I can't stay here."

Now Craig's cousin looks up. "What are you talking about?"

"I can't stay here with him around. I can't."

"You wanna leave? Go home?"

"I have to."

Craig's cousin goes over, pulls Son's arms away from his face and sits down beside him. "What are you talking about? You don't have to do anything.

Fuck, Son, do you ever think anything through? Something happens an' you react. Or you get yourself so fucked up you don't have to think about it."

"I don't wanna think about it. I want you to."

"Am I doin' that for you now? You say you wanna go."

Son struggles up, sitting back against the cabinet behind the bed. "You know, I'm the fuckin' victim here. I didn't do anything."

"You aren't a victim an' your dad didn't do anything either. You aren't thinking. This is drivin' me crazy the way you are with him. There is no fuckin' way he can win with you. You set people up to fail you, Son, an' if God fuckin' forbid they don't, you just make it up that they did anyway."

"I can't believe you're talkin' to me like this."

"Why not?"

"Because you're supposed to be on my side. Who else can I count on?"

"You wanna leave."

"Not without you."

"You want me to leave my job, my friends, my family."

"I can't stay here. Please don't make me stay here."

"Jesus Christ." Craig's cousin sits sideways on the bed, his head in his hands. "I can't believe you're doing this to me."

"I don't wanna stay."

"Don't want to? Can't? What?"

"Please."

Craig's cousin shakes his head and gets up. "I have to think."

"Where are you going?"

Craig's cousin is kicking out of his pajama bottoms, pulling his pants on. "I just have to think."

"Trevor…You won't…I mean, you can't…you won't leave me?"

Angrily, he turns back, putting his face close to Son's. "I told you. I won't. You won't. I saw that. Before I saw you. Do you fucking get that?"

"I'm not like you, Trevor. I'm not always sure of things."

"Why aren't you fucking sure of this?"

"I don't know."

"You know. You think everybody's gonna fuckin' leave you. Your dad. Your mom. You're so fucked up about that you want me to leave everything I love. I was born here, Son. I have a job here. Who in hell's gonna support us? You don't work. An' that's okay. I can do that for us. But this is where I do it. You think you can just pick up an' go anytime you want cuz all you have to do is call your daddy. Please send money. You might not like it, but he got that right. Well, I don't have that, an' you don't either anymore cuz you're with me. That shit stops. My mom an' dad work hard already. I can't ask. An' what the hell am I gonna do about Will? I owe him too. You're askin' me to leave everything an' you don't even have a good reason. That pisses me off."

He can tell Son is angry too. His face is red, his breathing heavy. "You're not gonna put this on me."

"You're the one asking."

"Okay, fine. You want me to not ask. I'm not asking anymore. Forget it."

"Just like that?"

"Jesus, Trevor, you said you don't wanna go. Okay. You made me think about it."

"I have to think about it too. I'll see you later."

"Trevor!"

"Fuckin' lay off me, Son. I need to be alone."

He grabs his jacket and keys, not wanting to look back where Son is sitting up on the bed now, staring after him with an expression that he knows will shred his insides if he looks back. Outside, he scrambles down the steps to his car. Cold air burns his nose, stings his eyes.

On the road he realizes he has nowhere to go and just drives without thinking.

Lights are on in the living room, bathroom and bedroom, but the inside of the house is still gray. It feels like dusk or dawn. Cold air blows through the open doors. Will is outside, stuffing Christmas paper into a garbage can, stomping down on it with a foot. Susie is inside, putting decorations away. Then she stops to hug her snowman, sitting on the couch with her mink bundled up under her chin. She's warm inside it. Yesterday, when Craig's cousin was here, he came up behind her and she shivered at the feel of him so close.

Then he put his lips against her ear and whispered, "Real enlightened, Susie."

She whipped her head around and her hair brushed across his lips. *My coat,* she realized. He didn't move and her heart was banging. Then he slipped around her and went out into the backyard.

Now she puts her mouth into the soft fur, thinking of him.

Outside, Will yells, *"Keep workin'!"*

One day, when Craig's cousin was working near town, he went to Candi's for pancakes. He can't remember which pancakes he got, but he remembers that Debby was going off shift and came to sit with him. He didn't know where Son was and didn't call him. They were only halfway living together then and even though he knew they would always be together, Son didn't, not really. Then Ray came in and Debby got up to go and bent down to kiss him. Craig's cousin was surprised, but he kissed her back and saw Ray watching. He came over with a smile and slid into the booth across from him. Maybe it was something about the kiss, the way it felt off to him because of Ray being there, but he wondered even then if Ray knew about Son and him.

The smile was mild, ironic, and not especially amused. But Craig's cousin couldn't really see anything anymore so he wasn't sure.

After ordering coffee and a chicken salad sandwich, Ray said, "Ever been to the Waffle Place?"

Craig's cousin was eating his pancakes, mumbled, "No," over a mouthful.

"You should check it out. It's in Enders. Place was made for you. A fuckin' wall of syrups."

Craig's cousin nodded, but said, "I kinda like Candi's."

"Definitely on friendly terms with the help."

"We used to go out."

"That's right. You brought 'er to Will's once."

"Could be."

"No doubt. I remember."

Ray stretched an arm across the top of the booth, drank his coffee, just studying him with that little smile. Craig's cousin caught himself shooting quick glances at him between bites of his pancakes, matching him up with Son, face, eyes, body. They were like mirror images in reverse, positive, negative, light, dark, everything about them alike, even the way they ate. Watching Ray chew aroused him and he focused on his food again at Ray's sudden stare, not wanting him to see that. But Ray just took a bite of his sandwich and Craig's cousin was sure he knew. The idea of that panicked Son. When Craig's cousin said to him, "You should just tell 'im, get it over with; my folks know," he jumped up off the couch and said, "Are you high? I'll never tell 'im. You don't know Ray. All he thinks about are women. To not be like him? I don't think he could take it. I mean, look at me. I'm inked up like him. I ride a Harley like him. I'm fucked up like him. I'm supposed to be bangin' chicks like him. He really, really likes women."

"He really likes sex, Son. He's oriented to women."

"What's the difference?"

"Well, there's kind of a lot of difference."

But Son was pacing the trailer, sweating anxiously. Astonished, Craig's cousin didn't say anything else. Even now, after the scene at home that morning, he doesn't think Ray really cares. Sex is the centerpiece of his life. He carries the aura of it, exudes it like an odor. Craig's cousin just doesn't think that Ray can be that inflexible with something that obsesses him. It isn't sex that obsesses Craig's cousin, just Son. In that way, he's like Ray because he knows that Ray feels that way about Miri. She's not a woman he'd choose. She's the one who lives in him, always has, a half-forgotten face, always recalled in the sadder moments of his life. Craig's cousin couldn't see Son's face until he met Ray and then he'd look at Ray in wonder. On the day he saw Son for the first time, walking across the sunlit parking lot at Candi's with Miri, he saw a face that was and wasn't Ray's. Son will never smile with Ray's ironic smile, never light up with a twinkle in his eyes, never fill a room with his presence, never attract people the way Ray can. His eyes are filled with darkness and there is a place inside him where there is only hurt. As good-looking as Ray is, it is Son's beat up, worn out soul Craig's cousin can't live without.

Acropolis makes him happy too, though. It always has. He doesn't see his family very often, but they are near. And he has Craig. He loves the mountains, the smell of the air, his familiar trailer.

Now he's driving through Enders on the long straight highway that bisects the town. The wind is blowing debris across the pavement and there are tall brown weeds, but no snow, on the shoulder of the highway. Up ahead, he sees the sign for the Waffle Place, slows and turns in. He hopes Son bothers to eat but knows he won't. He often thinks of the man who took him, of how scared Son must have been. Inside, he sees the rows of syrups and sits in a booth in back so he can look out at the almost empty highway. A waitress pours him a cup of coffee and pulls a menu out from under her arm.

"What's your best?" he asks. "Sweet being the deciding factor."

"A little sweet or a lot?"

"A lot sweet."

She's a redhead like him, blue eyes. Thinking makes her nose wrinkle. He likes that.

"Banana butterscotch."

"Okay. Bring it on. Better be sweet though."

She tucks the menu back under her arm. "Like a banana split."

"Cool."

The grayness of the day remains, low clouds that sometimes thin, then gather up again like dingy cotton balls. Sipping his coffee, he removes his phone from his pocket with his other hand, thumbing through his pictures. There is one of Son grinning at him that makes him happy. Being here, away from him, makes his heart hurt, but it's a good feeling, a strain that he knows he'll relieve just by going home. The image of that trailer in his mind makes him sad though and he sets his phone down and concentrates on the lonely looking sight outside, the bits of garbage blowing up against the dead brown weeds across the highway.

Almost all the lights are on at the shop. Ray's in the office in back, staring blankly at the computer screen, occasionally remembering to drink his beer. To his annoyance, the bar is closed again. Stirring himself finally, he gets up and looks outside. Through the gaps in the back fence he can see the flashing lights of the cars on Oly Way. The beer tastes sour in his mouth. He wants a real drink in a bar, a woman he doesn't know sitting beside him. His eyes close at a sudden feeling of pain. It's distracting him because he isn't really sure of its source. It might be in his belly or even lower. But there is a pain in his temples too, pain in his throat. His eyes roll up and he grimaces at the ceiling. All he needs to do is get in the car and go. She'd never know. She suspects him anyway. In the hallway, he pauses, looks out the side door at her car in the alley, then continues the other way down the hall, gets another beer and goes outside to sit on the porch.

Across the lot, Christmas lights, Rudolph. There's a light on at Carl's, struggling up to the shadows under the eaves. A shape in the window. The thought of Carl looking out at him mesmerizes him. He is sorry for Carl, but he doesn't want to die either. He isn't good at sacrifice, of that much empathy. He wouldn't give up his life for Carl's. He isn't even sorry about it. He is sorry for smaller things, things he can't take back.

Thinking brings back the taste of vomit on his tongue and he spits out a mouthful of beer. A night with somebody not his wife, that hardly makes him sorry, but he stays sitting in the dull gloom, eyes rising occasionally to Carl's window.

Then he sees his son's face, feels the shifting of bones.

Anger moves its way through him, pushing out the pain. He takes a long swallow of his beer. His life isn't about being sorry. The idea of it angers him. Looking up at Carl, he can see the evidence of the quickness of his days, days he won't waste, won't sacrifice, won't regret. Getting up, he sets the empty bottle inside the doorway, gets his keys, and switches off the lights.

Outside, underneath the faint whistling of the wind, he can hear bells. The sound surprises him. They must be Miri's and he guesses he left a window open. For a minute, he considers going back inside, then slides into Miri's car and starts it up.

Upstairs Carl can hear the bells too, but he knows they belong to Mr Torch.

Son is sitting on the couch in jeans and a sweatshirt, barefoot still, an empty beer bottle on the coffee table, a half full bottle in his hand, staring at him without speaking. Craig's cousin gets a beer too, goes over to stand near him. "Are you mad?"

"You left."

"I came back."

"Yeah. I see you."

Craig's cousin takes a swallow of his beer and says, "You don't have to be a shit about this."

"I told you I'd stay."

"An' make me pay for it."

"That's bullshit. I wouldn't do that."

"You're doin' it now."

"I can be mad, okay? Fuck, Trevor. I'm givin' in. Just let me be mad. Is that fuckin' okay?"

"I like it a lot better than givin' me an ultimatum."

"Goddammit, Trevor. I was pissed off. I thought about it. You don't have to go."

"That's big a you."

"Yeah. Kinda."

Craig's cousin pushes the empty bottle away and sits down on the coffee table.

"I tell you this all the time, Son. You tell me. How do you feel about me?"

"How do I feel about you? Seriously? Don't you know?"

"Tell me."

"You mean like we're girls?"

"Christ, you're a total shit, you know that? I mean, things change an' we fell for each other pretty quick."

"Are you tryin' to tell me somethin', Trevor?"

"The same thing I always tell you. I won't leave you."

"I won't leave you either."

"Tell me in your own words."

Son drinks his beer, staring at him, the skin around his eyes tight with irritation. Then he takes another swallow of beer, sets his bottle on the back of the couch and says, "Okay. You want sappy. I can do that. I fell the minute I saw you." He moves slowly on the couch, pushing himself to its edge. Then he takes the front of Craig's cousin's shirt and pulls him close, face to face. Craig's cousin can feel his lips moving. "I love you, Trevor. I love you." His hand on the back of Craig's cousin's neck pulls him closer, the force of his mouth forcing open Craig's cousin's. He can hear Son's words inside him. "I love you, Trevor. I fuckin' think about you all the time. I have to have you. I want you. I feel clean—"

"Baby—"

"—with you. You want me to say this? I love you with all my heart an' soul, Trevor. I don't feel good without you. I don't work without you. You fuckin' drive me crazy. Your lips…." He bites one, pulling it into his mouth. "I love watchin' people listen to you. I get all shaky inside. I want you to fuck me right there in front of everybody." Craig's cousin opens his mouth, feels Son's teeth, his tongue. He tries to swallow it and Son is pulling him closer, breathing through his nose, his voice vibrating inside of Craig's cousin's mouth. Then, suddenly he pulls his head away and Craig's cousin feels bereft for a moment, almost dizzy.

"I love you, Trevor. You're so fuckin' good inside. You said it. I'm a shit. I could never be that good. I look up to you."

Craig's cousin cups Son's face in his hands and pulls him back. He holds him close, just to feel the pounding of his heart, and pushes a hand up the back of his shirt until he reaches the place where he knows the sun tattoo is. It's his imagination, he knows, but Son's skin feels warmer there, pulsing with life.

"Okay, baby. We'll go."

"We don't have to, Trevor. I'll do anything you want."

"Anything?"

"Anything."

"Marry me."

He is shocked by Son's tears, the sudden sobs that erupt and shake him. He pulls him off the couch, holding him between his legs, rocking him and rubbing his back. The sounds of the sobs are like knives in his chest. "Baby...baby...." He closes his eyes, feeling Son grow sweaty in his arms. His skin is sticky. Craig's cousin presses his face into his neck, waiting him out.

"Are you okay?" he asks after a while. Son nods, sits back on his heels. His face is flushed, swollen, pain-filled. "I didn't mean to hurt you."

"You didn't. I...." He starts to cry again and his head rocks back and forth. "Fuck. This is fuckin' sick. I'm really losin' it here."

"What are you talking about? What is it?"

"You wanna be with me like that. That's so fuckin' real. I didn't think anybody would ever want me like that."

"Jesus, Son, why are you so damn down on yourself? What were we just sittin' here talkin' about? I love you. I can't live without you. You are fucking everything to me. You count, goddammit. You matter. I will take care of you every day of your life and be fuckin' grateful I get to do that. You're perfect just like this."

"I love you, Trevor."

"I'm going to marry you."

Son nods. "Okay."

"Come lie down with me now. I'm really tired."

In the bedroom, he feels a vague fear he won't let on to. They lie down with their clothes on and he holds Son in his arms, inhales the scent of his hair, looks at the room in the fading light. He bought this trailer when he was twenty-three, found garage sale and thrift store furniture for it. Kmart dishes and cookware. Things he needed to live, but seven years later, no decorations, no personal touches. He never put plants outside or a chair to sit on. He moves his head, follows the shadows on the ceiling. The light out the window is dismal and gray. He feels Son growing heavy, falling asleep. He wants to sleep too, but his eyes stay open on the sad gray light for a long time.

24

◆ Love, Please ◆

"Tell me about your home...."

The house Son grew up in is built close to the sidewalk, painted white with gingerbread trim and a round window under the roof. There's a veranda with delicate white spindles and honeysuckle vines below. A driveway at the side of the house ends in boggy gravel. There's a porch out back, and across the street oleander and morning glory poke through chain-link. On the other side of the fence, Goschke's Salvage, all glitter and sparkle in the chilly sun.

"I know what we can do," says Son. "I know where you can work."

In winter, cool pale light bounces off the sidewalks and the rooftops of cars like glitter on glass. The sun makes a blurry circle in a cloudy sky. Windows shine and birds chatter.

A long time ago there was no street between the house and the salvage yard, no other houses. In places, ivy grows up the chain-link between the oleander and morning glory. On the corner of the street is Goschke's Gas, a white stucco building with a red tile roof. Weeds grow in the cracks of asphalt and plywood covers up the windows. Between the gas station and the entrance to the salvage yard, giant cedars droop over piles of dark, damp needles.

"I don't know anything about running a junk yard," says Craig's cousin.

"You can do it. You can do anything. An' it'll be ours," says Son. "We'll own it."

A place where wrecked and discarded cars rise like a futurist cityscape and cats lie in wait for careless bluejays and metal and glass glitter or gleam in the light.

At Will's, Ray sits on the steps out back and laughs. Will's car is spinning in a circle under the porch light and Will is laughing too. "Ain't it cool!" On his own porch there's a welcome mat with sunflowers painted on it and a green watering bucket, glass bottles from an antique store called Whatchamacallits, and rubber flip-flops that remind him of ladies in curlers sitting in laundromats.

At home later on, he grabs a beer on his way out to the living room. The refrigerator hums, a low rumble. Even though the TVs on, the house is quiet and the sound of the refrigerator, the heater, the creak of the floor as he crosses the linoleum magnifies the emptiness of the house. Miri and him. No other people. It doesn't always bother him. Tonight, though, he wants the sounds of laughter, of busyness, longing for Vicki or Serena or any other woman he isn't seeing anymore. Something, anything else. His ears ache, ringing with pressure.

She's sitting slumped on the couch with her feet on the coffee table, knees up. He takes a swallow of beer, wipes his mouth with the back of his wrist, focuses on the feel of his hairy skin against his lips. A part of him doesn't know why he doesn't go over and drop down between her legs. Another part knows that it's because it's her, not somebody strange and safe from knowing him. The minute he goes over, she'll feel something on him, something he doesn't want to give away.

The pressure in his ears builds.

She drops her magazine on the coffee table and there's something about it, something that tells him she was waiting for him.

"What?" he asks.

She frowns at him, pulling her feet up on the couch. "Whadda you mean, what? What's wrong?"

"Nothing's wrong."

"Are you sure?"

"Are you deaf?"

"Jesus, Ray."

"What?"

"Are you trying to start a fight with me?"

"I know what you're thinking."

"What am I thinking?"

"I'm not callin' 'im."

She runs a hand through her hair and he sees the way it doesn't fall back in her face anymore. He wishes she would turn into the Snake Lady. He aches to open up her thighs and disappear inside her. All he'd think about is her, her taste and smell, and forget about everything else.

She twists on her hip, her hand on her ankle, pulling her legs closer to her. "I don't like seeing you unhappy."

"I'm not unhappy."

"You're mad."

"You keep buggin' me."

"I don't bug you."

"You bug me," he mutters.

"I love you."

A Snake Lady, green and pain-filled, oblivious to him. He could slip into her darkness unseen and disappear.

"I have to go."

"Ray, don't."

But he does anyway, out the door, leaving his empty bottle on the counter as he goes.

After work, Craig's cousin stops by Will's house. There is nobody home so he goes around back and through the window into the bedroom. Jumping off the bed he lands on, he goes out into the kitchen, gets a beer, then sits down on the couch to wait. He drinks half the bottle, staring at the wall. He rubs his throat once and grimaces, then cocks his head to the side, cracking his neck. As time passes, he begins to feel nervous. It is already dark and he is hungry. After a while, he sees a pair of headlights swing across the front window, but it is just Susie. She comes in through the back door.

"Trevor?"

"Yeah."

She doesn't come out into the living room until she hears his voice. He smiles at her. She's wearing a skirt and suit jacket, pink, with a white blouse and a string of pearls he guesses are fake. Generally, skimpy and shiny is her style, but he likes her in a suit. Something about it reminds him of Mrs Cleaver.

"Drink a beer with me, Susie?"

"Okay. You want another one too?"

"Sure."

He finishes the one he's drinking and sets the empty bottle down on the coffee table. Susie comes out a moment later, stretching a bottle out. He takes it, watches her plop down and kick her shoes off. Her legs swing over the arm of her chair and she wiggles her toes.

"You don't come around like you used to."

"I've been pretty busy."

"You should relax. Whadda you do to relax, Trevor?"

She is tilting her head at him, twirling her string of pearls around her finger. She has that appraising look that always amuses him. He isn't particularly offended for Will. He knows Susie isn't living a happy life. She stays for some reason that isn't his business, but he feels sorry for her. He smiles again.

"I dunno. TV. The usual."

"You need some variety."

"You mean get high with you guys?"

Her toes curl and a flush rises up her neck. "That's Will, not me."

"Do you know where he is today?"

"No."

Neither does Craig's cousin. He isn't sure what kind of Will he'll see, but he's running out of time and telling Will he's leaving isn't going to be a good idea on any of the days he can see. He isn't getting a positive feel for today either, but it's better than the others. He gets up, looks outside, drinking the rest of his beer. The house on the corner has its Christmas lights on. Then as he downs the last swallow of beer, Will's car appears and zooms over half the yard before stopping with a squeal of brakes on the driveway.

"Guess that's Will," murmurs Susie, getting out of her chair.

He looks back. "Stay, Susie."

"I need to change."

She sounds grumpy now, out of sorts, maybe because of Will, but Craig's cousin has the feeling she won't be coming back out again. He scowls, sets his empty bottle beside the first one and sits down.

When Will comes in, Jimbo is behind him, lighting up at the sight of Susie's empty chair. Kicking out his legs, he drops into it and sighs. Will looks over. "Beer, man. Get us some beer."

"I'm okay," says Craig's cousin.

"No, you're not. You're drinkin' with me. Christ, Trev, where have you been?"

"Around. I saw you at Christmas."

"Yeah," he says, sitting down on the couch. "When was that?"

"Just a couple weeks ago, Will." Will nods. He's wearing a pair of sunglasses and Craig's cousin wonders if he was driving in them which could explain missing the driveway by half a yard. "How can you see in those? It's dark."

"I have acute eyesight," says Will.

Craig's cousin nods. "Acute."

"Yeah." He tips the glasses down, looks over the top, examines the room, then tosses them onto the coffee table. "This is okay, though."

Jimbo passes the beers over and drops back into Susie's chair again.

"Drink," says Will, tapping his bottle against Craig's cousin's. "Seriously. I want you to drink with me. I miss you, Trev."

"Come on, Will. You didn't even think about me 'til you saw me."

"I think about all a my crew all the time. I keep that in my brain all at once."

"I'm not a part of your crew, Will."

"Well, you're in a fucked up mood. Here I am glad to see you, complimentin' you. Drink your fuckin' beer, Trev. Chill for a while."

"I came here to talk, Will."

"About what?"

Craig's cousin sighs and stares into Will's eyes, eyes that stare calmly back at him like the remains of a mirror where a kaleidoscope of colors wink on the splinters of glass and there's a meaningless darkness beyond.

"About what?" he asks again.

"I'm leaving. Moving away. I already quit my job, sellin' my place."

"You can't do that." Will looks at him with a slightly chiding expression, maybe a little annoyed at having to tell him that.

Craig's cousin's voice is gentle. "Yeah, Will, I can. I'm doin' this. This is for real."

Will sets his beer down, rubs his cheeks with his fingertips, frowning introspectively, a distant look in his eyes. Craig's cousin sits quietly, feeling the sweat under his arms, trying to hide his worry for Will. Jimbo scoots up on the edge of Susie's chair, a happy grin on his face. Will refocuses and his lids are low on his eyes. Craig's cousin sighs again.

"Take it back."

"Take what back, Will? Take back livin' my own life? I'm not gonna do that."

Will's tiny pupils constrict to pinpoints, then his hand suddenly shoots out and grabs Craig's cousin by the neck. The edge of his hand connects with Craig's cousin's larynx and he gags.

"Take it the fuck back," says Will.

Craig's cousin rasps. "Fuck you."

Will shakes him. "Take it back."

Jumping up to loom above them on the other side of the coffee table, Jimbo glows. "Choke the little faggot! Choke 'im, Will!"

"Will!" Coming up over the coffee table, skirt hitching up, Susie wraps her arms around Will's shoulders, kissing him frantically. "Will, honey. Will. Stop. Stop it!"

He tries to shrug her off, fingers loosening. Craig's cousin pulls free and Susie sits behind Will, still holding on.

"You can't fucking leave," says Will.

Craig's cousin sits back against the end of the couch, rubbing his throat.

"Fuckin' faggot," Jimbo says again.

Will's head swivels slowly, a frown building on his face. "Why do you keep callin' him that?"

"Cuz that's what 'e is, right? Ain't that right, Trev? You an' that little twink a yours. Baby Wycowski?"

Will's head whips back to Craig's cousin. "Fuck, Trevor. Tell 'im off. You aren't that way." He looks back at Jimbo. "That's fuckin' bullshit, Jimbo."

"You hear 'im denyin' it?"

"Trevor?" Will asks again.

The pain in his throat isn't as bad as the pain in his forehead, a pinched feeling tightening up. "I'm not saying anything."

"That's cuz you're a fuckin' chicken shit faggot," says Jimbo and Craig's cousin can see the pieces of a puzzle clicking together in Will's eyes. It hurts Craig's cousin's feelings. He wonders why he never saw that, that it matters to Will. The day he met him, they were instant friends. He felt sorry for Will and Will gave off a charming faith in Craig's cousin's talent, a belief that it was almost peculiar to their friendship. As if Craig's cousin saw things only because he needed to for Will's sake. Now the look in Will's eyes makes him feel sick to his stomach. Will was fooled by all the girlfriends he brought over, women close to his heart at the time, women Will didn't question. No reason to. He was affectionate. He wasn't playing. They weren't a lie, but they weren't all the truth either. Maybe he always knew not to tell Will the truth.

Craig's cousin is embarrassed by all the things he knows Will is thinking about him now and he can feel the blood in his face. Sitting back on the edge of Susie's chair, Jimbo is staring at him, a smile playing on his mouth, enjoying this, ready to jump back up again. Craig's cousin feels worn out. He can sense his slowness, his unwillingness to set them off and that angers him. The blood in his face grows hotter. His vision contracts and he can feel his pulse pounding, hear a ringing in his ears. A moment later he is standing without realizing he stood up. Will is leaning back against Susie, Jimbo beginning to frown. Rounding the coffee table, Craig's cousin looks at Will, says, "You fucker," and lunges at Jimbo. Leaning on one leg, all his weight follows his fist. The shock of the connection jolts up his arm. Jimbo howls, clapping both hands to his smashed nose. "An' you, you fucker. I better never even hear his fuckin' name come outta your mouth." Then he kicks him in the knee and backs away, breathing heavily, afraid he is missing something.

Will is stiff, wary. Craig's cousin catches Susie's eye. She is staring at him over Will's head. Slowly, her lips move in a friendly smile. There is kindness in her eyes. Almost panting, Craig's cousin can feel himself calm. He smiles back, but he knows his smile is sad. "See you, Susie."

"Bye, Trevor."

A boy on a red bike is riding by the shop, warm breath puffing into the air. His cheeks are a bright pink, eyes shining. He's wearing jeans and a big blue and white parka, legs pumping him down the road, around the corner at Errol's and out of sight.

Ray continues up the stairs of the porch and goes inside. He checks all the windows. Closed. The memory of the bells is still in his ears. Unlocking the front door, he looks outside, sees the boy again on the far side of the empty lot.

He bought Son a silver bike one Christmas. Back then he spent a lot of Christmases with Kathy. It was a dark house, usually noisy, but he always felt at home in it. After he stopped waiting for Horace's wife, Sadie, to let him in when he knocked, he just went in. Nobody ever minded. The summer after the Christmas he gave Son the bike, Son built a ramp on the sidewalk out of sight of the house, riding his bike off of it until the wheels shot out from under him one day and he fell on the edge of the curb and broke his arm. When Ray got to the house later, Son was sitting on a couch in the dark living room downstairs with a cast on his arm, crying helplessly. Kathy was yelling at him, bending down to look into his face.

"You went a block away to do this! You went where nobody could see you because you knew it was wrong! You knew that! You knew that an' you did it anyway! Sneaking off like that is the same as lying! That was sneaking off! You lied to me doing that!"

From the door to the living room couch, Ray went from cool to boiling mad. Without a look at her, he pushed his arm under Son's good one, clasped him around his back, picked him up and went back outside with him. On the sidewalk he set him down and they walked several blocks away to a McDonald's where he bought him a bag of fries and a strawberry milkshake, and they sat in a booth and stared at each other. Then Ray grinned at him.

"You got me beat, kid. I never broke my arm. Did it hurt?"

Son's brows drew into a frown that would soon be almost plastered on him and said, "Yeah. Kind of."

"You cry?"

"No."

"Took it pretty good?"

"Yeah. I got my bike home."

"Tough kid."

He drank his milkshake, still frowning, then said, "Dad?"

"Yeah, baby."

"I didn't lie."

"You knew your mom wouldn't want you doin' that. You went where nobody'd see you, didn't you?"

"Yeah."

"You scared 'er."

"I never get to do anything."

"I'm not sorry for you."

He loved the way Son stared at him, studying him, disapproving or disbelieving. Cynical, but halfway gullible too. The cynical part charmed him, the gullible part woke up every protective cell in his body. "You like that shake?" Son nodded. "Better than chocolate?"

"I don't like chocolate."

"You don't like chocolate? Why not?"

"Cuz everybody else does."

Ray's laughter roared and he knew heads were turning. "That's my boy."

White ice rims the edges of the road, the blades of dead straw-like weeds in the lot across from Ray's. Other than the boy on the bike, the day has nothing cheerful in it. The occasional Christmas lights look desolate. Ray rolls open the warehouse doors and drinks his coffee outside. Next door, Henry comes out to take the wreath off the bar door and then goes back in again. Ray's phone vibrates in his pocket, but he ignores it, drinking his coffee in the cold air. As the sun rises higher, the ground starts to steam and the light grows bright and reflective. Back inside, he pours another cup of coffee and takes his phone out of his pocket and looks at the display. No message, just Craig's cousin's call. Eight calls in two days. Grimacing over his too hot coffee, he sets the cup down and calls Craig's cousin back.

"Fuck, Ray."

"What the fuck do you want?"

"C'mon. You're just gonna let us go? No talkin'?"

"I don't have anything to say to either a you."

"That's such bullshit, Ray."

He tries his coffee again. Craig's cousin is silent, waiting him out. "Why is this so important to you?"

"You make or break 'im. Not me. You always fuckin' have. An' this is total bullshit that you would just cut 'im off. You don't care about us bein' together."

"You think?"

"I know it, Ray. You forget. I know things."

"You know what I know, Trev? I got it right here on my phone. You're the only one callin' me, so I don't think I'm really carryin' the weight you think I do."

"C'mon, Ray. Jesus Christ. Just cut me a break, will you? I'm askin' you. I'm fuckin' beggin' you, okay?"

"Don't. This isn't about you two. This is about that little shit showin' me no goddam respect. An' you aren't explainin' that away. I'm fuckin' fed up."

Craig's cousin's voice is thick, almost not his. "You can fix this."

"I'm not the only player."

"C'mon, Ray."

"Get over here, Trevor. I have somethin' to give you. I'm just not talkin' about this anymore."

He disconnects the call, drops the phone on the counter and puts his head in his hands for a moment. It aches, a pain just above his eye. He pushes at it with the heel of his palm, then straightens up and takes a swallow of his coffee. Outside, the edges of the road are damp and dark, the ice gone. A black streak of birds crosses the sky. He sees Wendy climbing the stairs at Errol's. She pulls at her feet like she's sinking in quick sand. Then a car pulls up and he goes inside.

Just before lunch, a delivery truck arrives, clanking and squealing. A few more customers. Then Craig's cousin.

He walks back across the shop, pauses up front until he sees Craig's cousin in the doorway and then says, "Wait here."

A moment later he comes back out again and tosses Son's jacket at him. Craig's cousin catches it with a small smile. "Thanks, Ray. This means a lot."

"I doubt it."

"You sure you don't wanna give it to 'im yourself?"

He can feel his annoyance again. "Real sure, Trev."

"You've got that one on me, Ray. I really don't think I could be so fuckin' sure all the time."

"You're turning this on me? Were you not fucking there?"

"I get why you're pissed, Ray. I just don't get why you're lettin' it go on this long. What if there's no comin' back?"

"I'm not lettin' anything go on."

"Fuck, man. You have all the goddam power. Give in a little."

Ray's eyes narrow, slitted with anger. "Jesus Christ, Trevor. You've got it bad."

Craig's cousin flares too. "So what?"

"I'm not givin' in. I can't do anything else to fix this."

"You can fix this. I'm beggin' you, okay? You want me on my fuckin' knees? I am beggin' you just to see 'im. Let 'im talk. Please."

The ache over his eyes is back. Craig's cousin's pale face irritates him. He wants him to go. He rubs his forehead, feeling the skin move over his brow. "Go on. You know where to find me if you need to."

Craig's cousin nods, backing up. "Okay…okay." His face looks drained, tired. Ray listens to the sound of his boots on the steps and then the sound of his car pulling away.

Getting out of the car beside the dark trailer, Craig's cousin goes slowly up the steps. He knows Son is inside, lying listlessly on the air mattress probably. His excitement at going home was temporary. Maybe he doesn't want to go home anymore, but he won't say so. He isn't happy, but Craig's cousin knows that he lets the flow of things take him. Inside, he sees Son's shape in the bedroom, a shadow that doesn't move. He lays the jacket on the counter, sets his keys down, flips on a light. Daylight barely filters through the windows. He switches on the lamp that's on the living room floor and hits the light on in the bedroom. Son peers up through a slitted eye. He turns the light in the bathroom on, then comes back out.

Son lies with his eyes open now, dully patient. Craig's cousin looks down at him. "Get up. Come out here a minute."

He rolls over, pushes up, follows him. Craig's cousin reaches over to the counter and turns back with the jacket, holding it out. Son stares in amazement, approaches slowly, takes it from him. He looks at it, squeezes the leather in his fist. "Where'd you get it?"

"Your dad."

"I thought—"

"I know what you thought. I told you he wouldn't do that."

"Why'd 'e give it back to you? Why'd you go over there?"

"I wanted to talk to 'im."

"About what?"

"About you."

Son abruptly drops the jacket on the floor and starts back to the bedroom. "I don't want it anymore."

Craig's cousin stops him in the short hall, turns him back around, holding onto his arm. "Wait a minute." He smells like soap. Craig's cousin tugs at his hair, curling it in his fingers, feeling the coolness and faint damp of his shower. "I'm not done talking."

"Nothing to say."

"I want you to go talk to him."

"No."

Craig's cousin holds onto him. "I want this for you."

Son's whips his head from side to side angrily. "Fuck that. Fuck him. Fuck you."

Craig's cousin sighs, looking into Son's face. "I don't wanna argue."

"I'm tellin' you."

"You're going."

"Hell I am."

"I mean it."

"Fuck you, Trevor."

"I mean it."

"No."

"Yeah."

"Fuck you," he says again and yanks away, dropping back on the air mattress with a whoosh of air from the valve, resting his head in the crook of his arm.

"C'mon. Get up."

"Fuck you."

"Yeah, yeah. You said that already. I heard you. You listen to me now. Get up an' take your clothes off."

Son looks up, staring at him, cheeks slowly flushing. Craig's cousin doesn't know if it's with desire or anger.

"I don't wanna go."

"I know."

A moment passes, then Son climbs back onto his feet and begins removing his clothes. His face is sullen, more angry than aroused, uncertain. Craig's cousin leans back against the wall, watching him. His fingers are clumsy, fumbling at his buttons. He shrugs out of his shirt, pulls his tee-shirt over his head, pulls off his socks, then drops his sweatpants, kicking them away. Craig's cousin just stares at him, trying to keep his face blank. Son's resistance in the hallway is still working at him, the sight of life sparking back into the angry eyes exciting him. He can sense Son's interest. But Son's afraid too. Too much emotion.

"Why am I doing this?"

"I want you to."

"Trevor?"

"C'mere."

Son's skin is hot. Craig's cousin takes his face, kissing him slowly, pulling him closer, and Son's arms come around him, warm, clutching at him. He pushes back until Son hits the edge of the mattress, another whoosh of air pushing out of the valve as he lies down. Craig's cousin goes down too, covering him up, inhaling his odor before he sucks in a breath and pushes back up, sitting between Son's legs. Color suffuses Son's chest and face. His eyes glitter and he bites his lip. Craig's cousin likes to look at him, roll him over and back, touch, kiss. Son's docility arouses him.

"Are you scared?" he asks.

Son frowns. "Of you?"

He nods.

"I love you, Trevor."

"Show me," he whispers and Son rolls onto hands and knees, waiting for him, glancing back anxiously. He wiggles his bottom and Craig's cousin gives it a sudden smack. Son sinks, face and chest down, bottom up. Craig's cousin mutters, "Fuck," and lies over him again, surrounding him, sweaty skin against sweaty skin. He's dimly aware of Son's gasps and the whoosh of the leaky valve. White light fills his eyes, happiness in his heart, the sound of laughter—"Oh fuck, yeah!" Then a bolt of lightening shoots through him and he blanks out, rolls as he falls, lying breathlessly. He feels Son's heart pounding against his arm, his sweaty skin spreading heat down his side.

His. A thing of value. Fragile.

"I love this with you," he says.

Son's fingers fumble for his and Craig's cousin rolls his head to look at him. "I meant it, though. About you goin' to see your dad."

"I know."

Craig's cousin doesn't want to think about the man who took Son, but for some reason he does. He thinks about the way the man didn't feed him, and the way he dropped him off on the curb like a bag of garbage. Not clean. Not beautiful. Not precious.

"I love you, baby."

"I love you, too, Trevor."

The ice is back, stinging bits blowing in the dark. The air smells like water, cold, astringent. Without the heater on, cold seeps in under the doors, through all the leaky window casements. Ray switches off the lights, ducks his face from the wind outside. His boots crunch on frozen gravel. Inside the bar, the air is warm and he relaxes, rolls his shoulders, slipping off his coat as he goes. At a table against the wall, he drinks by himself, rocking his chair backwards, eyeing the room through lowered lids. He isn't tired anymore. He feels good, just vaguely antisocial. The thought of that brings a smile to his face. Grace looks at him curiously.

"How you doin', sweet pea?"

"I'm okay. Another?"

"Yeah. Make that two," he adds, seeing Son come through the front door, face set in his usual scowl.

Ray drops his chair down, pushes at the one across the table from him. Son comes over, takes it, sitting stiffly.

"I ordered you a drink."

"Thanks."

"You're welcome."

Son's mouth twists, a look of concentration in his eyes. Then he slumps in his chair, apparently deciding not to follow through with whatever he was thinking about. A moment later, after Grace sets down their drinks, he straightens up, lifting his hands inside the pockets of his jacket. "Thanks for this."

"Couldn't bring myself to do it."

"You pawned something."

"Nothing important," he says, looking at the finger he used to wear Cora's ring on.

Son nods, shifts in his chair, then takes a hand out of his jacket and rubs his face. "Look, I don't wanna go like this. I want us to be okay."

"Up to you. You're my kid. You can always come to me."

"Except you're mad an' you don't like me."

Ray doesn't reply right away, takes a slow swallow of his drink, eyes still lingering on his finger. Then he sets his glass down and says, "I'm not mad anymore. An' it's your attitude I don't like. You've got a fuckin' chip on your shoulder an' no real reason for it. Christ, kid. You're young. You're good looking. You've got nothin' weighing you down. You should be happy. You want Trevor, you love 'im, whatever, fine. Fuck each other stupid. I don't care about that. Take advantage. Christ, when I was your age, I couldn't get enough of every fuckin' day. Life is great. Use it up. Every damn thing you come across, every experience, everything you have, everything you can take. You're not gonna get many more chances. You lose out real quick, believe me."

Son leans back in his chair, grips the arms and nods. "I know the way I am. I don't mean to be. I just get all worked up."

"Over what?"

"You."

"Christ, kid. I say I'm sorry 'til I'm sick a hearin' myself. I'd do it different, I really would. I just don't learn that quick, I guess."

"You did okay. I keep thinkin' an' I get scared. I think about all the things I did, not even tryin' to be careful, not thinkin' about you an' mom. I get chills sometimes, just out a the blue, an' then I get mad. I don't want to think about what I did, so I think about what you did. I wish you were around more. I'm not gonna lie about that. I just…I just can't blame you. I was askin' to die—"

"Jesus, kid."

"I was. An' I wonder why I'm here. An' I know I don't deserve to be."

"Don't fuckin' say that!" Ray's voice is sharp. "Don't you ever say that. You're the only good thing I have a claim to. You have everything to live for. Don't be scared anymore. That doesn't help. You don't need to be scared. You don't need to feel guilty about anything. You sure as hell don't need to be takin' any shit that ain't gonna fix it anyway an' I sure as hell don't need to put you in the middle of that life anymore."

"Whadda you mean?"

"I'm gettin' out. I already told Ed."

"Are you shittin' me? Just like that?"

"Pretty much."

"What will you do? Just work at the shop?"

"I doubt it. I'll probably be comin' home in a couple months too."

"With Miri?"

"Yeah, with Miri. Whadda you think?"

"Are you doin' it for me?"

"Are you upset about this?" There's a tinge of anger in Ray's voice.

"No, I just…I just never thought you'd change."

"Well, I guess you were wrong. Which means there's no fuckin' excuse for you."

Son looks nonplussed. He moves his gaze around the bar as if looking for something. Then his eyes come back to rest on Ray and he lifts his shoulders, drops them again. "Okay."

"Okay with what I'm doin' or okay you're gonna try an' enjoy your damn self for a change?"

"Especially the enjoy part."

"Good. That's my boy. Now go get me another drink. An' you better get goin'. Trev's waitin' for you, isn't 'e?"

"Yeah. I told 'im I might be a while."

After he gets Ray's drink, he sits back down and takes a swallow out of his glass. Then his other hand comes out, cupping the glass on the table, and he almost jumps when Ray grabs his wrist and twists it. "Hell's that?"

He's looking at the ring on Son's finger. Son's face goes white, then turns a slow red. "We got married."

"Are you shittin' me?"

"No."

"You don't think that was a little quick?"

"No."

Ray sighs, sitting back again. "Your life."

Son nods. "Yeah. That's what you said, right? Take everything. Enjoy it. Well, I hit the jackpot with Trevor. Fuck everybody else. An' you know what?" he adds, pointing at Ray's ring finger. "The best thing? I beat you on this. I did it first."

Ray's mouth works up a small smile. "Yeah, kid, you beat me on this."

"You know it's a competition, right?"

Ray's smile broadens. "From the day you were born."

Son smiles back, starts to get up, then stops, settles down again and says, "I love you, Dad, okay?"

Ray grimaces at him. "Yeah, yeah. Now go on. Get out a here."

Son doesn't say anything else, just smiles again, and a moment later walks out the front door.

After he leaves, Ray sets his glass down and twists at his bare finger with an unease that takes a long time to go away.

25

♦ Panic ♦

Warmth seeps away, coolness coming under the covers. No sound. Waking up, Miri feels at the empty side of the bed and rolls over, facing the door. There's no light in the hallway or out in the kitchen. The coolness grows, his warmth gone. Pushing the covers back, she creeps to the side of the bed, listening for him. Then she hears him, sees a glimmer of light that disappears with the sound of the refrigerator door closing. The dark gleam of the mirror over the dresser faces her, over the drawer that used to keep Cora's pictures. But there are no pictures of Cora anymore. Thinking about that, she feels a strange worry. Loving him is easy for her.

In the hall, she feels the chill of a draft. The back door is open, Ray outside on the porch, drinking his coffee. A few pale stars splatter the dark sky. At the sound of her, he glances back, his irritation slow to leave his face.

"Hey, babe. Wake you?"

"No."

She knows she keeps nothing she thinks secret. Even Will can see into her. At the Club the other night, he dropped onto a stool and had a sympathetic smile, cocking his head in a fashion she used to love. His face was calm in a way it seldom is anymore, in his eyes a momentary lucidity. His fear, though, was like an oil slick shining on the surface. He was aware of the moment, aware of his clarity, aware of his swiftly receding sanity. Under his sympathy, his old malice rose, stronger than the fear.

"Ain't seen Ray lately."

She shrugged. "Try calling 'im."

"No answer."

"Leave a message."

"Personal."

She straightened her arm against the counter, putting distance between them. "Whadda you want, Will?"

He squinted at her. "I'm just talking."

"To drink."

"Oh. Grey Goose." She poured it for him, set it down, started to move away. "I can tell you, though."

Resigned, she sighed and came back. "I thought it was personal."

"Well, you know, right? I'm not judgin' Ray. I love the man." The last made him squirm uncomfortably and he added, "You know, in a normal way. I cut Trevor off. You know what kind of a friend Trevor was? No fuckin' kind. I don't blame Ray for keepin' a low profile, but like I say, I'm not judgin'."

"Really? You cut Craig's cousin off an' that's not you judging?"

He set his empty glass down and tapped it with his finger, gesturing for her to pour another one. "Trevor's sick. I meant I wasn't judging Ray about that kid a his. Who I never fuckin' liked anyway. Ray didn't really raise 'im, no way to man 'im up. Too late now. That's all I'm sayin'."

Her eyes rolled a little. Setting the bottle back on the counter behind her, she said, "There's your drink," and started to move off again.

"I keep drivin' by your house. Think I'll see 'im an' stop in, talk in person. But I never do."

His sympathy was back, but so was that look of fractured glass in his eyes. A thousand pieces of Will.

"We're fine, Will."

But they weren't and they weren't the minute Ray gave her a ring, doing what his heart wanted, but what every other part of his being told him to run away from. He put away Cora's pictures, those pictures he has carried around with him for most of his life, symbols of everything he gave up.

On the porch, she watches him watching her over his cup of coffee, seeing in his eyes the slow calculation that comes up with nothing that he's getting from her.

"You okay, lady?"

Screaming at herself to shut up, she says, "I hardly see you anymore, Ray."

"You're seein' me now."

She leans back, resting the bottom of her foot against the doorsill, lifting her eyes up. "This isn't seeing you."

"Well, whadda you want me to say? I have a lot a work without the kid around. I can't just take off like before."

"You used to."

He puts his cup on the railing and says, "I don't have the same income I used to have."

"Are you blaming me for that?"

"I'm tellin' you. You asked. You want, we'll go out. You arrange it. Just tell me where to be."

"You don't get it, do you?"

In the growing light she can see his face, pale, expressionless, unrelievedly cool, anger in place of love. An anger he carries with an energy that is thrumming inside him. She knows he battles for that coolness, for the cheerful good humor that never cares about anything. His real life, not with her, is somewhere safe with Cora's pictures.

"I guess not," he says. "An' I don't have time to talk about it."

With that, he turns, quick on the steps, slower out to the driveway. She rolls her foot against the door jamb, waiting until all the sounds of him leaving have faded away.

On his way home the night he saw Miri, Will drove by her house, dark on a dark street. In back though, a lamp over the garage door bled a thin watery light over Ray's bike. Surprised to see it, Will shut off his headlights, idling by the driveway. The idea of Ray asleep brought him a strange pleasure. At the bar, he was marveling at Miri's face, her allure growing on him again. He liked her tired look, the shadows under her eyes, the colorlessness of her skin. He wanted to be the one who wore her out, who gave her a vision of life that was real, not happily ever after. His life wasn't happily ever after anymore. He lost Craig's cousin. Ray was Son's, Miri's, not Will's.

Will wanted Miri again. At the Club, he felt the stool underneath him, even tasted a medicinal sharpness on his tongue when he drank his vodka. Other times, he floated, adrift, the world around him contracting against his pinpoint pupils. Once he tried opening his eyes with his fingers, but everything stayed small, confined in a circle that made him imagine he had paper towel tubes attached to his eyes. He blamed Craig's cousin. Darkness began to rim the scene at the moment of Craig's cousin's betrayal. His vision was shrinking. Craig's cousin could see. Staring at Miri and Ray's house, he saw Son's face filling the confines of his vision, transforming into Ray's.

A longing to leave his car and go quietly into the house came over him. He saw the short hall to the bedroom. He felt his feet sinking soundlessly into carpet, saw himself push gently at the bedroom door. He wanted Ray to see like him, to understand him. Dying, he would. He would see through Will's eyes, his world slowly pulling in, a rim of deepening darkness. Will didn't know how to kill him. It would have to be sudden, a shock that let him slip in. Then, sitting in the car, he panicked at the thought of losing Ray too.

His breath choked him and he panted in little whines.

The garage light grew into a giant blue halo, damp and blurry. Whispers rose in the air, *"Trevor, Trevor,"* but he didn't hear them. His panic eased though. Switching his lights back on, he drove home and ran inside. Jumping on the bed, he woke Susie up. She grabbed him as she came floundering out of the covers. He kissed her, holding her head, and she swatted at him and switched on the bedside lamp.

"Ow," he muttered.

She was squinting at him. "Jesus, Will."

He didn't feel welcome. She looked pasty in that light anyway and there were creases on her cheek. She was always complaining that he didn't kiss her, didn't make her happy, and when he came home and kissed her, thinking she'd be happy and he didn't really like Miri anymore anyway, she complained about that too.

He felt himself growing cool.

"I was with somebody better anyway."

When she burst into tears, he didn't care.

"Teach you," he muttered.

Now it's morning and she opens up the curtains and the sun comes in through the spruce outside.

Will blinks, looks up at the light above him and blinks again, trying to find Susie in the glare. He can't see and gropes at the air. "Susie!"

He thinks he hears her and swipes in a panic at the room, fumbling for her, hearing a faint, faraway, niggling laughter. A sound that rises and recedes, chuckles, titters, a mix of delight and malice.

"You better shut those!"

She doesn't.

At the stop light, Jonah looked and didn't see her. The bowling pin's shadow lay across the parking lot and the glass doors to the alley were dark under the eaves. A car was parked on the shoulder of the road by a chain link fence across from Kurt's; and that's where he saw her, sitting on the other side of the car where the asphalt rose in a ridge against the remains of a sidewalk. She was sitting with her feet on either side of a puddle, her fingers in a knot at the back of her head, holding her hair back.

He thought of Mavis again. It was something about the way she sat there. Later, after he took her home, he waited until he saw her light come on upstairs. She stayed in the light for a moment and he knew Mavis did that too, stood there looking out her window until she finally left, even though there was nothing she was going to.

Alone with her at Kurt's, he said, "What were you doin' down there?"

"Waiting for you."

There was a tone of surprise in her voice. He didn't think she understood him anymore. He was alone again despite her. At the kitchen table he sat with a beer, his shirt already off and she sat on the side of the bed, all of her clothes, even her jacket still on, her hands shoved into her jacket pockets. It was cold in the room and he was aware that he didn't feel it, even though when he looked, he noticed goose bumps on his bare skin. He slumped back with his beer, looking at her.

"You don't wanna do this?"

She shook her head. "No. Not right now."

"We don't have a lotta time."

"That's okay."

"That's okay that we don't do it?"

"We don't have to."

He shrugged. "Then why are we here?"

"I like seeing you. Can't we just be here?"

He stared at her, imagining her picturing other lives revealed in that puddle she had been staring into, her mother's daughter. Slowly, he reached for his sweatshirt, pulled it back on. Oddly, he felt colder than before. "Are you tired of this?" he asked, watching for her expression.

She looked startled, surprised at him, then cautious. "Are you?"

After a moment, he said, "No, I guess not."

"Then I'm not either."

Later, at home, he sat half in, half out of his pickup. Steam was rising off the trees and the sun felt almost warm. He imagined there was once a meadow like Ira's where the house was now. A meadow with wild flowers and the sound of the wind and almost nothing else.

At the bowling alley, the rising sun lights a shower of glass on the pavement. The sun is brightening, losing winter's cool, but the tiny bits of glass still look like slivers of ice. Cars are parked in the parking lot, but a wide open space surrounds the car without any windows. This is the only damage to the cars now, no drain opener, just blasted windshields.

Sitting in a booth at Candi's, Andy can see Jimbo cruise slowly by the bowling alley, make a turn at the signal light and come back again, pulling into the diner's parking lot. Andy sighs, elbows on the table, rubbing the back of his neck. By the time Jimbo enters, his breakfast has arrived and he chews on a piece of bacon, ignores Jimbo as he slips into the booth on the other side of him.

Jimbo grimaces as Andy sticks his bacon into the yolk of one of his eggs.

"That's sick."

Andy doesn't answer. But when Jimbo orders blueberry pancakes, he says, "Channelin' Trev?"

"That little shit," says Jimbo, jerking his arm halfway up to his face, then dropping it again. Craig's cousin broke his nose and now there's a scar across the dented bridge. Jimbo won't admit that Craig's cousin broke it though. "Just the skin," he says. "Fuckin' faggot." It shames him. Even now his skin flushes.

Andy starts in on another piece of bacon, eliciting a repeated grimace from Jimbo. "You know," says Andy, bringing the dripping bacon to his mouth. "You shouldn't've been drivin' by over there. That's what people do all the time. Return to the scene of the crime."

Jimbo shoots a quick glance around. His face turns red and he tries not to look back through the window at the bowling alley. A man is sweeping bits of glass into a pile. Jimbo tries to look confused. "What crime?"

Andy looks at him carefully, worriedly. Not that he likes Jimbo. He isn't worried out of any concern for him. He doesn't really worry about Will for Will's sake either, but without Craig's cousin around there isn't a lot of sanity. Will is like a balloon bouncing off the bottom of a ceiling. He's never going to reach the sky, but he doesn't seem to know that. Jimbo is as cracked as the glass he keeps shattering. Andy doesn't get that at all and he's pretty sure Jimbo doesn't either.

"Are you fuckin' stupid?" he asked when Jimbo came over with Andy's crow bar, just walking through the apartment complex with it, bragging to Andy about it, crowing out loud. "You should come, dude. It is way cool."

"Two words, Jimbo. Surveillance cameras."

That shut Jimbo up, but as with any compulsion, he couldn't stop. Andy can tell that he wants to though. He eats his pancakes almost furtively, eyeing Andy petulantly. He wants Andy's amazement, jealousy even. A feeling of malice at not getting that rises up in Jimbo, but he only says, "I'm layin' low for a while. Get back to it later."

Andy gapes at him. "It's not a fucking chore, man. You don't have to get back to it. You guys are fuckin' nuts."

"What guys?"

"You," says Andy, but he sees Jimbo thinking about that. He doesn't think it would take a rocket scientist to know he meant Will though. Andy never thought Will was normal and now he doesn't think Jimbo is either.

After breakfast, Jimbo follows him home, slumping on his couch, watching TV. He leaves at night, but in the morning he is back. This goes on for a few days before Andy says, "What's with you, man? You don't even like me."

Jimbo looks surprised. "I like you. Takin' your advice."

"What advice?"

"About layin' low."

Andy doesn't remind him that that was his own advice. Instead, he says, "Sure, no prob. Just tryin' to help." Then after a moment, he adds,

"Thinkin' a that. You oughta give me that crow bar back. Keepin' it's kinda risky."

Jimbo gives him a canny look, points the remote at the TV and says, "Might need it again."

Andy scowls at him, then says, "Be right back. We need some beer."

He walks across the street to the liquor store beside Quality Videos. Stepping up on the curb, he stops and steps back again, looking at the telephone pole beside him. The wooden pole is wearing a sleeve of paper notices stapled to it. Andy looks at one with a picture of a windowless car and the word REWARD in block letters at the top. He laughs abruptly, then continues into the liquor store. At home, he tells Jimbo about it, laughing again while Jimbo's face turns red.

"Sure aren't offerin' a lot to catch you. Hell, even I wouldn't turn you in for that."

"Ain't offerin' nothin' for you," says Jimbo.

"An' you know what, Jimbo? I'm thinkin' that's a good thing."

For some reason Jimbo doesn't go home that night and Andy goes to sleep listening to him snore on the couch. In the morning, he scratches at his belly and stares at Jimbo watching TV while he eats a bowl of cereal.

"This sucks," he mutters.

"It's the news," says Jimbo. "Gotta keep up, man."

Getting dressed, Andy says, "I'm goin' out," grabbing his keys and feeling petulant. His skin is beginning to twitch with irritation at everything Jimbo does.

"Need some more beer," says Jimbo.

He slams the door. At Will's, he sits down and Will says, "Wanna hit?" He reaches for Will's pipe. He's sitting in Susie's chair, sinking into the cushions. Softness surrounds him and he begins to realize why Jimbo likes her chair. Will is wearing sunglasses in a room that's dark except for the TV and a beam of light through the crack in the curtains. Andy's eyes follow the specks of dust up the beam of light.

Will peers at him over the tops of his glasses. "Where's Jimbo?"

"Layin' low."

"Hell's that mean?"

"You know. Keepin' a low profile."

"A low profile?"

"Yeah."

"Cuz?"

"Cuz a those cars. You know? The windows an' shit?"

"No way. Jimbo? Our Jimbo?"

Andy nods and Will laughs. Then he stops laughing and says, "How come you know about it an' I don't?"

The conversation is making Andy uncomfortable. He squirms in Susie's chair. "I was there the first time. Son's car."

"Don't say that fucker's name in my house."

"You asked me."

"Call 'im."

"Call who?" asks Andy, momentarily confused.

"Jimbo."

"Oh."

He wishes he didn't come over but sitting around listening to Jimbo slurp cereal was even worse. He rolls out of Susie's chair so Jimbo won't yank him out of it. Will is flipping through channels with a ferocious look of focus on his face. The light from the TV doesn't seem to bother him. Colors flash. Will is mesmerized. He doesn't even look up at the sound of Jimbo's car.

Andy stares uneasily. Will is cycling through the channels, never pausing. He seems trapped until all of a sudden the door opens and light floods in. Will's arms fly up, circle around his head. "Fucker!"

Jimbo stares at him.

"Shut the door," says Andy.

"Shut the door!" Will yells.

Jimbo shuts it. He stares at Andy. Andy shrugs. "Geez, man. You okay?"

Will's arms come down. The face that appears is familiar, cold, and blank. Without frailty. He pulls his sunglasses off and his eyes are wide open. "You fuckers keep screwin' with me an' I don't like that. You. Trev."

Jimbo looks back at Andy angrily. "What the fuck?"

"You don't keep secrets from me, Jimbo. Shit I need to know. You don't trust me anymore?"

"You asshole," says Jimbo, still staring at Andy.

"I don't get it," says Will. "You tell Andy an' not me. That hurts my fuckin' feelings."

Jimbo tries to explain. "I was—"

"Scared," says Andy.

Jimbo's face puffs. His eyes sink in reddening pits and he moves, first with a lurch, then with slow soundless steps. Andy backs away, runs up against Susie's chair. He jerks at the jab of Jimbo's fingers in his chest, swats his arm away. The next thing he knows he's flying backwards into Susie's chair. The bottom almost drops out, sucking him in. Jimbo grabs his collar, lifts, and shoves him back down again. Andy grabs at the arm of the chair and holds on, kicking Jimbo away. The sound of laughter deafens him, Will's joining Jimbo's. Jimbo grabs Andy's foot and pulls while Andy clutches at the sides of Susie's chair and feels it scoot up. Jimbo stops, inhales, and pulls again. Andy shoots a plaintive look at Will, but Will just keeps laughing at him because Andy knows Will likes Jimbo better than he likes Andy. Jimbo gave him reindeer ears for Christmas.

Andy grimaces. "C'mon, Jimbo. Back off."

Jimbo's face is blank. He jerks at Andy's foot and then Will gets up and says, "Wait a sec."

Jimbo twists back to look and Andy twists too, sinking to the bottom of Susie's chair. Will's at the door, opening it up. "Vamoose," he says.

Andy thought that was always Jimbo's idea in the first place and he can tell by Jimbo's pause that Jimbo thought so too and is a little discombobulated at Will's interference.

"C'mon," says Andy. "I let you stay with me. I bought you chips. Kept you in fuckin' cereal an' beer."

"Vamoose!" yells Will.

"Yeah," murmurs Jimbo.

Will grins and steps back as Jimbo yanks Andy out onto the porch and scrambles up and over the arm of the chair to get back inside. The door slams.

Andy can hear them inside.

"Vamoose!"

"Vamoose!"

Susie's earrings are white cubes dangling on silver chains. She blows a bubble, watching Will over the purple top. Will's sunglasses lower and he peers at her, beginning to smile. He taps an earring, cool as marble.

"I like these."

Her bubble starts to shrink and she sucks it in with tiny snapping noises.

"Christmas present."

Will's delighted. "From me!"

It was from her mother actually, but she snaps her gum again and says, "Yeah."

"Cool."

Outside, he swings his arm over her shoulders and she walks at a tilt, hugging him at the waist with her cheek against his shoulder, ignoring the strain on her neck. In the car, she sits close too. She is looking forward to Candi's, but then they are passing it and she twists to stare back over Will's shoulder. She doesn't say anything though. She doesn't want to break the mood. A minute later, Will is on the side street by Mulligan's, passing that too to pull up in front of Ray's.

"Closed," says Ray when they come in the door.

"Social," says Will.

"Lock it."

"Lock it," says Will to Susie, swinging his arm up and over her head. She falls back and Will follows Ray.

"I'm not botherin' you, am I? You don't fuckin' call me anymore. You should be more sensitive, man."

Susie sees a smile playing on Ray's mouth as he glances back. "I'm havin' a tough time," says Will. "You know. It's like somebody died. Fuckin' little—"

The smile drops off of Ray's mouth. He grows still, a hand above the light switch in back. "Yeah?"

Will shrugs. "Man, it's just Trev. I didn't mean your kid."

"I take Trev personally, Will."

"I'm just sayin' you should come around. Like before."

"Things aren't like before. I told you that."

His hand flips off the lights and Susie stands in the dark until a light in back goes on. It reaches down the hall and past the door. She hears Will say, "You're gonna love this. Jimbo's been keepin' busy."

She feels for the latch on the door. Flips it. Then she goes in back too and sees Will standing by a dark window with Ray leaning against a counter across from the door. Ray's arms are folded and he's beginning to smile.

"Jimbo, huh?"

"Yeah," says Will. "Dude didn't even tell me. Andy didn't either. Fuckers. Vamoose, man? You like that word?"

Ray shrugs, not drinking his beer. "It's a word."

"Jimbo was pissed an' Andy was just sittin' in Susie's chair like it was a goddam carnival ride, holdin' on like this—" He pushes Susie away, beer bottle between his knees, gripping both sides of his chair, hunched up, grinning at Ray, who recrosses his ankles and looks at his boots, smile growing more amused. Will sits up, opening his arm for Susie again. She leans in. It wasn't that funny a story to Susie, but she's smiling too, squeezing Will's shoulders. "Anyway, I open up the door an' Jimbo's draggin' Andy out, goin—"

"Vamoose, Andy!"

Susie's face blanches at the sound of her voice. Ray laughs and tips his bottle up to drink and Will stares at her with his own bottle halfway up, frozen, as she slowly lets him go.

"*I* was tellin' the *goddam story!*" Susie backs away, pulls her mink up, trying to duck inside it. Will gets up slowly. His tiny pupils grow. "Get out!"

"Will—"

"Out! Out!"

He is pushing her. She stumbles into the dark and hears Ray say, "Not here, man," but she doesn't see him pull Will's bottle away.

Will is following her. "You goddam piss me off!"

But then Ray is behind him, an arm dropping over his shoulder, pulling him back. Susie skitters on her heels down the hallway, Ray's quiet voice behind her. "C'mon, man. Get you another beer."

The side door is locked. She fumbles at it, stumbles outside, pulls the door shut behind her. The screen door eases back halfway. She pushes. It has a spring to it. It pushes back at her. Through the glass in the door, she can see the kitchen light in back. Will doesn't appear. Her hands shake. She bundles up in the collar of her coat again. It's cold and clear out and the air smells green and sweet. The weeds in the lot are making a soft susurration. Letting go of her coat, she pushes at the screen door again. It creaks, stiff against her fingers, swings back.

"Fuckin' door," she mutters.

"Susie."

She whirls, a dark figure outside the reach of the bar's light coming closer. She squints at it. "Kurt?"

"Yeah."

Coming down the stairs, she skips a step and staggers across the gravel, catching onto the arm Kurt throws out for her. Her weight spins them in a circle. Kurt laughs and she laughs a little too and throws her arms out for balance. He grabs her again, feels the cool softness of her mink.

"Wow."

She likes Kurt's tone of awe and pulls up the collar to rub her cheek against it. "I got it for Christmas."

"Cruella De Vil without spots," Will told her. The toy car she gave him for Christmas is covered in scratches and dirt. Seeing it that way, his favorite toy, makes her uneasy. When Kurt says, "Buy you a drink," she has to come back from that unease and feels off balance.

"Buy me a drink?"

"Yeah."

She scrunches up her collar again. "Yeah, okay."

With a swing of his arm at the door, Kurt says, "Ladies first," and she walks by in a light-headed dream-like daze.

At home, Kurt has a bottle of champagne that he isn't drinking because he really bought it to drink with Joy on New Year's Eve. After work, he came right home and her apartment was dark. He guessed she'd be going out but not that early. He kept finding reasons to come outside and run into her. Once he took out the garbage and another time remembered a pair of boots he left in his car. Between times she came home and he heard people laughing. In the morning, he saw pieces of confetti outside her door. At the bowling alley, after he got his donut and coffee, he felt a sudden embarrassment and didn't know where it came from.

Now, sitting with Susie and drinking champagne, he remembers that and says, "Happy New Year's, Susie."

Susie looks a little startled because, of course, it isn't really New Year's and Kurt blushes slightly, but then she gives him a bright 'who cares' kind of smile and says, "Yeah. Happy New Year's, Kurt."

Outside, stars sparkle and car lights swoop over jewel-like weeds and a milky, paper-like moon comes up and doesn't care about champagne or

Joy's confetti or winter flowers that look just like spring or jars of cold cream or fake crystal doorknobs or lawns cut in crisp diagonals.

Mr Torch is sitting against the wall at Carl's with his hands clasped in his lap and Scott is looking at Carl without really hearing anything he says because he doesn't want to. Carl is looking frustrated. His heart feels fast and he can see multicolored dots in the air and the air feels light and ticklish.

"Okay?!"

Scott jumps and Mr Torch sighs in disapproval this time. Carl sneers at him and Mr Torch looks away. Scott just stares.

"I want Val to have my parrot."

Scott hears him now and notices that Carl glows as luminously as moonlit bones. Val is the gardener at the Acropolis Inn. Scott swallows and looks for the parrot which sits on a shelf above Mr Torch. Mr Torch looks up too, smiles.

Carl knows he isn't enough for Mr Torch anymore. Mr Torch wants Scott now too.

Scott frowns. "Okay."

Even though it was Wendy's parrot, which she bought on a cruise and gave to Carl to match a pair of tropical fish earrings he bought for her in the same bright blue and green colors.

A reminder of sandy beaches and deep blue water and soft warm breezes and a little palm tree on a cold winter's day.

Scott looks down and Carl stares and Mr Torch looks outside.

Tires squeal, leave black streaks on the pavement. A slight fishtail before Will straightens out the car. Inside, Susie hugs herself. Will's knuckles are yellow white on the steering wheel. The car squeals again onto Oly Way, then stops at the signal light by Candi's and Susie wants to run inside where it's bright and warm and full of people.

Will's bellow suddenly fills the car. "You were makin' time!"

She wails back at him. "I was not!"

Cold turns all the lights around town sharp and bright. A few stray Christmas lights still shine in random places.

Inside the Club, Miri is rubbing her bare arms. She's wearing a pink and green check skirt and a flimsy pink top, dangly earrings with pink plastic balls in her ears. "I'm *cold!*"

Otis sighs. "Win-ter-time."

She has goose bumps on her arms, and when Ray comes in, he gives her a wry smile.

"Hey, babe."

He taps the bar where she's standing as he passes and after a moment she goes over to an empty table and drops shot glasses inside of beer mugs and wipes off the table top. The tables are covered in a heavy varnish and she can see her face looking back up at her. Straightening, she picks up the beer mugs and hears Ray's laugh. He is talking to Otis. At the bar, she drops the mugs in a plastic tub and he says, "I can always use a good idea," before looking over at her.

She brushes her hands off and smooths her skirt.

After a moment, he looks back at Otis and says, "I keep runnin' out of 'um."

Andy can't find the walkway at Jimbo's. His apartment complex has a pool in the middle with gated walkways between the buildings. The outside of the complex is surrounded by ivy. Andy is looking for a light that's always on in the clubhouse by the pool. When he finds it, flickering through more ivy crawling up the side of one of the buildings, he can see the pale gleam of the walkway too.

He gets in through the sliding glass door Jimbo always forgets to lock. The sound seems loud but it stays dark and quiet inside. He leaves the door open and goes soundlessly across the living room floor. At the end of the hall, he reaches in through a partly open door and flips on a light. Jimbo jerks up onto his elbows, blinking furiously, and the covers flip up as his girlfriend ducks underneath. Andy can hear her.

"Who is that?"

Jimbo blinks again, focusing. "Andy?"

His voice sounds like he isn't sure Andy's real and he pinches at the lids of his eyes and squints in the light. The fixture that's on is the one in the ceiling over the bed. Jimbo has a waterbed with shelves built into either side of a heavy headboard and a mirror in the center. The bed is still moving, sloshing slowly.

Jimbo is beginning to scowl.

"Fuck you want?"

"I got a message for you."

Jimbo rolls sideways and the water underneath him slaps against the sides. He is looking for his clock, forgetting in this surreal moment where it is. When he sees the time, his chest heaves and a hurt look crosses his face. "Jesus, Andy...."

When Will told Ray about Jimbo, Ray just smiled. He almost laughed at Will's story too. But after Susie left and they drank another beer, he sighed, set his empty bottle in the sink, and repeated from earlier:

"Jimbo, huh?"

There was a tightness to Ray's jaw when he smiled, meaning it wasn't really a smile. Will didn't care about Son's car because it wasn't his anymore and he didn't even relate to the fact that it once was. He forgot something though in the fun of telling his story and looked a little embarrassed.

"Oh yeah. I guess I owe ya. No problem."

"Jimbo owes me." Ray thought it wouldn't have irritated him so much except it was just another sign of the disrespect everything he gives Son brings him. "The dude's got no fuckin' sense."

Will nodded. "That's true."

Jimbo's girlfriend is named Charlotte, although Jimbo likes to call her Charley because she always responds to that by slugging him in the shoulder and giving him an excuse to wrestle her to the floor where they both end up laughing and thrashing at each other. She has blonde hair with dark roots, a big nose, pitted skin, and an attractiveness that makes Jimbo take her with him to Ray's the next day. On the way over, he puffs up, deflates, puffs up again. Charlotte never asks him anything. That's another thing he likes about her. He suspects Ray will like her too. He might ignore her, but Jimbo is guessing she'll keep him peaceable. Usually, Ray behaves around women, but maybe not always, a thought that unsettles Jimbo a little, puffs him back up. Swinging around the corner of the bar though, he just deflates again, an angry flutter in his belly.

Wisps of steam uncurl from the rooftops where the sun is shining. The sound of Jimbo's slamming door carries in the quiet. His heavy steps crunch on the gravel. Charlotte hurries to catch up to him before they even reach the porch and Ray comes out and says, "Close enough."

His voice sounds normal, but Jimbo stops. His eyebrows contract and he starts to feel as put upon as when Andy woke him up. "You know how fuckin' early it is?" asks Jimbo.

"Ten thirty."

"That's early," he mutters. "I'm doin' Will a favor. Said you needed to see me."

"You know why you're here. You better have the cash."

"Or what?"

Ray just stares and Jimbo's face puffs and there's a kind of desperate belligerence in the way he shuffles from foot to foot. Ray stays cool, his eyes unnaturally flat. "Trust me, Jimbo. This is the best way."

Jimbo sneers but takes a wad of money out of his pocket and Ray nods at the railing beside him. He doesn't even uncross his arms and Jimbo steps in a patch of bare dirt that gives underfoot and never grows anything but weeds anymore and smacks the money down on the peeling board. After that, he says, "C'mon," and takes Charlotte's hand. She swings it as they walk, releasing it at the car with a grin. Jimbo likes that about her too. She's fun, but she isn't really interested in him. At least not in details or personal things. He could tell her he's a serial killer or a bank robber and it might only marginally register. Ray's insults don't. Jimbo doesn't even bother to puff up this time as he drives off.

A door slams at Errol's. At first Ray can't see anything, then Errol appears with a mattress that he's dragging across the soggy grass. Ray watches him struggle with it. As it tips away, Errol scurries around it to the other side, scoots it up, scurrying back around again.

Near the road, the grass gives way to gravel and Errol pushes and slides the mattress into his carport, letting it drop with a thump. Ray smiles appreciatively. Errol doesn't have a car and doesn't use the carport. It's just an open box of cinderblock with a roof like a giant bus stop and not much good for anything but cars. Or a bike, he thinks. But he never leaves his bike out anywhere, even without Jimbo's new hobby. Besides, Errol has a garage, doesn't need the carport that just fits Scott's and Fin's cars.

Watching Errol return with a pair of garbage cans that he sets beside the mattress, Ray guesses he doesn't feel like sharing his carport anymore. Ray figures Fin will just take it, the way he takes everything, but Scott's got a temper. Ray has only seen him up close a few times, but the repressed way he kept snapping the cap of his lighter up and down each time amused him. He shakes his head as Errol disappears around the front of the house, going back inside.

Sighing, Ray sits up, stretching stiffly. The idea of working all day depresses him. He moves slowly, leaving the door open behind him.

Cars and pickups pull into the factory parking lot. Swiveling in his chair, Fin looks out, watching people heading for the factory door below. He reaches back for his coffee, leaning sideways, then faces forward to look outside again. He doesn't worry about the coffee keeping him awake. He doesn't particularly want to sleep. Headlights keep swooping in. He can't hear anything but imagines the slam of doors, voices. He must be visible in the window, featureless probably. That thought appeals to him, to be without a face, to live in oblivion and anonymity.

Sitting on the edge of the chair, he rests his forearms on the windowsill, leaning his weight forward, forehead almost touching the cold glass. The heat from his coffee and breath cloud the window. For a moment, he lets the cloud grow, relishing the vagueness it brings. Almost reluctantly, he swipes it clear again, leans back a little. He isn't sure why he is waiting. His heart quickens nervously. He swallows some coffee and grimaces at the sourness. Acid rises in his throat. He swallows it and its familiarity haunts him. He wants a drink again. Setting the cup on the desk behind him, he looks back out the window. The activity below is slowing down. A couple of lone figures hurry across the parking lot. Then another set of headlights swings in, a pickup making an almost erratic zigzag across the lot. He sees Jonah briefly when the interior light pops on. His breathing is rapid, shallow. He doesn't know what he's doing.

Almost jumping up, he bumps against the window, feeling its cold thrum. Below him, alone in the parking lot, Jonah stops and Fin knows he's looking up, seeing him. His eyes bear down, but he can't see Jonah's face or tell anything from his stance. He's just a dark shape, a shape like Fin's against the light. Anger makes him shake. He wants a drink, wants to smash a fist into Jonah's face, to keep hitting him until he begins to laugh, a weak, brittle laugh that sounds like something breaking inside. Then they will be alike and Fin won't have to remember. But the fantasy doesn't make his anger disappear and he grows sick and looks away from the window.

He rubs his face, then picks up the coffee cup and walks out to the break room. Back in his office, he looks outside again and the parking lot is empty.

The other day, out running, he scooted up to the side of the road as Jonah's pickup blew past him, then he whirled around and ran almost without thinking back up the road to Jonah's. His heart was racing faster than the run accounted for. His ears were buzzing. Swiping at his sweat, he stopped once to listen. There was no sound but the sound of the river, of his heart and bellowing lungs. Walking slowly, he drew up near a scoop in the road where the shoulder slid away in a rooty tangle. Water gleamed down below, dark and glassy. He backed away, shaking, feeling dizzy. Up higher, the rising road breached open air. He could see the house but it was dark and lifeless looking.

No cars. No listlessly rising smoke from the chimney.

He came out into the open. The house was a dingy white with a good sized porch, deeper near one of the two doors. Moving quietly, he stepped up on the porch. One of the doors was a front door, he guessed. He saw a living room through the window beside it. There were no windows by the other door, but he knew that was the one everybody came in and out of. This is where he saw Sissy for the first time, standing with one bare foot on top of the other. On the same day, Jonah sitting shirtless, offering him a drink from the bottle he promised him earlier at Orly's. The taste of bourbon came clearer to him than any other memory, warm and sweet and burning, fumes just as warm, just as sweet, filling his nose as he drank. He remembered Jonah's smile after he gave him the bottle back, surprised and friendly.

His mouth filled with saliva, remembering that, tasting bourbon again, and he spat onto the gravel. Then the sound of the river grew louder until he realized it wasn't the river and he ran, barely breaking into the trees before Jonah's pickup came flying up, sliding to a sudden stop. He didn't pause to look back, just ran, slipping, picking himself up, until he burst out on the road by the river. Then he kept running until his legs began to wobble and the thoughts of his mother's gin faded away.

Sitting at his usual table at Mulligan's, Ray feels his phone vibrate and takes it out, looking without real interest, then he answers it and says, "Hey, bub."

"Are you home?"

"No. Why? What's up?"

"Have you eaten?"

"No. Hungry though."

"Meet me at Marjorie's?"

"Sure. You headin' out now?"

"Yeah. I'm comin' from work."

"Okay. See ya in a few."

He pushes his phone back in his pocket, finishes his drink, and sets his glass on the counter on his way out. The eerie blue light from the bar's rooftop sign pushes back at the dark. The empty lot just across the street is like a black hole, a watchful, hidden presence. The wind is still and the air is sharp with moisture. It's better on Oly Way, warm with the heat of the passing cars.

He rubs his hands inside of Marjorie's, sitting at a table in back. The Chevelle pulls in a few minutes later. It occurs to him that he hasn't seen Fin since Jimbo started on his rampage. He doesn't blame him with a car like that. The sight of Fin's face surprises him though. His eyes are deep inside dark purple hollows. Sitting down, he looks around quickly with a flitting motion of his eyes. They flicker over to Ray, warm up with a quick smile.

"Thanks for coming out."

Ray shrugs. "Gotta eat."

Fin nods. "How're you doin'?"

"Good."

"Good," he answers back.

"You okay?"

"Yeah, sure. Why?"

"You're sweatin'."

"I am?" He feels his face. The sides of his nose and cheeks are wet. "Fuck. I am. Weird."

"You an' your girl okay?"

His fingers move dismissively. "That's fine. I keep wakin' 'er up though. I can't sleep. I should probably take something."

"Why don't you?"

He shrugs. Ray doesn't push him. It's not really his business. He sits back in his chair as the waitress approaches, a thin worn out woman with her eyebrows penciled in. She reminds him of his mother's friend, Marie, and he realizes he isn't even sure if Marie's alive anymore. He orders the crab ravioli.

"I'll have that, too," says Fin. "An' water. Just water."

Ray can hear the dryness in his throat. It's a painful sound that makes him look away, giving him privacy for something only they can see. Gestures and colors move on the glass. He looks back at the other people in the room. Wine glasses clink, rims hitting the edges of plates as people lift them, drinking.

"You've got it bad," he says quietly and Fin looks at him in shock. His pupils dilate, nostrils flaring as he draws in a breath. Then his eyes lower and his lids squeeze shut for a moment. His voice is low. "Pretty bad, I guess."

"Anything I can do?" He's not used to helping people. It feels strange on him.

"No. I called you. That's all."

"Glad you did."

"What can you do?"

"I dunno, bub. But I've got time. No worries."

Fin breathes in, gives him a slight, ironic smile. "Well," he says. "At least the ravioli's supposed to be pretty good."

Ray grins back at him. "At these prices? Goddam better be."

That night, Scott comes home, swings into the carport, headlights catching the garbage cans before he can stop. They fly backwards at the impact, hit the wall and careen back into his front grill.

The sound of the crash wakes Errol, but he doesn't come out to see.

After the metallic echoes fade, it grows quiet again.

Coming home, she sees all the lights on, Fin's Chevelle in the driveway. She pulls in beside it, goes inside, dropping her purse on the counter. Fin's on the couch, watching TV. Ray's asleep in a chair, feet up on the coffee table. There's a glass of orange juice on the table by Fin.

"Hi," she whispers.

"Hi. Is this okay? My being here?"

"Why not?" She smiles, bending down to kiss Ray's forehead. He stirs but doesn't wake. "I'm going to bed though."

"Okay. Thanks."

Lying down, she smiles, feeling almost happy again. They leave before she gets up. In the morning, she straightens up the house, goes out for groceries, watches TV, makes a sandwich that she puts in the refrigerator for Ray. After that though, she loses her feeling of happiness. She probably won't see him. She thinks sometimes about quitting her job, but then she almost panics because she likes her job and she's pretty sure she wouldn't be good at anything else. She can serve drinks and she usually makes people smile. She likes to make people smile. She used to be able to do that for Ray.

With his sandwich made, she sits on the side of the bed, playing that game that he's going to leave her again. She'll come home and he'll be sitting where she is now, just waiting for her. Then he'll get up and touch her face and say, "I'm sorry, lady. I just can't do it."

She looks in his drawers, hesitantly, pulling the top drawer open slowly. She looks again as if Cora's pictures will miraculously reappear. She pulls out the ones that remain. Ed in a suit. Son with his arm around the waist of a smiling girl. Ed on Ray's couch, staring fixedly into the camera. She worries about Cora, but his demons are really here. She tries to remember the sound of Ed's voice, that strange timbre.

And then, all of a sudden, she feels the worry drain away.

Cora's pictures belong here, with Ed's. They are a part of a whole that isn't whole anymore. Like an ice flow breaking off, thunderously exploding into the ocean, free, rootless.

She puts the pictures away and picks up one of his tee-shirts and breathes him in, filling herself with the life force that is the whole everyone else attaches to.

The house is dark, only the porch light on, and Ray starts to pace before he remembers Irene with her cigarettes, pacing, thinking of Wayne maybe, who was maybe thinking of her while he sat on his own porch, drinking a beer without her in St. Louis. Irene always made Ray painfully aware of Wayne's absence.

By the door he sees the flip-flops with the flowers Miri doesn't wear anymore and doesn't throw away either. The chaise lounge on the lawn is covered in rust like the doughboy pool at home.

In the kitchen, he opens a beer and takes a swallow and thinks of going back out to see her. The window over the sink is open, but the cold feels good. He drinks some more and doesn't go out, and not going out becomes a real thing like her flip-flops or the lounge chair or her arms, real and skinny, not Cora's or Kathy's or anybody else's.

Then his beer is gone. He puts the bottle in the sink, squeezes the sink's cold rim for a moment, then goes back out and rides over to the Club.

The air is colder, the stars are a bright white, and the light coming through the gaps in the shutters at the bar look warm. He rides around to the back where it's darker and sits quietly for a while. Music comes muffled through the walls, then blasts out through the door as somebody emerges. Muffled again, footsteps. Then the sound of an engine and tiny rocks popping as the car pulls out. When the quiet returns, he goes inside, catches sight of her quickly. She's wearing a shirt with little red hearts, a red denim skirt and her red go-go boots. It isn't cold inside, but she has a frozen look he remembers on Kathy's face when he left with Ed for the last time. He thinks of the flip-flops she won't throw away and swivels on the stool he sits down on as she comes around the bar and starts to wipe at a spot that doesn't need wiping.

"Hey."

"Hi, Ray."

She comes over to pour him a drink. He is resting his weight on his forearms, looking at the scoop neck of her shirt, the freckles on her chest. She starts to blush and he says, "I can't see you bein' a stripper."

Then her blush deepens and she looks at the other people at the bar, picks up her cloth again and says, "I have to work."

He shrugs and she takes her cloth, going over to a table near the door. He follows and sits down, putting his drink down after she wipes the table and leaves again. He drinks slowly and she keeps looking at him. Once he winks at her and laughs when she shakes her head and looks away. After a while, he gets up, letting Otis pour him another drink, stares at her, and then goes back to his table. She opens a bottle of water and looks over at him. He pushes a chair out with his foot. She hesitates but then approaches and sits down. "Cute top," he says.

She nods without saying anything and starts to play with a button in the shape of a heart.

"I saw this dude the other day," he says, making her eyes rise back up. She stares at him while he talks about Errol and his mattress and garbage cans. "I don't think I could get that worked up about somethin' I wasn't even using even if I did own it. Who the fuck has that kind of energy? I mean the dude must be sittin' inside plottin' this out. I take what I want," he says, leaning a little closer to her, resting some of his weight on the arm of his chair. "You know that. I own shit, sure. I want the stuff I use. The stuff I don't use? Fuck it. Anything else? That's just hella crazy." Smiling, he says the word 'crazy' again in a sing song voice, making her think of the Patsy Cline song.

"Say that again," she says. "That word. Like you're singing it."

"That word?"

"Crazy."

His smile grows and he leans closer to her, singing, "Crazy," in a voice she can barely hear, breathing his warm, bourbon-sweet breath at her. His warmth fills her and her body feels heavy. He grins. "You like that?"

"Yes," she murmurs, leaning closer. Her lips touch his.

"That's a real song, right?"

"Patsy Cline."

"Yeah."

He cups the back of her neck, kissing her slowly before he sits back up. He thinks again about the song his mother used to sing every morning. The sound of her voice drawing him awake, mixing with the sounds of running water, the heater, the ticking clock.

He was humming it once, catching Otis's smile. "What?"

"That's an oldie. Way before your time. Mine too."

"What is it?"

"Judy Garland. I'm Nobody's Baby."

"Yeah, yeah. That's right."

When they leave, Miri follows him, but he gets home first and sits on the porch outside, light on above the door, waiting for her. A few minutes later, she stops at the bottom of the steps and smiles up at him.

"Hi, Ray."

"Hiya, lady."

———————

In the morning, Jimbo goes over to Will's, but Susie won't open the door all the way. He puts his foot in and she pushes at it and sounds like she's crying.

"Get out!"

"Fuck you. Just tell me where Will is."

"I don't know!"

He backs up and almost kicks the door, but it isn't glass so he doesn't. At Andy's he starts into the apartment complex, then jogs suddenly across the street to the liquor store where he rips the paper about the reward off the telephone pole. When Andy answers his door, Jimbo pushes it open because he can and Will's there on the couch with a pillow against the arm and a blanket on his lap.

Jimbo stops.

"You sick?"

"No." His voice sounds weak though.

Andy's straddling the other arm of the couch, cupping the end of it in his hands. He looks at Will, looks glad there's somebody else there too now.

"You look sick."

"I am sick."

Andy shrugs, then smiles, looking at the paper Jimbo brought in. "You collectin' those?" Jimbo balls it up and throws it at him and Andy catches it and opens it back up. "Like I said, man, you aren't goin' for a whole lot."

Will's laugh surprises him. He looks over and Will sits up, takes the paper away and then says, "We have to go to Kmart, man. Jimbo's on sale."

Andy doesn't want to laugh in front of Jimbo, but he can't help it. Jimbo sits down, awkwardly, his face put-upon. Then Will yawns, gets up and pours a bowl of cereal. But he doesn't eat it. Instead, he sets it on the coffee table and says, "I need a Fry Baby."

When Will starts patting at his pockets, looking for his keys, Andy jumps up and says, "Yeah, yeah. Me too," because Will is leaving and Jimbo isn't.

Outside, Will's sudden good humor dissolves again though and he throws his arms up over his face.

"Goddam sun."

At the shop, Ray is sitting outside and Carl is leaning against the windowsill across the street, looking up at a cloudless blue sky. Cars on Oly Way rush by like water.

Across the street, Errol is looking for his garbage cans. They are half collapsed now, smashed by Scott's fender and the wall they flew into, but

Errol can only see the rings they made in the slightly damp dirt. He backs away. At the garage he throws the door up and Scott stops in the middle of the living room and says, "What was that?"

Carl shrugs. Mr Torch knows. He can see things over the sill and under doors. He can hear a pin drop.

"I heard you might be sellin' this place," says a man below.

Carl can only hear Ray's laugh, but Mr Torch can hear him agree. "Price is right, I will."

Carl's window fills with light, warm bright sunlight slipping low. Shadows stretch. On the street below, Ray is standing in cool shade. The man he is talking to leaves, then he goes inside, comes back out again a moment later, starts to get on his bike and then stops and looks into the dark behind the shop where there is a twinkle of light on something that wasn't there the day before. He goes around his bike and crosses over, boots crunching on gravel before the dirt starts up again, pulls back a bush and sees a pair of garbage cans behind it. There is a pause, maybe while he thinks about what he's looking at, and then he starts to laugh.

Mr Torch smiles.

Carl's eyes close, hearing him laugh fleetingly inside his head, light and soft, a sound that never ends. He settles back, sensing Mr Torch's pity. He doesn't need Mr Torch's pity though. He needs that laugh and wishes he could have lived his whole life laughing.

At Errol's, Ray sets the garbage cans down and Errol peeks out with a sense of wonder. Ray grins.

"Have a good day, bub."

As the sun begins to fall, Jonah looks outside and pictures Agnes coming out of the trees, backs away and closes the door on her image. She fades at the steps, though, not knocking or coming in, so he goes into the living room again and stares at the TV. The light is quiet and gray. He sees a jar or just a glass on top of the TV.

Later, at Kurt's, he hugs her and smells her shampoo. "Your hair's wet," he says.

"I just washed it."

At Kmart, Will points at everything with a 'For Sale' sign. "Jimbo!" Andy grimaces a smile at him. Will likes the slow way Andy follows him, hands stuffed in the pockets of his jeans, pushing them down on his hips, a strip of skin showing between pants and sweatshirt. He is scruffy, blue eyes puffy and sullen, and people veer away from him. This is what Will likes, to be followed by somebody other people are afraid of. Will likes people to be afraid of him too. He is pretty sure Jimbo is. Not Andy though. Andy just wants drugs and Will is the Pied Piper. That makes him happy too.

Andy follows him. Sullenly. Glowering. Always in control though.

Will admits that. Jimbo doesn't use the way Andy does, but he's never really in control.

"You must have a high metabolism," Will says, looking back at Andy's cautious face.

"I dunno."

"Get a Fry Baby."

"I don't wanna Fry Baby. I like cereal."

"You're like a fuckin' grocery store," says Will, breezily, happily going up and down the aisles.

Andy's cupboards are full of cereal boxes. Cap'n Crunch. Cocoa Puffs. Rice Krispies. Trix. Will is suddenly hungry. Outside he pulls his sunglasses off, blinking cautiously in the dark. The parking lot lights emit a light bluish glow that doesn't really bother him. Coming out of the parking lot, he turns in the opposite direction of home. Beside him, Andy stiffens and looks over. "Where we goin'?"

"Ray's."

"Fuck, man."

"What? Poker. Chill."

Will can feel Andy's nerves the way Craig's cousin could always sense things with him. Thinking of Craig's cousin, though, makes him clench up angrily. His knuckles are white on the steering wheel, voice rough. "Fuck is it with you an' him anyway?"

"Nothin'. I just don't like gettin' lectured."

"Lectured?" Will likes the idea of lecturing. "Lectured about what?"

"About my fuckin' sister an' that Joe Clay dude."

"Your fault."

Andy looks away with a glower, ignoring him. Will doesn't care. Now he can't get the thought of Craig's cousin out of his mind and it's upsetting him. His fingers squeeze and roll on the steering wheel. He begins to feel light-headed and rocks up and back. Sometimes he thinks he's about to float away and grabs onto whatever's near him to hold on. He remembers the feel of Craig's cousin's throat in his fingers. His knuckles ache. At Ray's, it takes him a moment to release the steering wheel. He can feel Andy's curious gaze.

"Get outta my car."

Andy does, slamming the door behind him. Will follows him inside. Ray is in the living room, sitting on the couch. "Getch yourselves a beer," he says.

"Food?" asks Will.

"Take what you want."

Andy stays in the kitchen, watching Will look around. There are chips on top of the refrigerator, but Will's eyes continue to roam. Then he sees the onions in a metal basket and opens a cupboard door.

"Wonder bread!"

Andy stares, watching him make a lettuce and onion sandwich. He scoops up mayonnaise with the biggest spoon in the drawer, notices Andy's stare. "What?"

"You're gonna eat that?"

"You don't like onions?"

"I like cereal. Taco Bell."

Will's eyes gleam and he jabs the spoon in Andy's direction, nodding, mouth full of raw onion.

In the other room, Ray says, "C'mon in, bub," before there's even a knock on the door. With its opening, a breeze blows straight through the house.

Will takes his sandwich out on a paper towel where Kurt is now sitting on the other end of the couch from Ray. Susie's friend. Will sits on a chair, thinking of Susie with a welling of grief. His eyes down, he reaches up to pat at the sunglasses that aren't there. He looks at Ray sitting with his ankle across his knee and his elbow on the arm of the couch, wiping at his smile with a thumb.

"Good onions." Will can always taste onions. "I got me a Fry Baby today," he says before he takes another bite.

"What for?"

"Fries."

"Oh."

The bread is soft, and even when he can't taste it, he likes the feel. The first time he realized he could taste onions even when he couldn't taste anything else was when his mother made tuna fish sandwiches. She added chopped onions to the tuna and he remembers eating slowly because he didn't want her to know that he could taste it.

"Real good onions," he says.

Ray gets up and goes into the kitchen. He takes a bottle of bourbon out of the cupboard and rubs his face. The table takes up most of the open space, but he pulls it out a little anyway and Kurt slips in against the wall. Andy is standing in the doorway, back against the frame. Ray pours a drink, takes a long swallow, and then another car pulls up outside. Andy can see Will's face droop, eyelids lowering as he looks out the window. Will gets up, swallowing the last of his sandwich and opens the door, letting in Craig.

Craig doesn't speak, edges around him. Will's heart hurts. Now he has to think about Craig's cousin. He walks sluggishly into the kitchen, sits down and says, "Get over here," to Andy. Andy sighs and pulls out the chair beside him.

Ray opens the cupboard door where the glasses are, sets a couple on the counter, pours another drink, sits down, and shuffles the cards. After he deals, Will looks at his cards, looks back at Ray, and says, "Pair."

"Wanna ante up first?"

"Preparatory."

Ray nods. "Preparatory." He looks at Kurt. Will looks at him too, then so does Andy, following Will's stare. Kurt looks back nervously. Ray taps gently at the deck of cards and says, "You're quiet, man. Everything okay?"

"Just thinkin'," says Kurt.

"Quit it," says Will.

Ray deals out a few more cards, smiling at Will. "Wouldn't catch Will doin' that."

"Hell, no," says Will.

Andy stares intently at the table.

"What's so interestin' anyway?" asks Ray.

"Nothin' really," says Kurt. "Just work."

"Give it a rest a while," advises Ray.

"I admire people who work for a living," says Will.

Andy can't help it. He laughs. Ray is laughing too, but it's Andy Will is staring at. "What're you laughing at?"

"That's a hell of a weird thing to say," says Ray.

"Not you," mutters Andy.

"Yeah, you were. Fuck's up with you lately, Andy?"

"C'mon, bub. Chill. We're supposed to be havin' fun here."

Will slowly shifts his eyes to Ray, Kurt, Craig. Craig meets his eyes nervously, face flushing with worry. He didn't laugh though. Will squints, feeling the light beginning to hurt his eyes. He slaps Andy hard on the arm. "Get my shades."

Andy gets up without a word, disappears outside, returns a few minutes later with Will's sunglasses. Will sighs, putting them on. He looks at Craig again.

Ray nudges him. "You out or in?"

"Out."

Craig gives Will a nervous, twitchy smile. Will squints behind his glasses, trying to see a resemblance to Craig's cousin. They are built alike maybe, tough and spare. Will misses Craig's cousin but he can't let on to that. He can't let on that Jimbo got the best of him. It was Jimbo's fault and he looks at Andy with a mildly fond expression. Andy squirms and looks away.

Ray sighs. "Will, man."

"What?"

"New round."

"Oh."

He plays distractedly. The room is growing dark, even when he dips his sunglasses down. Without Craig's cousin he won't be able to see at all. He didn't always like it that Craig's cousin could see things, though. When they first met, their families had just moved into the neighborhood. Craig's cousin was rolling up and down the street on a skateboard. When he saw Will, he jumped off, flipped up one end to catch hold of it and said, "Okay."

Will was just about to offer him some Cocoa Puffs out of the box he was already stretching out to him. He remembers the bareness of that neighborhood, no fences between the houses yet, spindly baby trees. Will always believed that Craig's cousin's gift was for him, but there was a time when he knew more about the things Craig's cousin could do, that he said, "That's special," in a tone that meant he didn't like special things. Special things weren't normal. They stood out. His mother almost stood out.

"Your mom looks like Mrs Cleaver," said Craig's cousin. "That's totally cool."

One day Will stood out too. That was when he hid behind the bushes at Craig's cousin's house and Will's mother came out and stood on the porch. She looked around for him and her eyes were worried. Maybe she got in trouble too. The thought made him antsy and he almost got up, but then he didn't. Instead, he waited for her to go back inside and then he came out from behind the bushy hedge and walked away. He was already dealing drugs, but Craig's cousin told him not to use any and for a long time he didn't. That night though he got so high that he floated off to a place that he sometimes went to even without drugs. The next day, he went home. This was after he realized that he could break a glass or rob a liquor store and he'd get the same belt, the same number of times. It didn't matter what he did. He supposed there was some principle involved, but he had long ago lost the energy to care. He liked floating, the blissful feeling of not really being there. But he always went home anyway because he really wanted them to love him even if he didn't know that.

"I'm out," he says, mainly because he can't see his cards. His eyes feel itchy and he blinks at a strange dampness. He thinks of Susie, pictures her face with a cramping pain in his gut.

"Our factory's got a new manufacturing site," says Kurt. "We can put in for a transfer if we want. I don't think I will, though."

"Where would you go?"

"Medford."

Ray shrugs. "Don't think I'd bother."

"I'm pretty good where I am."

On the day Will went back home, his mother called his father and his father came home from work. When he came into Will's room and started to take his belt off, Will said, "You'll be sorry when I choke you to death with it." After a moment his father backed out and closed the door. When he came out that evening, his father got up and they sat down in the dining room and began to eat. After that, his father never came into his room again, but he still couldn't taste things.

"I had a job once," says Will suddenly. "I bought my car with that money."

An amused smile slowly lights Ray's face. "Lemme guess where. Jack-in-the-Box?"

"Yeah!"

In the dark, fir needles skitter. Around the front of the apartment building, Joy's wind chimes catch the light inside and glitter like ovals of milky glass. The colored ones are shades of dark.

Upstairs, Jonah's eyes move as Kurt comes in, sucking up pop through a straw. "Hey," he says, pushing himself up higher on the pillows. A bottle of beer rests on his chest. Kurt opens one too, setting his pop in the sink, and looks at the TV.

"News?"

"Yeah."

"Hear about the new site?"

"What's it to me?" he says quietly.

Kurt takes a drink and swallows. "What if it's a bust? Expandin' like this? Think it'll come back on us?"

Jonah smiles, rolling his head toward him. "Who's askin' us?"

Kurt sighs. "That's kind of the thing. I wish somebody would."

"No use sweatin' it."

"I guess not."

Tossing the clothes on a chair onto the floor, Kurt sits down and puts his feet up on the corner of the bed. Jonah looks away, back at the TV. A flutter of light and movement across his eyes, a low drone in his ears. It is Agnes he sees, her wooly hair, her eyes rising up, the glitter of the stars that fade to a dim flicker above all the lights, as phantom pale as the moon he saw earlier. A moon like a moon he saw over the roof of the garage at home one day a long time ago. Wispy and pale with light gray shadows. It loomed in the dawn sky. He went into work sick that day and then Ira took him back home, letting him out at the bottom of the road. After Ira drove off, he walked up a ways and then stopped at the place where Samuel first wanted to make Ivy's pond and where he saw the grouse on the day of Job's funeral. Looking down there at the glassy black water, he recalled that still, almost paper-like shape below and could almost feel Aster's breath of wonder at it like a ghost against his cheek.

"Look," she whispered.

Pulling himself away, he started walking again and when he got to the house, he took his boots off. The TV was on, the volume up, an explosion, cartoon-like, as he pushed through the screen door. A *Road Runner* cartoon. Sissy's favorite. She wasn't watching though. The living room was empty, a jar of Aster's homemade cold cream that Abel gave to Sissy on top of the TV. The air smelled a little like strawberries. The shadows of snowflakes decorated the floor. He got his coat halfway off, heard the heater thump and felt the air blowing out. It made a muffled sound, or maybe it wasn't the air. He went down the hall with his coat half off. Sissy's door was ajar, and when he pushed it all the way open Abel froze for a moment and then got off her and pulled his pants up.

There was no surprise, he felt no surprise at all, just gravity, a sky as gray and heavy as iron, breaking him underneath its weight. His voice broke too, the voice he grew into, slow and slumberous. "You sick fuck."

Then Abel hit him, catching him with his arms still inside his coat. He fell against the wall, twisting to get free, foot up, kicking back at Abel. Fingers grabbed his ankle and pulled. He fell onto the floor, got one arm out of his coat and whipped it through the air. Abel grabbed it and yanked him over, kicking him in the side of the head. He fell, suddenly groggy and hot. He got his other arm free, rolled over, and felt that gray sky crashing down on him, except the sky was as bony as Abel's knees, iron knobs breaking him into pieces. He sucked at the air, face in the carpet, lungs full of grime and dust.

"You fuck!"

He thought he yelled, or Abel did. He got an elbow under him, freed it, slamming it back into Abel's face. The weight rose and he felt light, scrambling away, hearing Abel grunt and thump up against the wall as he rose, Sissy's cartoons on the TV, bright light flashing, snowflake shadows moving across the floor. Jonah got up, felt the air burst out of him, Abel slamming him back down again. He dug his fingers into the carpet, Abel's fingers on the back of his pants, pulling. He kicked out, twisting half over, Abel's foot stomping him in the belly. He grabbed at chair legs, the corner of a wall, feeling his shirt pull up as Abel dragged him, feeling the coolness of linoleum, the rough wood of the door to the service porch. His fingers grabbed on, his body suspended in air as Abel pulled, abruptly stopped, grabbed a bottle of Gatorade off one of the shelves and smashed Jonah's fingers with it. Jonah let go, kicked up into Abel's crotch and sent him staggering back. He got up just as Abel picked up the bottle again and flung it. It hit him under the eye, knocking him back against the wall and down onto the floor again. He heard crying sounds, a wailing, "Fucker!"

The puffiness of his eye half-blinded him. Abel was the shade of utter blackness. He swung and felt his fist hit Abel's face. Then his head hit the floor. Abel was pulling him again, down the steps, Jonah's head hitting every board. The gray sky turned bright with color and sparks. The gravel underneath him was ice. His pants rode low on his hips, his shirt bunched up. Abel's knees dropped heavily onto his bare belly. He retched, blinded by sparks and colored motes. Again, he heard that crying, wailing sound and pain filled his head and he retched again. The weight lifted and he rolled over. Fingers pulled him up by the hair and he felt his face smashed down. Gravel, like bits of ice, cut him open. A singing sound filled his head, a whistling wind that was icy and numbing so that everything he felt came from far away, and in some sense, always remained that way. Then he felt Abel's fingers growing still in his hair and there was a moaning sound that wasn't his.

"Fuck, fuck, fuck."

Abel thought he was dead, but he wasn't. He felt cold air underneath him, his head lolling back and the ground dragging at him as Abel pulled him across the gravel. He wanted to tell Abel that he wasn't dead, but nothing came out. Wails filled his chest, howls of terror, but the only sounds came from Abel, grunts as Abel pulled on him. Jonah's lolling head kept bouncing off the ground, dragging. On the inside, he was begging, blubbering, *"Don't let me die! Please don't let me die!"* His heart beat in a thunderous panic.

But Abel didn't answer, just kept dragging him. Urine flooded his jeans, but Abel didn't stop. Then he fell again, not far, lying with his head and neck twisted sideways. He couldn't move. He heard footsteps recede, then the light faded out.

"*Pleeeease....*"

Alone, his heart beat itself into exhaustion.

In the dark, he woke up again. His eyes and mouth were filled with blood. It covered his face and it was cold and dark and he saw the moon and the edges of a shingleless hole in the roof and the silver sides of the rafters and a deep empty dark.

In his memory though, it's always the way he told Orly. He's always on the roof with his frozen fingers grabbing onto air, always falling through to some place so far below he never seems to reach it.

When Jonah leaves in the morning, Joy is coming outside with a bucket of water. They look at each other when they pass but don't say anything.

In the lot at Ray's, the weeds are the color of limes, willowy curves as sparrows swoop and flutter.

Inside, dust floats as bright as gold.

On a couch that isn't his, Will is covering his face with his arms. The drapes are open and this is the side of the house the sun comes up on. It's warm and feels good, but he rolls away anyway.

Will's sure the sun's reflecting off the cushion into his face.

"Hey, babe!" After a moment, Miri comes out in one of Ray's tee-shirts and he rolls back over and says, "Close the drapes, will ya?"

Then he sits up, squinting, because she doesn't come over. "You have no heart," he bleats, then covers his face with a hand and grabs at the drapes with the other.

"Use the cord."

He can't see through his fingers though and grabs a fistful of drapes and cord, pulling both as he tries to twist away from the sun. A slight resistance pulls him back and then the rod pops off the wall and the drapes drop on top of him and pull him down to the carpet where the sun shines underneath. He hears a slapping sound, Miri's hands on her thighs, and then she says, "Great, Will" and leaves to get dressed.

He hears that too and sits up in a muggy glare.

"Hey!"

When Miri tells Ray he doesn't even laugh, just shakes his head and says, "Moron."

At home, Will goes in with a Kmart bag and a white box, puts the bag down on the floor, and goes into the living room with the box. The TV in the bedroom is on. Going in, he stops, seeing Susie scoot away. She covers up her face, fat lip, puffy nose. Will sucks in a breath, then holds the box out in both hands.

"Coconut cream," he says.

Then she sees the name Candi's in hot pink letters on the top of the box and climbs slowly off the bed, swiping at her eyes. He inches over, his chest hitching with sobs. Susie takes the box, almost awestruck.

"I love coconut cream."

"I love you," he says plaintively, his face scrunched up in misery. She puts the box on the bed and goes back over to him. His arms open and she pulls his face down and rubs his neck, feeling him grow softer and warmer. His tears dampen her skin.

"I love my boy," she whispers.

He rubs his face against her and picks her up, going over to the bed. Letting him lay her down, she wraps her legs around him and holds his face above hers, memorizing the look of his damp cheeks and tender eyes.

At the end of the day, Miri gets onto Ray's bike, and when he says, "Where to?" she's quiet for a moment, then she presses up against him and says, "The ocean."

"Pretty far."

"I don't care," she says. "That's where."

It's dark when they get there. All they can see are misty lights and the gray of the fog; the only sound is of waves, deep and rolling.

"Like it?"

"I love it," she murmurs, remembering foggy days when she was growing up, seagulls flying by, misty gray and lonely sounding.

26

◆ Going...Going...Goodbye ◆

They don't really talk anymore. Ally looks at the things in the house, sometimes at just the way the light comes in under the eaves, always dim and soft. It only shines in fully in the mornings. One day he sees her like that, sitting on the edge of the couch with her coffee cup on her knees and Asa on a blanket on the floor.

"Are you okay?"

When she looks up, she smiles slowly.

"This is such a pretty place."

Maybe he's wrong: maybe she won't leave. Maybe she'll stay, only want to go.

His feelings confuse him. In his mind, Ally and Agnes are always together.

On the porch one day when he says, "Goodbye, baby," it doesn't sound like forever. There's a stillness in her though. She stares for a moment, almost comes back to the steps, then smiles like always, and he thinks maybe she didn't hear it. It's a sunny day, windy and bright. "Bye, Mister."

"Bye," he murmurs again and then she is running off through Clover's flowers.

At the river, she feels the air grow cool and damp and goes through dark and wintry shadows, glimpses silver blue and sunlit water. At home, she sees Doug's car and begins to slow.

Above, there's a tiny sliver of a moon.

The sky is bluish and the stars aren't out yet. Kurt is happy at this time of year. Outside, Wes says, "Bingo tonight," and Kurt gives him a look. Wes doesn't fit his image of a bingo player.

"I won the football pool," says Kurt, and that reminds him to go to Ray's house after work.

"I always lose at those," says Wes. "Bingo an' the lottery. Pure luck."

"Yeah. Which I never have."

Wes laughs. "I think this might be your year though. I have a pretty good feelin' about that."

Kurt perks up. Even though there's still the problem of the football pool. When George asked Ray if he wanted to play too, Ray said, "No cash on me," and George said, "No problem. Pay when you can." Now, weeks later, Kurt is waiting for Ray to remember.

On his way past the bowling alley and his apartment, he rolls his window down. The air is soft and pleasant feeling and the moon looks as white as snow.

He can tell Ray isn't home because his bike isn't there, but he goes up to the door anyway and Miri smiles when she sees him. "Hi."

"Hi."

Inside, she takes a glass of wine off the coaster where she usually has her orange juice. "Want some?"

"Sure."

She pours him a glass and brings the bottle back out with her. He can see the freckles on her face when she sits back down. He drinks his wine, remembering that Jonah's supposed to come over to his place later, and almost out of reflex, pictures Joy's door being open. It almost always is, TV on, with something like a glass or a plate he can see on the coffee table that makes him think she really lives there, that she's really like other people, maybe lonely like him.

"Where's Ray?"

"Will's. There's a party," she adds.

Jimbo's guarding it and people are keeping out of his way. He goes from the kitchen to the living room, outside and back in again, drinking as he makes his circuit.

When Ray arrives, he starts to grin and stops in the front door, spreading his legs across the threshold. He never manages to say, "Invite only," though. The minute he opens his mouth, Ray slugs him in the solar plexus and pushes on through. Jimbo's immobilized. At first, the momentum of Ray's punch swung him away and slowly back again to fill up the door; now he stands without moving, just staring outside.

Andy comes up behind him, peering over his shoulder. "Okay, Jimbo?"

There's a laugh in his voice, but Jimbo can't hear it over the buzzing in his ears. "'Kay," he finally manages. After that he takes another breath, blinks in surprise.

The trees are darker against the sky.

At Miri's, Kurt drinks the last of the wine and gets up. She scoots out of her hollow on the couch and he can tell she wants him to stay. He wants to too, but he also wants to go. He is thinking about Joy but feels a strange lack of interest in her now. One more night, he thinks, of walking by her door. He thinks he is starting to resent her.

Miri gets up too. "Are you going by Will's?"

"Probably."

He knows he doesn't sound too enthused. It's the same feeling Joy's beginning to give him and for no reason he knows of. On the porch Miri watches him go, arms crossed in front of her.

Now the trees are lost against the sky.

"See ya, Miri."

"Bye."

At home, Jonah puts his boots on and goes out to the living room where Ally's sitting with the side of her face lit by the lamp beside the couch. Her eyes follow him to the chair where he sits on the arm and holds his keys with a finger through the ring.

"Think 'e likes that?" He means Asa, asleep in his car seat.

"I think so," she says, reaching out to slowly rock it.

"Almost like a swing," he observes, and thinks she almost pauses before she nods. He looks down at the carpet for a moment and then gets up. "Guess I better go."

Now she looks up too and seems to hesitate again and then says, "Are you working long?"

"Couple hours. Meetin' Kurt after though."

"Okay."

She looks pale or maybe it's just the color of the light beside her. He glances at the TV and then at the afghan on the floor at her feet. The couch is the one she wanted. The one from before was beige and brown.

"Anything you want me to bring home?"

She seems to think about it and even looks into the kitchen for ideas. "Cheese."

"What kind?"

"American."

"Okay." It makes him think of Aster's soup and sandwiches every day.

At work, he lights a cigarette and says, "Remind me to get some cheese."

"Cheetos," says Wally, who is leaning up against a car he parks under a light, reminding Jonah of Kurt in a way.

Everything feels the same and not the same anymore. He starts across the parking lot and Wally pushes away from his car to come too.

"Wish we didn't sign up," says Wally.

"Me either."

At the door, Jonah drops his cigarette and blows his smoke away. It drifts in the lamplight and a moth swoops like gold in the clear air. Inside, he sees some day people he doesn't know. Wally stops for coffee and Jonah waits for him to drink it.

"You goin' out tonight?" asks Wally.

"Yeah."

After work, Jonah gets another cup of coffee, sipping it as he goes down the hall. Outside, the air is still clear and a moth still swoops like spun gold under the lamps. It smells good out, like fir trees. At Kurt's he walks slowly, quietly, wondering if Joy hears his footsteps. It is past midnight, but her door is open and she is watching, waiting for him.

"I know your walk," she says.

"Yeah?" He is pushing open her screen with the toe of his boot.

"Come on in."

She sits up, scooting over to make room for him on the couch. He sits with his arm across the top and remembers Clete. He can tell Joy does too, just as she's aware of Agnes and smiles slowly, leaning sideways with her arm over his. Her eyes are a cool, pale blue like water that never ripples.

"Whach ya doin'?" he asks.

She smiles again.

"Nothing."

Kurt stares. There's a girl at a cooler with a beer. She yells at him, but the sounds in her mouth drown in the thunderous noise pounding inside Will's house. The girl looks wispy and dreamlike in the layers of smoke that surround her. As she waits, people jostle her.

Kurt yells back. *"What?!"*

His voice warbles. Other people in other solar systems are probably listening to Will's party. He imagines the model of the solar system he got for Christmas years ago spinning in the blasts of Will's speakers. The girl yells again, head cocked in a curious tilt, eyes alight and friendly.

Kurt laughs for no reason. When he arrived a few minutes ago, he went around back where a sudden burst of people came outside and one sat on the steps and said, "Fuck. Hot in there."

It was cold to Kurt, who looked into the dark and then said, "I'm looking for a guy named Ray."

"Yeah, I know 'im. Inside I think."

Then he was pushing by people he didn't know and stopping to talk to the girl by a cooler full of beer.

"*Lookin' for Ray!*"

Now she frowns and gives him a beer. He smiles at her, but she only waves her fingertips at him now and walks away.

People push past and he pushes too, trying to get through the living room. At the next door he stops and looks up at Jimbo, who is stooping under the door jamb, glowering at everybody in the room until he sees Kurt and points a bottle of bourbon at him. "*Wait up!*"

Kurt nods, but tries to get by anyway, thinks he sees the girl from the cooler in the other room.

"*Wait a minute!*"

Jimbo is wiping bourbon off his chin, scowling at Kurt's scowl. Kurt lifts his beer can into the air, squeezing by, almost through before Jimbo grabs him around the neck and pulls him up on his toes. His lips are close to Kurt's ear. "*I know you!*"

After the echoes dim, Kurt nods. "*Yeah!*"

Then Jimbo swings away and Kurt throws a palm up, just missing a door sill and slips outside when Jimbo stops to drink. A moment later though Jimbo is beside him again.

"Said wait up."

He isn't smiling anymore, coming up close to stare into Kurt's eyes. The porch that was crowded a moment before begins to empty. Jimbo is blinking across the yard. Kurt looks too, sees a patch of white. He thinks for a moment that it's the girl from the cooler, then decides it isn't. Stepping away quietly, he almost makes it back to the door.

Jimbo sways sideways, scowling at him.

"Whadda ya doin', anyway?"

"Lookin' for Ray."

A sudden flush colors Jimbo's face. "Hell for?"

Kurt thinks. "Owes me money."

Jimbo blows out a gust of air and wobbles for balance. "Fucker."

"Yeah," Kurt agrees.

Taking another step back, he's over the threshold. Bodies bob against him and he slips in-between. He keeps looking for the girl from the cooler. Her face was like a cartoon character's, all exaggerated liveliness. Shiny eyes, bow-shaped, mobile lips. He liked that, but he can't find her. Then he thinks he hears Ray's laugh and squeezes his way back outside again. Jimbo's spinning a circle on the back porch. His arm swings back for a punch at Ray and he smashes Kurt in the face with his elbow. Kurt flies back and bounces off the side of the house. His face hits the porch.

Jimbo says, "Ow," then Kurt rolls over, staring airlessly up into Jimbo's look of pain. Ray is looking down at him too, then at Jimbo. "Hell you do that for?"

Jimbo just rubs his elbow, glowering at Ray.

"Asshole."

She will lull herself away, disappear in the way that spirits can't. A wispy breath that will float off with the morning mists.

Jonah looks at her, cheek against her palm on the doorframe, lips in a cool smile, eyes on the dark beyond, moonless, her birdbath in shadow, all that awaits, waiting for her.

She will fade almost peacefully into the dawn.

Coming back a step, he leans in closer to her. "You know Kurt's favorite name?"

"Angeline."

"Yeah."

Upstairs, he lies down and dreams about Agnes and strawberries and windy, sunny skies and tomato soup and Aster's eyes and angels with Sissy's face and a spirit like Joy's that rises up and vanishes in sunshine; and rainbows and cool, green water and empty, blue skies. And in his dream, he hears Abel laughing again.

It's windy out, all of a sudden, fir and spruce needles blowing, a whoosh in the air.

Sinking down onto Will's back porch with a yawn, Jonah looks sideways at Kurt's puffy nose, then swipes a sudden smile off his face and looks away again.

"Thought you were too tanked to drive?"

"I am."

"Looks a little worse than that."

Kurt snuffles, only stopping to drink out of the bottle of bourbon he's holding onto until Jonah pulls it away, drinking too. Then Jonah lets the bottle swing between his knees, following Kurt's stare to a wisp of white across the yard. Jonah thinks of Clover in her slip, thin as a veil, on the day she died. She lives in the stories Job told, following him, a movement under the trees, swelling like a sheet on the line, filling with the breeze, then settling again. He takes a drink and looks up as Will goes by and stops on the grass with his arms wide open. Andy comes out too and leans on the railing. He is laughing under his breath. Susie is crossing the grass, wearing her slippers and a white and yellow flannel nightgown. It billows as she walks.

Andy laughs again. "Cool party dress."

"Screw you."

Jonah watches her pull Will back to the chaise lounge under the fir trees, then glances sideways at Kurt, who is pushing cautiously at his nose.

Jonah feels the urge to laugh. Instead he just shakes his head and says, "You're a fuckin' shit magnet, you know that?"

Kurt nods, almost agreeably. "Yeah, I know."

Ally is home, surprising him in a way. He feels tired and his steps are slow. He stopped for a while at the place where Abel died. There was light down below and he whispered, "Pops," and imagined the wind, almost still, as motionless as the water.

As the screen closes, he hears the creak of wood in the garage and smells the dampness of old pipes. She moves away as he comes closer. Then she stops and he does too. She folds her hands underneath her chin and he can see the whiteness of her knuckles, a blanching under her eyes.

"Please understand," she says. "I waited to tell you."

"Tell me what?"

"That I'm leaving."

He imagines the whiteness of his own knuckles, clenched tightly, the scars on his face beginning to flame.

"Just like that? You're leaving me?"

"It's not just like that, Jonah."

"Then what's it like?"

"I want you to be happy."

He gives a quick laugh. "Happy?"

"I don't make you happy."

"You never tried."

"Jonah—" He slams a fist into the wall, making her jump back, hands at her mouth now. "Jonah, please...."

"Where's Asa?"

"Home."

"Home? This is home." His knuckles hurt. He brings his hand up, flexing his fingers, feeling a stiffness in his jaw, a burning in his face. "Just like that?"

Her head moves slowly, back and forth. "This happened a long time ago."

Her words have a distant feel to them too and he feels himself deflate. "Don't go, Ally."

She backs up into the hall where the light never comes in all the way and a dark, disembodied shape appears in the bedroom door, and for a moment, without knowing it, he is at home. He follows her, her hands coming free to feel for the walls, brushing against Sissy's doorknob. But he doesn't look at that, only at her. The light in the hall is the faint light he saw at Joy's when he thought of spirits disappearing. Now he'll be alone again. Then his fingers close on her arm. But his face is cooling and he feels sleepy and languorous as if he's swum for a long time, fought the silty lure of Ivy's green water for days.

He pulls her to him and hugs her, feeling her arms come tentatively around him. "I never meant to hurt you."

She is quiet, but she stays in his arms, hugging him back.

They don't move for a while and then he straightens and looks into their room that once was Clover's and Job's and Aster's and Abel's, where a drawer in the dresser in open and empty with violets on the paper inside.

At Ivy's the sky is clear and moonless. He sinks and looks up and it's dark and sunless too. He comes up with a gasp and hears the stir of needles.

Outside of the house, Ally stares up into the dark, cool trees and then gets into her car. It starts and Jonah floats. His chest in the air feels like ice. In the wind, fir needles drop and scatter, an echo blowing away.

"Pops!"

27

✦ Godspeed ✦

Mr Torch shimmers with benevolence, a light against the shadowless wall. At Carl's, the curtains stir and flowers bloom outside and golden motes of pollen blow away. At springtime, Mr Torch is philosophic at silver windswept puddles, at the smell of water in the air.

George and Ray are outside, Ray with an arm over the top of his sign. "Make 'um keep my name," he says with a laugh.

"Don't even sell. Get a manager."

He shrugs and taps his sign with the tops of his fingers. He's thought of it, especially now with the feel of the sun on the rustling air and the weed-choked lot beginning to bloom. The cool shadows in the shop dwell in familiar places, the smell of the house and the heater that still kicks in every morning. He'll think about this place the way he thinks about the house he grew up in, Ed, even Cora. The pain in his gut every time he thinks of this is new though and irritates him like the ache in his fingers.

"Too much work," he says finally.

At Mr Torch's, it's sunny. At Will's, it's dark inside and milky at Carl's and full of shadows at Grace's and dusty gray beams at George and Henry's.

At the factory, softness spreads across the sky and birds make dark specks in the distance. Inside Wes says, "This OT's pure torture."

Kurt just swallows his milk and takes a bite of pickle, which makes him twitch in his chair and screw up his face every time. Afterwards, he sighs and says, "I like the money though."

He is floating on happiness.

Upstairs, Ally's violets are abloom and sunshine pours in and an angel with a big smile glows in Kurt's heart. "Seen the new girl?" he asks.

Wes nods. "Cute."

"Nice smile," says Kurt. When he first saw her, he stood by his cubby with his mouth half open.

"Ask 'er out," says Wes.

Kurt finishes his pickle. "I was just commentin'," he says and thinks of Joy with her parakeet on her finger and her face in the coolness by her door. Outside her doves coo and puffy clouds blow by.

At the market, Agnes drinks her tomato juice with her bare feet on the cool stoop out back. Under the firs, it is dark and damp. At the river, gold and silver and purple dots sparkle on the watery surface.

In the lot by Ray's, the weeds are purple and white and yellow with flowers. At the pond, a faint warmth moves in the depths. Come dusk, the air is soft and Will squints at it over the tops of his sunglasses. The TV is full of little dots of light. He sniffles and looks sideways. Susie is eating.

"Susie...."

She gets up with her cookies and plastic crackles, the rest of her chocolate pinwheels weighing down one side of the tray. "Want one?"

She is sitting on the couch now. He's still mad at her but he says, "Okay."

She peeked out a side of the drapes earlier and a soft brightness touched the wall over the TV he was watching and even his sunglasses didn't help.

Will wears his sunglasses all the time, never notices the way Andy is always watching him with his tongue stuck into his cheek now, contemplating a change of scenery. Assuming he could convince Jade to go with him. They're all the family each other has anymore. Will is worrying him. He even went to Ray at the Club and said, "Man, this dude is goin' to pieces."

"Hell you want me to do about it?" asked Ray in surprise.

Andy took a breath, watching Ray's attention go back to the reflection of the room in the mirror. He spoke in a rush. "I thought maybe you could talk to Trev an' ask 'im to call Will."

"Fuck that," said Ray without even looking at him.

His tongue poked at his cheek a moment before he sat down and got a drink. Ray swiveled his head at him a moment later and said, "That was advice, you know?"

Yeah, thinks Andy every time he sees Will now. *Fuck this.*

At the shop still, George says, "The guy's name's Van. Seems real interested in the place."

Ray nods.

It's dark on the porch and all of a sudden the curtains on the door make him imagine a dusty old foyer with doilies and porcelain figurines.

"One sixty."

George nods too. "You paid fifty."

Ray smiles and pulls his arm off the top of the sign. "That's my askin' price."

Carl is aghast. "For sale!"

One day he woke up and saw only a dull, gray blur. It was unexpected and anticipated all at the same time. He froze, waiting to see, and felt that soft, warm air again and saw not even a lesser shade of gray.

All at once he needed Mr Torch.

"I can't see!"

But after that, he could see, because Mr Torch could see. Mr Torch sat by Carl and Carl saw with him. Sometimes Scott would almost sit on top of Mr Torch and Mr Torch would raise his eyebrows at Carl and Carl would smile back in victory. Carl is a special case to Mr Torch, who isn't in the foyer of the white building with the green lawn cut in crisp diagonals. Even though it's cool and smells sweet there. Even though the birds sing in the trees and the bells ring in soft chimes Wendy will hear forever and ever.

Wendy can't forget that sound. Sometimes she even stops in the middle of the living room and listens, sometimes for so long that she even distracts Al from the TV and he stares at her, half suspiciously, with his brow furrowing up.

"That bell again?"

"Do you hear that?" she asked once.

"What?"

"A bell."

She thought about Clarence trying to get his wings in *It's A Wonderful Life* and a bell ringing when he finally did. She was afraid she was hearing Carl die.

Her expression bothered Al and he went back to his TV. After all, there was nothing he could do.

Mr Torch likes Wendy and he reminds Carl of her all the time.

Carl sees her in a purple dress on a wooden dance floor with his father. There are paper lanterns in the trees, not Mr Torch's bells and urns, icy and dark. She has stars in her eyes and John still loves her.

Mr Torch shows him that and things like the luminous drops of water that ran off of Scott's face in the pool at the Acropolis Inn and glows in Carl's eyes.

Mr Torch smiles and George switches on the sign at the bar.

At Ray's, Kurt pulls on the screen door at the side of the shop and it pops off its hinges.

Mr Torch laughs silently into his fingers. "Delightful!"

Carl cringes and pulls his blankets up.

Later, after Ray arrives, he mutters, "Fuck," then leans the broken door against the side of the porch. Inside, he drinks a beer in one breath, then draws in a lungful of air and lets it out slowly. Everything in this place, except for the box with his gun and money under the floorboards, he'll leave. At home, the cupboards are empty and there's a box on the coffee table with Miri's cat statue and sunflower clock inside. The sight of it makes him feel the same thing he did watching Irene smoke her cigarettes on the porch.

With another slow breath, he stands still, waiting for some answer to come that he doesn't think ever will.

The pictures on the wall are gone too.

When Will saw it, he grew afraid and his heart began to pump. There was a rag and a bowl of water on top of the TV and that gave him an idea.

"Paintin'?" he asked.

"No."

That was all Miri said and then she left him alone in the room. He went closer to the TV. The water in the bowl was dirty.

At home, he half covered his eyes, turned on a light and said, "Do you ever wash our walls?"

Susie looked at him as if she thought he'd gone insane. "No."

Now he lies under a damp rag she gives him and tries not to think anything until she gets up and he looks over at her. She's back in her chair again, squinting at her fingernails. "Go get me a beer."

"We're out."

"Go get some. Fuck you doin'?"

"Working, Will. Working."

He throws his rag at her. "Get me a beer!"

He relaxes after the door slams. The air stills, softens to a pale gray. Everything is quiet, peaceful. Then a rumble growing louder and louder. His eyes snap open and he rolls off the couch, scrambling on the floor for the rag he threw at Susie. The rumble dies, a ringing silence following. He opens the door, clamping the rag over his eyes. The only light on is in the kitchen.

Ray flips the switch and Will drops back onto the couch.

"I almost didn't stop, man. Fuck you doin' in the dark?"

"Nothin'."

"You eat yet?"

"No."

"Gimme your keys. I have to eat an' you're not drivin'. C'mon an' get up."

Will drops the rag, gets up, and comes back out of the kitchen with his keys. "Jack-in-the-Box?"

"Yeah, whatever, man. Sure."

Outside, a moon and starlight and the cool, kind dark Mr Torch sees in Carl's eyes.

Scott is up again, annoying Mr Torch until he sips Carl's grape juice with a look of wonder. Mr Torch smiles at him, almost kindly.

Mr Torch's Mortuary is aloft with spirits that only Mr Torch can see. Carl saw a woman he didn't know give Scott a bottle of morphine and Mr Torch gave her a gentle smile.

Now Carl blinks at Scott, who bends over him and says, "Wendy's here."

Carl frowns.

Later, Scott looks out at the top of the palm tree at the Acropolis Inn and pictures Carl in the lobby again.

At home, Carl looks at Wendy and sees her sit in the chair across from him and turn on the TV. "I brought ice cream. Butter Pecan. Your favorite."

At home, she used to come out in a robe and pink slippers every morning and point a Pop Tart box at him. "Sweets for my sweet."

One night, she twirled in a new dress and gave him a wink and caught his face in her palms and spun away again in a swirl of gardenia. "Wish me luck!"

Carl sees with Mr Torch's eyes to distant places beyond his lawn with the crisp diagonal cuts and its bright white walkway and its warm and glossy wood and its peaceful emptiness. Carl sees himself on the curb with a red fire engine in the gutter. Wendy is there too. Her eyes are red though and her face is puffy.

"Wish me luck," she cries and John looks back and laughs.

Outside, the ball of sun drops away and Carl follows it, swooping through a sky of stars, rising up again into a blue, empty space.

Mr Torch smiles.

It is morning again and the sun is yellow and the weeds are dewy below the deep green firs and there are flowers and fragrance in the cool air.

Carl can hear footsteps at Ray's. Will's are soundless.

Will stops to look in at Susie and all the cool air inside the house fills him up. She rolls over and sees him. He leans to the bedroom a little, fingers on the jamb, slipping off. He circles her and she scoots up against her pillows and smiles.

"Hi, honey."

He stops. Her face is grayish in the shade of the big spruce outside.

"I love you," he says and she shivers and uses her feet to push up against the headboard. "I said *I fuckin' love you!*"

Her whisper is toneless. "I love you too."

Will laughs.

Outside of the shop, Ray pulls up in Miri's car with a screen door tied to the roof.

Carl smiles at Scott's smile.

At Candi's, Debby sits down in the back of the diner with a cup of coffee. She rubs her eyes, then pulls her phone out of her purse, smiling at one of her messages. "Cherry Jubilee pancakes. Whipped cream. Maple syrup. Yeah, baby!"

At the shop, Ray sits back with his elbows on a step above him. After a while, George comes over with a man named Van and Ray gets up and Carl sees a butterfly disappear like a yellow leaf on a cool day. It swirls, he thinks, like leaves, like other butterflies, under the little urns in Mr Torch's trees and catches currents at dusk to rise up again and blow on.

Carl sighs.

Mr Torch is a shadow.

A ball of sun like the sun in Carl's dream fills up the sky with orange.

At the river, Agnes sees dots of color like marbles and imagines Aster's and Sissy's hair floating like reeds. She puts her toes in the water and feels the coldness underneath and sees the sky up above, orange and pink, and stays until the sun sinks below the trees and all the shadows deepen and cool.

At Carl's, a last pale glow rises up the wall and absorbs Mr Torch.

At the Acropolis Inn, the palm tree rustles and the fountain splashes below. Carl sees specks of orange float up like fairy dust. Mr Torch appreciates the imagery. Carl's smile is mild and peaceful.

Val is out with the lawnmower. Scott is in the pool. A big blue fish is swimming in circles in a tank in the lobby of the Jade Palace where Ray gives the glass a tap as he goes by.

"Cool fish."

Fin nods.

"You order?"

He nods again. "Octopus."

"Great," says Ray with a blank face.

At Jack-in-the-Box, Will burst into tears. "You can't move!"

Ray just sat there, not looking away, pretty sure everybody else in the place was looking over. Then Will said, "Oh fuck," and dropped his forehead onto his palms. Ray just drank his soda and saw him again the way he did at Candi's that first time with Andy and Craig's cousin following behind him, twitching fingers drumming against the back of the vinyl booth, a foot bobbing over a knee. Quick moving eyes that didn't glitter with grief-stricken craziness.

"You should get outta town too, you know? Try somethin' new."

Will's fingers came down slowly, face pale and lifeless. He sighed heavily. "This is my place," he said quietly. "I'm a king here."

Ray didn't even want to laugh at that, just slowly rolled his empty cup in his fingers, staring down at a chip on the table, a lonely king in a grimy Jack-in-the-Box sitting on the other side. "You need to lay off the drugs, Will, I'm tellin' ya. You're too fuckin' young to die."

"I'm thirty," said Will, watching him roll his cup. "I won't die."

Ray leaned in. "I got off the stuff."

Will's lids lowered and a dark look came on his face. "You sound like Trevor."

"Yeah? You should listen to 'im. The dude's psychic, remember?"

"No," he said, shaking his head. "Trevor's a liar."

Ray raised his palms up. "Okay, man. You win. I leave you to your kingdom."

Will nodded, smiling again. "Yeah. My kingdom."

There are no bells at Carl's, no little urns in the dark. Mr Torch's fingers make a steeple and he is quiet.

Below him, Errol peeks out his curtains and sees the car he just heard outside with its lights on the wall of cinder block and concrete he just put up across the front of the carport. It's a true box now with a roof where he can store things.

The lights of the Chevelle stay on, but Fin gets out and looks over.

Errol fades back.

Mr Torch smiles patiently.

Fin sits slowly on the hood of his car and rubs his face. A pain grows behind his eyes.

In the parking lot of the Jade Palace, Ray shook his hand and said, "You be good, my friend."

"You too."

That got him a laugh. Before he rode away Ray said, "See ya sometime," and Fin said, "Sure," and saw the faces of Ginny and Blossom and Sally and Sissy right before Ray looked back over and grinned at him. Then, for some inexplicable reason, he said, "No regrets, man," and rode away.

When Fin gets up he tugs on a stone at the top of Errol's wall and the curtains closest to him flutter madly.

A dawn mist floats up from the river under a cloudless sky. The air is damp and sweet. The Chevelle ticks as it cools. Shadows fill the house and the floor boards creak.

At the door, Fin looks back inside, feeling a wistfulness he can't explain. It's not fear that he won't be coming back, but it's close to that. His eyes roam up the stairs, grayish white with the pale light seeping in through the back window. Scanning the living room as he turns, his wistfulness becomes sorrow and the sorrow closes around his throat, fills his mouth with the remembered taste of bourbon.

Quickly, he closes the door and starts to run. His shoes thump pleasantly on the gravel driveway and he focuses on the mist rising from the river, the way it keeps to the firs. Then he staggers, all of a sudden boneless, slamming down to the ground, onto his hands and knees before he even rounds the curve in the driveway. He pants through his open mouth and stares blankly, numbly at the gravel, the shades of gray, the seepage of moisture. A pain like no other is crushing him. He makes noises he can't stop. The memories that come with the pain steal his sight. He gasps and tries to get up. Resisting him, his body curls up, pushing his forehead into the gravel. He stays like that until the pain recedes, leaving only memory. Memories that make him moan, things he doesn't want to see. The amorphous shapes that used to float through his consciousness, distant things he didn't need to touch are now concrete, made of stone. Slowly, he pulls his hands to his temples and squeezes in. His eyelids flutter open and he can see again. He rises up on shaky arms, stares at the mist still clinging to the trees, the paleness of the sky.

A sky unlike the skies on any of the days he remembers, days evocative of nothing here. A clear sky above him, no rain, a cold foggy midnight, not dawn. His eyes grow dark and he is on a roof, sitting in a chair under a dark sky. Drinking for a long time, he finally sets the bottle down and gets up. He can see himself doing this, a frozen image like a snapshot. He sees himself on the edge of the roof, barefoot, his toes in the air. No sensation of falling though, nothing to be afraid of. He can think on this, hold this in his memory, a memory that doesn't matter. He lets it roll by again, the roof, the sky, the chair, the roof, the sky, the chair.

Then he sees sunshine lighting the trees. He is sitting on his heels now and, slowly, he is able to get up. His joints ache. He staggers again. The sky is blue, the mist burned away.

Looking back at the house, he stares at it for a long time. White paint, black shutters, black door. A porch with a roof. A chimney, dark windows, beams of pale sun shining over the roof. He feels that sorrow again, the longing for a place that's gone. The emptiness inside is a weight. His eyes roam the colorless rooms, the stairway that rises up to the dead eye of a window. His body is nerveless. He takes his shoes off, holding onto the banister, slipping sideways to sit on the steps. His socks lie beside his shoes. He sits with his face in his hands, quietly following the memory of the roof, the sky, the chair. He is crying, but that has nothing to do with the roof. His tears are hot on his palms and he sits up, breath catching.

Slowly, he gets back up and goes down the hall to the kitchen. Opening the back door, he sees his mother, one of his first memories, staring back at him through gasoline fueled flames. He shivers in the cold. His feet are numb. Turning, he crosses the room and opens the door to the basement. He flips the light switch and shadows push back against the walls. He runs quickly down the stairs, then crouching in the corner by the box of his mother's gin, he opens a bottle and takes a long swallow. The relief makes him shake. He can't hold himself up and sits down. He doesn't feel the cold or his rigid grip on the bottle. He keeps drinking and pictures his mother, the smiles she never gave him, the fingers she never ran through his hair, the laughter she never shared. Gasping, he leans sideways on one arm, keeping the bottle close to his body. Her face appears, floating in the dim basement light, the face in his dreams. He raises her bottle, looking up at the rafters laced with cobwebs, thinking that wherever she is, maybe she loves him now.

Cold seeps out of the cinder block walls, up from the floor, rolls over him like a frozen wave. His arms and legs shake, the bottom of a bottle clunking against the floor. He hugs the bottle, tries to warm himself with a swallow. It burns and he coughs, searing his throat. His nose burns too, beginning to run. Slowly, he rocks, rocks again, gets up on his knees. The basement spins and he throws his hands underneath him, skinning his knuckles underneath the bottle. Sitting back up, he holds the bottle to his mouth. Now his lips burn and he shudders. He looks at another bottle gleaming in the light, empty, the flutter of broken cobwebs above the crate. He crawls, not feeling the rough concrete abrade his skin. At the stairs, he grabs on, tries to stand, swings away and lets go, tumbling onto his back, gin splashing his chest. He moans angrily, rolls onto his side and reaches up for the staircase. The wood creaks. He pulls anyway, rising, staggering onto the steps. He crawls again and sprawls through the door at the top in relief. It is almost dark out, a wedge of pale light at the open back door. He tries to drink lying down, gags and sputters, sits up and pushes his back against a wall. His vision is constricted by a dark band squeezing in, his swimming head heavy, dragging him down, pulling his chin to his chest. Sleep fills him with dread. He throws his head back suddenly, slamming it against the wall, crying out at the shock of it. He gasps several times, his head pounding, then pulls the bottle up, drinking again. He is vaguely aware that this is killing him, that he is drinking too much. He doesn't even think he wants it anymore. He wants to hurt before the hurt stops. He drops his head against the wall again and the pain makes him moan. He half dreams of a roof, sees his toes poke over the edge, slides a foot into the open air. The sensation of falling makes him drop the bottle and he grabs onto the floor. His eyes squeeze shut and he holds himself still, hunched over his bent legs, sweating, feeling sudden heat melt the cold inside him. His body shakes. Breathless, he opens his eyes, sees the bottle on the floor under the kitchen table, resting against a chair leg, and crawls over, picking it up out of a puddle of gin. The bottle looms up and recedes, bigger, smaller, meeting his lips with a crack against his teeth. He swallows and doesn't want it, but drinks anyway, forcing it down over a sudden retching, holding it in.

His nose is running again. He swipes at it, his breath bubbling. Setting the bottle down carefully, watching the way it totters and tips, he gently releases it upright, pulls his tee-shirt off and scrubs at his face, the fabric rough or soft, he isn't sure. He keeps rubbing and then he is shivering; he drops his shirt and carefully, delicately lifts the bottle up again. He takes several quick swallows and feels a sudden rush back up into his nose. He shudders, shakes his head and almost falls over again. The pain doubles him up. He feels the top of his head resting on the cold floor. A humming sound reaches him and he realizes it's coming from him. It soothes him and he starts to rock, humming louder. He thinks he goes to sleep, but he isn't sure. It bothers him. Sitting up again, holding onto the leg of the table, he tips up the bottle and drinks until he can't swallow anymore and spits it up. His skin is wet, his hair clinging to him. He is looking out the open back door. He wants to get onto his feet. The quiet house grows darker and the window at the end of the hall upstairs turns luminously pale. Sorrow and tenderness fill every room. The fragrance of flowers grows in the air. But it isn't real. There is no laughter, no memory of celebration, just the heat-buffeting waves of her burning dahlias.

He can't get up. His feet won't work.

The dark is creeping up to the door. A blue light he can't see fills his eyes. Water washes the color away. He knows he is crying. His feet scramble under him, but he just falls back, lets go of the bottle and watches it roll away. Then, with a sudden loud cry, he throws himself after it, falling hard on his belly. The gin inside him rushes up and spews out. In a panic, unable to breathe, he throws up again. His fingers claw at the floor. He drags himself away, groans and curls up, vomit splashing the floor in a bitter puddle. Scared, he rolls backwards, kicking himself across the room, pulling himself into the hallway where he throws up again. His stomach is on fire, innards stretched out in agony. A wheezing cry of pain emerges. He retches again and reaches up to a table, grabbing onto the runner under the lamp. Dragging it down with him, the lamp comes crashing down on top of him. He yelps and pushes it away. Without really understanding how, he is wedged underneath the table with his back to the wall.

He relaxes a little now, feeling oddly safe. His breathing settles, not too quick. He pulls into himself, curls up, arms across his chest, waiting, preternaturally alert now. His eyes roam to the front door.

It is dark.

He fixes on the windows on either side of the door, just waiting.

Upstairs, Mr Torch rolls his eyes with a sigh. Carl's are dim. Outside, the coolness seeps in under the window sashes and Mr Torch gets up and sits by the wall again.

In the blue light, he is shadowless.

Carl is at the Acropolis Inn. In wintertime. With the pool blue and empty. Outside, bells ring and water splashes in the fountain. He looks up at ghostly clouds through the fronds of the palm. All he can hear are bells and all he can see is an empty motel. As he stares, all the lights go off and the water in the pool turns dull and gray. He is looking for Scott and Wendy as the sun tops the trees and curls of steam come off the rooftops and the damp green weeds in the lot and Ray comes out of his shop and looks at Carl's where there's a shadow he thinks is Carl.

Carl is looking at a shadowless wall again.

At Mr Torch's mortuary, wind chimes and bells ring in the soft air. Mr Torch's fingers make a steeple under his chin.

Outside, Ray is standing on the porch at his open front door, working at one of the screws holding Miri's bells in place. Getting it off, he drops it into his pocket, starting on the other one. The shop has a particular smell that's strong in the open air. He doesn't look inside though, just unscrews the screw, slips it into his pocket and pulls the bells away from the door. The wood bears the imprint of the diamond hasp, and when he sees it, that strange pain starts knotting up his guts again. He stares inside, past the shelves to the counter, half imagining himself there day after day, and he's not really sure if the panic he suddenly feels is because he almost stayed or because he isn't going to. A moment later, he pulls the door shut behind him and turns away.

Upstairs, Mr Torch departs, only a smile above his steeple of fingers as Carl goes too.

Goodbye, Mr Torch.

Goodbye, Carl.

28

◆ Ghosts ◆

His eyes are full of sunshine and blue skies. At Ira's, all the weeds are in bloom and winter's puddles are silver mirrors. At the market one day, Jonah sees Agnes spinning in slow circles on her stool with her sandals on the footstep below, dusty summertime toes. She never swam in Ivy's pond or came out of the shadows of the firs into yellow green sunshine.

"Just some coffee," he says and hears her feet drop softly as she goes.

On his way past Ira's again, he remembers Ira's Christmas lights and the pillowcases in the windows and the stool he sat on, waiting for Ira to wake up, and the loose, gray pants Ira died in.

At work, Wally grins.

"I am T.O.'d, man. Ticked off at no time off. You hear me?!" he yells at the ceiling. "Wally Work-a-Lot! Cheap Taiwanese toy!"

A couple of people look over and Jonah laughs. Then Gus comes up and says, "Hear about the Cultural Awareness class we're havin'?"

"No."

"Yeah. After OT's over."

"No way."

"Ask Wes. Awareness of Others. An' I bet you're the reason why," he adds with a look at Wally before he walks away.

Wally looks hurt.

"I was jokin'!"

At home, clouds puff up in a sky as blue as Aster's eyes while Ally's geraniums bloom like Aster's once did and a wind he can't hear blows through the garage. A board or a hinge creaks. Sunshine flashes on the living room window and a sheet Ally put up still flaps on the clothesline. Outside, he stares back through the screen at the stove where Aster once made him tomato soup, where Clover put flowers in her bell, and Ally put yellow knobs on the cupboard doors and new curtains that stir and throw shadows in the gray air.

At the pond, he puts his head back and watches the soundless clouds grow into piles of soft white cotton.

Coming through the firs, the light is thin, lies in pale patches on the ground. The house is split into two levels, built into an incline. The upper level is a wall of windows, shady dark, shining with light at a corner. Cedar shakes, an orange red door. On the other side of the road, in front of the house, the lake twinkles in the sunshine.

Standing on the driveway, Fin feels a moment of almost lethargic peacefulness. His eyes close briefly and he feels the stir of the wind. Grace looks back at him, eyes curious.

"You really want to sell your house?"

"Do you like this?"

"I love this."

"Well?"

She comes back to him and he knows she doesn't believe any of the times he tells her he's feeling good, even though he really is. Even though he woke up under the foyer table in a stink of vomit that just made him throw up again. A thin watery drool that his stomach kept trying to heave up anyway. Sleeping the rest of the day, he thought he dreamed. He kept waking up, thrashing, just to roll over and sleep again. Later, at Grace's, he came in and sat on the couch, eyes roaming the room, settling on the remote. He picked it up and her shadow appeared in the kitchen door, moved into the corner of his eye.

"No hi?"

His eyes flickered up. "Sorry. I'm out of it today. Gettin' a cold, I think."

Her face was pale, strained. She moved back into the kitchen. He found *I Love Lucy* on TV, sat with a knee bobbing, feeling jittery and nervous.

"What are you cooking?"

"Chili."

Bile rose, burning the back of his throat. He swallowed it back down. Sitting at the table a while later, he chewed slowly on a piece of corn bread. It went down with a painful swallow and he sat quietly, looking at his chili. He felt her stare, saw the whiteness of her knuckles across the table.

"Fin?" He met her eyes, waiting. "Are you okay?"

"Yeah. Why?"

"Are you drinking again?"

"No," he said quickly." No…I'm…I'm not. I…I just…I can't sleep. I'm just tired. I swear to God I'm not—"

"Fin—"

"Jesus, Grace. Don't do this. Don't ask. I'm sorry. I don't…I can't do this again. I can't. I can't."

He was staring down at his bowl, the smell of food making his stomach spasm. He swallowed loudly, didn't hear her get up but felt her arms around his head, pulling his face in. He breathed out, wrapped his arms around her, pulling her into him, lips moving against her.

"God, I love you."

Her fingers ran through his hair, soothing him, making him sleepy.

"Why, Fin?"

"I don't know, Grace. Please."

"I have to ask. You won't talk to me. I'm scared. You have all these secrets I don't know anything about. All I know is it's killing you. I thought everything was okay. But then all of a sudden it wasn't anymore. You look like you're dying, Fin, an' I have to watch that. I can't take watching that."

"Please don't leave me."

He felt her cheek come to rest on top of his head. "I won't leave you. I can't leave you."

"I made a mistake. I fucked up. I won't do it again."

She sighed and her fingers grew slow. "You can't promise that."

Pulling away, he looked up at her, his green eyes swallowed in darkness. "I won't cut you out. I can promise that. I just…I have to figure things out."

She smiled sadly and the backs of her fingers came down to his stubbly cheeks, stroking gently. His head bent, pushing against her again, and she held him close. "I'm sorry," he said.

"I don't want you to be sorry. I want you to be happy. You deserve that."

"No," he said softly. "I don't."

He felt her begin to cry. "Yes, you do, Fin. I love you. I don't want to love anybody else. I don't want anybody else. I want you. I'm afraid of losing you."

"You won't." He sat up, pulling her into his lap, hugging her tightly. "I promise you. I swear to God I'll get better. I'll make you happy. I won't drink again. I'll come out of this. I swear to God. I swear it…." He murmured that over and over, rocking her in his lap. "I swear to God…I swear to God…."

It struck him as strange, because he didn't believe, but he felt a sense of happiness come over him, warmth from Grace's body, her arms around him, and his pain floated away on the same peaceful wave that later carried him into a dreamless sleep.

No lawn chairs. No graves.

The woozy feeling stayed with him until he found the house by the lake with the lights, not far from Sully's. He is clearer about things now. That he's even here is miraculous to him, even though he knows he doesn't deserve it, that he was careless, always careless. Occasionally, he feels suddenly cold and afraid. His heart pounds and he grows sweaty. A moment later, the feeling of peace returns and the picture of his mother's gin fades away. He knows that he didn't want to come out of that basement alive, wanted to die down there in the dark and the dirt. But with Grace's touch or the sound of Sully's gruff voice, the fear always fades.

He knows he doesn't want to die now. Not really.

Wrapping his arms around Grace in front of the house, he kisses the top of her head and says it again, "Well?"

"I like this house, Fin. Are you sure though?"

"I'm sure. I don't want to go back. I don't think I can."

She moves in his arms, turning around to look at the house again, leaning back against him. The sun shifts and spreads across the windows. The thickness of the fir trees will soon hide the light, but even the darkness here doesn't bother him. It's only the absence of light, not the presence of other things.

He rocks her again. "Well?"

She wraps her arm around his and leans her face back, smiling up at him. "Okay, Fin."

Then he smiles too, and for a moment, the shifting sun shines on his face, banishing the shadows from his eyes.

At home again, Jonah opens a beer and sits on the couch with the TV on. At dusk a softness comes on, a mistiness like the start of rain. After a while, he gets up and goes into the bedroom, setting his beer on top of his dresser. Wriggling open the stiff top drawer, he takes out Kurt's gun, picks up his beer and goes back out to the living room. For a moment though, he feels uncertain and stares into the thin light coming through the window, spreading a faint rectangle on the carpet. A blue carpet, but he thinks it was a gold carpet once. Gold or beige. It bothers him strangely that he can't picture that old carpet anymore.

Stirring himself, he puts the gun down on top of the TV and backs away. Lying down, he rests up against the arm of the couch and drinks his beer and watches cartoons. Memory washes over him, a thing of the light, the sound of the TV, the time of day. He isn't really sure of time or seasons anymore. Sometimes he isn't even sure if Aster died in summer. Maybe it was winter and rainy like the day Abel came home with Jonah's pickup full of wood. Maybe the carpet was not gold or beige. Maybe cream. A dirty, worn out cream. He was lying on the couch in his memory though, like he is now. He got up when he heard the pickup and Abel saw him at the window and pointed at the wood in back. His mouth moved soundlessly, "Get out here." It came to Jonah from faraway, like a lot of things then.

Outside, the day was like glass, silver gray, ready to rain.

It's really dusk though, growing darker. He hears a car coming, its sound close and faraway at the same time. It sounds like water, slow and quiet, then loud and fast. Maybe it's Ally coming home with a grocery bag in her arms and flowers coming out of the top.

He takes Kurt's gun into the bedroom and puts it under the covers, then sits on the end of the bed and waits, picturing Ally's worryless smile. A smile she never smiled at anyone. She was always worried because she imagined things like seeing Clover's ghost where she picked her flowers or hearing Sissy's quiet when she went into her room or seeing Aster's bewilderment everywhere or that he never loved her.

In a minute though he hears a knock, but he doesn't get up. Then the door opens and he hears footsteps that aren't hers, then sees Kurt in the door, staring at him before he takes a swallow of the beer he got out of the refrigerator on his way back and says, "You better not be canceling out. I'm starved."

"No," he says.

"Good. I'm meetin' Angie for ice cream after."

A new girl came to work at the factory one day. Standing by his cubby, Kurt stared at her in amazement. A face full of life, twinkling with humor. A dimple winking with her smiles. Almost numbly, he came out of the alcove and her smile grew.

"Hi," she said. "I'm Angela."

Angeline, he thought.

"Kurt," he said, going over.

He took her to Candi's after a movie one night and she ate her slice of pickle right away and said, "This is the best part."

She likes pickles and the giant bowling pin on the roof of the bowling alley. Her TV is little and she can blow real bubbles with the bubble gum pieces in her ice cream. At work, Kurt leans his elbows on the counter and watches her come and go, sudden smiles flashing over at him, and he's happy like that. A pause with Joy was always a void to fill up. Maybe to Joy too, with her wind chimes and her TV always on.

Upstairs, in the early sun, he looks at the windowsills and sees circles in the layers of luminous dust, reminders of the pots of violets that aren't there anymore. All the strings like cobwebs shimmer against the glass.

At home a soundless wind blows through the tops of the trees. It smells like strawberries and summer air. Sitting on the porch, Jonah drinks his beer and thinks about Agnes. After a while the sun grows hot and the clouds disappear too and he swims in soft green water.

At night he sees her come to a warm, lit window and look out into the dark. Her hair is a golden halo, her face as soft as memory.

He dreams on hot sunny days of dusk and bourbon, stillness and strawberries, Orly slurping coffee at dawn.

At the pizza parlor, he stares at a jukebox against a dark wood wall and Kurt wipes his mouth and says, "I have some news. Not Wes's either," he adds when Jonah looks over. "Angie's."

"What is it?"

"Ally's going away. Transferring to the new site."

Jonah nods and looks off across the room again where the juke box flashes orange and yellow and blue lights like a Christmas tree or the eaves of Ira's trailer. He frowns slightly.

"You sure?"

"Yeah."

He stares at a girl putting on strawberry lip gloss as she goes by. Her hair catches a flash of yellow light, shines like sunshine, like Agnes's as she runs in his dreams through Ira's meadow. Like Aster's under a blue and white sky, sunlit and shiny.

He can sense Kurt's stare, looking up under his brows, head dipped down to hide it. He looks back over, takes a long swallow of his beer. "You know," he says. "It's kind of a relief."

"Yeah?"

"Yeah. I don't want it draggin' on. This is better," he says.

Except he can't hear the wind blow.

The porch light is on again. He forgets to turn it off.

At dawn, it looks cool like the sun when it shines on the pond in the morning. Later on, it just looks left on, forgotten, like Ally's colorless geraniums on the porch.

Coming through the door, he can see the kitchen taking on a pale and fuzzy definition, like a picture made of gray and white pin dots. Unreal. Dreamlike.

The top drawer in the dresser is still open, empty, a corner of the paper beginning to pull up. She came back the other day when he was gone and took Asa's toys and the rocker her mother gave her.

In the hallway, he stops at Asa's room to flip on the light and looks in at the yellow walls and the fluffy clouds she painted on the ceiling. It keeps reminding him of Aster and he wonders now about the day he found her. It was clear maybe, maybe winter, maybe with a sun so big and white it made the air hum. He wonders about Ally's eyes, a dreamy blue, full of wonder, and

Ira's eyes at Christmastime or in summers with a bowl full of Oreos, remembering too.

Always.

The flowers that Aster painted on the bathroom wall look paler than before. One day there will be nobody left who remembers her. On the way up to Ivy's pond Jonah always stops near the top and looks back through the trees at the lights below the way Abel probably always looked at Aster's flowers every morning. It was a long time before they began to fade.

On the day Abel died, Sissy's hair was blowing in a wind that came up from the river. The air smelled like water and she wore her coat with the fluffy collar. Maybe there was a lot of Clover in Abel at that moment and maybe the sadness he felt wasn't really over Sissy. It was just that she looked so much like Aster when she was a girl and he went over to her house to pick her up, her smile full of love at first; except that Sissy was looking sideways with that smile, giving it to Fin, who was walking beside her. They were coming up the road, out of the trees, down by the river, doing things Abel didn't want her doing with anybody else. Aster got pregnant with Jonah before they were married and Abel remembered her half-excited, half-anxious expression.

"Please don't be mad."

"I'm not mad." Even though he was only seventeen, Aster nineteen. For all his life, Abel saw himself a part of the place he grew up in, that the house was his more than Job's with every day that he got stronger and Job got older. A family just made his thoughts more real. His family, his Sissy with a half-excited, half-anxious look, her fingers entwined with Fin's until Fin saw him and pulled away. Then she stopped too, staring between them. The cold brought color to their faces, but Fin's was going slowly white.

"Where'd you come from?" asked Abel.

"We were just walking."

"Where?"

"By the river," said Fin.

"Doing what?"

"Walking."

A smile grew on Abel's face and then he laughed a laugh that mixed with the sounds of the growing wind, blowing louder than before, filling the air with sounds like water.

"I know what you were doing."

Then they all stood there, frozen in a moment stilled in the cold and wind. A wind that blew at Sissy's hair, masking her face, bit at Jonah's hands and eyes, cut across Fin's and Abel's locked stares. Fin would've run if he could, but Abel saw that he was too scared. He just stood there frozen until he made his mistake of slowly turning to look at Sissy.

"I know what you were doing!"

Abel's outrage rose and swirled above them. There was a drop of rain maybe.

Abel was waiting for thunder. He thought it had to come.

Clouds loomed and a soundless wind bent the trees.

Jonah saw the billowing of gray up above, the evidence of a force he couldn't hear. Then he saw Abel pick up a hammer lying on top of the pile of wood and rush across the gravel at Fin, breaking the frozen spell that held everybody still, so that Fin jumped back, hands up, almost running before he stopped to look back at Sissy. He froze again and Abel came up with the hammer raised and Fin sank to his knees. And then Abel stumbled with an image flashing across his eyes of Clover lying in her white slip, looking at him across the silvery ground where he hid under the porch. Behind him, Jonah stood with a piece of wood in both of his hands. On the ground, Abel grunted, scrabbled at the gravel a little, and then Jonah swung the board back up and brought it down on Abel's head again with a dull, soggy thump. Blood sprayed up and Fin rolled away and threw up.

Jonah wheezed. "I couldn't...couldn't...." But he couldn't get it out, what it was he couldn't do or see or give in to. His heart pounded. Then he grew colder and colder until he felt nothing. "I couldn't," he said again, trying to explain.

But nobody answered. Fin was bent over, his hands on the gravel, and Sissy stood with her arms over her head, not looking.

Then the sky grew darker and the rain started, bouncing up in silver and gray balls as the clouds parted and came together again.

They put Abel onto a blue tarp and rolled him over the side of the road, hearing the splash of water below as he landed. Fin slipped in the mud, stayed on his hands and knees, head down, rain dripping from his hair. At the edge of the road, just as the truck went over, Jonah saw Abel's eyes come open, dark blue mirrors of his own eyes, snapping wide. That's when he tried to grab the truck, stop it going over, and then felt Fin grab onto him, holding him back as he grappled at empty air. A crushing boom sent birds flying into the sky, wings whipping all around, an echo following, fading slowly away. Then Fin let him go and Jonah rocked in the mud, bent over his knees with his head in his hands.

At the cemetery, Fin walks up to a pair of gravestones and crouches down near the ground. Needles fall and the wind gently buffets him. It feels cool and the sun shines pale and white on the stones, reminding him of snowflakes or Sissy's moonlit eyes. At night, she appears and smiles at him. Rising up again, he looks down the hillside, catching a glimpse of his house.

Outside, his mother's dahlias are coming up and hydrangeas bloom in the shade.

Once upon a time only flowers
        bloomed in Ira's meadow,
        and Ivy's pond was a dark, woodsy pool.
        This was Clover's place
        where Asa lives now,
        where Jonah swims
        in a dark, cold pond under a starry sky.

And this is where the ghosts come,
        where Abel hid under a dark porch
        and saw Clover fall without a sound,
        where Job stood silently beside her
        and saw her rise above
        a slippery patch of gravel.

And this was Aster's place,
        with her windblown hair,
        where she fell in love with Abel
        and came to live with Clover's ghost.

And this was Sissy,
        who looked like Aster,
        who fell in love with Abel,
        who was left with only the memory of his mother.

And this is Jonah,
        who looks up at stars that look like snowflakes,
        who smells strawberries blowing on soundless winds
        and lives with all the ghosts,
        Sissy's and Aster's,
        and Abel's,
        who once saw Clover fall in a gown of white
        and lie on rocks of silver.

And this is Ally kissing Asa's cheek
        in a moonlit room,
        once in love with Jonah,
        who hugged her
        under stars like snowflakes
        and remembers Sissy,
        whose hair blew like Aster's one day,
        and whose smile was like Clover's,
        good and gentle.

And this is Agnes,
       who took Ally's love
       and Jonah's too,
       and never saw the stirrings of his memories
       of Aster's pale flowers,
       a garden of irises,
       where Abel used to come
       and watch her with eyes like Job's.

And this is Asa,
       who sleeps with Ally's kisses.
       And this is Ally,
       who lives in Jonah's dreams
       with all the ghosts
       that rise as misty white
       as a winter's day.

www.ingramcontent.com/pod-product-compliance
Lightning Source LLC
Chambersburg PA
CBHW030533260626
47157CB00006B/2013